A TEXT BOOK OF

FUNDAMENTALS OF ELECTRICAL ENGINEERING

FOR

(SEMESTER – I & II)

FIRST YEAR DEGREE COURSE IN B. TECH.

(COMMON FOR ALL BRANCHES)

Strictly According to Syllabus of

Bharati Vidyapeeth Deemed University, Pune

(EFFECTIVE FROM ACADEMIC YEAR 2014)

A. N. SARWADE
M. Tech. (Electrical)
Sinhgad College of Engineering, Pune

S. J. THANEKAR
M. E. (Electrical)
Singhad College of Engineering, Pune

V. V. SANGAMNERKAR
B.E. (Electrical)
Smt. Kashibai Navale College of Engineering, Pune

NIRALI PRAKASHAN
ADVANCEMENT OF KNOWLEDGE

N1060

FUNDAMENTALS OF ELECTRICAL ENGINEERING (F.Y.B.Tech. SEM. I BVDU)

Second Edition :   January 2015   ISBN: 978-93-5164-106-3

© : Authors

Published By :
PRAGATI BOOKS PVT. LTD.
Abhyudaya Pragati, 1312, Shivaji Nagar,
Off J.M. Road, PUNE – 411005
Tel - (020) 25512336/37/39, Fax - (020) 25511379
Email : niralipune@pragationline.com

DISTRIBUTION CENTRES
PUNE

Nirali Prakashan
119, Budhwar Peth, Jogeshwari Mandir Lane
Pune 411002, Maharashtra
Tel : (020) 2445 2044, 66022708, Fax : (020) 2445 1538
Email : bookorder@pragationline.com

Nirali Prakashan
S. No. 28/25, Dhyari,
Near Pari Company, Pune 411041
Tel : (022) 24690204 Fax : (020) 24690316
Email : dhyari@pragationline.com
bookorder@pragationline.com

MUMBAI
Nirali Prakashan
385, S.V.P. Road, Rasdhara Co-op. Hsg. Society Ltd.,
Girgaum, Mumbai 400004, Maharashtra
Tel : (022) 2385 6339 / 2386 9976, Fax : (022) 2386 9976
Email : niralimumbai@pragationline.com

DISTRIBUTION BRANCHES

NAGPUR
Pratibha Book Distributors
Above Maratha Mandir, Shop No. 3, First Floor,
Rani Jhanshi Square, Sitabuldi, Nagpur 440012,
Maharashtra, Tel : (0712) 254 7129

BENGALURU
Pragati Book House
House No. 1, Sanjeevappa Lane, Avenue Road Cross,
Opp. Rice Church, Bengaluru – 560002.
Tel : (080) 64513344, 64513355,
Mob : 9880582331, 9845021552
Email:bharatsavla@yahoo.com

JALGAON
Nirali Prakashan
34, V. V. Golani Market, Navi Peth, Jalgaon 425001,
Maharashtra, Tel : (0257) 222 0395
Mob : 94234 91860

KOLHAPUR
Nirali Prakashan
New Mahadvar Road,
Kedar Plaza, 1st Floor Opp. IDBI Bank
Kolhapur 416 012, Maharashtra. Mob : 9855046155

CHENNAI
Pragati Books
9/1, Montieth Road, Behind Taas Mahal, Egmore,
Chennai 600008 Tamil Nadu, Tel : (044) 6518 3535,
Mob : 94440 01782 / 98450 21552 / 98805 82331, Email : bharatsavla@yahoo.com

RETAIL OUTLETS
PUNE

Pragati Book Centre
157, Budhwar Peth, Opp. Ratan Talkies,
Pune 411002, Maharashtra
Tel : (020) 2445 8887 / 6602 2707, Fax : (020) 2445 8887

Pragati Book Centre
Amber Chamber, 28/A, Budhwar Peth,
Appa Balwant Chowk, Pune : 411002, Maharashtra,
Tel : (020) 20240335 / 66281669
Email : pbcpune@pragationline.com

Pragati Book Centre
676/B, Budhwar Peth, Opp. Jogeshwari Mandir,
Pune 411002, Maharashtra
Tel : (020) 6601 7784 / 6602 0855

PBC Book Sellers & Stationers
152, Budhwar Peth, Pune 411002, Maharashtra
Tel : (020) 2445 2254 / 6609 2463

MUMBAI
Pragati Book Corner
Indira Niwas, 111 - A, Bhavani Shankar Road, Dadar (W), Mumbai 400028, Maharashtra
Tel : (022) 2422 3526 / 6662 5254, Email : pbcmumbai@pragationline.com

www.pragationline.com   info@pragationline.com

PREFACE

It is with great pleasure that we present the book of **"Fundamentals of Electrical Engineering"** for First Year Engineering Students. This text book has been prepared in accordance with the syllabus prescribed by the Bharati Vidyapeeth Deemed University.

Each chapter has been dealt within detail. Sufficient number of problems have been given and exercises have been set. Emphasis has been given to Solved Numericals and Questions.

We take this opportunity to thank a number of colleagues and our teachers who have helped us in clearing a concept.

Our thanks are due to the Publisher Shri. Dineshbhai Furia, Shri Jigneshbhai Furia and Co-ordinator Shri. M. P. Munde who has been instrumental in bringing out this most needed book at the most opportune time. We are thankful to the entire staff of Nirali Prakashan, Pune. Last but not the least our thanks are due to our families and friends who have also contributed in no small measure to the publishing of this book.

Constructive suggestions, criticisms and comments are always welcome from our well wishers, patrons, colleagues and students for the further improvement of this book.

PUNE.   **– Authors**

❖ ❖ ❖

SYLLABUS

Unit – I : Basic Concepts (06 Hours)

Concept of EMF, Potential Difference, Current, Resistance, Ohm's law, Resistance temperature coefficient, SI units of Work, Power, Energy, Conversion of energy from one form to another in Electrical, Mechanical and Thermal systems.

Unit – II : Network Theorems (06 Hours)

Voltage source and current sources, Ideal and practical, Kirchhoff's laws and applications to network solutions using mesh analysis, Simplifications of networks using series – parallel, Star/Delta transformation. Superposition theorem. Thevenin's theorem, Maximum Power Transfer theorem.

Unit – III : Electrostatics (06 Hours)

Electrostatic field, Electric field intensity, Electric field strength, Absolute permittivity, Relative permittivity, Capacitor composite, Dielectric capacitors, Capacitors in series and parallel, Energy stored in capacitors, Charging and discharging of capacitors, Batteries – Types, Construction and Working.

Unit – IV : Magnetic Circuit and Transformer (06 Hours)

Magnetic effect of electric current, Cross and dot convention, Right hand thumb rule, Concept of flux, Flux linkages, Flux Density, Magnetic field, Magnetic field strength, Magnetic field intensity, Absolute permeability, Relative permeability, B-H curve, Hysterisis loop, Series-parallel magnetic circuit, Composite magnetic circuit, Comparison of electrical and magnetic circuits.

Faraday's law of electromagnetic induction, Statically and dynamically induced emf, Self inductance, Mutual inductance, Coefficient of coupling.

Single-phase transformer : Construction, Principle of operation, EMF equation, Voltage ratio, Current ratio, kVA rating, Losses in transformer, Determination of efficiency and regulation by direct load test.

Unit – V : A.C. Fundamentals and A.C. Circuits (06 Hours)

AC waveform definitions, Form factor, Peak factor, Study of R-L, R-C, RLC series circuit, R-L-C parallel circuit, Phasor representation in polar and rectangular form, concept of impedance, admittance, active, reactive, apparent and complex power, Power factor, 3-ph A.C. circuits.

Unit – VI : Electrical Wiring and Illumination System (06 Hours)

Basic layout of distribution system. Types of Wiring System and Wiring Accessories, Necessity of Earthing, Types of Earthing, Different types of Lamps (Incandescent, Fluorescent, Sodium Vapour, Mercury Vapour, Metal Halide, CFL, LED), Study of Electricity Bill.

CONTENTS

UNIT – IV

4. MAGNETIC CIRCUIT AND TRANSFORMER   4.1 – 4.36

5. ELECTROMAGNETIC INDUCTION 5.1 – 5.22

6. SINGLE PHASE TRANSFORMER 6.1 – 6.30

7. A.C. FUNDAMENTALS AND A.C. CIRCUITS   7.1 – 7.40

UNIT - I

$\mathbf{C}$hapter $\mathbf{1}$

BASIC CONCEPTS

This unit deals with the fundamentals of electrical parameters such as current, voltage and resistance.

1.1 FUNDAMENTALS OF ELECTRICITY

1.1.1 Concept of Current (I)

Generally, all pure metals are good conductors of electricity as they contain excess (free) electrons. The flow of these free electrons is nothing but electric current. Higher the number of flowing electrons, higher is the value of current.

In another sense, **the electric current is also defined as "the rate of flow of charge".**

So, $$\text{Current (I)} = \frac{\text{Charge (Q)}}{\text{Time (t)}}$$

The unit of current is Ampere (A). Where, 1 Amp.= 6.24×10^{18} electrons.

The electrons can be drifted (transferred) by certain force which is called as "electromotive force" (e.m.f.).

1.1.2 Concept of E.M.F. (E)

The force which is required to drive the current or drift the electrons from one point to another in an electrical circuit is called EMF.

It is denoted by a symbol (E) and its unit is volts (V).

Sources of EMF:

1. The electrodes of dissimilar material immersed in an electrolyte as in primary and secondary cells.
2. Relative motion of the conductor and a magnetic flux in electric generators, transformers.

1.1.3 Concept of Potential Difference (Voltage)

The potential difference (p.d.) or voltage is the difference in potential existing between two points. **The potential difference is defined as work done in bringing out unit positive charge from one point in the field to the other point.**

The unit of potential difference is volt.

Current always flows from higher potential level to lower potential level.

1.1.4 Difference Between Emf and Potential Difference

The unit of EMF and Potential difference is same i.e. volt but these two terms are different.

For example, if a load (lamp) is connected across battery terminals, the current starts flowing instantly and lamp glows. Here in battery due to chemical action electrical energy is produced, and desired voltage is made available across battery terminals. This voltage will act as source voltage(EMF).

But, when the lamp glows, light energy is produced. Here electrical energy is converted into other form of energy. When such energy conversion takes place, their exists a potential difference (p.d.) at load (lamp) connecting terminals.

1.1.5 Concept of Resistance (R)

It is defined as, "**Actual opposition made by the material specimen on account of its dimension to the current flowing through it.**"

Different specimen having different physical dimension materials but made up of same material, will have different resistance, although resistivity is same in each case.

It is denoted by a symbol (R) and it's unit is ohm (Ω). The mathematical expression for resistance is,

$$R = \rho\,\frac{l}{a}$$

where, ρ = Resistivity or specific resistance of material (Ω - m)

l = Length of material (m);   a = Cross-sectional area (m²)

1.1.6 Factors Governing the Resistance Value

From the expression of resistance, $R = \rho\,\dfrac{l}{a}$

(1) Length (l) : $R \propto l$, it means as the length of conductor increases, it's resistance also increases. The electrons in the conductor have to cover more and more distance as length increases, which increases the resistance.

(2) Cross-sectional area (a) : $R \propto \dfrac{1}{a}$, it means as the cross-sectional area of conductor increases, it's resistance decreases.

Resistance of thick conductor is lower than thin conductors. Thick conductor provides more space for the electrons to move through it freely than the thin conductor.

(3) Resistivity : The resistivity of material depends on the material used.

(4) Temperature : Resistance of material depends on temperature. As the temperature changes the resistance of the material also changes. Generally, for conducting materials, as temperature increases, the resistance also increases and for insulating materials resistance decreases with increase in temperature.

Conductance : It is the reciprocal of resistance.

It is denoted by G, where $G = \dfrac{1}{R}$. It's unit is mho ($\mho$) or siemens (S).

1.1.7 Resistivity or Specific Resistance

As the resistivity is the property of material by virtue of which it opposes the flow of current. Being property it is independent of physical dimensions. It can be measured by considering the specimen of the same material having unit length and unit cross sectional area. It is attributed by the composition of the material.

Factors governing the Resistivity Value :

1. **Temperature :** As the temperature of the material increases, it is found that resistivity also increases.

2. **Addition of Impurity :** Resistivity also changes by adding impurity in the material.

3. **Cold Working :** Cold work produces mechanical stresses in the material, which disturbs the crystal structure. This affects resistivity.

4. **Age Hardening :** Due to age hardening, the resistivity of the material also changes.

1.2 OHM'S LAW

As long as the physical condition of conductor remains the same (temperature is maintained constant to maintain the resistance i.e. circuit parameter constant), the current flowing through the conductor is directly proportional to the potential difference or voltage across it.

Explanation: $\qquad I \propto V \qquad\qquad\qquad \ldots(I)$

$$I = \frac{V}{R} \qquad \text{(Proportionality constant is 1/R)}$$

Thus we can write $\boxed{V = I.R}$

NUMERICALS ON RESISTANCE

Example 1.1 :

Find the resistances of the following copper wires.

(1) 1 mm^2 cross section, 100 m long

(2) 25 cm^2 cross section, 200 m long

Given : ρ is 1.73 $\mu\Omega$ cm.

Solution : (1) $R = \rho\dfrac{l}{a} = 1.73 \times 10^{-6} \times \dfrac{100 \times 10^2}{1 \times 10^{-2}} = 1.73 \ \Omega$

(2) $R = \rho\dfrac{l}{a} = 1.73 \times 10^{-6} \times \dfrac{200 \times 10^2}{25} = 0.001384 \ \Omega$

Example 1.2 :

Calculate the resistance of 100 m length of aluminium wire having uniform cross-sectional area of 0.01 mm^2 and having resistivity of 50 $\mu\Omega$ cm.

If the wire is drawn three times to its original length, calculate the value of new resistance.

Solution : Given : $\rho = 50 \ \mu\Omega$ cm $= 50 \times 10^{-6} \ \Omega$ cm, $l = 100$ m $= 100 \times 10^2$ cm

$a = 0.01$ mm$^2 = 0.01 \times 10^{-2}$ cm^2

$$R = \rho\dfrac{l}{a} = 50 \times 10^{-6} \times \dfrac{100 \times 10^2}{0.01 \times 10^{-2}} = 5000 \ \Omega$$

New length $l' = 3 \ l$. New cross-sectional area $= a'$.

After drawing the volume of the wire remains same,

Volume $=$ Cross-sectional area $\times$ Length

$= a \times l = a' \times l' = a' \times 3l$

Thus we get, $a' = \dfrac{a}{3} = \dfrac{0.01 \times 10^{-2}}{3}$ cm^2

and $l' = 3l = 3 \times 100 \times 10^2$ cm

New resistance, $R' = \rho\dfrac{l'}{a'}$

$= 50 \times 10^{-6} \times \dfrac{300 \times 10^2}{\dfrac{0.01 \times 10^{-2}}{3}}$

$= 45000 \ \Omega$

1.3 CONDUCTOR, INSULATOR AND SEMICONDUCTOR

(A) Conductor : The metal in which there are 1, 2 or 3 electrons in valence shell of their atom are known as conductors of electricity. The presence of large number of free electrons makes it good conductor. Such type of materials offer very less resistance (opposition) to the flow of current. In case of good conductor, i.e. copper, there are so many electrons available at room temperature. The best conductors are silver, copper, gold etc.

(B) Insulators : Materials in which there are 5, 6 or 7 electrons in the valence shell of their atom are called as insulators, because in such materials valence electrons are tightly held to their parent atom to produce few free electrons. Such materials offer very large resistance to the flow of current, hence are called as insulators. The various insulating materials are plastic, ceramic, rubber, paper, most liquids and gases etc.

(C) Semiconductors : Semiconductors are a special class of materials which, as their name implies, are neither good conductors nor good insulators. Semiconductor elements have four valence electrons. The best known semiconductors are silicon and germanium. Basically these are insulators, but by some changes, they can act as conductors.

1.3.1 Effects of Temperature on Resistance

As we know that the temperature changes the resistance of material, but this variation of the resistance also depends on type of the material. Let us see the effects of temperature on the resistance of different materials like

(A) Pure metals, (B) Insulators, (C) Semiconductors, (D) Alloys.

(A) Pure Metals (Conductors) : The conductor has more number of free electrons. When such conductor is connected across some voltage, ions get formed inside it and the electrons which are moving randomly, will get aligned in certain direction. At low temperature ions are stationary, but as soon as temperature increases, the unmovable ions gain energy and start oscillating about their mean position. More the temperature more will be the magnitude of oscillation. This will cause obstruction to flow of free electrons; which lead to increase in resistance.

So in case of conductor, increase in temperature will increase its resistance. So the conductors have positive temperature coefficient of resistance (Fig. 1.1). e.g. Gold, Silver, Copper etc.

(B) Insulator : In insulator the number of free electrons are less. With increase in temperature, vibration of ions will increase but simultaneously the electrons from the atoms gain extra energy and made available as free electrons. This will reduce the resistance.

So in case of insulator, increase in temperature will decrease its resistance. The insulators have negative temperature coefficient of resistance (Fig. 1.1). e.g. Mica, Rubber, Plastic etc.

(C) Semiconductor : At low temperature, the resistance of semiconductor is high. But dominant increase in temperature causes a greater number of free electrons. Increased temperature gives valence electrons additional energy necessary to escape from their parent atom.

So in case of semiconductor, after certain rise in temperature the resistance drastically reduces to small value and remains constant thereafter (Fig. 1.1). e.g. Silicon, Germanium.

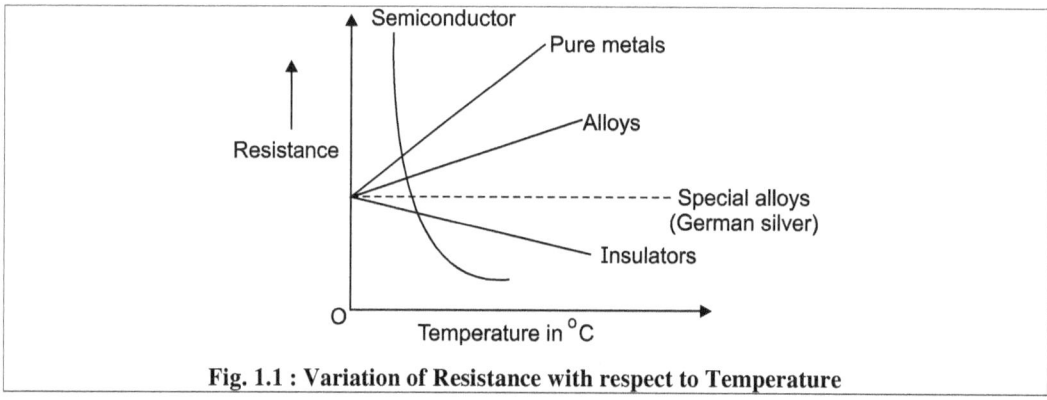

Fig. 1.1 : Variation of Resistance with respect to Temperature

(D) Alloy : The resistance of alloy increases as the temperature increases, but the rate of increase is very small and irregular. In some alloys an increase in temperature not only causes an obstruction to the electron movement but also compensates for this by increase in number of free electrons where the number of free electrons is about equal to the obstruction to the thermal energy gained. The temperature change may have little effect on resistance e.g. Manganin, Eureka show almost no change in resistance with change in temperature.

So such types of alloys are used to make resistance boxes. Alloys have positive temperature coefficient of resistance.

1.4 RESISTANCE TEMPERATURE COEFFICIENT (R.T.C.)

As discussed in previous section, resistance of different materials will change (increase, decrease or remain constant) with change in temperature.

This change in resistance depends on :

(1) Initial resistance.

(2) Change in temperature.

(3) Type and nature of material.

If R_0 - Initial resistance i.e. resistance at 0°C

R_t - final resistance i.e. resistance at t° C

Then $R_t - R_0 \propto R_0$

as well as $\qquad R_t - R_0 \propto (t - 0)$

so $\qquad R_t - R_0 \propto R_0 (t - 0)$

$$R_t - R_0 = \alpha_0 R_0 t \qquad \qquad ...(1)$$

where α_0 is constant of proportionality depends on type and nature of material.

From (1), $\qquad \qquad \alpha_0 = \dfrac{R_t - R_0}{R_0 t} \qquad \qquad ...(2)$

where α_0 = Temperature coefficient of resistance (R.T.C.) at 0°C

Definition : It is defined as the change in resistance per ohm initial resistance per degree celcius change in temperature.

Unit : $\qquad \qquad \alpha_0 = \dfrac{R_t - R_0}{R_0 t}$

$$= \dfrac{Ohm}{Ohm°C}$$

$$= \dfrac{1}{°C} \quad \text{or} \ / \ °C \text{ per degree Celsius}$$

If the initial temperature is t_1°C and final temperature is t_2°C. If R_1 and R_2 are the resistances at t_1°C and t_2°C, then,

$$R_2 - R_1 = R_1 \alpha_1 (t_2 - t_1)$$
$$R_2 = R_1 + R_1 \alpha_1 (t_2 - t_1)$$
$$= R_1 (1 + \alpha_1 (t_2 - t_1))$$
$$= R_1 (1 + \alpha_1 \Delta t)$$

where $\quad \alpha_1$ = R.T.C. at t_1°C and $\quad \Delta t = t_2 - t_1$

1.4.1 Effect of Temperature on R.T.C.

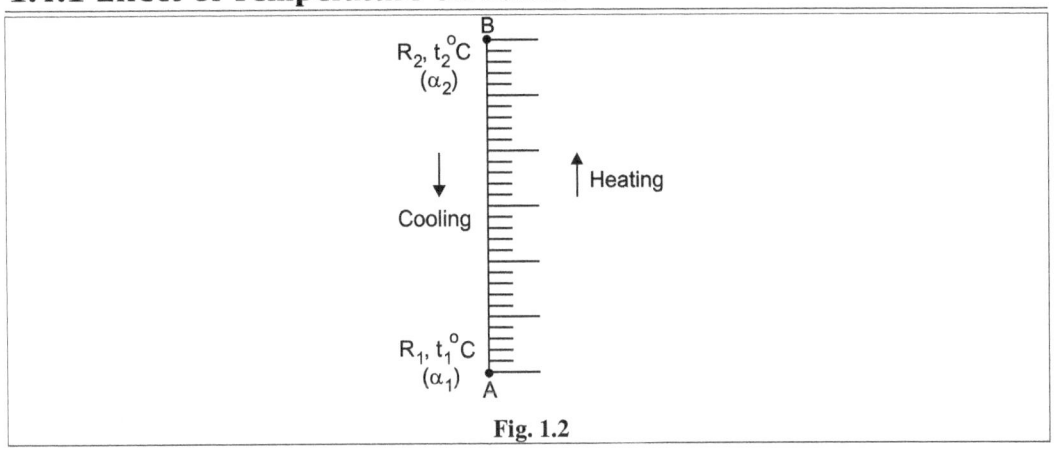

Fig. 1.2

Let us consider a conducting material whose initial resistance is R_1 at temperature $t_1°C$ i.e. at point A. Now, if the temperature of the material is gradually increased by heating process upto temperature $t_2°C$ i.e. at point B, then it's resistance will be R_2.

We can write expression as, $R_2 = R_1 \left[1 + \alpha_1 \cdot (t_2 - t_1) \right]$ ...(1)

where α_1 is R.T.C. at $t_1°C$

Now consider that, the material is having resistance R_2 at t_2 °C and if the temperature of conducting material is gradually reduced by cooling process upto initial temperature $t_1°C$ i.e. upto point A, then we can write,

$$R_1 = R_2 \left[1 + \alpha_2 \cdot (t_1 - t_2) \right]$$ ...(2)

where α_2 is R.T.C. at $t_2°C$

From equations (1) and (2), taking ratio of $\dfrac{R_1}{R_2}$

$$\frac{R_1}{R_2} = 1 + \alpha_2 (t_1 - t_2)$$

$$= \frac{1}{1 + \alpha_1(t_2 - t_1)}$$

$$\alpha_2 (t_1 - t_2) = \frac{1}{1 + \alpha_1 (t_2 - t_1)} - 1$$

$$= \frac{1 - 1 - \alpha_1 (t_2 - t_1)}{1 + \alpha_1 (t_2 - t_1)}$$

$$= \frac{-\alpha_1 (t_2 - t_1)}{1 + \alpha_1 (t_2 - t_1)}$$

Multiplying both sides by negative sign and rearranging the equation,

$$\alpha_2 (t_2 - t_1) = \frac{\alpha_1 (t_2 - t_1)}{1 + \alpha_1 (t_2 - t_1)}$$

$$\boxed{\alpha_2 = \frac{\alpha_1}{1 + \alpha_1 (t_2 - t_1)}}$$ ...(3)

If we consider $t_1 = 0°$ C and $t_2 = t°$ C , $\alpha_1 = \alpha_0$ and $\alpha_2 = \alpha_t$

then, $$\boxed{\alpha_t = \frac{\alpha_0}{1 + \alpha_0 (t - 0)} = \frac{\alpha_0}{1 + \alpha_0 t}}$$ ...(4)

From equation (3) making cross multiplication, we get

$$\alpha_2 + \alpha_1 \, \alpha_2 \cdot (t_2 - t_1) = \alpha_1$$

$$\boxed{\alpha_1 - \alpha_2 = \alpha_1 \, \alpha_2 (t_2 - t_1)}$$ ...(5)

NUMERICALS ON R.T.C.

Example 1.3 :

An aluminium conductor has resistivity of 2.6 micro-ohm-cm at 20°C and the resistance temperature co-efficient of 0.0039 per °C at 20°C. Find its resistivity and resistance temperature co-efficient at (i) 0°C, (ii) 50°C.

Solution : Given : $\rho_{20} = 2.6$ micro-ohm-cm, $\alpha_{20} = 0.0039/°C$

(1) R.T.C. at 0°C i.e. α_o

as
$$\alpha_t = \frac{\alpha_o}{1 + \alpha_o t}$$

$$\alpha_{20} = \frac{\alpha_o}{1 + \alpha_o (20)} \qquad \text{where } t = 20\ °C$$

$$0.0039 = \frac{\alpha_o}{1 + \alpha_o (20)}$$

$$\alpha_o = 0.00423/°C$$

Let resistivity at 0°C is ρ_o and resistivity at t °C is ρ_t

$$\rho_t = \rho_o (1 + \alpha_o t)$$
$$\rho_{20} = \rho_o (1 + \alpha_o (20)) \qquad \text{where } t = 20\ °C$$
$$2.6 = \rho_o (1 + (0.00423 \times 20))$$
$$\rho_o = 2.3972\ \mu\Omega\text{-cm}$$

(2) R.T.C at 50° C
$$\alpha_{50} = \frac{\alpha_o}{1 + \alpha_o (50)}$$

$$= \frac{0.00423}{1 + (0.00423 \times 50)}$$

$$= 0.003419/°C$$

Resistivity at 50° C i.e. ρ_{50}
$$\rho_{50} = \rho_o (1 + \alpha_o 50)$$

$$= 2.3972 (1 + (0.00423 \times 50)$$

$$= 2.9042\ \mu\Omega\ \text{cm}$$

Example 1.4 :

A resistance element having cross-sectional area of 10 mm² and a length of 10 m, takes a current of 4 A from a 220 V supply at an ambient temperature of 20°C. Resistance temperature coefficient at 20°C is 0.0003/°C

Find : (i) The resistivity of the material.

(ii) Current it will take when the temperature rises to 60°.

Solution : Given : $V = 220$ V, $I = 4$ A, $a = 10$ mm²

Resistance at 20°C, $R_{20} = \dfrac{V}{I} = \dfrac{220}{4} = 55\ \Omega$

$$R_{20} = \rho \times \frac{l}{a}$$

$\therefore$

$$\rho = \frac{R \times a}{l}$$

$$\text{Resistivity } \rho = \frac{55 \times 10 \times 10^{-6}}{10}$$

$$= 55 \ \mu\Omega m$$

At 60°C temperature,

$$R_{60} = R_{20} (1 + \alpha_{20} \times \text{temperature difference})$$

$$= 55 \ [1 + 0.0003 \times (60 - 20)]$$

$$= 55.66 \ \Omega$$

$$I_{60} = \frac{V}{R_{60}} = \frac{220}{55.66}$$

$$= 3.9525 \ A$$

Example 1.5 :

At 0°C, a specimen of copper wire has its resistance equal to 4mΩ and its temperature coefficient of resistance equal to (1/234.5) per 0°C. Find the values of its resistance and temperature coefficient of resistance at 70°C.

Solution : Given : Resistance at 0°C = R_0 = 4 mΩ, Temperature co-efficient of resistance at 0°C = $\alpha_0 = \dfrac{1}{234.5}$ /°C.

$$\alpha_t = \frac{\alpha_0}{1 + \alpha_0 t}$$

$\therefore$ α at 70°C

$$\alpha_{70} = \frac{\dfrac{1}{234.5}}{1 + \dfrac{1}{234.5} \times 70}$$

$$\alpha_{70} = 0.003284/°C$$

Now,

$$R_t = R_0 (1 + \alpha_0 t)$$

R at 70°C

$$R_{70} = 4 \left[1 + \frac{1}{234.5} \times 70 \right]$$

$$R_{70} = 5.194 \ m\Omega$$

Example 1.6 :

Determine the current flowing at the instant of switching a 100 watt lamp on 230 V supply. The ambient temperature is 25°C. The filament temperature is 2000°C and the resistance temperature coefficient is 0.005/°C at 0°C.

Solution : Given : P = 100 W, V = 230 V, t_1 = 25°C, t_2 = 2000 °C, α_0 = 0.005/°C

$$R_2 = \text{Resistance of filament in ON condition}$$

$$= \frac{V^2}{P} = \frac{(230)^2}{100} = 529 \ \Omega$$

$$\alpha_1 = \text{R.T.C. at } t_1 = 25°C$$

$$= \frac{\alpha_0}{1 + \alpha_0 \, t_1} = \frac{0.005}{1 + 0.005 \times 25}$$

$$\alpha_1 = 4.44 \times 10^{-3}/°C$$

Now, $$R_2 = R_1 (1 + \alpha_1 \, \Delta t)$$

∴ $$529 = R_1 [1 + 4.44 \times 10^{-3} \times (2000 - 25)]$$

∴ $$R_1 = 54.15 \ \Omega$$

$$I = \text{Current at the instant of switching}$$

$$I_{25} = \frac{V}{R_1} = \frac{230}{54.15} = 4.25 \ A$$

Example 1.7 :

The filament of 240 V of metal filament lamp is to be constructed from a wire having a diameter of 0.03 mm and a resistivity of 4.3 μΩcm. If the RTC of the filament material is 0.005/°C at 20°C, what length of the filament is necessary for the lamp to dissipate 60 watt at a filament temperature of 2420°C. Assume room temperature as 20°C.

Solution : V = 240 V, d = 0.03 m, ρ = 4.3 μΩ cm, α_{20} = 0.005/°C, t_1 = 20°C, t_2 = 2420 °C

R at 2420°C = $R_{2420;}$ $$R_{2420} = \frac{V^2}{P} = \frac{240^2}{60} = 960 \ \Omega$$

$$R_2 = R_1 (1 + \alpha_1 (t_2 - t_1))$$

$$R_{2420} = R_{20} [1 + \alpha_{20} (2420 - 20)]$$

$$960 = R_{20} [1 + 0.005 (2400)]$$

$$R_{20} = \frac{960}{1 + 0.005 \times 2000}$$

$$= 73.84 \ \Omega$$

$$R_{20} = \rho \frac{l}{a} = \frac{4.3 \times 10^{-6} \times 10^{-2} \times l}{\pi \, d^2/4}$$

$$l = 73.84 \times \pi \times \frac{(0.03 \times 10^{-3})^2}{4} / \, 4.3 \times 10^{-8}$$

$$= 1.21 \text{ m or } 121.25 \text{ cm}.$$

Example 1.8 :

A certain copper winding has a resistance of 100 Ω at room temperature. If resistance temperature coefficient of copper at 0°C is 0.00428/°C, calculate the winding resistance if temperature is increased to 50°C. Assume room temperature as 25°C.

Solution : Given: t_1 = 25°C, R_1 = 100 Ω, t_2 = 50°C, α_0 = 0.00428/°C

Now,
$$\alpha_t = \frac{\alpha_0}{1 + \alpha_0 t}$$

∴
$$\alpha_1 = \frac{\alpha_0}{1 + \alpha_0 t_1} = \frac{0.00428}{1 + 0.00428 \times 25}$$
$$= 0.003866/^\circ C$$

Use
$$R_2 = R_1 [1 + \alpha_1 (t_2 - t_1)]$$
$$= 100 [1 + 0.003866 (50 - 25)]$$
$$= 109.6657 \ \Omega \qquad \ldots \text{Resistance at } 50^\circ C$$

1.5 SOME IMPORTANT CONVERSIONS

1. Current   1 milli Amp (1 mA) $= 1 \times 10^{-3}$ Amp.
2.   1 micro Amp (1 μA) $= 1 \times 10^{-6}$ Amp.
3. Voltage   1 milli volts (1 mV) $= 1 \times 10^{-3}$ volt
4. Resistance   1 milli ohm (1 mΩ) $= 1 \times 10^{-3}\Omega$
5.   1 mega ohm (1 MΩ) $= 1 \times 10^{6} \ \Omega$
6. Power   1 kilo watt (1 kW) $= 1 \times 10^{3}$ watts
7.   1 Horse power (1 HP) $= 746$ watt
8. Length (l)   1 mm $= 1 \times 10^{-2}$ cm or 1×10^{-3} m
9.   100 cm $= 1$ metre (1 m)
10.   1000 mm $= 1$ m
11. Area (a)   1 mm^2 $= 1 \times 10^{-6}$ m^2
12.   1 cm^2 $= 1 \times 10^{-4}$ m^2
13. Energy   (1 kJ) $= 1 \times 10^{3}$ joule
14.   (1MJ) $= 1 \times 10^{6}$ joule
15.   1 calorie $= 4.1869$ joule
16.   1 kWh $= 860$ kcal $= 1$ unit $= 36 \times 10^{5}$ joule
17.   1 tonne $= 1000$ kg
18.   1 cubic metre (1 m^3) $= 1$ tonne $= 1000$ kg
19.   1 cm^3 $= 1$ gm
20.   1 kg mass of water $= 1$ litre (1 ltr.)
21.   Boiling temperature of water $= 100^\circ C$

1.6 WORK, POWER, ENERGY

Study of Three Important Systems :

(1) Thermal System,

(2) Mechanical System,

(3) Electrical System.

1.6.1 Thermal System

This system relates with the production of heat.

(1) Calorie : It is the thermal unit of energy. A calorie is the amount of heat energy required to raise the temperature of 1 gm of water through 1°C. The thermal energy is measured in calories. The relation between calorie and joule is

1 calorie = 4.1869 joules

Important Terms involved in Thermal System :

(2) Heat Capacity : The amount of heat required to produce a given temperature rise in a given mass of the material.

$$\text{Heat capacity} = \frac{Q}{T_2 - T_1}$$

where, Q = Heat supplied in joules

$T_2 - T_1$ = Change in temperature in K

Unit of heat capacity = J/K

(3) Specific Heat : It is defined as the heat capacity of a body per unit mass.

$$\therefore \qquad \text{Specific heat (s)} = \frac{Q}{m\,(T_2 - T_1)}$$

The unit of specific heat (s) is J/kg K. Specific heat for certain materials is as follows.

Sr. No.	Material	Sp. heat in J/kg K
1.	Water	4186
2.	Iron	500
3.	Aluminium	950
4.	Copper	390

(4) Sensible Heat : The amount of heat gained or lost due to change in temperature, without change in the form of substance.

$$\text{Sensible heat} = \text{Mass} \times \text{Specific heat} \times \text{Change in temperature}$$

$\therefore$ $\quad\quad\quad\quad\quad\quad\quad\quad H = \text{m.s. } (T_2 - T_1)$

$\therefore$ $\quad\quad\quad\quad\quad\quad\quad\quad H = \text{m.s. } \Delta t \text{ joule}$

This change in temperature can be sensed, so it is called as sensible heat.

(5) Latent Heat : It is defined as the amount of heat energy required to change the form of the substance. The heat is not sensed by the body, in terms of temperature rise, hence it is called as latent heat.

(a) Latent heat of fusion or liquification : It is the heat required to convert a body from solid state to liquid state.

(b) Latent heat of vaporisation : It is the heat required to convert liquid state to gaseous state.

$\therefore$ $\quad\quad\quad\quad\quad\quad \text{Latent heat} = \text{m} \times \text{L}$

where, $\quad\quad\quad\quad\quad\quad\quad\quad \text{m} = \text{Mass in kg}$

$\quad\quad\quad\quad\quad\quad\quad\quad\quad\quad L = \text{Latent heat or specific enthalpy in J/kg.}$

$\quad\quad\quad\quad \text{So total heat} = \text{Sensible heat} + \text{Latent heat}$

Calorific Values : Heat is produced by burning the fuels such as coal, petrol, diesel etc. For such fuels, the calorific value is specified. It is defined as the amount of heat energy produced in joules by burning the unit mass of the fuel. It is measured in J/kg.

$\therefore$ $\quad\quad\quad \text{Heat energy produced (J)} = \text{Mass in (kg)} \times \text{Calorific value (J/kg)}$

Water Equivalent of a Container : While heating any liquid (generally water), its container is also heated. This is wastage of heat. To take into account this wastage of heat, the container body is assumed to be equivalent to some quantity of water, which is called as water equivalent of the container.

In short, additional mass of water is considered along with the actual mass of water to be heated; if water equivalent of container is mentioned.

Radiation Loss : The heat energy escaping to the surroundings due to radiation is called radiation loss. It is measured in joules (J).

Practical Examples of Thermal System :

(1) Immersion water heater or Geyser, (2) Furnace, (3) Thermal power plant

1.6.2 Key Points for Solving Numericals on "Thermal System"

Case I : If certain mass of water is to be heated from T_1 to T_2 and efficiency of system is given.

Then, calculate output (heat) energy $= \text{m} \times \text{s} \times (T_2 - T_1)$

$$\text{Input energy} = \frac{\text{Output heat energy}}{\text{Efficiency}}$$

Case II : If certain mass of water is to be heated from T_1 to T_2 and water equivalent of container is given and efficiency of system is given.

Then, First calculate total mass (m) = $\dfrac{\text{Actual mass}}{\text{of water}} + \dfrac{\text{Water equivalent of}}{\text{container mass}}$

Calculate, Output (heat) energy = Total mass (m) $\times$ s $\times$ ($T_2 - T_1$)

$$\text{Input energy} = \frac{\text{Output heat energy}}{\text{Efficiency}}$$

Case III : If mass of water is to be evaporated and efficiency of system is given. Then,

First calculate output heat energy required (H_1) = msΔt

Also calculate, Latent heat energy required (H_2) = m $\times$ L

So,   Total output heat energy required = $H_1 + H_2$

Then, calculate input energy required = $\dfrac{\text{Total output heat energy}}{\text{Efficiency of system}}$

Case IV : If mass of a water is evaporated and if water equivalent of container is given and also efficiency of system is given.

Then, first to calculate output heat energy required.

Total mass = Mass of actual water + Water equivalent mass

Output heat energy required (H_1) = m $\times$ s $\times$ Δt

Then,   latent heat energy required = Actual mass of water (m) $\times$ L

Total output heat energy required = $H_1 + H_2$

so, Input heat energy required = $\dfrac{\text{Total output heat required}}{\text{Efficiency}}$

Case V: If a certain mass of ice is to be evaporated and efficiency of system is given then,

Step I : $\dfrac{\text{Output heat energy required}}{\text{to convert ice (solid state)}}$ = m $\times$ Latent heat of liquification
into water (liquid state) (H_1)

Step II : $\dfrac{\text{Output heat energy required}}{\text{to boil the water } (H_2)}$ = m $\cdot$ s $\cdot$ Δt

Step III : $\dfrac{\text{Output heat energy required}}{\text{to evaporate the water } (H_3)}$ = m $\times$ Latent heat of fusion

Now, calculate total output heat energy required (H) = $H_1 + H_2 + H_3$

Then calculate input heat energy required = $\dfrac{\text{Total output heat energy}}{\text{Efficiency}}$

SOLVED EXAMPLES

Example 1.9 :

An immersion heater supplied at 250 V D.C. is placed in a bucket containing 5 litres of water. The temperature of water goes up by 50°C in 20 min. The water equivalent of the bucket is 500 g. Calculate the heater resistance. Specific heat of water is 4180 J/kg K and heat lost due to radiation is negligible.

Solution : Given : V = 250 V, Specific heat of water = 4180 J/kg K, Water equivalent of the bucket = 500 gm, $(t_2 - t_1)$ = 50

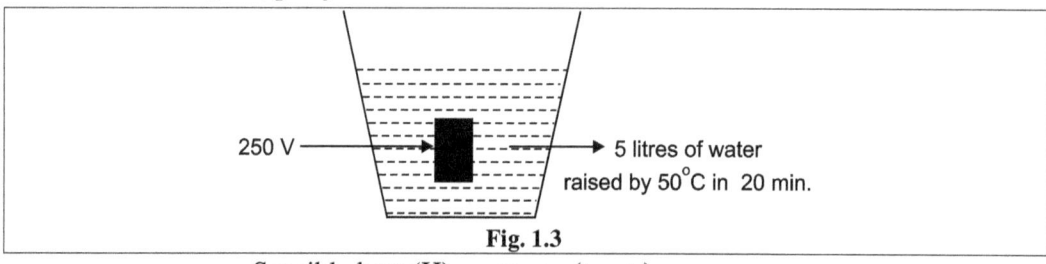

Fig. 1.3

$$\text{Sensible heat (H)} = \text{m . s . } (t_2 - t_1)$$

$$\text{Total Output energy} = (5 + 0.5) \times 4180 \times 50$$

$$= 1149500 \text{ J}$$

$$= \text{Input energy (as radiation losses are absent)}$$

$$\text{Input power} = \frac{\text{Sensible heat}}{\text{Time}} = \frac{1149500}{20 \times 60} = 957.916 \text{ W}$$

If R is the heater resistance, $\dfrac{250^2}{R} = 957.916$ (as P = $\dfrac{V^2}{R}$)

∴   R = 65.246 Ω.

Example 1.10 :

An electric kettle supplied from 230 V D.C. supply is required to heat 0.5 kg of water from 20°C to boiling point in 5 minutes. If the efficiency of the kettle is 80%, calculate the resistance of the heating element of the kettle. The specific heat of water is 4180 J/kg K.

Solution : Given : V = 230 V, Specific heat of water = 4180 J/kgK,

Efficiency of kettle = η = 80%.

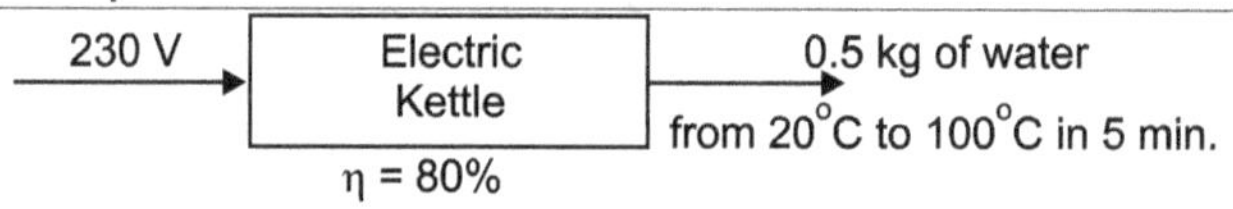

```
                  230 V    ┌──────────┐    0.5 kg of water
                      ─────▶│ Electric │─────▶
                            │  Kettle  │  from 20°C to 100°C in 5 min.
                            └──────────┘
                              η = 80%
```

Fig. 1.4

$$\text{Output energy of the kettle} = ms\Delta t = 0.5 (100 - 20) \times 4180 = 167200 \text{ J}$$

$$\text{Input to the kettle} = \frac{\text{Output energy}}{\eta} = \frac{167200}{0.8} = 209000 \text{ J}$$

$$\text{Input power} = \frac{\text{Input energy}}{t} = \frac{209000}{5 \times 60} = 696.67 \text{ W}$$

If R is the resistance of heater element

$$P = 696.67 = V^2 / R = \frac{230^2}{R}$$

∴   R = 75.93 Ω

Example 1.11 :

An electric geyser is used to heat 5 litres of water from 13°C to 83°C. Heat lost to atmosphere in radiation is 40 kJ and water equivalent of the geyser is 100 gm. Determine geyser efficiency. Specific heat of water is 4200 J/kg-K.

Solution : Given : $t_1 = 13°C$, $t_2 = 83°C$, Heat lost = 40 kJ, m = 5 litres = 5 kg, Specific heat of water = 4200 J/kg-K, $m_2 = 100$ gm

$$\text{Useful output energy} = m_1 s \Delta t = 5 \times 4200 \times (83 - 13) \text{ J}$$
$$= 1470000 \text{ J}$$

$$\text{Loss of heat in the container} = m_2 s \Delta t = \frac{100}{1000} \times 4200 \times (83 - 13) = 29400 \text{ J}$$

$$\text{Loss of heat due to radiation} = 40 \times 1000 \text{ J} = 40000 \text{ J}$$

$$\text{Efficiency} = \frac{\text{Output energy}}{\text{Input energy}}$$

$$= \frac{1470000}{1470000 + 29400 + 40000} \times 100 = 95.5\%$$

Example 1.12 :

A bucket contains 15 litres of water at 20°C. A 2 kW immersion heater is used to raise the temperature of water to 95°C. The overall efficiency of the process is 90% and the specific heat capacity of water is 4187 J/kg K. Find the time required for the process.

Solution : Given : m = 15 kg (1 litre = 1 kg),

Specific heat capacity of water (s) = 4187 J/kg K, $t_1 = 20°C$, $t_2 = 95°C$,

Input power = P_{in} = 2 kW, efficiency = η = 90%.

Energy required to heat the water is the output energy.

$\therefore$

$$\text{Output energy} = m s \Delta t$$
$$= 15 \times 4187 \times (95 - 20)$$
$$= 4.7103 \times 10^6 \text{ J}$$

$$\text{Input energy} = \frac{\text{Output}}{\eta}$$

$$= \frac{4.7103 \times 10^6}{0.9} = 5.2337 \times 10^6 \text{ J}$$

$$P_{in} = \frac{\text{Input in J}}{\text{Time in sec.}}$$

$\therefore$

$$2 \times 10^3 = \frac{5.2337 \times 10^6}{\text{Time}}$$

$\therefore$

$$\text{Time} = 2616.875 \text{ sec.} = 43.614 \text{ minutes}$$

Example 1.13 :

An electric furnace is used to melt aluminium. Initial temperature of the solid aluminium is 32°C and its melting point is 680°C. Specific heat capacity of aluminium is

0.95 kJ/kg.K and the heat required to melt 1 kg of aluminium at its melting point is 450 kJ. If the input power drawn by the furnace is 20 kW and its overall efficiency is 60%, find the mass of aluminium melted per hour.

Solution : Given : $t_1 = 32°C$, $t_2 = 680°C$, Specific heat capacity of aluminium(s) = 0.95 kJ/kg K, $P_{in} = 20$ kW, efficiency = 60% = 0.6, Latent heat (L) = 450 kJ/kg

Heat required to melt 1 kg of aluminium at melting point is 450 kJ is the information related to latent heat.

$$\text{Total heat} = \text{Sensible heat} + \text{Latent heat}$$
$$= m \, s \, \Delta t + mL$$
$$\therefore \quad \text{Total output energy} = m \, [s \, \Delta t + L]$$
$$= m \, [0.95 \times (680 - 32) + 450]$$
$$= m \times 1.0656 \times 10^3 \text{ kJ}$$
$$P_{in} = 20 \text{ kW}$$

and time = 1 hour (as mass of Al melted per hour is to be obtained)

$\therefore$ Input energy = $P_{in} \times$ time = $20 \times 10^3 \times 3600 = 72 \times 10^6$ J

$\therefore$ Output energy = input $\times \eta = 72 \times 10^6 \times 0.6 = 43.2 \times 10^6$ J $= 43.2 \times 10^3$ kJ

Equating with total output energy required,
$$m \times 1.0656 \times 10^3 = 43.2 \times 10^3$$
$$m = 40.5405 \text{ kg}$$

Example 1.14 :

In a thermal generating station, the heat energy obtained by burning 1 kg of coal is 16,000 kJ. Find the mass of coal required to get an output electrical energy of 1 kWh from the station, if its overall efficiency is 18%.

Solution : Given : m = 1 kg, Heat energy = 16000 kJ, Output = 1 kWh, efficiency = η = 18%.

$$\text{Calorific value of coal} = 16000 \text{ kJ/kg.}$$
$$\text{Total input energy} = m \times 16000 \times 10^3 \text{ J} \qquad \ldots(i)$$
$$m = \text{mass of coal burned}$$
$$\text{Output required} = 1 \text{ kWh} = 1 \times 10^3 \text{ Wh}$$
$$= 1 \times 10^3 \times 3600 \text{ W sec. i.e. J}$$
$$\text{Input required} = \frac{\text{Output energy}}{\eta} \text{ in J.}$$
$$= \frac{1 \times 10^3 \times 3600}{0.18}$$
$$= 20 \times 10^6 \text{ J} \qquad \ldots(ii)$$

Equating (i) and (ii),
$$\therefore \qquad m \times 16000 \times 10^3 = 20 \times 10^6$$
$$\text{Mass of coal required, m} = 1.25 \text{ kg}$$

1.6.3 Mechanical System

Basic terms related with mechanical system are :

(a) Mass (m) : The matter possessed by a body. The unit of mass is kg.

(b) Velocity (v) : Rate of change of displacement is called velocity. The unit of velocity is metre/sec i.e. m/s.

(c) Acceleration (a) : Rate of change of velocity is called acceleration. The unit of acceleration is m/s^2.

(d) Force (F) : It is the push or pull required to change the state of rest or uniform motion of body.

$$\text{Force (F)} = \text{Mass} \times \text{Acceleration}$$

$$\boxed{F = m \times a}$$

The unit of force is Newton (N).

(e) Weight (W) : It is the product of mass and gravitational acceleration.

$$\text{Weight (W)} = m \times g$$
$$g = 9.81 \ m/s^2$$

(f) Torque (T) : It is the product of force and perpendicular distance between the line of action of force and the axis of rotation.

∴ $$\text{Torque (T)} = \text{Force (F)} \times \text{Radial distance (r)}$$

∴ $$\boxed{T = F \times r}$$

The unit of torque is Newton metre i.e. N-m.

(g) Mechanical Work Done (W) : When a force (F) acts on a body, then it moves through a certain distance which is called as mechanical work done.

∴ $$\boxed{\text{Work (W)} = \text{Force (F)} \times \text{Displacement (d)}}$$

The unit of work done is (N-m) or Joules (J).

(h) Power (P) : Rate of doing work is called power.

∴ $$\boxed{\text{Power (P)} = \frac{\text{Work done}}{\text{Time}}}$$

Unit of power (P) is watt (W), $1 \ watt = 1 \ J/s = 1 \dfrac{N\text{-}m}{s}$

(i) Energy (E) : Capacity to do the work is called as energy.

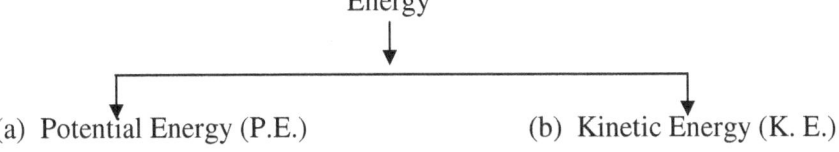

   (a) Potential Energy (P.E.)   (b) Kinetic Energy (K. E.)

(a) Potential energy (P.E.) : It is the energy possessed by a body due to its position.

$$\boxed{\text{P.E.} = \text{m.g.h. i.e. } W \times h} \ \text{Joule}$$

(b) Kinetic energy (K.E.) : It is the energy possessed by a body due to its motion.

$$\boxed{\text{K.E.} = \frac{1}{2}\, m\, v^2}\ \text{Joule}$$

Also, $\boxed{\text{Energy (E)} = \text{Power} \times \text{Time} = \text{Work done}}$

The unit of energy (E) is Joule (J).

Relation between Power and Torque :

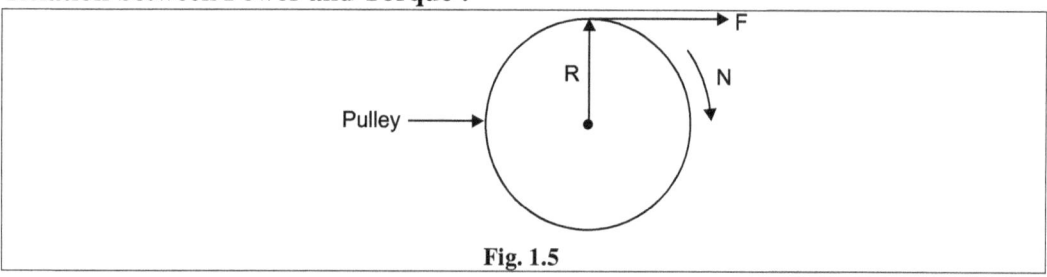

Fig. 1.5

Consider a pulley with radius R and is free to rotate. If 'F' is the force applied, then,

$$\text{Torque (T)} = F \times R$$

Let, the pulley rotate at 'N' revolution per minute. Hence, work done in one revolution is,

$$W = \text{Force} \times \text{Distance travelled}$$
$$= F \times 2\pi R$$

where, $2\pi R$ is pulley circumference. The time required for one revolution is $\frac{60}{N}$ seconds.

∴ $\text{Power (P)} = \dfrac{\text{Work done (W)}}{\text{Time (t)}}$

∴ $P = \dfrac{F \times 2\pi R}{60/N}$

∴ $P = (F \times R) \cdot \dfrac{(2\pi N)}{60}$

∴ $\boxed{P = T \cdot \omega}\ \text{watt}$

where, $T = \text{Torque}$

                  $\omega = \text{Angular velocity, rad/sec.}$

Practical Examples of Mechanical System:

(1) Work done by motor pump set in lifting the water.

(2) Upward and downward journey of lift or cage.

(3) Motion of train/car on horizontal and inclined plane.

1.6.4   Key Points for Solving Numericals on Mechanical System

(A) **Motor–Pump Set : Case I :** Water is to be lifted from tube well and if overall efficiency of system is given.

First calculate output work done by pump = m.g.h. (J)

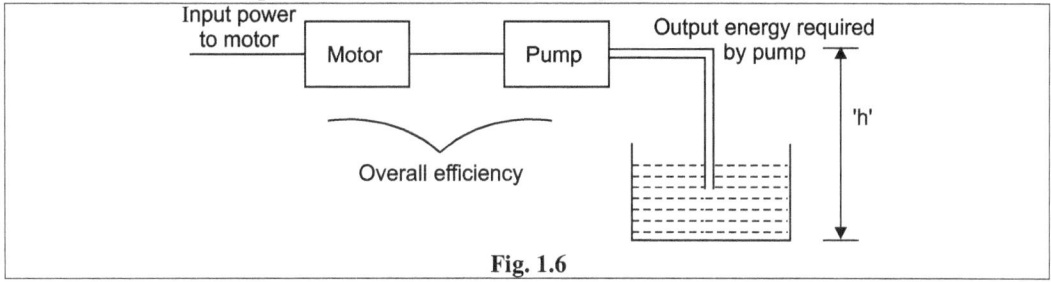

Fig. 1.6

$$\text{Output power of pump} = \frac{\text{Output energy i.e. work done}}{\text{Time}}$$

$$P = \frac{m.g.h.}{t}$$

Then, calculate input power required by motor,

∴ $\text{Input power to motor} = \dfrac{\text{Output power}}{\text{Overall efficiency}}$ …(I)

Use, $\text{Power (P)} = V \times I$ …(II)

Equating equations (I) and (II), we can calculate current taken by the motor.

Case II : If water is to be lifted and the efficiencies of pump and motor are mentioned separately, then,

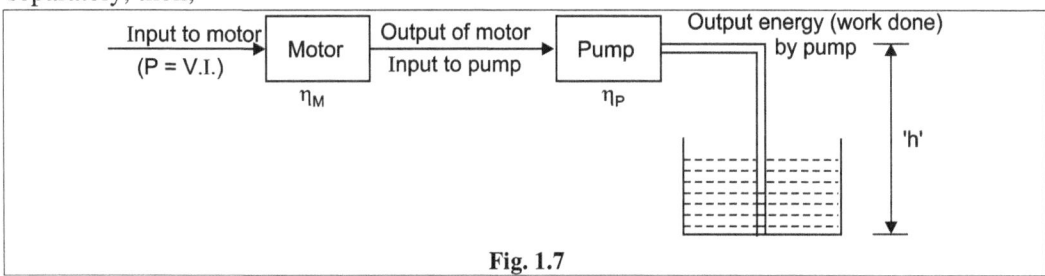

Fig. 1.7

First calculate,

Output energy (work done) by pump = m.g.h

$$\text{Output power of pump} = \frac{\text{Output work done (J)}}{\text{Time (sec.)}}$$

$$\text{Input power to pump} = \frac{\text{Output power of pump}}{\eta_p} = \text{output power of motor,}$$

where, η_p = Efficiency of pump

so, $\text{Input power required by motor} = \dfrac{\text{Output power of motor}}{\eta_m}$ …(I) where, η_m = Efficiency of motor

Input electrical power to motor = $V \times I$ ...(II)

Equating equations (I) and (II), we can calculate current taken by motor.

Case III : If water is to be lifted and efficiencies of pump and motor are given separately and friction loss in pipeline is given.

Note : Frictional loss is mentioned as either loss of water head (i.e. height) or sometimes percentage of water head.

We have to consider the additional height, that is why more work is done by pump.

Total height through which water is lifted = Actual height in 'm' + Loss of water head in 'm'.

Remaining calculations are as per case II.

(B) Upward and Downward Journey of lift or cage :

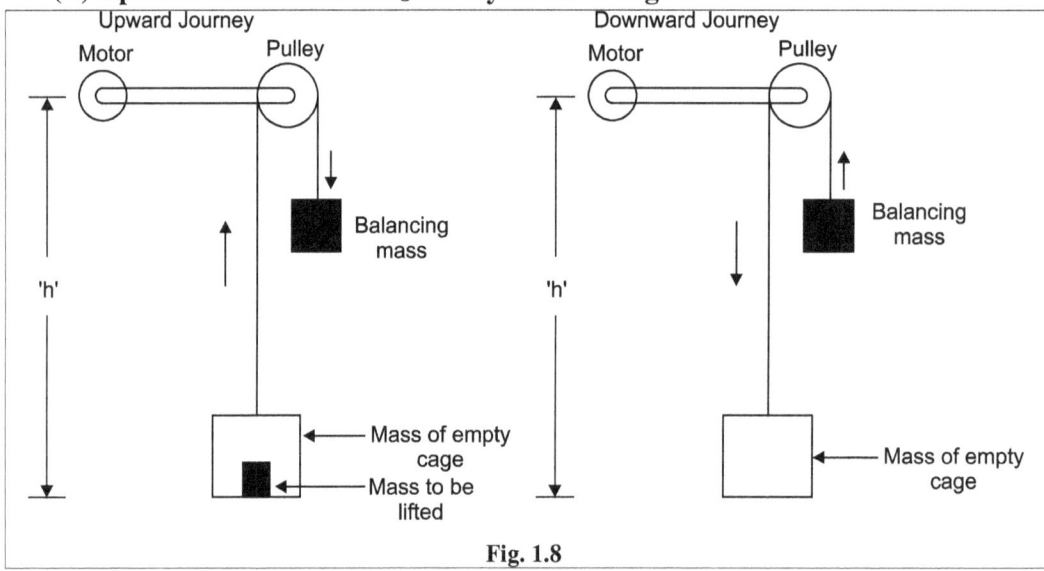

Fig. 1.8

Net mass lifted upwards during upward journey,

m = Mass of empty cage + Actual mass to be lifted – Balancing mass

Calculate output energy during the upward journey,

$$E_1 = m.g.h.$$ ...(I)

Then downward journey,

Net mass coming down = Balancing mass – Mass of empty cage

E_2 i.e. output energy during downward journey,

$$E_2 = m.g.h.$$ ...(II)

$$\text{Total output energy} = E_1 + E_2$$

$$\text{Total input energy} = \frac{\text{Total output energy}}{\text{Efficiency of system } (\eta)}$$

To calculate power rating of motor,

Then   Power input to motor during up journey (P_{up}) $= \dfrac{E_1}{Time_{(up)} \times \eta}$

Similarly, calculate,

Power input to motor during down journey (P_D) $= \dfrac{E_2}{Time_{(down)} \times \eta}$

Note : When power rating of motor is to be calculated then the power required during upward journey (P_{up}) has to be considered as motor does more work while going upwards.

1.6.5   Motion of Train / Car on Horizontal and Inclined Plane

Horizontal Plane	Inclined Plane

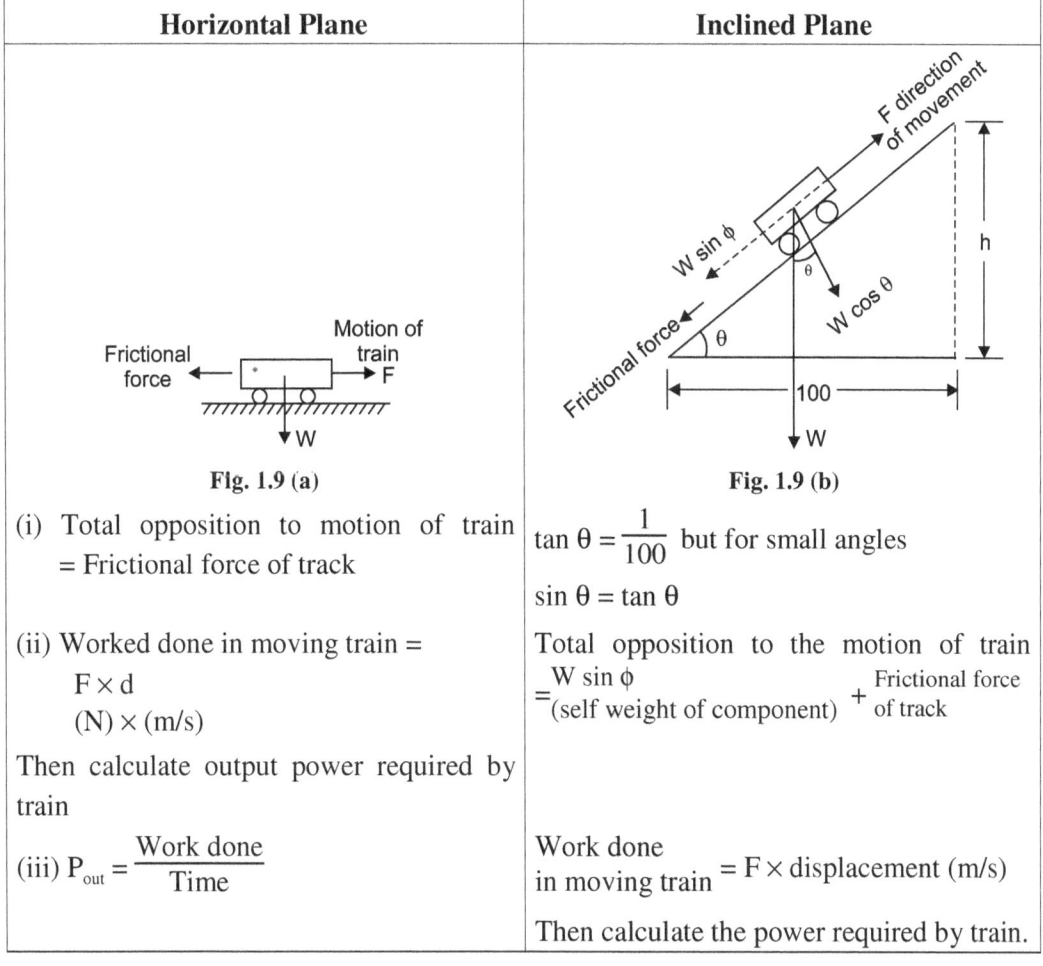

Fig. 1.9 (a)	Fig. 1.9 (b)

(i) Total opposition to motion of train = Frictional force of track

$\tan \theta = \dfrac{1}{100}$ but for small angles

$\sin \theta = \tan \theta$

(ii) Worked done in moving train =

    $F \times d$

    $(N) \times (m/s)$

Then calculate output power required by train

Total opposition to the motion of train

$= \dfrac{W \sin \phi}{(self\ weight\ of\ component)} + \dfrac{Frictional\ force}{of\ track}$

(iii) $P_{out} = \dfrac{Work\ done}{Time}$

Work done in moving train $= F \times$ displacement (m/s)

Then calculate the power required by train.

Horizontal Plane	Inclined Plane
(iv) $P_{in} = \dfrac{P_{out}}{\eta \text{ (efficiency)}}$ (v) P_{in} for electrical motor $= V \times I$ So $\qquad I = \dfrac{P_{in}}{V}$	$P_{out} = \dfrac{\text{Work done}}{\text{Time}}$ $P_{in} = \dfrac{P_{out}}{\eta}$ P_{in} for electrical motor $= V \times I$ So $\qquad I = \dfrac{P_{in}}{V}$

Example 1.15 :

Find the current and energy input to a crane driving motor when raising a load of 1 tonne through a height of 16 m in 10 sec. Motor efficiency is 85% and crane efficiency is 60% . Supply voltage is 400 V D.C.

Solution : Given : Motor efficiency = 85%, Crane efficiency = 60%, V = 400 V, h = 16 m, t = 10 sec.

$$\text{Output energy} = mgh = 1000 \times 9.81 \times 16 \text{ N-m}$$

$$\text{Input energy} = \frac{\text{Output energy}}{\eta_{crane} \times \eta_{motor}} = \frac{1000 \times 9.81 \times 16}{0.6 \times 0.85}$$

$$= 307764.7 \text{ W.sec.} = 0.0855 \text{ kWh}$$

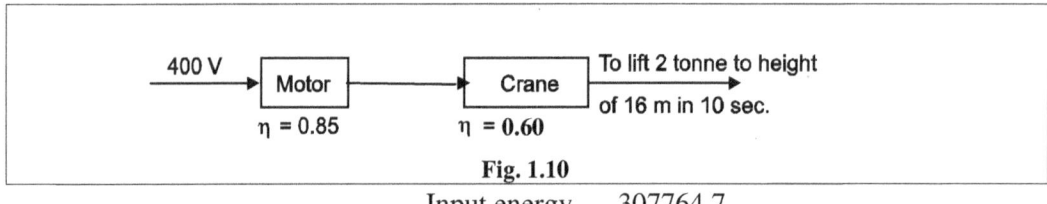

Fig. 1.10

$$\text{Input current} = \frac{\text{Input energy}}{t \times \text{voltage}} = \frac{307764.7}{10 \times 400} = 76.94 \text{ A}$$

Example 1.16 :

A 500 V D.C. motor drives a pump to lift 14 cubic meter of water to a height of 27 m in one min. Motor efficiency is 90% and pump efficiency is 75%. Allow a height of 3 m for pipe friction. Determine motor current.

Solution : Given : V = 500 V, h = 27 m, η = 90%, η_p = 75%, h_1 = 3m

Remembering that 1 m^3 water has mass of 1 tonne i.e. 1m^3 = 1000 kg.

$$\text{Output energy} = mg (h + h_1)$$

$$= 14 \times 1000 \times 9.81 \times (27 + 3)$$

$$= 4120200 \text{ J}$$

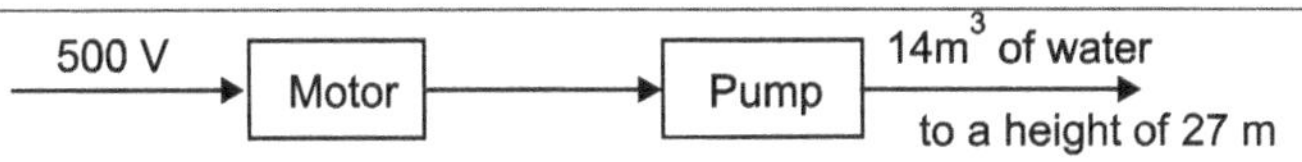

500 V → Motor → Pump → 14m³ of water to a height of 27 m

Fig. 1.11

$$\text{Input energy} = \frac{\text{Output energy}}{\eta_m \times \eta_p} = \frac{4120200}{0.9 \times 0.75}$$

$$= 6104000 \text{ J}$$

$$\text{Motor current} = \frac{\text{Output energy}}{V \times t} = \frac{6104000}{500 \times 60} = 203.46 \text{ A}$$

Example 1.17 :

A water tank 1 m × 1 m × 1 m is filled to its 85% capacity five times daily. The water is heated from 20°C to 65°C. Loss of heat takes place throughout the day due to radiation at an average rate of 300 W per sq. m of tank surface. Find electrical loading of the tank and its efficiency. Electrical power input to a device is known as its electrical loading.

Solution : Given : $t_1 = 20°C$, $t_2 = 65°C$, Loss of heat = 300 W per sq. m., $1m^3 = 1000kg$

$$\text{Output energy/day} = ms\Delta t \times 5$$

$$= 1000 \times 0.85 \times 4180 \times (65-25) \times 5$$

$$= 799.42 \text{ MJ}$$

$$\text{Output power} = \frac{\text{Output energy}}{\text{time}}$$

$$= \frac{799.42 \times 10^6}{24 \times 3600 \times 1000} = 9.2526 \text{ kW}$$

The tank has six surfaces and loss of power due to radiations from each surface is 300 W. Thus, total loss is 1800 W = 1.8 kW.

$$\text{Power input i.e. electric loading} = 9.2526 + 1.8$$

$$= 11.0526 \text{ kW}$$

$$\text{Efficiency} = \frac{\text{Output}}{\text{Input}} = \frac{9.2526}{11.0526} \times 100 = 83.71\%$$

Example 1.18 :

An electric motor is driving a train weighing 100 thousand kilograms upon an inclined track of 1 in 100 at a speed of 60 km/h. The frictional force of tracks is 10 kg per 1000 kg of its weight. If the motor operates on 11 kV, find the current taken by the motor assuming the overall efficiency of the system as 70%.

Solution : Given : $\eta = 70\%$, V = 11 kV.

Force trying to pull the train downward is W sin θ

$$= 100 \times 1000 \times 9.81 \times \frac{1}{100} = 9810 \text{ N}$$

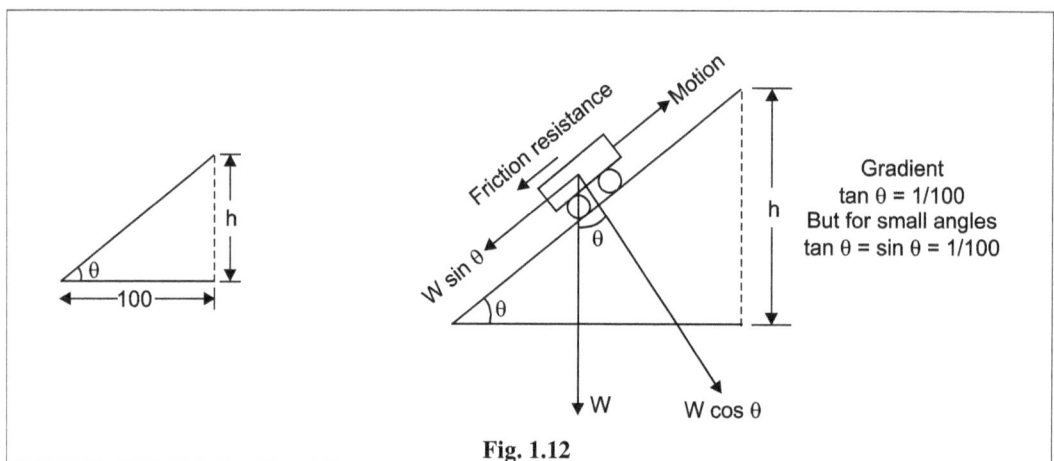

Fig. 1.12

$$\text{Frictional force} = 10 \times 9.81 \times 100$$

$$= 9810 \text{ N}$$

$$\text{Total opposing force} = 9810 + 9810$$

$$= 19620 \text{ N}$$

Work done against this force at a speed of 60 km/hr. $= \dfrac{60 \times 1000}{3600}$ m/sec. is

$$= \text{force} \times \text{distance/sec} = 19620 \times 60 \times \dfrac{1000}{3600}$$

$$= 327000 \text{ J/s or watts} = 327 \text{ kW}$$

$$= \text{Output power}$$

$$\text{Input power} = \dfrac{\text{Output power}}{\eta} = \dfrac{327}{0.7}$$

$$= 467.1428 \text{ kW}$$

But, $\text{Input} = V \times I$

$\therefore$ $I = \dfrac{467.1428 \times 1000}{11 \times 1000} = 42.467 \text{ A}$

Example 1.19 :

An electric lift raises a load of 5 tonnes to a height of 50 m while going upwards and returns empty. A balance weight is of 3 tonnes and weight of empty cage is 500 kg. The time taken by either up and down journey is 1 minute. Calculate the current taken by the lift, when it operates on 220 volt. Also calculate daily cost of energy at a rate of ₹ 2.35/- per unit if lift makes 100 double journeys in a day and H.P. rating of lift motor. (Assume efficiency of installation as 60%)

Solution: Given: V=220 volt, $\eta = 60\%$

Net mass lifted upwards during upward journey,

m_1 = Mass of empty cage + Actual mass to be lifted − Balancing mass

  = 500 + 5000 − 3000 = 2500 kg

Output energy during the upward journey,

$$E_1 = m_1.g.h. \qquad \qquad ...(I)$$

$$= 2500 \times 9.81 \times 50 = 1226250 \text{ J}$$

Then for downward journey,

  Net mass coming down; m_2 = Balancing mass − Mass of empty cage

  = 3000 − 500 = 2500 kg

Output energy during downward journey,

$$E_2 = m.g.h. \qquad \qquad ...(II)$$

$$= 2500 \times 9.81 \times 50 = 1226250 \text{ J}$$

$$\text{Total output energy} = E_1 + E_2 = 1226250 + 1226250$$

$$= 2452500 \text{ J}$$

$$\text{Total input energy} = \frac{\text{Total output energy}}{\text{Efficiency of system } (\eta)}$$

$$= \frac{2452500}{0.6} = 4087500 \text{ J}$$

$$\text{Input power} = \frac{\text{input energy for upward journey}}{\text{time for upward journey}} = \frac{2452500}{60} = 34062.5 \text{ Watt}$$

$$\text{Motor current} = \frac{\text{Total input power}}{\text{voltage}} = \frac{34062}{220} = 154.82 \text{ Amp}$$

Lift makes 100 double journeys means it works for 200 minutes in a day

$$\text{Energy consumption per day in kWh} = 34.0625 \times \frac{200}{60} = 113.54 \text{ kWh}$$

To calculate power rating of motor,

Then   Power output of motor during up journey (P_{up}) = $\dfrac{\text{ouput energy during upward journey}}{\text{Time}_{(up)}}$

$$= \frac{1226250}{60} = 20437.5 \text{ watt}$$

$$\text{H.P. rating of motor} = \frac{\text{output power}}{746} = \frac{20437.5}{746} = 27.4 \text{ H.P}$$

Example 1.20 :

An electric pump lifts 12 m³ of water per minute to a height of 15 m. If its overall efficiency is 60%, find the input power. If the pump is used for 4 hours a day, find the daily cost of energy at ₹ 2.25 per unit.

Solution : Given : m = 12 m³ = 12 × 1000 kg (1 m³ = 1000 kg), h = 15 m, η = 60%, time = 1 minute = 60 sec.

$$\text{Energy output} = \text{m.g.h}$$
$$= 12 \times 1000 \times 9.81 \times 15$$
$$= 1.7658 \times 10^6 \text{ J}$$
$$\text{Energy input} = \frac{\text{Energy output}}{\eta}$$
$$= \frac{1.7658 \times 10^6}{0.6}$$
$$= 2.943 \times 10^6 \text{ J}$$
$$\text{Time for lifting} = 1 \text{ min.} = 60 \text{ sec.}$$
$$P_{in} = \frac{\text{Energy input}}{\text{Time}}$$
$$= \frac{2.943 \times 10^6}{60} = 49.05 \text{ kW}$$

$$\text{For 4 hours, pump consumes } P_{in} \times 4 = 196.2 \text{ kWh}$$
$$\text{Thus, total units per day} = 196.2$$
$$\text{Daily cost} = 196.2 \times 2.25$$
$$\therefore \qquad = \text{Rs. } 441.45/-$$

Example 1.21 :

An electric pump lifts 60 m³ of water per hour to a height of 25 m. The pump efficiency is 82% and the motor efficiency is 77%. The pump is used for 3 hours daily. Find the energy consumed per week, if the mass of 1 m³ of water is 1000 kg.

Solution : Given : m = 60 m³ = 60000 kg, h = 25 m, η_m = 77%, η_p = 82%, Time = 1 hour = 3600 sec.

$$\text{Output energy per hour} = \text{m.g.h}$$
$$= 60000 \times 9.81 \times 25$$
$$= 14.715 \times 10^6 \text{ J/hour}$$
$$\text{Output power in watts} = \frac{\text{Output energy in J}}{\text{Time}}$$
$$= \frac{14.715 \times 10^6}{3600}$$
$$P_{out} = 4087.5 \text{ W}$$
$$P_{in} = \frac{P_{out}}{\eta_m \times \eta_p} = \frac{4087.5}{0.77 \times 0.82}$$
$$= 6473.7092 \text{ W}$$
$$= 6.473 \text{ kWh}$$

Per day 3 hours running hence,

$$\text{Daily consumption} = 6.473 \times 3 = 19.42 \text{ kWh}$$

$\therefore$ $$\text{Weekly consumption} = 7 \times 19.42 = 135.94 \text{ kWh}$$

1.7 LIST OF FORMULAE

1. $$\text{Current (I)} = \frac{\text{Charge (Q)}}{\text{Time (t)}} \text{ Amp. (A)}$$

2. $$\text{Resistance (R)} = \rho \frac{l}{a} \text{ Ohm } (\Omega)$$

3. $$\text{Ohm's law, V} = \text{I.R.}$$

4. $$\text{Conductance (G)} = \frac{1}{R} \ (\Omega)^{-1} \text{ or Siemens}$$

5. $$\text{Insulation resistance } (R_i) = \frac{\rho}{2\pi l} \ \log_e (R_2/R_1) \text{ in mega ohm } (M\Omega)$$

6. $$\text{R.T.C. } \alpha_0 = \frac{R_t - R_0}{R_0 \cdot t}$$

$$= \frac{\Delta R}{R_0 \cdot t} \ /^\circ C$$

7. $$R_t = R_0 (1 + \alpha_0 \cdot t)$$

OR $$R_2 = R_1 [1 + \alpha_1 (t_2 - t_1)]$$

8. $$\alpha_t = \frac{\alpha_0}{1 + \alpha_0 \cdot t}$$

OR $$\alpha_2 = \frac{\alpha_1}{1 + \alpha_1 (t_2 - t_1)}$$

1.7.1 Thermal System

(a) $$\text{Heat capacity} = \frac{Q}{T_2 - T_1} \ \text{J/K}$$

$$Q = \text{Heat supplied in joules}$$

$$T_2 - T_1 = \text{Temperature difference}$$

(b) $$\text{Specific heat (s)} = \frac{Q}{m (T_2 - T_1)} \ \text{J/kg K}$$

(c)   Sensible heat (H) = m.s. Δt (J)

(d)   Latent heat = m $\times$ L (J)

(e)   Total heat = Sensible heat + Latent heat

(f)   Heat energy produced by fuel = mass $\times$ calorific value

1.7.2 Mechanical System

1.   Mass (m) = in kg

2.   Velocity (v) = dx/dt in m/s

3.   Acceleration (a) = dv/dt in m/s^2

4.   Force (F) = m $\times$ a Newton (N)

5.   Weight (W) = m $\times$ g

6.   Torque (T) = F $\times$ R   N-m

7.   Mechanical work done = F $\times$ d   (N-m) or joules

8.   Power (P) = $\dfrac{\text{Work done}}{\text{Time}} \cdot \dfrac{\text{N-m}}{\text{sec}}$.

9. Energy (E) : (a)   Kinetic energy = $\dfrac{1}{2}$ mv^2 joule

          (b) Potential energy = m.g.h.

                                        = W $\times$ h Joule

                          Energy (E) = Power $\times$ Time

10. Relation between power and torque, P = T $\times \omega$

11.   Angular velocity (ω) = $\dfrac{2\pi N}{60}$ rad/sec.

12.   Mass = Volume $\times$ Density

1.7.3 Electrical System

1.   Electrical work (W) = Q $\times$ V = V $\times$ I $\times$ t Joules (J)

2.   Power (P) = V $\times$ I watt = I^2 $\times$ R watt

                                        = V^2/R watt

3.   Energy (E) = V $\times$ I $\times$ t (kWh)

                                        = Power $\times$ Time

Efficiency (for thermal, mechanical and electrical system)

$$\% \, \eta \;=\; \frac{\text{Output energy}}{\text{Input energy}} \times 100$$

$$\% \, \eta \;=\; \frac{\text{Output power}}{\text{Input power}} \times 100$$

REVIEW QUESTIONS

1. An electric kettle is required to heat 500 gm of water from 10°C to the boiling point in 5 minutes, the supply voltage being 230V. if the efficiency of kettle being 80%. Calculate the resistance of the heating element.   **(67.17 ohm)**

2. An electric geyser is used to heat 5 liters of water from 15°C to 85°C. If the heat lost due to radiation is 35 kJ and water equivalent of the container is 100gm. Determine the efficiency of geyser. Take specific heat of water as 4200 J/kg.K

    (95.80%)

3. A 100 MW hydroelectric station is supplying full load for 8 hours per day. Calculate the volume of the water which has been used. Assume effective head of station as 200 meters and overall efficiency of station as 78%.   **(1881910.14 m^3)**

4. In a station the difference in head between the water surface and the turbine driving generator is 425 meters. If 1250 liters of water is required to generate 1 kWh of electric energy, find the overall efficiency.   **(69.69%)**

5. An electrically driven pump lifts 50m^3 of water per minute through a height of 15 meters. Efficiency of motor and pump are 70% and 80% respectively calculate :

    (a) Current drawn by motor if it works on 230v supply.

    (b) Energy consumption in kWh and cost of energy at the of 3 Rs/kWh if pump operates 2 hour per day for 30 days.   **(952 A, ₹ 39415/-)**

6. An electric furnace can melt 120 kg of aluminium in one hour. The room temperature is 26°C. find:

    (a) Power rating of the furnace

    (b) Cost of electric energy per month if the furnace works for 8 hours per day and 30 days per month.

    Assume melting point of aluminum :650 ^{0}C, specific heat of aluminum: 950J/kg.K, latent heat of fusion: 450 kJ/kg, efficiency of furnace:0.8, cost of electrical energy: Rs.3/kWh.   **(34.760 kW, ₹ 25027.2/-)**

7. An electric lift makes 12 double journeys per hour. During upward journey it carries a load of 5000 kg in 2 minutes to a height of 50m and it returns empty in 90 seconds. The weight of empty cage is 550 kg and balance weight is 2500 kg. The efficiency of lift and motor are 0.7 and 0.85 respectively. Find

    a) Electrical energy input to the system in one double journe;y.   **(1.14 kWh)**

    b) Operating cost for 5 hours in a day if cost per kWh is Rs. 3.50/-.   **(Rs.240.40/-)**

8. A motor drives a load torque of 250 N-m at 750 rpm drawing 20 kW from mains. Assuming constant temperature. Determine:

    a) Efficiency of motor.   **(98.12%)**

    b) losses   **(375 W)**

9. A filament lamp has normal rating of 230 V, 60 W. If it is switched on at room temperature of 26°C to 230 V supply, it draws a current of 2.5 A. Calculate the temperature of the filament in normal (hot) condition if the temperature coefficient at 26°C is 0.0055/°C.   **(t = 1586.6°C)**

10. A single core copper cable has conductor diameter of 2.6 cm and insulation thickness of 2 cm. The resistivity of insulation is 8×10^{12} ohm-m. Determine the insulation resistance of the cable for 200 meter length.   **(5933.5 MΩ)**

UNIT - II

Chapter **2**

NETWORK THEOREMS

2.1 NETWORK TERMINOLOGY

Let us define some basic terms which are closely related with an electrical network.

(1) Network : An arrangement of one or more energy sources with different circuit elements forms an 'electrical network' or 'electric circuit'.

(2) Circuit Elements : Circuit element may be active or passive. Active elements supply energy to the network, while passive elements either store or dissipate energy. Inductor and capacitor stores energy, while resistor dissipates energy in the form of heat. In this unit, we are only concerned with resistance.

(3) Branch : Part of the network which connects various junction points with each other, is called 'branch'.

(4) Node or Junction : It is the point in a network at which two or more branches meet.

(5) Mesh or Loop : A set of branches forming a closed path in a network, such that, if one branch is removed, then remaining branches do not form a closed path. It is called 'Mesh' or a 'Loop'.

(6) Open Circuit : Two points in a network are said to be open circuited, if there is no direct electrical connection or branch between them. There exists a voltage or potential difference between such points.

Ideally, open circuit means zero current or infinite resistance.

(7) Short Circuit : Two points in a network when connected by a good conducting wire are said to be short circuited. As resistance is very low, high current flows.

Ideally, short circuit means zero potential difference or zero resistance.

Consider a network shown below in Fig. 2.1.

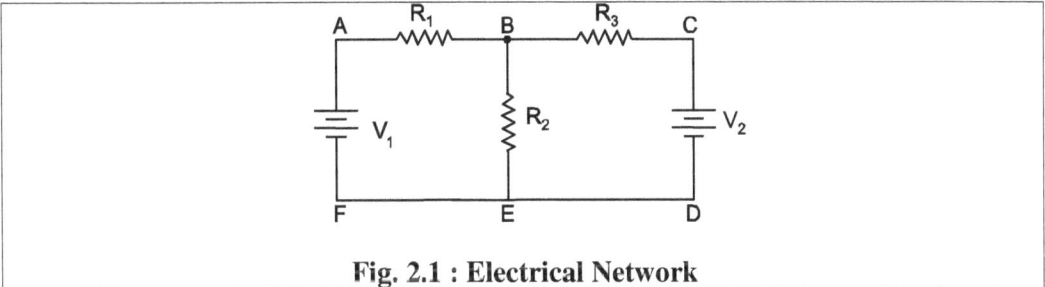

Fig. 2.1 : Electrical Network

In this network, there are 6 nodes, namely A, B, C, D, E and F. Similarly, AB, BC, CD, ... etc. are branches. There are 3 loops namely ABCDEFA, ABEFA and BCDEB and two meshes namely ABEFA and BCDEB.

2.2 CLASSIFICATION OF ELECTRICAL NETWORKS

Following are the various classifications of electrical networks :

(1) Linear and Non-Linear : A network in which values of the circuit elements (resistance, inductance and capacitance) remain constant, irrespective of change in voltage or current, is known as *'linear network'*. Ohm's law is applicable to such network. Linear network also obeys homogeneity and superposition principle.

On the other hand, if values of the circuit elements change with change in voltage or current, such a network is called *'Non-linear network'*. Ohm's law is not applicable to such a network. Even it does not obey superposition principle.

Circuit consisting of diode is the best example of non-linear circuit, because variation of diode current with respect voltage applied is non-linear.

(2) Bilateral and Unilateral : If characteristics or behaviour of the circuit is independent of direction of current through various elements, such a network is called *'bilateral'*. Network comprised of pure resistance is bilateral one.

Conversely, if characteristic or behaviour of the circuit depends on direction of current through one or more elements it is called *'Unilateral'*.

A diode allows flow of current only in one direction when it is forward biased, circuit consisting of diode is unilateral one.

(3) Active and Passive : If electric circuit contains at least single energy source, it is called *'active network'*. It may be either voltage or current source.

A circuit in absence of an energy source containing only passive elements is called *'Passive network'*.

(4) Lumped and Distributed : If all the network elements are physically separable, such a network is called *'lumped network'*. Most of the electrical networks are lumped in nature.

A network in which elements are not physically separable is known as *'distributed network'*.

As resistance inductance and capacitance of a transmission line are uniformly distributed over it's length, it is a 'distributed network'.

2.3 ENERGY SOURCES

Basically, there are two types of energy sources, namely 'voltage sources' and 'current sources'.

(1) Voltage Source : An ideal voltage source is one which gives constant voltage across it's terminals, irrespective of current drawn. Symbol for ideal voltage source and it's V-I characteristic are shown in Fig. 2.2 (a) and (b).

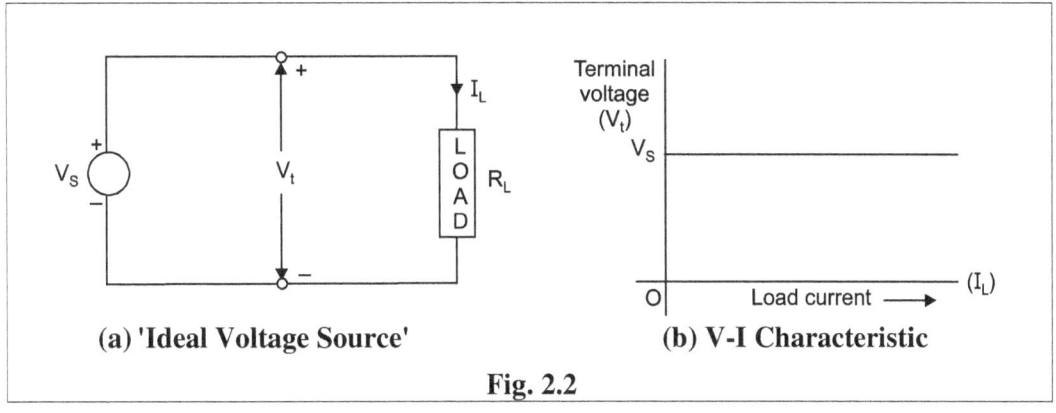

(a) 'Ideal Voltage Source'   **(b) V-I Characteristic**

Fig. 2.2

Let, V_t = Terminal voltage, R_L = Load resistance

V_s = Source voltage I_L = Load current

From V-I characteristic it can be seen that whatever is the value of load current, terminal voltage remains constant. In practice, it is not possible because every voltage source has small internal resistance.

Symbol of practical voltage source and it's V-I characteristic are shown in Fig. 2.3 (a) and Fig. 2.3 (b) respectively.

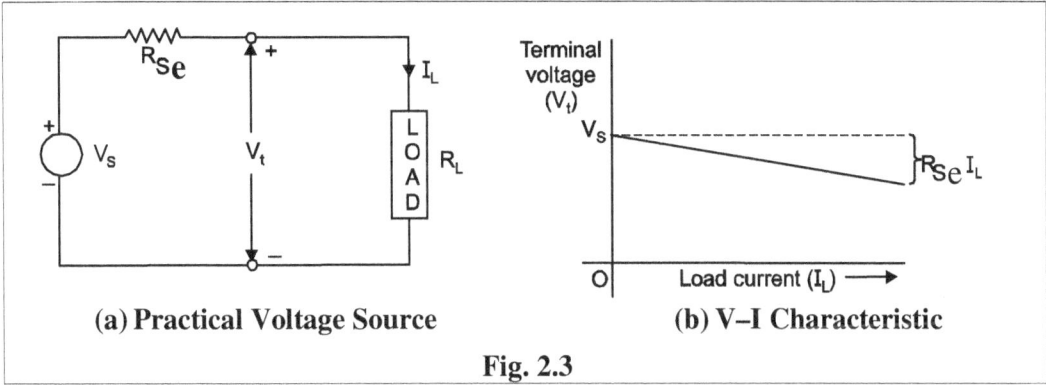

(a) Practical Voltage Source   **(b) V–I Characteristic**

Fig. 2.3

As load current increases, $(R_{se} \times I_L)$ drop increases and terminal voltage reduces.

Terminal Voltage

$$V_t = V_S - (R_{se} \cdot I_L) \qquad \ldots(2.1)$$

Thus, ideal voltage source has zero internal resistance, while practical voltage source has small internal resistance.

(2) Current Source : An ideal current source is one which delivers constant current irrespective of voltage across it's terminals.

Symbol for ideal current source and it's V-I characteristics are shown in Fig. 2.4 (a) and Fig. 2.4 (b) respectively.

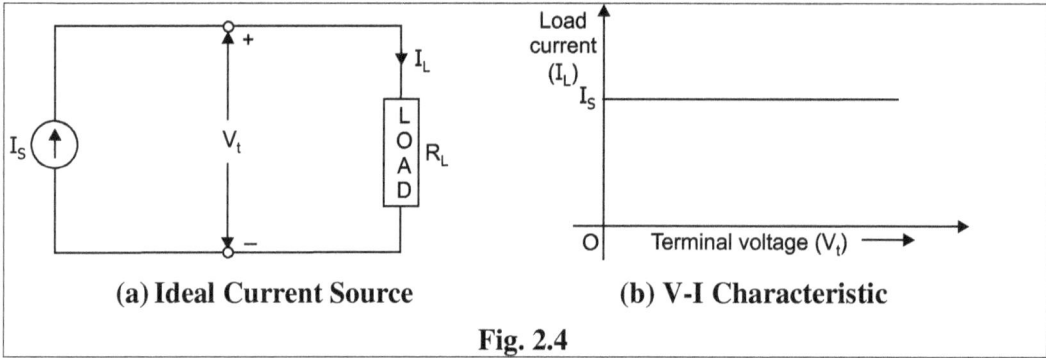

(a) Ideal Current Source   **(b) V-I Characteristic**

Fig. 2.4

Internal resistance of ideal current source is infinity. But practical current source has high (finite) internal resistance. Hence, with increase in terminal voltage, current delivered by such a source decreases. Symbol for Practical Current Source and it's V-I characteristics are shown in Fig. 2.5 (a) and Fig. 2.5 (b) respectively.

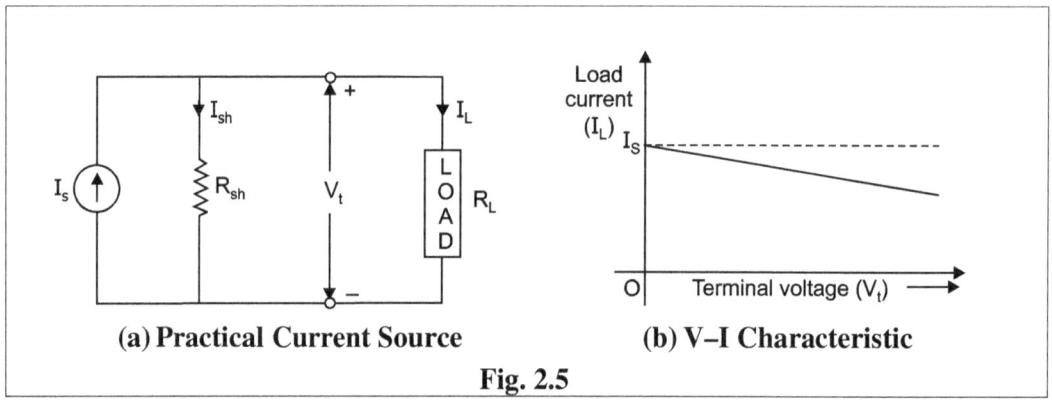

(a) Practical Current Source   **(b) V–I Characteristic**

Fig. 2.5

2.4 SERIES AND PARALLEL CIRCUITS

Two circuit elements are said to be connected in series when current flowing through them is same. Consider a circuit shown in Fig. 2.6

Let three resistances of values R_1, R_2 and R_3 Ω (ohm) be connected in series across a voltage source of V volt. Current flowing through each of them be I ampere.

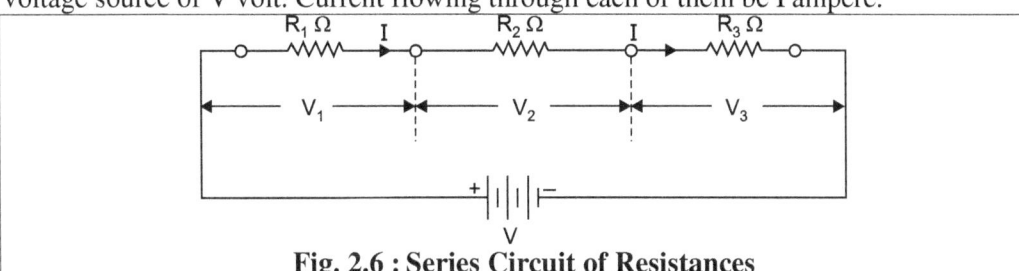

Fig. 2.6 : Series Circuit of Resistances

According to Ohm's law,

Voltage across R_1	$V_1 = IR_1$	... (2.1)
Voltage across R_2	$V_2 = IR_2$	... (2.2)
Voltage across R_3	$V_3 = IR_3$	... (2.3)

But, $V = V_1 + V_2 + V_3$ ...(KVL)

Put $V = I\,R_{eq.}$

Where

$R_{eq.}$ = Equivalent resistance

$\therefore$ $I.R_{eq.} = I.R_1 + I.R_2 + I.R_3$

$\therefore$ $R_{eq.} = R_1 + R_2 + R_3$ ...(2.4)

Thus, equivalent resistance of series connection is the largest of all individual resistance.

Conversely, two circuit elements are said to be in parallel, when same potential difference or voltage exists across them.

Consider a circuit shown in Fig. 2.7.

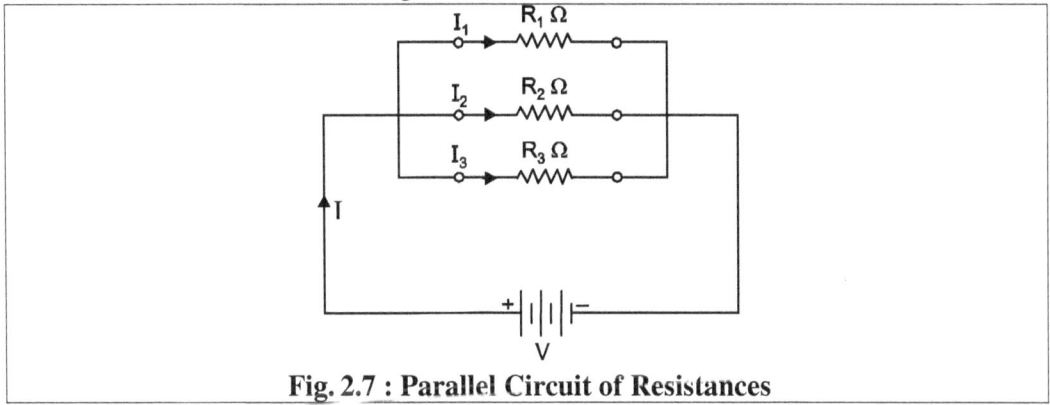

Fig. 2.7 : Parallel Circuit of Resistances

Let three resistances having values R_1, R_2 and R_3 Ω (ohm) be connected in parallel across a voltage source of V volt. Let I_1, I_2 and I_3 be the currents in ampere flowing through R_1, R_2 and R_3 respectively.

Voltage across each of them is V volt.

Let I ampere be the total current delivered by source.

By Ohm's law,

$$\left(I_1 = \frac{V}{R_1} , I_2 = \frac{V}{R_2} , I_3 = \frac{V}{R_3} \right) \qquad \qquad ...(2.5)$$

Also, $$R_{eq} = \frac{V}{I}$$

$$\therefore \qquad \qquad I = \frac{V}{R_{eq}} \qquad \qquad ...(2.6)$$

By KCL,

$$I = I_1 + I_2 + I_3$$

$$\therefore \qquad \frac{V}{R_{eq}} = \frac{V}{R_1} + \frac{V}{R_2} + \frac{V}{R_3}$$

$$\therefore \qquad \frac{1}{R_{eq}} = \frac{1}{R_1} + \frac{1}{R_2} + \frac{1}{R_3} \qquad \qquad ...(2.7)$$

where R_{eq} = Equivalent resistance of parallel connection.

Thus, equivalent resistance of parallel connection is the smallest of all resistances.

2.5 CURRENT DIVISION IN PARALLEL RESISTANCES

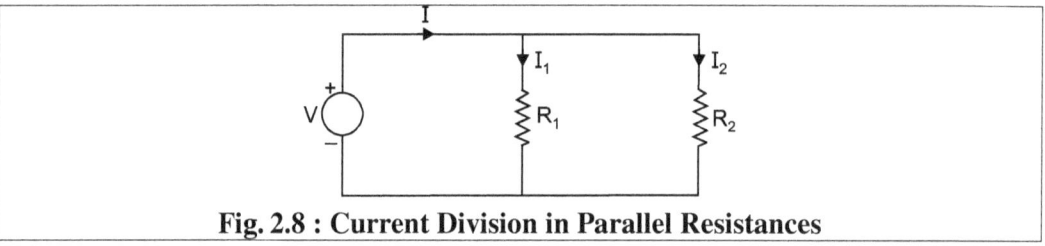

Fig. 2.8 : Current Division in Parallel Resistances

Let two resistances R_1 and R_2 be connected in parallel across voltage source of V volt, as shown in Fig. 2.8. Let currents flowing through R_1 and R_2 be I_1 and I_2 (ampere) A respectively.

Let I A be the total current delivered by a voltage source.

By Ohm's law,

$$I_1 = \frac{V}{R_1}$$

and $$I_2 = \frac{V}{R_2}$$

$\therefore$ $$V = I_1 R_1 = I_2 R_2 \qquad \dots (2.8)$$

$\therefore$ $$I_1 = \frac{R_2}{R_1} . I_2 \qquad \dots(2.9)$$

By KCL,

Total current, $$I = I_1 + I_2 \qquad \dots(2.10)$$

Put equation (2.9) in equation (2.10)

$\therefore$ $$I = \left(\frac{R_2}{R_1}\right) . I_2 + I_2$$

$\therefore$ $$I = \left(\frac{R_2 + R_1}{R_1}\right) I_2$$

$\therefore$ $$I_2 = \left(\frac{R_1}{R_1 + R_2}\right) I \qquad \dots(2.11)$$

Similarly, $$I_1 = \left(\frac{R_2}{R_1 + R_2}\right) I \qquad \dots(2.12)$$

Thus, by knowing values of resistance in parallel and total current one can easily find currents flowing through individual resistance. This is called 'Current Division' in parallel resistances.

2.6 KIRCHHOFF'S CURRENT LAW (KCL)

Statement : Algebraic sum of currents meeting at any junction point in an electric circuit is always zero.

$$\sum I = 0$$

In other words, at any junction or node in an electric circuit, sum of incoming currents is equal to sum of outgoing currents.

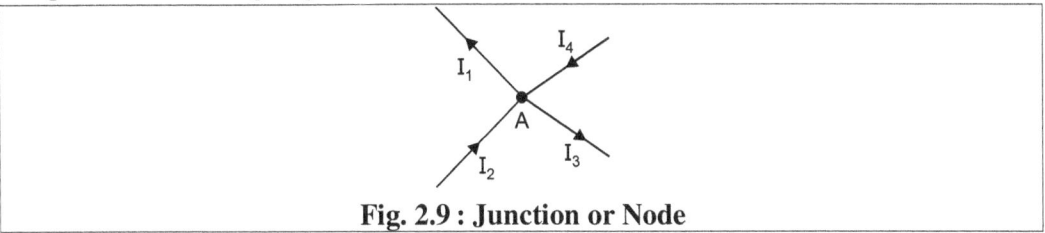

Fig. 2.9 : Junction or Node

Explanation : Consider a node A as shown in Fig. 2.9.

Four branches meet at junction or node A.

By KCL, $$I_2 + I_4 = I_1 + I_3 \qquad \dots(2.13)$$

where I_2 and I_4 are incoming currents while I_1 and I_3 are outgoing currents.

2.6.1 Kirchhoff's Voltage Law (KVL)

Statement : In any electrical network, algebraic sum of voltage drops across various elements around any closed loop or mesh is equal to algebraic sum of e.m.f.s in that loop.

$$\sum E = \sum IR$$

In other words, if we trace any closed path or loop in an electrical network an algebraic sum of branch voltages is always zero.

i.e. $$\sum V = 0$$ ...(2.14)

Also, sum of potential rises must be equal to sum of potential drops, while tracing any closed path of the circuit.

Sign Conventions:

(1) For IR voltage drop

Direction of current through a circuit element decides polarity of voltage. Current always flows from higher potential to lower potential where higher potential and lower potential terminals are marked as positive and negative respectively.

While tracing a closed path if we travel from positively marked terminal of resistor to negatively marked terminal then it indicates 'potential drop'. This is shown in Fig. 2.10.

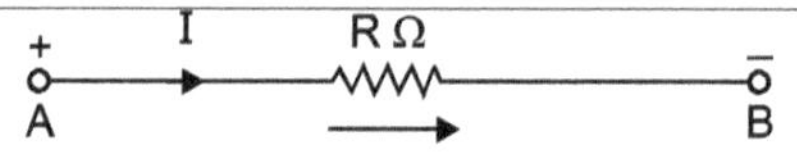

Fig. 2.10 : Potential Drop

If we travel from negatively marked terminal to positively marked terminal, then it indicates potential rise. This is shown in Fig. 2.11.

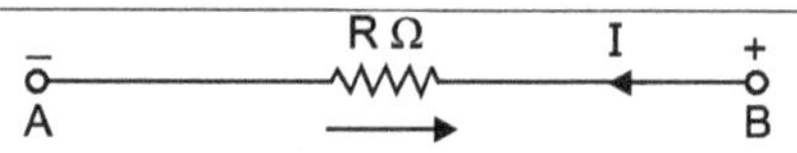

Fig. 2.11 : Potential Rise

(2) For the Sources of E.M.F.

If the source is traced from its positive terminal to negative terminal, it is considered as potential drop and when it is traced from its negative terminal to positive terminal, it is considered as potential rise. While writing the voltage equation for any closed loop, potential rise is taken as positive and potential drop is taken as negative.

Mesh or Loop Analysis : It can be performed by following two methods.

(1) Loop current method : Consider a network shown in Fig. 2.12.

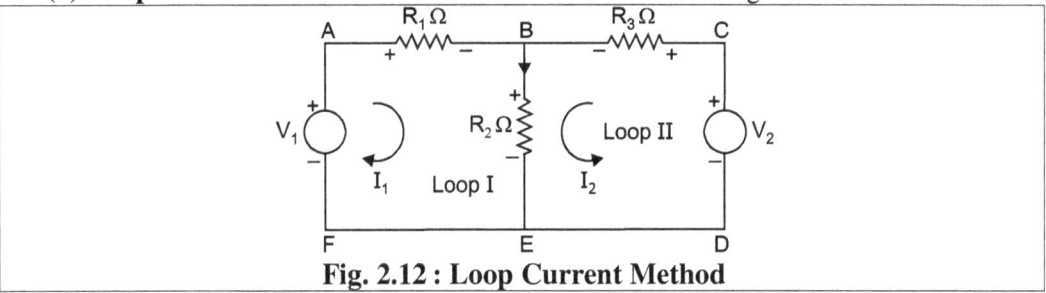

Fig. 2.12 : Loop Current Method

Let us assume loop currents I_1 and I_2 for loops ABEFA and CBEDC respectively. Loop current is restricted to flow within that loop only. Also by applying KVL to loop ABEFA, polarities of voltage drops

$$R_1 . I_1 + R_2 (I_1 + I_2) = V_1 \qquad \qquad ...(2.15)$$

Above two equations can be easily solved by Cramer's rule or any other method to find loop currents.

(2) Branch Current Method : Consider a network shown in Fig. 2.13.

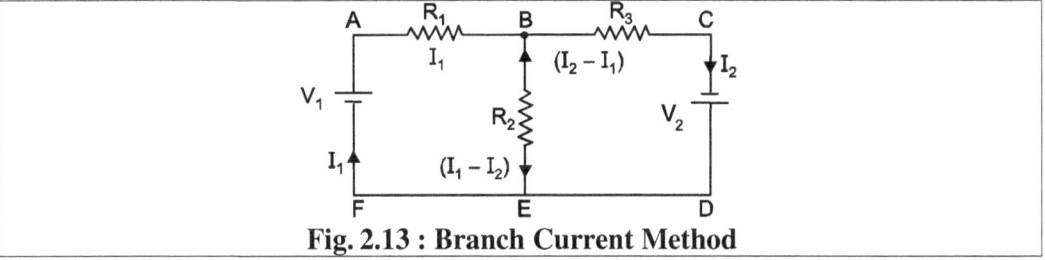

Fig. 2.13 : Branch Current Method

Let us assume that sources V_1 and V_2 deliver currents I_1 and I_2 respectively.

Now, let us decide various branch currents. According to KCL either current $(I_1 - I_2)$ flows from B to E through R_2 or current $(I_2 - I_1)$ flows from E to B through R_2. Applying KVL to loop ABEFA yields

$$-R_1 I_1 - R_2 (I_1 - I_2) - V_1 = 0$$
$$(R_1 + R_2) I_1 - R_2 I_2 = V_1 \qquad \qquad ... (2.16)$$

Similarly, for loop EDEBC,

$$+ V_2 - R_2 (I_2 - I_1) - R_3 I_2 = 0$$
$$R_2 I_1 - (R_2 + R_3) I_2 = V_2 \qquad \qquad ... (2.17)$$

Solving above two equations we can easily find various branch currents.

Voltage drops across resistances depend on direction of currents through them. It can be observed that number of equations to be solved is always equal to number of loops. In a given electrical network if number of loops are less then mesh or loop analysis is preferred. On the other hand if number of nodes are less then nodal analysis is preferred. Solved examples in the end of this unit will help for better understanding of KCL and KVL.

SOLVED EXAMPLES

Example 2.1 :

Using Kirchhoff's laws, calculate the current flowing in 2 ohm resistance for the circuit shown in Fig. 2.14.

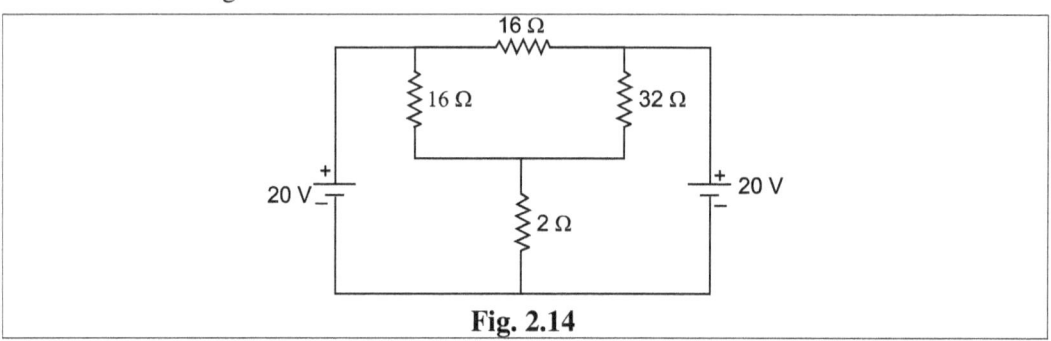

Fig. 2.14

Solution : The various branch currents are shown in Fig. 2.15 below :

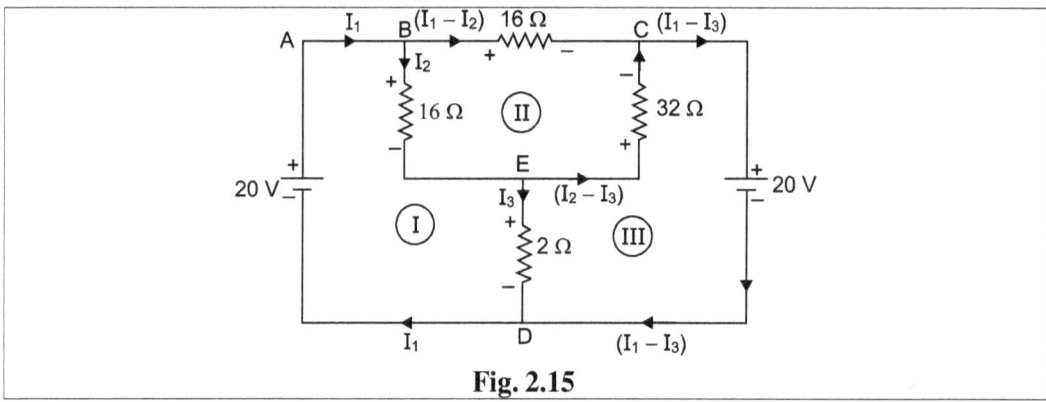

Fig. 2.15

Loop I : (ABEDA)
$$-16\,I_2 - 2\,I_3 + 20 = 0$$
$\therefore$
$$16I_2 + 2\,I_3 = 20 \qquad\qquad\qquad ...(1)$$

Loop II : (BCEB)
$$-16\,(I_1 - I_2) + 32\,(I_2 - I_3) + 16\,I_2 = 0$$
$\therefore$
$$-16\,I_1 + 64\,I_2 - 32\,I_3 = 0 \qquad\qquad\qquad ...(2)$$

Loop III : (CDEC)
$$-20 + 2\,I_3 - 32\,(I_2 - I_3) = 0$$
$\therefore$
$$-32\,I_2 + 34\,I_3 = 20 \qquad\qquad\qquad ...(3)$$

By Cramer's rule,

$$\Delta = \begin{vmatrix} 0 & 16 & 2 \\ -16 & 64 & -32 \\ 0 & -32 & 34 \end{vmatrix}$$

$$= -16\left[(-16 \times 34) + 0\right] + 2\left[(-16) \times (-32) - 0\right]$$
$$= 8704 + 1024$$
$$= 9728$$

$$\Delta_3 = \begin{vmatrix} 0 & 16 & 20 \\ -16 & 64 & 0 \\ 0 & -32 & 20 \end{vmatrix}$$

$$= -16\left[-320 - 0\right] + 20\left[(-16 \times -32) - 0\right]$$
$$= 5120 + 10240$$
$$= 15360$$

$$I_3 = \frac{\Delta_3}{\Delta} = \frac{15360}{9728}$$

$$\boxed{I_3 = 1.5789 \text{ A} \downarrow}$$

Example 2.2 :

Find the V_{CE} and V_{AG} for the circuit shown below.

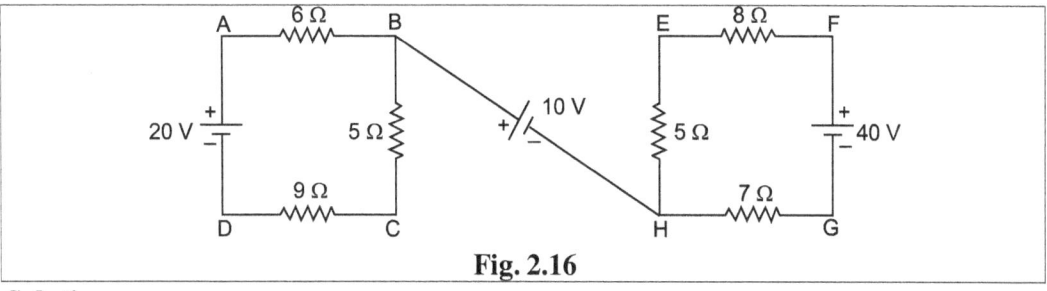

Fig. 2.16

Solution :

Applying KVL, for Loops ABCDA and EHGFE (Fig. 2.17(a))
$$-6I_1 - 5I_1 - 9I_1 + 20 = 0$$
$$-8I_2 - 5I_2 - 7I_2 + 40 = 0$$

$$\therefore \qquad\qquad I_1 = 1A$$

and $\qquad\qquad I_2 = 2A$

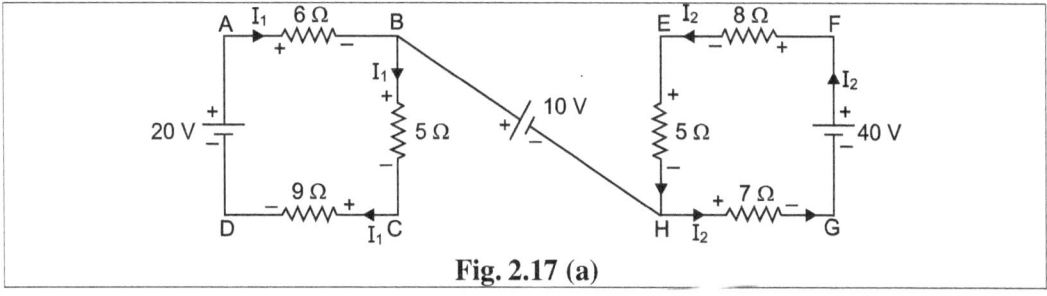

Fig. 2.17 (a)

(i) V_{CE}

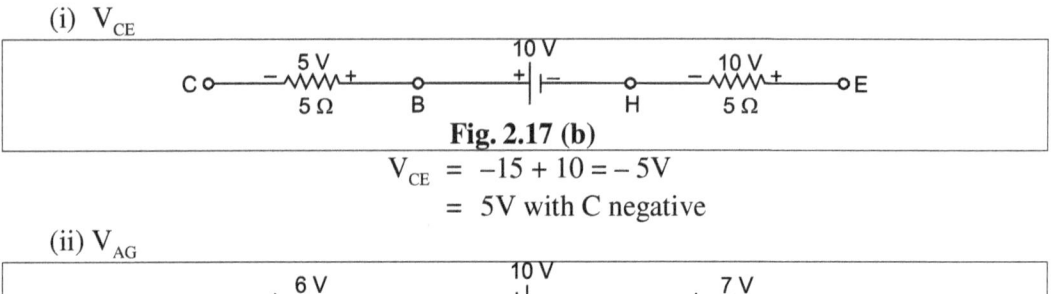

Fig. 2.17 (b)

$$V_{CE} = -15 + 10 = -5V$$
$$= 5V \text{ with C negative}$$

(ii) V_{AG}

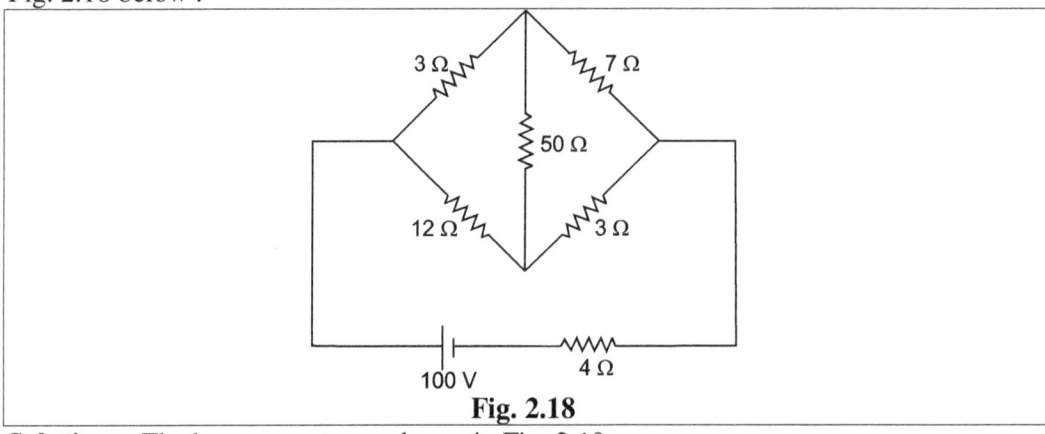

Fig. 2.17 (c)

$$V_{AG} = 6 + 10 + 7$$
$$\boxed{V_{AG} = 23 \text{ V}}$$

Example 2.3 :

Use Kirchhoff's law to find current supplied by the battery for the circuit shown in Fig. 2.18 below :

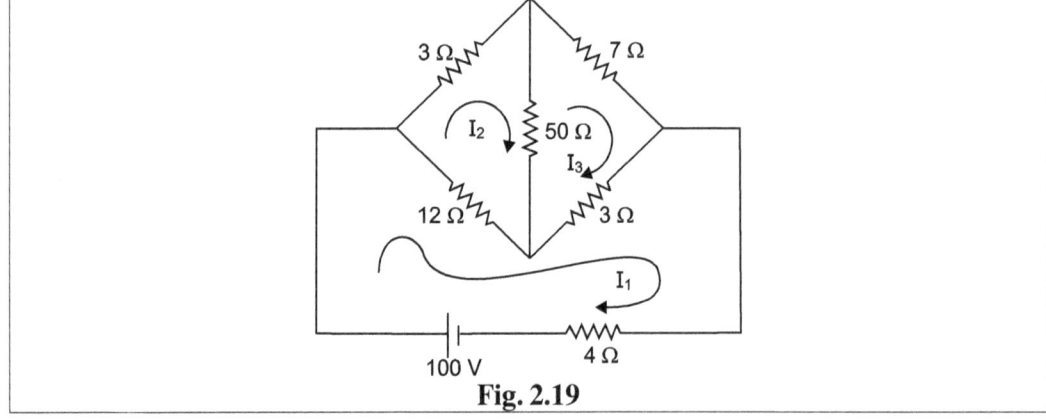

Fig. 2.18

Solution : The loop currents are shown in Fig. 2.19.

Fig. 2.19

Applying KVL to the three loops 1, 2 and 3,

$$- 12\,(I_1 - I_2) - 3\,(I_1 - I_3) - 4\,I_1 + 100 = 0$$
$$-19I_1 + 12\,I_2 + 3I_3 + 100 = 0$$

∴ $$19\,I_1 - 12\,I_2 - 3\,I_3 = 100 \qquad \ldots(1)$$

$$-3I_2 - 50\,(I_2 - I_3) - 12\,(I_2 - I_1) = 0$$

∴ $$- 12\,I_1 + 65\,I_2 - 50\,I_3 = 0 \qquad \ldots(2)$$

$$-50\,(I_3 - I_2) - 7\,I_3 - 3\,(I_3 - I_1) = 0$$

∴ $$- 3\,I_1 - 50\,I_2 + 60\,I_3 = 0 \qquad \ldots(3)$$

Solving equations (1), (2) and (3) by Cramer's rule,

$$\Delta = \begin{vmatrix} 19 & -12 & -3 \\ -12 & 65 & -50 \\ -3 & -50 & 60 \end{vmatrix}$$

$$= 13775$$

$$\Delta_1 = \begin{vmatrix} 100 & -12 & -3 \\ 0 & 65 & -50 \\ 0 & -50 & 60 \end{vmatrix} = 140000$$

∴ $$I_1 = \frac{\Delta_1}{\Delta}$$

$$= \frac{140000}{13775}$$

$$\boxed{I_1 = 10.1635\ \text{A}} \qquad \text{…Current supplied by battery}$$

Example 2.4 :

Determine the current supplied by each battery in the circuit shown in Fig. 2.20 using Kirchhoff's laws.

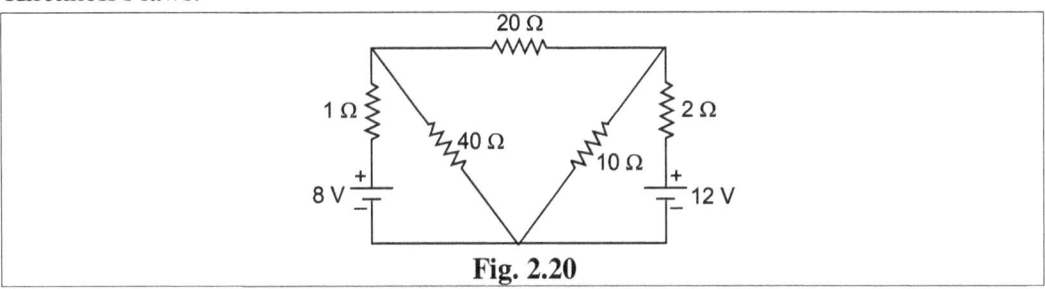

Fig. 2.20

Solution : Using branch current method

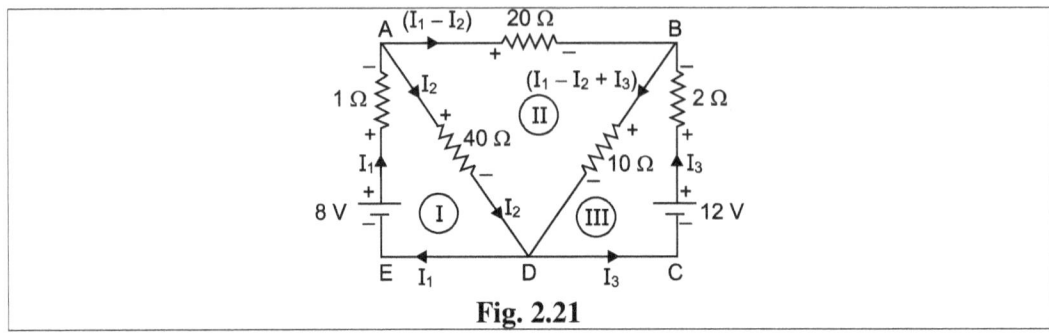

Fig. 2.21

Applying KVL to the loops (I), (II) and (III) i.e. ADEA, ABDA and BCDB

$$-I_1 - 40\,I_2 + 8 = 0$$

∴ $$I_1 + 40I_2 = 8 \qquad\qquad ...(1)$$

$$-20\,(I_1 - I_2) - 10\,(I_1 - I_2 + I_3) + 40\,I_2 = 0$$

∴ $$-30\,I_1 + 70\,I_2 - 10\,I_3 = 0 \qquad\qquad ...(2)$$

$$2\,I_3 - 12 + 10\,(I_1 - I_2 + I_3) = 0$$

∴ $$10\,I_1 - 10I_2 + 12\,I_3 = 12 \qquad\qquad ...(3)$$

Solving equations (1), (2) and (3) by Cramer's rule we get,

$$\boxed{\begin{array}{l} I_1 = 0.1005A \\ I_3 = 1.0807\ A \end{array}}$$

(I_1 is current supplied by 8 V battery and I_2 is current supplied by 12 V battery)

Example 2.5 :

For the circuit shown in Fig. 2.22 write the Kirchhoff's law equations for loops BCDB, CEDC and ABDEFA in terms of the branch currents I_1, I_2 and I_3 as shown. Find current I_1 by solving these equations.

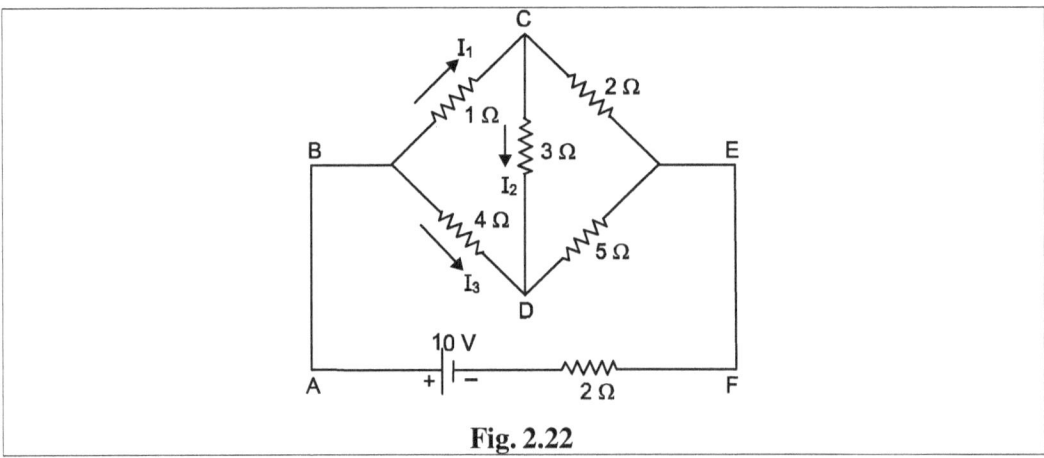

Fig. 2.22

Solution :

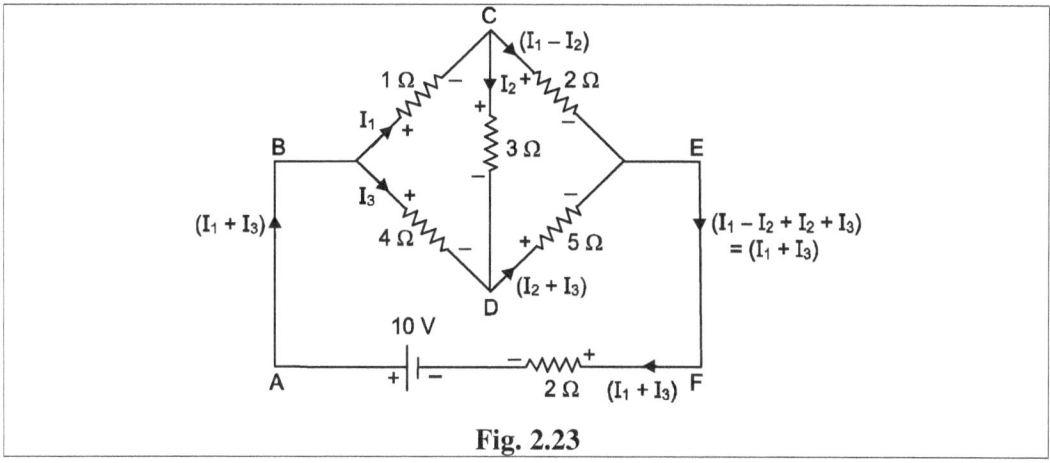

Fig. 2.23

Apply KCL to loop BCDB,

$\therefore$ $\qquad\qquad\qquad\qquad -I_1 - 3I_2 + 4I_3 = 0$ $\qquad\qquad\qquad$ ...(1)

Apply KCL to loop CEDC,

$\qquad\qquad -2(I_1 - I_2) + 5(I_2 + I_3) + 3I_2 = 0$ $\qquad\qquad\qquad$ ...(2)

$\therefore$ $\qquad\qquad\qquad\qquad -2I_1 + 10I_2 + 5I_3 = 0$

Apply KCL to loop ABDEFA

$\qquad\qquad -4I_3 - 5(I_2 + I_3) - 2(I_1 + I_3) + 10 = 0$

$\therefore$ $\qquad\qquad\qquad\qquad 2I_1 + 5I_2 + 11I_3 = 10$ $\qquad\qquad\qquad$ ...(3)

By solving equations (1), (2) and (3) by Cramer's rule we get,

$$\Delta = \begin{vmatrix} -1 & -3 & 4 \\ -2 & 10 & 5 \\ 2 & 5 & 11 \end{vmatrix} = -301$$

$$\Delta_1 = \begin{vmatrix} 0 & -3 & 4 \\ 0 & 10 & 5 \\ 10 & 5 & 11 \end{vmatrix} = -550$$

$\therefore$ $\qquad\qquad I_1 = \dfrac{\Delta_1}{\Delta} = \dfrac{-550}{-301} = 1.8272 \text{ A}$

$$\boxed{I_1 = 1.8272 \text{ A}}$$

Example 2.6 :

Write the Kirchhoff's voltage equations for the circuit shown in Fig. 2.24 and hence find current flowing through 4 Ω resistance.

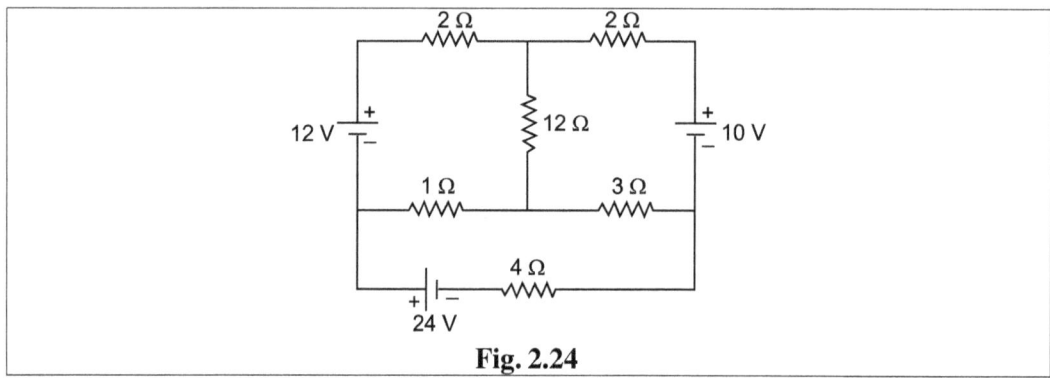

Fig. 2.24

Solution : Apply loop current method,

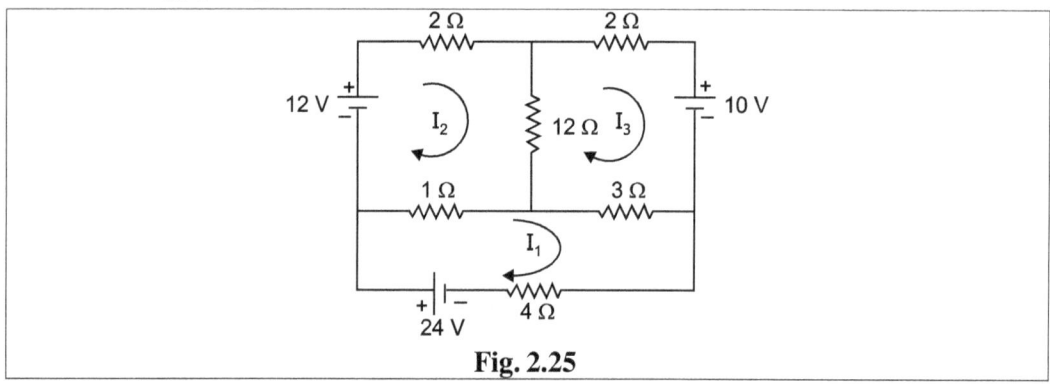

Fig. 2.25

Applying KVL to loops 1, 2 and 3

$$- (I_1 - I_2) - 3 (I_1 - I_3) - 4I_1 + 24 = 0$$

i.e.
$$8I_1 - I_2 - 3I_3 = 24 \qquad \qquad ...(1)$$

$$-2I_2 - 12 (I_2 - I_3) - 1 (I_2 - I_1) + 12 = 0$$

i.e.
$$- I_1 + 15 I_2 - 12 I_3 = 12 \qquad \qquad ...(2)$$

$$-2 I_3 - 10 - 3 (I_3 - I_1) - 12 (I_3 - I_2) = 0$$

i.e.
$$3 I_1 + 12 I_2 - 17 I_3 = 10 \qquad \qquad ...(3)$$

To find current through 4 Ω i.e. to find I.

By solving equations (1), (2) and (3) by Cramer's rule we get,

$$\Delta_1 = \begin{vmatrix} 24 & -1 & -3 \\ 12 & 15 & -12 \\ 10 & 12 & -17 \end{vmatrix} = -2730$$

$$\Delta = \begin{vmatrix} 8 & -1 & -3 \\ -1 & 15 & -12 \\ 3 & 12 & -17 \end{vmatrix} = -664$$

$$I_1 = \frac{\Delta_1}{\Delta} = \frac{-2730}{-664} = 4.11$$

$$\boxed{I_1 = 4.111 \text{ A}}$$

Example 2.7 :

For Fig. 2.26, a d.c. two source network, the branch currents I_1 and I_2 are as marked in it. Write using Kirchhoff's laws two independent simultaneous equations in I_1 and I_2. Solve these to find I_1.

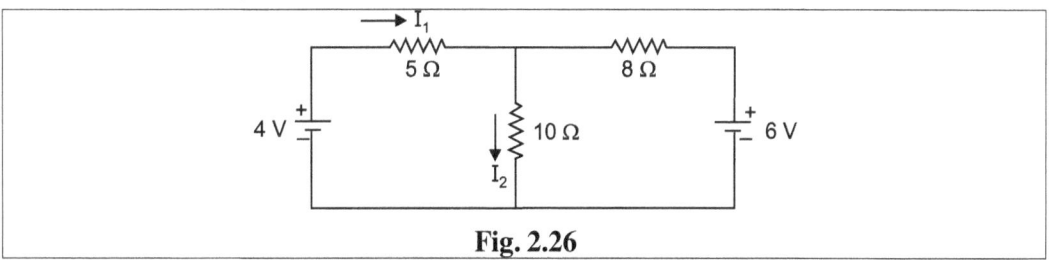

Fig. 2.26

Solution : The branch currents, current distributions are shown in Fig. 2.27.

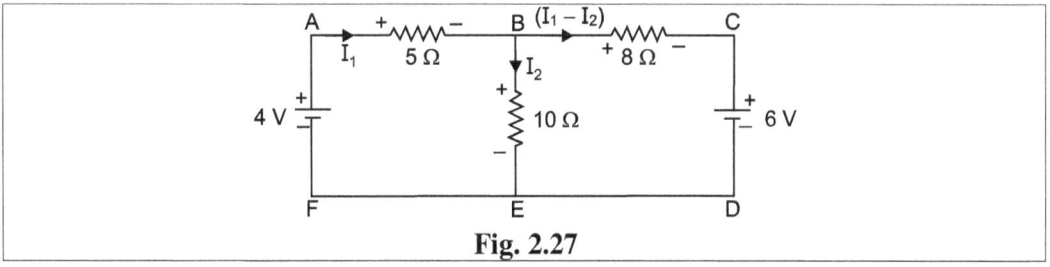

Fig. 2.27

Apply KVL to the two loops.

Loop ABEFA,

$$-5I_1 - 10I_2 + 4 = 0$$

∴
$$5I_1 + 10I_2 = 4$$

∴
$$I_1 + 2I_2 = 0.8 \qquad \qquad \text{...(1)}$$

Loop BCDEB,

$$-8(I_1 - I_2) - 6 + 10I_2 = 0$$

$$-8I_1 + 18I_2 = 6 \qquad \qquad \text{...(2)}$$

Solving equations (1) and (2) by variable reduction we get,

$$\boxed{I_1 = 0.0705 \text{ A}}$$

Example 2.8 :

For d.c. circuit shown in Fig. 2.28 write the Kirchhoff's law equations in the branch currents I_1, I_2 and I_3 as shown, for loops ABGHA, BCFGB and CDEFC. Solve these equations to find current I_2.

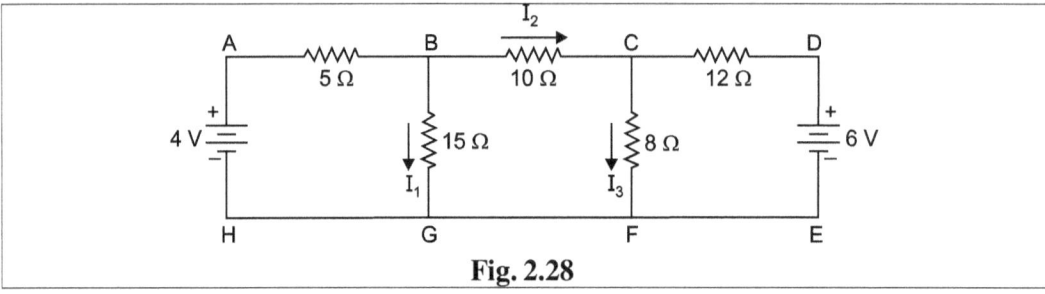

Fig. 2.28

Solution : The branch currents and their distributions are shown in Fig. 2.29.

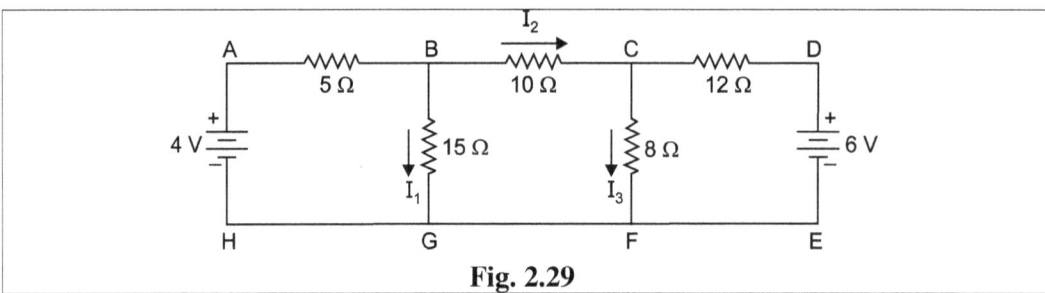

Fig. 2.29

Apply KVL to loops.

Loop ABGHA,

$$-5 (I_1 + I_2) - 15 I_1 + 4 = 0$$

$\therefore$
$$20 I_1 + 5 I_2 = 4 \qquad \qquad ...(1)$$

Loop BCFGB,

$$-10 I_2 - 8I_3 + 15 I_1 = 0$$
$$15 I_1 - 10 I_2 - 8I_3 = 0 \qquad \qquad ...(2)$$

Loop CDEFC,

$$-12 (I_2 - I_3) - 6 + 8I_3 = 0$$
$$- 12 I_2 + 20 I_3 = 6 \qquad \qquad ...(3)$$

Solving equations (1), (2) and (3) to find I_2.

$$\Delta = \begin{vmatrix} 20 & 5 & 0 \\ 15 & -10 & -8 \\ 0 & -12 & 20 \end{vmatrix} = -7420$$

$$\Delta_2 = \begin{vmatrix} 20 & 4 & 0 \\ 15 & 0 & -8 \\ 0 & 6 & 20 \end{vmatrix} = -240$$

$$I_2 = \frac{\Delta_2}{\Delta} = \frac{-240}{-7420} = \boxed{0.03234 \text{ A} \rightarrow}$$

Example 2.9 :

Use Kirchhoffs laws to find the value of unknown resistance R such that 2 Amp current flows through it. The directions of the current in Fig. 2.30 are given below. All resistances are in ohm.

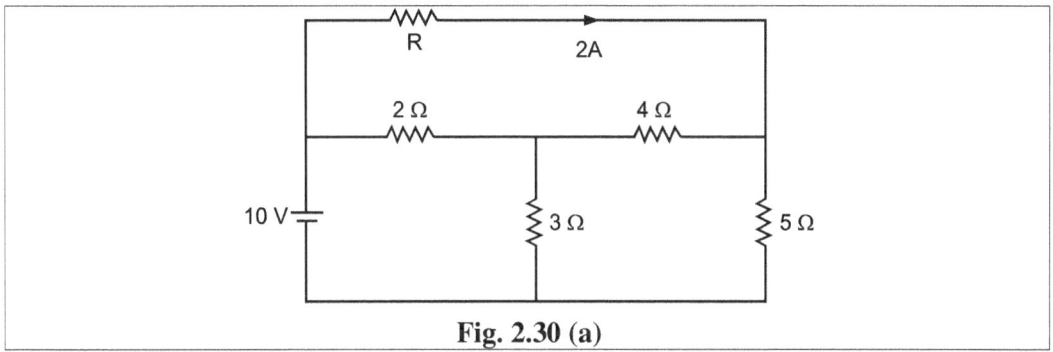

Fig. 2.30 (a)

Solution :

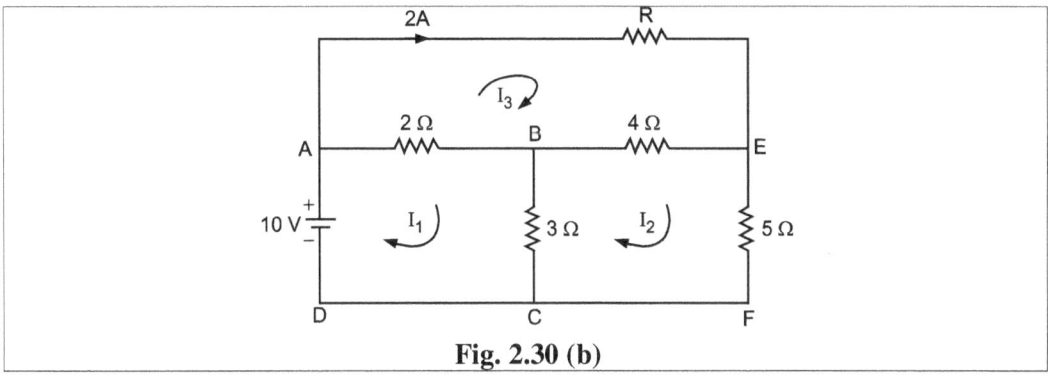

Fig. 2.30 (b)

For loop ABCDA,

$$5I_1 - 3I_2 - 2I_3 = 10 \qquad\qquad (I_3 = 2A \text{ given})$$
$$5I_1 - 3I_2 - 4 = 10$$
$$5I_1 - 3I_2 = 14 \qquad\qquad\qquad ...(1)$$

For loop BEFCB,

$$-3I_1 + 12I_2 - 4I_3 = 0$$

$$-3I_1 + 12\,I_2 - 8 = 0$$
$$-3\,I_1 + 12I_2 = 8 \qquad \qquad ...(2)$$

For loop AEBA,

$$-2I_1 - 4I_2 + (R + 2 + 4)\,I_3 = 0$$
$$-2I_1 - 4I_2 + (R + 6)\,2 = 0$$
$$2\,(R + 6) = 2I_1 + 4I_2 \qquad \qquad ...(3)$$

Solving (1) and (2) simultaneously,

$$5I_1 - 3I_2 = 14$$
$$-3I_1 + 12I_2 = 8$$

Multiply equation (1) by 4

$$20I_1 - 12I_2 = 56$$
$$-\,3I_1 + 12I_2 = \quad 8$$
$$\overline{17\,I_1 = 64}$$

$$I_1 = \frac{64}{17} = 3.76 \text{ Amp}$$

As
$$5I_1 - 3I_2 = 14$$
$$5\,(3.76) - 3I_2 = 14$$
$$3I_2 = 18.8 - 14 = 4.8$$
$$I_2 = 1.60 \text{ Amp}$$

Put value of I_1 and I_2 in equation (3)

$$2\,(R + 6) = 2I_1 + 4I_2 = 2\,(3.76) + 4\,(1.6)$$
$$2R + 12 = 13.92$$
$$2R = 1.92$$
$$\boxed{R = 0.96\ \Omega}$$

Example 2.10 :

Using Kirchhoff's laws, calculate the current delivered by the battery shown in Fig. 2.31

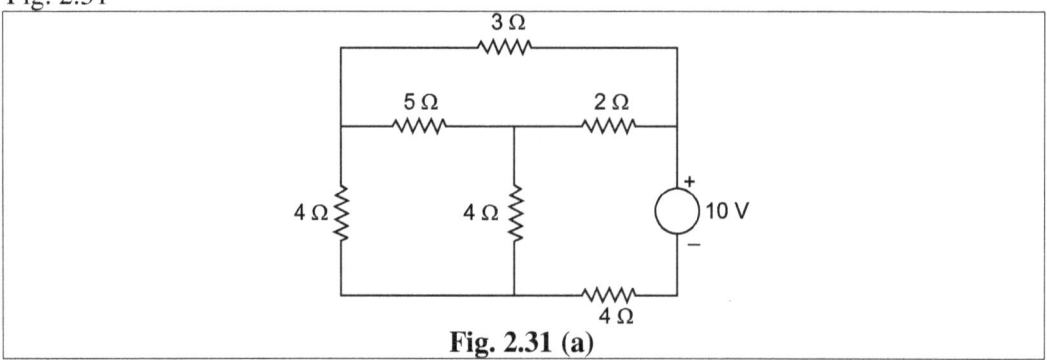

Fig. 2.31 (a)

Solution :

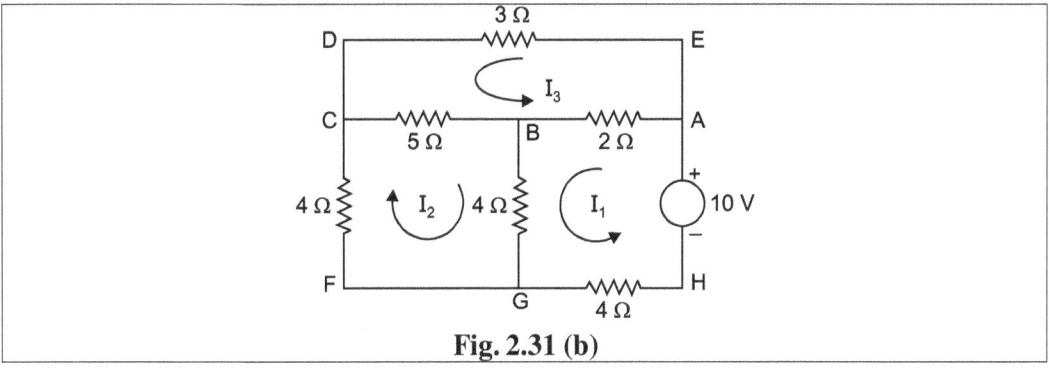

Fig. 2.31 (b)

For loop ABGHA, according to KVL,

$$2.(I_1-I_3) + 4.(I_1 +I_2) + 4.I_1 = 10$$

$\therefore$ $\qquad 10.I_1 + 4.I_2 - 2.I_3 = 10$ ...(1)

For loop CBGFC,

$$5.(I_2+I_3) + 4.(I_2+I_1) + 4.I_2 = 0$$

$\therefore$ $\qquad 4.I_1 + 13.I_2 + 5.I_3 = 0$ ...(2)

For loop DCBAED,

$$3.I_3 + 5.(I_2+I_3) + 2.(I_3-I_1) = 0$$

$\therefore$ $\qquad -2.I_1 + 5.I_2 + 10.I_3 = 0$ ...(3)

System determinant,

$$\Delta = \begin{vmatrix} 10 & 4 & -2 \\ 4 & 13 & 5 \\ -2 & 5 & 10 \end{vmatrix}$$

$$= 10 (130-25) - 4 (40+10) - 2 (20+26)$$
$$= 1050 - 200 - 92$$
$$= 758$$

$$\Delta_1 = \begin{vmatrix} 10 & 4 & -2 \\ 0 & 13 & 5 \\ 0 & 5 & 10 \end{vmatrix}$$

$$= 10(130-25) - 4(0) - 2(0) = 1050$$

Here, $\qquad\qquad I_1 = \dfrac{\Delta_1}{\Delta}$

$$= \dfrac{1050}{758} = 1.3852 \text{ A}$$

$\therefore$ Current delivered by 10 V battery $\boxed{I_1 = 1.3852 \text{ A}}$

Example 2.11 :

For the circuit shown determine the voltages (i) V_{df} and (ii) V_{ag}.

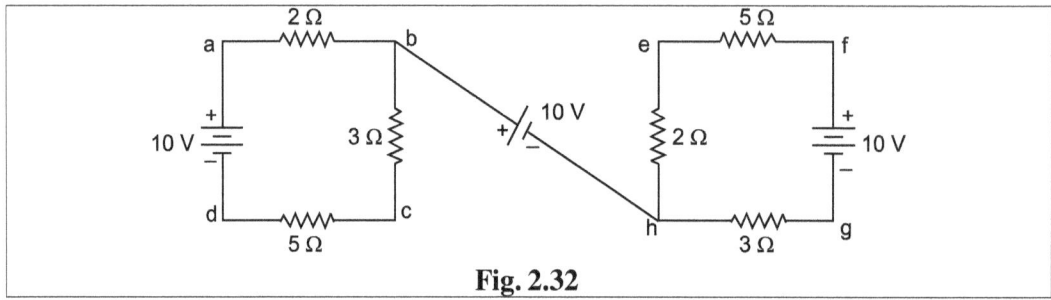

Fig. 2.32

Solution :

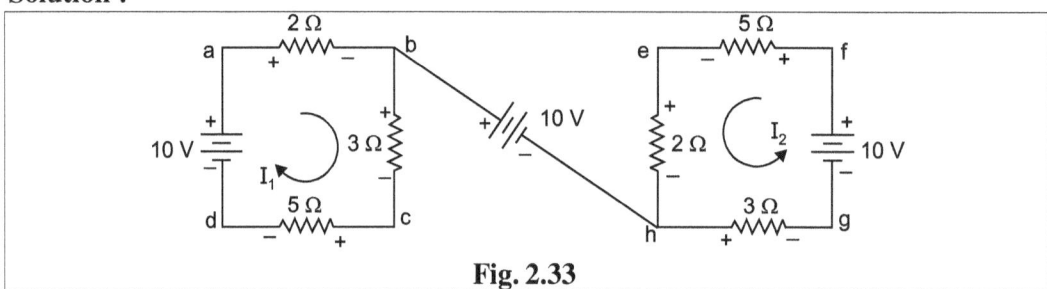

Fig. 2.33

For loop abcda,

According to KVL,

$$2.I_1 + 3.I_1 + 5.I_1 = 10$$

$$\therefore \qquad 10.I_1 = 10$$

$$\therefore \qquad I_1 = 1 \text{ A}$$

For loop ehgfe,

According to KVL,

$$5.I_2 + 2.I_2 + 3.I_2 = 10$$

$$\therefore \qquad 10.I_2 = 10$$

$$\therefore \qquad I_2 = 1\text{A}$$

(i) $\qquad V_{df} = -5.I_1 - 3.I_1 + 10 - 2.I_2 - 5.I_2$

$$= -5 - 3 + 10 - 2 - 5$$

$$= -15 + 10$$

$$\boxed{V_{df} = -5 \text{ V}}$$

Thus, $\qquad V_{df} = 5$ V with d negative w.r.t. f.

(ii) $\qquad V_{ag} = 2.I_1 + 10 + 3.I_2$

$$= 2 + 10 + 3$$

$$\boxed{V_{ag} = 15 \text{ V}}$$

Example 2.12 :

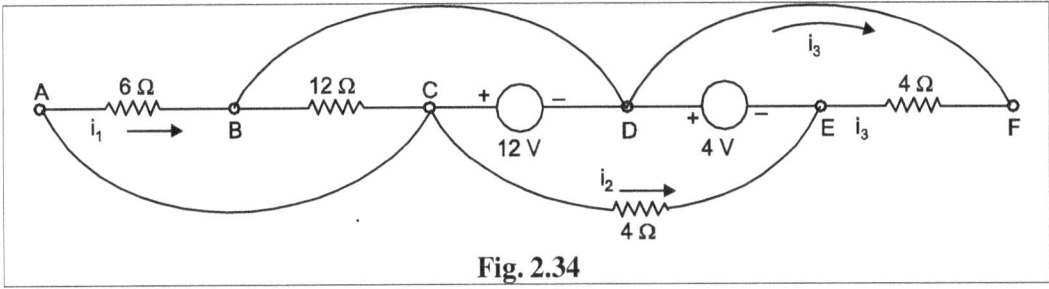

Fig. 2.34

Find the currents i_1, i_2 and i_3. Also find power delivered by each source.

Solution :

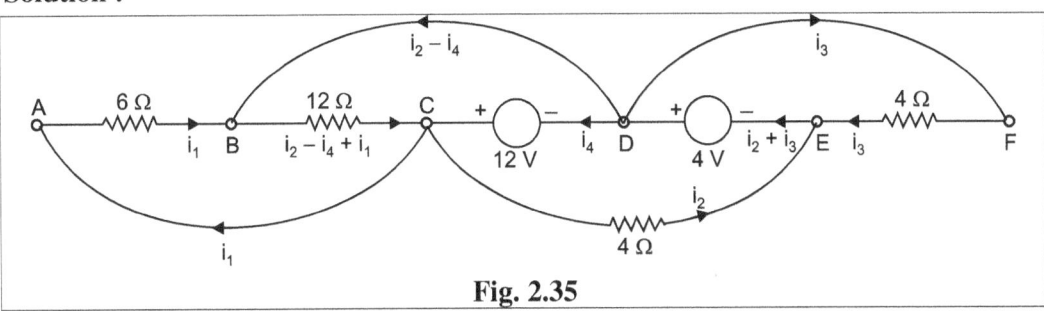

Fig. 2.35

For loop ABCA, according to KVL,

$$6i_1 + 12(i_2 - i_4 + i_1) = 0$$

∴ $$18.i_1 + 12.i_2 - 12.i_4 = 0 \qquad \qquad \text{...(1)}$$

For loop CDEC,

$$4.i_2 = 12 + 4$$

∴ $$4i_2 = 16$$

∴ $$\boxed{i_2 = 4\,A}$$

For loop DEFD,

$$4.i_3 = 4$$

∴ $$\boxed{i_3 = 1A}$$

For loop BCDB,

$$12.(i_2 - i_4 + i_1) = -12$$

∴ $$i_2 - i_4 + i_1 = -1$$

Put value of i_2

∴ $$i_4 - i_1 = 5 \qquad \qquad \text{...(2)}$$

Also, put value of i_2 in equation (1)

∴ $$18.i_1 + 12.(4) - 12i_4 = 0$$

$$18i_1+48-12.i_4 = 0$$

$$\therefore \qquad 3i_1+8-2i_4 = 0$$

$$\therefore \qquad 2.i_4-2.i_1 = 8 \qquad\qquad\qquad ...(3)$$

Solving equations (1) and (2)

$$2.i_4-2.i_1 = 10$$

$$2.i_4-3i_1 = 8$$

$$\overline{\qquad\qquad i_1 = 2A \qquad}$$

Put in equation (3) $\boxed{i_1 = 2A}$

$$\therefore \qquad 2i_4-3(2) = 8$$

$$\therefore \qquad 2i_4 = 14$$

$$\therefore \qquad \boxed{i_4 = 7\,A}$$

$$4\text{ V source} = 4\,(i_2+i_3)\text{ W}$$

$$= 4\,(4+1)$$

$$= 20\text{ W}$$

Power delivered by 12 V source $= 12\,(i_4)$

$$= 12\times7$$

$$\boxed{P_{12v} = 84\text{ W}}$$

Example 2.13 :

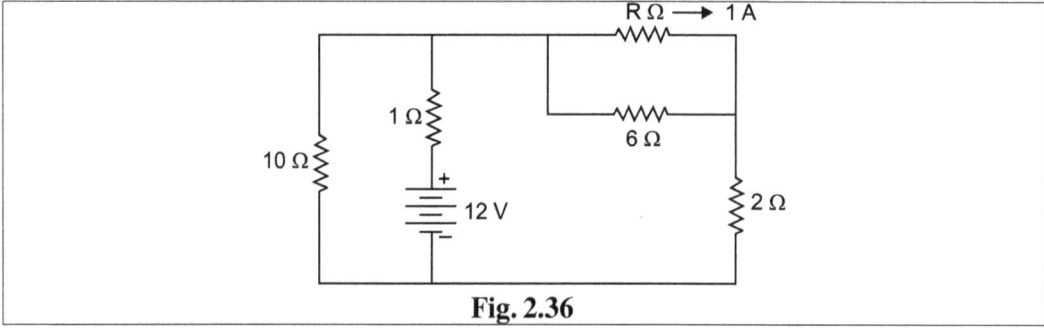

Fig. 2.36

Find the value of R such that 1 A would flow through it.

Solution :

Let us assume the various branch currents as shown in Fig. 2.37.

For loop ABGHA, by applying KVL,

$$1.(I_1)+10.(I_2) = 12 \qquad\qquad\qquad ...(1)$$

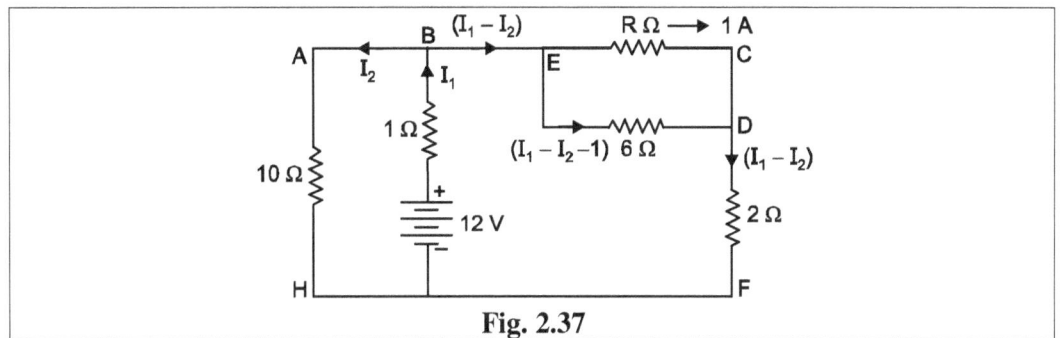

Fig. 2.37

Similarly for loop BEDFGB,

$$1 \, (I_1) + 6.(I_1 - I_2 - 1) + 2.(I_1 - I_2) = 12$$

$$\therefore \qquad 9.I_1 - 8.I_2 - 6 = 12$$

$$\therefore \qquad 9I_1 - 8.I_2 = 18 \qquad \qquad \ldots(2)$$

Solving equations (1) and (2),

$$9.I_1 + 90.I_2 = 108$$

$$9.I_1 - 8.I_2 = 18$$

$$- \qquad + \qquad -$$

$$\rule{4cm}{0.4pt}$$

$$\therefore \qquad 98 \, I_2 = 90$$

$$\therefore \qquad 98 \, I_2 = 90$$

$$\therefore \qquad I_2 = 0.9183 \text{ A}$$

Put in equation (1)

$$\therefore \qquad I_1 + 10.(0.9183) = 12$$

$$\therefore \qquad I_1 = 2.8163 \text{ A}$$

As R Ω and 6 Ω resistances are in parallel,

p.d. across both of them should be same.

$$\therefore \qquad R.(1) = 6.(I_1 - I_2 - 1)$$

$$\therefore \qquad R = 6 \, (2.8163 - 0.9183 - 1)$$

$$\therefore \qquad \boxed{R = 5.388 \ \Omega}$$

Example 2.14 :

Find current in branch AB using Kirchhoff's laws.

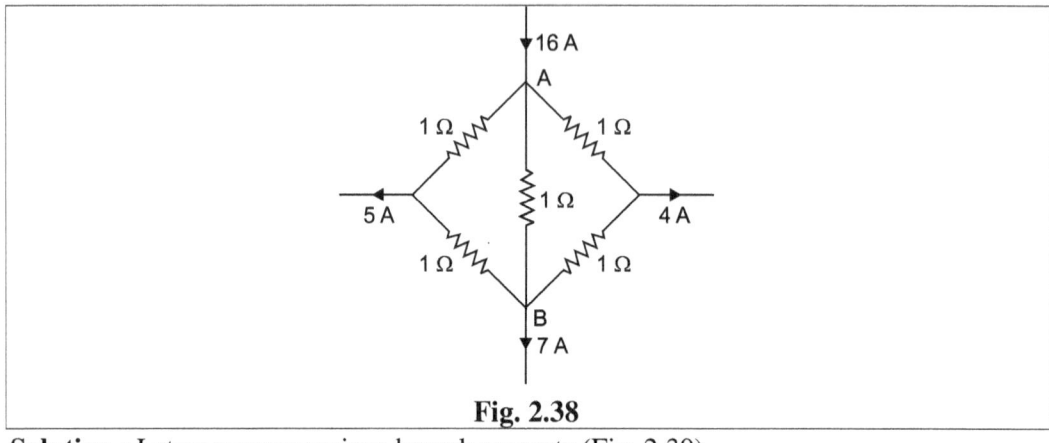

Fig. 2.38

Solution : Let us assume various branch currents.(Fig. 2.39)

According to KVL, for loop ABCA,

$$1.(I_1) - 1.(12 - I_1 - I_2) - 1.(16 - I_1 - I_2) = 0$$

∴ $I_1 - 12 + I_1 + I_2 - 16 + I_1 + I_2 = 0$

∴ $3.I_1 + 2.I_2 = 28$ ...(1)

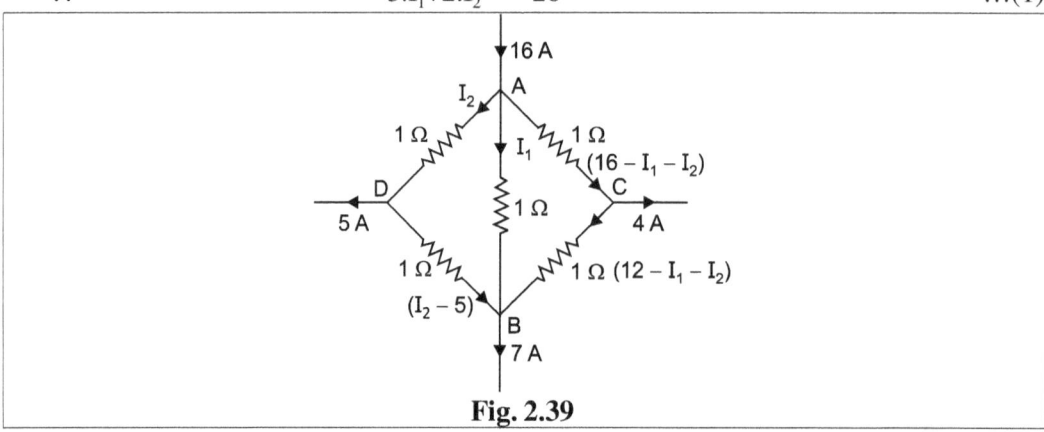

Fig. 2.39

Similarly for loop ABDA,

∴ $1.(I_1) - 1.(I_2 - 5) - 1.I_2 = 0$

∴ $I_1 - I_2 + 5 - I_2 = 0$

∴ $I_1 - 2.I_2 = -5$ ...(2)

Solving equations (1) and (2),

$$3.I_1 + 2.I_2 = 28$$
$$I_1 - 2.I_2 = -5$$
$$\overline{}$$
$$4.I_1 = 23$$

∴ $\boxed{I_1 = 5.75\ A}$

∴ Current flowing through branch AB = 5.75 A (from A to B)

Example 2.15 :

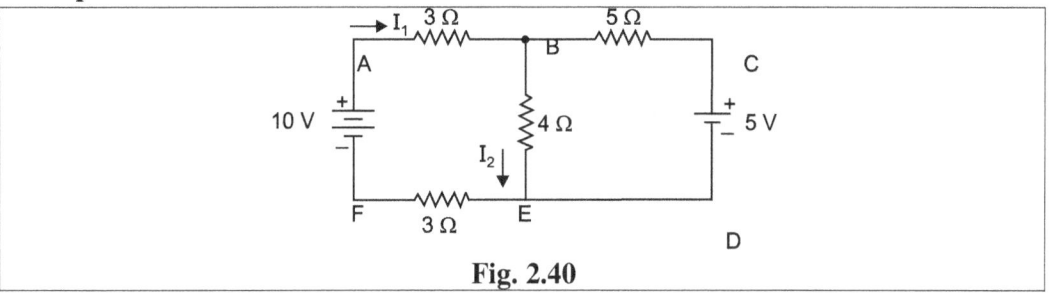

Fig. 2.40

Use Kirchhoff's laws to find current in 4 Ω resistance. Use branch currents as shown and not loop currents.

Solution :

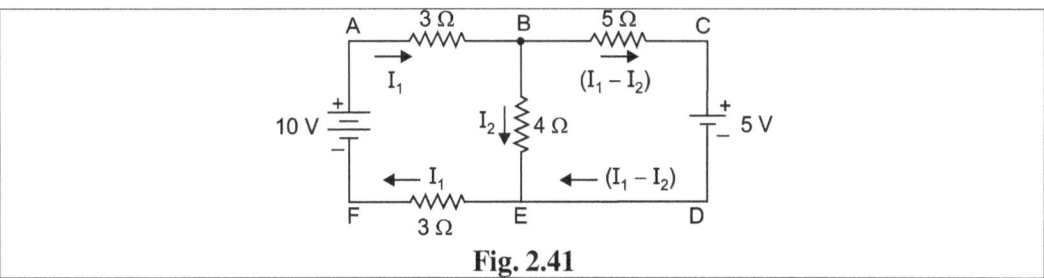

Fig. 2.41

According to KVL,

For loop ABEFA,

$$3.I_1 + 4.I_2 + 3.I_1 = 10$$

∴ $$6.I_1 + 4.I_2 = 10$$

∴ $$3I_1 + 2.I_2 = 5 \qquad \qquad ...(1)$$

Similarly for loop BCDEB,

$$5.(I_1 - I_2) - 4.I_2 = -5 \qquad \qquad ...(2)$$

∴ $$5\,I_1 - 9\,I_2 = -5$$

Solving equations (1) and (2)

$$15.I_1 + 10.I_2 = 25$$

$$15.I_1 - 27.I_2 = -15$$

$$\underline{\quad - \qquad + \qquad \qquad + \qquad}$$

∴ $$37.I_2 = 40$$

∴ $$\boxed{I_2 = 1.081 \text{ A}}$$

2.7 STAR AND DELTA CONNECTION

Application of Kirchhoff's laws in complicated network gives complex set of simultaneous equations. It is tedious and time consuming. In such situations *Delta Star* or *Star-Delta* transformation brings the network in simpler form.

Star Connection :

When three resistances are connected in such a manner that one end of each is connected together to form a junction keeping remaining three terminals open, it is known as *'Star Connection'*. Such a connection is shown in Fig. 2.42.

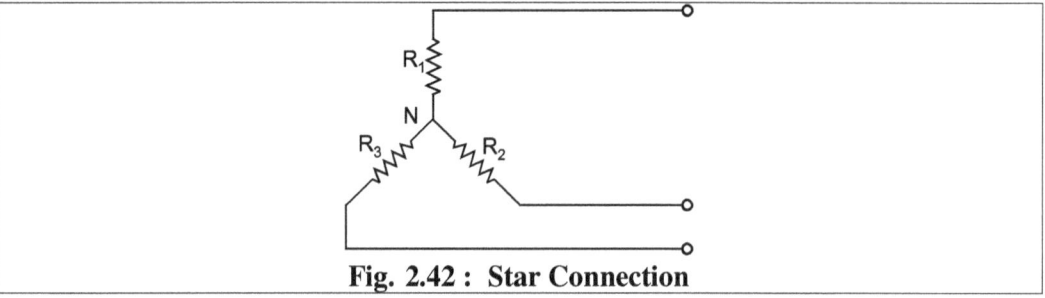

Fig. 2.42 : Star Connection

Delta Connection :

When three resistances are connected to form a mesh or loop and three terminals are taken away from three junction points, it becomes *'Delta Connection'*. It is shown in Fig. 2.43.

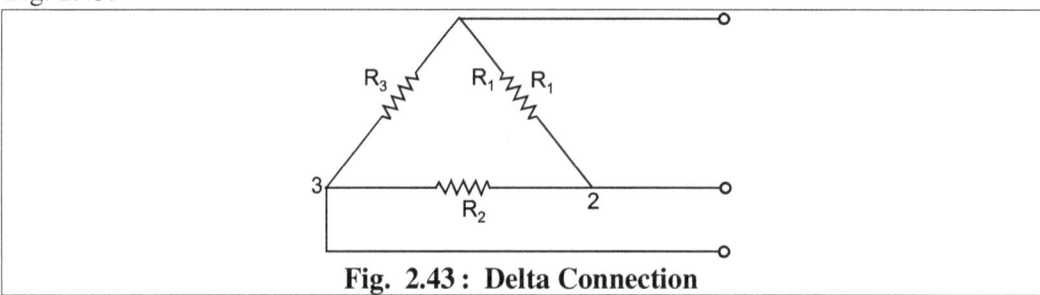

Fig. 2.43 : Delta Connection

2.7.1 Delta-Star Transformation

Let three resistances R_{12}, R_{23} and R_{31} be connected in delta as shown in Fig. 2.44.

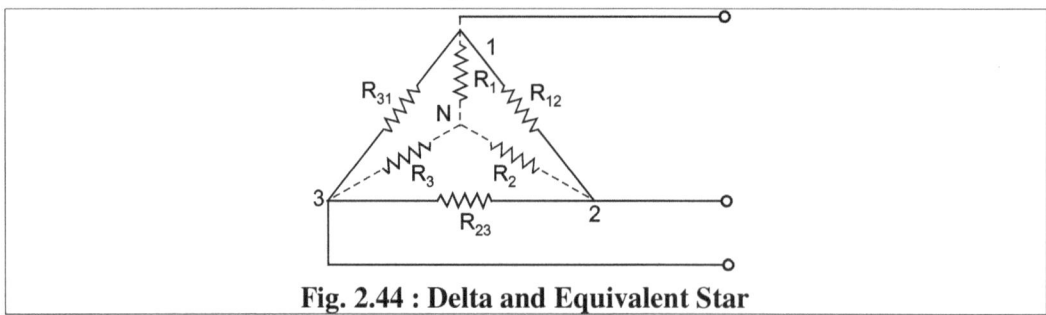

Fig. 2.44 : Delta and Equivalent Star

Let us convert this delta connection into an equivalent star connection. Let equivalent star resistances be R_1, R_2 and R_3.

To call these arrangements as equivalent of each other, resistance between two terminals must be same in both types of connections.

Resistance between terminals 1 and 2 will be

$$\text{For delta connection } = \frac{R_{12}.(R_{23}+R_{31})}{R_{12}+R_{23}+R_{31}} \qquad \text{... (1)}$$

and $\qquad\qquad\qquad$ for star connection $= R_1+R_2 \qquad\qquad$ ... (2)

Equating (1) and (2)

$$\frac{R_{12}(R_{23}+R_{31})}{R_{12}+R_{23}+R_{31}} = R_1+R_2 \qquad \text{...(3)}$$

Similarly for resistances between terminals 3 and 1, we get

$$\frac{R_{31}.(R_{12}+R_{23})}{R_{12}+R_{23}+R_{31}} = R_1+R_3 \qquad \text{... (4)}$$

Also for resistances between terminals 2 and 3 we get,

$$\frac{R_{23}.(R_{31}+R_{12})}{R_{12}+R_{23}+R_{31}} = R_2+R_3 \qquad \text{... (5)}$$

Let us find R_1, R_2 and R_3 in terms of R_{12}, R_{23} and R_{31}

Subtracting Equation (4) from equation (5) we get,

$$\frac{R_{23}(R_{31}+R_{12})-R_{31}(R_{12}+R_{23})}{R_{12}+R_{23}+R_{31}} = R_2-R_1 \qquad \text{...(6)}$$

Adding equations (3) and (6) we get,

$$\frac{R_{12}(R_{23}+R_{31})+R_{23}(R_{31}+R_{12})-R_{31}(R_{12}+R_{23})}{R_{12}+R_{23}+R_{31}} = 2.R_2$$

$\therefore \qquad\qquad\qquad$
$$\frac{2.R_{12}.R_{23}}{R_{12}+R_{23}+R_{31}} = 2.R_2$$

$\therefore \qquad\qquad\qquad$
$$R_2 = \frac{R_{12}.R_{23}}{R_{12}+R_{23}+R_{31}} \qquad \text{...(7)}$$

Similarly,

$$R_1 = \frac{R_{12}.R_{31}}{R_{12}+R_{23}+R_{31}} \qquad \text{...(8)}$$

and

$$R_3 = \frac{R_{23}.R_{31}}{R_{12}+R_{23}+R_{31}} \qquad \text{... (9)}$$

2.7.2 Star-Delta Transformation

Let 3 resistances R_1, R_2 and R_3 be connected in star as shown in Fig. 2.43.

Making use of equations (7), (8) and (9) we get,

$$R_1.R_2 = \frac{R_{12}^2.R_{31}.R_{23}}{(R_{12}+R_{23}+R_{31})^2} \qquad \ldots (10)$$

$$R_2.R_3 = \frac{R_{23}^2.R_{12}.R_{31}}{(R_{12}+R_{23}+R_{31})^2} \qquad \ldots (11)$$

and $$R_3.R_1 = \frac{R_{31}^2.R_{12}.R_{23}}{(R_{12}+R_{23}+R_{31})^2} \qquad \ldots (12)$$

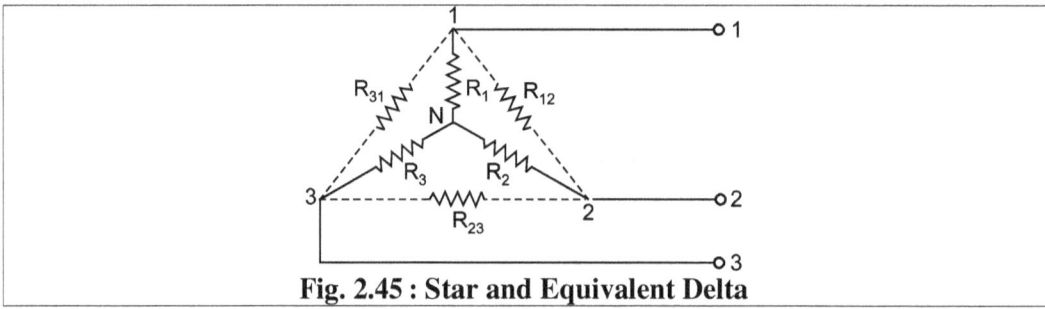

Fig. 2.45 : Star and Equivalent Delta

Adding equations (10), (11) and (12) we get,

$$R_1.R_2+R_2R_3+R_3R_1 = \frac{R_{12}^2R_{31}R_{23}+R_{23}^2R_{12}R_{31}+R_{31}^2R_{12}R_{23}}{(R_{12}+R_{23}+R_{31})^2}$$

$\therefore$ $$R_1R_2+R_2R_3+R_3R_1 = \frac{R_{12}.R_{23}.R_{31}(R_{12}+R_{23}+R_{31})}{(R_{12}+R_{23}+R_{31})^2}$$

$\therefore$ $$R_1R_2+R_2R_3+R_3R_1 = R_{12}.\left(\frac{R_{23}.R_{31}}{R_{12}+R_{23}+R_{31}}\right) \qquad \ldots (13)$$

Put $$\frac{R_{23}.R_{31}}{R_{12}+R_{23}+R_{31}} = R_3 \text{ in equation (13)}$$

$\therefore$ $$R_1R_2+R_2R_3+R_3R_1 = R_{12}.R_3 \qquad \ldots (14)$$

$\therefore$ $$R_{12} = \frac{R_1.R_2+R_2.R_3+R_3.R_1}{R_3} = R_1 + R_2 + \frac{R_1R_2}{R_3} \qquad \ldots (15)$$

Similarly,

$$R_{23} = \frac{R_1.R_2+R_2.R_3+R_3.R_1}{R_1} = R_2 + R_3 + \frac{R_2R_3}{R_1} \qquad \ldots (16)$$

and

$$R_{31} = \frac{R_1.R_2+R_2.R_3+R_3.R_1}{R_2} = R_3 + R_1 + \frac{R_3R_1}{R_2} \qquad \ldots (17)$$

Example 2.16 :

Determine the resistance between the terminals X and Y as shown in Fig. 2.46.

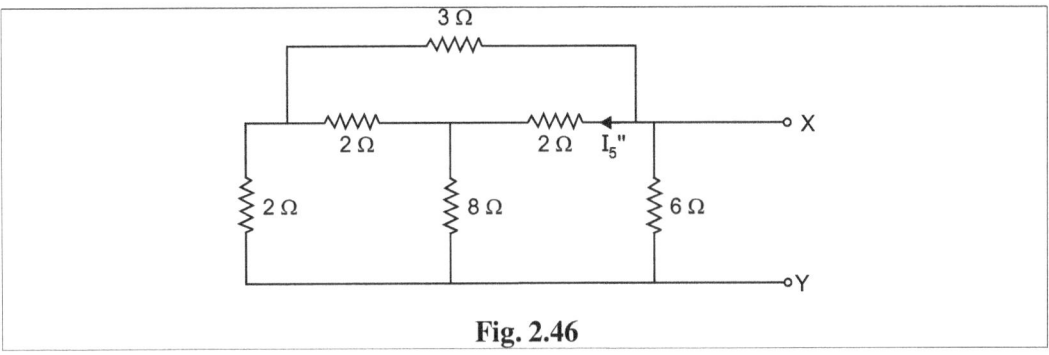

Fig. 2.46

Solution : Convert delta of 3 Ω, 2 Ω and 2 Ω to star.

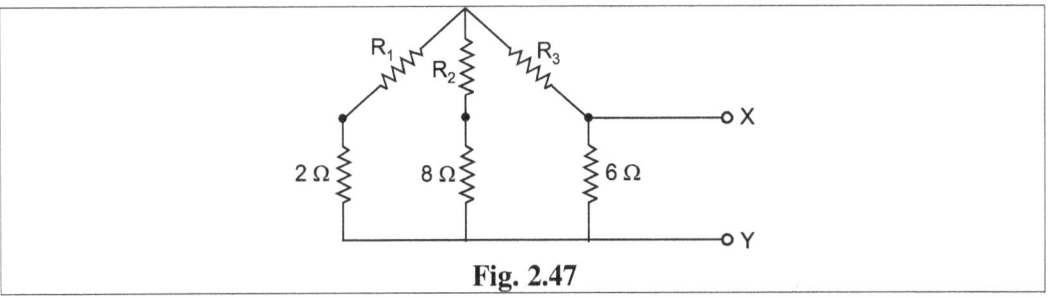

Fig. 2.47

$$R_1 = \frac{3 \times 2}{3+2+2} = 0.8571 \ \Omega$$

$$R_2 = \frac{2 \times 2}{3+2+2} = 0.5714 \ \Omega$$

$$R_3 = \frac{3 \times 2}{3+2+2} = 0.8571 \ \Omega$$

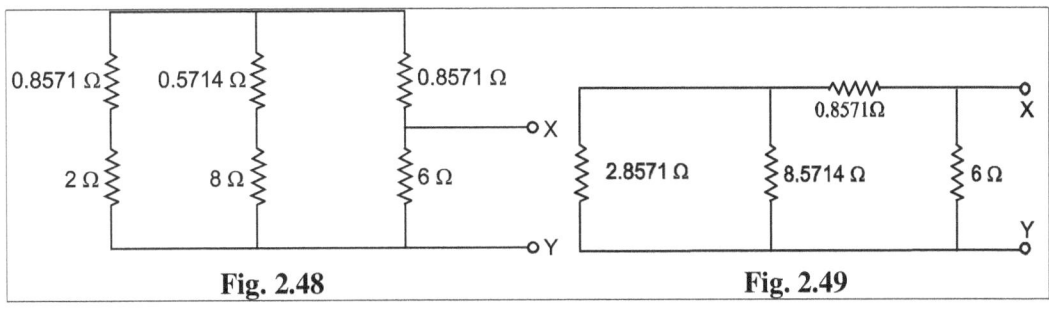

Fig. 2.48   **Fig. 2.49**

$2.8571 \parallel 8.5714 - 2.1428 \ \Omega$

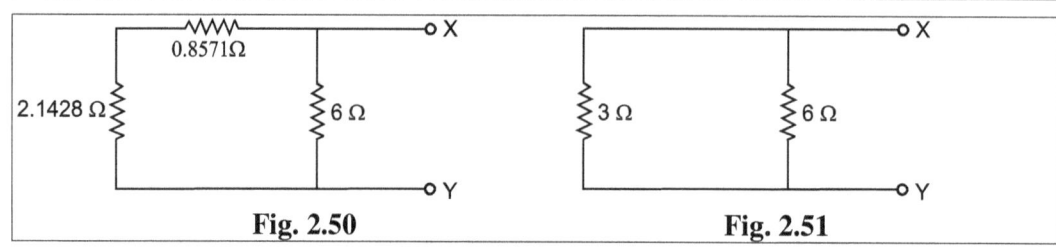

Fig. 2.50   Fig. 2.51

$$R_{XY} = 3 \parallel 6$$

$$= \frac{6 \times 3}{6 + 3} = 2\ \Omega$$

Example 2.17 :

Determine the resistance between the terminals X and Y for the circuit shown in Fig. 2.52 below.

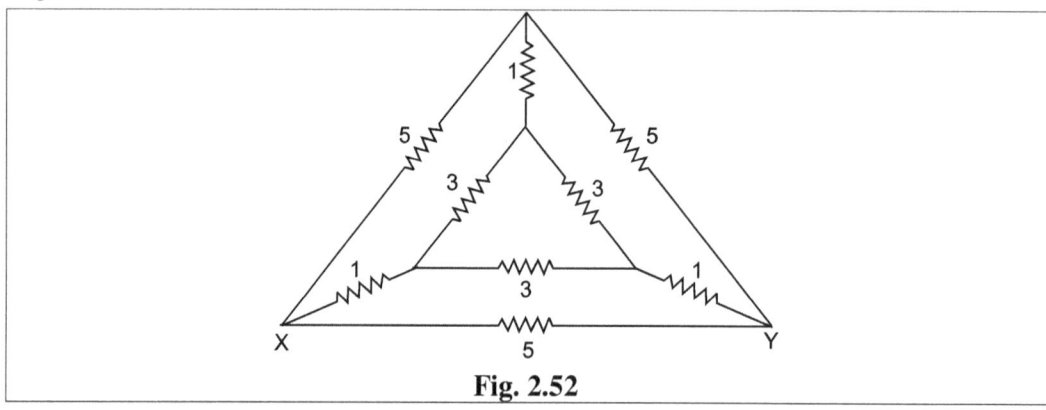

Fig. 2.52

Solution : Converting inner delta to star : Each resistance $= \dfrac{3 \times 3}{3 + 3 + 3} = 1\ \Omega$

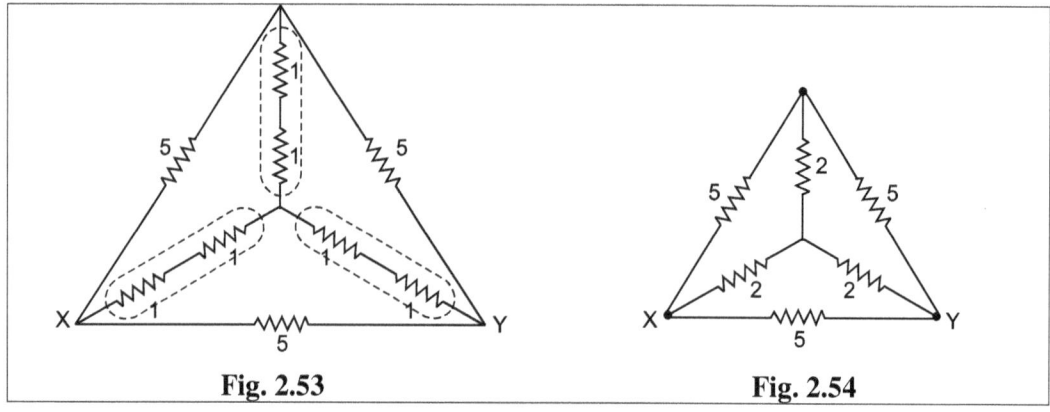

Fig. 2.53   Fig. 2.54

Converting inner star to delta.

Each resistance $= \dfrac{(2 \times 2) + (2 \times 2) + (2 \times 2)}{2} = 6\ \Omega$

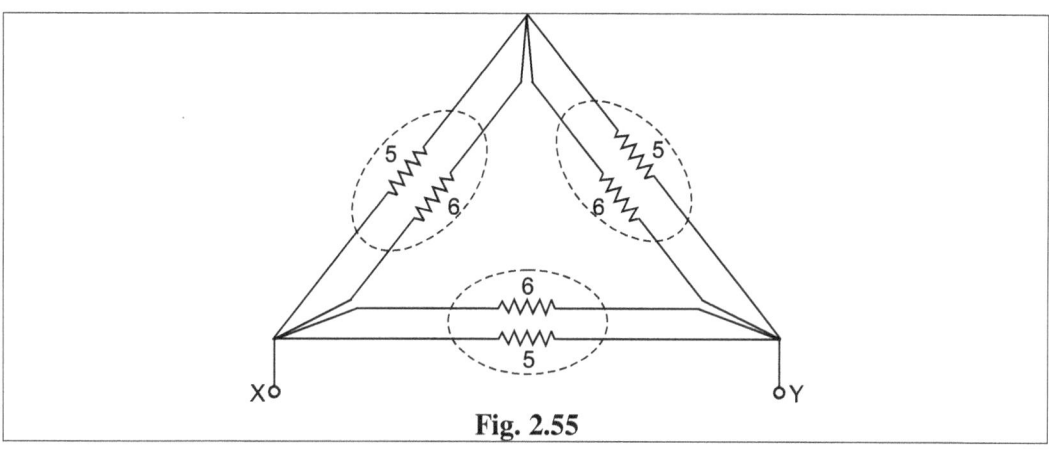

Fig. 2.55

$$5 \parallel 6 = \frac{5 \times 6}{5 + 6} = 2.7272 \ \Omega$$

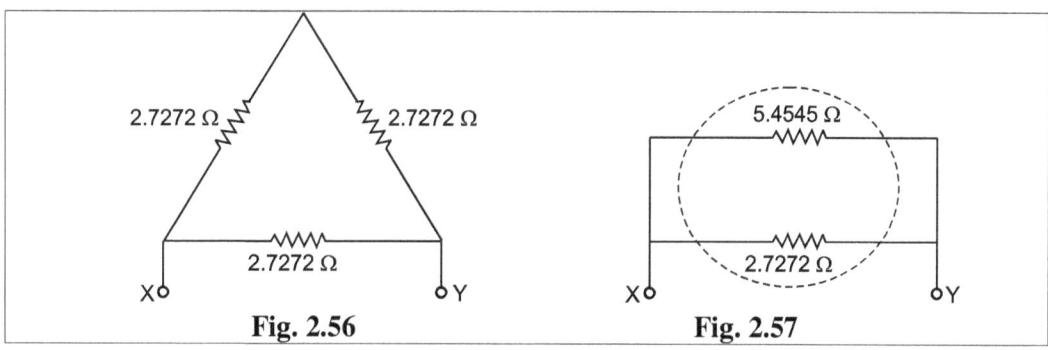

Fig. 2.56   **Fig. 2.57**

$$R_{XY} = 5.4545 \parallel 2.7272 = 1.8181 \ \Omega$$

Example 2.18 : Find the source current by the method of simplification of network.

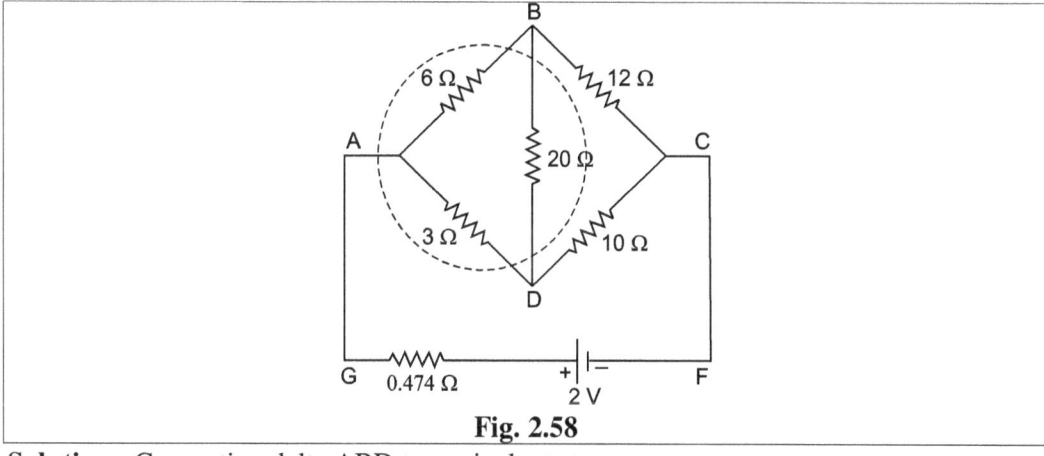

Fig. 2.58

Solution : Converting delta ABD to equivalent star we get,

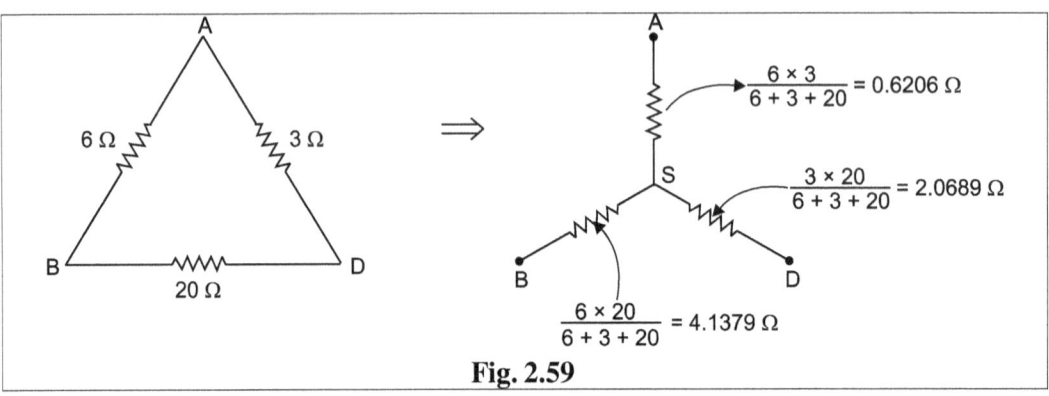

Fig. 2.59

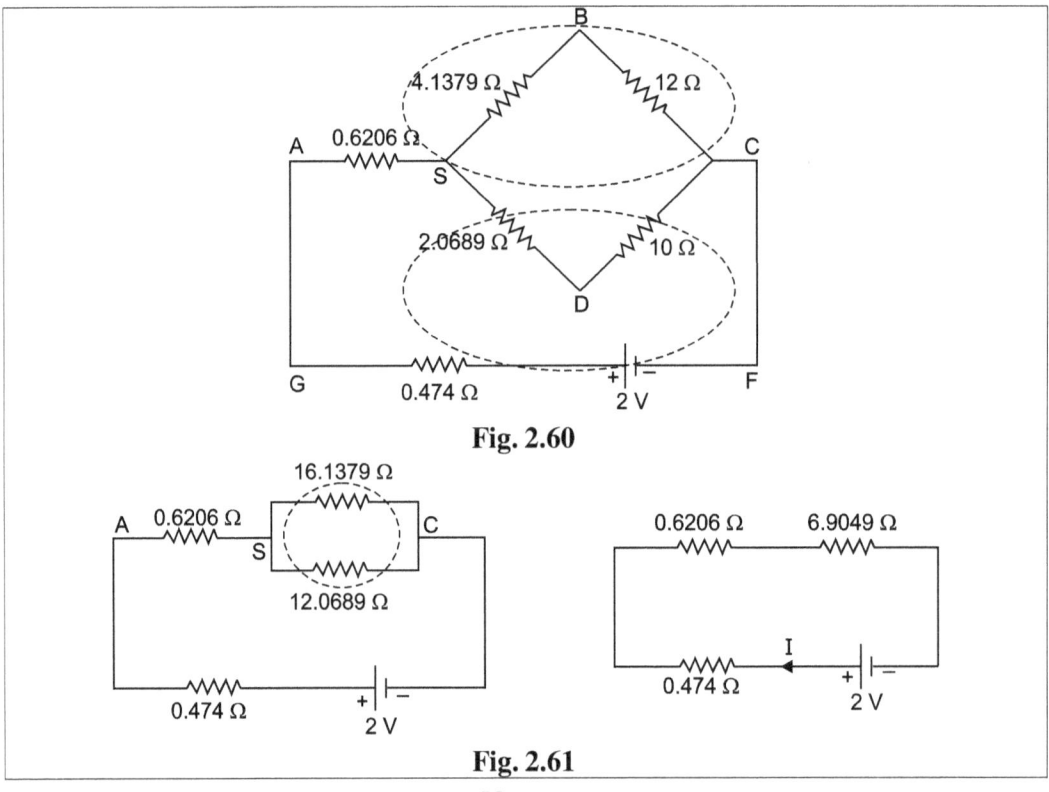

$$I = \frac{V_{Total}}{R_{Total}} = \frac{2}{0.6206 + 6.9049 + 0.474} = 0.25 \text{ A}$$

Example 2.18 :

Find the effective resistance across terminals M-N of the resistive network given below.

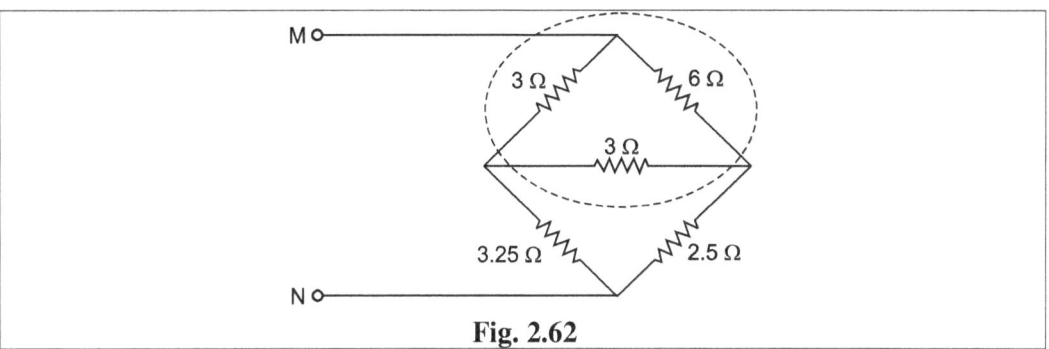

Fig. 2.62

Solution : Converting upper delta 3 Ω, 3 Ω and 6 Ω to equivalent star.

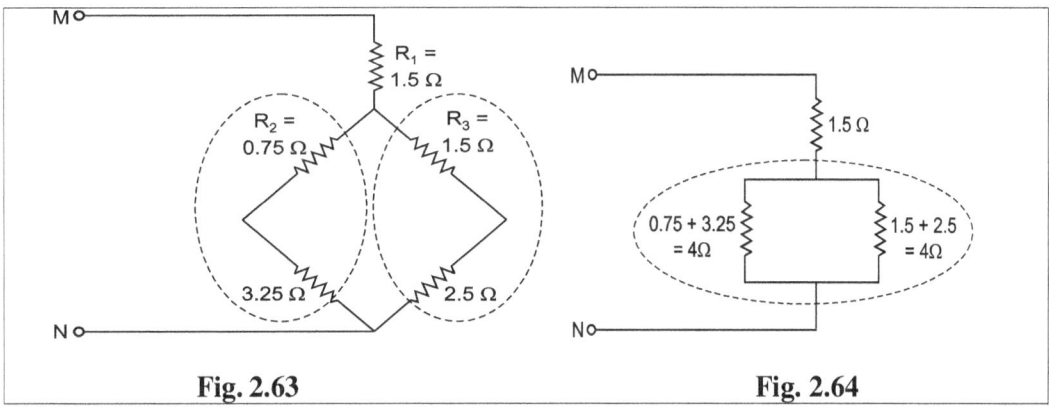

Fig. 2.63   **Fig. 2.64**

$$R_1 = \frac{3 \times 6}{3 + 3 + 6} = 1.5 \ \Omega, \quad R_2 = \frac{3 \times 3}{3 + 3 + 6} = 0.75 \ \Omega, \quad R_3 = \frac{3 \times 6}{3 + 3 + 6} = 1.5 \ \Omega$$

$$R_{MN} = 1.5 \ (4 \parallel 4) = 1.5 + 2 = 3.5 \ \Omega$$

Example 2.19 : Calculate the effective resistance between points A and B.

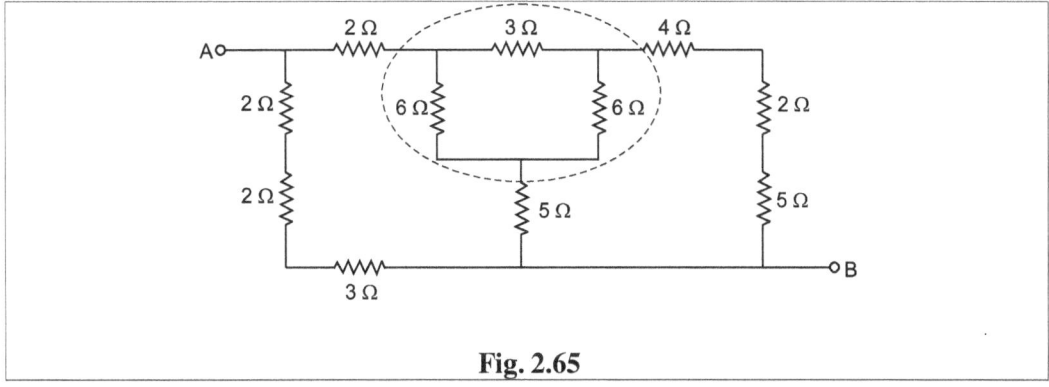

Fig. 2.65

Solution :

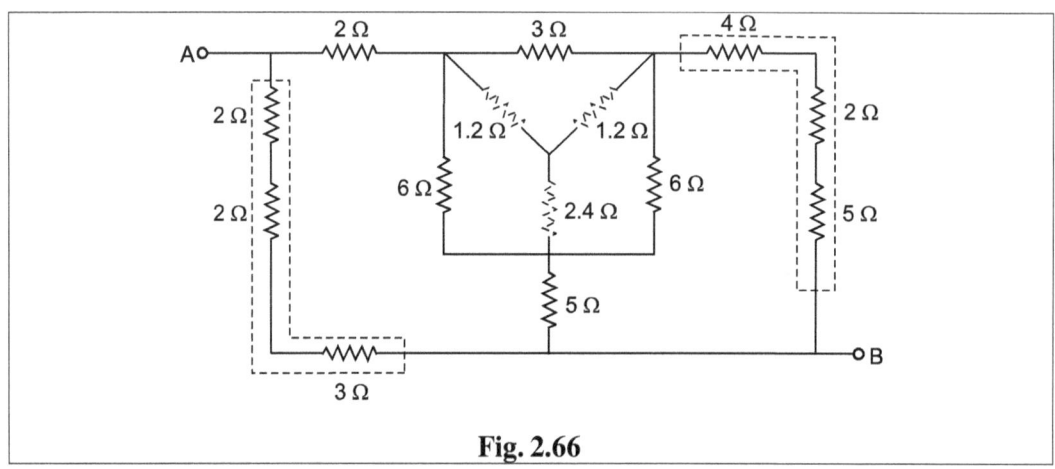

Fig. 2.66

Convert delta into equivalent star.

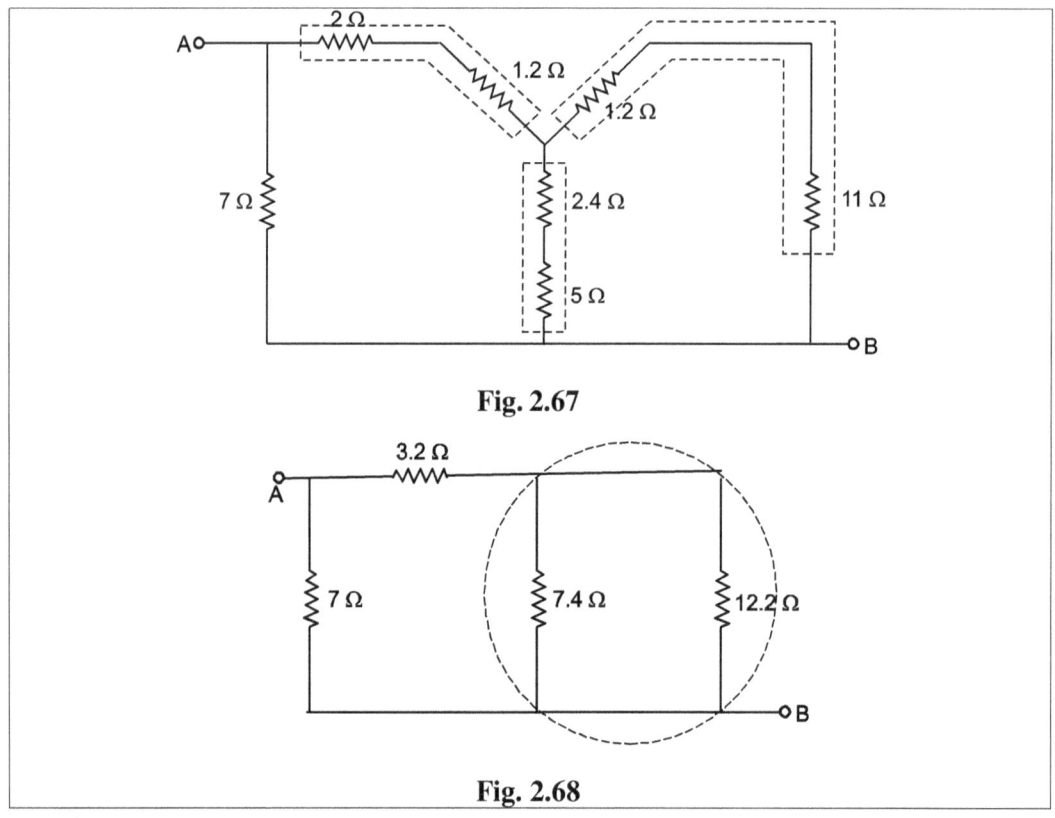

Fig. 2.67

Fig. 2.68

7.4 Ω and 12.2 Ω are in parallel.

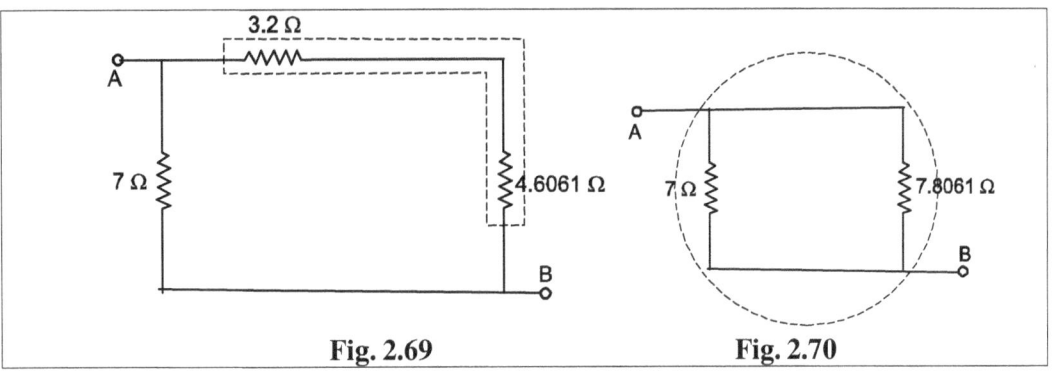

Fig. 2.69   Fig. 2.70

7Ω and 7.8061Ω are in parallel across A and B. Hence, equivalent resistance,

Across terminals A and B, $R_{AB} = \dfrac{7 \times 7.8061}{(7+7.8061)} = 3.69\ \Omega$

Example 2.20 :

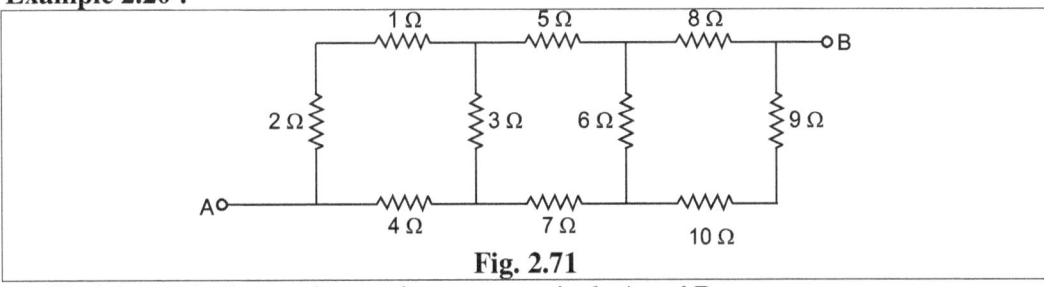

Fig. 2.71

Find the equivalent resistance between terminals A and B.

Solution :

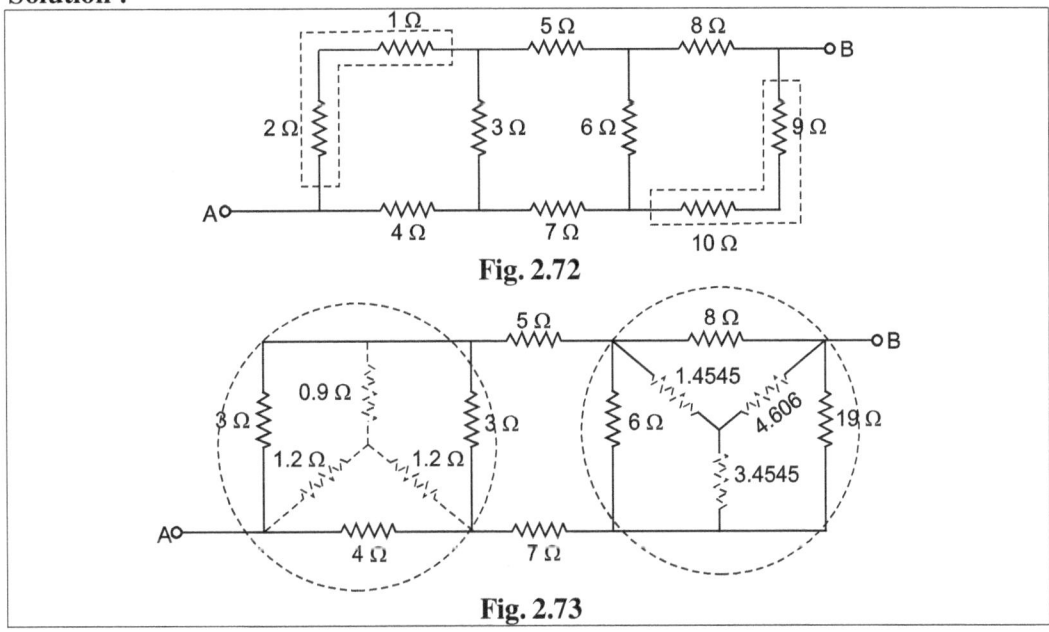

Fig. 2.72

Fig. 2.73

Convert both the delta into equivalent star.

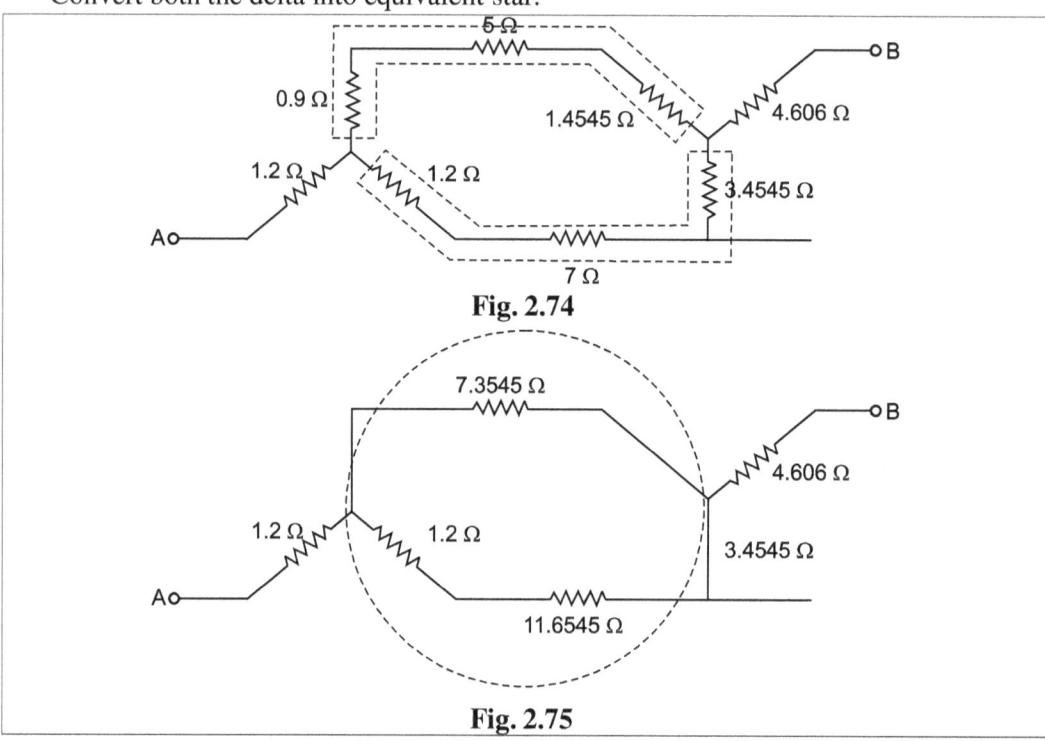

Fig. 2.74

Fig. 2.75

Here 1.2 Ω and 11.6545 Ω are in series. Resistances 7.3545Ω and 12.8545 Ω are in parallel.

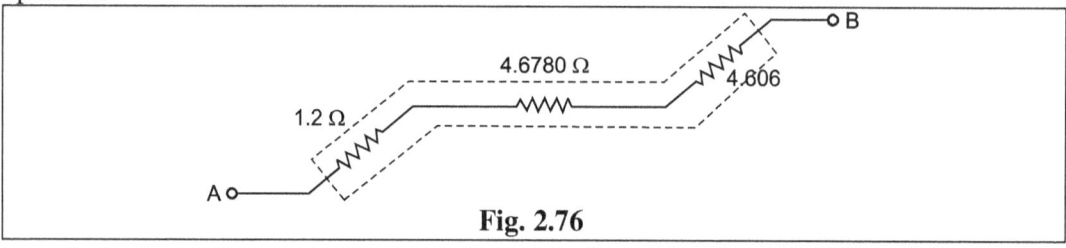

Fig. 2.76

$\therefore$ Equivalent resistance between terminals A and B $R_{AB} = 10.4840\ \Omega$

Example 2.21 : Find the equivalent resistance across the terminals A and B.

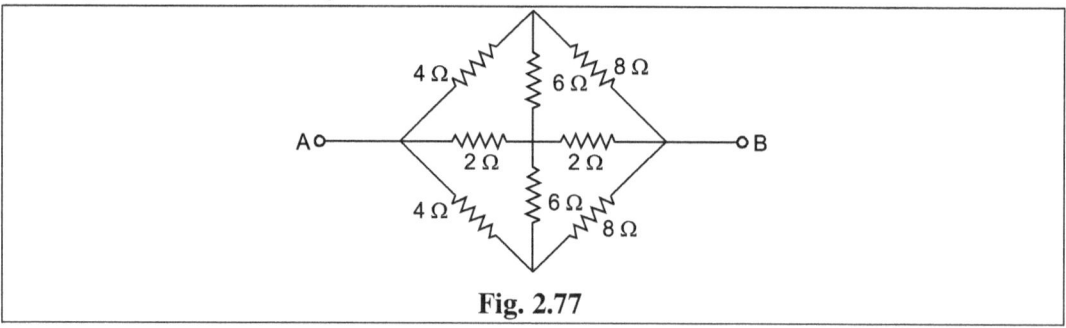

Fig. 2.77

Solution :

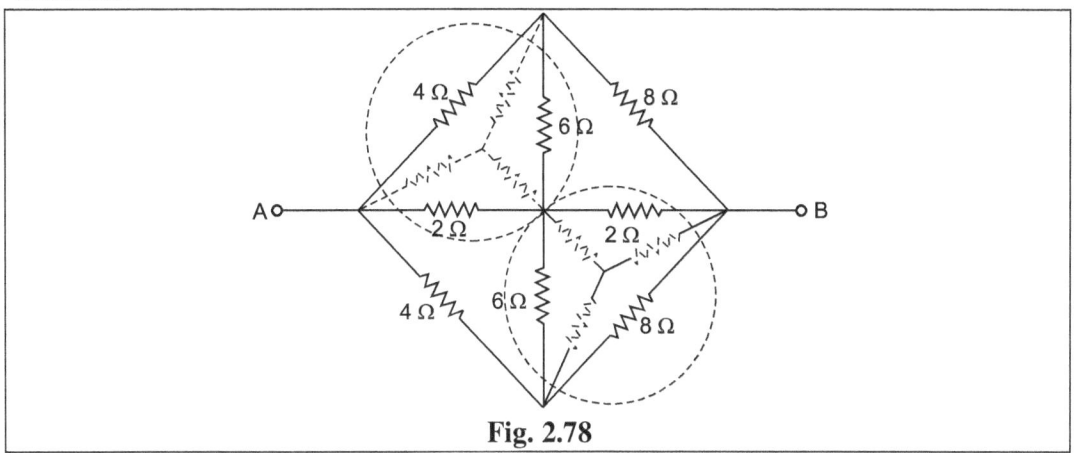

Fig. 2.78

Convert delta into equivalent star.

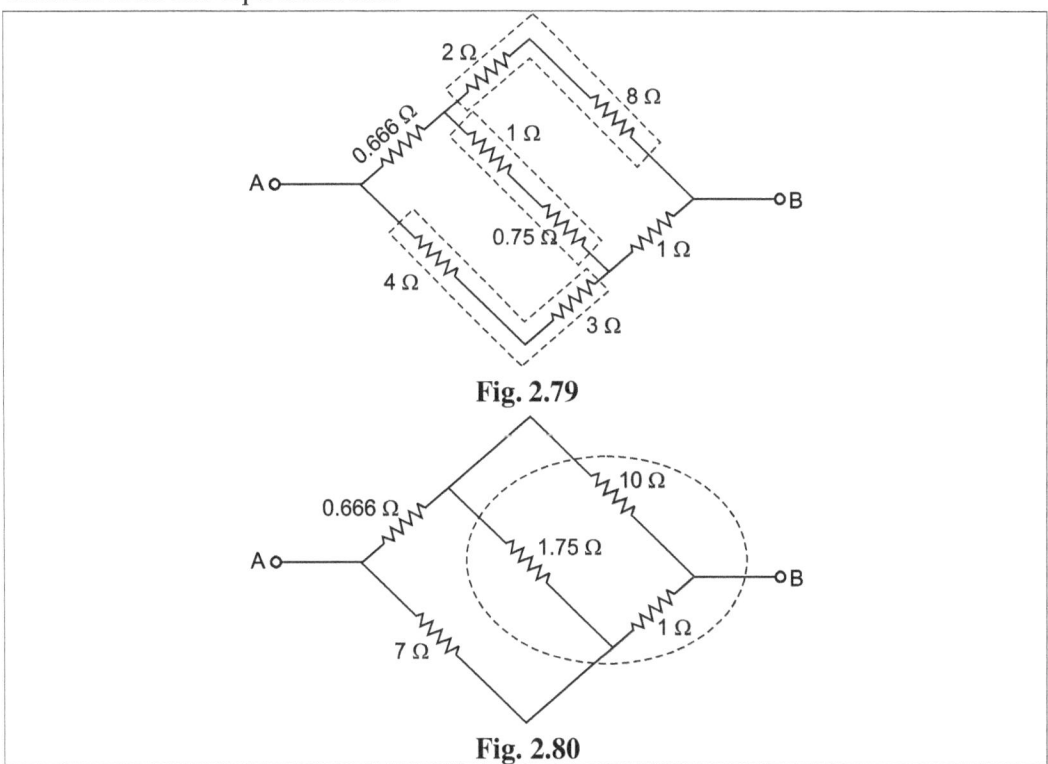

Fig. 2.79

Fig. 2.80

Convert delta into star.

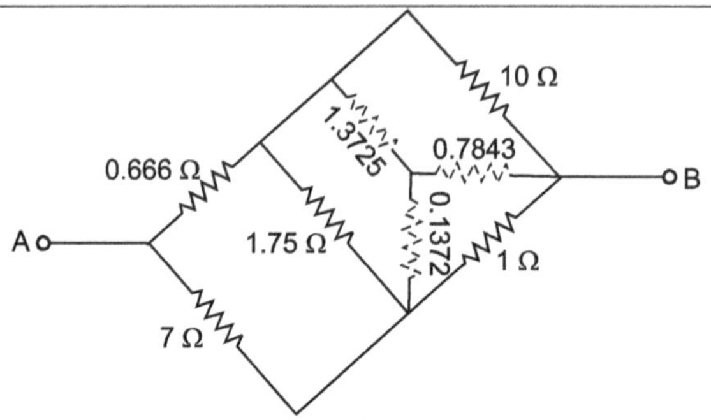

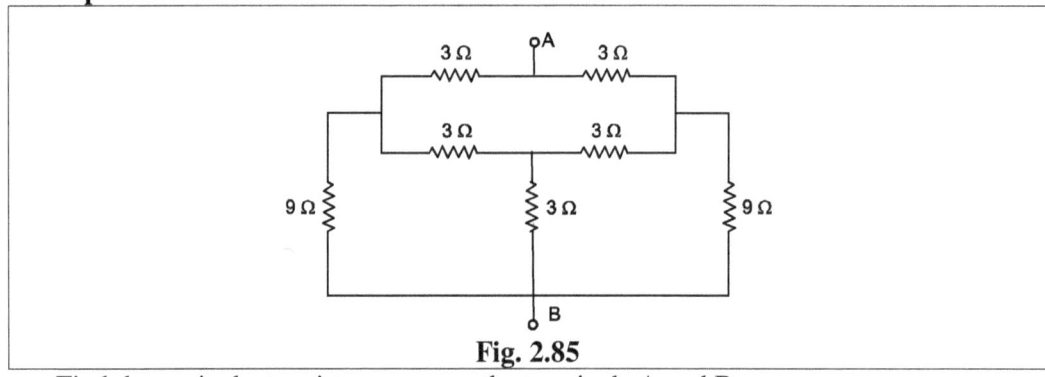

Fig. 2.81

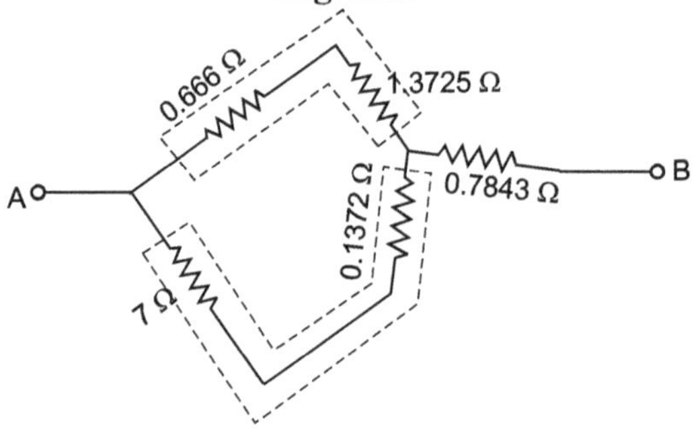

Fig. 2.82

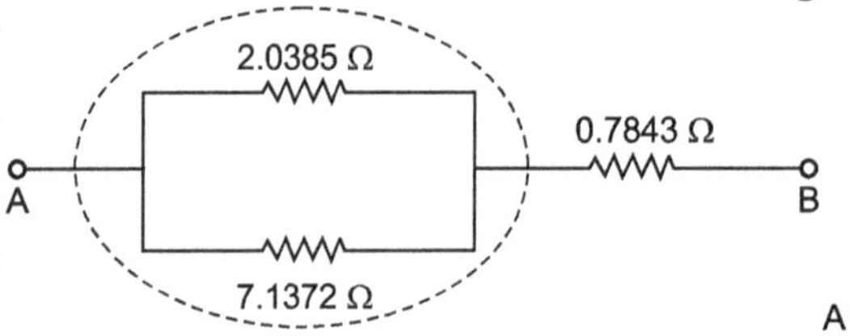

Fig. 2.83   **Fig. 2.84**

$$R_{AB} = [(2.0385 \,\|\, 7.1372) + 0.7843] = 1.6377 + 0.784 = 2.422 \ \Omega$$

Example 2.22 :

Fig. 2.85

Find the equivalent resistance across the terminals A and B.

Solution :

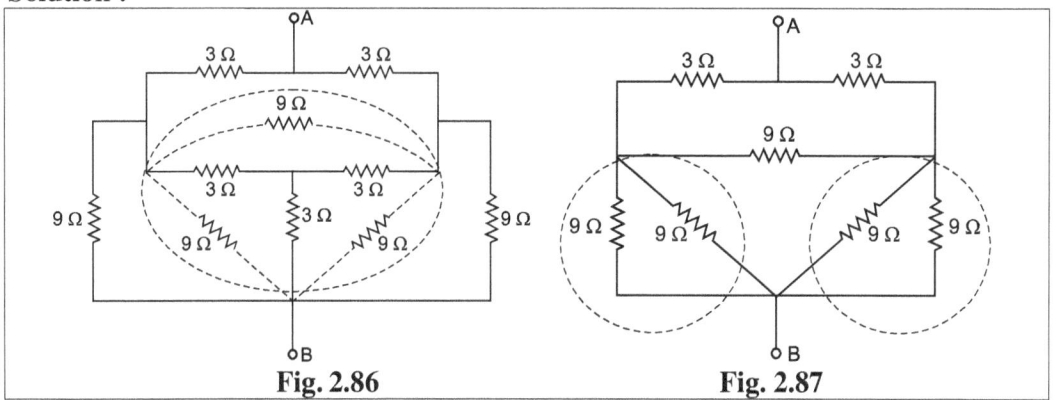

Fig. 2.86   **Fig. 2.87**

Convert inner star into equivalent delta.   Here 9Ω resistances are in parallel.

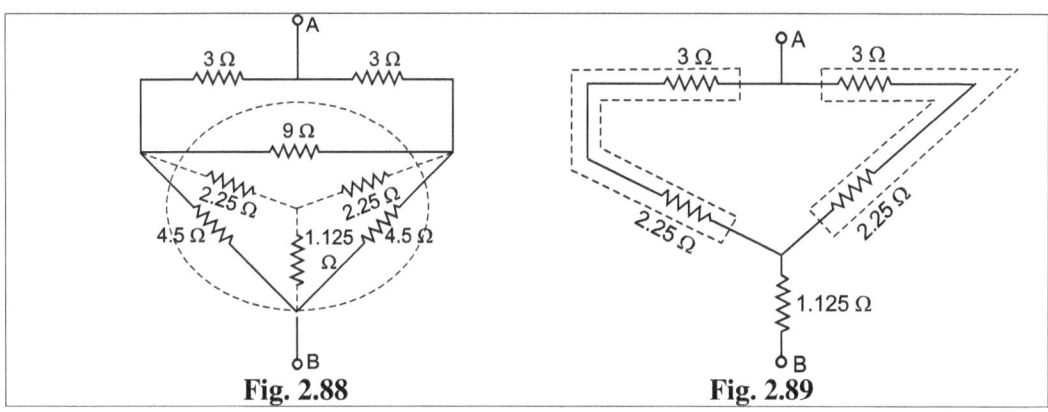

Fig. 2.88   **Fig. 2.89**

Hence,

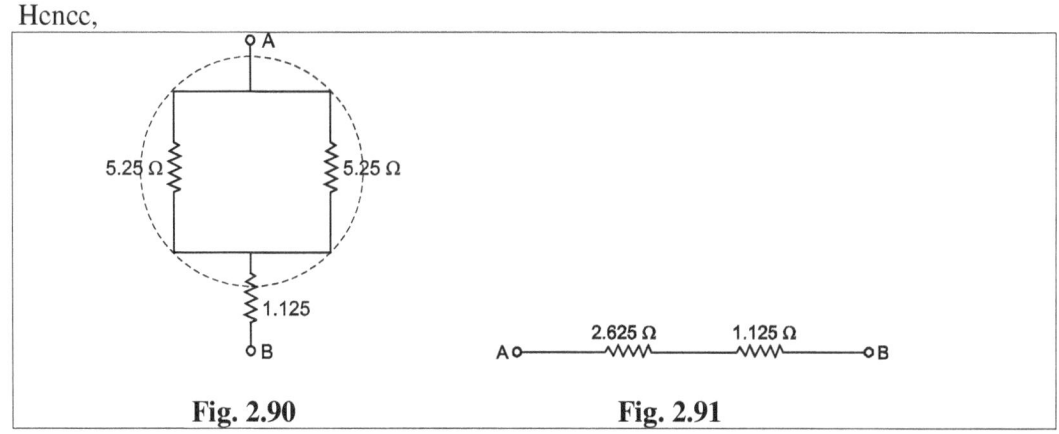

Fig. 2.90   **Fig. 2.91**

$$R_{AB} = 2.625 + 1.125 = 3.75 \ \Omega$$

Example 2.23 :

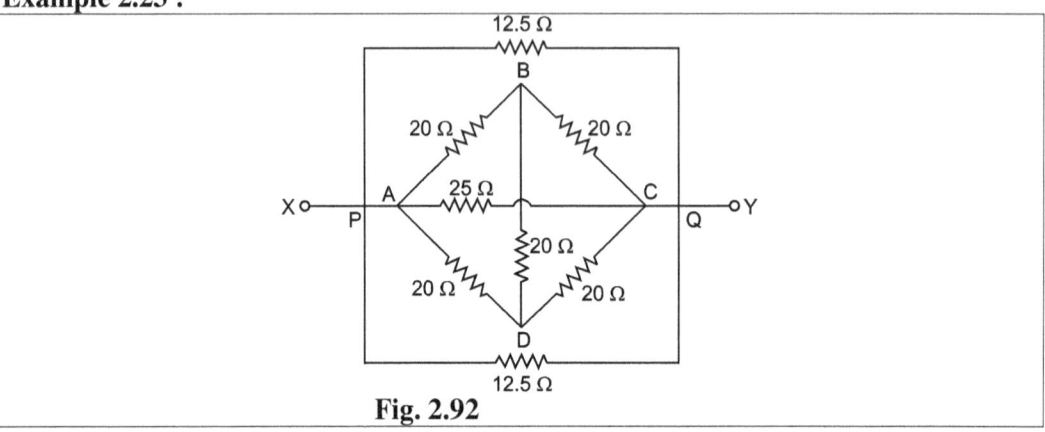

Fig. 2.92

Find the equivalent resistance between the terminals X and Y.

Solution :

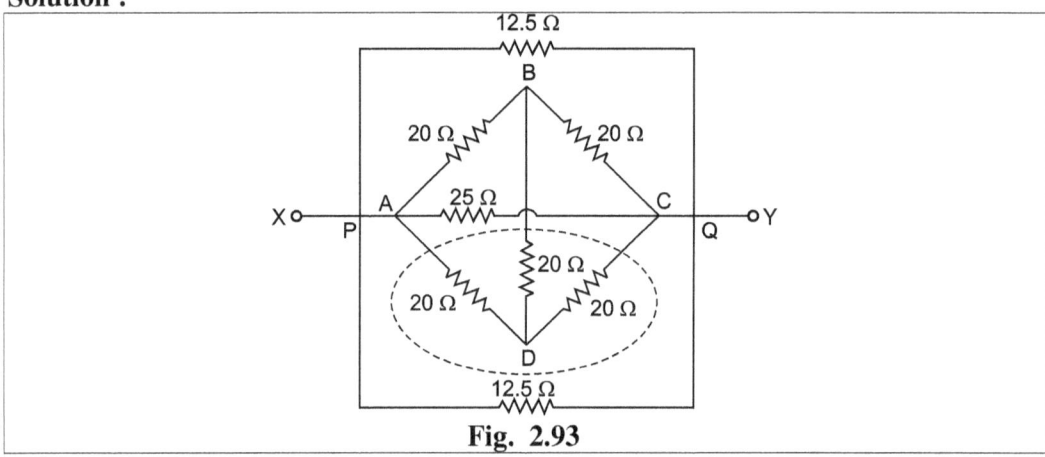

Fig. 2.93

Convert star into equivalent delta. Then circuit will become as shown in Fig. 2.94.

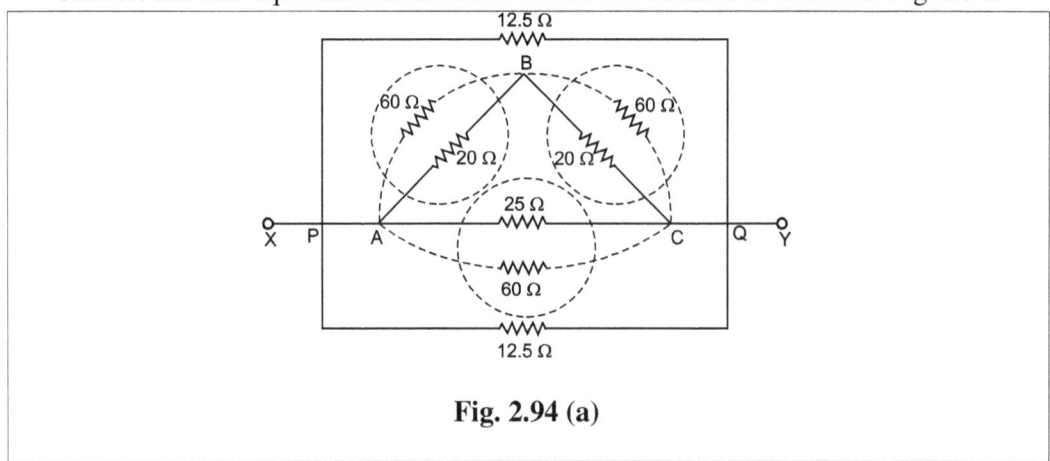

Fig. 2.94 (a)

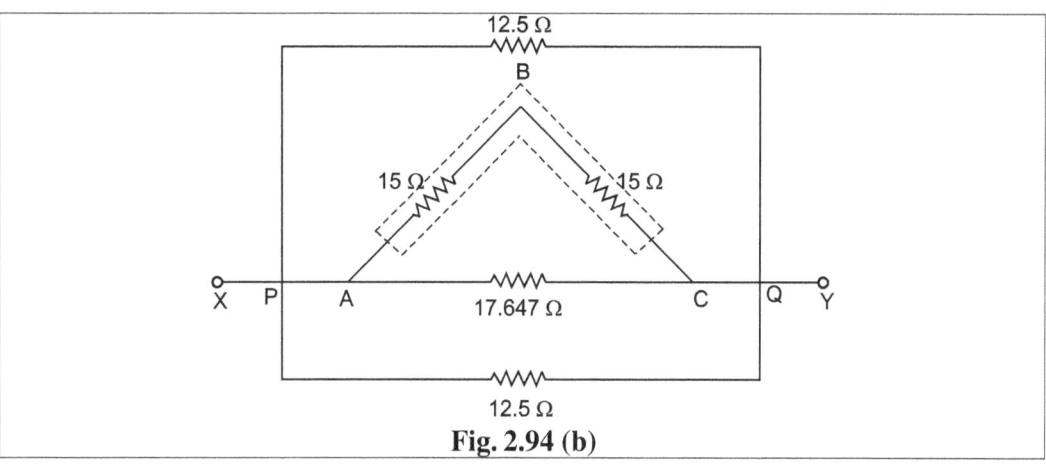

Fig. 2.94 (b)

Two 12.5 Ω resistances are in parallel. While two 15 Ω resistances are in series.

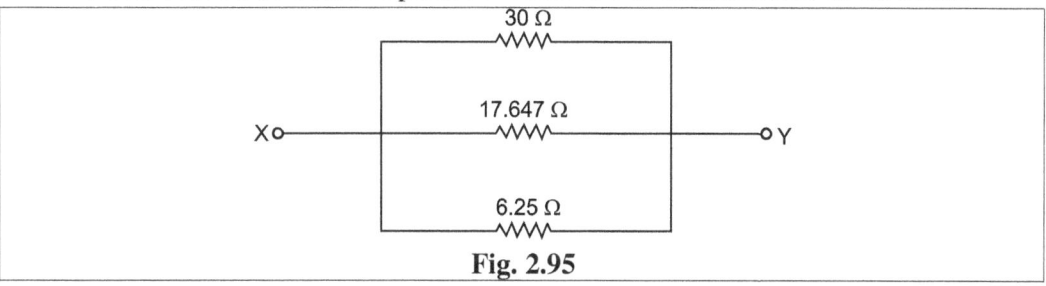

Fig. 2.95

All the resistances are in parallel.

$$\therefore \qquad \frac{1}{R_{XY}} = \frac{1}{17.647} + \frac{1}{30} + \frac{1}{6.25}$$

$$\therefore$$

$$\therefore \qquad R_{XY} = 4 \ \Omega$$

Example 2.24 :

Find the equivalent resistance across the terminals A – B for the network shown in figure given below. All resistances are in ohm.

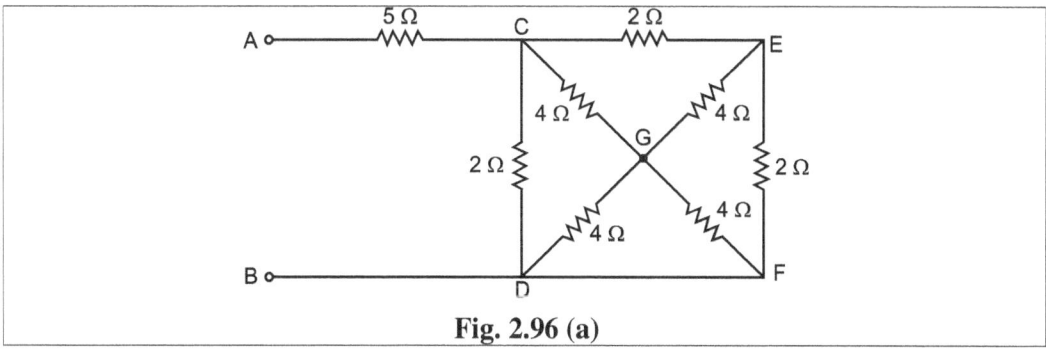

Fig. 2.96 (a)

Solution : Convert CGD and EGF (Delta) into star.

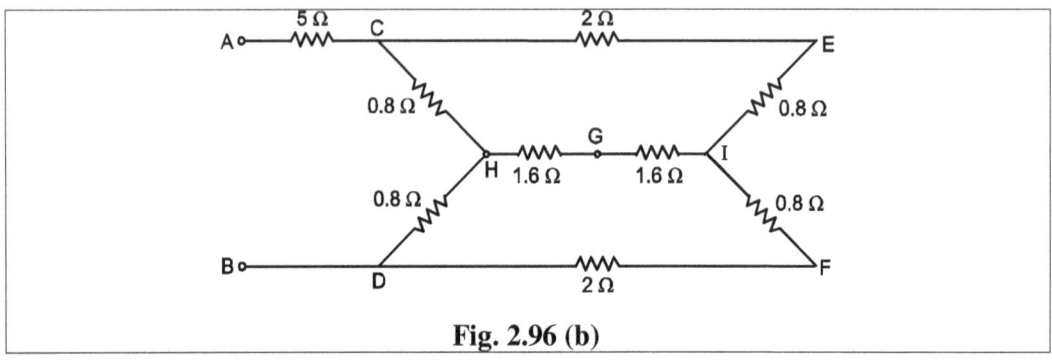

Fig. 2.96 (b)

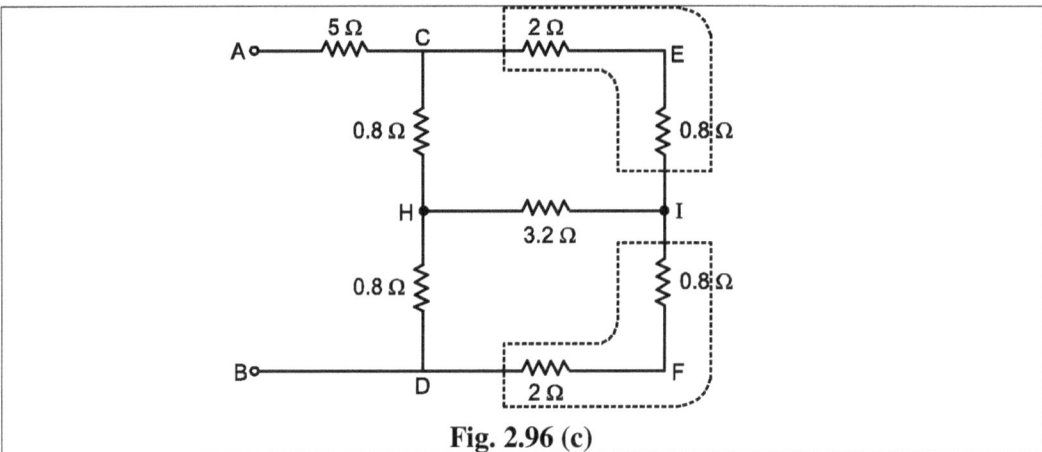

Fig. 2.96 (c)

Convert either CHI or DHI into star.

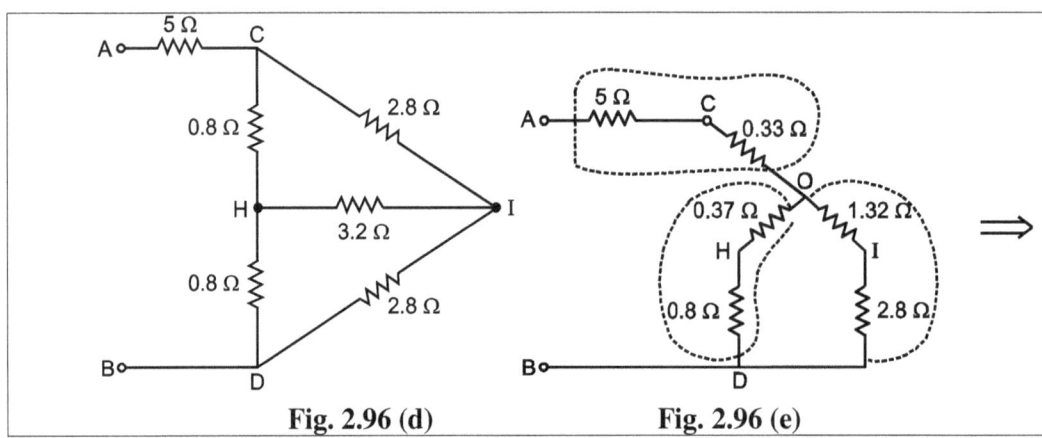

Fig. 2.96 (d)   **Fig. 2.96 (e)**

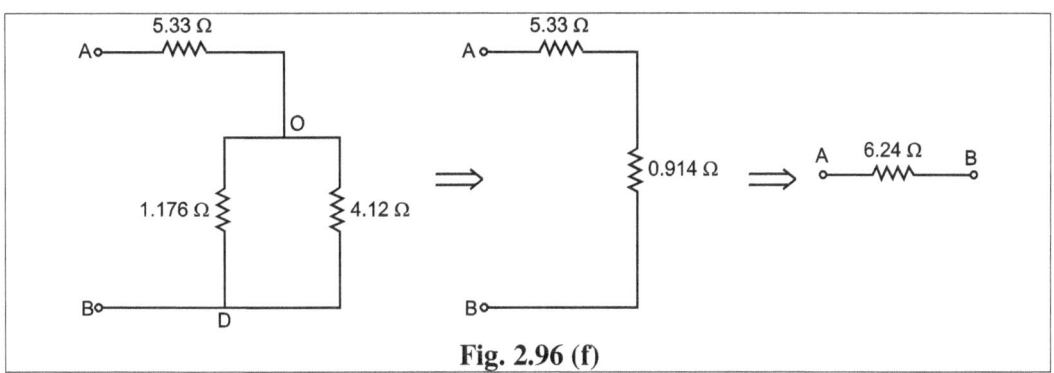

Fig. 2.96 (f)

2.8 NETWORK THEOREMS

Let us study following theorems one by one.

2.8.1 Superposition Theorem

Statement : In any linear, bilateral network containing atleast two energy sources, response in any element is equal to algebraic sum of responses caused by individual sources acting alone, making all other energy sources inactive or inoperative i.e. replacing the remaining sources by their internal resistance (if any).

Explanation : Consider a network shown in Fig. 2.97.

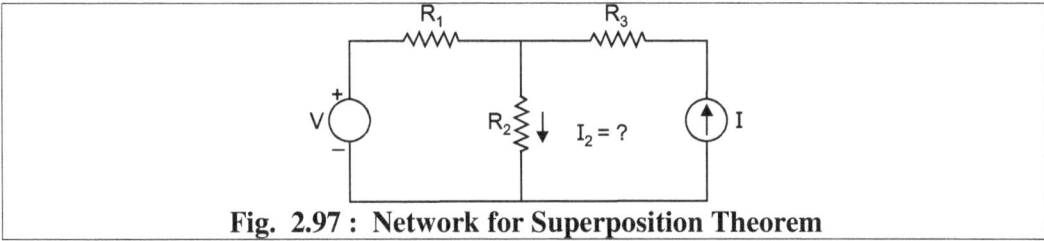

Fig. 2.97 : Network for Superposition Theorem

We are interested in finding I_2 i.e. current flowing through R_2.

Note : Consider voltage source acting alone. Make current source inactive i.e. replace it by it's internal resistance. As internal resistance of an ideal current source is infinite, it is replaced by open circuit. Circuit will be as shown in Fig. 2.98.

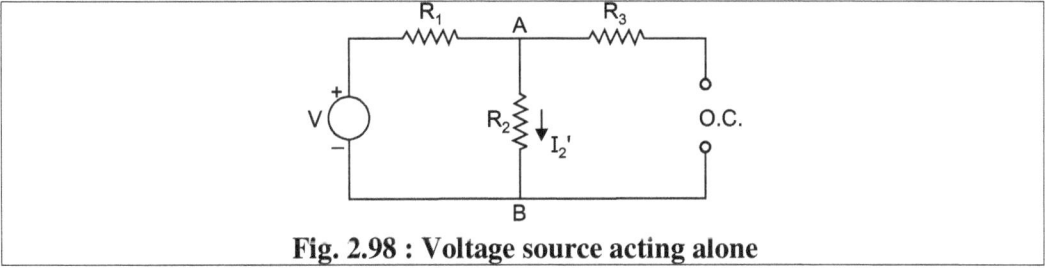

Fig. 2.98 : Voltage source acting alone

Let corresponding response through R_2 be I_2'.

$\therefore$ $$I_2' = \frac{V}{R_1+R_2} \text{ (from A to B)}$$

Now consider current source acting alone. Replace ideal voltage source by short circuit, because it's internal resistance is zero. Circuit will be as shown in Fig.2.99.

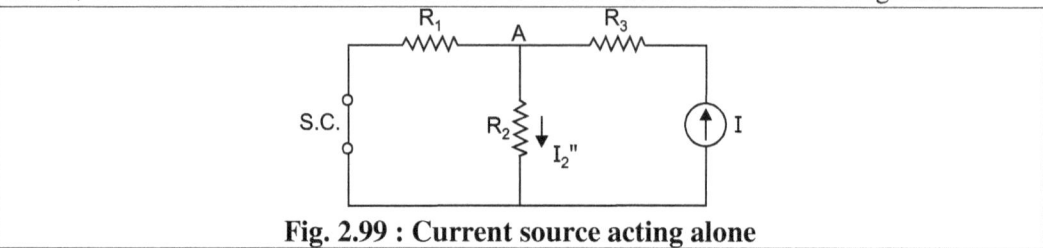

Fig. 2.99 : Current source acting alone

Let corresponding response through R_2 be I_2''.

Using current division,

$$I_2'' = \left(\frac{R_1}{R_1+R_2}\right) . I \quad \text{(from A to B)}$$

According to superposition theorem, current through R_2 when both sources act simultaneously i.e. net response will be

$$I_2 = I_2' + I_2''$$

How to apply superposition theorem ?

Steps :

(i) Consider single energy source at a time.

(ii) Replace all remaining energy sources by their internal resistances.

(iii) Find out corresponding response through a given element.

(iv) Repeat above procedure for all energy sources to find remaining individual response.

(v) Add all individual responses algebraically considering directions to find net response through a given element.

Limitations :

(i) Not applicable to non-linear circuits.

(ii) Not applicable to unilateral circuits.

(iii) Network must contain at least two energy sources.

SOLVED EXAMPLES

Example 2.25 :

Find the current flowing through 5 ohm resistance by superposition theorem.

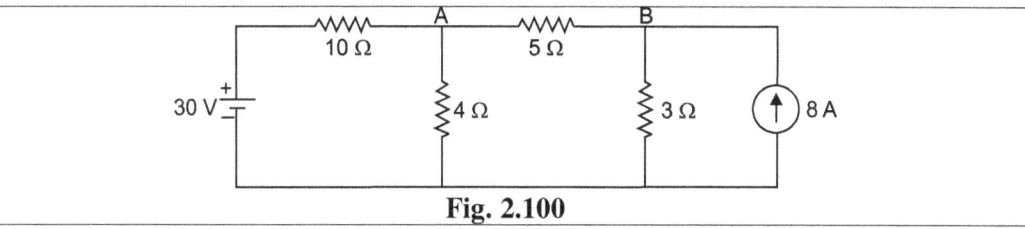

Fig. 2.100

Solution : Case 1 : Consider 30 V source alone and open 8 A source.

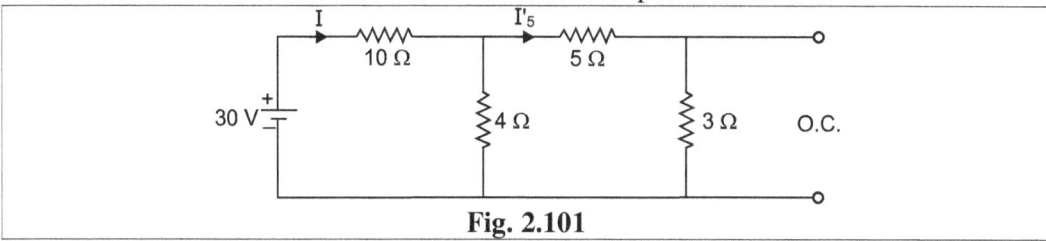

Fig. 2.101

To find total current I, equate series resistance 5 Ω and 3 Ω.

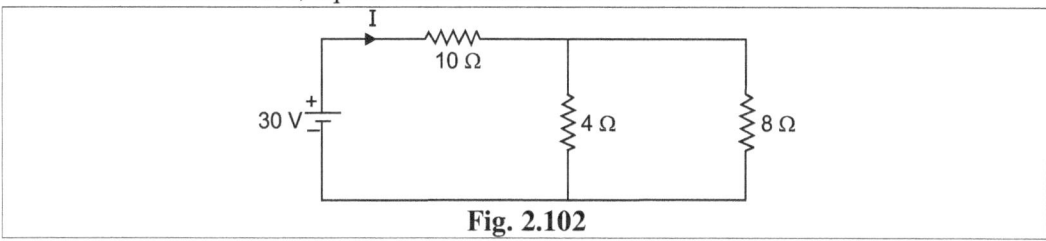

Fig. 2.102

$$I = \frac{30}{10 + [4\| 8]}$$

$$= 2.3684 \rightarrow$$

Using current division rule,

$$I'_5 = I \times \frac{4}{4 + 8}$$

$$= 2.3684 \times \frac{4}{12} = 0.78946 \text{ A} \rightarrow$$

The direction is from left to right.

Case 2 : Consider 8A source alone, short 30 V source.

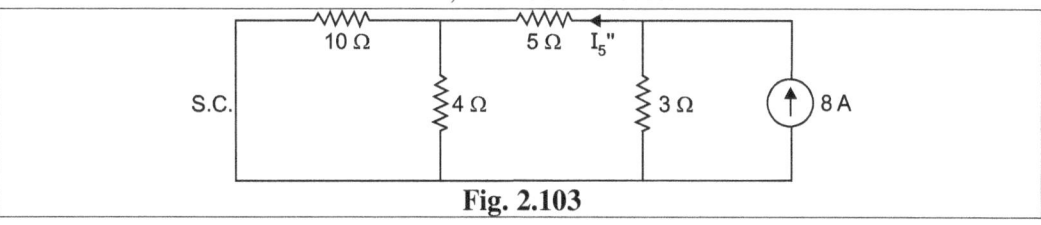

Fig. 2.103

10 Ω parallel to 4 Ω = $(10 \times 4)/(10 + 4)$

$$= 40/14 = 2.857 \text{ Ω}$$

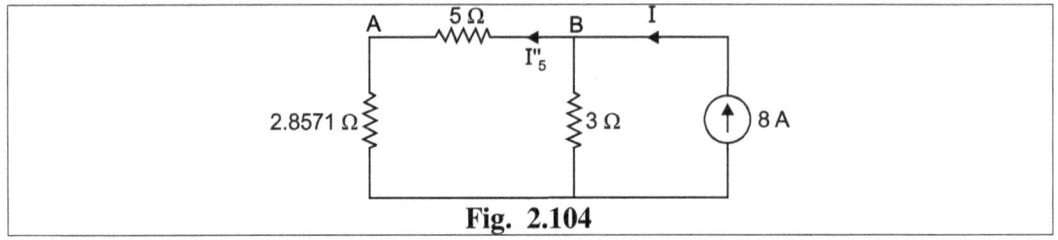

Fig. 2.104

By current division rule,

$$I_5^{''} = 8 \times \frac{3\Omega}{5 + 2.8571 + 3}$$

$$= 2.21053 \text{ A} \leftarrow$$

Case 3 : According to superposition theorem,

$$I_5 = I_5^{'} + I_5^{''}$$

$$= 0.78946 \rightarrow + 2.21053 \leftarrow$$

$$= (2.21053 - 0.78946) \leftarrow$$

$$\boxed{I_5 = 1.42107 \text{ A} \leftarrow}$$ from right to left.

Example 2.26 :

Find current flowing through 3 Ω resistance by superposition theorem for the circuit shown in Fig. 2.105.

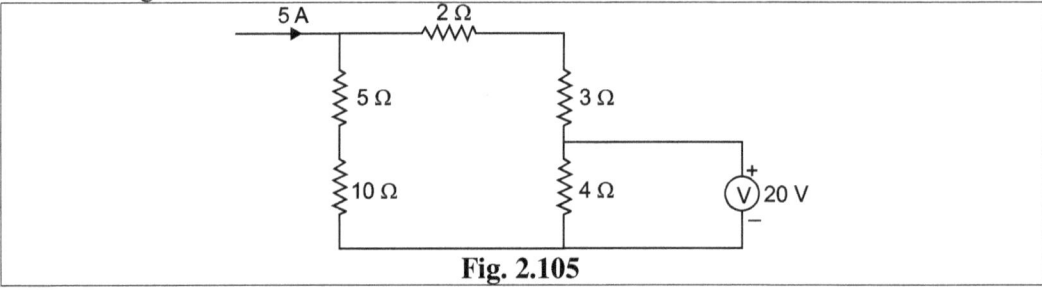

Fig. 2.105

Solution : Case 1 : Consider 5 A alone, short 20 V source.

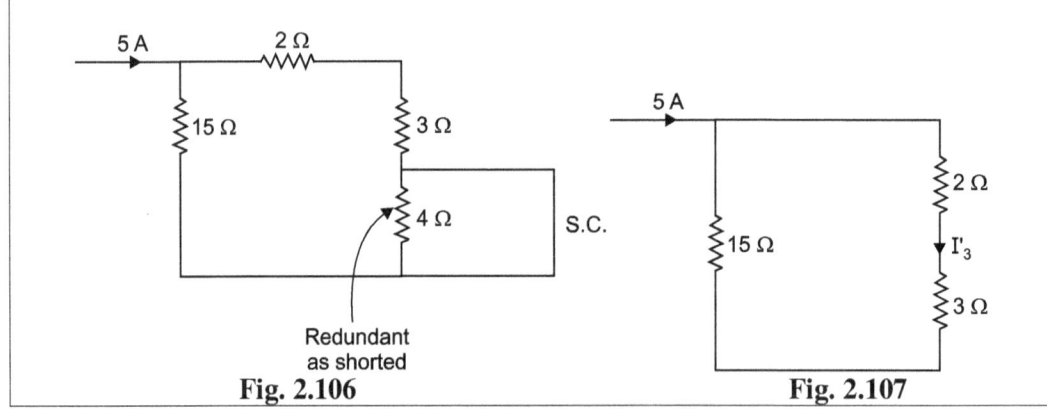

Fig. 2.106   **Fig. 2.107**

Using current division rule,

$$I_3' = 5 \times \frac{15}{15 + 2 + 3}$$

$$= 3.75 \text{ A} \downarrow$$

Case 2 : Consider 20 V alone, open 5 A.

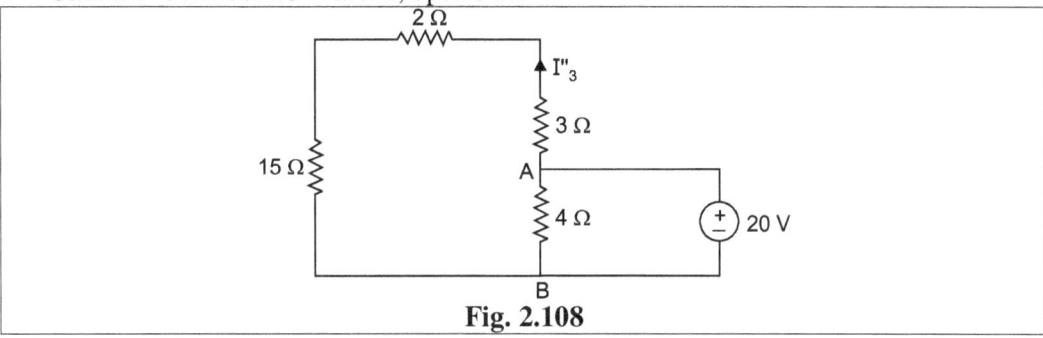

Fig. 2.108

15 Ω, 2 Ω, 3Ω are in series.

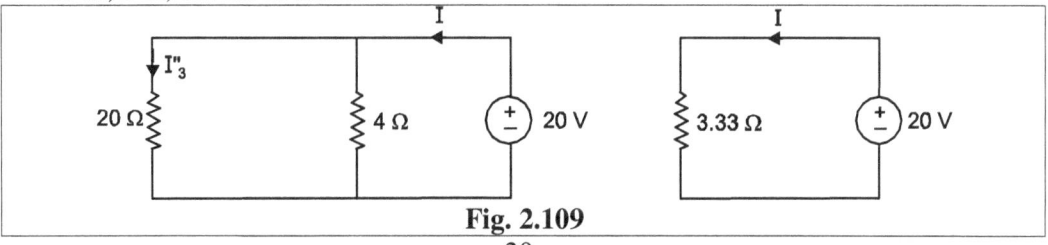

Fig. 2.109

Total current, $I = \dfrac{20}{(20\|4)}$

$$= 6 \text{ A}$$

Using current division rule, $I_3'' = I \times \dfrac{4}{4 + 20} = 6 \times \dfrac{4}{24} = 1 \text{ A} \uparrow$

∴   From case 1 and case 2, $I_3 = 3.75 \text{ A} \downarrow + 1 \text{ A} \uparrow = 2.75 \text{ A} \downarrow$

Example 2.27 :

Using superposition theorem, calculate the current flowing in 1 Ω resistance for the network shown in Fig. 2.110.   **(Dec. 05)**

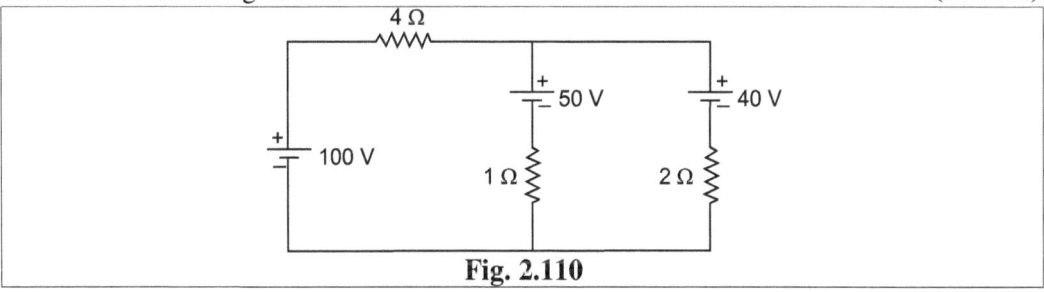

Fig. 2.110

Solution : Case 1 : Consider 100 V battery alone, other sources are shorted.

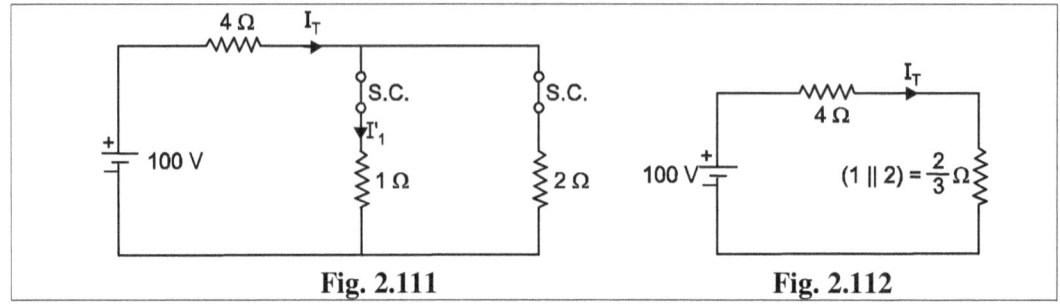

Fig. 2.111   **Fig. 2.112**

$$\text{Total current,} \qquad I_T = \frac{100}{4 + \dfrac{2}{3}} = 21.4285 \text{ A}$$

Using Current Division Rule, $I_1^{'} = I_T \times \dfrac{2}{(2 + 1)} = 14.2857 \text{ A} \downarrow$

Case 2 : Consider 50 V alone and other sources are shorted.

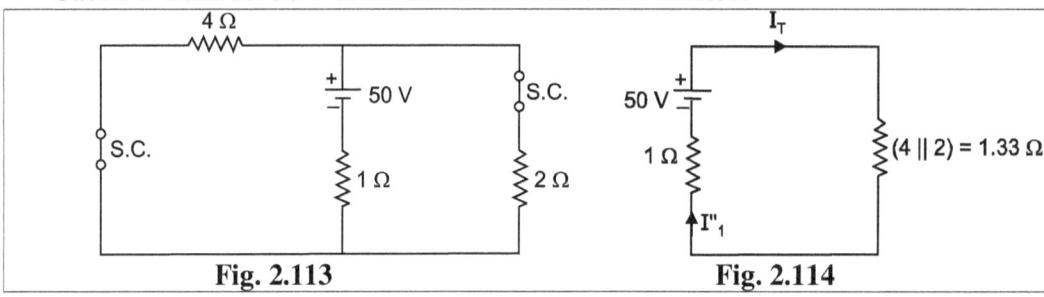

Fig. 2.113   **Fig. 2.114**

$4\,\Omega$ and $2\,\Omega$ are in parallel.

$$I_T = \frac{50}{1 + 1.33} = 21.43 \text{ A}$$

$\therefore \qquad\qquad I_1^{''} = I_T = 21.43 \text{ A} \uparrow$

Case 3 : Consider 40 V alone, shorting other sources.

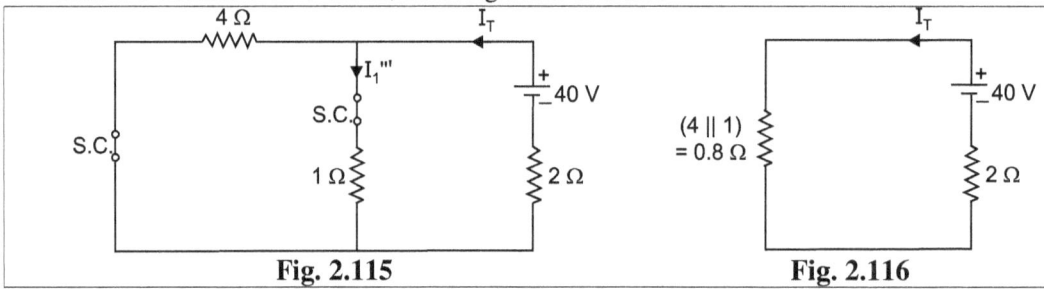

Fig. 2.115   **Fig. 2.116**

$\therefore \qquad\qquad I_T = \dfrac{40}{2.8} = 14.29 \text{ A}$

Using Current Division Rule, $\qquad I_1^{'''} = I_T \times \dfrac{4}{4 + 1} = 11.42 \text{ A} \downarrow$

∴ Using Superposition Theorem, $I_1 = I_1' + I_1'' + I_1'''$

$$= 14.28 \text{ A} \downarrow + 21.43 \text{ A} \uparrow + 11.42 \text{ A} \downarrow$$

$$\boxed{I_1 = 4.28 \text{ A} \downarrow}$$

Example 2.28 :

Find by superposition theorem, the current I_3 in the 8 ohm resistance in the circuit shown in Fig. 2.117.

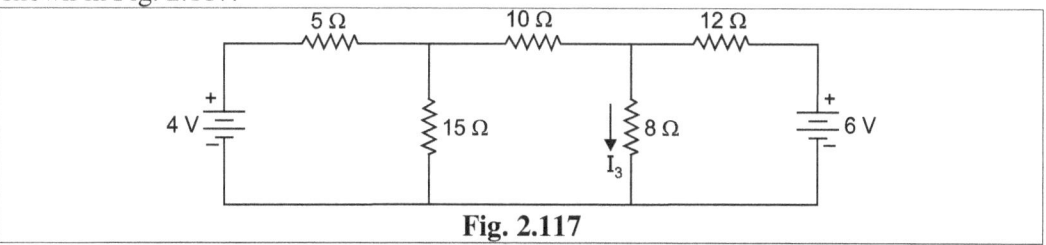

Fig. 2.117

Solution : Case 1 : Consider 4 V source alone and 6 V source shorted.

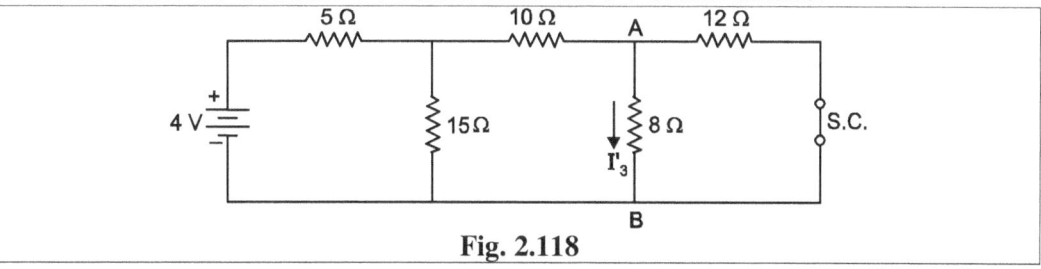

Fig. 2.118

Let, corresponding response through 8 Ω be I_3' .

Let first find total current delivered by 4 V, so that 12 Ω and 8 Ω are in parallel.

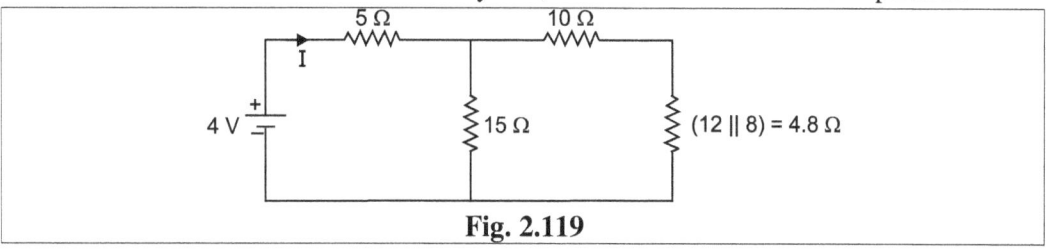

Fig. 2.119

10 Ω and 4.8 Ω are in series and 15 Ω and 14.8 Ω are in parallel.

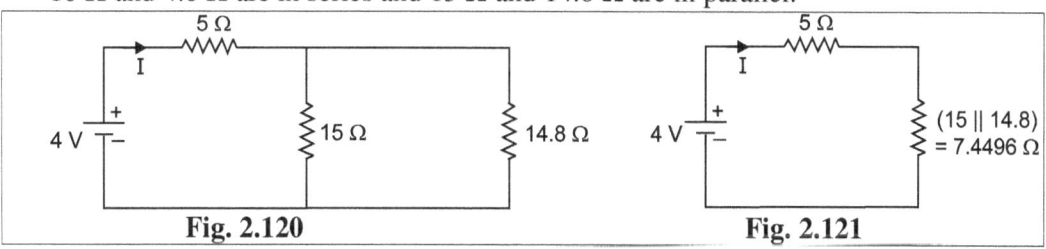

Fig. 2.120   **Fig. 2.121**

Total current, $I = \dfrac{4}{5 + 7.4496} = 0.3212 \text{ A}$

∴ Current through 10 Ω resistor using current division rule

$$= 0.3212 \times \frac{15}{(15 + 14.8)} = 0.1617 \text{ A}$$

Again using current division rule, current through 8 Ω,

$$I_3' = 0.1617 \times \frac{12}{(12 + 8)}$$

$$= 0.09703 \text{ A} \quad \text{(from A to B)} \downarrow$$

Case 2 : Consider 6 V source acting alone and replace 4 V source by short circuit.

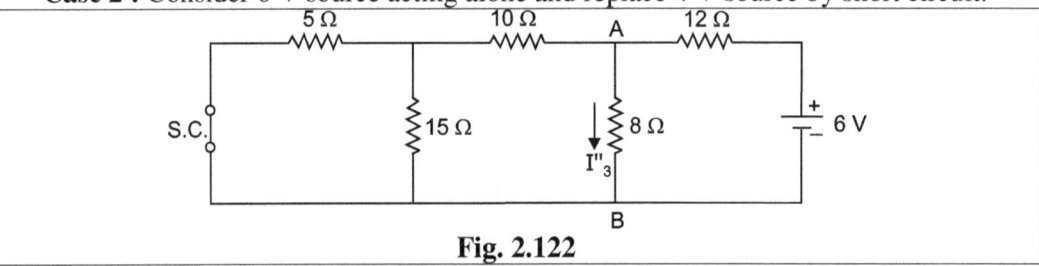

Fig. 2.122

Let, corresponding response through 8 Ω be I_3'', 5 Ω and 15 Ω are in parallel.

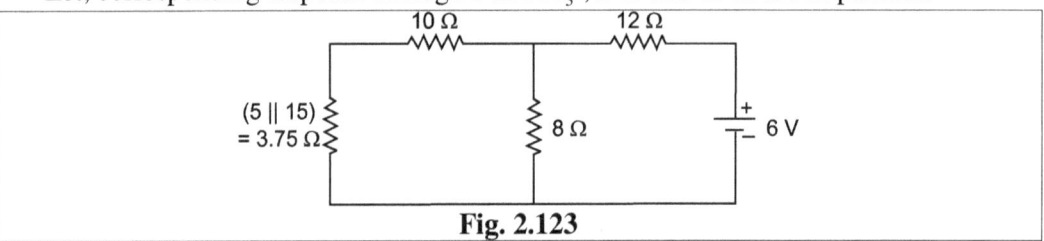

Fig. 2.123

3.75 Ω and 10 Ω are in series i.e. $(3.75 + 10 = 13.75 \text{ Ω})$ and 8 Ω are in parallel.

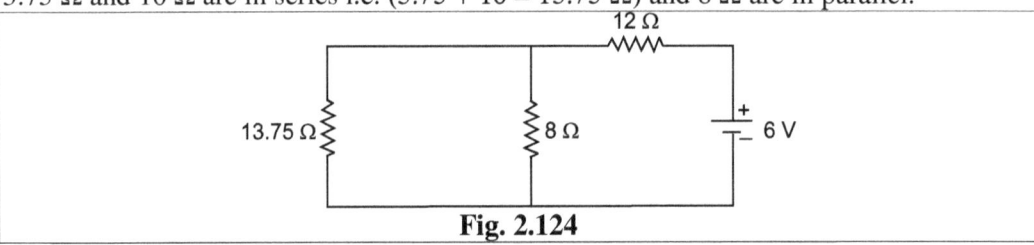

Fig. 2.124

$$(8 \parallel 13.75) = \frac{8 \times 13.75}{8 + 13.75} = 5.05747$$

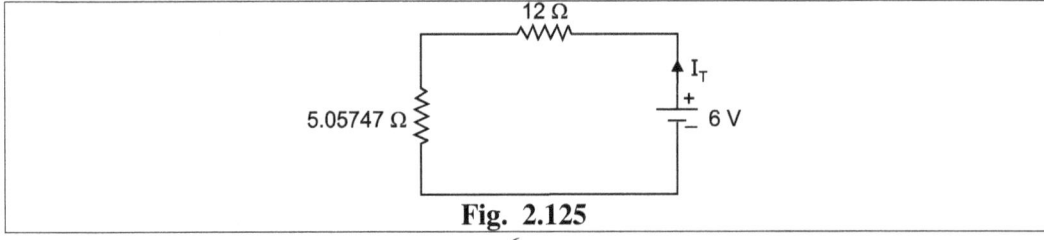

Fig. 2.125

$$I_T = \frac{6}{12 + 5.05747} = 0.3517 \text{ A}$$

Using current division rule, current through 8 Ω,

$$I_3'' = \frac{13.75}{8 + 13.75} \times 0.3517 = 0.2223 \text{ A} \qquad \text{(from A to B)}$$

∴   According to superposition theorem,

$$I_3 = I_3' + I_3'' = 0.09703 \text{ A} \downarrow + 0.2223 \text{ A} \downarrow$$

$$\boxed{I_3 = 0.3194 \text{ A} \downarrow \text{ (from A to B)}}$$

Example 2.29 :

Find the current flowing through 8 Ω resistor using superposition theorem for the network shown.

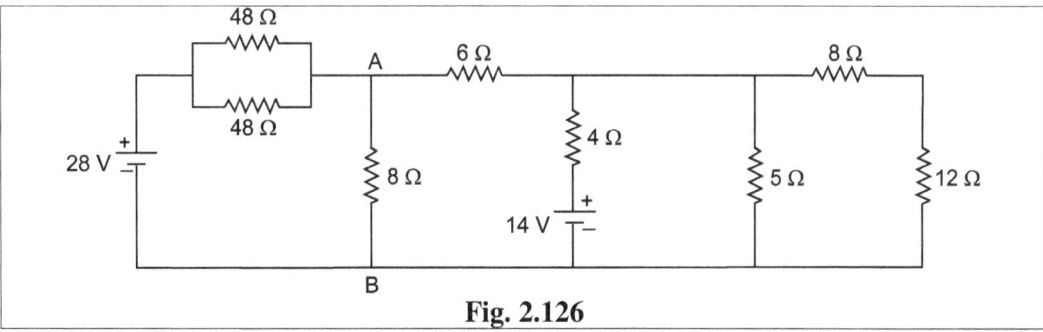

Fig. 2.126

Solution : Let us first obtain the network in simplified form.

Two 48 Ω resistors are in parallel. 8 Ω and 12 Ω are in series.

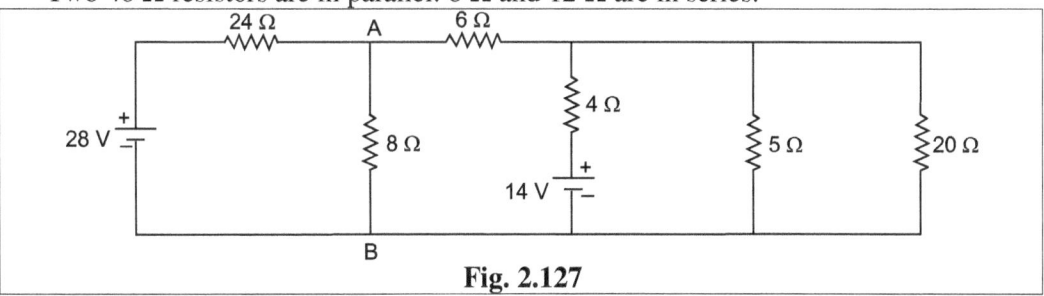

Fig. 2.127

5 Ω and 20 Ω are in parallel.

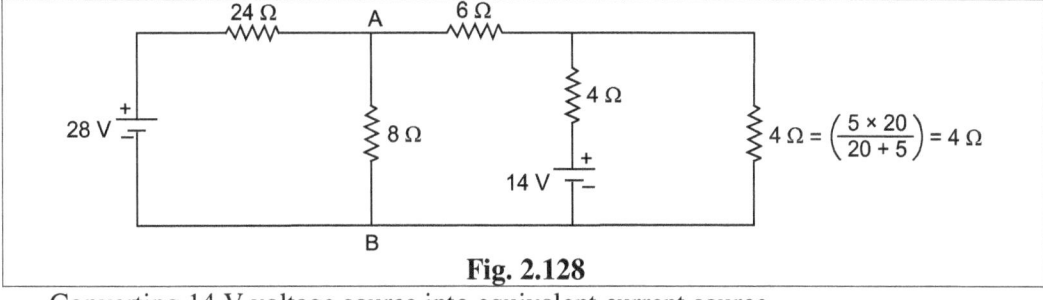

Fig. 2.128

Converting 14 V voltage source into equivalent current source.

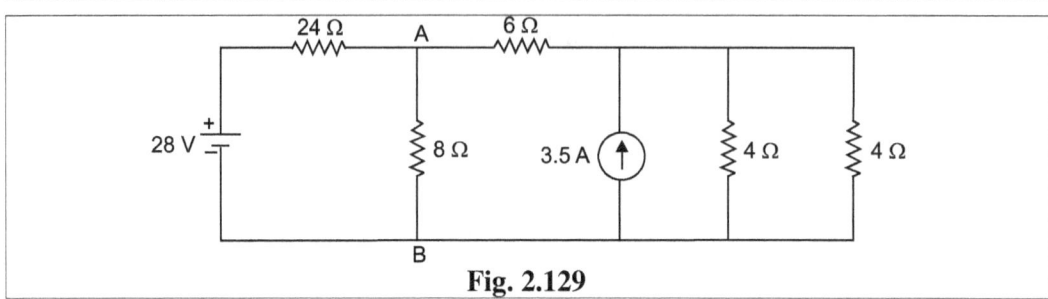

Fig. 2.129

Two 4 Ω resistors are in parallel.

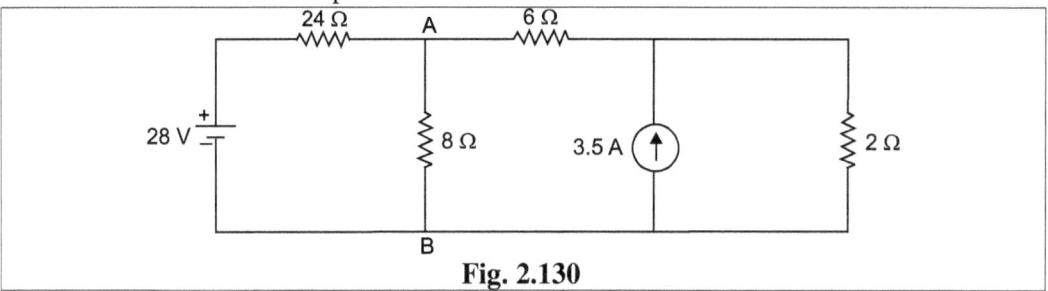

Fig. 2.130

Converting 3.5A current source into equivalent voltage source.

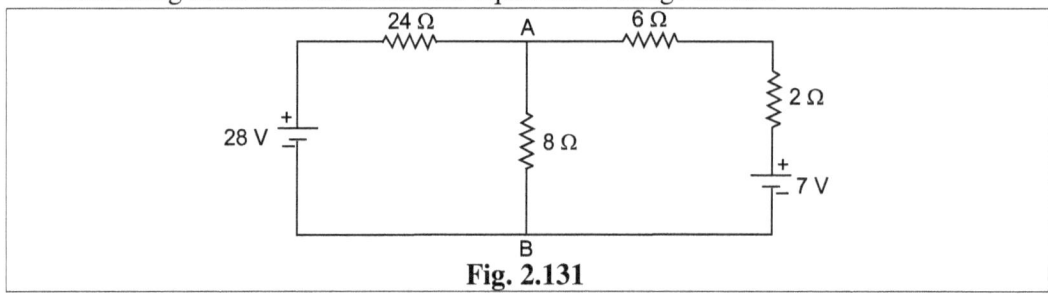

Fig. 2.131

6 Ω and 2 Ω are in series.

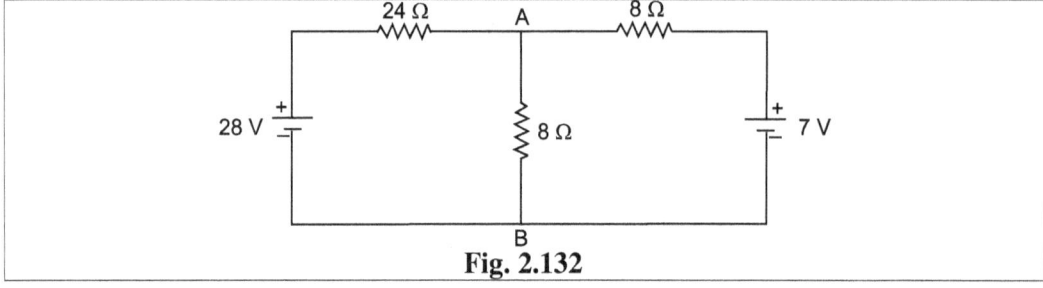

Fig. 2.132

Let us apply superposition theorem.

Case 1 : Consider 28 V acting alone and 7V is shorted.

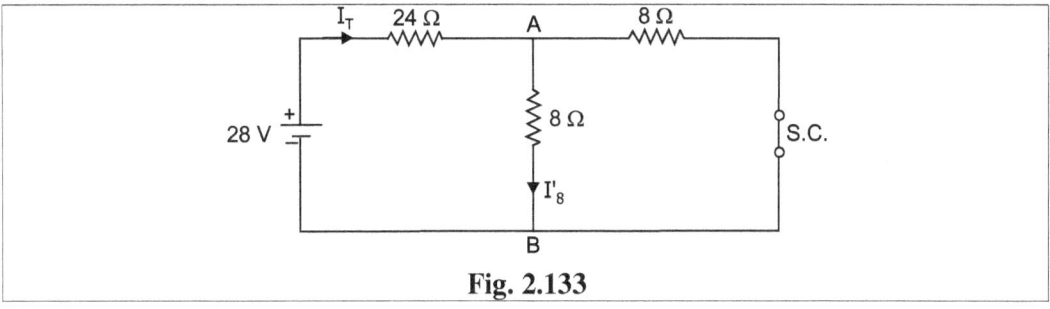

Fig. 2.133

Let corresponding response through 8 Ω be I_8' and total current be I_T .

$$I_T = \frac{28}{24 + (8 \parallel 8)} = \frac{28}{24 + 4} = 1 \text{ A}$$

∴   Using current division rule,

$$\text{Current through } 8\,\Omega = I_8' = I_T \times \frac{8}{8 + 8} = 1 \times \frac{1}{2}$$

$$\boxed{I_8 = 0.5 \text{ A} \downarrow} \qquad \qquad \qquad \dots(1)$$

Case 2 : Consider 7 V source is acting alone and 28 V is shorted. Let corresponding response through 8 Ω be I_8'' and total current be I_T.

$$I_T = \frac{7}{8 + (24 \parallel 8)} = 0.5 \text{ A}$$

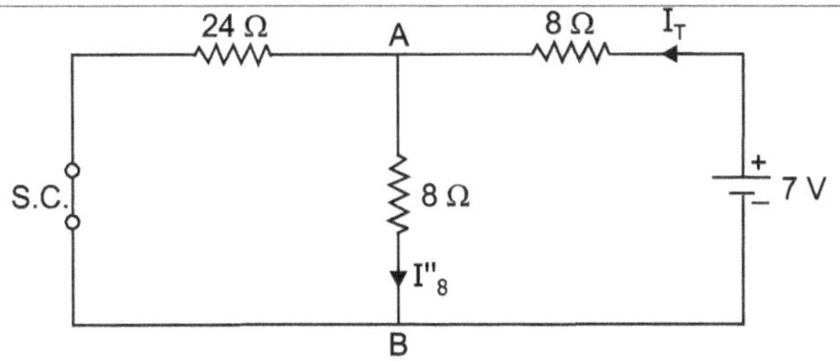

Fig. 2.134

∴ $$I_8'' = 0.5 \times \frac{24}{24 + 8}$$

$$= 0.375 \text{ A} \qquad \qquad \qquad \dots(2)$$

From equations (1) and (2),

$$\text{Current through } 8\,\Omega = I_8 = I_8' + I_8'' = 0.5 + 0.375$$

$$\boxed{I_8 = 0.875 \text{ A} \downarrow}$$

Example 2.30 :

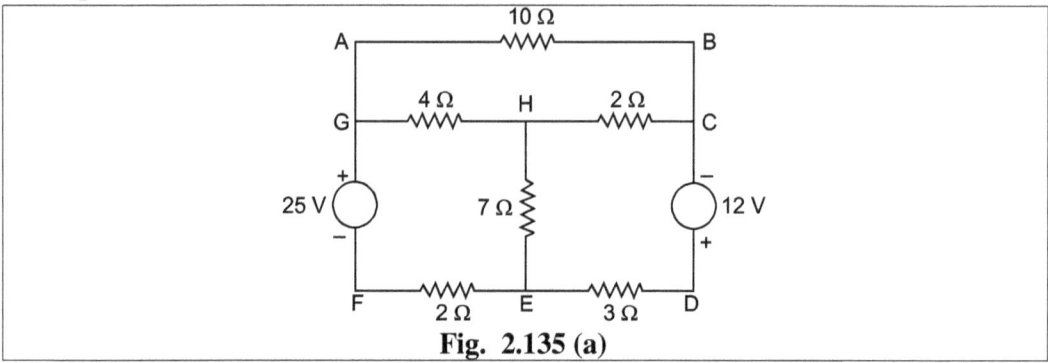

Fig. 2.135 (a)

Calculate current through 10 Ω resistance using superposition theorem.

Solution :

Case (i) : First consider 25 V source. Let us find current through 10 Ω resistance due to 25 V source acting alone. For this replace 12 V source by short circuit.

Let us assume various loop currents as shown in Fig. 2.135 (b).

According to KVL,

For mesh GHEFG,

$$4.(I_1' - I_3') + 7.(I_1' - I_2') + 2.I_1' = 25$$

$\therefore$ $\qquad\qquad 13.I_1' - 7.I_2' - 4.I_3' = 25$ $\qquad\qquad$ ...(1)

For loop HCDEH,

$$2.(I_2' - I_3') + 3.I_2' + 7.(I_2' - I_1') = 0$$

$\therefore$ $\qquad\qquad -7.I_1' + 12.I_2' - 2.I_3' = 0$ $\qquad\qquad$ ...(2)

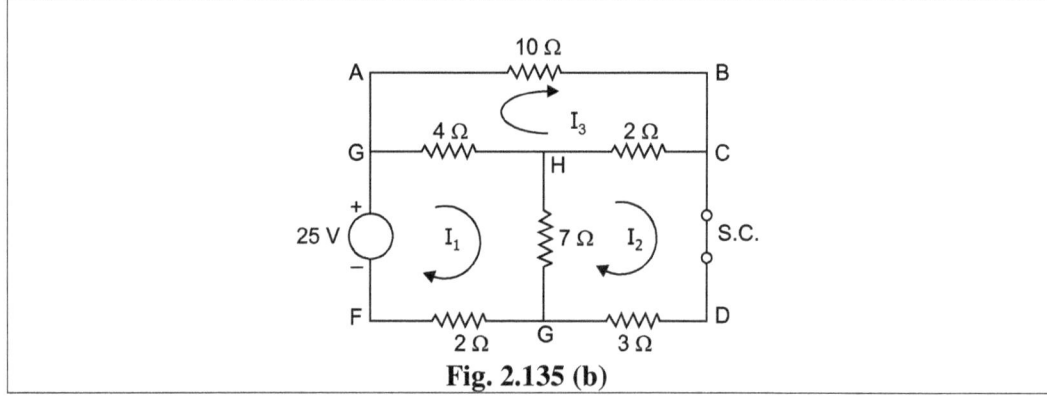

Fig. 2.135 (b)

For loop ABCHGA,

$$4.(I_3' - I_1') + 10.I_3' + 2(I_3' - I_2') = 0$$

$\therefore$ $\qquad\qquad -4.I_1' - 2.I_2' + 16.I_3' = 0$ $\qquad\qquad$ ...(3)

According to Cramer's rule,

System determinant,

$$D = \begin{vmatrix} 13 & -7 & -4 \\ -7 & 12 & -2 \\ -4 & -2 & 16 \end{vmatrix}$$

$$= 13\,[192 - 4] + 7\,[-112 - 8] - 4\,[14 + 48]$$

$$= 2444 - 840 - 248$$

$$= 1356$$

and

$$D_3 = \begin{vmatrix} 13 & -7 & 25 \\ -7 & 12 & 0 \\ -4 & -2 & 0 \end{vmatrix}$$

$$= 13\,[0 - 0] + 7\,[0 - 0] + 25\,[14 + 48]$$

$$= 1550$$

Hence,

$$I_3 = \frac{D_3}{D}$$

$$= \frac{1550}{1356}$$

$$= 1.143 \text{ A}$$

Let current through 10 Ω resistance when 25 V source is acting alone

$$= I_{10}'$$

$$= 1.143 \text{ A (from A to B)} \qquad\qquad ...(4)$$

Case II : Consider 12V source only. Replace 25V source by its internal resistance i.e. zero resistance. Therefore, 25V source acting as a short circuit. Now find current through 10Ω resistance due to 12V source acting only.

Let us assume various loops as shown in Fig. 2.135 (c).

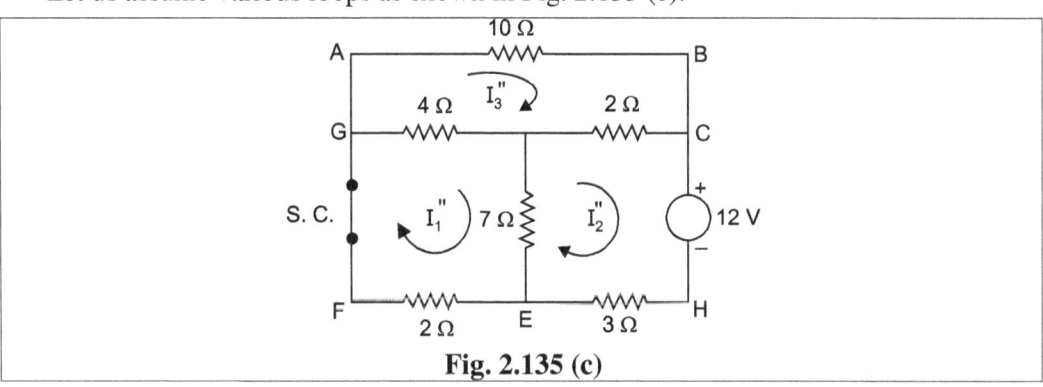

Fig. 2.135 (c)

For loop GHEPG,

$$4 (I_1'' - I_3'') + 7 (I_1'' - I_2'') + 2I_1'' = 0$$

$$\therefore \qquad 13 I_1'' - 7 I_2'' - 4 I_3'' = 0 \qquad\qquad ...(5)$$

For loop ABCHGA

$$10 I_3'' + 2 (I_3'' - I_2'') + 4 (I_3'' - I_1'') = 0$$

$$-4 I_1'' - 2 I_2'' + 16 I_3'' = 0 \qquad\qquad ...(6)$$

For loop HCDEH

$$2 (I_2'' - I_3'') + 7 (I_2'' - I_1'') + 3I_2'' = 12$$

$$-7 I_1'' + 12 I_2'' - 2 I_3'' = 12 \qquad\qquad ...(7)$$

According to Cramer's Rule,

System Determinant,

$$D = \begin{vmatrix} 13 & -7 & -4 \\ -4 & -2 & 16 \\ -7 & 12 & -2 \end{vmatrix}$$

$$= -2444 + 840 + 240 = -1364$$

$$D_3 = \begin{vmatrix} 13 & -7 & 0 \\ -4 & -2 & 0 \\ -7 & 12 & 12 \end{vmatrix}$$

$$= -312 - 336 = -648$$

Hence, $\qquad\qquad I_3'' = \dfrac{D_3}{D} = \dfrac{-648}{-1364} = 0.4750 \text{ A} \qquad\qquad$ From (A to B) ... (8)

From equations (4) and (8) we get current through 10 Ω resistance when both sources are acting.

$$\therefore \qquad\qquad I_{10} = I_3' + I_3'' = 1.143 \text{ A} + 0.4750 \text{ A}$$

$$= 1.62 \text{ A}$$

$$\boxed{I_{10\Omega} = 1.62 \text{ A}} \qquad\qquad\qquad \text{(From A to B)}$$

Example 2.31 :

Using superposition theorem, calculate current flowing in branch A-B for the circuit shown in Fig. 2.136 (a). **(May 09)**

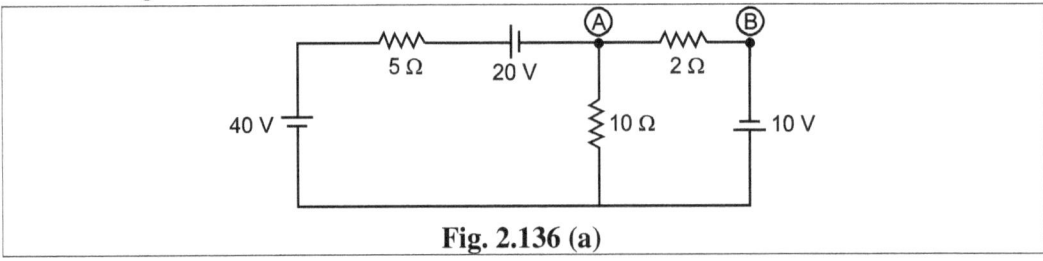

Fig. 2.136 (a)

Solution : Case 1 : Consider 20 V battery alone, other sources are inactive.

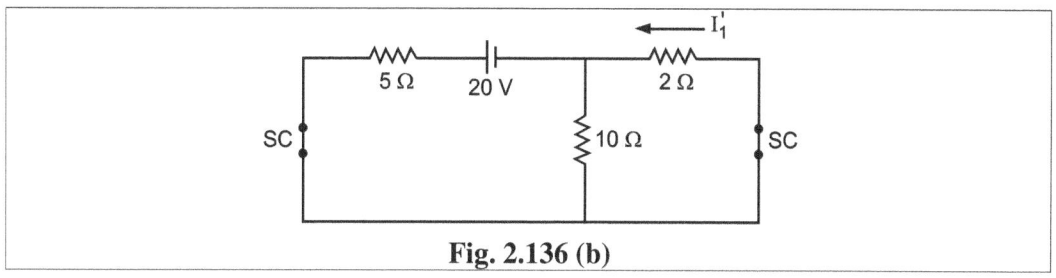

Fig. 2.136 (b)

$$R_{eq} = 5 + (10 \parallel 2) = 6.66 \ \Omega$$

$$I_{total} = \frac{20}{6.66} = 3A$$

By current division rule,

$$\therefore \qquad\qquad I_1' = 3 \times \frac{10}{12}$$

$$= 2.5 \text{ Amp} \leftarrow \qquad\qquad …(1)$$

Case 2 : Consider 40 V battery alone, other sources are inactive.

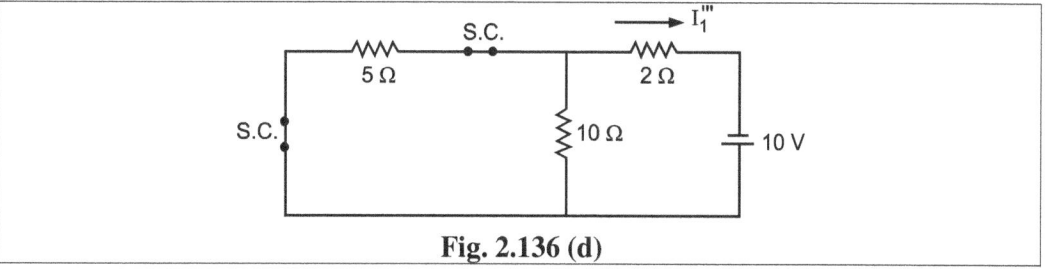

Fig. 2.136 (c)

$$\text{Total current } I_{total} = \frac{40}{5 + (2 \parallel 10)} = 6 \text{ Amp}$$

By current division rule,

$$\therefore \qquad\qquad I''_1 = 6 \times \frac{10}{12} = 5 \text{ Amp} \rightarrow \qquad\qquad …(2)$$

Case 3 : Consider 10 V battery alone, other sources are inactive.

Fig. 2.136 (d)

$$\text{Total current } I_{Total} = \frac{10}{2 + (5 \parallel 10)} = 1.875 \text{ Amp.} = I_1''' \qquad\qquad …(3)$$

∴ By superposition theorem,

$$I_{AB} = I_{2\Omega} = -I_1' + I_1'' + I_1''' = -2.5 + 5 + 1.875$$
$$= 4.375 \text{ Amp}$$
$$\boxed{I_{AB} = 4.375 \text{ Amp}} \rightarrow$$

2.8.2 Thevenin's Theorem

Statement : Any linear, bilateral network containing energy sources and circuit elements can be replaced by an equivalent circuit containing a voltage source V_{Th} and a series resistance R_{Th} or R_{eq} across the terminals under consideration. Value of voltage source V_{Th} is equal to the open-circuit voltage across the terminals under consideration while R_{Th} or R_{eq} is the equivalent resistance measured between the same terminals replacing all the energy sources by their internal resistances.

Explanation of Thevenin's theorem : This theorem is applicable to

(i) Linear circuits (ii) Bilateral circuits.

By using this theorem we can easily find current flowing through any particular circuit element or voltage across a particular circuit element.

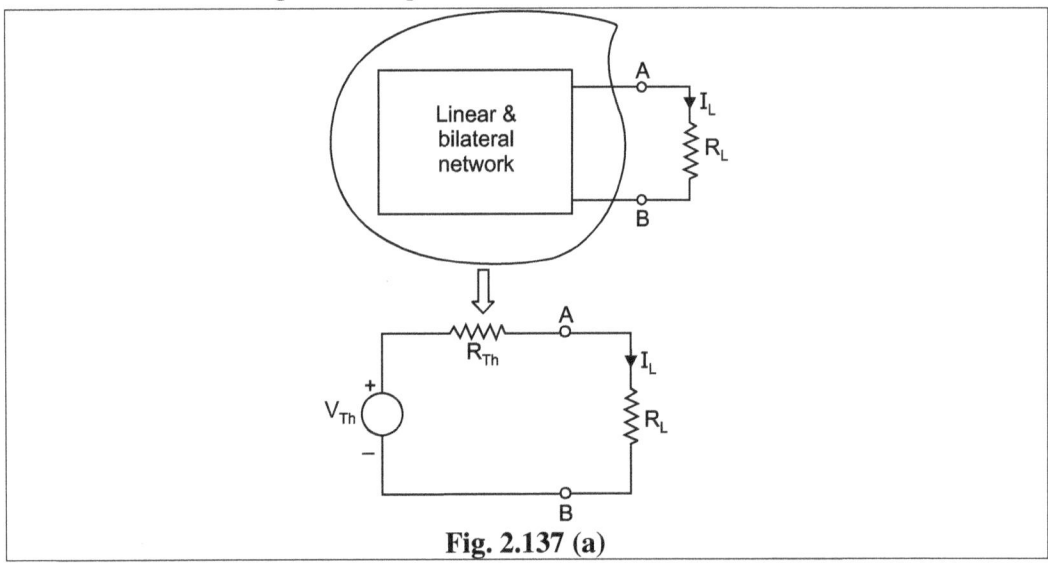

Fig. 2.137 (a)

How to apply Thevenin's theorem ?

(i)   Remove the circuit element under consideration from the network.

(ii) Find the value of open-circuit voltage across those terminals. This is nothing but Thevenin's voltage source.

(iii) Find the equivalent resistance between the same terminals replacing all energy sources by their internal resistances. Ideal voltage sources are replaced by short circuit, while ideal current sources are replaced by open circuit. This resistance is R_{Th} or R_{eq}.

   (iv) Replace the given network across terminals under consideration by Thevenin's equivalent circuit, which is Thevenin's voltage source in series with an equivalent resistance.

   (v) Reconnect original element across Thevenin's equivalent circuit and find current through it.

Limitations :

   (i) Not applicable to non-linear circuits and unilateral circuits.

   (ii) There should not be magnetic coupling between load element and the element in the circuit to be replaced by Thevenin's equivalent circuit.

   (iii) In the load side, there should not be dependent or controlled sources, controlled from some part of the circuit.

Steps for solving Thevenin's theorem :

Given network :

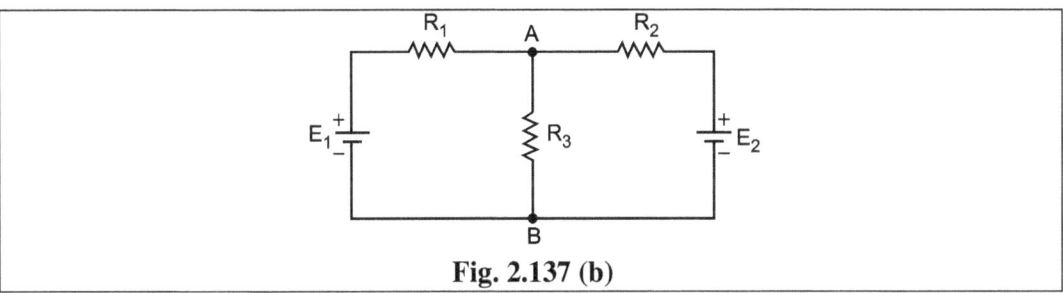

Fig. 2.137 (b)

It is asked to calculate current flowing through R_3 resistance.

Step I : Remove load resistance $R_L = R_3$ and redraw the network.

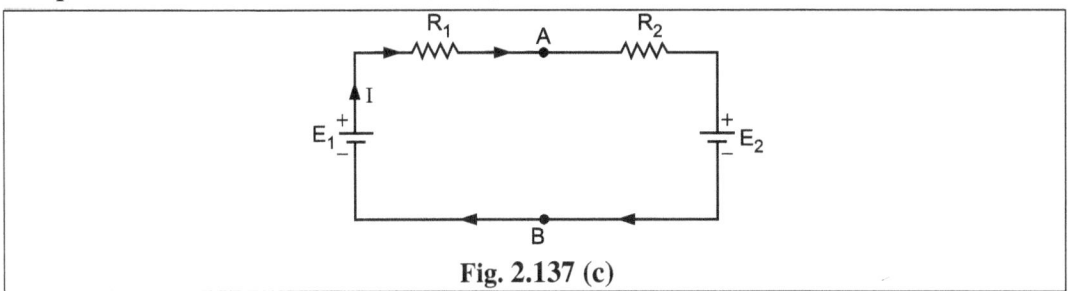

Fig. 2.137 (c)

By applying KVL

$$-IR_1 - IR_2 - E_2 + E_1 = 0$$

Calculate the value of current I

Step II : Consider a battery between points A and B find V_{th}.

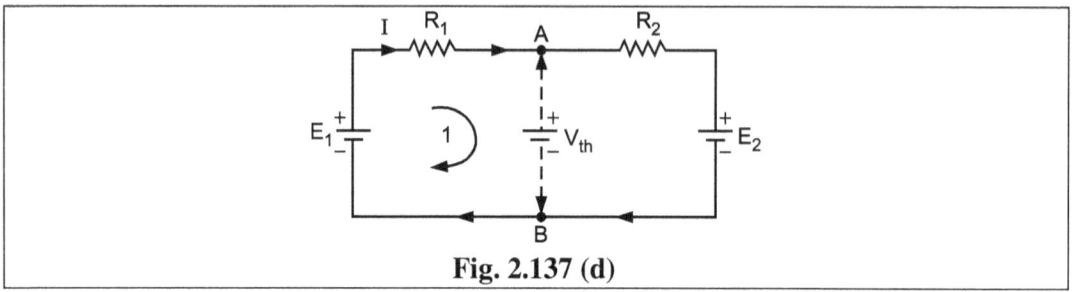

Fig. 2.137 (d)

Considering only mesh I and applying KVL

$$-IR_1 - V_{th} + E_1 = 0$$

$$E_1 - IR_1 = V_{th}$$

Note : If V_{th} is +ve then the polarities of V_{th} are correct and if V_{th} is − ve, then the assumed polarities are to be reversed.

Step III : Determine R_{th}

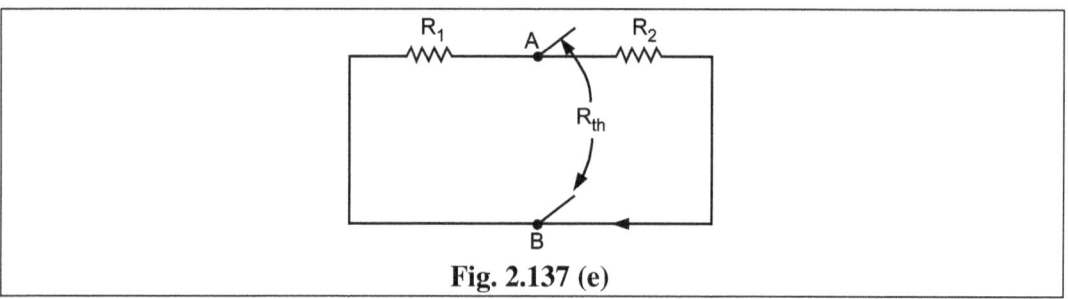

Fig. 2.137 (e)

$$R_{th} = R_1 \parallel R_2 = \frac{R_1 . R_2}{R_1 + R_2}$$

Note : Voltage sources are short circuited, while current sources are open circuited.

Step IV : Prepare Thevenin's equivalent network and find the value of load current (I_L)

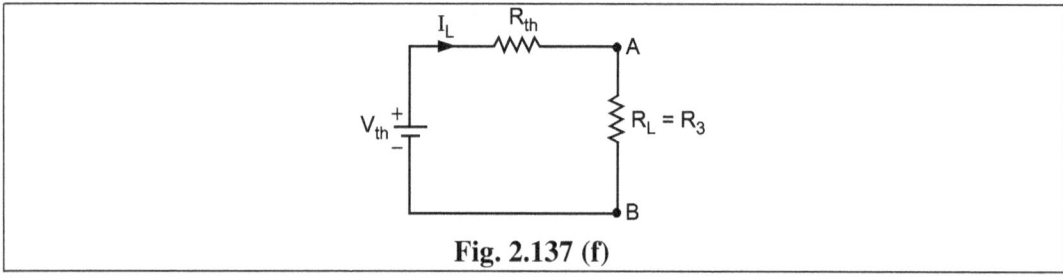

Fig. 2.137 (f)

$$I_L = \frac{V_{th}}{R_{th} + R_L}$$

SOLVED EXAMPLES

Example 2.32 :

For the circuit shown in Fig. 2.138 find the current flowing through 5 Ω resistance by Thevenin's theorem.

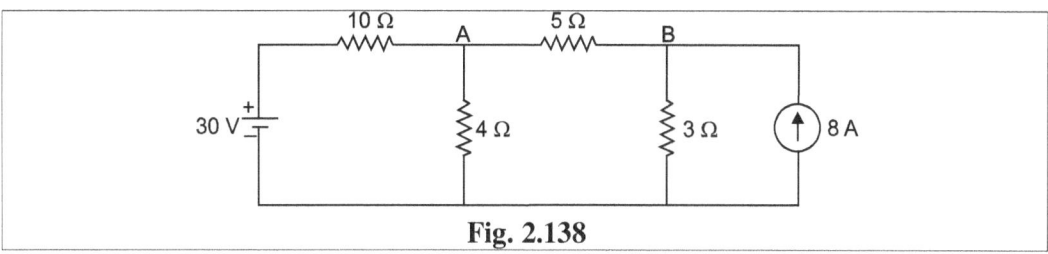

Fig. 2.138

Solution : First remove 5 Ω resistance and open circuit the terminals AB. Let us find open- circuit voltage across terminals AB i.e. V_{TH}.

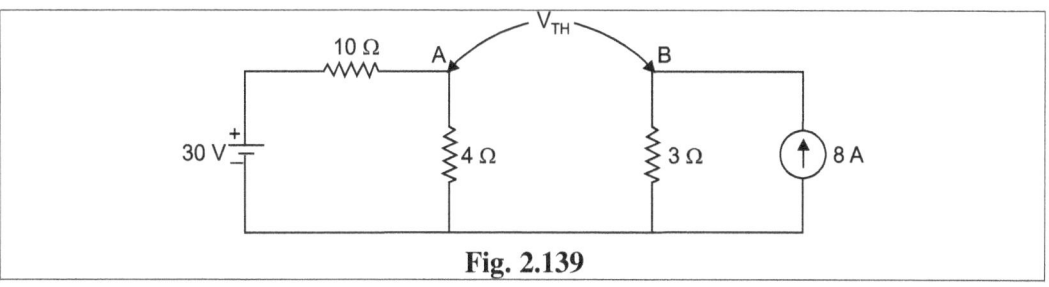

Fig. 2.139

Potential at node B,

$$V_B = 3 \times 8 = 24 \text{ V}$$

Potential at node A,

$$V_A = I \cdot R$$

$$= \frac{30}{10 + 4} \times 4 = 8.5714 \text{ V}$$

$\therefore$
$$V_{TH} = V_{BA} = 24 - 8.5714$$
$$V_{TH} = 15.4285 \text{ V}$$

Let us find R_{TH} across terminals A–B. Replace 30 V source by short circuit and 8A source by open circuit.

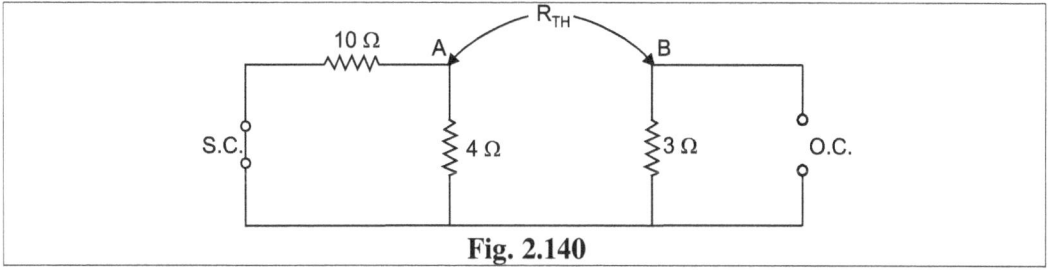

Fig. 2.140

10 Ω and 4 Ω are in parallel.

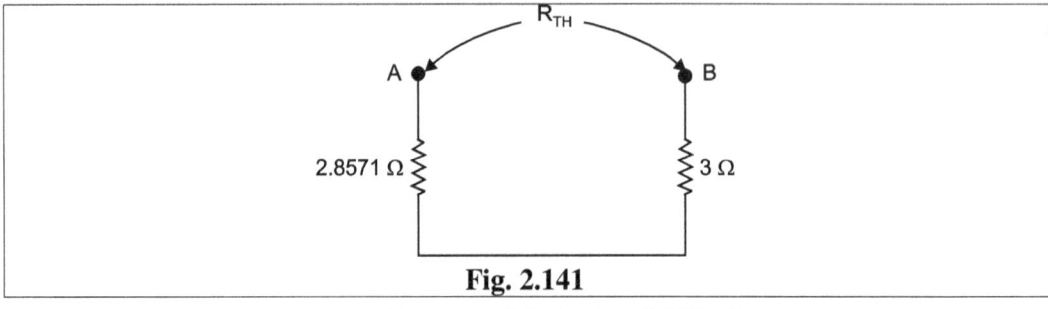

Fig. 2.141

∴ R_{TH} = 2.8571 + 3 = 5.8571 Ω

Replace given network across terminals AB by Thevenin's equivalent circuit and reconnect 5 Ω resistance.

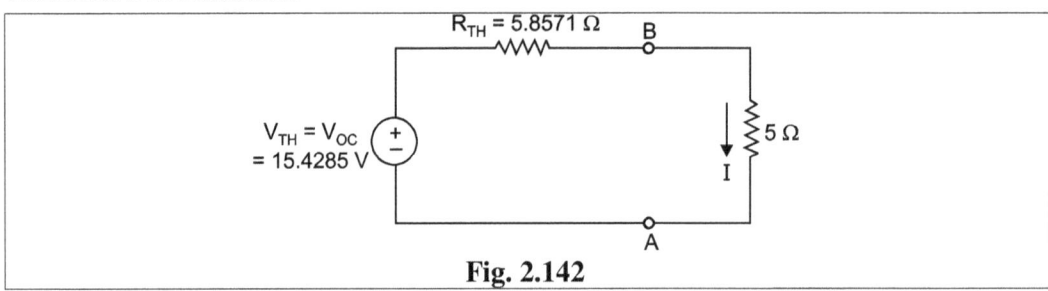

Fig. 2.142

Current through 5 Ω resistor

$$I = \frac{15.4285}{(5.8571 + 5)}$$

$$= 1.421 \text{ A} \text{ (From B to A)}$$

Example 2.33 :

Apply Thevenin's theorem to calculate current through branch AB for the circuit shown in Fig. 2.163.

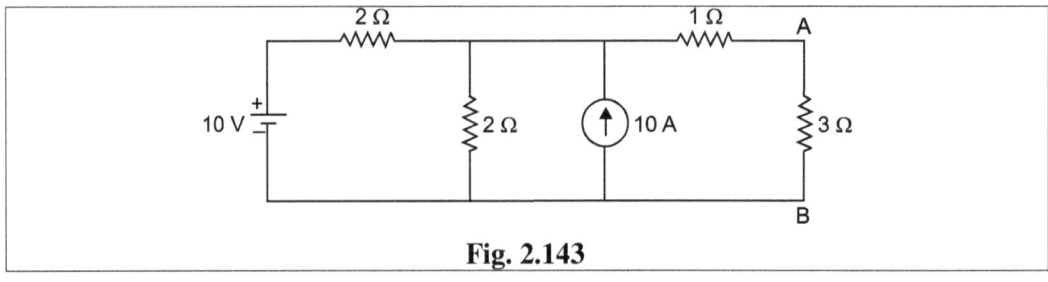

Fig. 2.143

Solution : First remove branch AB.

Calculate $V_{AB} = V_{TH}$,   open-circuit voltage

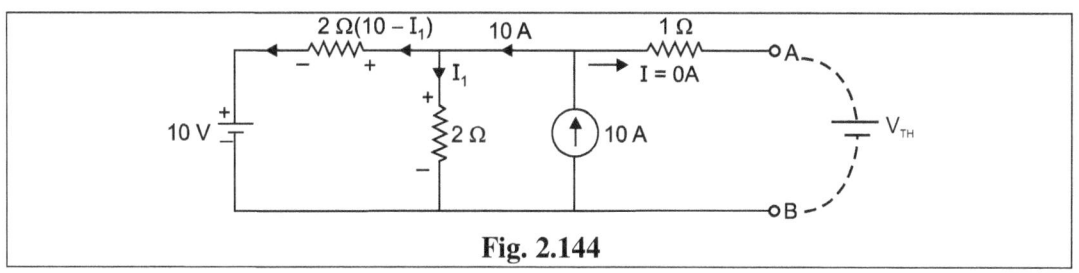

Fig. 2.144

$$-2(10 - I_1) - 10 + 2I_1 = 0$$

i.e. $$I_1 = 7.5 \text{ A}$$

$2\,\Omega$ and 10 A sources are in parallel across AB.

Applying KVL for loop ABCDA,

$$-V_{TH} + 2I_1 + 0 = 0$$
$$-V_{TH} + 2 \times 7.5 = 0$$
$$V_{TH} = 15 \text{ volt}$$

Calculate R_{TH} or R_{eq} by open circuit 10 A and short circuit 10 V source.

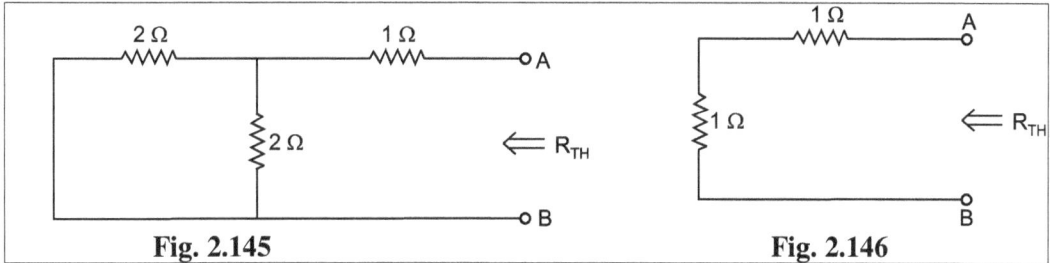

Fig. 2.145   **Fig. 2.146**

$$R_{TH} = R_{eq} = 1 + 1 = 2\,\Omega$$

Draw Thevenin's equivalent circuit.

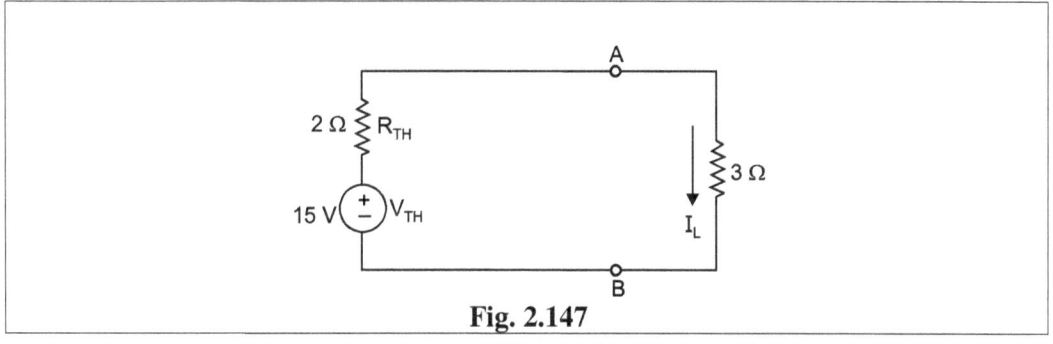

Fig. 2.147

∴ $$I_L = \frac{V_{TH}}{R_{TH} + R_L} = \frac{15}{2 + 3}$$

$$I_L = 3 \text{ A (A to B)}$$

Example 2.34 :

Use Thevenin's theorem to find current in 1 Ω resistance for the circuit shown in Fig. 2.148.

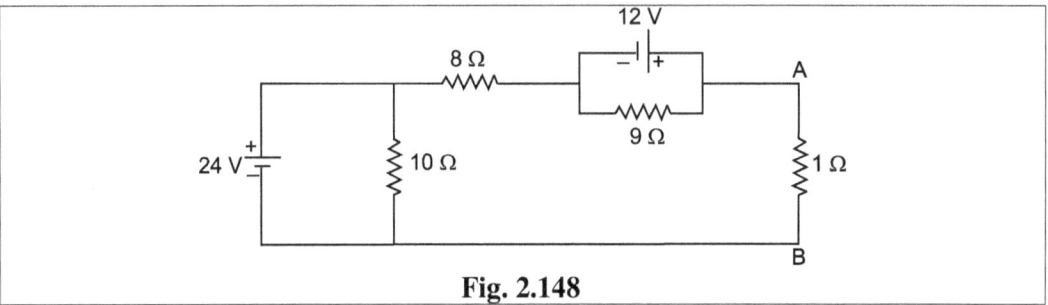

Fig. 2.148

Solution : Remove the 1 Ω resistance and find open-circuit voltage V_{TH} .

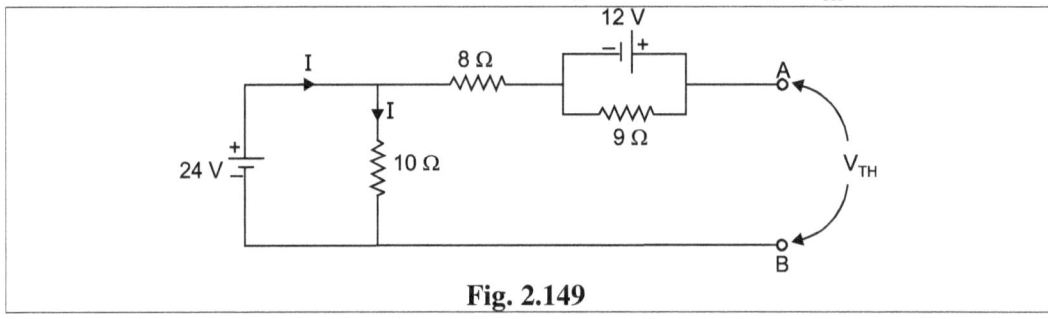

Fig. 2.149

$$I = \frac{24}{10} = 2.4 \text{ A}$$

and voltage drop across 10 Ω is 24 V. Voltage drop across 8 Ω is zero because no current can flow through 8 Ω. Tracing path from A to B

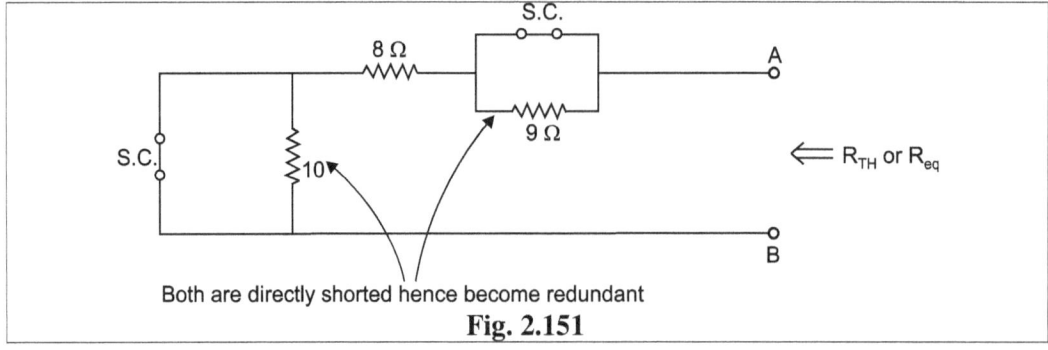

Fig. 2.150

∴ $V_{TH} = 12 + 0 + 24 = 36$ V   with A positive

Finding R_{TH} by short circuiting all voltage sources.

Fig. 2.151

$\therefore$ $R_{eq} = R_{TH} = 8\ \Omega$

The Thevenin's equivalent circuit is shown below :

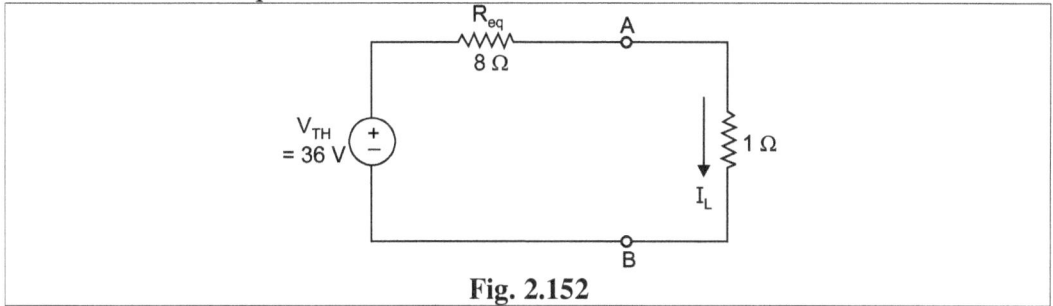

Fig. 2.152

$\therefore$ $I_L = \dfrac{V_{TH}}{R_{eq} + 1} = \dfrac{36}{8 + 1}$

$\therefore$ $I_L = 4\ A$

Example 2.35 :

Using Thevenin's theorem determine the current flowing through 2 Ω resistance in the network shown in Fig. 2.153.

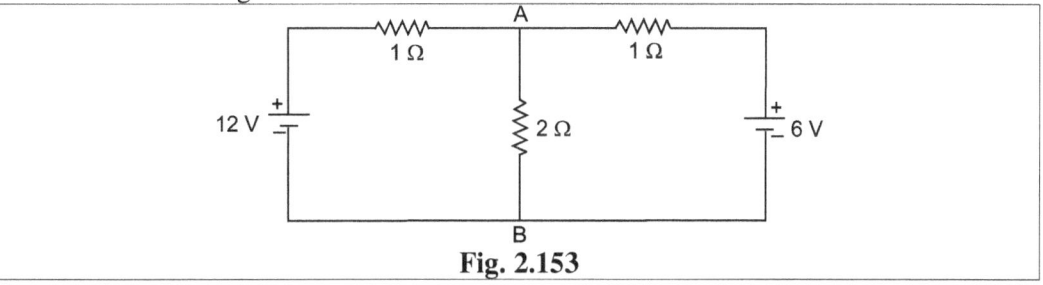

Fig. 2.153

Solution : Remove 2 Ω resistance and find open-circuit voltage V_{TH}.

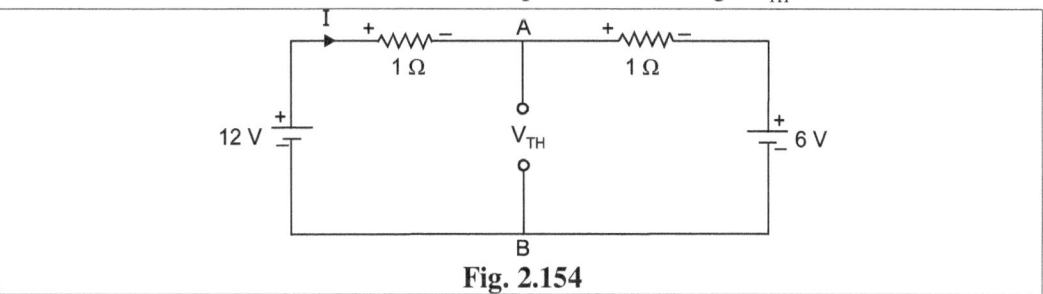

Fig. 2.154

Applying KVL to the loop,

$$-I - I - 6 + 12 = 0$$

$\therefore$ $I = 3\ A$

Drop across 1 Ω = 3×1 = 3 V

Tracing the path from A to B through 12 V source

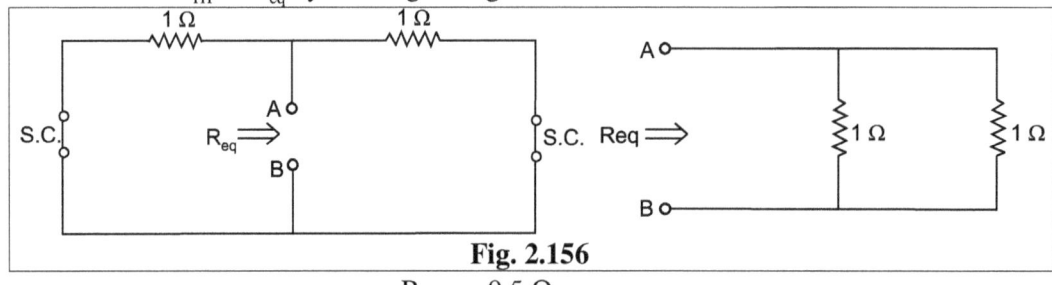

Fig. 2.155

∴ $V_{AB} = V_{TH} = 12 - 3 = 9$ V   with A positive

Calculate R_{TH} or R_{eq} by shorting voltage sources.

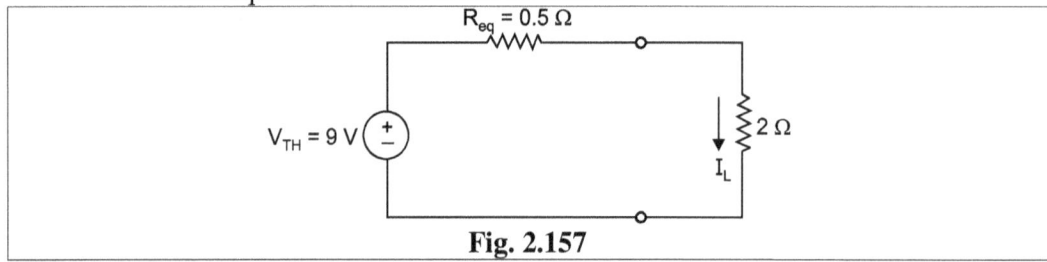

Fig. 2.156

∴ $R_{eq} = 0.5\ \Omega$

∴   Thevenin's equivalent circuit is shown below.

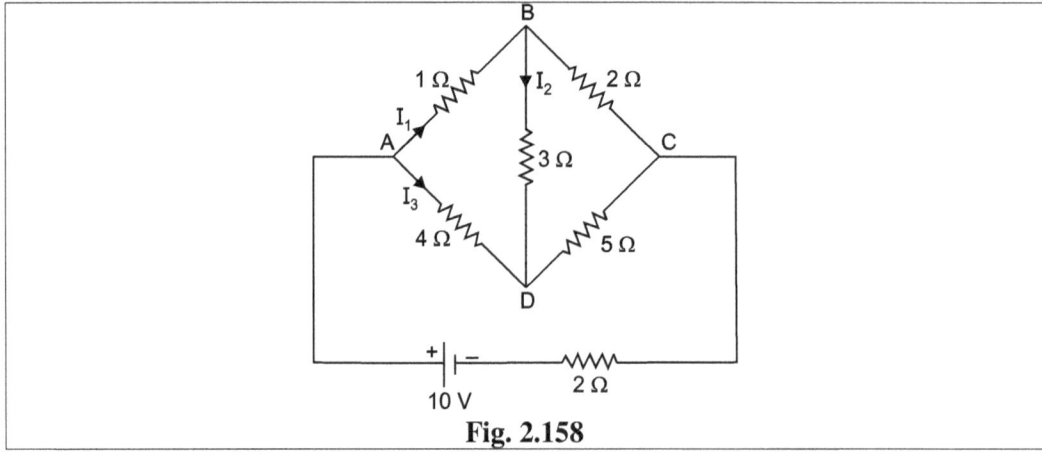

Fig. 2.157

∴   Current through 2 Ω is

$$I_L = \frac{V_{TH}}{R_L + R_{eq}} = 3.6\ A$$

Example 2.36 :

For the network shown in Fig. 2.158 find the current I_2 in the 3 Ω resistance by applying Thevenin's theorem.

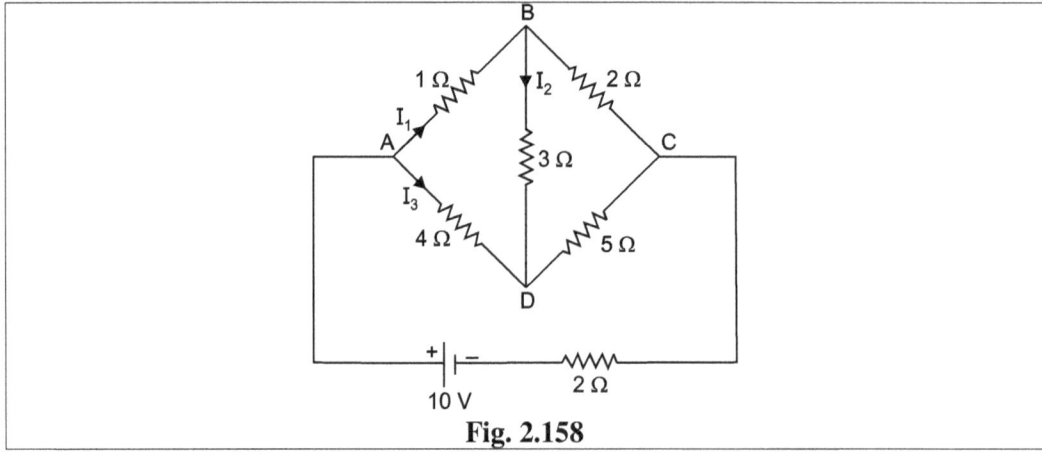

Fig. 2.158

Solution : Let us first remove 3 Ω resistor and find the value of open-circuit voltage V_{OC} or V_{TH}.

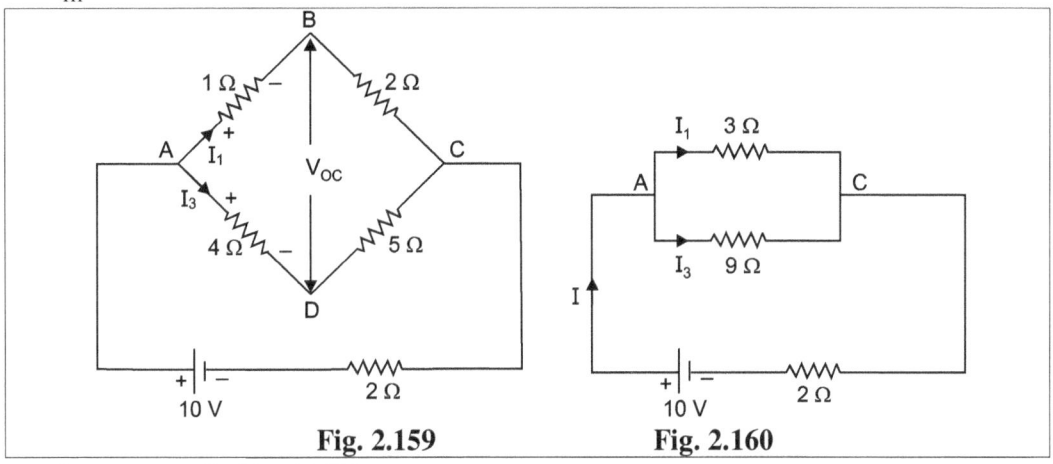

Fig. 2.159   Fig. 2.160

Current supplied by 10 V battery,

$$I = \frac{10}{2 + (3 \parallel 9)} = \frac{10}{4.25} = 2.35 \text{ A}$$

$$I_1 = 2.35 \times \frac{9}{9+3} = 1.76 \text{ A}$$

and,

$$I_3 = 2.35 \times \frac{3}{9+3} = 0.5875 \text{ A}$$

$$V_{TH} = V_{BD}$$

$$= -1\, I_1 + 4\, I_3 = -1.76 + (4 \times 0.5875)$$

$$= 0.59 \text{ V} \qquad\qquad \text{with B +ve w.r.t. D}$$

Now, find Thevenin's equivalent resistance.

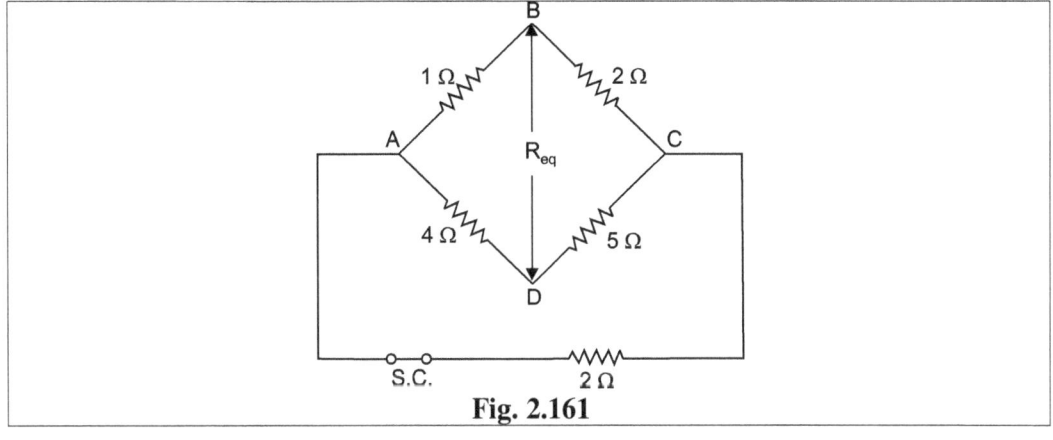

Fig. 2.161

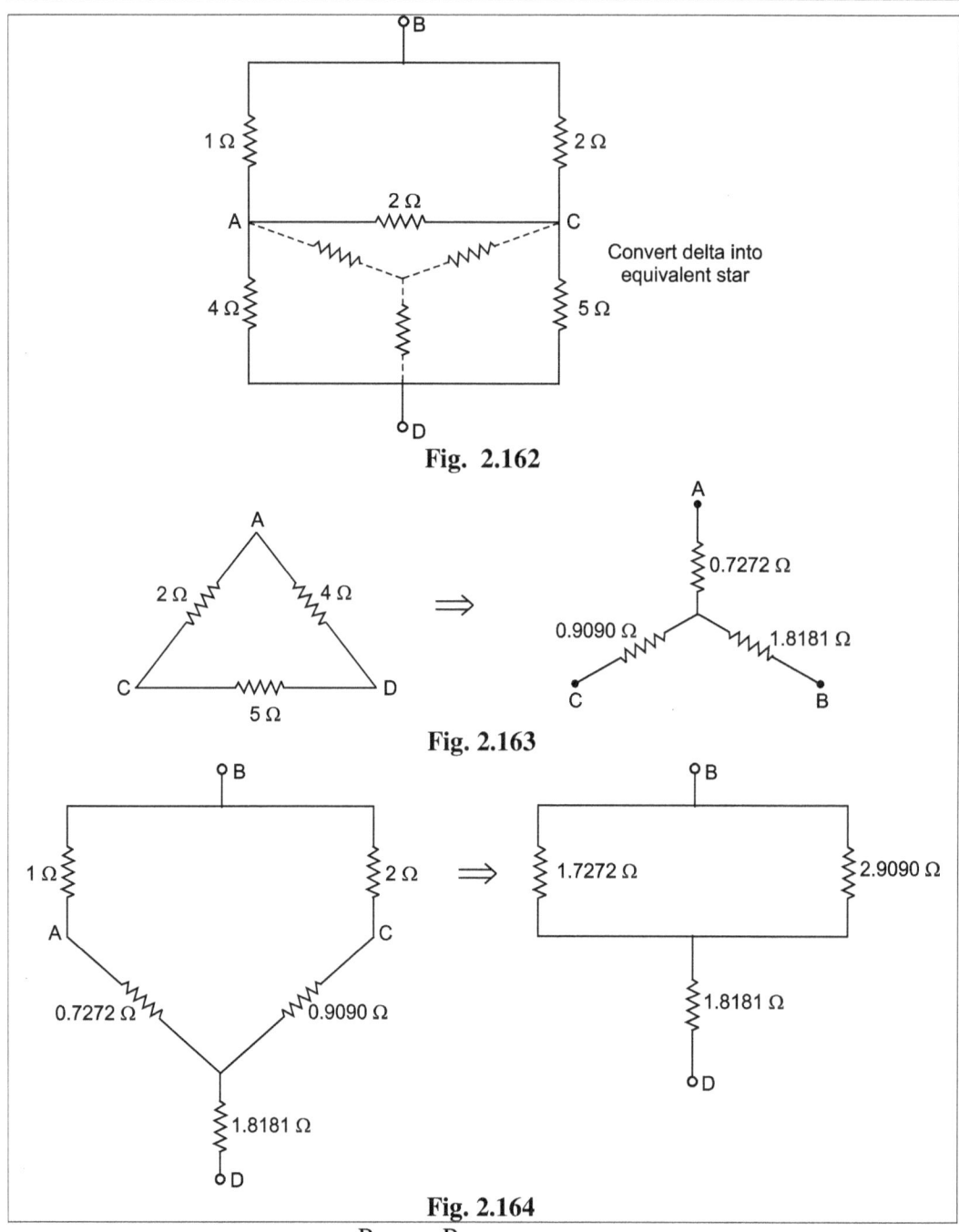

Fig. 2.162

Fig. 2.163

Fig. 2.164

$$R_{TH} = R_{eq}$$
$$= 1.8181 + (1.7272 \parallel 2.90890) = 2.9018 \ \Omega$$

Let us draw Thevenin's equivalent circuit.

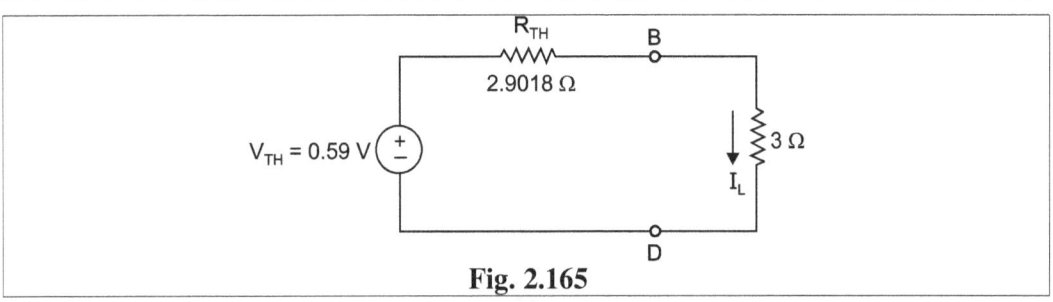

Fig. 2.165

Current through 3 Ω is $\quad I_2 = \dfrac{V_{TH}}{R_{TH} + R_L} = \dfrac{0.59}{2.9018 + 3} = 0.09996$ A

Example 2.37 :

Use Thevenin's theorem to find the current in the branch BD of the network shown in Fig. 2.166.

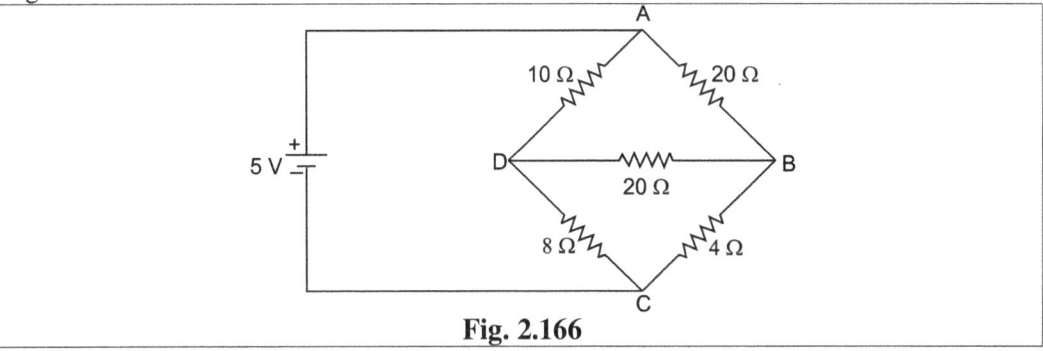

Fig. 2.166

Solution : Remove branch BD and find the open-circuit voltage $V_{TH} = V_{BD}$.

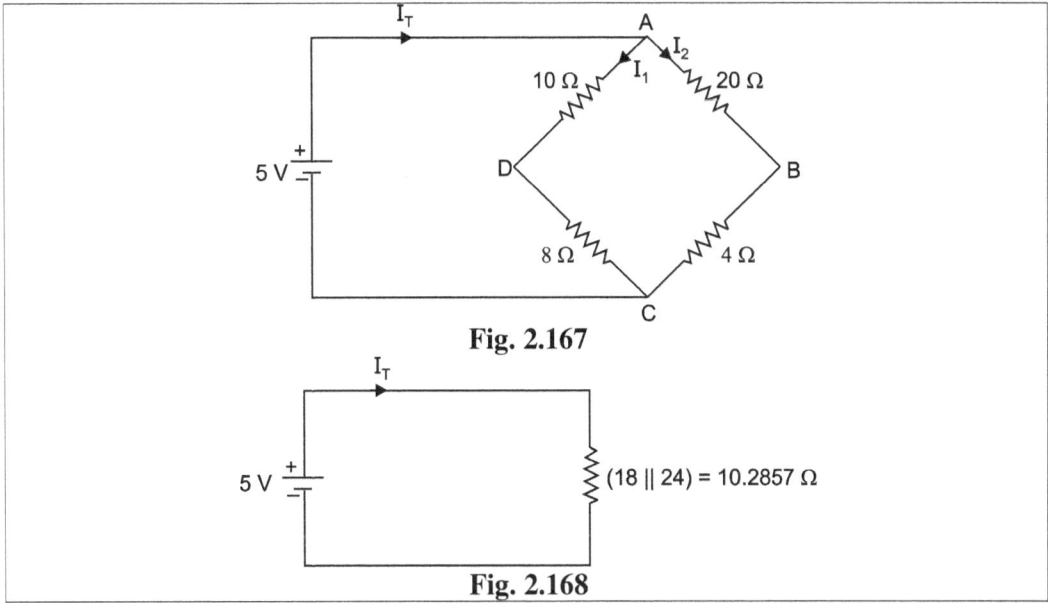

Fig. 2.167

Fig. 2.168

$$I_T = \frac{5}{10.2857} = 0.48611 \text{ A}$$

Using current division rule,

$$I_1 = I_T \times \frac{24}{24 + 18} = 0.2778 \text{ A}$$

$$I_2 = I_T - I_1 = 0.20833 \text{ A}$$

The various voltage drops due to I_1 and I_2 are shown in Fig. 2.169 :

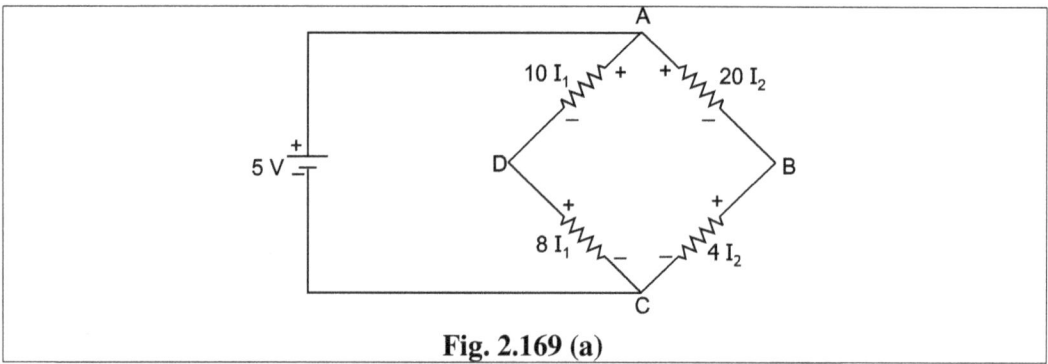

Fig. 2.169 (a)

Trace path BCD,

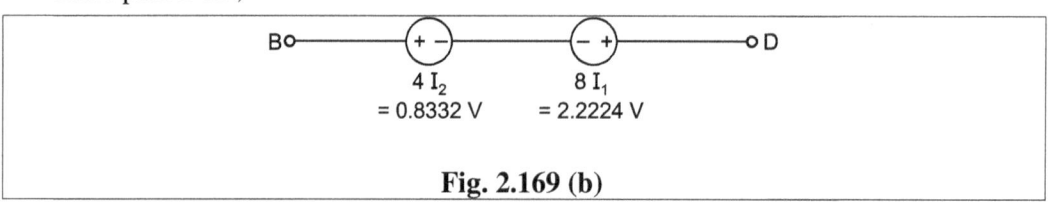

Fig. 2.169 (b)

$$V_{BD} = 2.2224 - 0.8332 = 1.3892 \text{ V} \qquad\qquad \text{B negative w.r.t. D}$$

$$\therefore \qquad\qquad V_{TH} = V_{BD} = 1.3892 \text{ V} \qquad\qquad \text{with B negative}$$

Find R_{TH} with shorting voltage source.

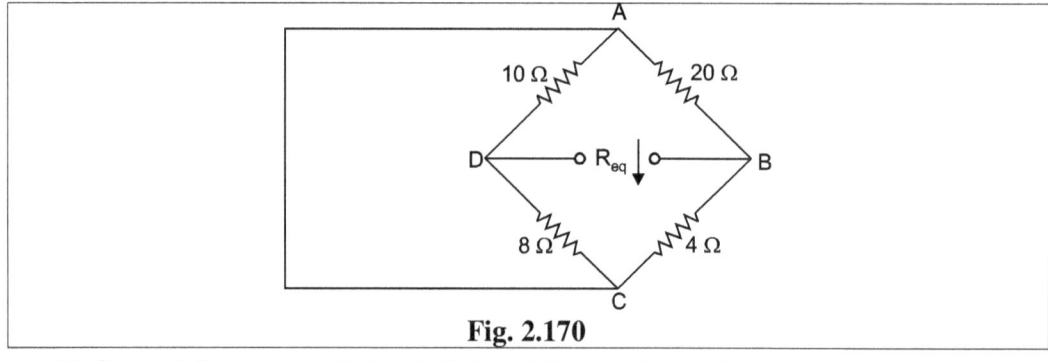

Fig. 2.170

$20 \ \Omega$ and $4 \ \Omega$ are in parallel and $10 \ \Omega$ and $8 \ \Omega$ are in parallel.

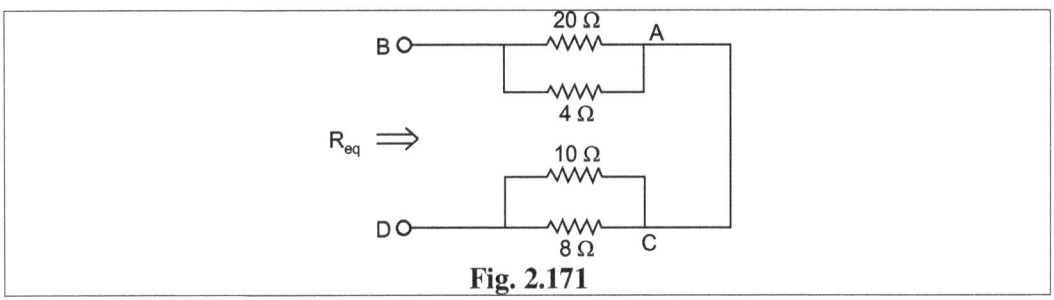

Fig. 2.171

$$R_{eq} = (20 \| 4) + (10 \| 8) = 3.33 + 4.44 = 7.77 \, \Omega$$

Thevenin's equivalent circuit is

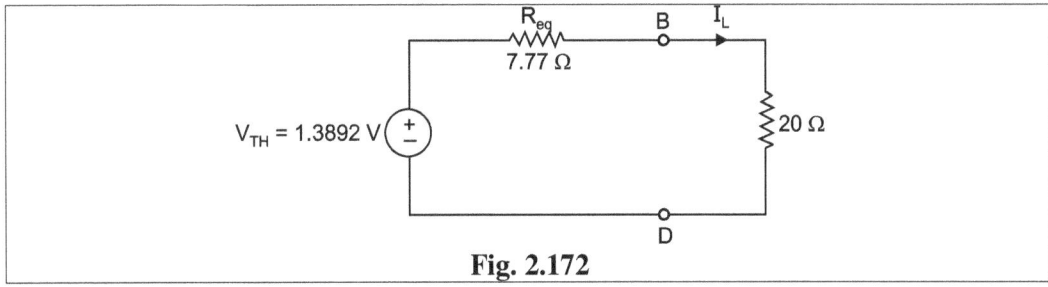

Fig. 2.172

$$I_L = \frac{V_{TH}}{R_{eq} + 20} = \frac{1.3892}{27.777} = 0.05 \text{ A (from D to B)}$$

Example 2.38 :

Find current I_2 shown in Fig. 2.173 by application of Thevenin's theorem.

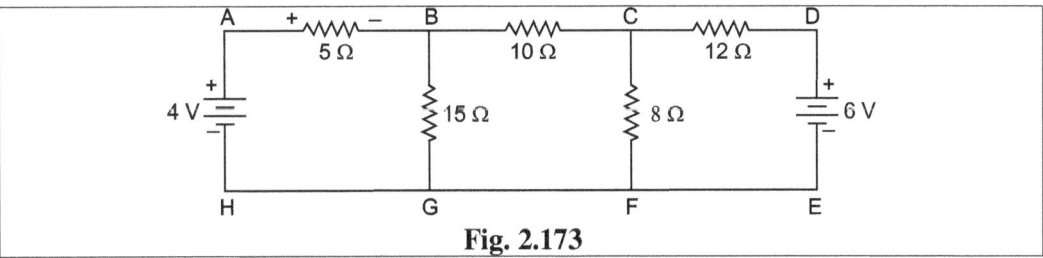

Fig. 2.173

Solution : Remove the branch of 10 Ω and find open-circuit voltage V_{TH}.

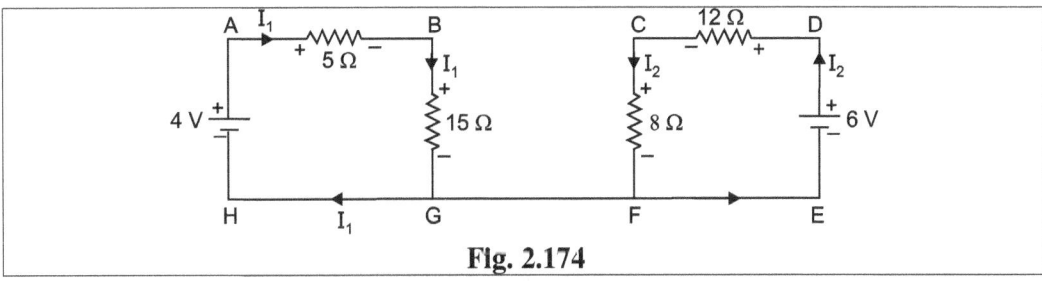

Fig. 2.174

Let I_1 and I_2 be the currents delivered by 4 V and 6 V sources.

Applying KVL to loop ABGHA,

$$-5\,I_1 - 15\,I_1 + 4 \;=\; 0$$

$$\therefore \qquad\qquad\qquad I_1 \;=\; 0.2 \text{ A}$$

Applying KVL to loop CFEDC

$$-8I_2 + 6 - 12\,I_2 \;=\; 0$$

$$\therefore \qquad\qquad\qquad I_2 \;=\; 0.3 \text{ A}$$

$$\therefore \qquad\qquad\qquad V_{TH} \;=\; 15\,I_1 - 8\,I_2$$

$$\;=\; 15\,(0.2) - 8\,(0.3)$$

$$\;=\; 0.6 \text{ V} \qquad\qquad \text{(with B positive w.r.t. C)}$$

To find R_{TH}, replace both voltage sources by short circuit.

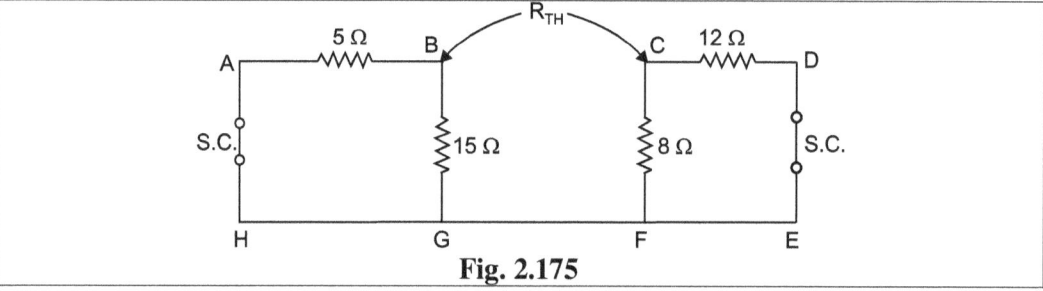

Fig. 2.175

15 Ω and 5 Ω are in parallel. Similarly, 8 Ω and 12 Ω are in parallel.

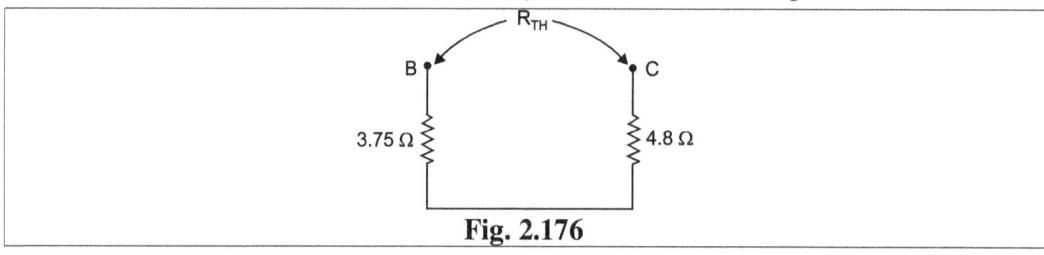

Fig. 2.176

$$\therefore \qquad\qquad R_{TH} \;=\; 3.75 + 4.8 = 8.55 \text{ Ω}$$

Replace given network by Thevenin's equivalent circuit & reconnect 10 Ω resistance.

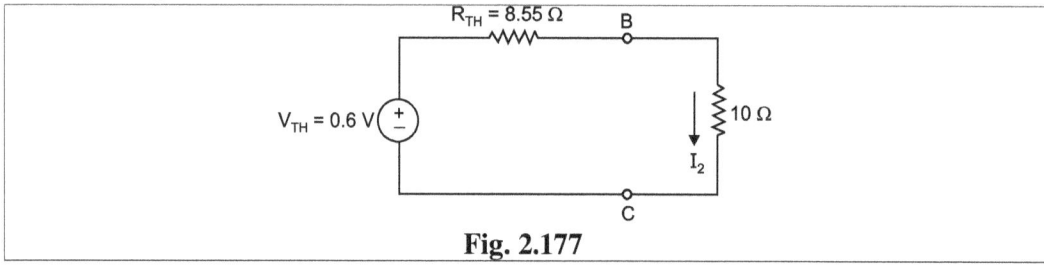

Fig. 2.177

$$I_2 \;=\; \frac{0.6}{8.55 + 10}$$

$$\;=\; 0.03234 \text{ A} \qquad\qquad \text{(from B to C)}$$

Example 2.39 :

Apply Thevenin's theorem to the circuit shown in Fig. 2.177 (a) to calculate the current flowing in Branch A–B.

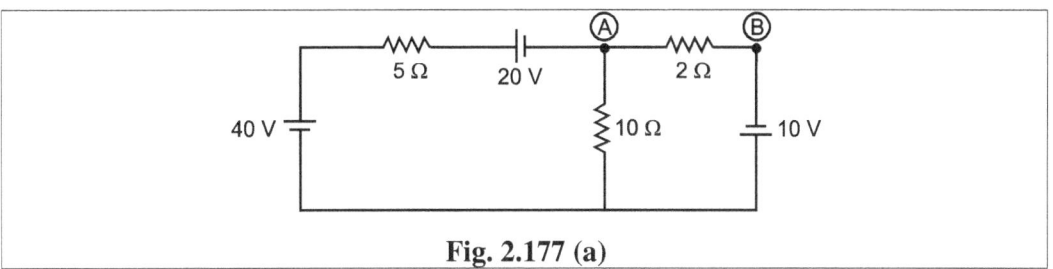

Fig. 2.177 (a)

Solution : First remove 2Ω resistance and open circuit the terminals AB. Let us find open circuit voltage across terminals AB i.e. V_{TH}.

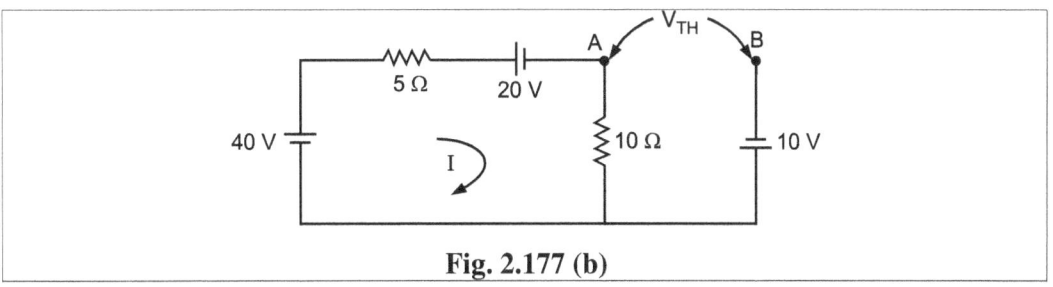

Fig. 2.177 (b)

$$I = \frac{40 - 20}{15} = \frac{20}{15}$$

$$= 1.33 \text{ A}$$

$$V_{AB} = V_{TH} = V_{OC} = 10 + 1.33 \,(10)$$

$$= 23.33 \text{ V}$$

To find R_{TH}, replace voltage sources by short circuit.

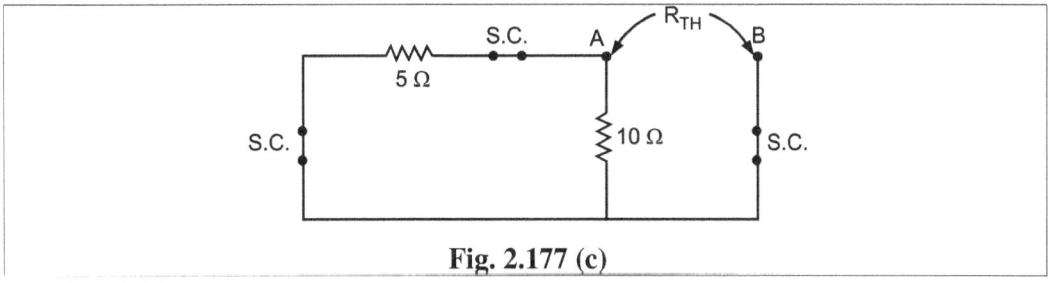

Fig. 2.177 (c)

$$R_{TH} = \frac{5 \times 10}{5 + 10} = 3.33 \ \Omega$$

Current flowing branch AB

i.e. $I_{AB} = I_{2\Omega} = \dfrac{V_{TH}}{R_{TH} + R_L} = \dfrac{23.33}{3.33 + 2} = 4.37$ A

Example 2.40 :

Use superposition theorem to find current in 4Ω resistance as shown in figure. Hence verify your results by Thevenins theorem. All resistances are in ohm.

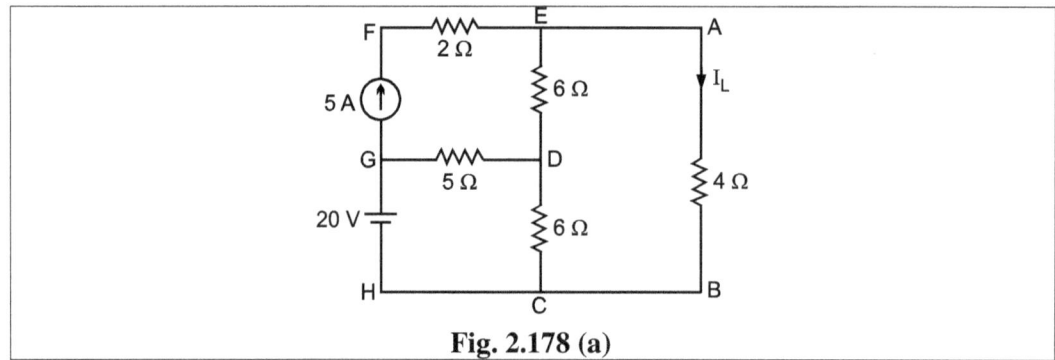

Fig. 2.178 (a)

Solution : Case (I) : Consider a source of 5 Amp acting alone, and 20 V source replaced by S.C.

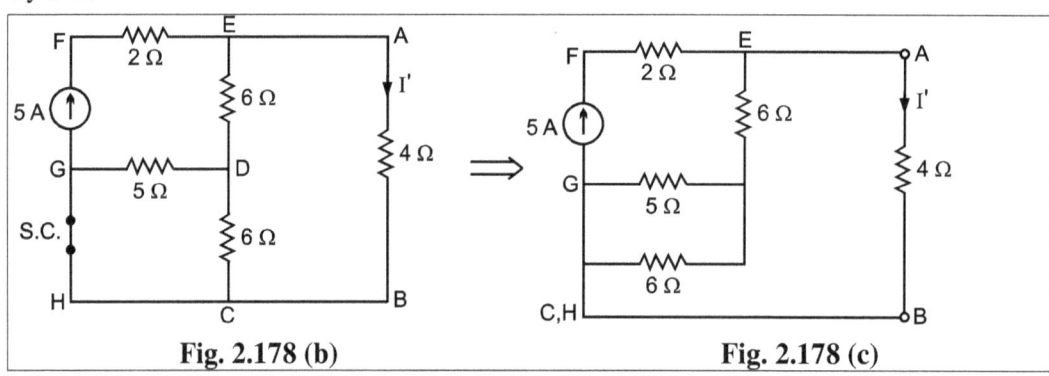

Fig. 2.178 (b)   **Fig. 2.178 (c)**

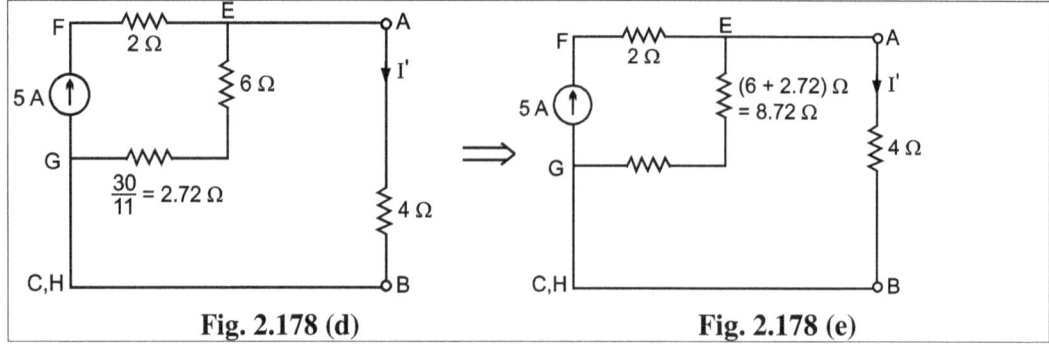

Fig. 2.178 (d)   **Fig. 2.178 (e)**

$$I' = 5 \times \frac{8.72}{8.72 + 4}$$

$$= 3.42 \text{ Amp (from A to B)}$$

Case (II) : Now consider a source of 20 V alone and a source of 5 Amp is replaced by opening it.

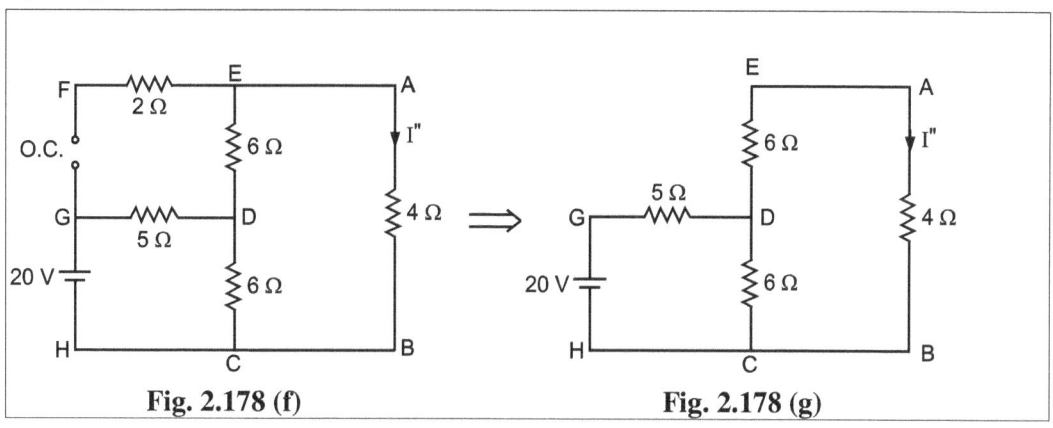

Fig. 2.178 (f)   Fig. 2.178 (g)

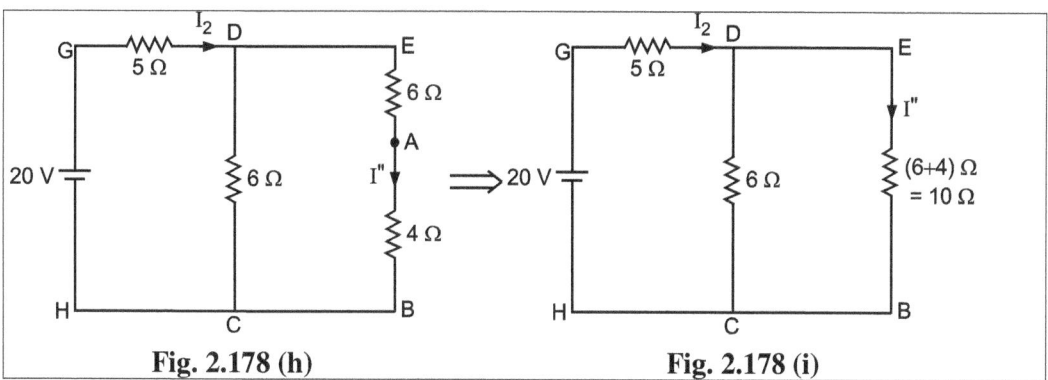

Fig. 2.178 (h)   Fig. 2.178 (i)

Fig. 2.178 (j)

$$I_2 = \frac{20}{(5 + 3.75)}$$

$$= 2.28 \text{ Amp}$$

Current through 4Ω

$$I'' = I_2 \times \frac{6}{6 + (6 + 4)} = 2.28 \times \frac{6}{16}$$

$$= 0.857 \text{ Amp (from A to B)}$$

Total current,

$$I = I' + I''$$

$$= 3.42 + 0.857$$

$$= 4.27 \text{ Amp (from A to B)}$$

Verification of the result by using Thevenin's Theorem

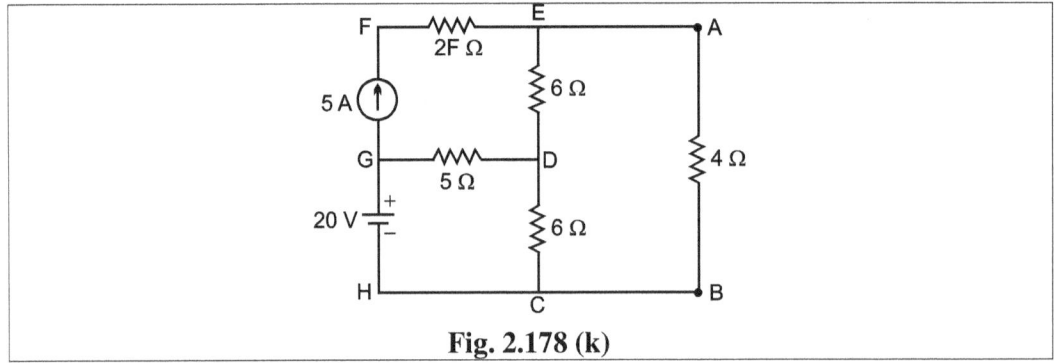

Fig. 2.178 (k)

(1) To find V_{TH} (O.C. Voltage)

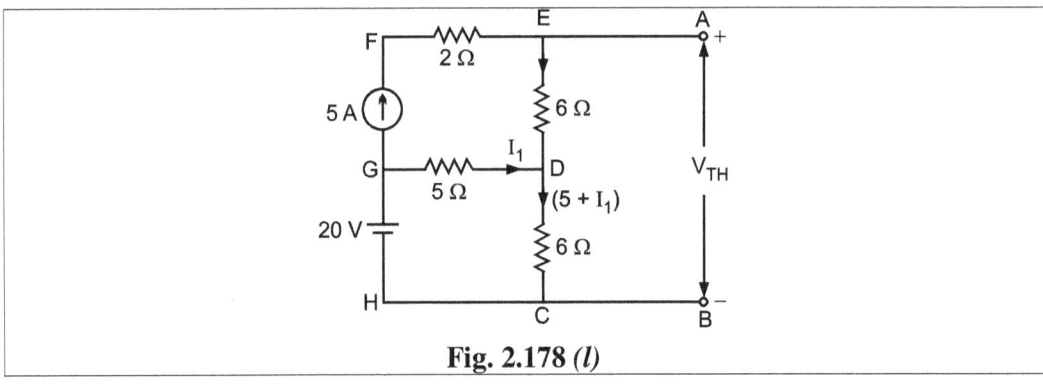

Fig. 2.178 (l)

Consider A is at higher potential with respect to B for loop, ABCDEA

$$-V_{TH} + 6 (5 + I_1) + (6 \times 5) = 0$$

$$V_{TH} = 30 + 30 + 6 I_1 \qquad \qquad \dots(1)$$

to find value of I_1 consider loop GDCHG

$$-5I_1 - 6 (5 + I_1) + 20 = 0$$

$$-11 I_1 - 30 + 20 = 0$$

$$I_1 = -\frac{10}{11}$$

$$= -0.909 \text{ Amp}$$

(actually flows form D to E)

Substitute value of I_1 in equation (1)

$$V_{TH} = 60 + 6(-0.909)$$

$$= 60 - 5.45$$

$$= 54.54 \text{ volt}$$

(2) To find R_{TH} : Replace the source by their interval resistance's i.e. current source by opening and voltage source by shorting it.

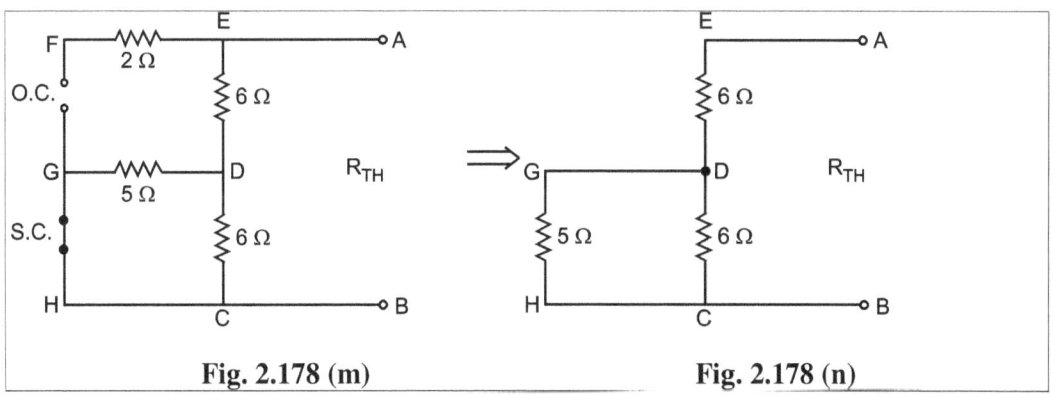

Fig. 2.178 (m)   Fig. 2.178 (n)

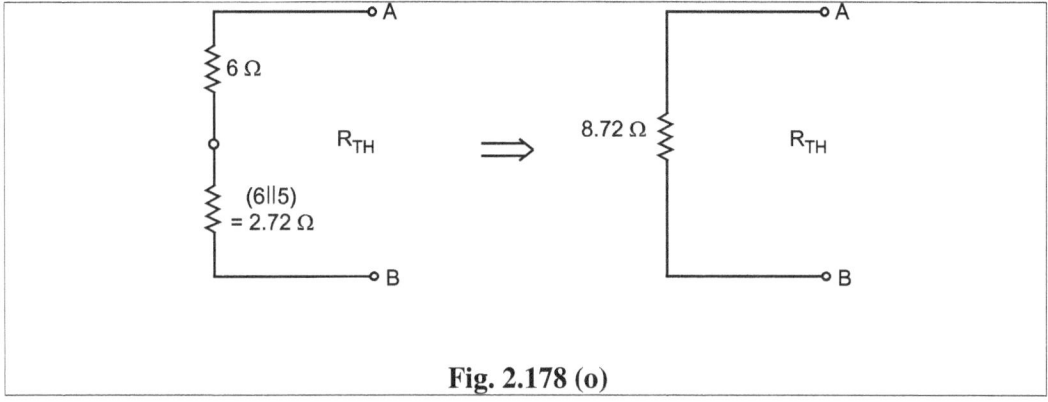

Fig. 2.178 (o)

$$R_{TH} = 8.72 \ \Omega$$

(3) Thevenin's equivalent circuit :

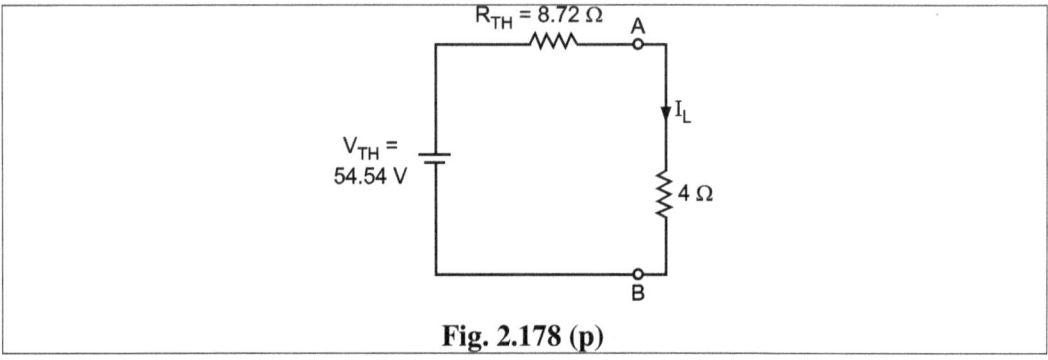

Fig. 2.178 (p)

$$I_L = \frac{V_{TH}}{R_{TH} + R_L} = \frac{54.54}{8.72 + 4} = \frac{54.54}{12.72} = 4.28 \text{ Amp}$$

2.8.3 Maximum Power Transfer Theorem

Statement : In an active, resistive network, maximum power transfer to the load resistance takes place when the load resistance equals the equivalent resistance of the network as viewed from the terminals of the load.

Proof : Consider a d.c. source of voltage V volts and having internal resistance of r Ω connected to a variable load resistance R_L as shown in Fig. 2.179. Load current I_L is given by,

$$I_L = \frac{V}{(r + R_L)} \qquad \qquad ...(1)$$

Power consumed by load resistance R_L is,

$$P = I_L^2 \, R_L = \left[\frac{V}{(r + R_L)} \right]^2 \cdot R_L \qquad \qquad ... (2)$$

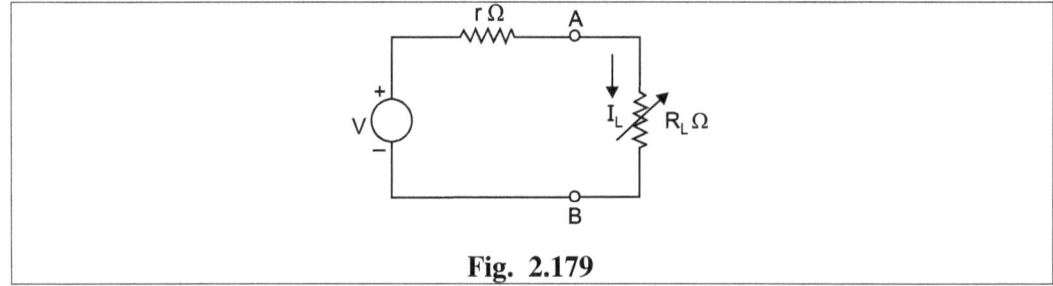

Fig. 2.179

If R_L is changed, I_L is also going to change and at a particular value of R_L, power transferred to the load is maximum. Let us find value of R_L for which power transfer to the load is maximum.

For that differentiate equation (2) with respect to R_L and equate it to zero.

i.e. $\dfrac{d}{dR_L}(P) = 0$

$\therefore \qquad\qquad \dfrac{d}{dR_L}\left\{\dfrac{V^2}{(r+R_L)^2}\cdot R_L\right\} = 0$

$\therefore \qquad\qquad V^2\dfrac{d}{dR_L}\left\{\dfrac{R_L}{(r+R_L)^2}\right\} = 0$

$V^2\left\{\dfrac{(r+R_L)^2\cdot 1 - R_L^2\,(r+R_L)}{(r+R_L)^4}\right\} = 0$

$(r+R_L)^2 - 2R_L(r+R_L) = 0$

$(r+R_L) - 2.R_L = 0$

$\therefore \qquad\qquad\qquad r = R_L \qquad\qquad\qquad\qquad …(3)$

Thus, when load resistance is equal to the internal resistance of source maximum power transfer takes place.

Now, any complex network can be represented with a single voltage source of V_{TH} volts with equivalent resistance R_{eq} in series with it, using Thevenin's theorem across load terminals. Thus, the variable resistance R_L, in such a case must be equal to R_{eq} to have maximum power transfer to the load.

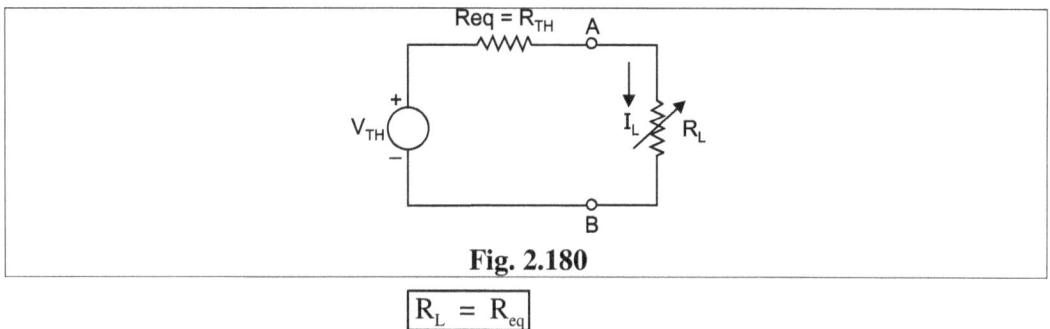

Fig. 2.180

$$\boxed{R_L = R_{eq}}$$

For maximum power transfer, let us calculate magnitude of maximum power transfer.

$$\therefore \qquad P_{max.} = \left(\frac{V_{TH}}{R_{eq.} + R_L}\right)^2 \cdot R_L$$

$$= I_L^2 \cdot R_L$$

But, $\qquad R_L = R_{eq}$

$$\therefore \qquad P_{max} = \frac{V_{TH}^2}{(2 \cdot R_{eq})^2} \cdot R_{eq}$$

$$= \frac{V_{TH}^2}{4 \cdot R_{eq}} \text{ watt}$$

$$\therefore \qquad \boxed{P_{max} = \frac{V_{Th}^2}{4 \cdot R_{eq}}}$$

How to apply maximum power transfer theorem ?

(1) Replace the given network across load terminals by Thevenin's or Norton's equivalent circuit. i.e. obtain V_{TH} or I_N and $R_{eq.}$

(2) $R_L = R_{eq.}$ gives condition for maximum power transfer to the load.

(3) If magnitude of maximum power is asked then only find it with the help of

$$P_{max} = \frac{V_{TH}^2}{4 \cdot R_{eq}}$$

If value of R_L for maximum power transfer is asked then only find R_{eq}. Don't find V_{TH} unnecessarily.

Example 2.41 :

Find the value of load resistance (R_L) for maximum power transfer and magnitude of maximum power dissipated in the resistor (R_L) shown in Fig. 2.181.

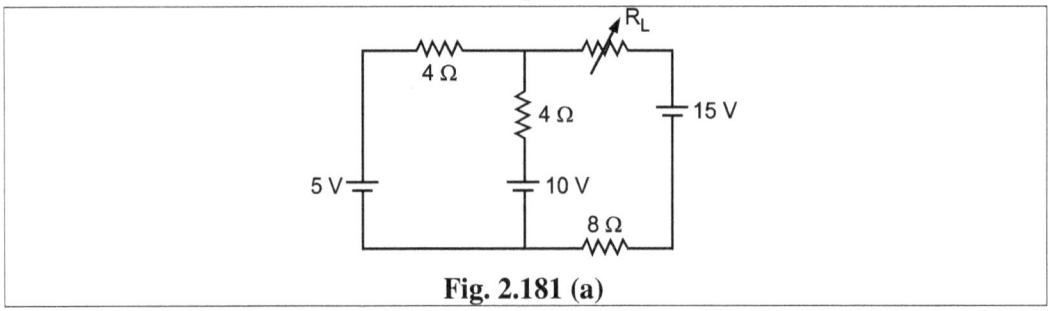

Fig. 2.181 (a)

Solution : Calculation of V_{TH}

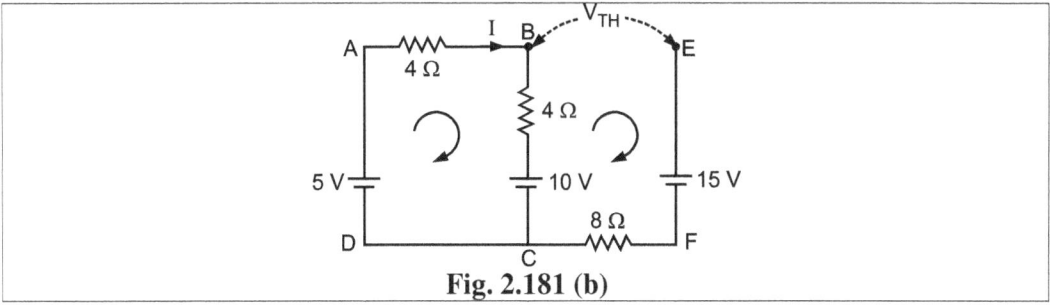

Fig. 2.181 (b)

Applying KVL to loop ABCDA

$$-4I - 4I - 10 + 5 = 0$$

$$-8I - 5 = 0$$

$$-8I - 5 = 0$$

$$-8I = 5$$

$$\therefore \qquad I = \frac{-5}{8} \text{ Amp}$$

Now, considering loop BEFCB

$$-V_{TH} - 15 + 10 + 4 \times I = -V_{TH} - 5 + 4 \,(-5/8)$$

$$- V_{TH} - 7.5 = 0$$

$$\therefore \qquad V_{TH} = -7.5 \text{ Volt} \qquad \text{(E is at higher potential than B)}$$

Calculation of equivalent resistance (R_{TH})

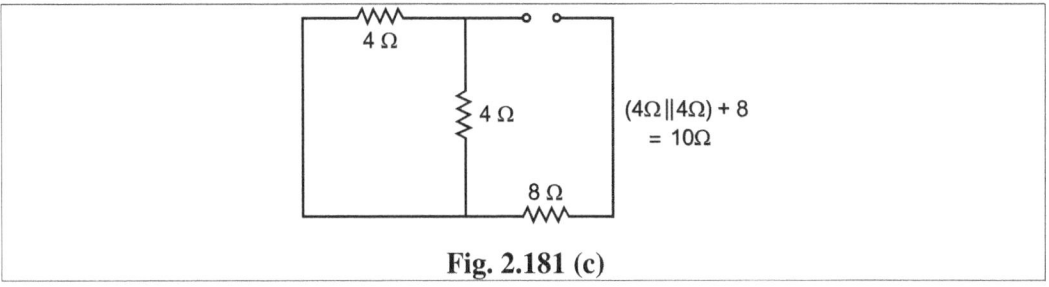

Fig. 2.181 (c)

(1) Thus for maximum power transfer load resistance (R_C) $= R_{TH} = 10\Omega$

(2) Maximum power transfer $\dfrac{V_{TH}^{\,2}}{4R_{TH}} = \dfrac{7.5^2}{4 \times 10} = 1.406$ watt

REVIEW QUESTIONS

1. Find the equivalent resistance between the terminals (i) B & C, (ii) A & C in the network shown.   **[Ans. : (i) $R_{BC} = 12\ \Omega$, (ii) $R_{AB} = 15\ \Omega$]**

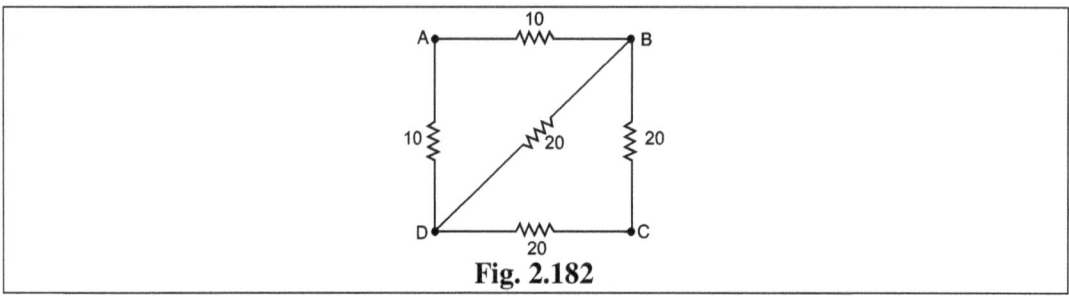

Fig. 2.182

2. Find the equivalent resistance between points P and Q for the network shown.

[Ans. : $R_{PQ} = 24.5\Omega$]

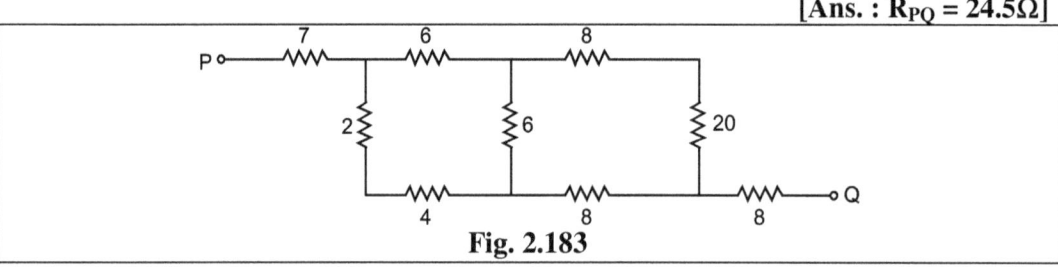

Fig. 2.183

3. Determine the resistance between the points X and Y for the network shown.

[Ans. : $R_{XY} = 0.5833\ \Omega$]

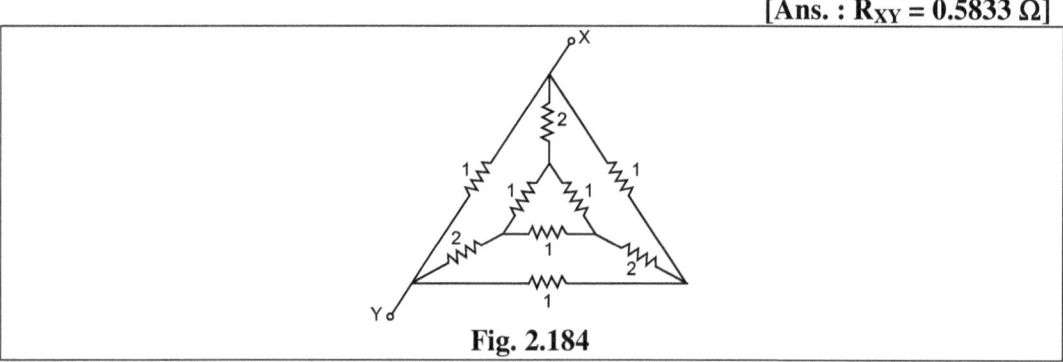

Fig. 2.184

4. Calculate the effective resistance between points A and B of the network shown :

[Ans. : $R_{AB} = 7\ \Omega$]

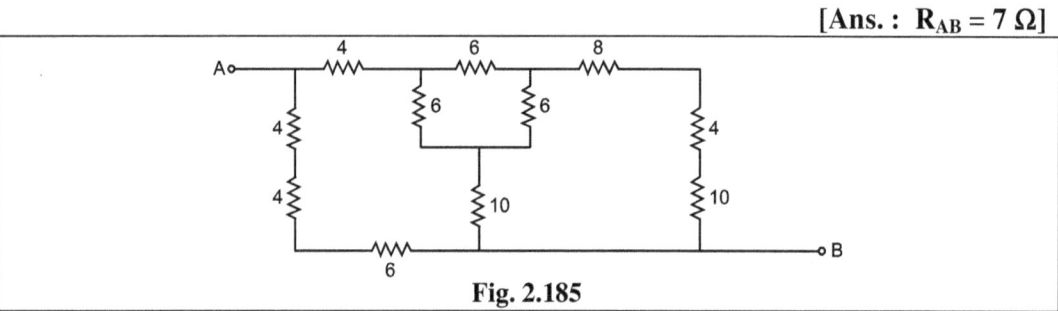

Fig. 2.185

5. Using Kirchhoff's laws, calculate the current delivered by the battery in Fig. 2.186.

[Ans. : I = 1.385A]

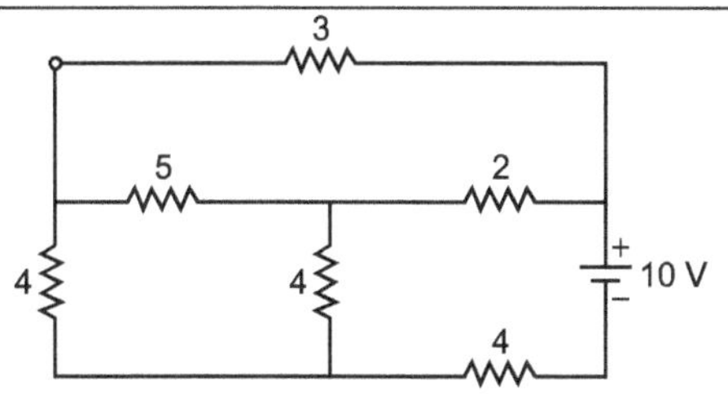

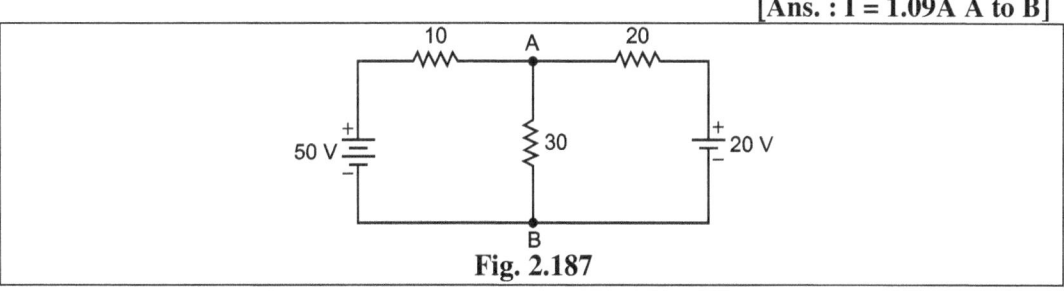

Fig. 2.186

6. Find the current through 30Ω resistance by KCL and KVL.

[Ans. : I = 1.09A A to B]

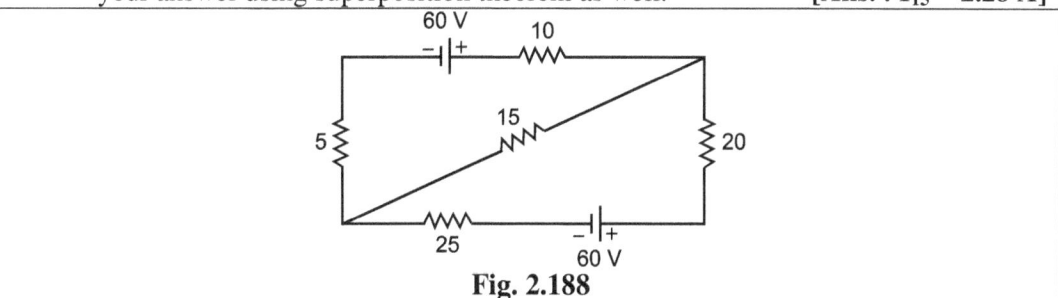

Fig. 2.187

7. Calculate the current through 15Ω resistance using Kirchhoff's laws and verify your answer using superposition theorem as well.   [Ans. : I_{15} = 2.28 A]

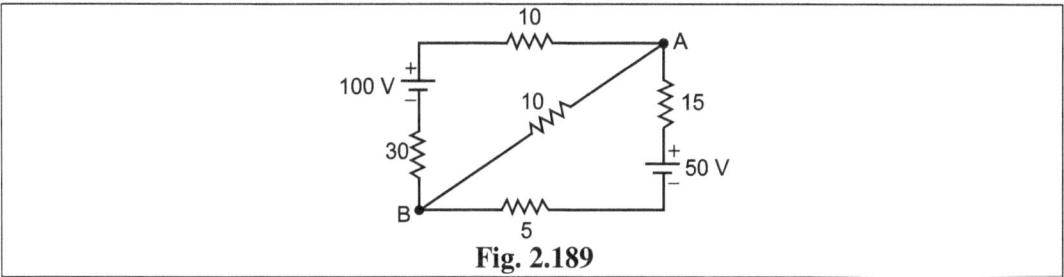

Fig. 2.188

8. For the circuit shown below, find the current in 10Ω resistance connected between terminals A and B by Kirchhoff's laws and verify the answer by superposition theorem.   [Ans. : I = 2.86A, I_1' 1.43 A, I_2' = 1.43 A]

Fig. 2.189

9. Find the current flowing in 1 Ω resistance using superposition theorem for given
   network.   [Ans. : I = 14 A ↑ ^A_B]

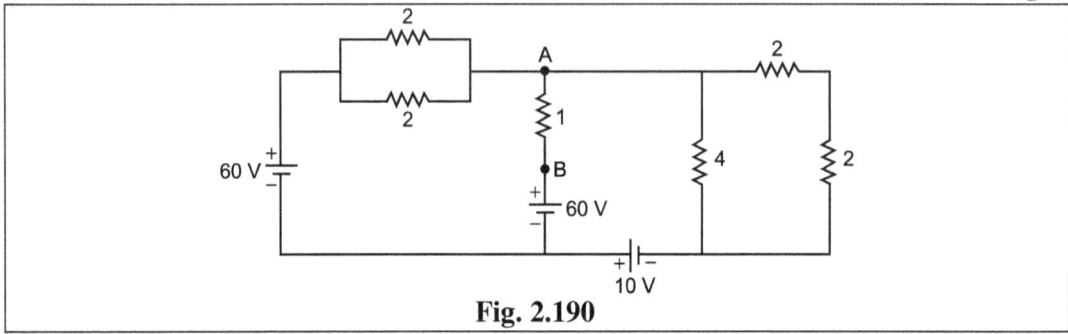

Fig. 2.190

10. Find the current in 10 Ω resistance using Thevenin's theorem.
    [Ans. : V_{th} = − 6.2857 V, R_{th} = 9.4286 Ω, I_L = 0.3235A B to A]

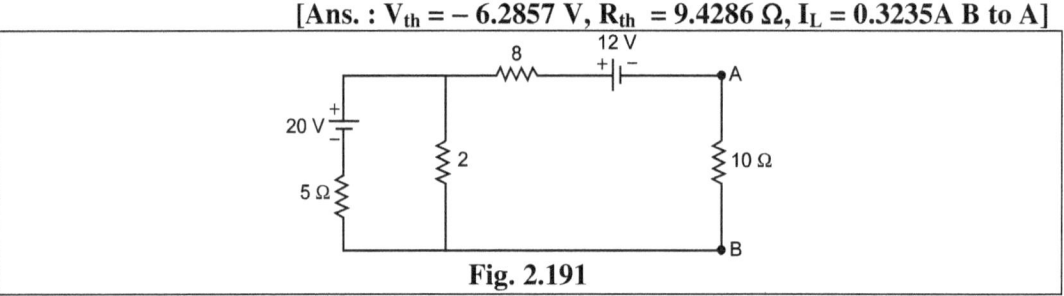

Fig. 2.191

11. Find the power dissipated in 10Ω resistance of the circuit shown.
    [Ans. : V_{th} = 4.762 V, R_{th} = 0.9524Ω, P = 1.89W]

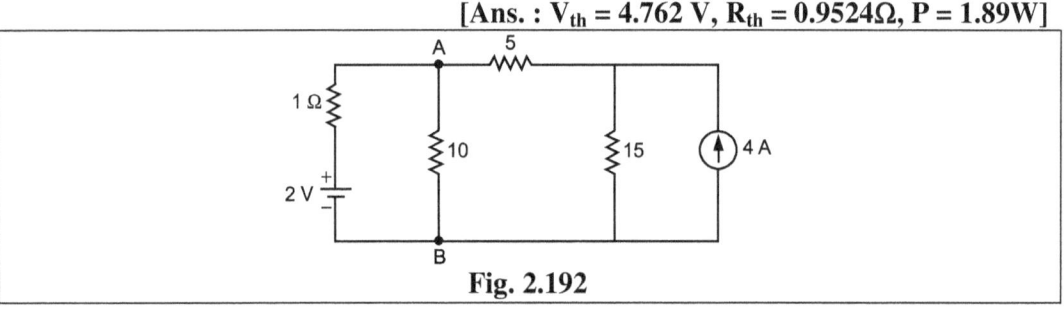

Fig. 2.192

12. Use Thevenin's theorem to find the current through 2 Ω resistance in the network
    shown.   [Ans. : I_L = 0.176 A]

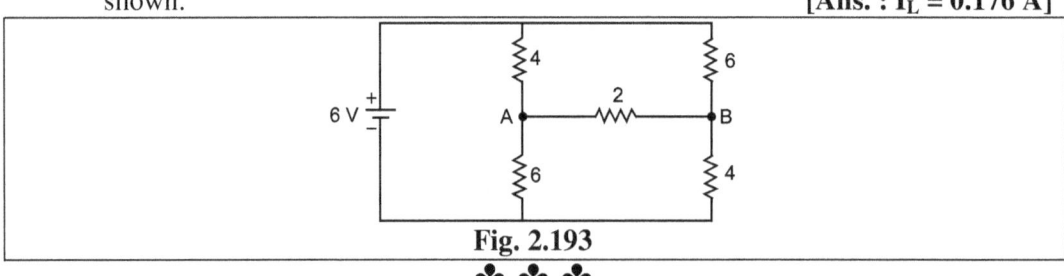

Fig. 2.193

❖ ❖ ❖

Chapter 3

ELECTROSTATICS

3.1 INTRODUCTION

Electrostatics is the branch of science which deals with electricity at rest. Under normal conditions, the atom is said to be electrically neutral. The atoms are said to be positively charged when they have deficit of electrons and negatively charged when they have excess of electrons on it.

Thus, charge is defined as total deficiency or excess of electrons in a body.

3.2 LAWS OF ELECTROSTATICS (COULOMB'S LAW)

First Law : Like charges of electricity repel each other and unlike charges attract each other.

Second Law : The force between two very small charged bodies separated by a distance is directly proportional to the product of the charges and inversely proportional to the square of distance between them. It can be expressed as,

$$F \propto \frac{q_1 \, q_2}{d^2}$$

$$F = K \cdot \frac{q_1 \, q_2}{d^2}$$

$$F = \frac{1}{4 \pi \in_o \in_r} \times \frac{q_1 \, q_2}{d^2}$$

where, q_1 , q_2 : be the two charges in coulombs.

F : be the force between the charges in Newton (N)

d : distance between the charges in meter (m)

$\in_o$: be the permittivity of free space

$\in_r$: be the relative permittivity of the medium.

But, $\in_o = 8.854 \times 10^{-12}$ F/m

∴ Hence, force becomes, $F = \dfrac{1}{4\pi \times 8.854 \times 10^{-12} \in_r} \cdot \dfrac{q_1 \, q_2}{d^2}$

$$= 9 \times 10^9 \frac{q_1 \, q_2}{\in_r d^2}$$

Hence, unit charge is defined as the charge which when placed one metre away from a similar charge in vacuum experiences a force of 9×10^9 N.

(3.1)

3.3 DIFFERENT QUANTITIES RELATING TO ELECTROSTATICS

3.3.1 Electric Field

It is defined as the space in which an electric charge experiences a force. The field configuration for isolated positive charge and negative charge are shown in Fig. 3.1.

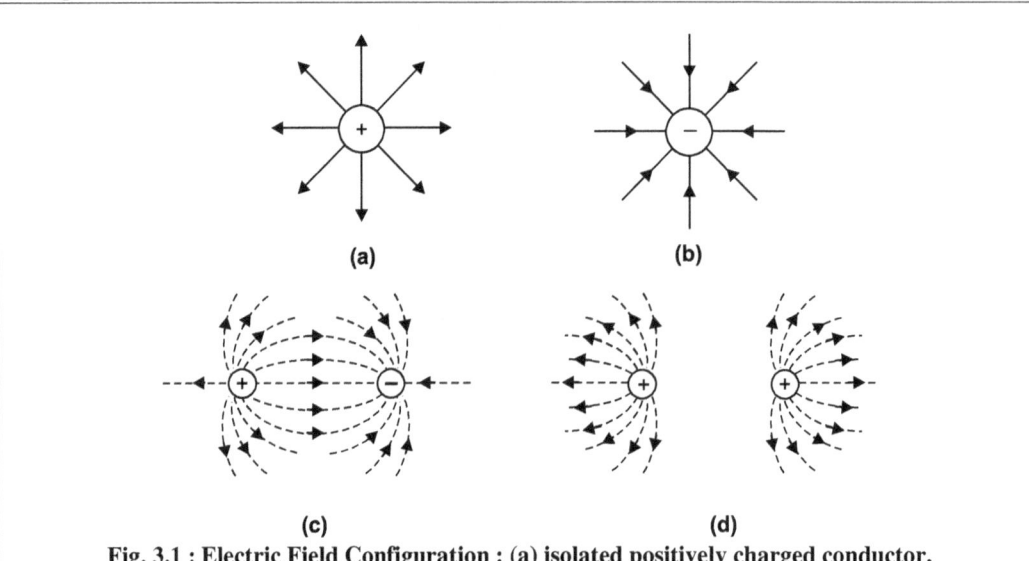

(a)   (b)

(c)   (d)

Fig. 3.1 : Electric Field Configuration : (a) isolated positively charged conductor, (b) isolated negatively charged conductor, (c) two equal unlike charges, (d) two equal like charges.

Properties of Electric Field Lines :

(i)   A line starts from positive charge and ends at negative charge.

(ii) The lines do not intersect each other.

(iii) The lines enter or leave a body at a right angle.

(iv) They always try to contract in length.

3.3.2 Electric Flux

It is defined as the total number of electric field lines. It is represented by the symbol ψ (psi). The unit of electric flux is Coulomb.

∴   Electric flux, ψ = Q Coulomb

3.3.3 Electric Flux Density

It is defined as the flux passing through unit area at right angle to the direction of field. The electric flux density is denoted by 'D'. It is measured in Coulomb per square metre. It is given as,

$$D = \frac{\psi}{A} \ C/m^2$$

3.3.4 Electric Field Strength

It is defined as the force experienced by unit positive charge at a particular point in a given electric field. It is denoted by 'E'. It is measured in Newton/Coulomb. It is given as,

$$E \ = \ \frac{F}{Q} \, N/C$$

It is also called as Electric Field Intensity. It is different at different point in a non-uniform electric field and same at all points in uniform electric field. It can also be expressed in volt/meter.

3.3.5 Permittivity

It is defined as readiness of a material or medium to allow passage of flux through it. The ratio of electric flux density in a vacuum or free space to the corresponding electric field strength is known as the permittivity of free space. It is denoted by ϵ_0. It is measured in Farad/meter. The permittivity of a vacuum or free space is 8.854×10^{-12} Farad/metre.

(a) Absolute Permittivity : It is defined as the ratio of electric flux density in a dielectric medium to the corresponding electric field strength. It is denoted by ϵ. It is measured in Farad/meter. It is given as,

$$\epsilon \ = \ \frac{D}{E} \ \ Farad/meter$$

where, D : be the electric flux density

E : be the electric field intensity.

(b) Relative Permittivity : It is defined as the ratio of electric flux density in a dielectric medium to that produced in free space by the same electric field strength under the same conditions. It is denoted by ϵ_r. Being a ratio it is unitless.

$$\epsilon_r \ = \ \frac{D}{D_0}$$

The relative permittivity of some of the insulating materials is given below :

Insulating Material	Relative Permittivity
Air	1.0006
Paper	1.8 – 2.6
Rubber	2.5 – 4
Oil	4 – 8
Mica	2.5 – 7
PVC	3.7
Glass	5 – 12
Bakelite	5
Porcelain	5 – 6.7
Vacuum	1

3.3.6 Electric Potential

Let us consider an isolated positive charge 'Q' placed in air in the electric field (Fig. 3.2). It has its own electrostatic field which can extend upto infinity. Now, consider charge 'P' far away from Q. If it is at infinity then practically force on it is zero. As 'P' is brought near to Q, force of repulsion acts on it. So, work or energy is required to bring it near to Q.

Hence, electric potential is defined as work done in bringing a positive charge of one coulomb from infinity to that point against the electric field. It is expressed in Joule/Coulomb.

Electric potential difference between two points in an electric field is the work done in moving a charge of one Coulomb from the point of lower potential to the point of higher potential. It is measured in volt.

$$\text{Electric potential, } V \ = \ \frac{W}{Q}$$

3.3.7 Potential Gradient

Let us consider the isolated charge. The field intensity at point P be E. The direction of E be along QP. The amount of work done in moving unit positive charge from P to Q is $-Edx$, where dx be the distance in m.

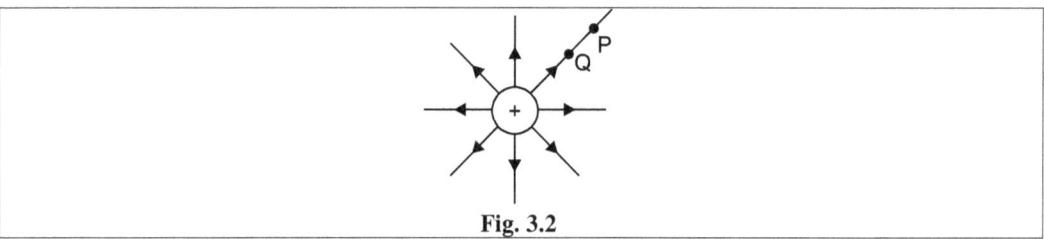

Fig. 3.2

Let dV be the potential drop.

Then, $dV \ = \ -E\,dx$

$\therefore$ $E \ = \ -\dfrac{dV}{dx}$

where $\dfrac{dV}{dx}$ is the voltage gradient. Hence, potential gradient is defined as the rate of change of potential with distance in the direction of electric field.

3.4 CAPACITOR

Two conductors separated from each other by an insulating material form capacitor. The insulating material is called as dielectric.

3.4.1 Capacitance

Capacitance is the property of capacitor to store the electric charge.

3.4.2 Action of a Capacitor

Consider the conducting plates P and Q separated by an air (Fig. 3.3).

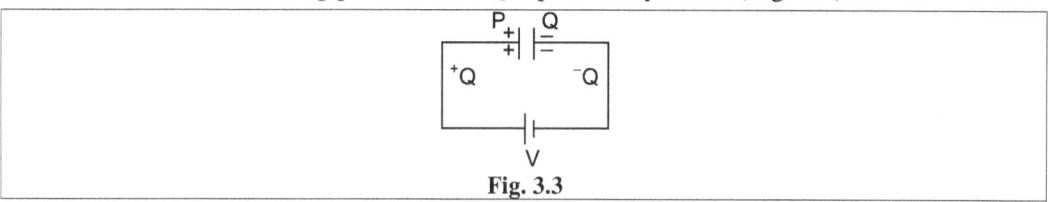

Fig. 3.3

Each plate has large number of free electrons. As soon as plates are connected to D.C. supply, electrons are attracted from plate P to the positive side of the battery. This causes the deficiency of electrons on the plate 'P', resulting into positive charge on plate 'P'. The electrons from the negative side of the battery are repelled and collected on plate Q. Thus, charge on plate 'P' is positive and on plate 'Q' is negative. When the charge on plate 'P' and 'Q' becomes equal, then potential difference between 'P' and 'Q' is equal to the supply voltage. Then capacitor is said to be fully charged.

3.5 RELATION BETWEEN VOLTAGE, CAPACITANCE AND CHARGE

Let,   V : be the applied voltage in volt.

Q : be the charge stored by capacitor in Coulomb.

As experimentally,

$$Q \propto V$$
$$Q = CV$$

where, C : be the constant called the capacitance of the capacitor

$$C = \frac{Q}{V}$$

Hence, capacitance can be defined as the ratio of stored charge to the applied voltage. It is measured in Farad.

3.6 DIELECTRIC STRENGTH AND BREAKDOWN VOLTAGE

When the applied voltage to a dielectric exceeds a certain value, then it breaks down. The electric current starts flowing through it. Hence, breakdown voltage is defined as the minimum voltage required to break it down.

The ability of dielectric medium to resist its breakdown when potential difference is applied across it, is called dielectric strength. It is measured in V/m. It is usually expressed in kV/mm. Its value depends on the following factors :

(i) thickness of the insulator, (ii) temperature, (iii) moisture, (iv) shape of the electrodes. The dielectric strengths of some material are given as below :

Material	Dielectric Strength (kV/mm)
Air	5.75
Paper	4 to 10
Glass	5 to 28.5
Bakelite	20 to 25
Mica	40 to 200

3.7 CAPACITORS IN SERIES

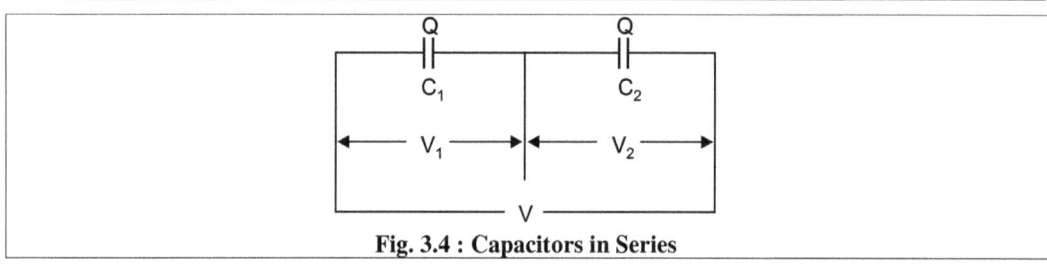

Fig. 3.4 : Capacitors in Series

Consider two capacitors in series connected across the supply voltage 'V'.

Let, Q be the charge on each capacitor.

Then, $Q = C_1 V_1$

and $Q = C_2 V_2$

$\therefore$ $V_1 = \dfrac{Q}{C_1}$

and $V_2 = \dfrac{Q}{C_2}$

Also, the charge stored by equivalent capacitor,

$Q = CV$

i.e. $V = \dfrac{Q}{C}$

As the charge on each capacitor and on equivalent capacitor is same, we have,

$$CV = C_1 V_1$$
$$= C_2 V_2$$

Now, the total voltage, $V = V_1 + V_2$

$$\dfrac{Q}{C} = \dfrac{Q}{C_1} + \dfrac{Q}{C_2}$$

$$\frac{1}{C} = \frac{1}{C_1} + \frac{1}{C_2}$$

If the number of capacitors are connected in series then equivalent capacitance,

$$\frac{1}{C} = \frac{1}{C_1} + \frac{1}{C_2} + \ldots \ldots \frac{1}{C_n}$$

3.8 CAPACITORS IN PARALLEL

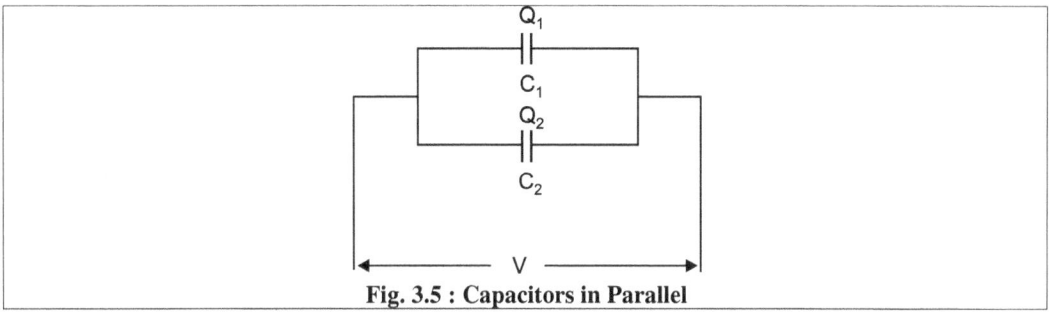

Fig. 3.5 : Capacitors in Parallel

Consider the two capacitors in parallel connected across the supply voltage 'V'.

Let, Q_1 be the charge on capacitor C_1

Q_2 be the charge on capacitor C_2

Then, $Q_1 = C_1\,V$

and $Q_2 = C_2 V$

Now, Q be the total charge in Coulomb.

$$Q = C.V.$$

Then, $Q = Q_1 + Q_2$

$$CV = C_1 V + C_2 V$$

$$C = C_1 + C_2$$

If the number of capacitors are connected in parallel then equivalent capacitance,

$$C = C_1 + C_2 + \ldots \ldots C_n$$

SOLVED EXAMPLES

Example 3.1:

Three capacitors of values 2 μF, 4 μF and 6 μF have an applied voltage of 60 volt across their series combination. Determine the voltage on each of the capacitor.

Solution : Given : $C_1 = 2\,\mu F$, $C_2 = 4\,\mu F$, $C_3 = 6\,\mu F$, $V = 60$ V.

Equivalent capacitance of series combination,

$$\frac{1}{C_{eq}} = \frac{1}{C_1} + \frac{1}{C_2} + \frac{1}{C_3}$$

$$= \frac{1}{2 \times 10^{-6}} + \frac{1}{4 \times 10^{-6}} + \frac{1}{6 \times 10^{-6}}$$

$$C_{eq} = 1.09 \ \mu F$$

∴   Charge on capacitor, $Q = C_{eq} \cdot V$

$$= 1.09 \times 10^{-6} \times 60$$

$$= 65.45 \times 10^{-6} \ \text{Coulomb} = 65.45 \ \mu C$$

∴ Voltage across each capacitor,

$$V_1 = \frac{Q}{C_1} = \frac{65.45 \times 10^{-6}}{2 \times 10^{-6}}$$

$$= 32.725 \ \text{volt}$$

$$V_2 = \frac{Q}{C_2} = \frac{65.45 \times 10^{-6}}{4 \times 10^{-6}}$$

$$= 16.36 \ \text{volt}$$

$$V_3 = \frac{Q}{C_3} = \frac{65.45 \times 10^{-6}}{6 \times 10^{-6}}$$

$$= 10.908 \ \text{volt}$$

Example 3.2 :

Two capacitors of 8 μF and 2 μF are connected in series across 400 volt supply. Calculate (i) Resultant capacitance, (ii) Charge on each capacitor, (iii) Potential difference across each capacitor.

Solution : Given : $C_1 = 8 \ \mu F$, $C_2 = 2 \ \mu F$, $V = 400 \ V$

(i) Resultant capacitance, $C_{eq} = \dfrac{C_1 \times C_2}{C_1 + C_2}$

$$= \frac{8 \times 10^{-6} \times 2 \times 10^{-6}}{8 \times 10^{-6} + 2 \times 10^{-6}} = 1.6 \ \mu F$$

(ii) Charge on each capacitor, $Q = C_{eq} \times V$

$$= 1.6 \times 10^{-6} \times 400$$

$$= 6.4 \times 10^{-4} \ \text{Coulomb}$$

(iii) Potential difference across each capacitor,

$$V_1 = \frac{Q}{C_1} = \frac{6.4 \times 10^{-4}}{8 \times 10^{-6}} = 80 \text{ volt}$$

$$V_2 = \frac{Q}{C_2} = \frac{6.4 \times 10^{-4}}{2 \times 10^{-6}} = 320 \text{ volt}$$

Example 3.3 :

When two capacitors A and B are connected across 210 V D.C. supply, the potential difference across A is 110 V. If this potential difference increases to 140 volt, when 3 µF capacitor is connected in parallel with B, calculate the capacitance of A and B.

Solution :

Let the capacitance of A and B in µF be C_1 and C_2.

(i) When they are in series, the charge on both remains same.

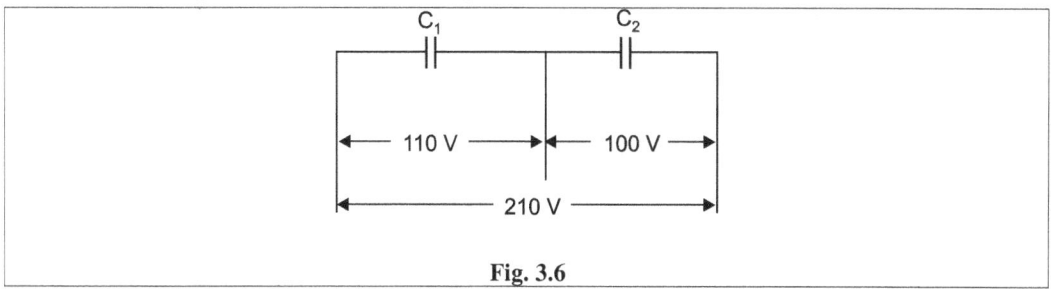

Fig. 3.6

$\therefore$ $C_1 V_1 = C_2 V_2$

$\therefore$ $110\, C_1 = 100\, C_2$

$\therefore$ $C_1 = \frac{100}{110} C_2$

                              $C_1 = 0.909\, C_2$

(ii) When 3 µF capacitor is connected in parallel with B then total capacitance of C_2 and 3 µF is $C_2 + 3 \times 10^{-6}$.

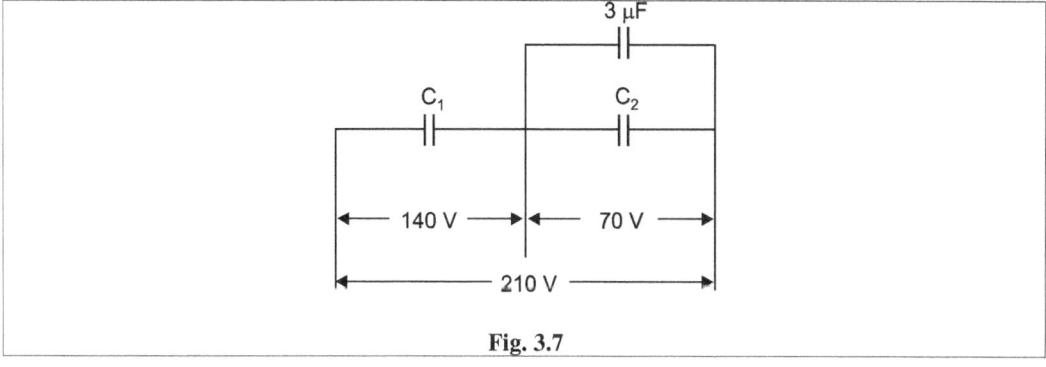

Fig. 3.7

Now, $(C_2 + 3 \times 10^{-6})$ and C_1 in series, hence charge on them remains same.

$$\therefore \qquad\qquad 140\, C_1 = 70\,(C_2 + 3 \times 10^{-6})$$

$$140\, C_1 = 70\, C_2 + 2.1 \times 10^{-4}$$

But, $\qquad\qquad\qquad C_1 = 0.909\, C_2$

$$\therefore \qquad 140 \times 0.909\, C_2 = 70\, C_2 + 2.1 \times 10^{-4}$$

$$57.26\, C_2 = 2.1 \times 10^{-4}$$

$$\therefore \qquad\qquad\qquad C_2 = 3.66 \times 10^{-6}$$

$$= 3.66\ \mu F$$

$$\therefore \qquad\qquad\qquad C_1 = 3.33 \times 10^{-6} = 3.33\ \mu F$$

3.9 CAPACITANCE OF A PARALLEL-PLATE CAPACITOR

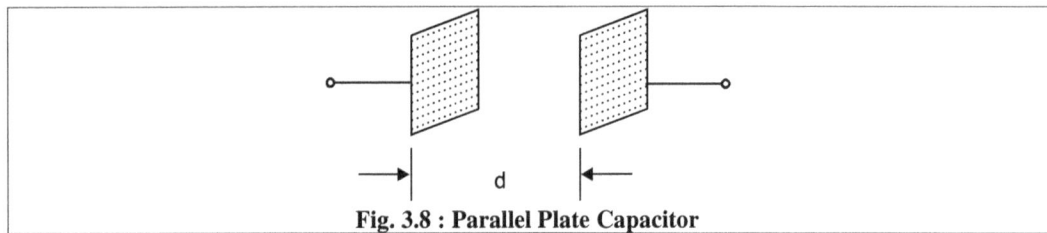

Fig. 3.8 : Parallel Plate Capacitor

Consider a parallel-plate capacitor as shown in Fig. 3.8.

Let,   A : be the area of each plate in m².

       d : be the distance between the plates in m.

       V : be the applied voltage between the plates.

and $\in_r$: be the relative permittivity

The electric field strength in the dielectric is given as,

$$E = V/d \qquad\qquad\qquad\qquad\qquad …(I)$$

The flux density in the dielectric is given as,

$$D = \frac{Q}{A} \qquad\qquad\qquad\qquad\qquad …(II)$$

Dividing equation (II) by (I), $\dfrac{D}{E} = \dfrac{Q}{A} \cdot \dfrac{d}{V}$

But, $\dfrac{D}{E} = \in_o \in_r$

$\therefore$

$$\epsilon_o \epsilon_r = \frac{Q \cdot d}{A \cdot V} = \frac{Cd}{A}$$

$$\epsilon_o \epsilon_r = \frac{Cd}{A}$$

$\therefore$

$$C = \frac{\epsilon_o \epsilon_r A}{d}$$

3.10 MULTI-PLATE CAPACITOR

The multiplate capacitor is used to get the large plate area into a small space. As shown in Fig. 3.9, alternate plates are connected together. If there are n number of plates, it is like (n – 1) capacitors in parallel.

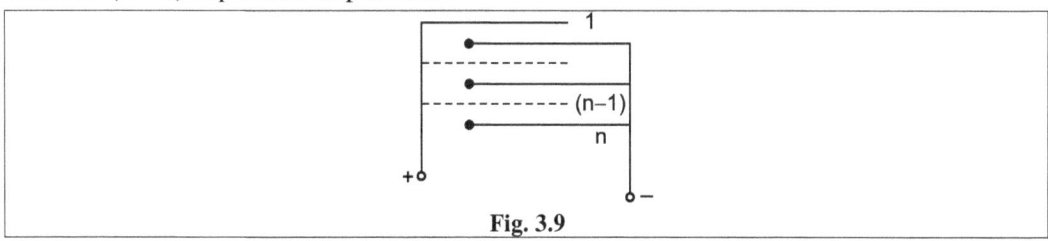

Fig. 3.9

Hence, total capacitance is given by,

$$C = \frac{\epsilon_o \epsilon_r A}{d} (n - 1)$$

where   A be the area of plate in m²
        d be the thickness of each dielectric or distance between the plates.

3.11 CAPACITORS WITH COMPOSITE DIELECTRICS

The capacitors are said to be composite dielectric capacitors when parallel-plate capacitor has two or more dielectrics between the plates.

Consider the capacitor with three dielectric materials as shown in Fig. 3.10.

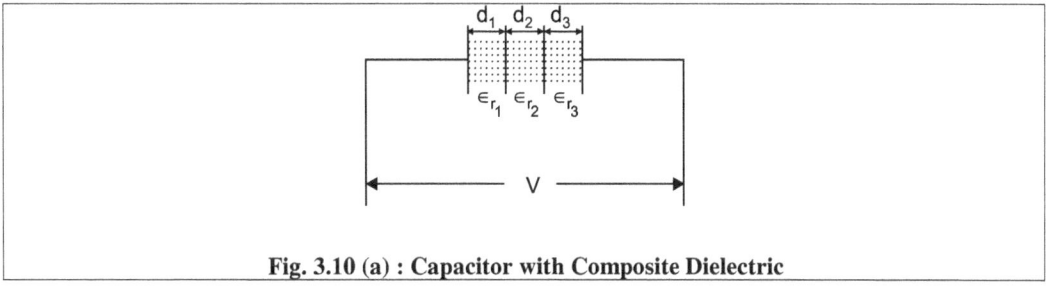

Fig. 3.10 (a) : Capacitor with Composite Dielectric

Let, d_1, d_2 and d_3 be the thicknesses of dielectric.

$\in_{r_1}$, $\in_{r_2}$, $\in_{r_3}$ be the relative permittivities of the dielectric.

E_1, E_2 and E_3 be the electric field intensities in the dielectric.

V_1, V_2 and V_3 be the voltages across the dielectric.

A : be the area of each plate.

Q : be the charge on each plate.

V : be the applied voltage.

As the capacitor is of parallel-plate type,

$$V = V_1 + V_2 + V_3$$
$$= E_1 d_1 + E_2 d_2 + E_3 d_3 \qquad \qquad ...(I)$$

Now, electric flux density on each dielectric,

$$D = \frac{Q}{A}$$

and field intensity $\qquad \qquad E_1 = \dfrac{D}{\in_o \in_{r_1}} = \dfrac{Q}{\in_o \in_{r_1} A}$

Similarly, we have $\qquad \qquad E_2 = \dfrac{D}{\in_o \in_{r_2}} = \dfrac{Q}{\in_o \in_{r_2} A}$

$$E_3 = \dfrac{D}{\in_o \in_{r_3}} = \dfrac{Q}{\in_o \in_{r_3} A}$$

Substituting the value of E_1, E_2 and E_3 in equation (I), we have,

$$V = \frac{Q}{\in_o \in_{r_1} A} d_1 + \frac{Q}{\in_o \in_{r_2} A} d_2 + \frac{Q}{\in_o \in_{r_3} A} d_3$$

$$= \frac{Q}{\in_o A}\left[\frac{d_1}{\in_{r_1}} + \frac{d_2}{\in_{r_2}} + \frac{d_3}{\in_{r_3}}\right]$$

But, $\qquad \qquad$ Capacitance $C = \dfrac{Q}{V}$

$\therefore \qquad \qquad$

$$C = \frac{Q}{\dfrac{Q}{\in_o A}\left[\dfrac{d_1}{\in_{r_1}} + \dfrac{d_2}{\in_{r_2}} + \dfrac{d_3}{\in_{r_3}}\right]}$$

$$C = \frac{\in_o A}{\dfrac{d_1}{\in_{r_1}} + \dfrac{d_2}{\in_{r_2}} + \dfrac{d_3}{\in_{r_3}}}$$

If there are 'n' number of dielectrics on composite capacitor then,

$$C = \frac{\in_o A}{\Sigma\, d/\in_r}$$

3.11.1 Composite Dielectric Capacitors (Type 2)

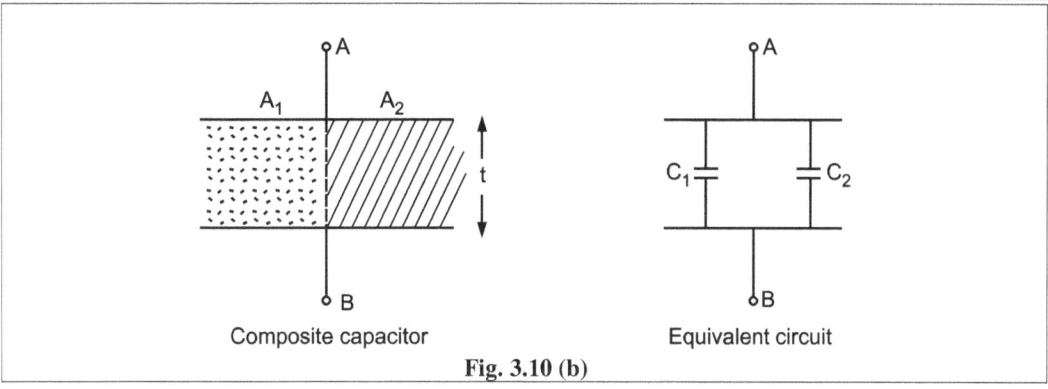

Composite capacitor   Equivalent circuit

Fig. 3.10 (b)

In this type, two dielectrics are arranged as shown in Fig. 3.10 (b). Let $\in_{r1}$, $\in_{r2}$ be the relative permittivities for two dielectrics. The thickness for both is same, but area is different.

As shown in equivalent circuit two capacitors exist in parallel due to two different dielectrics.

$$\therefore \qquad C_{eq} = C_1 + C_2 = \frac{\in_0 \in_{r1} A_1}{t} + \frac{\in_0 \in_{r2} A_2}{t}$$

$$= \frac{\in_0}{t} (\in_{r1} A_1 + \in_{r2} A_2)$$

For n dielectrics arranged in same thickness 't',

$$C_{eq} = \frac{\in_0}{t} (A_1 \in_{r1} + A_2 \in_{r2} + \dots\dots\dots\dots + A_n \in_{rn})$$

3.11.2 Composite Dielectric Capacitors (Type 3)

In practice we can have capacitor which is a combination of above two types as shown in Fig. 3.10 (c)

Where $\in_{r1}$, $\in_{r2}$ and $\in_{r3}$ are the relative permittivites of three dielectrics used in capacitor and t_1 and t_2 are dielectric thicknesses.

As shown in equivalent circuit there are two capacitors C_1 and C_2 in parallel.

C_1 is having thickness t_1, relative permittivity $\in_{r_1}$ and area A_1

$$\therefore \qquad C_1 = \frac{\in_0 \in_{r_1} A_1}{t_1}$$

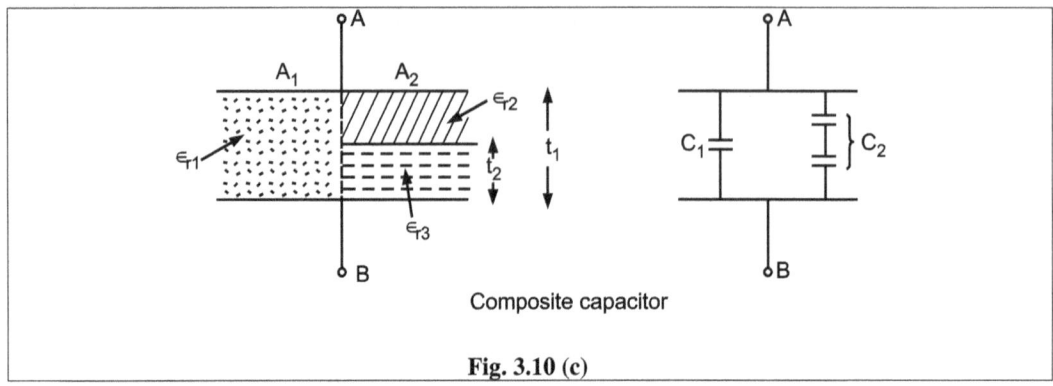

Composite capacitor

Fig. 3.10 (c)

C_2 is again a composite capacitor which is itself made up of two capacitors in series (Type 1 case).

From the result of Type 1, we can write

$$C_2 = \frac{\epsilon_0 A_2}{\dfrac{(t_1 - t_2)}{\epsilon_{r_2}} + \dfrac{t_2}{\epsilon_{r_3}}}$$

Hence the total capacitance is a parallel combination of C_1 and C_2.

∴ $$C_{eq} = C_1 + C_2$$

$$= \frac{\epsilon_0 \epsilon_{r_1} A_1}{t_1} + \frac{\epsilon_0 A_2}{\dfrac{(t_1 - t_2)}{\epsilon_{r_2}} + \dfrac{t_2}{\epsilon_{r_3}}}$$

SOLVED EXAMPLES

Example 3.4 :

A capacitor is composed of two plates separated by a sheet of insulating material of 3 mm thick and relative permittivity of 4. The distance between plates is increased to allow the insertion of second sheet of 5 mm thick and relative permittivity ϵ_r. If the capacitance of capacitor so formed is one half of the original capacitance, find the value of ϵ_r.

Solution : Given : $d_1 = 3$ mm, $\epsilon_{r_1} = 4$, $d_2 = 5$ mm, $C_2 = \dfrac{1}{2} C_1$, $\epsilon_{r2} = $?

Now, capacitance of original capacitor,

$$C_1 = \frac{\epsilon_0 \epsilon_{r_1} \cdot A}{d_1} = \frac{8.854 \times 10^{-12} \times 4 \times A}{3 \times 10^{-3}} \text{ Farad} \qquad \ldots(1)$$

∴ Capacitance of the new capacitor,

$$C_2 = \frac{\epsilon_0 A}{\left(\dfrac{d_1}{\epsilon_{r_1}} + \dfrac{d_2}{\epsilon_{r_2}}\right)} = \frac{8.854 \times 10^{-12} \times A}{\left(\dfrac{3 \times 10^{-3}}{4} + \dfrac{5 \times 10^{-3}}{\epsilon_{r_2}}\right)} \qquad \ldots(2)$$

But, $$C_2 = \frac{1}{2} C_1$$

∴ $$\frac{8.854 \times 10^{-12} \times A}{\left(\dfrac{3 \times 10^{-3}}{4} + \dfrac{5 \times 10^{-3}}{\epsilon_{r_2}}\right)} = \frac{1}{2} \frac{8.854 \times 10^{-12} \times 4 \times A}{3 \times 10^{-3}}$$

∴ $$\epsilon_{r_2} = 6.67$$

Example 3.5 :

The capacitance of capacitor of two parallel plates each of 200 cm² area separated by a dielectric 4 mm thick is 0.0004 µF. A potential difference of 20 kV is applied across it. Calculate (i) the total charge on the plates, (ii) potential gradient in V/m, (iii) dielectric flux density, (iv) relative permittivity of dielectric.

Solution : (i) Total charge on the plate,

$$Q = CV = 0.0004 \times 10^{-6} \times 20 \times 10^3 = 8 \times 10^{-6} \text{ C}$$

(ii) Potential gradient, $$E = \frac{V}{d} = \frac{20 \times 10^3}{4 \times 10^{-3}} = 5 \times 10^6 \text{ V/m}$$

(iii) Dielectric flux density, $$D = \frac{Q}{A} = \frac{8 \times 10^{-6}}{200 \times 10^{-4}} = 4 \times 10^{-4} \text{ C/m}^2$$

(iv) Relative permittivity, $$E = \frac{D}{\epsilon_0 \epsilon_r}$$

∴ $$\epsilon_r = \frac{D}{\epsilon_0 E}$$

∴ $$\epsilon_r = \frac{4 \times 10^{-4}}{8.854 \times 10^{-12} \times 5 \times 10^6}$$

$$= 9$$

3.12   ENERGY STORED IN A CAPACITOR

Let us consider a capacitor having capacitance 'C' Farad and charged to voltage 'V' volt (Fig. 3.10(d)).

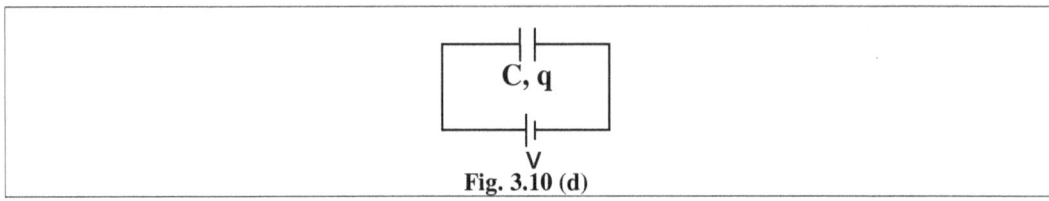

Fig. 3.10 (d)

Let 'q' be the charge on capacitor in Coulomb. Then potential difference across the capacitor,

$$v = \frac{q}{C}$$

Now, the work done to move the charge of one Coulomb from one plate to another,

$$dw = v \, dq = \frac{q}{C} \, dq \text{ Joule}$$

This work done is stored in the form of potential energy in the electric field. Now, total energy stored in the capacitor when it is charged to 'Q' Coulomb,

$$\int dw = \int_{0}^{Q} \frac{q}{C} \, dq$$

$$W = \frac{1}{C} \left[\frac{q^2}{2} \right]_{0}^{Q} = \frac{1}{C} \frac{Q^2}{2}$$

But, $Q = CV$

Substituting this in above equation, we have

$$W = \frac{1}{2} CV^2 \text{ Joule}$$

3.13 TYPES OF CAPACITORS

Capacitors can be classified based on the nature of dielectric used.

(1) Air Capacitor : It has two sets of metal plates. One set is fixed and other set is movable. The fixed set is spaced and connected in parallel and is mounted rigidly on to an insulating framework. The movable set is also spaced, connected in parallel and is mounted on the shaft with bearing. The movable plate is adjustable. The air capacitors are available with working voltage range of 150 to 3000 volt. Air capacitors are used in high frequency radio tuning.

(2) Paper Capacitor : Paper capacitors consist of a long spring of tin or aluminium or copper foil, interleaved with them oil or wax impregnated paper. The strips are rolled up spirally into a compact form and then soaked in melted wax and cooled to get solid construction. Paper capacitors are available with working voltage of 100 V to 100 kV. They are used in by-pass and coupling capacitors of signal communication system.

(3) Mica Capacitor : It consists of a series of plates of aluminium or tin foil, separated by thin mica sheets. The plates are alternatively connected to form two sets and two terminals are brought out. The entire assembly is homed in a sealed metallic container. They are in a range of 5 to 1000 pF. They are used in high frequency radio and electronic circuits.

(4) Ceramic Capacitors : It consists of discs of ceramic material whose parallel surfaces are coated with metallic silver. They are in the range of 3 pF to 2 μF. They are available in the working voltage range of 3 V to 6,000 volt. They are used in short wave network.

(5) Electrolytic Capacitor : In this capacitor, electrolyte can be used as a dielectric. It can be of dry type or wet type. In dry type capacitor, two aluminium foil electrodes are separated by a porous paper soaked in a electrolyte paste. In wet type capacitor, aluminium cylinder containing an electrolyte which acts as a cathode. They are available in the range of 1 μF to 10 F and voltage ranging from 1 V to 1 kV. They are used in smoothening circuits of communication system, reducing the ripple in the voltage wave obtained from a rectifier and filter circuit.

3.14 CHARGING OF A CAPACITOR

Consider a circuit as shown in Fig. 3.11, where capacitor C is connected in series with a resistance R across a battery having voltage V and with switch 'S'.

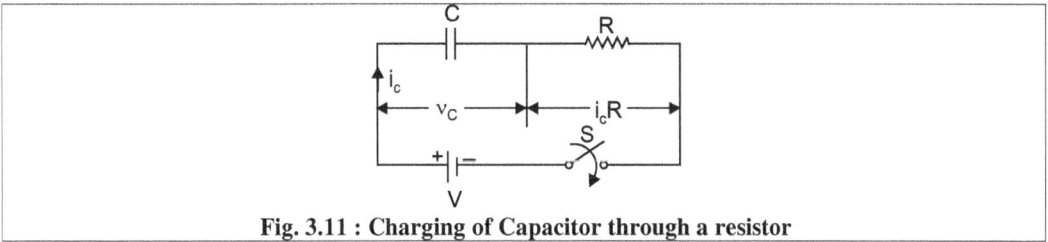

Fig. 3.11 : Charging of Capacitor through a resistor

When the switch 'S' is closed, charging currents start flowing in the circuit. At start it is maximum and thereafter decreases.

At any given instant, $V = i_c R + v_c$ ...(I)

where, i_c = be the charging current

                                         v_c = be the voltage across capacitor

But, $i_c = C \dfrac{dv_c}{dt}$

Now, $V = C \dfrac{dv_c}{dt} R + v_c$

$$V - v_c = RC \frac{dv_c}{dt}$$

$$\therefore \qquad \frac{dv_c}{V - v_c} = \frac{dt}{RC} \qquad \qquad \dots(\text{II})$$

Integrating above equation (II) we have,

$$\int \frac{dv_c}{V - v_c} = \int \frac{dt}{RC}$$

i.e. $\qquad \qquad -\log(V - v_c) = \frac{t}{RC} + \text{constant (K)}$

where K be the constant of integration.

$\therefore \qquad \qquad$ When $t = 0$, $\quad v_c = 0$

$\therefore \qquad \qquad -\log(V) = 0 + K$

$\therefore \qquad \qquad K = -\log(V)$

$\therefore$ Equation (II) becomes $\quad -\log(V - v_c) = \frac{t}{RC} - \log(V)$

$$\therefore \qquad \qquad \frac{t}{RC} = \log(V) - \log(V - v_c)$$

$$\therefore \qquad \qquad \frac{-t}{RC} = \log(V - v_c) - \log(V)$$

$$\therefore \qquad \qquad \frac{-t}{RC} = \log\left(\frac{V - v_c}{V}\right)$$

$$\therefore \qquad \qquad \frac{V - v_c}{V} = e^{-t/RC}$$

$$\therefore \qquad \qquad V - v_c = Ve^{-t/RC} \qquad \qquad \dots(\text{III})$$

$$\therefore \qquad \qquad v_c = V - Ve^{-t/RC}$$

$$= V\left(1 - e^{-t/RC}\right) \qquad \qquad \dots(\text{IV})$$

As total charge on capacitor,

Now, $\qquad \qquad V = \frac{Q}{C}$

and $\qquad \qquad v_c = \frac{q}{C} \qquad \qquad$ at any instant

Substituting this in equation (IV), we have,

$$\frac{q}{C} = \frac{Q}{C}\left(1 - e^{-t/RC}\right)$$

$$q = Q\left(1 - e^{-t/RC}\right)$$

From equation (I), $V - v_c = i_c R$ ...(V)

From equation (IV), $V - v_c = V e^{-t/RC}$ ...(VI)

Thus, from equations (V) and (VI),

$$i_c R = V e^{-t/RC}$$

$$i_c = \frac{V}{R} e^{-t/RC}$$

But, at $t = 0, \frac{V}{R} = I$ i.e. maximum

∴ $i_c = I e^{-t/RC}$

The variation of voltage and current with time during charging is shown in Fig. 3.12 (a) and (b).

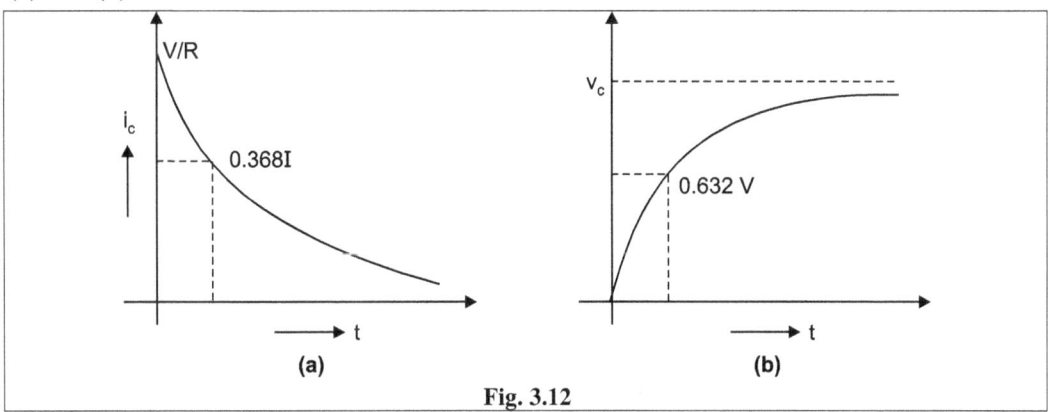

Fig. 3.12

3.14.1 Time Constant

Time constant may be defined as the time during which the capacitor voltage actually reaches to its 63.2% of its final value.

i.e. $v_c = V\left(1 - e^{-t/RC}\right)$, if $t = RC$ then $v_c = V(1 - e^1) = 0.632$ V. Similarly as $i = \frac{V}{R}$ $e^{-t/RC}$, if $t = RC$ then $i_c = I e^{-1} = 0.368$ I

It can also be defined as the time during which the capacitor current actually falls to 36.8% of its initial maximum value.

3.15 DISCHARGING OF A CAPACITOR

Consider a circuit as shown in Fig. 3.13, where capacitor 'C' is being discharged through a resistor 'R'. Capacitor is fully charged to voltage V volts and discharges through resistor R. The current flowing through the circuit is in the opposite direction to that of charging.

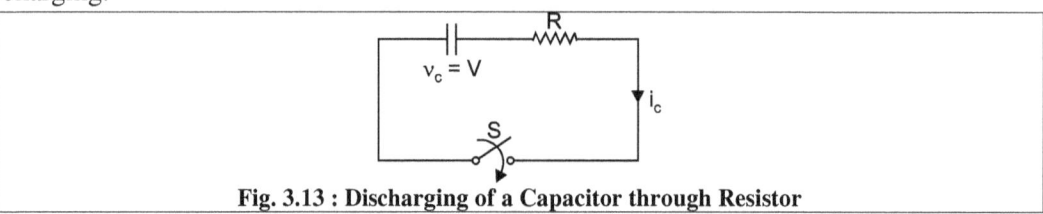

Fig. 3.13 : Discharging of a Capacitor through Resistor

When the switch is closed, the current starts flowing through the circuit. The voltage equation of the circuit is,

$$V = RC\frac{dv_c}{dt} + v_c \qquad \ldots(I)$$

Now,   at t = 0, V = 0

∴ Equation becomes,

$$0 = RC\frac{dv_c}{dt} + v_c$$

$$v_c = -RC\frac{dv_c}{dt}$$

i.e.

$$\frac{dv_c}{v_c} = -\frac{dt}{RC}$$

Integrating both sides we have,

$$\log v_c = \frac{-t}{RC} + K$$

where K be the constant of integration.

At   t = 0, v_c = V

∴ $\log V = 0 + K$

∴ $K = \log V$

Using this in above equation,

$$\log v_c = -t/RC + \log V$$

∴ $-t/RC = \log\left(\frac{v_c}{V}\right)$

∴ $\frac{v_c}{V} = e^{-t/RC}$

∴ $v_c = Ve^{-t/RC} \qquad \ldots(II)$

Now, at any instant, $v_c = \frac{q}{C}$

and at the starting, $V = \dfrac{Q}{C}$

Using these values in above equation (II),

$$\dfrac{q}{v_c} = \dfrac{Q}{V}\, e^{-t/RC}$$

i.e. $q = Q\, e^{-t/RC}$

Equation for instantaneous values of discharging current,

$$i_c = -\dfrac{V}{R}\, e^{-t/RC}$$

3.15.1 Time Constant

As $v_c = Ve^{-t/RC}$

If $t = RC$ then $v_c = Ve^{-1} = 0.368\ V$

Hence, time constant can be defined as time required for the capacitor voltage to fall 36.8% of its initial maximum value.

Similarly, for current as, $i_c = -Ie^{-t/RC}$

i.e. if $t = RC$

then $i_c = -Ie^{-1} = 0.368I$

Also, time constant can be defined as the time required during which the capacitor discharge current falls to 36.8% of its initial maximum value. The variation of voltage and current with time during discharge is shown in Fig. 3.14 (a) and (b).

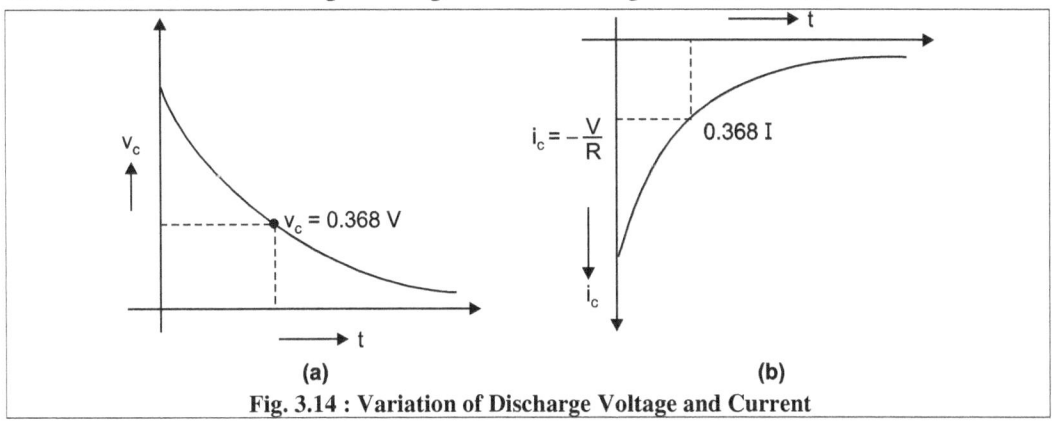

(a)   (b)

Fig. 3.14 : Variation of Discharge Voltage and Current

SOLVED EXAMPLES

Example 3.6 :

A capacitor having capacitance of 4 μF is connected in series with a resistance of 1 MΩ across 200 volt d.c. supply.

Calculate : (i) The time constant, (ii) The initial charging current, (iii) The time taken by capacitor to raise upto 160 volt.

Solution : Given : $C = 4 \ \mu F$, $R = 1 \ M\Omega$, $V = 200$ volt.

(i)   Time constant $= $ R.C.

$$= 1 \times 10^6 \times 4 \times 10^{-6}$$

$$= 4 \ sec$$

(ii) Initial charging current,

At $t = 0$

$$i = \frac{V}{R}$$

$$= \frac{200}{1 \times 10^6}$$

$$= 200 \times 10^{-6} \ Amp.$$

$$= 200 \ \mu A$$

(iii) Time taken by capacitor to raise the voltage upto 160 V

$$v_c = V \left(1 - e^{-t/RC} \right)$$

$$160 = 200 \ (1 - e^{-t/4})$$

$$e^{-t/4} = 0.2$$

$$-t/4 = \log_e (0.2)$$

$\therefore$ $t = 6.437 \ sec$

Example 3.7 :

A 2 μF capacitor in series with a 2 MΩ resistance is joined to 100 V D.C. supply. Calculate (i) the current flowing, (ii) energy stored in the capacitor at the end of 4 seconds from the start.

Solution : (i) Current flowing, $i = I e^{-t/RC}$

$$= \frac{V}{R} \ e^{-t/RC}$$

$$= \frac{100}{2 \times 10^6} \cdot e^{-4/2 \times 10^6 \times 2 \times 10^{-6}}$$

$$= 18.393 \ \mu A$$

(ii)   Energy stored (E) $= \frac{1}{2} CV^2$

But the voltage after 4 seconds, $v_c = V \ (1 - e^{-t/RC})$

$$= 100 \ (1 - e^{-4/2 \times 10^{-6} \times 2 \times 10^{-6}})$$

$$= 63.21 \ volt$$

$\therefore$ Energy stored $= \dfrac{1}{2}CV_c^2$

$$= \dfrac{1}{2} \times 2 \times 10^{-6} \times (63.21)^2$$

$$= 3995.764 \times 10^{-6} \text{ Joule}$$

Example 3.8 :

A capacitor of 10 μF is charged upto 200 V D.C. and then discharged through 2 MΩ, resistor. During discharge find (i) equation for voltage across capacitor, (ii) time required to reach a voltage of 100 V across capacitor, (iii) voltage across the capacitor after 20 seconds.

Solution : (i) Equation for voltage across capacitor,

$$v_c = V \cdot e^{-t/RC} = 200\, e^{-t/2 \times 10^6 \times 10 \times 10^{-6}}$$

$$= 200\, e^{-t/20}$$

(ii) Time required to reach a voltage of 100 V

$$v_c = V\, e^{-t/RC}$$

$$100 = 200\, e^{-t/20}$$

$\therefore$ $\qquad\qquad t = 13.86 \text{ sec.}$

(iii) Voltage across the capacitor after 20 seconds

$$v_c = 200\, e^{-20/20} = 73.576 \text{ volt}$$

Example 3.9 :

Two capacitors C_1 and C_2 are connected once in series and then in parallel. The equivalent capacitance of series combination is 0.4 μF and parallel combination is 0.2 μF. Calculate values of C_1 and C_2.

Solution : When capacitors are connected in series,

$$C_{eq} = \frac{C_1 C_2}{C_1 + C_2} = 0.4 \ \mu F$$

When capacitors are connected in parallel,

$$C_{eq} = C_1 + C_2 = 0.2 \ \mu F$$

$$C_1 = 0.2 - C_2$$

$$\frac{C_1 C_2}{C_1 + C_2} = 0.4$$

$$\frac{C_1 C_2}{0.2} = 0.4$$

$$C_1 C_2 = 0.2 \times 0.4$$

$$C_1 C_2 = 0.08$$

$$C_2 = \frac{0.08}{C_1}$$

$$C_1 = \frac{0.2\, C_1 - 0.08}{C_1}$$

$$C_1 = 0.2 - C_2$$

$$C_1 = 0.2 - \frac{0.08}{C_1}$$

$$C_1^2 = 0.2\, C_1 - 0.08$$

$$C_1^2 - 0.2\, C_1 + 0.08 = 0$$

$$C_1 = \frac{0.2 \pm \sqrt{(0.2)^2 - 4\,(0.08)}}{2}$$

After solving above quadratic equations one value is negative, so only solved upto quadratic equation.

3.16 BATTERIES (CELLS)

The device which converts chemical energy into electrical energy is called a Cell. This will act as a source of electromotive force (EMF). Voltage of this cell is very less. To get desired voltage, number of cells are connected in series, parallel or in series-parallel. This combination is called as *Battery*.

Classification of Cells

(1) Primary Cell,

(2) Secondary Cell.

3.16.1 Primary Cell

The chemical reaction taking place in these cells is irreversible. Hence, when the terminal voltage goes down, we have to replace by new one.

e.g. Alkaline cell, Zinc-chloride cell.

Applications : Hearing aids, Electronic calculators, Electronic clocks, Guided missiles, Audio devices, Camera, Medical electronic equipments such as Pace maker.

3.16.2 Secondary Cell

The chemical reaction taking place in these cells is reversible. i.e. these cells can be recharged. These are also called as storage cells, accumulators or rechargeable cells.

e.g. Lead acid cell, Nickel cadmium cell, Nickel metal hydride cell.

Applications : Emergency lighting, Automobile for starting, UPS, Railway signaling, Power stations.

3.17 CONSTRUCTION, WORKING, CHARGING METHODS AND MAINTENANCE OF SECONDARY CELL

(A) **Lead - Acid Cell :** This battery consists of following parts :

(1) Anode (positive plate), (2) Cathode (negative plate), (3) Electrolyte, (4) Separators, (5) Container.

(i) **Anode (positive plate) :** The material used for this is lead peroxide (PbO_2). Its colour is dark brown.

(ii) **Cathode (negative Plate) :** The material used for this is spongy lead (Pb) and its colour is grey. The positive and negative plates are arranged in groups.

(iii) **Electrolyte :** The electrolyte (liquid conductor) used is dilute sulphuric acid (H_2SO_4) whose specific gravity is 1.2. The anode and cathode both are immersed in the electrolyte.

(iv) **Separators :** These are thin plates of porous insulating material like rubber. These are placed between main plates, which prevent the plates to come in contact with each other.

(v) **Container :** The container is made up of plastic or ceramic. The anode, cathode and electrolyte is placed in container. The material of container is such that no chemical action should take place on container.

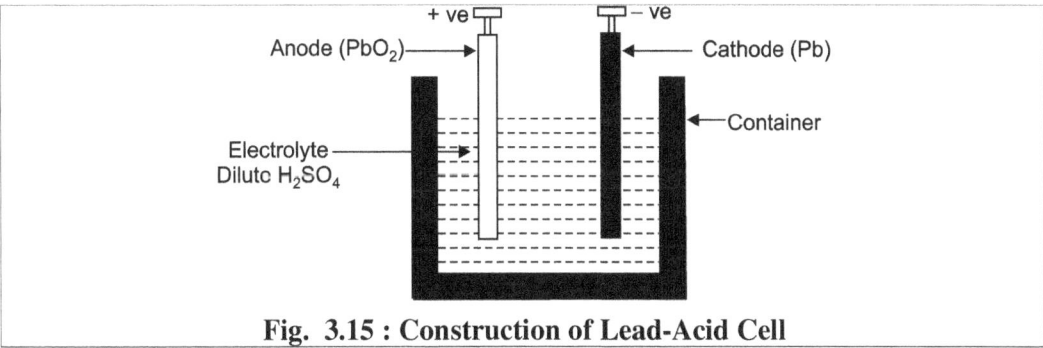

Fig. 3.15 : Construction of Lead-Acid Cell

3.18 CHARGING AND DISCHARGING OF LEAD-ACID BATTERY

3.18.1 Charging

When the cell is in use, after its utilization it will get discharged. It is required to recharge to maintain desired voltage level.

During the charging process a positive terminal of external charging voltage is applied to anode and negative terminal is applied to cathode as shown in Fig. 3.16. Due to externally connected voltage source, the current flows from anode to cathode inside the electrolyte.

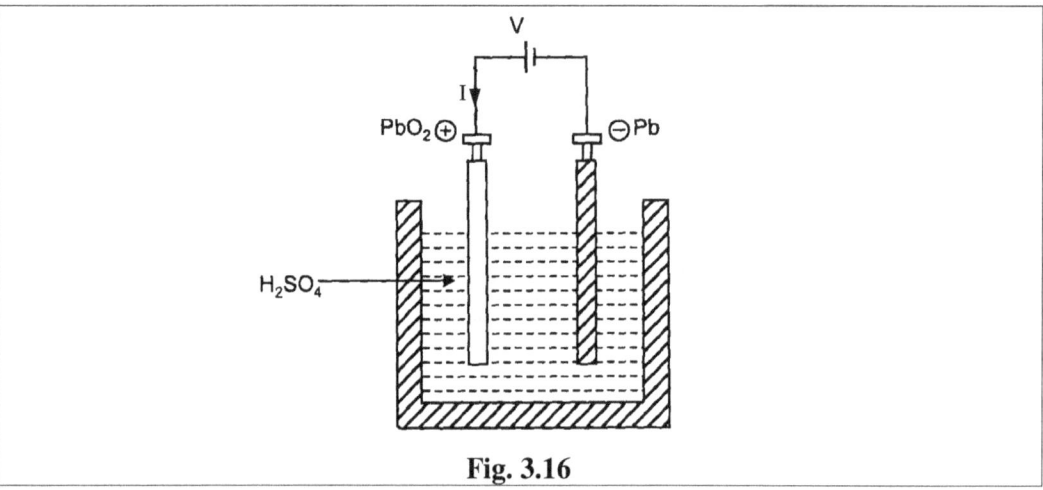

Fig. 3.16

Due to the passage of electric current, the electrolysis process takes place and results in following chemical action.

At Anode : $PbSO_4 + SO_4 + 2H_2O \rightarrow PbO_2 + 2H_2SO_4$

At Cathode : $PbSO_4 + H_2 \rightarrow Pb + H_2SO_4$

As water is consumed and H_2SO_4 is created, the specific gravity of H_2SO_4 increases, the energy is absorbed and voltage on the cell increases. So it is a charging process.

3.18.2 Discharging

When the cell is fully charged, then it is ready to use. When it starts discharging, the current starts flowing from the battery to the external load as shown in Fig. 3.17.

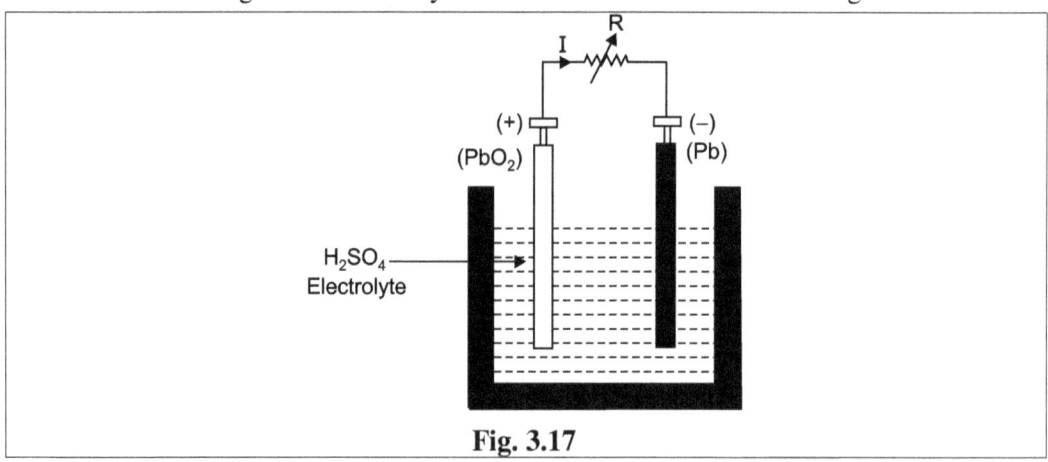

Fig. 3.17

Due to the current I, H_2SO_4 is dissociated into positive H_2 and negative SO_4 ions. The load current flows from anode to cathode externally but internally from cathode to anode. Therefore, the +ve (H_2) ions move to the cathode. The chemical reactions during discharging are as follows :

At Anode : $PbO_2 + H_2 + H_2SO_4 \longrightarrow PbSO_4 + 2H_2O$

At Cathode : $Pb + SO_4 \longrightarrow PbSO_4$

Due to formation of $PbSO_4$, both electrodes become whitish and due to the water formation the specific gravity of electrolyte reduces. So the output voltage decreases. This is called as discharging of battery.

Testing of Lead Acid Batteries :

(1) Remove the dirt and clean the battery terminals and tighten them.

(2) Check the specific gravity of electrolyte and it should be maintained to adequate level by adding distilled water.

(3) Check voltage per cell and it should not be less than 1.8 V.

Applications :

(1) In uninterrupted power supplies (UPS).

(2) In telephone system.

(3) In automobile for starting.

(4) Emergency lighting system.

3.19 NICKEL - CADMIUM CELL

It consists of anode made up of nickel hydroxide $[Ni(OH)_3]$ which acts as anode (positive plate) and cathode of spongy cadmium (Cd) (negative plate). The electrolyte used is potassium hydroxide (KOH) in distilled water.

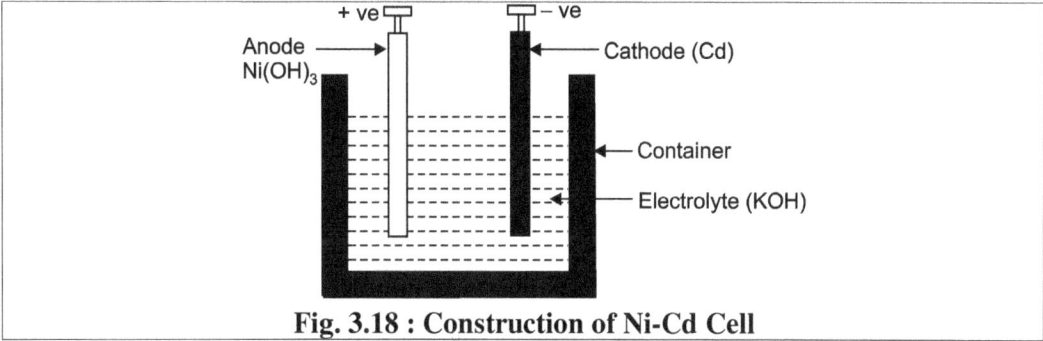

Fig. 3.18 : Construction of Ni-Cd Cell

Charging and Discharging of Ni-Cd Cell :

During charging of the cell positive (+ve) element is $Ni(OH)_3$ and negative element (–ve) is cadmium. When the cell is discharged the (positive) element becomes nickel hydroxide while negative (–ve) element becomes cadmium hydroxide. The charging and discharging equations are as follows :

$$2\,Ni(OH)_3 \quad + 2\,KOH \quad + \ Cd \qquad \underset{\overleftarrow{Charge}}{\overrightarrow{Discharge}} \qquad 2\,Ni(OH)_2 \ + 2\,KOH + \ Cd(OH)_2$$

↑	↑	↑		↑	↑	↑
Positive plate	Electrolyte	Negative plate		Positive plate	Electrolyte	Negative plate

Applications :

    (1) In military aeroplanes and helicopters.

    (2) The photographic equipments i.e. photoflash.

    (3) In electric shavers.   (4) In automobiles.

    (5) In traction for lighting.

3.20 CHARGING TECHNIQUES

    (1) Constant current charging method.   (2) Constant voltage charging method.

    (3) Rectifier method.

(1) Constant Current Charging :

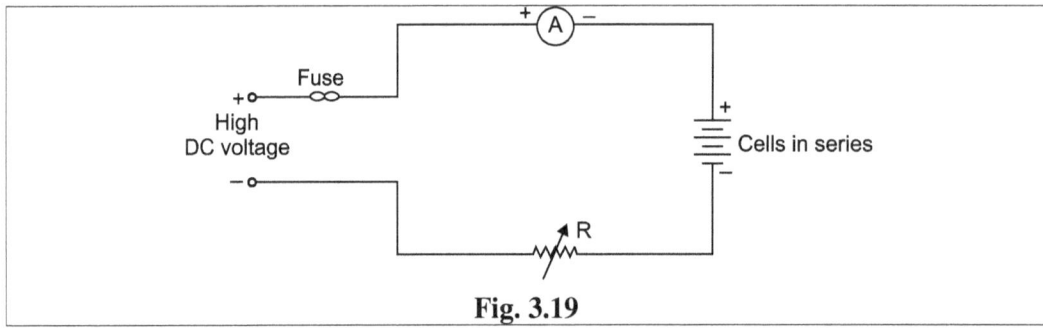

Fig. 3.19

    When the supply voltage is high and battery is to be charged is of low voltage, then this method is used. Number of batteries which can be charged are connected in series across a D.C. voltage and constant current is maintained with the variable resistor (R).

(2) Constant Voltage Charging :

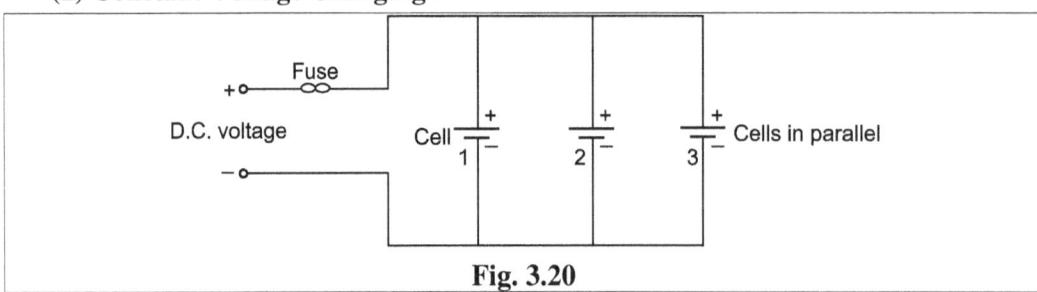

Fig. 3.20

In this method, constant voltage is applied across each cell. Generally, the batteries to be charged are connected to 6 V or 12 V D.C. supply. Charging process continues till cells will achieve same voltage as supply.

(3) Rectifier Method : Generally, bridge rectifier is used.

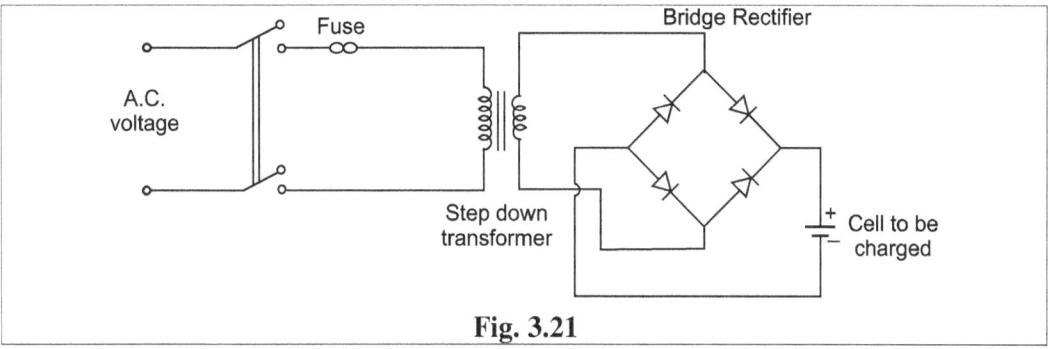

Fig. 3.21

A single phase A.C. voltage is step down to suitable voltage, which is rectified by using full wave bridge rectifier. The D.C. voltage is applied to the cell, which is to be charged.

(4) Trickle Charging : It is always necessary to keep the battery fully charged. The charging current is maintained slightly more than the load current, through the battery. It is used for compensating the charge lost due to the internal discharge of the battery.

(5) Boost Charging : When the battery is being charged for the first time or when it is being used after a long time, boost charging is used. Here the cell voltage is raised to 2.4 to 2.6 V. It is used for breaking down the crystalline $PbSO_4$ which is formed in lead acid batteries when the battery is not used for a long period.

Indications of Fully Charged Battery :

(1) **Specific Gravity :** The specific gravity of the fully charged cell increases upto 1.28 from about 1.18.

(2) **Gassing :** When the cell is fully charged, it starts liberating the gas freely. In lead acid battery hydrogen is liberated at cathode while oxygen is at anode. Gassing is a good indication of fully charged battery.

(3) **Voltage :** The voltage of fully charged cell is about 2.7 V.

(4) **Colour :** The colour of the plate changes when the cell is fully charged. As the plates are immersed in electrolyte, this indication is not clearly visible.

3.21 COMPARISON BETWEEN LEAD ACID CELL AND NICKEL CADMIUM CELL

Sr. No.	Parameter	Lead Acid Cell	Nickel Cadmium Cell
1.	Material used		
	Positive plate	Lead peroxide (PbO_2),	Nickel hydroxide Ni $(OH)_3$
	Negative plate	Lead (Pb)	Cadmium (Cd)
2.	Electrolyte used	H_2SO_4	KOH
3.	Average e.m.f.	2 V per cell	1.2 V per cell
4.	Internal resistance	Low	Low
5.	Amp-hour capacity	Depends on discharge rate and temperature	Depends on temperature only
6.	Weight	Medium	Heavy
7.	Life	Moderate	Long
8.	Efficiency	High	Moderate
9.	Maintenance requirement	Frequent	Less
10.	Cost	Less expensive	Expensive (twice the lead acid cell)
11.	Watt-hour-eff	72 – 80%	55 – 60%
12.	Ampere-hour eff	90 – 95%	70 – 80%

3.22 BATTERY MAINTENANCE

The maintenance procedure for batteries is as follows :

1. Keep the container surface dry.
2. Remove dirt, clean the battery terminals and tighten them.
3. Battery should not be discharged below a minimum voltage.
4. Never keep the battery in discharged condition for a longer time.
5. Check the specific gravity of electrolyte and maintain the level by adding distilled water.
6. The electrolytes should not be exposed to air.
7. Battery should not be overcharged.
8. Avoid contact with spark and flame.
9. Store in cool and dry place.
10. Avoid short circuit of plates, overcharging and sulphation.
11. Charge the battery at specific rate.

3.23 GROUPING OF CELLS

To get desired voltage level, it is required to connect cells in series, parallel or in series-parallel.

(a) Series connection, (b) Parallel connection, (c) Series-parallel connection.

3.23.1 Series Connection

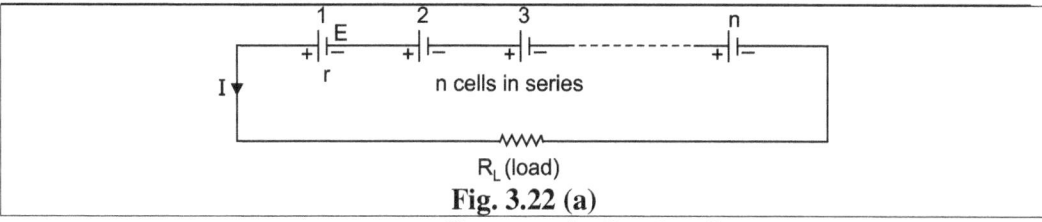

Fig. 3.22 (a)

$$E = \text{e.m.f. of each cell}$$
$$r = \text{Internal resistance of each cell}$$
$$\text{Total voltage available} = n \times E = \text{Volt}$$
$$\text{Total resistance of circuit} = R_L + nr$$
$$\text{Total current} = \frac{\text{Total voltage}}{\text{Total resistance}}$$
$$I = \frac{n \times E}{R_L + nr} \text{ Ampere}$$

3.23.2 Parallel Connection

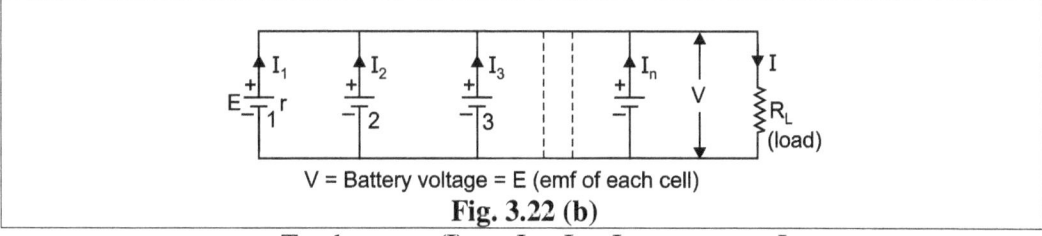

V = Battery voltage = E (emf of each cell)

Fig. 3.22 (b)

$$\text{Total current (I)} = I_1 + I_2 + I_3 + \dots\dots + I_n$$

Voltage remains same, but current capacity can be increased.

3.23.3 Series Parallel Connection

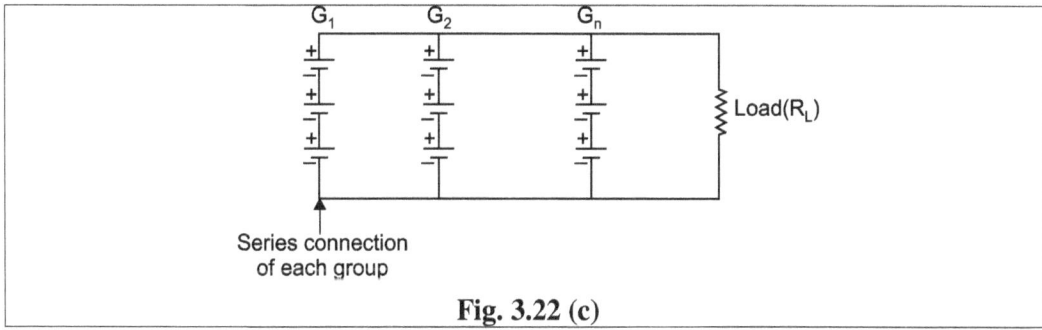

Series connection of each group

Fig. 3.22 (c)

G_1, G_2 upto G_n : Series group.

These groups are connected in parallel.

Such type of connection is used to get desirable voltage and current.

3.24 BATTERY CAPACITY AND EFFICIENCY

(A) Battery Capacity : The capacity of battery is expressed in (1) Ampere Hour (AH), (2) Watt Hour (WH).

(B) Battery Efficiency : It is nothing but amount of electricity which a battery can supply at specified rate, till its voltage falls to a specified value.

(1) Ampere-Hour Efficiency (AH) :

$$\% \text{ AH efficiency} = \frac{\text{AH during discharge}}{\text{AH during charge}} \times 100$$

$$= \frac{\text{Current} \times \text{time for discharge}}{\text{Current} \times \text{time for charge}} \times 100$$

The typical value of AH efficiency is 90 to 95%

(2) Watt-Hour (WH) efficiency :

$$\% \text{ WH efficiency} = \frac{\text{AH during discharge} \times \text{Average cell voltage at discharge}}{\text{AH during charge} \times \text{Average cell voltage while charging}} \times 100$$

$$= \frac{\text{Energy supplied by battery during discharging}}{\text{Energy taken by battery during charging}} \times 100$$

Typical value of WH is 75 to 80%.

3.25 Nickel-Metal Hydride (Ni-MH) Battery

Mobility is increasingly viewed as an essential attribute of todays life-style, both personal and professional. Advanced electronic devices such as cellular phones and portable computers now permit people on go to operate more efficiently than was possible in home and office-bound environments of a generation ago. But the price of mobility has been increasing demands and dependence on portable power sources.

Fortunately, with the development of new nickel-metal hydride (Ni-MH) battery options, improvements in electronics have now been matched by significant improvements in the batteries that power them. Nickel-metal hydride battery cells provide more power (in equivalently sized packages) than nickel-cadmium (Ni-Cd) cells while also eliminating some of the concerns over use of heavy metals in the cell.

Advantages :

(i) Improved energy density (upto 40% greater than nickel-cadmium cells) which can be translated into either longer run times from existing batteries or reductions in the space necessary for the battery.

(ii) Elimination of the constraints on cell manufacture, usage and disposal imposed because of concerns over cadmium toxicity.

(iii) Simplified incorporation into products currently using nickel cadmium cells because of many design similarities between the two chemistries.

Applications :

Electronic products like cellular phones, portable computers due to reductions in weight and volume coupled with improvement in performance.

3.25.1 Construction of Ni-MH Cell

(i) Anode (+ve plate) : The +ve electrode is Nickel oxyhydroxide (NiOOH).

(ii) Cathode (–ve plate) : The –ve electrode is metal hydride (MH).

(iii) Electrolyte : The electrolyte is used in an aqueous solution of potassium hydroxide (KOH).

In Ni-MH battery, the minimum amount of electrolyte is used as most of the liquid being absorbed by the separator and the electrode. The Ni-MH battery is designed with discharge and charge reserve in negative electrode (Fig. 3.33).

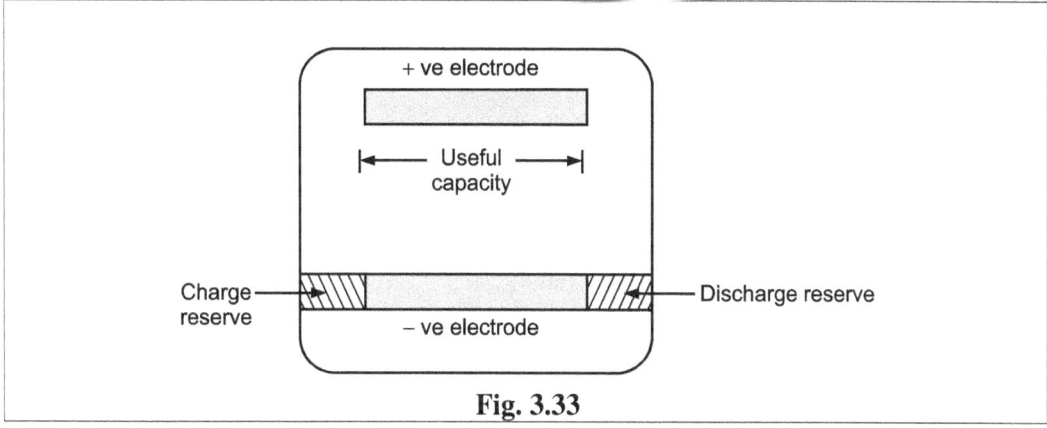

Fig. 3.33

The standard size of Ni-MH batteries are designed with cylindrical and prismatic type of Nickel-Metal hydride cells.

3.25.2 Charging and Discharging of Ni-MH Cell

(1) **Charging :** The +ve electrode reaches to the bulk charge before negative electrode and causes the oxygen to evolve.

$$2OH^- \rightarrow H_2O + \frac{1}{2}O_2 + 2e^-$$

$$2MH + \frac{1}{2}O_2 \rightarrow 2M + H_2O$$

The oxygen reacts with metal hydride of the negative electrode to produce water.

(2) **Discharging :** The nickel oxyhydride is converted into nickel hydroxide.

$$NiOOH + H_2O + e^- \rightarrow Ni(OH)_2 + OH^-$$

While the metal is oxidized to the metal alloy.

$$MH + OH^- \rightarrow M + H_2O + e^-$$

Thus the overall reaction on discharge is

$$MH + NiOOH \rightarrow M + Ni(OH)_2$$

3.25.3 Comparison Between Ni-Cd and Ni-MH Cells

Sr. No.	Parameter	Nickel-Cadmium (Ni-Cd)	Nickel-Metal Hydride (Ni-MH)
1.	Positive electrode	Nickel hydroxide $Ni(OH)_3$	Nickel oxyhydroxide $NiOOH$
2.	Negative electrode	Cadmium (Cd)	Metal hydride alloy (MH)
3.	Electrolyte	Potassium hydroxide (KOH)	Potassium hydroxide (KOH)
4.	Internal resistance	Low	Very low
5.	Life	Very long	Very very long
6.	Weight	Heavy	Light
7.	Mechancial strength	Good	Very good
8.	Gravimetric energy density	50 Wh/kg	55 Wh/kg
9.	Volumetric energy density	140 Wh/L	180 Wh/L
10.	Self discharge at 20°C	15-20% per month	20-30% per month
11.	Cost	Best cost as per performance value	Very high

REVIEW QUESTIONS

1. Three capacitors are connected in series across a 200 V D.C. supply. The potential differences across the capacitors are 40 V, 70 V and 30 V respectively. If the capacitance of A is 8 μF, what are the capacitances of B and C ?

    (**Ans. :** 4.57 μF and 3.56 μF)

2. A capacitor of 4 μF capacitance is charged to a potential difference of 400 volt and then connected in parallel with an uncharged capacitor of 2 μF capacitance. Calculate the potential difference across parallel combination of capacitors and the energy stored in the capacitor before and after being connected in parallel.

    (**Ans. :** 267 V, 0.32 J, 0.213 J)

3. A capacitor consists of two square metal plates of side 200 mm separated by an air space 2.0 mm wide. The capacitor is charged to a potential difference of 200 volt and then sheet of glass of 2 mm thickness having relative permitivity of 6 is placed between the metal plates and immediately they are disconnected from the supply. Calculate (i) the capacitance with air dielectric, (ii) capacitance with glass dielectric, (iii) potential difference across the capacitor after the glass plate has been inserted, (iv) charge on the capacitor.

    (**Ans. :** (i) 177 pF, (ii) 1.062 pF, (iii) 33.33 V, (iv) 0.0354 μC)

4. A 100 μF capacitor is connected in series with an 8000 Ω resistor Determine the time constant of the circuit. If the combination is connected suddenly to a 100 D.C. supply, find (i) initial rate of rise of potential difference across the capacitor,
    (ii) initial charging current, (iii) charge on the capacitor, (iv) energy stored in the capacitor.   (**Ans. :** (i) 0.85, (ii) 125 V/s, (iii) 12.5 mA, (iv) 0.01 C, (v) 0.5 Joule)

5. The energy stored in a certain capacitor when connected across a 400 volt d.c. supply is 0.3 joule. Calculate (i) the capacitance and (ii) charge on the capacitor.

    (**Ans. :** (i) 3.75 μF, (ii) 1.5 μC)

6. A 0.1 mF capacitor charged to a potential difference of 100 V between the plates. It is thereafter discharged through a resistor of 1 MΩ. Calculate (i) the initial value of discharge current, (ii) its value after 0.1 sec, (iii) initial value of decay of capacitor voltage.   (**Ans. :** (i) 100 μA/s, (ii) – 36.8 μA, (iii) 100 V/s)

7. A capacitor consists of two parallel rectangular plates each 120 mm square separated by 1 mm in air. When the voltage of 100 V is applied between the plates, an average current of 12 mA flows for 5 sec. Calculate (a) charge on

capacitor, (b) electric flux, (c) electric flux density, (d) electric field strength in the dielectric.   (**Ans. :** (a) 60 mC, (b) 60 mC, (c) 4.167 C/m², (d) 1 MV/m)

8. The two capacitors having capacitance of 6 µF and 10 µF respectively are connected in parallel. A 16 µF capacitor is connected in series with this parallel combination and whole circuit is connected across a 400 volt d.c. supply. Calculate : (i) total capacitance of the circuit, (ii) voltage across each capacitor, (iii) total charge in the circuit, (iv) charge on each capacitor.

   (**Ans. :** (i) 8 µF, (ii) $Q = 3.2$ mC, (iii) 200 V, 200 V (iv) $Q_6 = 1.2$ mC, $Q_{10} = 2$ mC)

9. A parallel-plate capacitor has plates of area 1.5 m². It has three dielectrics 1 mm, 1.6 mm and 2 mm thick. The relative permittivities of these dielectrics are 2, 4 and 5 respectively. Calculate the capacitance of the capacitor and the electric field strengths in the dielectrics if a voltage of 2.5 kV is applied between the plates.

   (**Ans. :** (i) $C = 10.21 \times 10^{-9}$ F, (ii) 0.961×10^6 V/m, 0.48×10^6 V/m,

   (iii) 0.38×10^{-6} V/m)

10. A 10 µF capacitor in series with an 1 MΩ resistor is connected across a 100 V d.c. supply. Determine (i) time constant of the circuit, (ii) initial value of charging current, (iii) the initial rate of rise of voltage across the capacitor, (iv) capacitor voltage after a time equal to the time constant, (v) the circuit current at this time, (vi) the voltage across the capacitor after 3 seconds, (vii) time taken for the capacitor voltage to reach 50 V.

   (**Ans. :** (i) 10 s, (ii) 0.1 mA, (iii) 10 V/s (iv) 63.2 V, (v) 0.0368 mA, (vi) 25.92 A,

   (vii) 6.931 s)

UNIT - IV

Chapter **4**

MAGNETIC CIRCUIT AND TRANSFORMER

4.1 LAWS OF MAGNETISM (COULOMB'S LAW)

There are two fundamental laws of magnetism which are as follows :

Law 1 : It states that 'like magnetic poles repel and unlike poles attract each other'.

Law 2 : This law is experimentally proved by scientist Coulomb and hence also known as Coulomb's law.

The force (F) exerted by one pole on the other pole is,

(a) Directly proportional to the product of the pole strengths.

(b) Inversely proportional to the square of the distance between them, and

(c) Nature of medium surrounding the poles. Mathematically, this law can be expressed as,

$$F \propto \frac{M_1 M_2}{d^2}$$

where, M_1 and M_2 are pole strengths of the poles while d is the distance between the poles.

$$\therefore \qquad \boxed{F = \frac{K M_1 M_2}{d^2}}$$

where, K depends on the nature of the surrounding medium.

4.2 DIFFERENT QUANTITIES RELATED TO MAGNETISM

4.2.1 Magnetic Field

The magnet has its influence on the surrounding medium. The region around a magnet within which the influence of the magnet can be experienced is called magnetic field. Existence of such field can be experienced with the help of compass needle, iron pieces or by bringing another magnet in the vicinity of a magnet.

4.2.2 Magnetic Lines of Force

The magnetic field of magnet is represented by imaginary lines around it which are called magnetic lines of force. Note that these lines have no physical existence, these are purely imaginary and were introduced by Michael Faraday to get the visualization of distribution of such lines of force.

4.2.3 Direction of Magnetic Field

The direction of magnetic field can be obtained by conducting a small experiment.

Let us place a permanent magnet on table and cover it with a sheet of cardboard. Sprinkle steel or iron fillings uniformly over the sheet. Slight tapping of cardboard causes fillings to adjust themselves in a particular pattern as shown in Fig. 4.1.

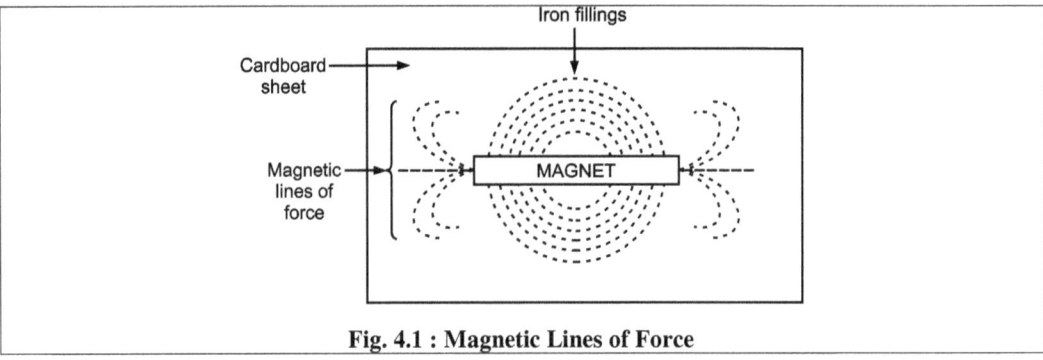

Fig. 4.1 : Magnetic Lines of Force

The shape of this pattern projects a metal picture of the magnetic field present around a magnet.

4.2.4 A Line of Force

Consider the isolated N pole (we cannot separate the pole but imagine to explain line of force) and it is allowed to move freely in a magnetic field. Then the path along which it moves is called line of force. Its shape is as shown in Fig. 4.2 and direction always from N-pole towards S-pole.

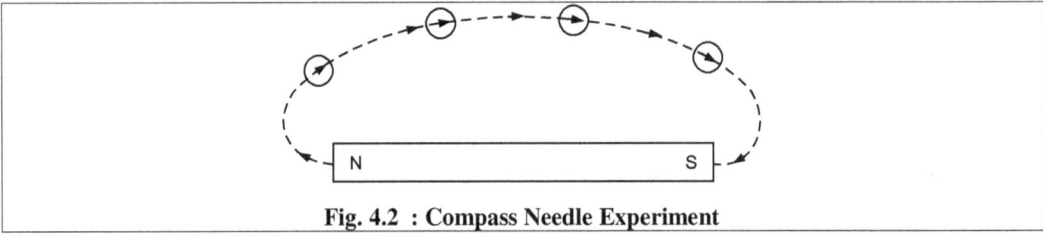

Fig. 4.2 : Compass Needle Experiment

The direction of lines of force can be understood with the help of small compass needle. If magnet is placed with compass needles around it, then needles will take positions as shown in Fig. 4.2. The tangent drawn at any point, to the dotted curve shown, gives direction of resultant force at that point. The N poles are all pointing along the dotted line shown, from N-pole to its S-pole.

The lines of force for a bar magnet and U-shaped magnet are shown in Fig. 4.3 (a) and (b).

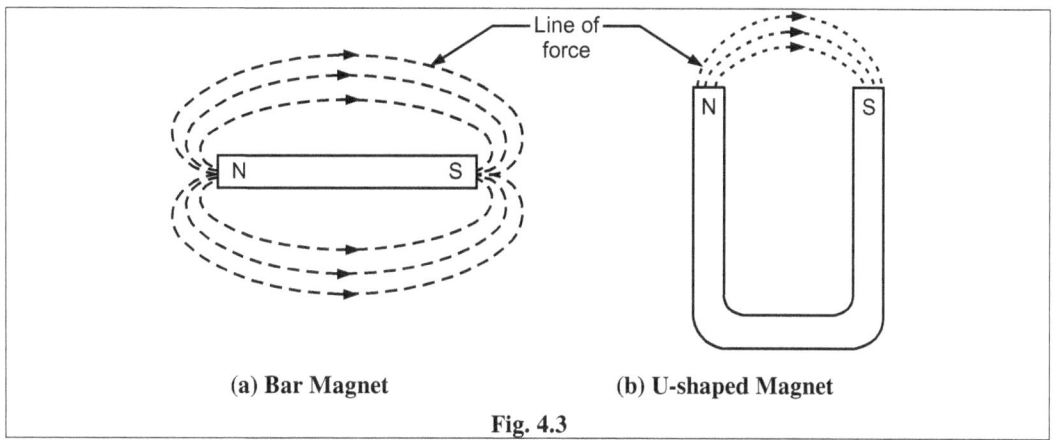

(a) Bar Magnet   **(b) U-shaped Magnet**

Fig. 4.3

Attraction between the unlike poles and repulsion between the like poles of two magnets can be easily understood from the direction of magnetic lines of force. This is shown in Fig. 4.4 (a) and (b).

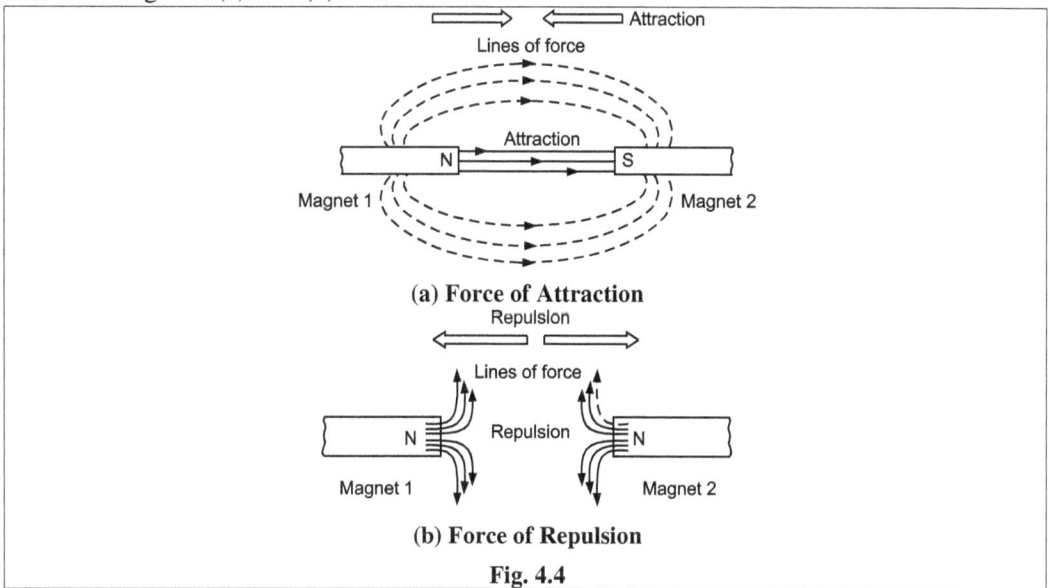

(a) Force of Attraction

(b) Force of Repulsion

Fig. 4.4

4.2.5 Properties of Lines of Force

Though the lines of force are imaginary, with the help of them various magnetic effects can be explained very conveniently. Let us see the various properties of these lines of force.

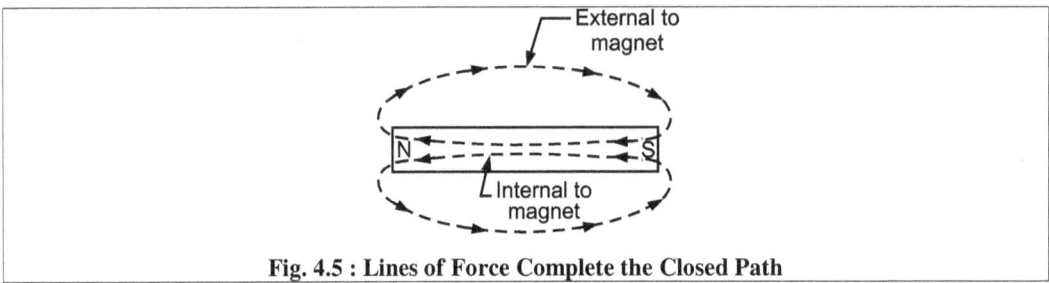

Fig. 4.5 : Lines of Force Complete the Closed Path

(1) Lines of force are always originating on a N-pole and terminating on S-pole, external to the magnet.

(2) Each line forms a closed loop as shown in Fig. 4.5.

Key Point : This means that a line emerging from N-pole, continues upto S-pole, external to the magnet while it is assumed to continue from S-pole to N-pole internal to the magnet completing a closed loop.

(3) Lines of force never intersect each other.

(4) The lines of force are like stretched rubber bands and always try to contract in length.

(5) The lines of force which are parallel and travelling in the same direction repel each other.

(6) Magnetic lines of force always prefer a path offering least opposition.

Key Point : The opposition by the material to the passage of lines of force is called reluctance. Air has more reluctance while magnetic material like iron, steel etc. have low reluctance. Thus, magnetic lines of force can easily pass through iron or steel but cannot pass easily through air.

4.2.6 Magnetic Flux (Φ)

The total number of lines of force existing in a particular magnetic field is called magnetic flux. The unit of flux is Weber and flux is denoted by symbol (ϕ). The unit Weber is denoted as Wb.

$$\boxed{1 \text{ Weber } = 10^8 \text{ lines of force}}$$

4.2.7 Pole Strength

The force between the poles depends on pole strengths. Every pole has a capacity to radiate or accept certain number of magnetic lines of force i.e. magnetic flux which is called its strength. Pole strength is a measurable quantity assigned to poles which depends on the force between the poles. If two poles are exerting equal force on one other, they are said to have equal pole strengths.

Unit of pole strength is Weber as pole strength is directly related to flux i.e. lines of force.

Key Point : A unit pole may be defined as that pole which when placed from an identical pole at a distance of 1 meter in free space experiences a force of $\dfrac{10^7}{16\pi^2}$ Newtons.

So when we say unit N-pole, it means a pole is having a pole strength of 1 Weber.

4.2.8 Magnetic Flux Density (B)

It can be defined as 'The flux per unit area (a) in a plane at right angles to the flux is known as 'flux density'. Mathematically,

$$B = \frac{\phi}{a} \ \frac{Wb}{m^2} \text{ or Tesla}$$

It is shown in Fig. 4.6.

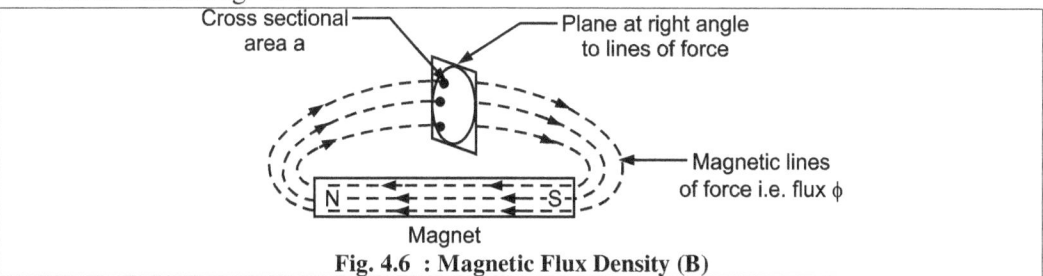

Fig. 4.6 : Magnetic Flux Density (B)

Key Point : The unit of flux density is Wb/m², also called Tesla denoted as T.

4.2.9 Magnetic Field Strength (H)

This gives quantitative measure of strongness or weakness of the magnetic field. Note that pole strength and magnetic field strength are different. This can be defined as 'the force experienced by a unit N-pole (i.e. N-pole with 1 Wb of pole strength), when placed at any point in a magnetic field is known as magnetic field strength at that point.

It is denoted by H and its unit is Newtons per Weber i.e. (N/Wb) or Amperes per meter (A/m) or Ampere Turns per meter (AT/m).

The mathematical expression for calculating magnetic field strength is,

$$H = \frac{\text{Ampere turns}}{\text{Length}}$$

∴
$$H = \frac{NI}{l} \text{ AT/m}$$

Key Point : More the value of 'H', more stronger is the magnetic field. This is also called magnetic field intensity.

SOLVED EXAMPLES

Example 4.1 :

A pole having strength of 0.5×10^{-3} Wb is placed in a magnetic field at a distance of 25 cm from another pole. It is experiencing a force of 0.5 N. Assume constant of medium as $\left(\dfrac{1}{36\pi^2 \times 10^{-7}}\right)$.

Determine (a) Magnetic field strength at that point.

(b) The strength of other pole.

(c) Distance at which force experienced will be doubled.

Solution : The given values are

$M_1 = 0.5 \times 10^{-3}$ Wb, d = 25 cm = 0.25 m, F = 0.5 N

$$K = \left[\dfrac{1}{36\pi^2 \times 10^{-7}}\right]$$

$$= 28144.773$$

(a) Magnetic field strength, $H = \dfrac{\text{Newton}}{\text{Wb}} = \dfrac{\text{Force experienced}}{\text{Pole strength}}$

$$= \dfrac{0.5}{0.5 \times 10^{-3}} = 1000 \text{ N/Wb.}$$

(b) According to Coulomb's law,

$$F = \dfrac{KM_1 M_2}{d^2}$$

$$0.5 = \dfrac{28144.773 \times 0.5 \times 10^{-3} \times M_2}{(0.25)^2}$$

∴ $M_2 = 2.22 \times 10^{-3}$ Wb   …(Pole strength of other pole)

(c) $F = 1$ N

$$1 = \dfrac{28144.773 \times 0.5 \times 10^{-3} \times 2.22 \times 10^{-3}}{d^2}$$

$$d = 0.1767 \text{ m}$$

$$= 17.67 \text{ cm}$$

At a distance of 17.67 cm from another pole, the first pole will experience a force 1N.

Key Point : When poles are brought nearer and nearer, force experienced by them increases.

4.3 MAGNETIC EFFECT OF AN ELECTRIC CURRENT (ELECTROMAGNETS)

When a coil or a conductor carries a current it produces the magnetic flux around it, then it starts behaving as a magnet. Such a current carrying coil or conductor is called an electromagnet (air cored). This is due to magnetic effect of an electric current.

If such a coil is wound around a piece of magnetic material like iron or steel and carries current then piece of material around which the coil is wound, starts behaving as a magnet, which is called as electromagnet (on cored). The flux produced and the flux density can be controlled by controlling the magnitude of the current. The direction and shape of the magnetic field around the coil or the conductor depends on the direction of current and shape of the conductor through which it is passing. The magnetic field produced can be experienced with the help of iron fillings on compass needle. Let us study two different types of electromagnets :

    (1) Electromagnet due to straight current carrying conductor.

    (2) Electromagnet due to circular current carrying coil.

4.3.1 Magnetic Field due to Straight Conductor

When a straight conductor carries a current, it produces a magnetic field all along its length. The lines of force are in the form of concentric circles in the planes right angles to the conductor. This can be demonstrated by a small experiment.

Consider a straight conductor carrying a current, passing through a sheet of cardboard as shown in Fig. 4.7. Sprinkle iron fillings on the cardboard. Small tapping on the cardboard causes the iron fillings to set themselves, in the concentric circuit pattern. The direction of the magnetic flux can be determined by placing compass needle near the conductor.

This direction depends on the direction of the current passing through the conductor. For the current direction shown in Fig. 4.7 i.e. from top to bottom, the direction of flux is clockwise around the conductor.

Conventionally such a current carrying conductor is represented by small circle (top view of conductor) shown in Fig. 4.7. Then current through such conductor will either come out of paper or will go into the plane of the paper.

When current is going into the plane of the paper, i.e. away from observer, it is represented by a 'cross' inside the circle indicating the conductors as shown in Fig. 4.8 (a).

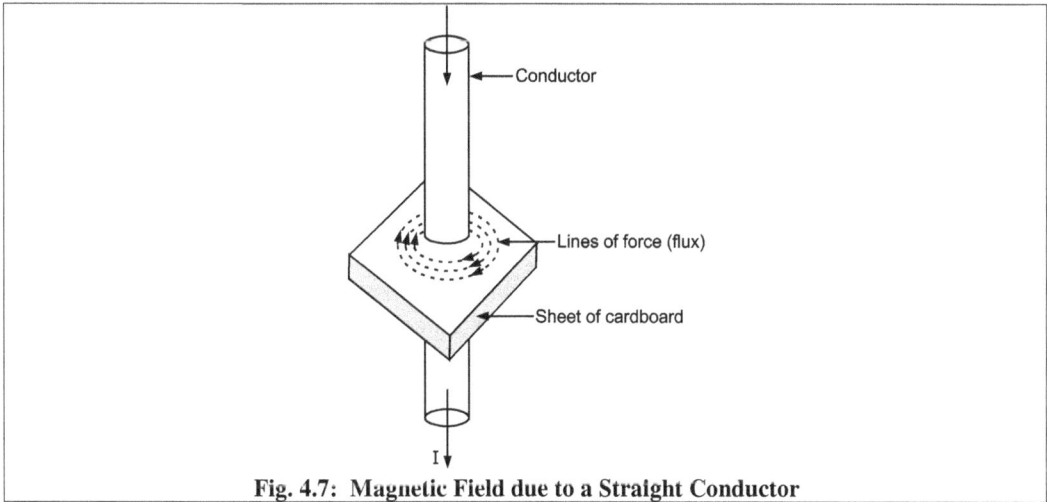

Fig. 4.7: Magnetic Field due to a Straight Conductor

The cross indicates rear view of feathered end of an arrow.

Key Point : The current flowing towards the observer i.e. coming out of the plane of the paper is represented by a 'dot' inside the circle.

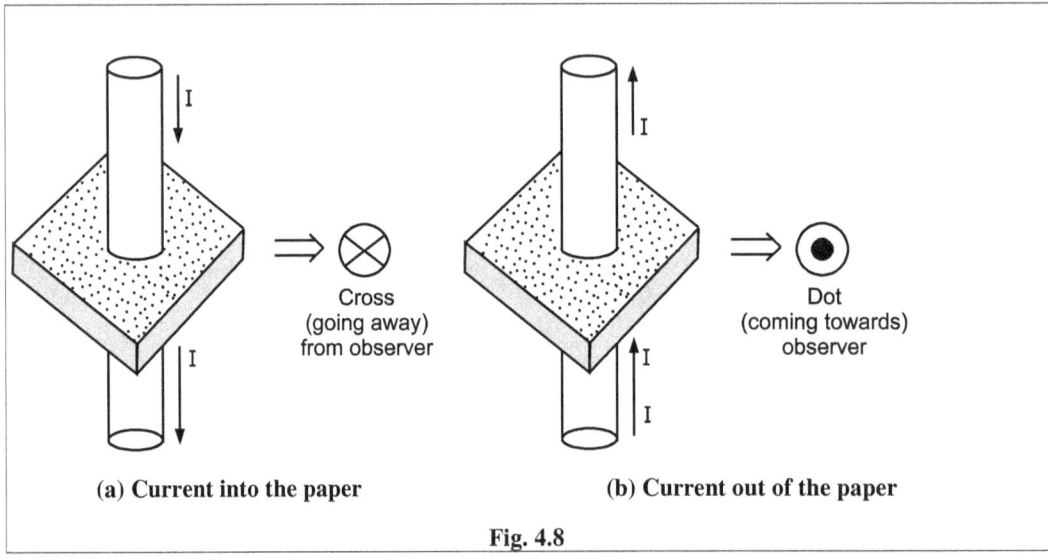

(a) Current into the paper   (b) Current out of the paper

Fig. 4.8

The dot indicates front view i.e. tip of an arrow. This is shown in Fig. 4.8 (b).

4.3.2 Rules to Determine Direction of Flux around a Conductor

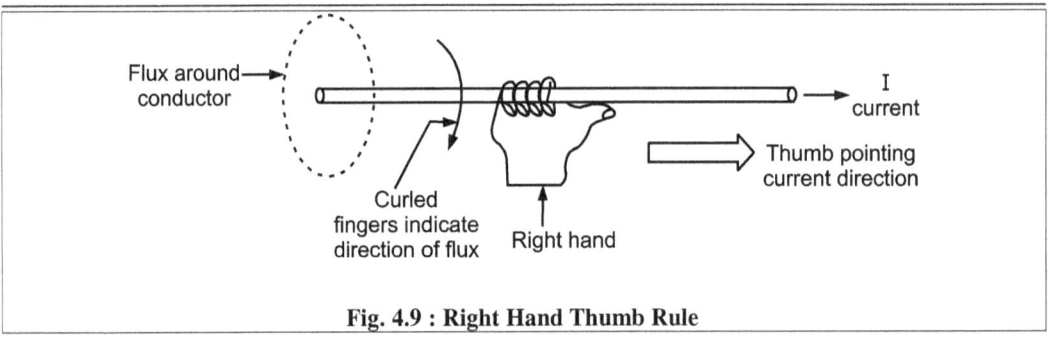

Fig. 4.9 : Right Hand Thumb Rule

4.3.2.1 Right Hand Thumb Rule

It states that, hold the current carrying conductor in the right hand such that the thumb pointing in the direction of current and parallel to the conductor, then curled fingers point in the direction of the magnetic field or flux around it. Fig. 4.9 explains the rule.

Let us apply this rule to the conductor passing through card sheet considered earlier.

This can be explained by Fig. 4.10 (a).

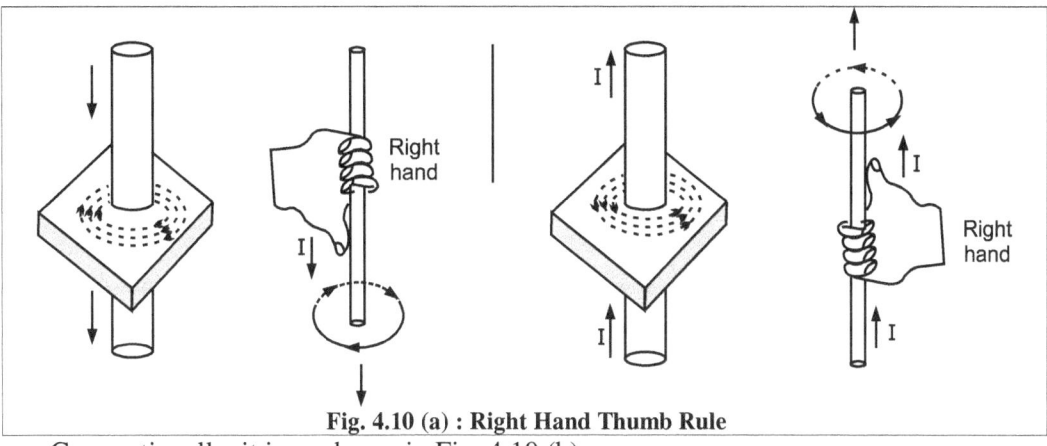

Fig. 4.10 (a) : Right Hand Thumb Rule

Conventionally, it is as shown in Fig. 4.10 (b).

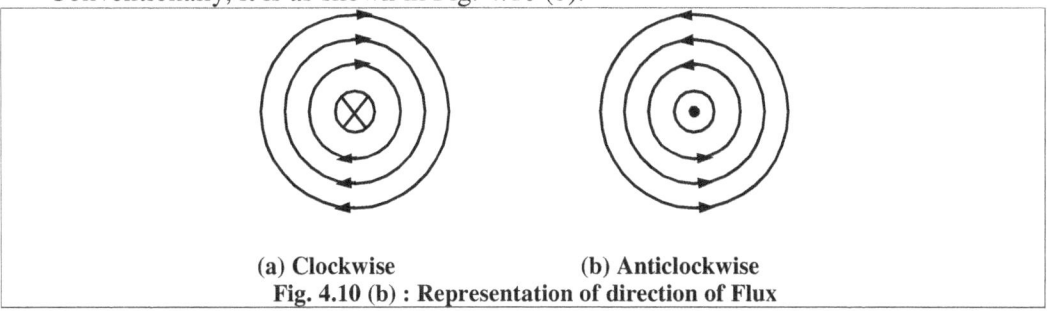

(a) Clockwise   (b) Anticlockwise

Fig. 4.10 (b) : Representation of direction of Flux

4.3.2.2 Corkscrew Rules

Imagine a right handed screw to be along the conductor carrying current with its axis parallel to the conductor and tip pointing in the direction of the current flow.

Then the direction of the magnetic field is given by the direction in which the screw must be turned so as to advance in the direction of the current.

This is shown in Fig. 4.11.

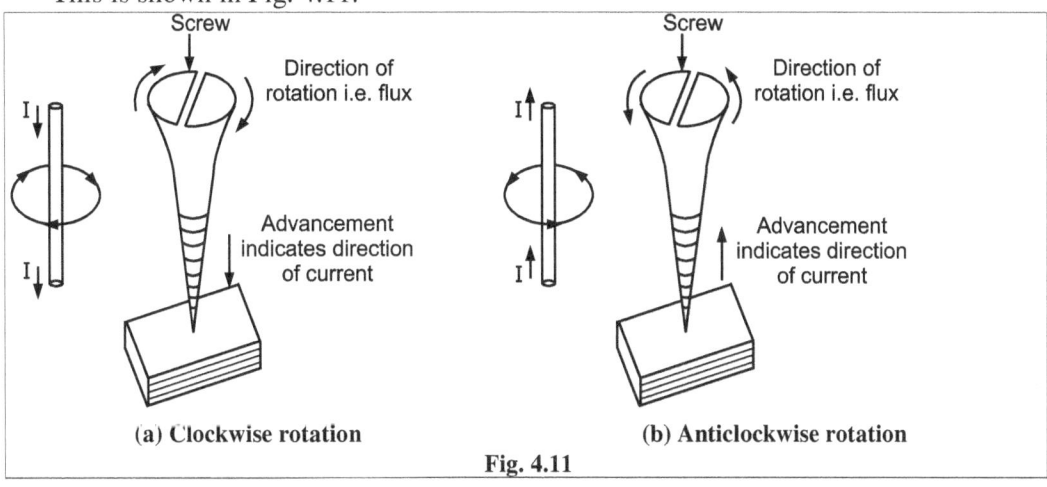

(a) Clockwise rotation   **(b) Anticlockwise rotation**

Fig. 4.11

4.3.3 Magnetic Field due to Circular Conductor i.e. Solenoid

A solenoid is an arrangement in which, long conductor is wound with number of turns close together to form a coil. The axial length of conductor is much more than the diameter of turns. The part or element around which the conductor is wound is called as core of the solenoid. Core may be air or may be some magnetic material. Solenoid with a steel or iron core as shown in Fig. 4.12 (a).

When such conductor is excited by the supply so that it carries a current then it produces a magnetic field, which acts through the coil along its axis and also around the solenoid. Instead of using a straight core to wound the conductor, a circular core can also be used to wound the conductor.

In such case, the resulting solenoid is called toroid. Use of magnetic material for the core produces strong magnet. This is because current carrying conductor produces its own flux. In addition to this, the core behaves like a magnet due to magnetic induction, producing its own flux. The direction of two fluxes is the same due to which resultant magnetic field becomes more strong.

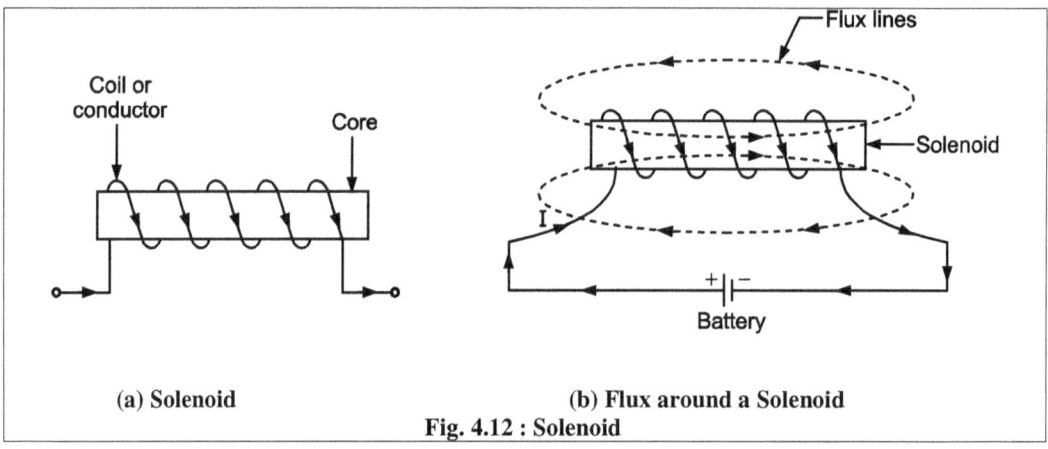

(a) Solenoid   (b) Flux around a Solenoid
Fig. 4.12 : Solenoid

The pattern of the flux around the solenoid is shown in Fig. 4.12 (b).

Hence, the rules to determine the direction of flux and poles of the magnet are formed.

4.3.3.1 The Right Hand Thumb Rule

Hold the solenoid in the right hand such that curled finger points in the direction of the current through the curled conductor, then the outstretched thumb along the axis of the solenoid points to the North pole of the solenoid or points to the direction of flux lines inside the core as shown in Fig. 4.13 (a) and (b).

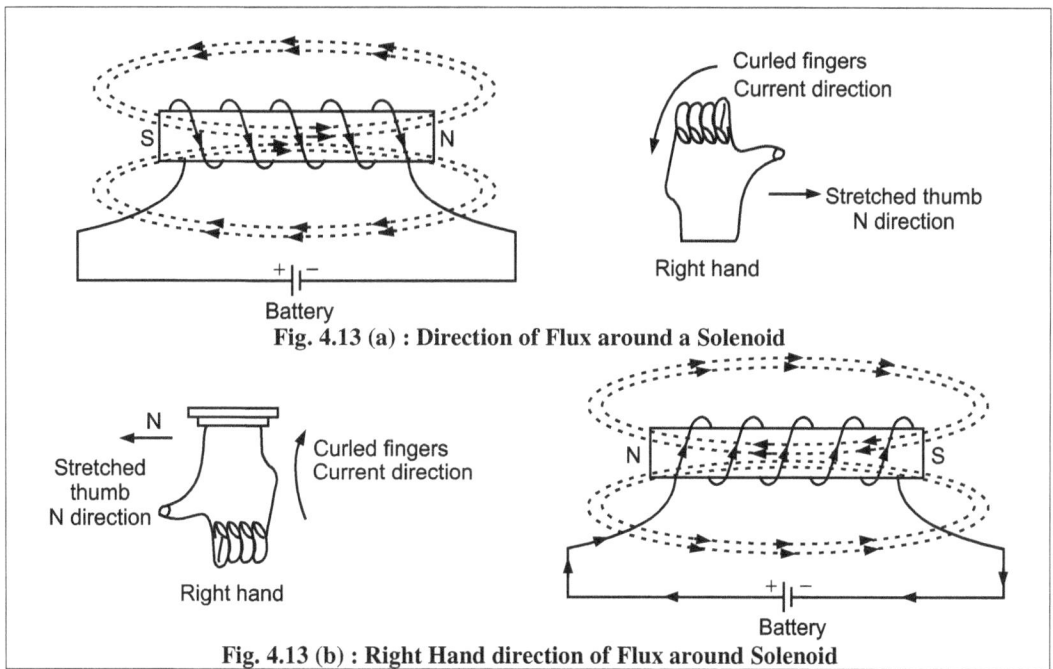

Fig. 4.13 (a) : Direction of Flux around a Solenoid

Fig. 4.13 (b) : Right Hand direction of Flux around Solenoid

In case of toroid, the core is circular and hence using right hand thumb rule, the direction of flux in the core, due to current carrying conductor can be determined. This is shown in Fig. 4.13 (c) and (d). In Fig. 4.13 (c), corresponding to direction of winding, the flux set in the core is anticlockwise while in Fig. 4.13 (d) due to direction of winding, the direction of flux set in the core is clockwise. The winding is also called magnetizing winding or magnetizing coil as it magnetizes the core.

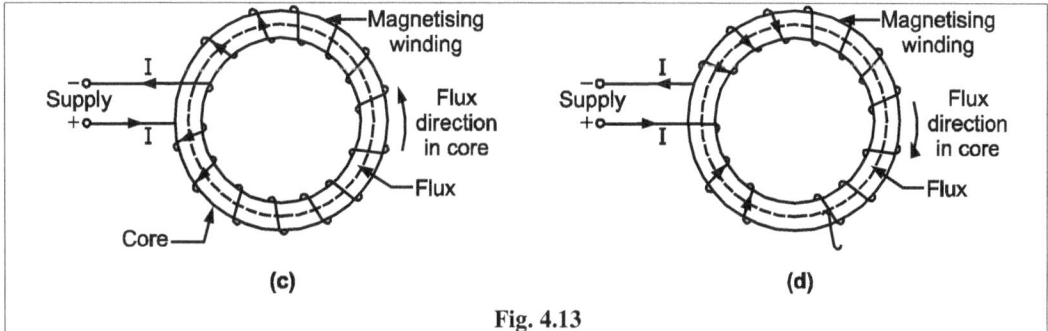

Fig. 4.13

4.3.3.2 Cork Screw Rule Solenoid

If axis of the screw is placed along the axis of solenoid and if screw is turned around in the direction of the current, then it travels towards the N-pole or in the direction of the magnetic field inside the solenoid.

4.4 PERMEABILITY

Permeability is defined as ability or ease with which the magnetic material forces the magnetic flux through a given medium.

For any magnetic material, there are two permeabilities :

(i) Absolute permeability (μ)

(ii) Relative permeability (μ_r).

(i) Absolute permeability (μ) : The ratio of magnetic flux density (B) in a particular medium (other than vacuum or air) to magnetic field strength (H) producing that flux density is called absolute permeability of that medium.

$$\mu = \frac{B}{H}$$

OR $B = \mu H$

It's unit is Henry per metre (H/m).

(ii) Permeability of free space or vacuum (μ_o) : If the magnet is placed in free space or vacuum or air then the ratio of flux density B_o and magnetic field strength H is called permeability of free space or vacuum or air.

$$\mu_o = \frac{B_o}{H} \text{ in vacuum}$$

$$= 4\pi \times 10^{-7} \, H/m \qquad \text{(always constant)}$$

(iii) Relative Permeability (μ_r) : Relative permeability of a material is equal to the ratio of the flux density produced in that material to the flux density produced in vacuum by the same magnetizing force (H).

$$\mu_r = \frac{B}{B_o}$$

$$= \frac{B \, (\text{Material})}{B_o (\text{Vacuum})}$$

OR $\mu_r = \dfrac{\mu H}{\mu_o H}$

OR $\mu = \mu_o \mu_r$

4.5 MAGNETIC FIELD STRENGTH OF A LONG SOLENOID

Let the magnetic field strength along the axis of the solenoid be H.

Let us assume that,

(i) The value of H remains constant throughout the length l of solenoid.

(ii) The value of H outside the solenoid is negligible.

Suppose a unit N pole is placed at point A outside the solenoid and is taken once around the complete path (shown dotted in Fig. 4.14) in the direction opposite to that of H.

Force of H Newton acts on N-pole only over length l. (H is negligible elsewhere)

The work done in one round = H $\times$ l Joule

The 'Ampere-turns' linked with path are NI where,

$$N = \text{Number of turns of solenoid.}$$
$$I = \text{Current in amperes passing through it.}$$

According to work law or Ampere's circuital law,

$$H \times l = NI \text{ OR } H = \frac{NI}{l} \text{ A/m}$$

Also,

$$B = \mu_o \frac{NI}{l} \frac{Wb}{m^2} \text{ or Tesla -------- (for air)}$$

$$= \mu_o \mu_r \frac{NI}{l} \frac{Wb}{m^2} \text{ or Tesla (medium other than air or vacuum)}$$

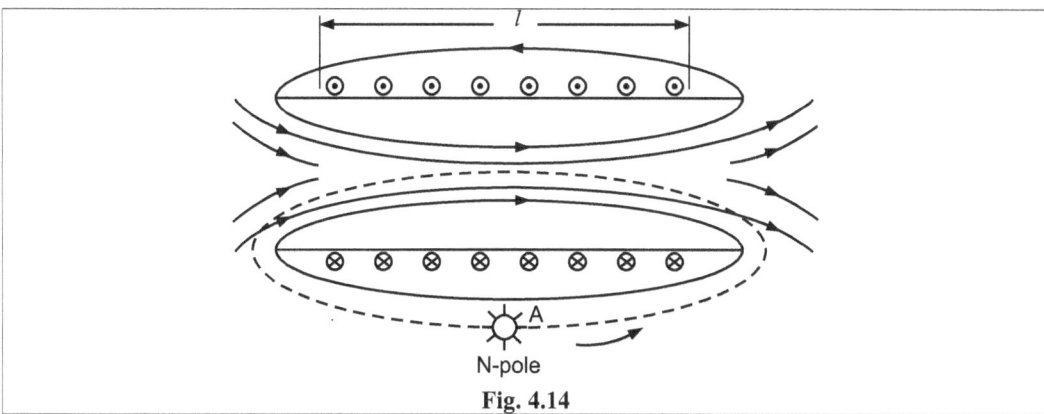

Fig. 4.14

4.6 EXPRESSION FOR THE FORCE EXPERIENCED BY TWO LONG STRAIGHT PARALLEL CONDUCTORS CARRYING CURRENT IN THE SAME DIRECTION

Consider the two long straight parallel conductors carrying current in the same direction as shown in Fig. 4.15.

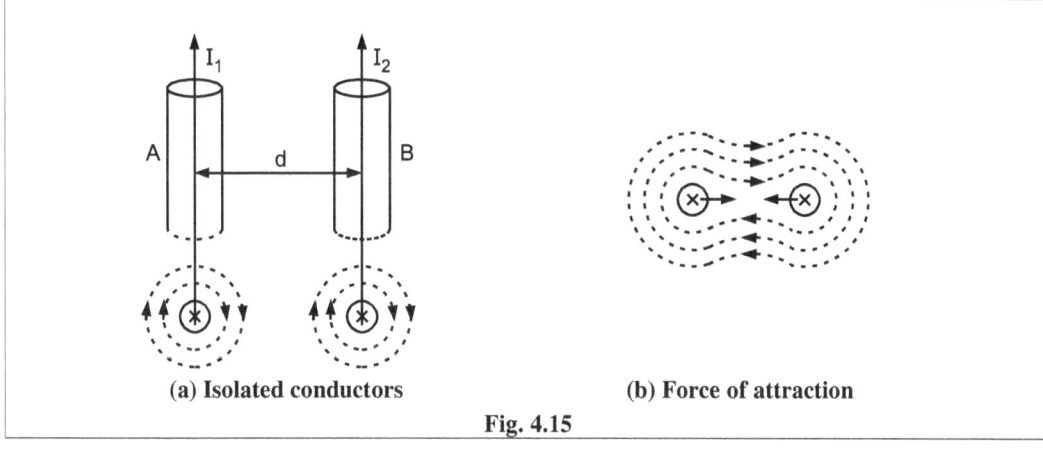

(a) Isolated conductors   (b) Force of attraction

Fig. 4.15

Let I_1, I_2 be the currents through conductors A and B, d the distance between the conductors.

Magnetic field strength at any point on conductor B due to the current in conductor A,

$$H = \frac{I_1}{2\pi d}$$

Corresponding flux density due to magnetic field strength,

$$B = \mu H$$

$$= \frac{\mu_o \mu_r I_1}{2\pi d} \qquad \qquad ...(1)$$

But force experienced by conductor B due to current I_2 ,

$$F = BI_2 l$$

$$= \frac{\mu_o \mu_r I_1}{2\pi d} \cdot I_2 \cdot l \qquad \mu_r = 1 \text{ for air}$$

$$= 4\pi \times 10^{-7} \times I_1 I_2 \frac{l}{2\pi d}$$

$$= 2 \times 10^{-7} \frac{I_1 I_2 l}{d} \text{ N}$$

If $l = 1$ m and $d = 1$ m and I_1, $I_2 = $ 1A

then,   force $= $ 2×10^{-7} N

Definition of Ampere :

It is defined as the force experienced per unit length between two long straight parallel conductors carrying the equal current, placed one metre apart is 2×10^{-7} N, then current in each of them is 1 Ampere.

Note : If the direction of current is opposite then force will be same and there will be force of repulsion between them.

SOLVED EXAMPLES

Example 4.2 :

Two parallel conductors A and B placed 140 mm apart in air, carry the currents 98 A and 77 A respectively in the opposite direction. Calculate (i) Force on each conductor per metre length, (ii) Magnetic field strength at a point C which is 90 mm from conductor A and 50 mm from conductor B.

Solution :

(i) Force between two parallel current carrying conductors :

$$F = 2 \times 10^{-7} \frac{I_1 I_2 l}{d}$$

$$F = \frac{2 \times 10^{-7} \times 98 \times 77 \times 1}{140 \times 10^{-3}} = 0.0107 \text{ N/m}.$$

(ii) Magnetic field strength at point C due to current 98 A in conductor A,

$$H_{CA} = \frac{I}{2\pi r} = \frac{98}{2\pi \times 90 \times 10^{-3}} = 173.38 \text{ A/m}$$

(iii)   Magnetic field strength at point C due to current 77 A in conductor B,

$$H_{CB} = \frac{I}{2\pi r} = \frac{77}{50 \times 10^{-3} \times 2\pi} = 245.22 \text{ A/m}$$

Now current in the two conductors is in opposite direction, both magnetic field strengths at point C act in the same direction.

∴   Resultant magnetic field strength,

$$H_C = H_{CA} + H_{CB}$$
$$= 173.38 + 245 = 418.55 \text{ A/m}$$

4.7 MAGNETIC CIRCUIT

It may be defined as the route or path which is followed by magnetic flux.

Consider a solenoid or a toroidal iron ring having a magnetic path of l meter, area of cross section a m^2 and a coil of N turns carrying I amperes wound on it as shown in Fig. 4.16.

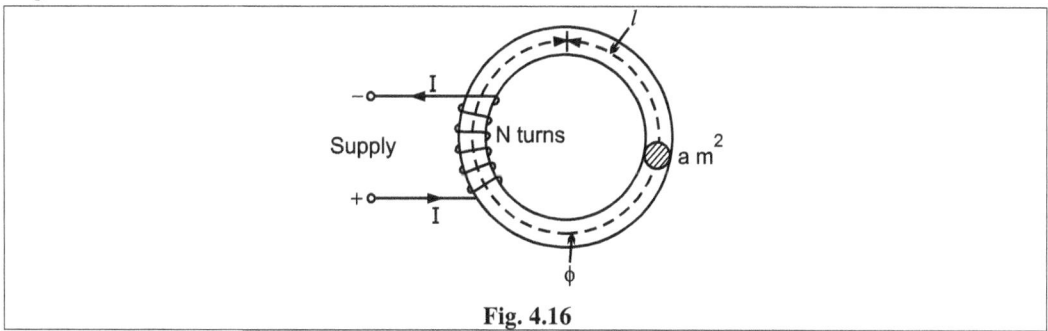

Fig. 4.16

The magnetic field strength inside the solenoid is

$$H = \frac{NI}{l} \frac{AT}{m}$$

Now, $$B = \mu_0 \mu_r H = \frac{\mu_0 \mu_r NI}{l} \text{ Wb/m}^2$$

Total flux $\phi = B \times a = \frac{\mu_0 \mu_r a NI}{l} \text{ Wb}$

∴. $$\phi = \frac{NI}{l/\mu_0 \mu_r a} \text{ Wb}$$

The numerator 'NI' which produces a magnetization in magnetic circuit is known as magnetomotive force (m.m.f.).

Obviously it's unit is Ampere Turn (AT). It is analogous to e.m.f. in an electric circuit.

The denominator $\dfrac{l}{\mu_o \mu_r A}$ is called the reluctance of the circuit and is analogous to resistance in electric circuits.

$\therefore$
$$\text{Flux} = \frac{\text{m.m.f.}}{\text{Reluctance}} \text{ i.e. } \phi = \frac{F}{S}$$

Sometimes, the above equation is called Ohm's law of magnetic circuit because it resembles a similar expression in electric circuits. i.e.

$$\text{Current} = \frac{\text{e.m.f.}}{\text{resistance}} \text{ i.e. } I = \frac{V}{R}$$

4.7.1 Definitions Concerning Magnetic Circuit

(1) Magnetomotive Force (m.m.f.) : It drives or tends to drive flux through a magnetic circuit and corresponds to electromotive force (e.m.f.) in an electric circuit. MMF is equal to work done in Joule in carrying a unit magnetic pole once through the entire magnetic circuit. It's unit is Ampere-Turns (AT).

(2) Reluctance : The opposition offered to the passage of magnetic flux through a material is called it's reluctance and is analogous to resistance in an electric circuit. It's unit is AT/Wb.

$$\text{Reluctance} = \frac{l}{\mu_o \mu_r a} = \frac{l}{\mu a}$$

(3) Permeance : It is reciprocal of reluctance and is defined as ease or readiness with which magnetic flux developed and is analogous to conductance in an electric circuit. It's unit is Wb/AT or Henry.

(4) Reluctivity : It is specific reluctance and corresponds to resistivity which is specific resistance.

4.8 COMPOSITE MAGNETIC CIRCUIT

4.8.1 Series Magnetic Circuit

Fig. 4.17 shows a composite series magnetic circuit consisting of three different magnetic materials A, B, C of different permeabilities μ_1, μ_2 and μ_3 and lengths l_1, l_2 and l_3 and one air gap ($\mu_r = 1$).

Each path will have its own reluctance.

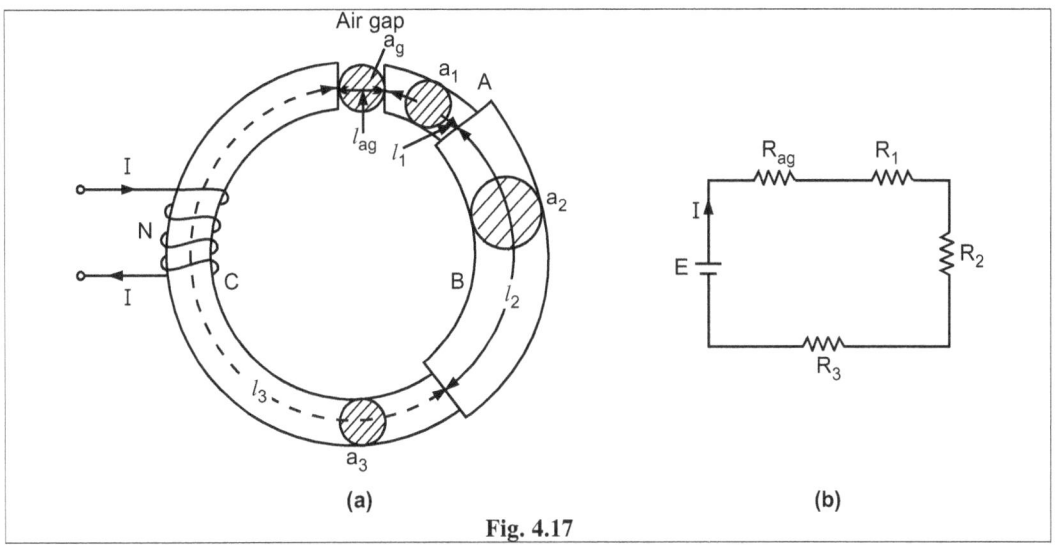

(a)   **(b)**

Fig. 4.17

The total reluctance is the sum of individual reluctances as they are joined in series.

$\therefore$ Total reluctance $S_T = \sum \dfrac{l}{\mu_a}$

= reluctance of A + reluctance of B + reluctance of C + reluctance of air gap

$= \dfrac{l_1}{\mu_o\mu_{r1}a_1} + \dfrac{l_2}{\mu_o\mu_{r2}a_2} + \dfrac{l_3}{\mu_o\mu_{r3}a_3} + \dfrac{l_{ag}}{\mu_o a_g}$

$\therefore$ $\qquad\qquad$ Flux $\phi = \dfrac{\text{m.m.f.}}{S_T}$

$$NI = \phi \cdot S_T$$

Total m.m.f. = m.m.f. for iron + m.m.f. of air gap

$$NI = \phi\,(\text{reluctance of iron}) + \phi\,(\text{reluctance of air gap})$$
$$= \phi\,[S_i] + \phi\,[S_{ag}]$$
$$= \phi\,S_i + \phi\,S_{ag}$$
$$= \phi\left[\dfrac{l_1}{\mu_o\mu_{r1}a_1} + \dfrac{l_2}{\mu_o\mu_{r2}a_2} + \dfrac{l_3}{\mu_o\mu_{r3}a_3}\right] + \left[\dfrac{l_{ag}}{\mu_o a_g}\right]$$

How to find Ampere turns: $H = \dfrac{NI}{l} \dfrac{AT}{m}$

Or $\qquad\qquad\qquad\qquad$ $NI = H \times l$

$\therefore$ $\qquad\qquad$ Ampere - turns $AT = H \times l$

Follow the procedure :

(i) Find H for each portion of the composite circuit.

For air, $H = \dfrac{B}{\mu_o}$ Otherwise $H = \dfrac{B}{\mu_o\mu_r}$

(ii) Find ampere-turns for each path separately by using the relation,

$$AT = H \times l$$

(iii) Add up these ampere - turns to get the total ampere - turns for the entire circuit.
Fig. 4.17 (b) shows electrical equivalent circuit of magnetic circuit.

4.8.2 Parallel Magnetic Circuits

Fig. 4.18 (a) shows the parallel magnetic circuit consisting of three parallel magnetic paths ACB, ADB and AB acted upon by the same m.m.f.

The flux produced by the coil wound on central core is divided equally at point A between the two outer parallel paths. Fig. 4.18 (b) shows the equivalent electrical circuit where the resistance offered to the e.m.f. source is $R \parallel R = \dfrac{R}{2}$.

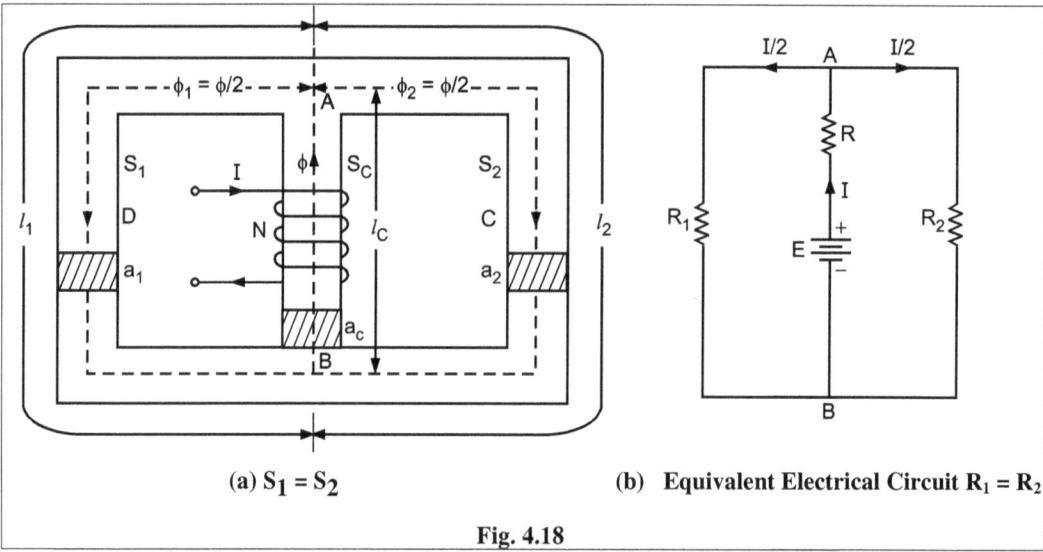

(a) $S_1 = S_2$ (b) **Equivalent Electrical Circuit $R_1 = R_2$**

Fig. 4.18

Flux ϕ divides equally at point A
Current I divides equally at point A
The mean length of path ADB $= l_1$ m , The mean length of path ACB $= l_2$ m
The mean length of path AB $= l_c$ m

The reluctance of path ADB $= S_1 \dfrac{AT}{Wb}$,   The reluctance of path ACB $= S_2 \dfrac{AT}{Wb}$

The reluctance of path AB $= S_c \dfrac{AT}{Wb}$,   Total m.m.f. produced $=$ NI AT

$\quad$ Flux $= \dfrac{m.m.f.}{Reluctance}$,   m.m.f. $= \phi \cdot S_1$

For path ADBA,   NI $= \phi S_c + \phi_1 S_2$
For path ACBA,   NI $= \phi S_c + \phi_2 S_2$

where, $S_1 = \dfrac{l_1}{\mu_{a1}}$, $S_2 = \dfrac{l_2}{\mu_{a2}}$ and $S_c = \dfrac{l_c}{\mu_{ac}}$

Total m.m.f. $= \phi S_c + \phi_1 S_1 = \phi S_c + \phi_2 S_2$

4.9 COMPARISON BETWEEN MAGNETIC CIRCUIT AND ELECTRICAL CIRCUITS

Similarities :

Magnetic Circuit	Electrical Circuit
 Fig. 4.19 (a)	 **Fig. 4.19 (b)**
1. Flux $= \dfrac{\text{m.m.f.}}{\text{Reluctance}}$	1. Current $= \dfrac{\text{e.m.f.}}{\text{Resistance}}$
2. m.m.f. = (Ampere – turns)	2. e.m.f. (volts).
3. Flux ϕ (Webers)	3. Current I (Amperes).
4. Flux density B (Wb/m^2)	4. Current density (A/m^2)
5. Reluctance $S = \dfrac{l}{\mu_o \mu_r a}$	5. Resistance $R = \rho \dfrac{l}{a}$
6. Permeance $= \dfrac{1}{\text{Reluctance}}$	6. Conductance $= \dfrac{1}{\text{Resistance}}$
7. Reluctivity	7. Resistivity.
8. Permeability $= \dfrac{1}{\text{Reluctivity}}$	8. Conductivity $= \dfrac{1}{\text{Resistivity}}$
9. Kirchhoff's m.m.f. and flux law is applicable to the magnetic circuit.	9. Kirchhoff's voltage and current law is applicable to the electric circuit.

Dissimilarities :

	Magnetic Circuit		Electrical Circuit
1.	Flux does not actually flow in the sense which current flows.	1.	The current actually flows i.e. there is movement of electrons in electric circuit.
2.	No magnetic insulator as flux can pass through all the materials, even air.	2.	Many insulators like air, P.V.C., synthetic resin etc. from which current cannot pass.
3.	Energy is required to create the magnetic flux, but not required to maintain it.	3.	Energy must be supplied to maintain the flow of current.
4.	Reluctance of a magnetic circuit depends on flux (and hence flux density).	4.	Resistance of an electric circuit is constant and is independent of the current (or current density) as long as temperature is kept constant.

4.10 MAGNETIC LEAKAGE AND FRINGING

4.10.1 Magnetic Leakage

The flux which does not follow the path intended for it is called as leakage flux.

The flux in the air gap is known as the useful flux because it is only the flux which can be utilized for various useful purposes.

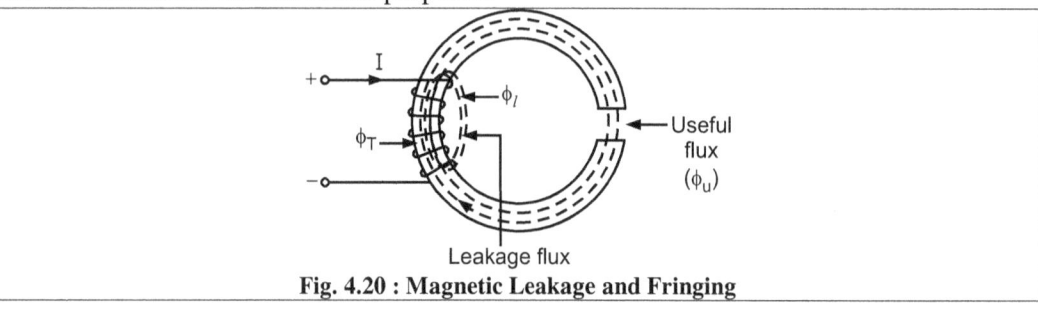

Fig. 4.20 : Magnetic Leakage and Fringing

If ϕ_T = Total flux produced

ϕ_u = Useful flux available in the air gap, then

ϕ_l = Leakage flux

Leakage coefficient, λ = $\dfrac{\text{Total flux}}{\text{Useful flux}}$ = $\dfrac{\phi_T}{\phi_u}$

and $$\boxed{\phi_T = \phi_u + \phi_l}$$

The value of λ for modern electric machines varies between 1.1 and 1.25.

4.10.2 Magnetic Fringing

The flux passing through the air gap is parallel to each other. So there will be force of repulsion between the magnetic lines of force which are parallel and having same direction.

Due to this repulsive force, the magnetic flux will spread out at the edge of air gap. This tendency of the magnetic flux to spread out (bulge out) at the edges of the air gap is called magnetic fringing.

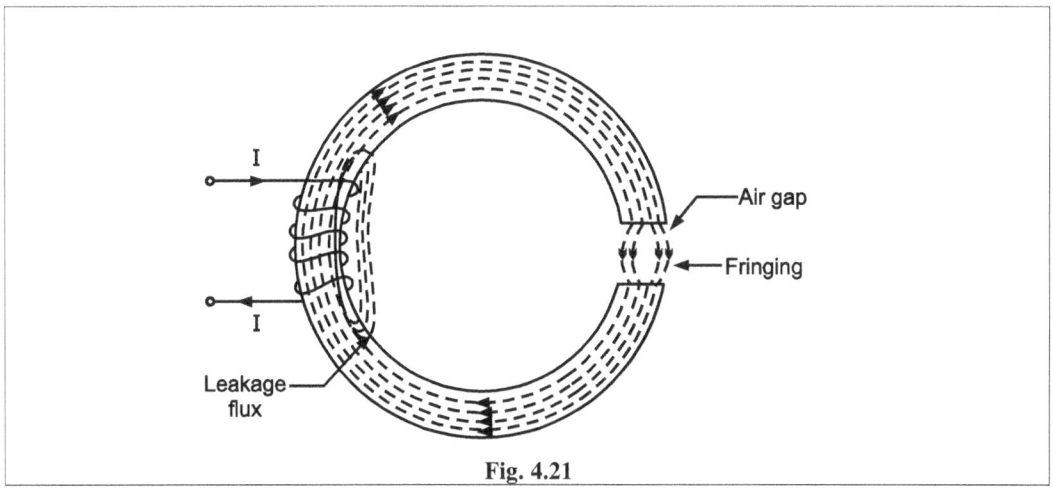

Fig. 4.21

It has following two effects :

(1) It increases the area of cross section of the air gap.

(2) Flux density $\propto \dfrac{1}{\text{area}}$, so it reduces the flux density.

Practically leakage, fringing and the reluctance of magnetic circuit should be as small as possible.

4.10.3 Magnetic Hysterisis

The phenomenon of lagging of flux density behind the magnetic field strength when a magnetic material subjected to a cycle of magnetization is called magnetic hysteresis.

Consider a coil wound on an iron core which is completely demagnetized.

(i) The field intensity in the coil is given as

$$H = \frac{NI}{l}$$

(ii) The value of 'H' can be increased or decreased by increasing or decreasing the current through the coil.

(iii) If the current in the coil is zero, then H = 0, and hence B = 0.

(iv) If the current in the coil increases, H also increases, gradually B also increases. The relationship between B and H is as shown below. Curve 'OA' be the normal magnetization curve.

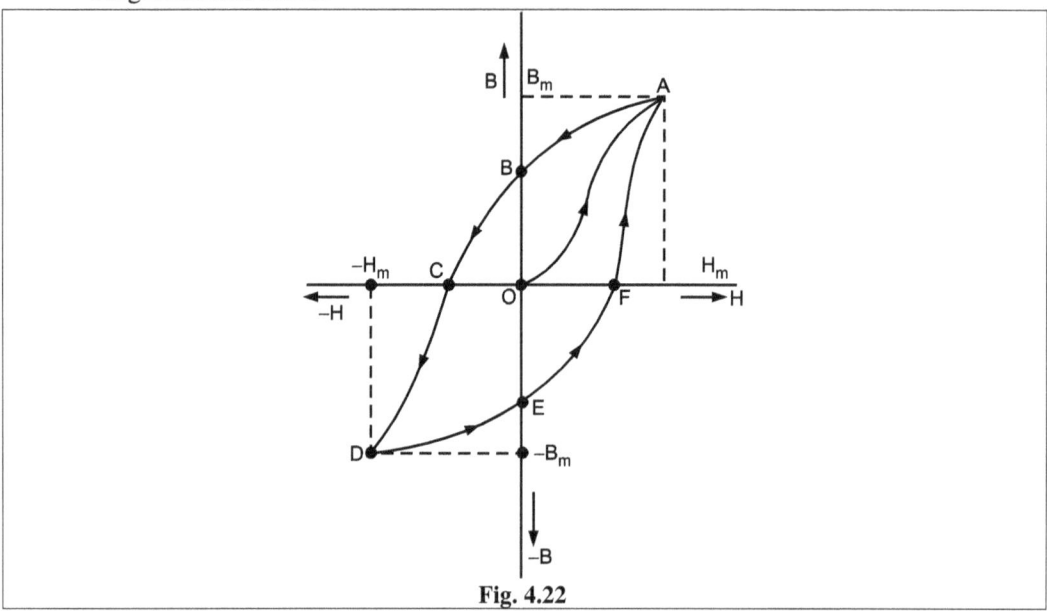

Fig. 4.22

(v) At point A the core becomes magnetically saturated and field strength reaches to its highest value to H_m. Also at this point flux density in the core is maximum i.e. 'B_m'.

(vi) If 'H' is gradually decreased then, curve 'OA' will follow another path i.e. AB.

(vii) At point B, H = 0 and OB = Br. 'OB' is called as residual flux density or remanent flux density.

(viii) To demagnetize the core completely H is reversed by reversing the current in the coil. Now, the flux density also decreases to zero as shown in Fig. 4.22 i.e. BC. At point C, B = 0 and H = OC. This is called as coercive force required to remove the residual flux density completely.

(ix) If H is further increased in reverse direction the curve follows the path CD. At point 'D' core becomes magnetically saturated in the reverse direction.

(x) Now if 'H' is again decreased then curve follows the path DE. At point E, H = 0 and B = – Bm.

(xi) Now, H is again increased in the +ve direction, curve follows the path EF. At point F, B = 0 and H = OF.

(xii) If H is further increased the curve follows the path FA. The closed loop ABCDEFA obtained when the magnetic core is subjected to one complete cycle of magnetization is called as hysteresis loop.

Hysteresis curves for different materials :

(a) Hard steel, (b) Cast steel, (c) Alloy of nickel and iron, (d) Non-magnetic material.

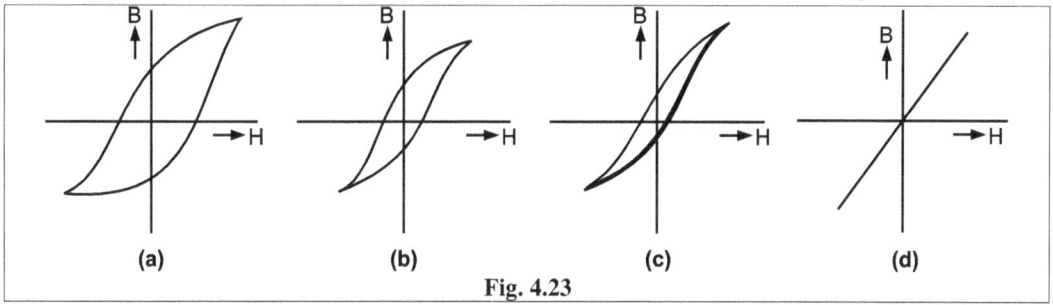

Fig. 4.23

$$\boxed{\textbf{SOLVED EXAMPLES}}$$

Example 4.3 :

A magnetic core in the form of a closed ring has mean length of 20 cm and a cross section of 1 cm². The relative permeability of iron is 2400. Find the current needed in the coil of 2000 turns uniformly wound on the ring to produce a flux of 0.2 mWb in the iron ring? Now if the air gap of 1 mm is cut through the core perpendicular to the direction of this flux, find the current required to maintain the same flux in the gap. Find the fraction of total ampere turns required to maintain the flux in the air gap.

Given : l = 20 cm, a = 1 cm², μ_r = 2400, N = 2000, ϕ = 0.2 mWb, l_{ag} = 1mm

Solution : (I) Reluctance of the ring :

$$S = \frac{l}{\mu_o \mu_r a} = \frac{20 \times 10^{-2}}{4\pi \times 10^{-7} \times 2400 \times 1 \times 10^{-4}}$$

$$= 663.48 \times 10^3 \ \text{A/Wb}$$

Now,   m.m.f. $= \phi S$

                 NI $= \phi S$

∴ $I = \frac{\phi S}{N} = \frac{0.2 \times 10^{-3} \times 6.63 \times 10^5}{2000}$

$$= 66.3 \times 10^{-3} A = 66.348 \ \text{mA}$$

(II) When air gap is introduced :

(i) m.m.f. required for iron ring,

$$\text{Flux density} = \frac{\phi}{a_i} \quad \text{(where } a_i = \text{area of iron ring)}$$

$$= \frac{0.2 \times 10^{-3}}{1 \times 10^{-4}} = 2 \ \text{Tesla}$$

and   Field strength H_i $= \dfrac{B_{iron}}{\mu_o \mu_r} = \dfrac{2}{4\pi \times 10^{-7} \times 2400} = 663.48$ AT/m

Therefore m.m.f. for iron ring $= H_i \times l_i$

$= 663.48 \times (0.20 - 0.001)$

$= 132$ Ampere turns

Now, m.m.f. required for air gap,

$$H_a = \dfrac{B_a}{\mu_o} = \dfrac{2}{4\pi \times 10^{-7}} = 0.159 \times 10^7 \text{ AT/m}$$

∴   m.m.f. for air gap $= H_g \times l_{ag}$

$= 0.159 \times 10^7 \times 1 \times 10^{-3} = 1592.35$ AT

Total m.m.f. for the magnetic circuit

$=$ m.m.f. of ring $+$ m.m.f. of air gap

$= 132 + 1592.35$

$= 1724.356$ AT

∴   Exciting current $= \dfrac{\text{m.m.f.}}{N} = 862.178$ mA

∴ Fraction of total ampere turns required to maintain the flux in the air gap

$$= \dfrac{1592.35}{1724.3563} = 0.924$$

Example 4.4 :

An iron ring made up of three parts has $l_1 = 10$ cm, $a_1 = 5$ cm², $l_2 = 8$ cm, $a_2 = 3$ cm², $l_3 = 6$ cm, $a_3 = 2.5$ cm². It is wound with a coil of 250 turns. Calculate the current required to produce a flux of 0.4 mWb in the ring. $\mu_{r1} = 2670$, $\mu_{r2} = 1050$, $\mu_{r3} = 650$.

Solution : Total reluctance of the ring,

$$S = \dfrac{l_1}{\mu_o \mu_{r1} a_1} + \dfrac{l_2}{\mu_o \mu_{r2} a_2} + \dfrac{l_3}{\mu_o \mu_{r3} a_3}$$

$$= \dfrac{1}{4\pi \times 10^{-7}} \left[\dfrac{0.1}{2670 \times 5 \times 10^{-4}} + \dfrac{0.08}{1050 \times 3 \times 10^{-4}} + \dfrac{0.06}{650 \times 2.5 \times 10^{-4}} \right]$$

$$= 5.555 \times 10^5 \text{ AT/Wb}$$

∴   Flux $\phi = \dfrac{\text{m.m.f.}}{\text{Reluctance}}$ m.m.f. $= \phi.S$

∴ $I = \dfrac{\phi.S}{N} = \dfrac{0.4 \times 10^{-3} \times 5.55 \times 10^5}{250} = 0.88$ Amp

Example 4.5 :

An iron ring of mean length 100 cm with an air gap of 2 mm has a winding of 500 turns. The relative permeability of iron is 600. When a current of 3 A flows in the winding, determine the flux density. Neglect fringing.

Solution : Given : $l_i = 100$ cm, $l_g = 2$mm, $N = 500$, $\mu_r = 600$

Total MMF required for the iron ring and air gap

$$\text{Total MMF} = (H_i \times l_i) + (H_g \times l_g)$$

$\therefore$
$$l_i = 100 \times 10^{-2} - 2 \times 10^{-3}$$

$$= 0.998 \text{ m}$$

$$l_g = 2 \text{ mm} = 2 \times 10^{-3} \text{ m}$$

$\therefore$
$$N \times I = \frac{B}{\mu_0 \mu_r} l_i + \frac{B}{\mu_0} l_g$$

$$500 \times 3 = \frac{B}{4\pi \times 10^{-7} \times 600} \times 0.998 + \frac{B}{4\pi \times 10^{-7}} \times 2 \times 10^{-3}$$

$$1500 = \frac{B}{4\pi \times 10^{-7}} \left[\frac{0.998}{600} + 2 \times 10^{-3} \right]$$

$$B = 0.514 \text{ Tesla or Wb/m}^2$$

Example 4.6 :

A steel ring has a mean diameter of 20 cm, cross section of 25 cm² and radial air gap of 0.8 mm cut across it. When excited by a current of 1 A through a coil of 1000 turns wound on the ring core, it produces an air gap flux of 1 mWb. Neglect leakage and fringing. Calculate (i) Relative permeability of steel, (ii) Total reluctance of the magnetic circuit.

Solution: (i) Total reluctance of the circuit,

$$S_T = \frac{\text{m.m.f.}}{\phi} = \frac{1 \times 1000}{1 \times 10^{-3}} = 10^6 \text{ AT/Wb}$$

(ii)
$$S_T = \frac{l_i}{\mu_0 \mu_r a} + \frac{l_g}{\mu_0 a}$$

$\therefore$
$$\text{m.m.f.} = \phi.S = \phi \left[\frac{l_i}{\mu_0 \mu_r a} + \frac{l_g}{\mu_0 a} \right] = \frac{\phi}{\mu_0 a} \left[\frac{l_i}{\mu_r} + l_g \right]$$

But,
$$l_i = \pi d - l_g$$

$$= \pi \times (0.2) - 8 \times 10^{-4}$$

$$= 0.6283 \text{ m.}$$

$\therefore$
$$\text{m.m.f.} = \frac{1 \times 10^{-3}}{4\pi \times 10^{-7} \times 25 \times 10^{-4}} \left[\frac{0.6283}{\mu_r} + 8 \times 10^{-4} \right]$$

$$1 \times 1000 = \frac{1 \times 10^{-3}}{4\pi \times 10^{-7} \times 25 \times 10^{-4}} \left[\frac{0.6283}{\mu_r} + 8 \times 10^{-4} \right]$$

$\therefore$
$$\mu_r = 268.504$$

Example 4.7 :

An iron ring of 100 cm mean diameter with an airgap of 2 mm width and 10 cm² cross section has 1000 turns of copper wire on it. If the permeability of the material is 1500 and it is required to produce a flux density of 1 Wb/m² in an air gap in the ring. Find : (i) Reluctance of ring, (ii) Flux produced, (iii) M.M.F. required, (iv) Current produced.

Solution : Mean diameter = 100 cm, l_g = 2 mm, a = 10 cm², N = 1000 turns, μ_r = 1500, B = 1 Wb/m²

1. Length of ring $= \pi d - l_g$

$= \pi \times 100 \times 10^{-2} - 2 \times 10^{-3}$

$= 3.1395$ m.

$\therefore$ Reluctance of the ring $= \dfrac{l_i}{\mu_0 \times \mu_r \times a}$

$= \dfrac{3.1395}{4\pi \times 10^{-7} \times 1500 \times 10 \times 10^{-4}}$

$= 1.6655 \times 10^6$ AT/Wb

2. Flux required $=$ B.a

$= 1 \times 10 \times 10^{-4}$

$= 10^{-3}$ Wb

3. MMF required $=$ $H_i \times l_i + H_g \times l_g$

$= \dfrac{B}{\mu_0 \mu_r} \times l_i + \dfrac{B}{\mu_0} \times l_g$

$= \dfrac{B}{\mu_0} \left[\dfrac{l_i}{\mu_r} + l_g \right]$

$= \dfrac{1}{4\pi \times 10^{-7}} \left[\dfrac{3.1395}{1500} + 2 \times 10^{-3} \right]$

$= 3257.10$ AT

4. Current produced :

As MMF $=$ N.I

$\therefore$ NI $= 3257.10$ AT

$\therefore$ I $= \dfrac{3257.10}{1000} = 3.257$ Amp.

Example 4.8 :

A magnetic circuit is excited by three coils as shown in Fig. 4.24. Calculate the flux produced in the air gap. The material used for core is iron having relative permeability of 800. The length of the magnetic circuit is 1000 with an air gap of 2 mm in it. The core has uniform cross-section of 6 cm².

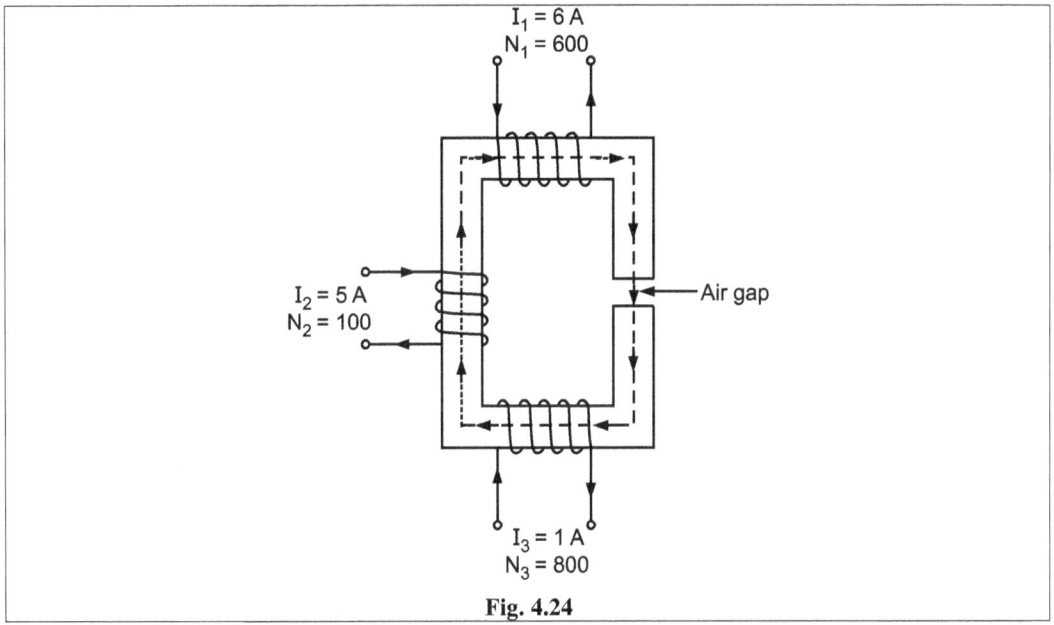

Fig. 4.24

Solution : $N_1 = 600$, $I_1 = 6A$, $N_2 = 100$, $I_2 = 5A$, $N_3 = 800$, $I_3 = 1A$, $l_g = 2$ mm, $l_T = 1m$,

$a = 6$ cm²

Length of the iron path $l_i = l_T - l_g = 1 - 2 \times 10^{-3} = 0.998$ m

Reluctance of the iron path

$$S_i = \frac{l_i}{\mu_0 \mu_r a}$$

$$= \frac{0.998}{4\pi \times 10^{-7} \times 800 \times 6 \times 10^{-4}}$$

$$= 1654548.26 \text{ AT/Wb}.$$

l_i = Reluctance of the air gap,

$$S_g = \frac{l_g}{\mu_0 a} = \frac{2 \times 10^{-3}}{4\pi \times 10^{-7} \times 6 \times 10^{-4}}$$

$$= 2652582.385 \text{ AT/Wb}.$$

Total reluctance $= S_i + S_g$

$$= 1654548.26 + 2652582.385$$

$$= 4307130.645 \text{ AT/Wb}$$

Let us find the direction of flux due to various coils using right hand thumb rule.

As shown in Fig. 4.25 the mmf of coils 1 and 2 are in same direction while mmf of coil B is in opposite direction.

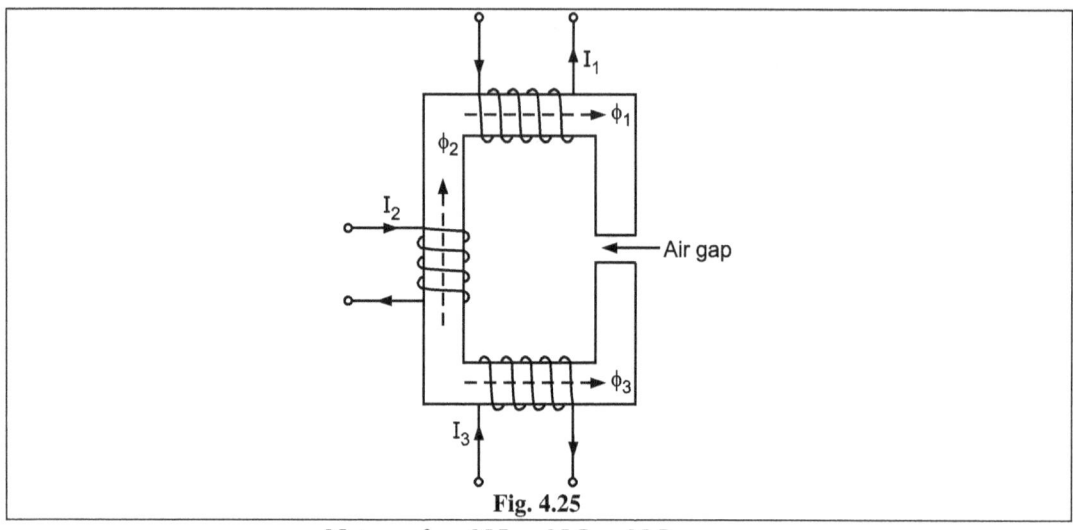

Fig. 4.25

$$\therefore \quad \text{Net mmf} = N_1I_1 + N_2I_2 - N_3I_3$$
$$= 600 \times 6 + 10 \times 5 - 800 \times 1 = 3300 \text{ AT}$$

$$\therefore \quad \text{Flux } (\phi) = \frac{\text{MMF}}{\text{Reluctance}} = \frac{NI}{S}$$

$$= \frac{3300}{4307130.645} = 766.17 \ \mu/\text{Wb}.$$

Example 4.9 :

An iron ring of cross-sectional area 5 cm² and mean length 100 cm has an air gap of 2 mm cut in it. Three separate coils having 100, 200 and 300 turns are wound on the ring and carry currents of 1 A, 2.5 A and 3 A respectively such that they produce additive fluxes in the ring. Relative permeability of the ring material is 1000. Calculate the flux in the air gap.

Solution: $a = 5 \text{ cm}^2 = 5 \times 10^{-4} \text{ m}^2$, $l_T = 100 \text{ cm} = 1 \text{ m}$, $l_g = 2 \text{ mm} = 2 \times 10^{-3}\text{m}$

$$l_i = l_T - l_g = 1 - 2 \times 10^{-3} = 0.998 \text{ m}$$

Total reluctance, $S_T = S_i + S_g$

$$S_i = \frac{l_i}{\mu_o\mu_r a}$$

$$= \frac{0.998}{4\pi \times 10^{-7} \times 1000 \times 5 \times 10^{-4}} = 1588366.332 \text{ AT/Wb}$$

$$S_g = \frac{l_g}{\mu_o a}$$

$$= \frac{2 \times 10^{-3}}{4\pi \times 10^{-7} \times 5 \times 10^{-4}} = 3183098.862 \text{ AT/Wb}$$

$$S_T = 1588366.332 + 3183098.862$$

$$= 4771465.194 \text{ AT/Wb}$$

$$\text{Net m.m.f.} = N_1 I_1 + N_2 I_2 + N_3 I_3$$
$$= 100 \times 1 + 200 \times 2.5 + 300 \times 3$$
$$= 1500 \text{ AT}$$

All m.m.f.s help each other as they produce additive fluxes in the ring.

$$\phi = \frac{\text{m.m.f.}}{\text{Reluctance}} = \frac{1500}{4771465.194} = 0.0003143 \text{ Wb}$$
$$= 0.3143 \text{ mWb}$$

Example 4.10 :

A magnetic circuit has mean length of flux path 20 cm and cross-sectional area of 1 cm^2. Relative permeability of its material is 2400. Find the m.m.f. required to produce a flux density of 2 Tesla in it. If an air gap of 1 mm is introduced in it, find the m.m.f. required for the air gap as a fraction of the total m.m.f. to maintain the same flux density.

Solution : $l_i = 20$ cm, a = 1 cm^2, $\mu_r = 2400$, B = 2T

$$S = \frac{l_i}{\mu_0 \mu_r a}$$
$$= \frac{20 \times 10^{-2}}{4\pi \times 10^{-7} \times 2400 \times 1 \times 10^{-4}}$$
$$= 663.145 \times 10^3 \text{ AT/Wb}$$
$$\phi = B \times a = 2 \times 1 \times 10^{-4} \text{ Wb}$$

Now,
$$\phi = \frac{\text{m.m.f.}}{S}$$

∴
$$\text{m.m.f.} = \phi \times S$$
$$= 2 \times 10^{-4} \times 663.145 \times 10^3 = 132.6291 \text{ AT}$$

Now,
$$l_g = 1 \text{ mm is introduced in it}$$

∴
$$l_i = 20 \text{ cm} - 1 \text{ mm} = 0.199 \text{ m}$$

∴
$$S_i = \frac{l_i}{\mu_0 \mu_r a} = 659.829 \times 10^3 \text{ AT/Wb}$$

and
$$S_g = \frac{l_g}{\mu_0 a} = 7.9577 \times 10^6 \text{ AT/Wb}$$

$$\phi = B \times a = 2 \times 10^{-4} \text{ Wb}$$

∴
$$(\text{m.m.f.})_{\text{iron path}} = S_i \times \phi = 131.9658 \text{ AT}$$

and
$$(\text{m.m.f.})_{\text{air gap}} = S_g \times \phi = 1591.5494 \text{ AT}$$

∴
$$\text{Total m.m.f.} = 1723.5152 \text{ AT}$$

∴
$$(\text{m.m.f.})_{\text{air gap}} = 0.9234 \text{ times total m.m.f.}$$

Example 4.11 :

A coil is wound uniformly with 300 turns over a steel of relative permeability 900, having a mean circumference of 40 mm and cross-sectional area of 50 mm^2. If a current of 5 A is passed through the coil, find (i) m.m.f., (ii) reluctance of the ring and (iii) flux.

Solution : Given : N = 300, μ_r = 900,

$$l = 40 \text{ mm} = 40 \times 10^{-3}\text{m}$$

$$a = 50 \text{ mm}^2 = 50 \times 10^{-6}\text{m}^2$$

$$I = 5 \text{ A}$$

(i) $\quad$ m.m.f. = NI = $300 \times 5 = 1500$ AT

(ii) $\quad S = \dfrac{l}{\mu_o\mu_r a}$

$$= \frac{40 \times 10^{-3}}{4\pi \times 10^{-7} \times 900 \times 50 \times 10^{-6}} = 707.714 \times 10^3 \text{ AT/Wb}$$

This is reluctance of the ring.

(iii) $\quad S = \dfrac{\text{m.m.f.}}{\phi}$

$\therefore \quad \phi = \dfrac{\text{m.m.f.}}{S} = \dfrac{1500}{707.714 \times 10^3} = 2.11 \text{ m Wb}$

Example 4.12 :

A ring shaped core is made up of two parts of same material. Part one is a magnetic path of length 25 cm and with cross-sectional area 4 cm^2, whereas part two is of length 10 cm and cross-sectional area of 6 cm^2. The flux density in part two is 1.5 Tesla. If the current through the coil is 0.5 Amp, calculate the number of turns of the coil.

Assume μ_r as 1000 for material.

Solution : Given : $\quad l_1 = 25$ cm

$$a_1 = 4 \text{ cm}^2$$

$$= 4 \times 10^{-4}\text{m}^2$$

$$l_2 = 10 \text{ cm}$$

$$a_2 = 6 \text{ cm}^2 = 6 \times 10^{-4}\text{m}^2$$

$$I = 0.5 \text{ Amp.}$$

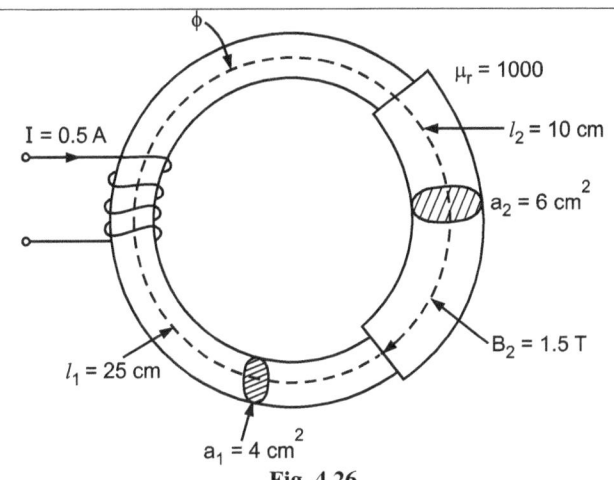

Fig. 4.26

$$B_2 = \frac{\phi}{a_2}$$

$$\phi = B_2 . a_2 = 1.5 \times 6 \times 10^{-4} = 9 \times 10^{-4} \, Wb$$

The flux ϕ is same through both the parts in series circuit.

$$S = S_1 + S_2$$

$$= \frac{l_1}{\mu_0 \mu_{r1} a_1} + \frac{l_2}{\mu_0 \mu_{r2} a_2} \qquad (\mu_r = \mu_{r1} = \mu_{r2} = 1000)$$

$$= \frac{25 \times 10^{-2}}{4\pi \times 10^{-7} \times 1000 \times 4 \times 10^{-4}} + \frac{10 \times 10^{-2}}{4\pi \times 10^{-7} \times 1000 \times 6 \times 10^{-4}}$$

$$= 629988.3164 \, AT/Wb$$

$$NI = \phi.S$$

$$N = \frac{\phi.S}{I} = \frac{9 \times 10^{-4} \times 629988.3164}{0.5}$$

$$N = 1133.97 \approx 1134 \, Turns$$

Example 4.13 :

An iron ring has circular cross-section of 4 cm in radius and the average circumference of 100 cm. The ring is wound with 700 turns.

Calculate :

(i) The current required to produce 2 mWb in the ring, if μ_r for the iron is 900.

(ii) If a saw cut of 1 mm is made in the ring, calculate the current which will give same value of flux in the ring.

Solution : Given : $\phi = 2 \, mWb = 2 \times 10^{-3} \, Wb$, $\mu_r = 900$, $l = 100 \, cm = 1 \, m$.

(i) Radius of circular cross-section $= 4 \, cm = 4 \times 10^{-2} m$

$$a = \pi r^2 = \pi \times (4 \times 10^{-2})^2 = 50.2654 \times 10^{-4} \, m^2$$

$$\phi = \frac{m.m.f.}{Reluctance} = \frac{NI}{S}$$

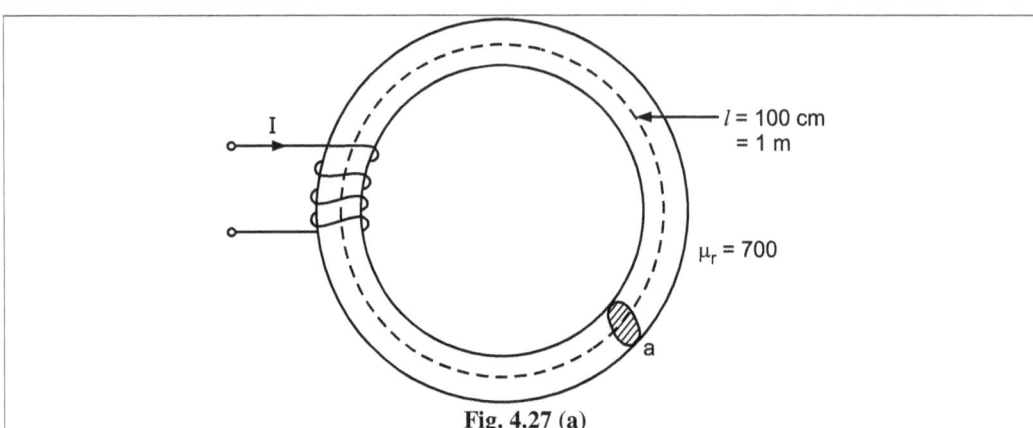

Fig. 4.27 (a)

where $S = \dfrac{l}{\mu_o \mu_r a}$

$$\phi = \dfrac{NI}{l} \times \dfrac{\mu_o \mu_r a}{1}$$

$$2 \times 10^{-3} = \dfrac{700 \times I \times 4\pi \times 10^{-7} \times 900 \times 50.2654 \times 10^{-4}}{1}$$

I = 0.5025 Amp.

(ii) Air gap of 1 mm cut in the ring :

length of iron l_i = l – length of air gap

$= l - l_{ag} = 1 - 1 \times 10^{-3}$

$= 99.9 \times 10^{-2}$ m

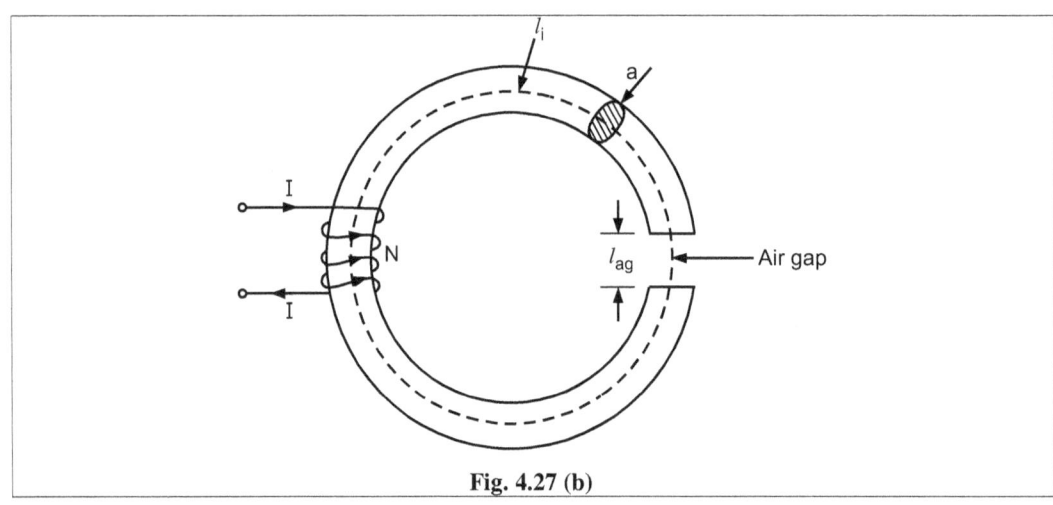

Fig. 4.27 (b)

Total reluctance $\qquad S_T = S_i + S_{ag} = \dfrac{l_i}{\mu_o \mu_r a} + \dfrac{l_{ag}}{\mu_o a}$

For air gap, $\qquad \mu_r = 1$

$$S_T = \frac{99.9 \times 10^{-2}}{4\pi \times 10^{-7} \times 900 \times 50.26 \times 10^{-4}} + \frac{0.001}{4\pi \times 10^{-7} \times 50.26 \times 10^{-4}}$$

$$S_T = 175748.1 + 158331.62$$

$$= 334079.72 \text{ AT/Wb}$$

$$\phi = \frac{NI}{S} = 2 \times 10^{-3} = \frac{700 \times I}{334079.72}$$

$$I = 0.9545 \text{ Amp.}$$

Example 4.14 :

An iron ring of mean length 50 cm has air gap of 1 mm and a winding of 200 turns. If the relative permeability of iron is 300, find the flux density when current of 1 Amp. flows through the coil.

Solution :

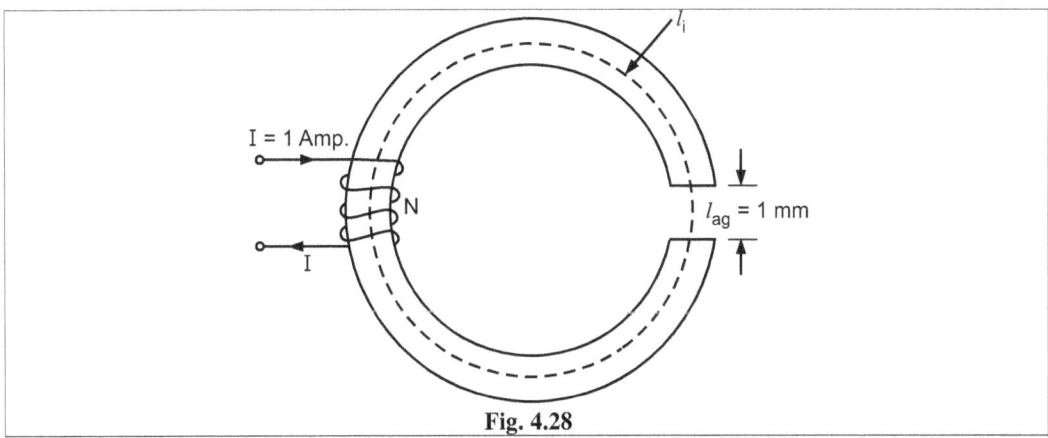

I = 1 Amp. N l_{ag} = 1 mm

Fig. 4.28

Total length $= 50 \text{ cm} = 0.5 \text{ m}$

$$= 50 \times 10^{-2} \text{m}$$

Length of air gap $l_{ag} = 1 \text{ mm} = 1 \times 10^{-3} \text{m} = 0.001 \text{ m}$

Length of iron path $= 0.5 - 0.001 = 0.499 \text{ m}.$

Total reluctance = Reluctance of iron path + Reluctance of air gap

$$S_T = \frac{l_i}{\mu_o \mu_r a} + \frac{l_{ag}}{\mu_o a}$$

$$NI = \phi \cdot S_T = \phi \left[\frac{l_i}{\mu_o \mu_r a} + \frac{l_{ag}}{\mu_o} \right]$$

$$= \frac{\phi}{a}\left[\frac{l_i}{\mu_o\mu_r} + \frac{l_{ag}}{\mu_o}\right]$$

$$= B\left[\frac{l_i}{\mu_o\mu_r} + \frac{l_{ag}}{\mu_o}\right]$$

$$= B\left[\frac{0.499}{4\pi \times 10^{-7} \times 300} + \frac{0.001}{4\pi \times 10^{-7}}\right]$$

$$200 \times I = B[1323.63 + 795.77]$$

$$B = \frac{200 \times 1}{2119.40} = 0.094 \text{ Tesla}$$

Example 4.15 :

A ring has mean diameter of 21 cm and cross-sectional area of 10 cm². The ring is made up of semi-circular section of cast iron and cast steel with each joint having a reluctance equal to an air gap of 0.2 mm. Find the ampere-turns required to produce a flux of 8×10^{-4} Wb. The relative permeabilities of cast steel and cast iron are 800 and 166 respectively.

Solution :

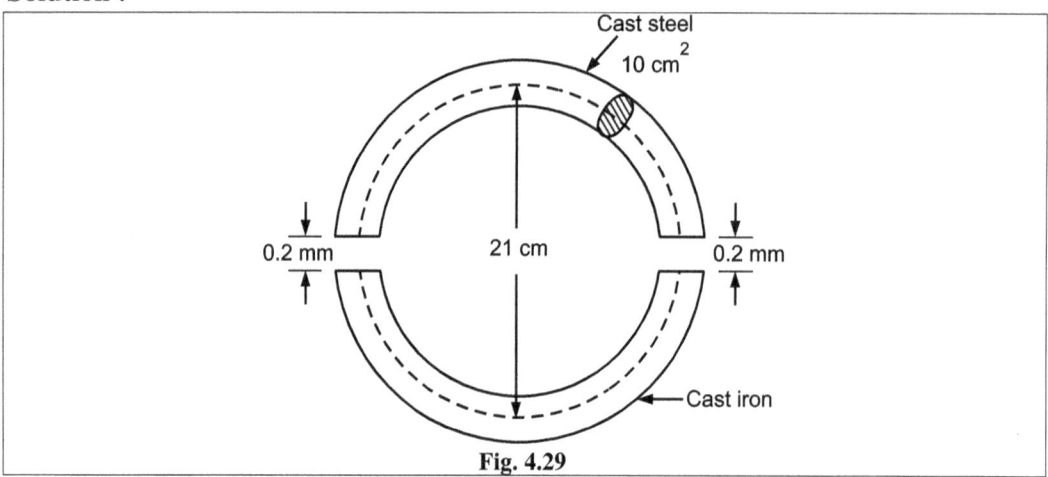

Cast steel
10 cm²
0.2 mm   21 cm   0.2 mm
Cast iron

Fig. 4.29

The total reluctance of a given arrangement

$$S_T = S_{iron} + S_{steel} + S_g + S_g$$

∴   Length of the iron ring $= \pi d$

$$= 65.973 \text{ cm.}$$

∴   Total air gap length $= 2 l_g$

$$= 0.4 \text{ mm}$$

∴   length of iron $=$ length of steel

$$= \frac{65.973 \times 10^{-2} - 0.4 \times 10^{-2}}{2}$$

$$\therefore S_T = \frac{l_{iron}}{\mu_0 \mu_{r1} a} + \frac{l_{steel}}{\mu_0 \mu_{r2} a} + 2 \frac{l_g}{\mu_0 \, a}$$

$$= \frac{1}{\mu_0 \times a} \left[\frac{l_{iron}}{\mu_{r1}} + \frac{l_{steel}}{\mu_{r2}} + 2 \, l_g \right]$$

$$= \frac{1}{4\pi \times 10^{-7} \, 10 \times 10^{-4}} \left[\frac{0.3296}{166} + \frac{0.3296}{800} + 2 \times 0.2 \times 10^{-3} \right]$$

$$= \frac{1}{4\pi \times 10^{-7} \times 10 \times 10^{-4}} [1.9855 \times 10^{-3} + 4.12 \times 10^{-4} + 2 \times 0.2 \times 10^{-3}]$$

$$= 2226179.766 \text{ AT/Wb}$$

$$\phi = \frac{MMF}{S_T}$$

$$MMF = \phi \times S_T$$

$$= 8 \times 10^{-4} \times 2226179.766$$

$$= 1780.94 \text{ A.T.}$$

REVIEW QUESTIONS

1. An iron ring of mean length 50 cm has an air gap of 1 mm and a winding of 100 turns. If the relative permeability of iron is 300, find the flux density when a current of 1.5 A flows through the coil. Neglect fringing.   **(Ans. 0.0707T)**

2. An iron ring of mean diameter 10 cm and cross sectional area of 6 cm^2 is wound with 200 turns of wire. Calculate :
   (i) Current required to produce a flux of 0.6 mWb in the ring if the relative permeability of iron is 2000.
   (ii) If a radial saw cut of 2 mm width is made in the iron ring find new value of current required to produce the same flux in the air gap. Neglect fringing and leakage.   **(Ans. (i) 625 A, (ii) 14.2 A)**

3. An iron ring of 50 cm mean circumference has a cross-sectional area of 10 cm^2 and has winding of 800 turns on it. The ring has an air gap of 1 mm. It is observed that a current of 3.18 A in the winding produces a flux density of 1.2 T in the air gap. Calculate the (i) relative permeability of iron, (ii) inductance of the coil.
   (Ans. : (i) 300, (ii) 0.30184)

4. A magnetic ring has mean circumference of 1.5 m and is of 0.01 m^2 in cross section. It is wound with 200 turns. A saw cut of 4 mm wide is made in the ring. Calculate the magnetizing current required to produce a flux of 0.8 mWb in the air gap. Assume relative permeability as 400 and leakage coefficient as 1.3.
   (Ans. : 3.207 A)

5. A magnetic circuit has mean length of iron as 50 cm and air gap of 1 mm. It is wound with a coil of 500 turns carrying current of 3 Amp. The cross-sectional area of the core is 10 cm². The m.m.f. required for air gap is 60% of the total m.m.f. Calculate : (i) magnetic flux, (ii) total reluctance, (iii) relative permeability of iron.   **(Ans. : (i) 1.131×10^{-4} Wb, (ii) 1.145×10^7 AT/Wb, (iii) 1334.5)**

6. A circular ring of 20 cm in diameter has an air gap of 1 mm cut in it. The cross-sectional area of ring is 3.6 cm². Calculate the current required to produce the flux of 5 mWb in the air gap. Assume relative permeability of iron to be 650 and number of turns of coil as 500.   **(Ans. 43.47A)**

7. A coil of 500 turns is wound on the central limb of a cast iron frame as shown below :

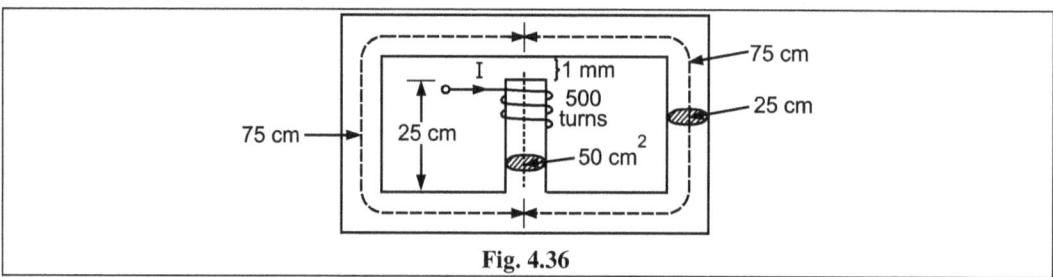

Fig. 4.36

Calculate the current required to produce flux of 2.5 mWb in the air gap, if the relative permeability of cast iron is 1000.   **(Ans : 11592 Amp)**

8. Two long straight parallel conductors placed 1.5 m apart in air, carry current of I_1 and I_2 ampere in the same direction. The magnetic field strength at a point midway between the conductors is 7.5 A/m. If the force on each conductor per metre length is 2.5×10^{-4} N, calculate the values of I_1 and I_2.

          (Ans. : (i) $I_1 = 64.44$ A, (ii) $I_2 = 29.1$ A)

9. A series magnetic circuit consists of three sections :

(i) Length of 80 mm with cross-sectional area 60 mm². (ii) Length of 70 mm with cross-sectional area 80 mm², (iii) An air gap of length 0.5 mm with cross-sectional area 60 mm².

For sections (i) and (ii) if material having magnetic characteristics given by following table :

H (A/m)	100	210	340	500	800	1500
B (T)	0.2	0.4	0.6	0.8	1	1.2

Calculate (i) the current required in a coil of 1000 turns wound on section, (ii) to produce a flux density of 0.7 T in the air gap.   **(Ans. : 82.9175 A)**

Chapter 6

SINGLE-PHASE TRANSFORMER

6.1 INTRODUCTION

Electrical energy is generated, at a place where it is easier to get water head for hydro, oil and coal, for diesel and thermal power stations respectively. This energy is transmitted over a long distance. As the transmission of power at high voltage is always economical, therefore it is required to step up or step down the voltage as and when required. This is possible with static device called as Transformer. Transformer transfers electrical energy from a certain voltage and current levels to another voltage and current levels keeping the frequency of supply same.

Hence, transformer can be defined as the static device which transfers electrical energy from one alternating current circuit to the another with desired change in voltage or current without change in frequency.

6.2 PRINCIPLE OF WORKING

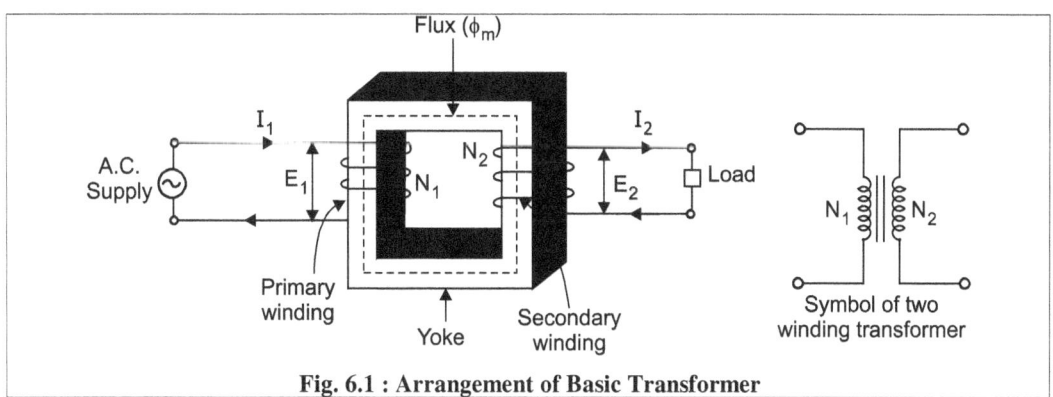

Fig. 6.1 : Arrangement of Basic Transformer

• Consider the two coils say 1 and 2 wound on simple magnetic circuit.

• These coils are insulated from each other, and there is no electrical connection between them.

• Consider N_1 and N_2 be the number of turns on coil 1 and 2 respectively.

• The coil which is connected across the supply voltage is called as primary winding.

- The coil which is delivering energy to the load is called as secondary winding.
- When the supply voltage is applied across the coil 1, the current starts flowing through it.
- This alternating current produces an alternating flux in the magnetic core.
- This alternating flux links the turns of coil 1 and hence induces a emf in it, by self induction.
- Assuming it is an ideal transformer, all flux produced by coil 1 links the turns of coil 2. Thus, induces an emf in coil 2 due to principle of mutual induction.
- Now, if the coil 2 is connected to load, the alternating current starts flowing through it, and energy will be delivered to it.

6.2.1 Transformer on D.C.

- Transformer should never be connected to direct current source. If the primary winding of the transformer is connected to a D.C. supply mains.
- The flux produced will not vary but remain constant in magnitude, therefore no emf will induce in the secondary winding except at the moment of switching.
- Also there will be no counter emf in the primary winding, hence primary will draw more current from the supply, which may damage the winding.
- Also the resistance of primary winding being small, primary draws heavy current from supply, which may damage the transformer.

6.3 CONSTRUCTION

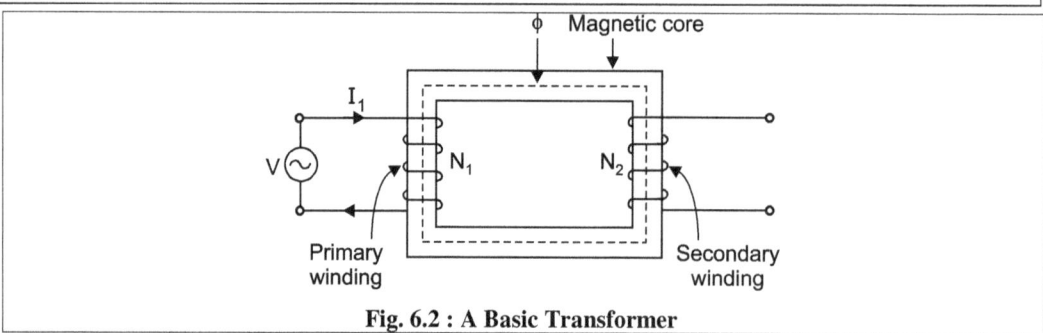

Fig. 6.2 : A Basic Transformer

As there are no rotating parts the construction of transformer is simple. It essentially consists of :

- Magnetic circuit, mainly consisting of limbs and yoke.
- Electrical circuit, consisting of windings, tappings and bushings.
- Tank consisting of cooling devices, conservators etc.

6.3.1 Magnetic Core

- It is made up of magnetic material such as high grade silicon steel.

- It is in the form of laminations with a thickness of about 0.35 to 0.5 mm.

- Vertical portion of the core on which the coils are wound are called as limbs.

- The top and bottom horizontal portion is called as yoke of the core.

- Laminations are provided in order to reduce the eddy current losses and high grade silicon steel is used to reduce the hysteresis losses.

- Laminations are insulated from each other by varnish.

- Yoke and limb laminations are usually interleaved to reduce reluctance and energy loss.

6.3.2 Windings

- In basic transformer, the primary and secondary winding is wound on the separate limbs. These are insulated from each other. They are made up of copper.

- If the two windings on separate limbs, then the flux produced by primary winding will not all link the secondary winding. Some of the flux leak out. Therefore, to reduce the leakage of flux, primary and secondary windings are placed on the same limb.

The windings may be classified as,

(i) Concentric winding,

(ii) Sandwiched winding.

Concentric winding is used in core type transformer and sandwiched winding is used in shell type transformer.

While placing the cylindrical coils concentrically around the limb, the low voltage coil is placed near to the core and high voltage coil is placed after that. It is always better to insulate the low voltage winding w.r.t. core.

6.4 TYPES OF TRANSFORMERS

Transformers are classified based on the arrangement of core and the windings. The types of transformers are as below :

(i) Core type transformer,

(ii) Shell type transformer.

6.4.1 Core Type Transformer

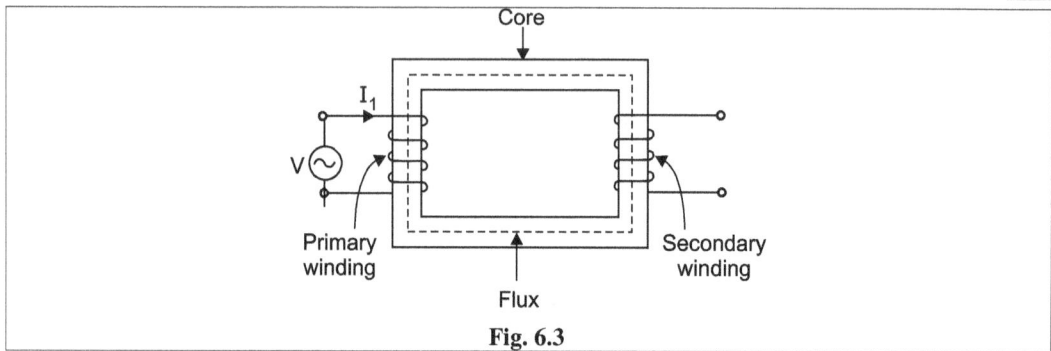

Fig. 6.3

Fig. 6.3 shows the actual arrangement of the core type transformer. The main features of the core type transformer are as follows :

- It has a single magnetic circuit.

- The coils i.e. windings used are cylindrical in form.

- The winding placed on separate limbs of the core, hence natural cooling is more effective.

- The winding surroundes major portion of the core.

- It is easy for repairing and maintenance as windings can be easily dismantled.

6.4.2 Shell Type Transformer

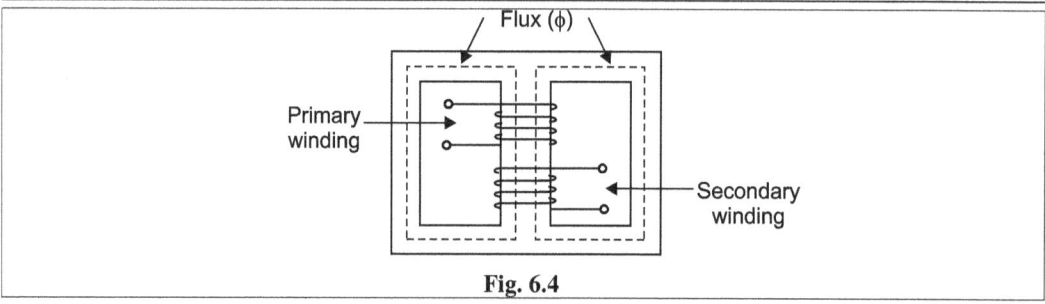

Fig. 6.4

Fig. 6.4 shows the actual arrangement of the shell type transformer. The main features of the shell type transformer are as follows :

- It has a double magnetic circuit.
- The primary and secondary windings are wound on the central limb and the outer limb provides the low reluctance path.
- The low voltage and high voltage windings are placed alternately like a sandwich. Therefore, such a winding is called as sandwich type winding.
- The core for shell type transformer is made up of U and T shape laminations.

- Natural cooling is poor as winding is surrounded by the core.
- It is difficult for repair and maintenance as winding can not be easily dismantled.
- The shell type transformer gives better support against electromagnetic forces.

6.4.3 Comparison between Core and Shell Type Transformer

Sr. No.	Core Type Transformer	Shell Type Transformer
1.	It has single magnetic circuit.	It has double magnetic circuit.
2.	Windings used in core type transformer are cylindrical in form.	Sandwich type windings are used.
3.	Core is surrounded by the winding.	The windings are surrounded by the core.
4.	It is easy for repair and maintenance.	It is difficult for repair and maintenance.
5.	Natural cooling is good.	Natural cooling is poor.

6.5 EMF EQUATION OF A TRANSFORMER

Let, N_1 : be the number of turns of primary winding

N_2 : be the number of turns of secondary winding

ϕ_m : be the maximum value of flux in weber

f   : be the supply frequency in Hz

E_1 : be the emf induced in primary winding

E_2 : be the emf induced in secondary winding

When primary winding is connected across the alternating current supply, the current starts flowing through it. This alternating current produces alternating flux in it. This alternating flux links the number of turns of primary winding, and hence emf (E_1) is induced in the primary winding due to phenomenon of self induction. Now, this flux also links the number of turns of secondary winding and hence emf (E_2) is induced in the secondary winding due to the phenomenon of mutual induction. Let us consider the flux waveform, as shown in Fig. 6.5.

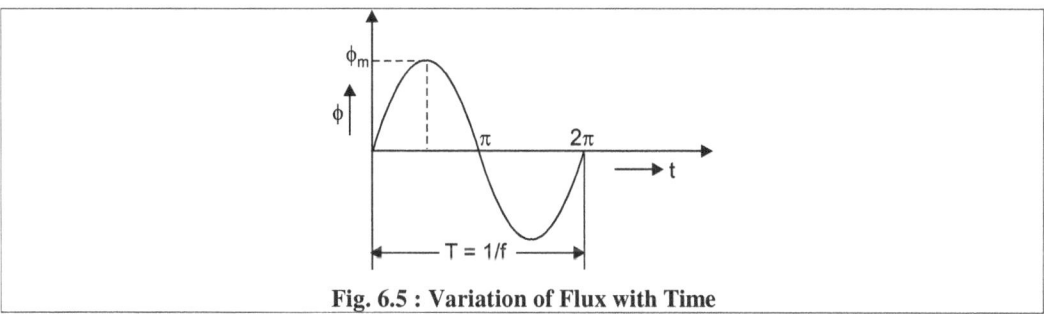

Fig. 6.5 : Variation of Flux with Time

According to Faraday's law of electromagnetic induction the average emf induced in each turn.

$$\text{Average emf induced in each turn} = \frac{d\phi}{dt}$$

where, $d\phi$: be the change in flux

dt : be the time required for change in flux

Now, considering quarter cycle of the flux waveform.

$$d\phi : \phi_m - 0 \quad \text{and} \quad dt : T/4$$

∴ Substituting this in above equation, average emf induced in each turn,

$$\frac{d\phi}{dt} = \frac{\phi_m - 0}{T/4} = \frac{4\,\phi_m}{T}$$

But,   Time period, $T = \dfrac{1}{f}$

∴ $\dfrac{d\phi}{dt} = \dfrac{4\,\phi_m}{1/f}$

$$= 4\,\phi_m f$$

But the flux considered very sinusoidally with time, the emf induced is also sinusoidal in nature.

For pure sinewave :Hence, Form Factor $= \dfrac{\text{RMS value}}{\text{Average value}} = 1.11$

∴ RMS value of emf induced in each turn,

$$= \text{Average value} \times 1.11$$

$$= 4\,\phi_m f \times 1.11$$

$$= 4.44\,\phi_m\, f \text{ volt}$$

Total emf induced in primary winding having N_1 number of turns $= 4.44\,\phi_m\, f\, N_1$ volt.

Similarly, total emf is induced in the secondary winding due to mutual induction.

$$E_2 = 4.44\,\phi_m f\, N_2 \text{ volt}$$

Alternate method for deriving emf. equation of Transformer.

The equation of alternating flux is

$$\phi = \phi_m \sin \omega t$$

If N_1 are the turns on primary winding of transformer, then

According to Faraday's law of electromagnetic induction,

$$E_1 = -N_1 \frac{d\phi}{dt}$$

∴ $E_1 = -N_1 \dfrac{d}{dt} (\phi_m \sin \omega t)$

$$\therefore \quad E_1 = -N_1 \phi_m \frac{d}{dt}(\sin \omega t)$$

$$\therefore \quad E_1 = -N_1 \phi_m \omega \cdot \cos \omega t$$

$$E_1 = N_1 \phi_m \omega (-\cos \omega t)$$

$$\therefore \quad E_1 = N_1 \phi_m \omega \sin\left(\omega t - \frac{\pi}{2}\right)$$

Comparing the above equation with $E = E_m \sin\left(\omega t - \frac{\pi}{2}\right)$

$$E_m = N_1 \phi_m \omega$$

The R.M.S. value of induced emf in primary

$$E_1 = \frac{E_m}{\sqrt{2}}$$

$$\therefore \quad E_1 = \frac{N_1 \phi_m \omega}{\sqrt{2}}$$

$$\therefore \quad E_1 = \frac{N_1 \phi_m \cdot 2\pi f}{\sqrt{2}} \qquad \qquad \dots \text{(As } \omega = 2\pi f)$$

$$\therefore \quad E_1 = 4.44 \ f \phi_m N_1 \qquad \qquad \dots \text{(I)}$$

Similarly if N_2 are the turns on secondary winding then

$$E_2 = 4.44 \ f \phi_m N_2 \qquad \qquad \dots \text{(II)}$$

Above equations (I) and (II) are called as the emf equations of transformer.

6.6 VOLTAGE AND CURRENT RATIO OF TRANSFORMER

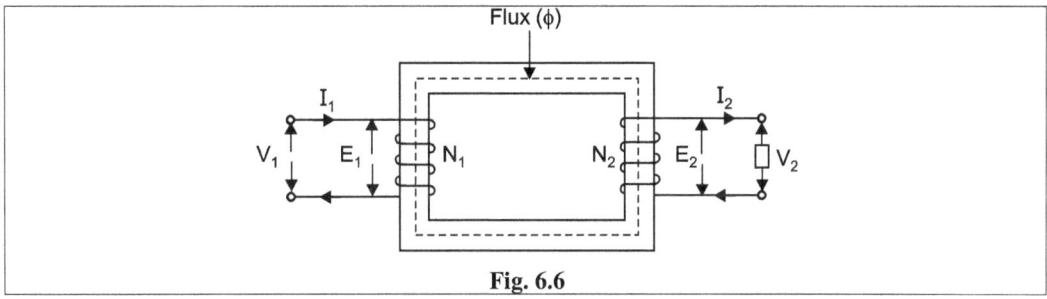

Fig. 6.6

(3) **Turns Ratio :** It is the ratio of primary number of turns to the secondary number of turns. It is given as,

$$\text{Turns ratio} = \frac{N_1}{N_2}$$

(4) Current Ratio : It is the ratio of primary current to the secondary current. It is given as,

$$\text{Current ratio} = \frac{I_1}{I_2}$$

(5) Transformation Ratio : The ratio of secondary voltage to primary voltage is equal to the ratio of secondary winding turns to the primary winding turns is termed as transformation ratio. It is denoted by K. It is given as,

$$K = \frac{V_2}{V_1} = \frac{N_2}{N_1} = \frac{E_2}{E_1}$$

6.6.1 Step Up Transformer

The transformer is said to be step up when transformation ratio (K) is greater than one or secondary voltage is greater than primary voltage.

i.e. $K > 1$ or $V_2 > V_1$ step up transformer

6.6.2 Step Down Transformer

The transformer is said to be step down, when the transformation ratio (K) is less than one or secondary voltage is less than primary voltage.

i.e. $K < 1$ or $V_2 < V_1$ step down transformer

6.6.3 One to One Transformer

The transformer is said to be one to one transformer only when the transformation ratio (K) is equal to one or secondary voltage is equal to primary voltage.

i.e. $K = 1$ or $V_2 = V_1$ one to one transformer

6.6.4 Ratings of the Transformer

(i) The primary voltage, secondary voltage, supply frequency and single phase or 3 phase is mentioned on the name plate.

(ii) **kVA rating (Kilo Volt-Ampere Rating) :** It is also mentioned on the name plate of a transformer.

If I_1 and I_2 be the rated full load current and V_1, V_2 be the rated primary and secondary voltages.

Then kVA rating of transformer,

$$\text{kVA rating} = \frac{V_1 I_1}{1000} = \frac{V_2 I_2}{1000}$$

The transformer rating is always expressed in kVA because:

The transformer is designed for a particular value of operating voltage and current for each of the winding not for particular value of out put power. The load connected across the secondary side of the transformer may be lagging, leading or unity. Thus, for the same operating voltage and current the out power can be different at different loading conditions. Hence, only the operating voltage and current are specified for transformer. This operating voltage and current are called as rated voltage and rated current of particular winding. Hence, product of rated voltage and rated current is called as 'Volt-Ampere' rating of transformer. In large transformer it is expressed in kVA i.e. Volt-Ampere devided by 1000.

SOLVED EXAMPLES

Example 6.1 :

A 3000 V/200 V, 50 Hz, single phase transformer is built on a core having an effective cross sectional area of 120 cm^2 and 60 turns on the secondary winding. Calculate (1) The value of maximum flux density, (2) The number of turns on the high voltage winding.

Solution : Given : $V_1 = 3000$ V, $V_2 = 200$ V, f = 50 Hz, $A_i = 120$ cm^2, $N_2 = 60$

(i) Using emf equation,

$$V_2 = 4.44 \, \phi f N_2 \qquad\qquad \text{As } B = \frac{\phi}{A}$$

$$V_2 = 4.44 \times B_m \times A_i \times f \cdot N_2$$

$$200 = 4.44 \times B_m \times 120 \times 10^{-4} \times 50 \times 60$$

$$B_m = 1.251 \text{ Tesla}$$

(ii) Using turns ratio and voltage ratio,

$$\frac{N_1}{N_2} = \frac{V_1}{V_2}$$

$$N_1 = \frac{V_1}{V_2} \times N_2 = \frac{3000}{200} \times 60$$

$$N_1 = 900 \text{ Turns}$$

Example 6.2 :

A 3300 V/250 V, 50 Hz, single phase transformer has to be worked at a maximum flux density of 1.1 web/m^2 in the core. The effective cross sectional area of the core is 145 cm^2. Calculate the primary and secondary turns.

Solution : Given : $V_1 = 3300$, $V_2 = 250$, f = 50 Hz, $B_m = 1.1$ Wb/m^2, $A_i = 145$ cm^2

Using the emf equation, $V_1 = 4.44 \, \phi f N_1 = 4.44 \times B_m \times A_i \times f \times N_1$

$$3300 = 4.44 \times 1.1 \times 145 \times 10^{-4} \times 50 \times N_1$$

$$N_1 = 931.966 \cong 932 \text{ Turns}$$

Now, using voltage and turns ratio equation,

$$\frac{V_1}{V_2} = \frac{N_1}{N_2} = \frac{3300}{250} = \frac{931.966}{N_2}$$

$$\therefore \qquad N_2 = 70.60 \cong 71 \text{ Turns}$$

Example 6.3 :

A 80 kVA, 6000 V/ 400 V, 50 Hz single phase transformer has 80 turns on the secondary winding. Calculate (i) the maximum flux in the core, (ii) the primary turns, (iii) primary and secondary current.

Solution : Given : 80 kVA, V_1 = 6000, V_2 = 400 V, f = 50 Hz, N_2 = 80

(i) Using emf equation,

$$V_2 = 4.44 \, \phi_m \, f \, N_2$$

$$400 = 4.44 \, \phi_m \times 50 \times 80$$

$$\therefore \qquad \phi_m = 22.522 \text{ m Wb}$$

(ii) Using turns ratio and voltage ratio,

$$\frac{V_1}{V_2} = \frac{N_1}{N_2}$$

$$N_1 = \frac{V_1}{V_2} \times N_2 = \frac{6000}{400} \times 80 = 1200$$

(iii) $\qquad$ Primary current $= \dfrac{kVA \times 1000}{V_1}$

$$= \frac{80 \times 1000}{6000} = 13.33 \text{ Amp.}$$

Secondary current $= \dfrac{kVA \times 1000}{V_2}$

$$= \frac{80 \times 1000}{400} = 200 \text{ Amp.}$$

Example 6.4 :

The voltage per turn of a single phase transformer is 1.1 V. When the primary winding is connected to 230 V, 50 Hz, A.C. supply, the secondary voltage is found to be 500 V. Find (i) primary and secondary turns, (ii) core area if the flux density is 1.2 T.

Solution : Given : voltage/turn = 1.1, V_1 = 230 Volt, f = 50 Hz, V_2 = 500 V

(i)   Voltage/turn = 1.1

$\therefore$ $\dfrac{V_1}{N_1}$ = 1.1

$N_1 = \dfrac{V_1}{1.1}$ = 209.09 Turns

Secondary turns : $\dfrac{V_1}{V_2} = \dfrac{N_1}{N_2}$

$\therefore$ $N_2 = \dfrac{V_2}{V_1} \times N_1 = \dfrac{500}{230} \times 209.09$ = 454.545 $\cong$ 455

(ii) Core area if flux density is 1.2 T, using emf equation :

$$V_1 = 4.44 \, \phi_m \, f \, N_1$$
$$V_1 = 4.44 \, B_m \times A_i \times f \times N_1$$
$$230 = 4.44 \times 1.2 \times A_i \times 50 \times 209.09$$
$$A_i = 4.129 \times 10^{-3} \text{ m}^2$$

Example 6.5 :

A 6600 V/220 V, 50 Hz, step down single phase transformer has 1500 turns on its primary side. Find (i) the secondary turns, (ii) effective cross sectional area of its core if the maximum flux density is 1.2 Tesla.

Solution : Given : V_1 = 6600 V, V_2 = 220 V, f = 50 Hz, N_1 = 1500, B_{max} = 1.2 Tesla.

(i) Using transformation ratio,

$$\dfrac{V_2}{V_1} = \dfrac{N_2}{N_1} = K$$

$\therefore$ $\dfrac{V_2}{V_1} = \dfrac{N_2}{N_1}$

$\therefore$ $N_2 = \dfrac{V_2}{V_1} \times N_1$

$\therefore$ $N_2 = \dfrac{220}{6600} \times 1500 = 50$

(ii) Using emf equation,

$$V \cong E_1 = 4.44 \, \phi_m \, f \, N_1$$

$$6600 = 4.44 \, B_m \times A_i \times f \times N_1$$

$\therefore$ $A_i = \dfrac{6600}{4.44 \times 1.2 \times 50 \times 1500}$

$= 16.516 \times 10^{-3} \text{ m}^2$

Example 6.6 :

A 10 kVA, 3300/240 V, single phase, 50 Hz transformer has a core area of 300 sq. cm. The flux density is 1.3 tesla. Calculate (1) Number of primary turns, (2) Number of secondary turns (3) Primary full load current.

Solution :
$$\text{Rating} = 10\,\text{kVA}$$
$$= 10 \times 1000\,\text{VA}$$
$$V_1 = 3300\,\text{V},\quad V_2 = 240\,\text{V}$$
$$A = 300\,\text{cm}^2 = 300 \times 10^{-4}\,\text{m}^2$$
$$B_m = 1.3\,\text{T},\quad f = 50\,\text{Hz}$$

find
$$N_1, N_2 \text{ and } I_{1\,(F.L).}$$

$$E_1 = 4.44\,f\,\phi_m\,N_1$$
$$E_1 = 4.44\,f\,(B_m \cdot A) \cdot N_1$$
$$3300 = 4.44 \times 50\,(1.3 \times 300 \times 10^{-4}) \cdot N_1$$

$\therefore$
$$N_1 = \frac{3300}{4.44 \times 50 \times 1.3 \times 300 \times 10^{-4}}$$

$\therefore$
$$\boxed{N_1 = 381.15 \cong 381\,\text{Turns}}$$

$$\text{using } \frac{E_2}{E_1} = \frac{N_2}{N_1}$$

$\therefore$
$$N_2 = \frac{E_2}{E_1} \times N_1 = \frac{240}{3300} \times 381 = 27.71\,\text{Turns}$$

$$\text{Full load primary current } (I_1) = \frac{kVA \times 1000}{\text{primary voltage } (V_1)}$$

$$= \frac{10 \times 1000}{3300} = 3.03\,\text{A}$$

6.7 CONCEPT OF IDEAL TRANSFORMER

An Ideal transformer is one whose windings have no ohmic resistances so there will be no copper losses in windings and no losses taking place in the core. The output power will be equal to Input power, so efficiency of Ideal transformer is always 100% and regulation is 0%. This is a imaginary transformer which has purely Inductive coils wound on a loss free core.

Comparison between Ideal and Practical Transformer

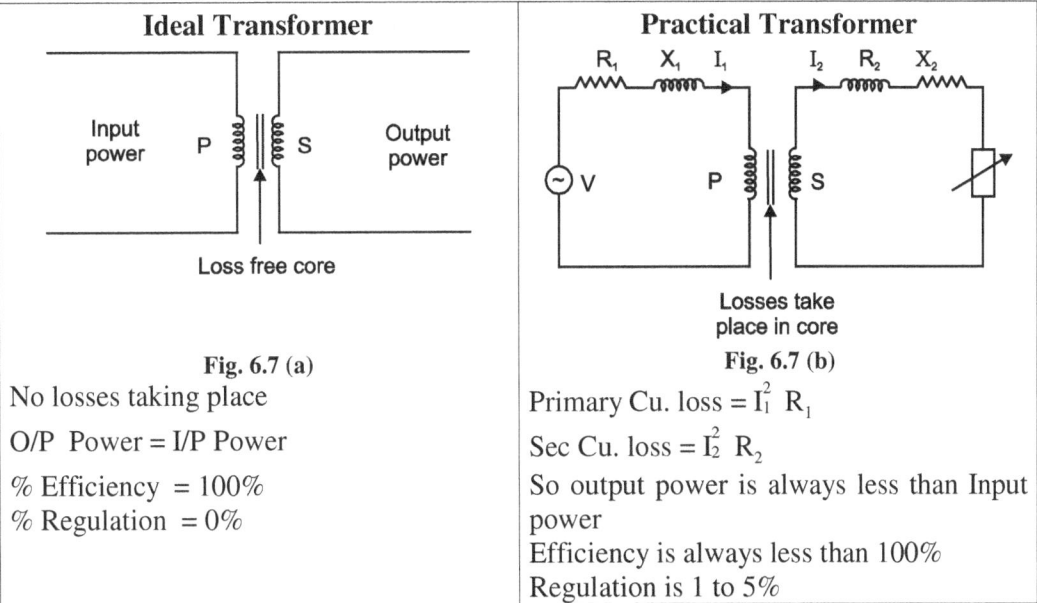

Ideal Transformer	Practical Transformer
Fig. 6.7 (a)	Fig. 6.7 (b)
No losses taking place	Primary Cu. loss = $I_1^2\, R_1$
O/P Power = I/P Power	Sec Cu. loss = $I_2^2\, R_2$
% Efficiency = 100%	So output power is always less than Input power
% Regulation = 0%	Efficiency is always less than 100%
	Regulation is 1 to 5%

6.7.1 Referred Values

Analysis of the transformer becomes simplified if the parameters are transferred to any one side i.e. either primary side or secondary side.

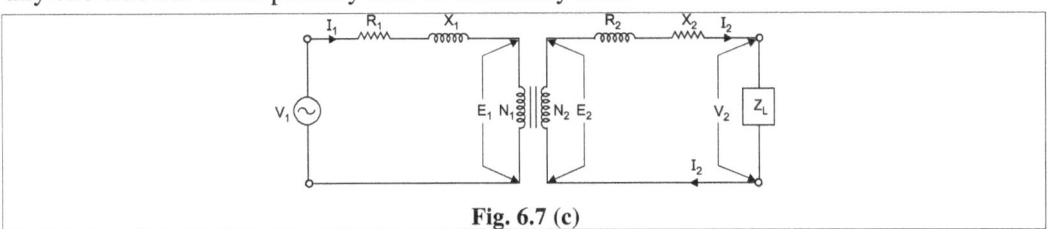

Fig. 6.7 (c)

Let, R_1 : be the resistance of primary winding

R_2 : be the resistance of secondary winding

X_1 : be the inductive reactance of primary winding due to leakage flux.

X_2 : be the inductive reactance of secondary winding due to leakage flux.

When the resistance is transferred to primary side from secondary side, then equivalent resistance of the winding.

$$R_{1e} = R_1 + R_2'$$

where, R_2': the transferred parameter to primary side.

$\therefore$

$$R_2' = \frac{R_2}{K^2} \quad \text{where K : transformation ratio.}$$

hence,
$$R_{1e} = R_1 + \frac{R_2}{K^2}$$

Similarly, if inductive reactance is transferred to primary side from secondary side its equivalent inductive reactance.

$$X_{1e} = X_1 + X_2' = X_1 + \frac{X_2}{K^2}$$

On the similar line the equivalent resistance and inductive reactance referred to secondary side.

$$R_{2e} = R_1' + R_2 = K^2 R_1 + R_2$$
$$X_{2e} = X_1' + X_2 = K^2 X_1 + X_2$$

Example 6.7 :

A 39 kVA transformer with ratio of 2200/240 V has primary winding resistance of 1.15 Ω and secondary winding resistance of 0.015 ohms. Calculate total resistance referred to primary side. Also calculate total copper loss.

Solution : Total resistance referred to primary side,

$\therefore$ $\qquad\qquad R_{1e} = R_1 + R_2' = R_1 + R_2/K^2$

$\therefore$ $\qquad\qquad K = \dfrac{V_2}{V_1} = \dfrac{240}{2200} = 0.109$

$\therefore$ $\qquad\qquad R_{1e} = 1.15 + \dfrac{0.0155}{(0.109)^2} = 2.452\ \Omega$

$\therefore$ $\qquad\qquad$ Total copper loss $= I_1^2\ R_{1e}$

$\therefore$ $\qquad\qquad$ Rated amount $I_1 = \dfrac{kVA \times 1000}{V_1} = \dfrac{39 \times 1000}{2200} = 17.727$ A

$\therefore$ $\qquad\qquad$ Total copper loss $= (17.727)^2 \times 2.452 = 770.556$ watt

---

6.8 LOSSES IN A TRANSFORMER

Since, the transformer is a static device and not a rotating machine, therefore friction and windage losses are not present. The losses which takes place in a transformer are of two types : (i) Iron losses or core losses (constant losses), (ii) Copper losses (variable losses).

6.8.1 Iron Losses

The loss occurs due to the alternating flux in the transformer core. These losses consist of : (a) hystersis loss, (b) eddy current loss.

These losses remains constant at any load condition.

(a) Hystersis Losses : When transformer core is subjected to a magnetic field, the molecules in the material are forced to get aligned in the direction of applied magnetic field. If the applied magnetic field is alternating in nature then, the molecules are forced to change the directions with the same frequency of applied magnetic field. But the molecules are very much reluctant to change their direction.

Hence, some energy is required in order to change their direction as per the applied alternating magnetic field. This loss of energy is called as hystersis loss. It is dissipated in the form of heat.

It is given by empirical formula as,

Hysteresis loss, $W_h = \eta \, B_{max}^{1.6} \, f. \, v. \, \text{watt}$

where, η :   be the Stenmitz constant

B_{max} :   be the maximum flux density in the core.

f :   be the frequency of alternating flux

v :   be the volume of core material.

(b) Eddy Current Losses : Due to the linking of alternating flux to transformer core, emf get induced in the transformer core. It gives rise to circulating, current in the core. These circulating currents are called as eddy currents. Now the every path of circulating current in the core has some resistance which causes the loss of energy. The total loss of energy due to the total eddy current is called as eddy current loss. It is also dissipated in the form of heat. It is also given by an empirical formula.

Eddy current loss $= \; K_e \, B_{max}^2 \; f^2 \, t^2 \, v \; \text{watt}$

where, K_e :   be the constant depending on the resistivity of core material

B_{max} :   be the maximum flux density

f :   be the frequency of alternating flux

t :   be the thickness of the lamination of the core

v :   be the volume of core material

The flux density in the core remains practically constant from no load to full load as well as supply frequency also remains constant therefore iron losses are also called as constant losses.

6.8.2 Copper Losses

The loss occurs in the primary and secondary windings due to resistance of primary and secondary winding.

Let I_1 and I_2 : the primary and secondary current.

R_1 and R_2 : the primary and secondary winding resistances.

$\therefore$ Hence,   Total copper loss $= \; I_1^2 \, R_1 + I_2^2 \, R_2$

$\therefore$ If the parameters are referred to primary side then total copper loss $= I_1^2 \, R_{1e}$

where, R_{1e} : equivalent resistance referred to primary side

and if parameters are referred to secondary side, the total copper loss $= I_2^2 \, R_{2e}$

where, R_{2e} : equivalent resistance referred to secondary side.

6.9 EFFICIENCY AND REGULATION OF A TRANSFORMER

Efficiency of a Transformer : It is the ratio of output power to the input power in a transformer.

$$\therefore \quad \text{Transformer efficiency, } \eta = \frac{\text{Output power}}{\text{Input power}}$$

$$= \frac{\text{Output power}}{\text{Output power + Losses}}$$

Output power of a transformer $= V_2 I_2 \cos \phi_2$

Losses in the transformer $= `W_i + W_c = W_i + I_2^2 \, R_{2e}$

where, W_i : the iron loss   and W_c : the copper loss

$$\eta = \frac{V_2 \, I_2 \cos \phi_2}{V_2 I_2 \cos \phi_2 + W_i + I_2^2 R_{2e}}$$

where, $V_2 \cdot I_2$ be the VA rating of transformer

Hence, for any loading condition,

$$\eta = \frac{x \cdot (\text{VA rated}) \cos \phi_2}{x \, (\text{VA rated}) \cos \phi_2 + W_i + x^2 \, W_c}$$

where, x be the degree of loading.

6.9.1 Condition for Maximum Efficiency

The efficiency of a transformer is given as,

$$\eta = \frac{V_2 \, I_2 \cos \phi_2}{V_2 \, I_2 \cos \phi_2 + W_i + I_2^2 \, R_{2e}}$$

From the above equation, the efficiency changes as the load current i.e. I_2 changes. Therefore, differentiating above equation with respect to I_2

$$\frac{d\eta}{dI_2} = \frac{(V_2 I_2 \cos \phi_2 + W_i + I_2^2 R_{2e}) \, V_2 \cos \phi_2 - V_2 I_2 \cos \phi_2 \, (V_2 \cos \phi_2 + 2I_2 R_{2e} + 0)}{(V_2 I_2 \cos \phi_2 + W_i + I_2^2 R_{2e})^2}$$

For maximum efficiency, $\dfrac{d\eta}{dI_2} = 0$

$$\therefore \quad \frac{(V_2 I_2 \cos \phi_2 + W_i + I_2^2 R_{2e}) \cdot V_2 \cos \phi_2 - V_2 I_2 \cos \phi_2 \, (V_2 \cos \phi_2 + 2I_2 R_{2e} + 0)}{(V_2 \, I_2 \cos \phi_2 + W_i + I_2^2 R_{2e})^2} = 0$$

$\therefore \ (V_2 I_2 \cos \phi_2 + W_i + I_2^2 \, R_{2e}) \, V_2 \cos \phi_2 - V_2 \, I_2 \cos \phi_2 \, (V_2 \cos \phi_2 + 2I_2 \, R_{2e} + 0) = 0$

$\therefore \ (V_2 I_2 \cos \phi_2 + W_i + I_2^2 \, R_{2e}) \, V_2 \cos \phi_2 = V_2 \, I_2 \cos \phi_2 \, (V_2 \cos \phi_2 + 2I_2 R_{2e})$

$\therefore \ V_2 I_2 \cos \phi_2 + W_i + I^2 R_{2e} = V_2 \, I_2 \cos \phi_2 + 2I_2^2 \, R_{2e}$

$$\therefore \qquad W_i + I_2^2 \ R_{2e} = 2I_2^2 \ R_{2e}$$

$$\therefore \qquad I_2^2 \ R_{2e} = W_i$$

$$\text{Copper loss} = \text{Iron loss}$$

Hence, efficiency of the transformer is maximum when copper loss is equal to iron loss. The variation of graph of efficiency against the load current is shown below.

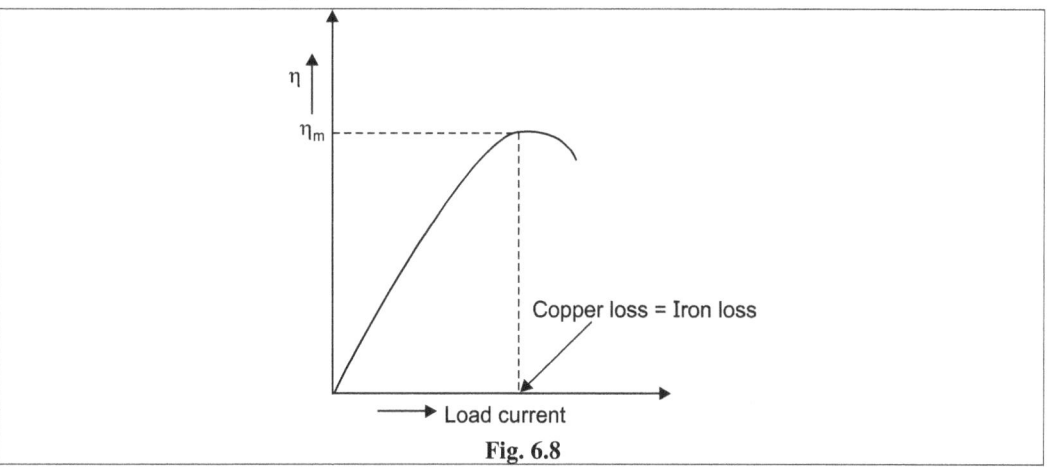

Fig. 6.8

6.9.2 Load Current and kVA at Maximum Efficiency

$$\text{Load current at maximum efficiency} = I_{2 \ (F.L.)} \sqrt{\dfrac{W_i}{W_{c \ (F.L.)}}}$$

where, I_2 :   be the full load current

  W_i :   be the iron losses

  $W_{c \ (F.L.)}$:   be the full load copper losses.

$$\text{kVA at Maximum Efficiency} = \text{kVA rating} \sqrt{\dfrac{W_i}{W_{c(F.L.)}}}$$

6.10 REGULATION OF TRANSFORMER

Load connected to the secondary of transformer operates at constant voltage. As soon as the current starts flowing through the load, the terminal voltage changes, because of the internal impedance of the transformer. Hence, the voltage regulation of transformer is defined as the variation of secondary voltage from no load to full load expressed as percentage of no load voltage, the primary voltage being assumed constant.

$$\therefore \qquad \text{Voltage regulation} = \dfrac{\text{No load voltage} - \text{Full load voltage}}{\text{No load voltage}}$$

$\therefore$ % regulation $= \dfrac{V_{2\,(N.L.)} - V_{2\,(F.L.)}}{V_{2\,(N.L.)}} \times 100$

$$= \dfrac{E_2 - V_2}{E_2} \times 100$$

Percentage of voltage regulation can also be expressed as,

$$= \dfrac{I_2\,R_{2e}\,\cos\phi \pm I_2\,X_{2e}\,\sin\phi}{V_{2\,(N.L.)}}$$

where, I_2 : the rated secondary current

$\qquad V_2$: the no load voltage

$\qquad R_{2e}$: the equivalent resistance referred to the secondary side

$\qquad X_{2e}$: the equivalent reactance referred to the secondary side

$\qquad \cos\phi$: the load power factor

It can also be expressed as,

$$\% \text{ of voltage regulation } = \dfrac{I_1 R_{1e}\,\cos\phi \pm I_1 \times X_{1e}\,\sin\phi}{V_1}$$

where, I_1 : be the rated primary current

$\qquad R_{1e}$: be the equivalent resistance referred to primary

$\qquad X_{1e}$: be the equivalent reactance referred to primary

$\qquad V_1$: be the primary voltage.

The voltage regulation may be positive or negative. In case of leading power factor i.e. capacitive load, the regulation is negative. In case of lagging power factor i.e. inductive load, the regulation is positive.

6.11 EFFICIENCY & REGULATION BY DIRECT LOADING METHOD

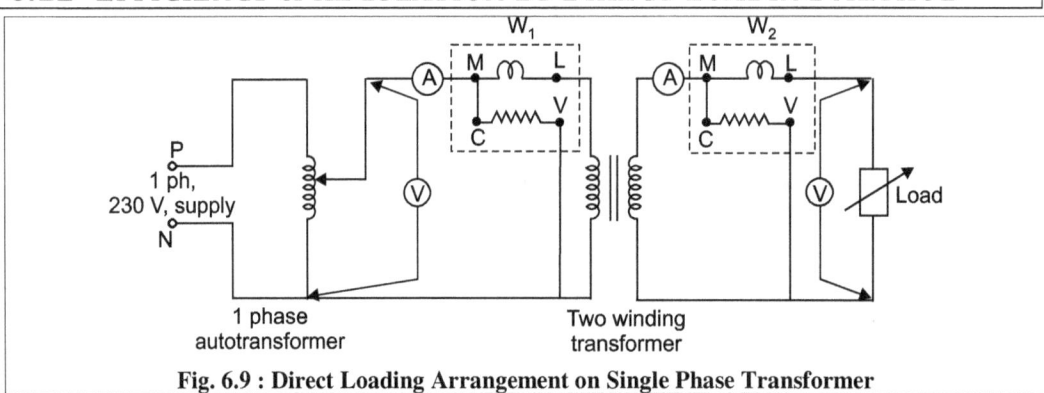

Fig. 6.9 : Direct Loading Arrangement on Single Phase Transformer

The efficiency and regulation of transformer can be found by direct loading method. The circuit diagram for direct loading method is as shown in Fig. 6.9.

Theory : For finding the efficiency and regulation of transformer, a single phase transformer is connected across the supply as shown in the above.

The primary winding is connected across the supply and the secondary winding is connected across the variable load. The wattmeters i.e. W_1 and W_2 are inserted in the circuit diagram in order to measure the power input and power output of the transformer. Ammeters and voltmeters are used for measurement of current and voltage in the circuit. The load on transformer is varied step by step and the readings are noted down. This test is useful only for small transformer and not for large ratings transformer, because the non availability of the load. The results obtained by this test are very accurate as the transformer is directly loaded for a particular load.

Procedure :
(1) Make the connections as per the circuit diagram.
(2) At start switch OFF the load.
(3) Switch ON the supply and slowly increase the voltage with the help of auto transformer.
(4) Adjust the voltage of transformer up to its rated value.
(5) Now slowly increase the load on secondary and note down the readings of ammeter, voltmeter and wattmeter.
(6) Load the transformer upto the rated capacity of transformer or 25% more than the rated capacity.

Observation Table :

Sr. No.	I_1	V_1	W_1	I_2	V_2	W_2
1.						
2.						

Formulae :

Efficiency : Efficiency of the transformer can be calculated as, $\eta = \dfrac{W_2}{W_1} \times 100$

Voltage Regulation :

Voltage regulation of a transformer can be calculated as,

$$\% \text{ regulation } = \frac{E_2 - V_2}{E_2} \times 100$$

When the secondary is open the secondary voltage $V_2 = E_2$.

Hence, for the start when the load is switched OFF regulation of transformer is zero. The subsequent regulations are calculated by using the above formulae.

List of Formulae

1. E.M.F. equations of Transformer are

$$E_1 = 4.44 \, f \, \phi_m \, N_1$$

$$E_1 = 4.44 \, f \, (B_m . A) \, N_1$$

and
$$E_2 = 4.44 \, f \, \phi_m \, N_2$$

$$E_2 = 4.44 \, f \, (B_m . A) \, N_2$$

2. Transformation Ratio (K)

$$\frac{E_2}{E_1} = \frac{N_2}{N_1} = \frac{V_2}{V_1} = \frac{I_1}{I_2} = K$$

for step up K > 1

for step down K < 1

3. Rating of Transformer is in kVA or MVA

$$1 \, kVA = 1 \times 10^3 \, VA$$

$$1 \, MVA = 1 \times 10^6 \, VA$$

4. (a) Full load primary current (I_1) = $\dfrac{kVA \times 1000}{\text{primary voltage } (V_1)}$

(b) Full load secondary current (I_2) = $\dfrac{kVA \times 1000}{\text{secondary voltage } (V_2)}$

5.

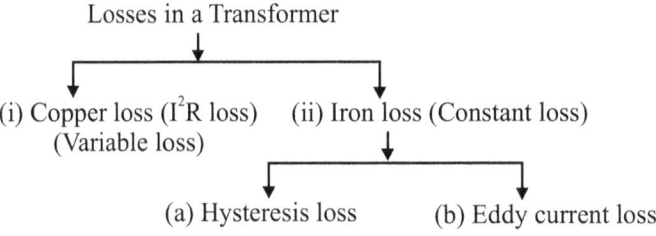

6. If the load is reduced to half then copper losses will be reduced by $\frac{1}{4}^{th}$ of full load copper losses.

7.   % Efficiency = $\dfrac{\text{Output power}}{\text{Input power}} \times 100 = \dfrac{W_2}{W_1} \times 100$

i.e. $\% \, \eta = \dfrac{V_2 \, I_2 \cdot \cos \phi}{V_2 \, I_2 \cos \phi + W_i + W_{cu}}$

At any loading

$$\% \, \eta = \frac{x \, V_2 \, I_2 \cdot \cos \phi}{x \, V_2 \, I_2 \cdot \cos \phi + W_i + (x)^2 \cdot W_{cu}}$$

where x is percentage of loading.

8. $\%\ \text{Regulation} = \dfrac{\text{No load sec. voltage} - \text{On load sec. voltage}}{\text{No load sec. voltage}} \times 100$

$\%\ \text{Regulation} = \dfrac{V_{02} - V_2}{V_{02}} \times 100$

Example 6.8 :

The iron loss of 80 kVA, 1000 V/250 V, 1 phase, 50 Hz, transformer is 500 W. The copper loss when the primary carries current of 50 A is 400 W. Find (i) Area of cross section of limb if working flux density is 1 T and there are 1000 turns on primary.

(ii) Primary and secondary full load current

(iii) Efficiency at full load and p.f. = 0.8 lag

(iv) Efficiency at 75% of full load and unity p.f.

Solution : Given : $W_i = 500$ W, kVA = 80, f = 50 Hz, 1000 V/250 V, Copper loss i.e. $W_c = 400$ W – for 50 A, flux density $(B_m) = 1$ T, $N_1 = 1000$.

(i) Using emf equation,

$$V_1 = 4.44\ \phi_m\ f\ N_1$$

$$V_1 = 4.44\ B_m \times A_i \times f \cdot N_1$$

$$1000 = 4.44 \times 1 \times A_i \times 50 \times 1000$$

$\therefore$ $A_i = 4.50 \times 10^{-3}\ \text{m}^2$

(ii)   Primary full load current $= \dfrac{\text{kVA} \times 10^3}{V_1}$

$$= \dfrac{80 \times 1000}{1000} = 80\ \text{A}$$

Secondary full load current $= \dfrac{\text{kVA} \times 10^3}{V_2}$

$$= \dfrac{80 \times 1000}{250} = 320\ \text{A}$$

(iii) Efficiency at full load and p.f. 0.8 (lag)

$$= \dfrac{x \cdot \text{kVA} \times 1000 \times \text{p.f.}}{x\ \text{kVA} \times 1000 \times \text{p.f.} + W_i + W_c\ (x)^2}$$

For 50 A loss $(W_c) = 400$ W

$\therefore$ Loss corresponding to the full load current

$\therefore$ $\dfrac{W_c \text{ on 50 A}}{W_c \text{ on F.L.}} = \dfrac{50^2}{80^2}$

$\therefore$ $$W_c \text{ on F.L.} = W_c \text{ on } 50 \text{ A} \times \left(\frac{80}{50}\right)^2$$

$$= 400 \times \left(\frac{80}{50}\right)^2$$

$$= 1024 \text{ watt}$$

$\therefore$ $$\% \eta = \frac{1 \times 80 \times 1000 \times 0.8}{0.8 \times 80 \times 1000 \times 1 + 500 + 1024} \times 100$$

$$= 97.67\%$$

(iv) Efficiency of the transformer at 75% of full load, unity p.f.

$$\% \eta = \frac{x \cdot \text{kVA} \times 1000 \times \text{p.f.}}{x \cdot \text{kVA} \times 1000 \times \text{p.f.} + W_i + x^2 W_{c \text{ (F.L.)}}} \times 100$$

$$= \frac{0.75 \times 80 \times 1000 \times 1}{0.75 \times 80 \times 1000 \times 1 + 500 + (0.75)^2 \times 1024} \times 100$$

$$= 98.23\%$$

Example 6.9 :

The iron loss of 100 kVA, 1000 V/250 V, single phase transformer, with 50 Hz, frequency is 1000 watt. The copper loss when primary carries current of 50 A is 500 watt. Calculate (i) Area of cross section of limb if working flux density is 0.9 T and primary has 1000 turns, (ii) Primary and secondary currents, (iii) Efficiency at full load and 0.8 p.f.

Solution : Given : 100 kVA, 1000 V/250 V, f = 50 Hz, W_i = 1000 watt, W_c on 50 A – 500 watt.

(i) Using emf equation of transformer,

$$V_1 = 4.44 \, \phi_m \, f \, N_1$$
$$V_1 = 4.44 \, B_m \times A_i \times f \times N_1$$
$$1000 = 4.44 \times 0.9 \times A_i \times 50 \times 1000$$

$\therefore$ $$A_i = 5 \times 10^{-3} \text{ m}^2$$

(ii)   Primary rated current $= \dfrac{\text{kVA} \times 1000}{V_1}$

$$= \frac{100 \times 1000}{1000} = 100 \text{ Amp.}$$

Secondary rated current $= \dfrac{\text{kVA} \times 1000}{V_2}$

$$= \frac{100 \times 1000}{250} = 400 \text{ Amp.}$$

(iii) Efficiency at full load and 0.8 p.f.

As W_c i.e. copper loss on 50 A – 500 W

$\therefore$ W_c on full load

$\therefore$ $$\frac{W_c \text{ on 50 A}}{W_c \text{ on F.L.}} = \frac{50^2}{100^2}$$

$\therefore$ $$W_c \text{ on full load} = W_c \text{ on 50 A} \times \left(\frac{100}{50}\right)^2$$

$$= 500 \times \left(\frac{100}{50}\right)^2 = 2000 \text{ watt}$$

$\therefore$ $$\% \eta = \frac{x \times kVA \times 1000 \times p.f.}{x \times kVA \times 1000 \times p.f. + W_i + W_{c\ (F.L.)}\ x^2} \times 100$$

$$= \frac{1 \times 100 \times 1000 \times 0.8}{1 \times 100 \times 1000 \times 0.8 + 1000 + (1)^2 \times 2000} \times 100$$

$$= 96.385\%$$

Example 6.10 :

A transformer is rated at 90 kVA at full load its copper loss is 1100 W and its iron loss is 950 W. Calculate :

   (i) Efficiency at full load, unity power factor.

  (ii) Efficiency at 60% of full load, 0.8 power factor.

 (iii) Efficiency at 75% of full load at 0.72 p.f.

 (iv) Load kVA at which maximum efficiency will occur.

  (v) Maximum efficiency at 0.8 power factor.

Solution : (i) The efficiency at full load unity power factor :

$$\% \eta = \frac{x \times kVA \times 1000 \times p.f.}{x \times kVA \times 1000 \times p.f. + W_i + x^2\ (W_{c\ (F.L.)})} \times 100$$

$$= \frac{1 \times 90 \times 1000 \times 1}{1 \times 90 \times 1000 \times 1 + 950 + (1)^2\ 1100} \times 100$$

$$= 97.77\%$$

(ii) The efficiency at 60% of full load and 0.8 p.f. 60% of full :

$$\% \eta = \frac{x \times kVA \times 1000 \times p.f.}{x \times kVA \times 1000 \times p.f. + W_i + (x^2)\ W_{c\ (F.L.)}} \times 100$$

$$= \frac{0.6 \times 90 \times 1000 \times 0.8}{0.6 \times 90 \times 1000 \times 0.8 + 950 + (0.6)^2\ 1100} \times 100$$

$$= 96.978\%$$

(iii) The efficiency at 75% of full load and 0.72 p.f. :

$$\% \, \eta = \frac{x \times kVA \times 1000 \times p.f.}{x \times kVA \times 1000 \times p.f. + W_i + x^2 \, W_{c \, (F.L.)}} \times 100$$

$$= \frac{0.75 \times 90 \times 1000 \times 0.72}{0.75 \times 90 \times 1000 \times 0.72 + 950 + (0.75)^2 \times 1100} \times 100$$

$$= 96.873\%$$

(iv) Load kVA at maximum efficiency :

$$kVA_{max} = kVA_{(F.L.)} \sqrt{\frac{W_i}{W_{c \, (F.L.)}}} = 90 \times \sqrt{\frac{950}{1100}} = 83.638 \, kVA$$

(v) Maximum efficiency at 0.8 p.f. :

$$\% \, \eta_{max} = \frac{kVA_{max} \times p.f. \times 1000}{1000 \times kVA_{max} \times p.f. + 2 \, W_i}$$

$$= \frac{83.638 \times 1000 \times 0.8}{83.638 \times 1000 \times 0.8 + 2 \times 950}$$

$$= 97.238\%$$

Example 6.11 :

A 80 kVA, 50 Hz, 400 V/11000 V, single phase transformer has an efficiency of 97.5% when supplying full load current at 0.82 power factor lagging and an efficiency of 98.5% when supplying half full load current at unity power factor. Find iron losses and copper losses corresponding to the full load current. Find the load current at maximum efficiency.

Solution : Given : 80 kVA, f = 50 Hz, 400 V/11000 V, η = 97.5% at p.f. = 0.82 and 98.5% at p.f. = 1.

The efficiency of the transformer is given as,

$$\% \, \eta = \frac{x \cdot kVA \times 1000 \times p.f.}{x \cdot kVA \times 1000 \times p.f. + W_i + x^2 \, W_{c \, (F.L.)}}$$

(i) When supplying full load,

$$0.975 = \frac{1 \times 80 \times 1000 \times 0.82}{1 \times 80 \times 1000 \times 0.82 + W_i + W_{c \, (F.L.)}}$$

$$\therefore \quad W_i + W_{c \, (F.L.)} + 65600 = \frac{80,000 \times 0.82}{0.975}$$

$$\therefore \quad W_i + W_{c \, (F.L.)} + 65600 = 67282.051$$

$$\therefore \quad W_i + W_{c \, (F.L.)} = 1682.051 \quad \quad \dots (I)$$

(ii) When supplying half load at unity p.f.

$$0.985 = \frac{0.5 \times 80 \times 1000 \times 1}{0.5 \times 80 \times 1000 \times W_i + \left(\frac{1}{2}\right)^2 W_{c(F.L.)}}$$

$$W_i + \frac{W_{c(F.L.)}}{4} + 40{,}000 = 40609.13$$

$$\therefore \quad W_i + \frac{W_{c(F.L.)}}{4} = 609.13 \quad \quad \quad ...(II)$$

Solving equations (I) and (II), we get

$$W_i = 251.48 \text{ watt}$$

$$\therefore \quad W_{c(F.L.)} = 1430.56 \text{ watt}$$

(iii) Load current at maximum efficiency :

$$I_{2\,max} = I_{2\,(F.L.)} \sqrt{\frac{W_i}{W_{c(F.L.)}}}$$

where,

$$I_{2\,(F.L.)} = \frac{80 \times 1000}{11000} = 7.272 \text{ Amp.}$$

$$I_{2\,max} = 7.272 \times \sqrt{\frac{251.48}{1430.56}} = 3.048 \text{ Amp.}$$

Example 6.12 :

A single phase transformer working at unity power factor has an efficiency of 89% at both half load and at full load of 450 watt. Determine the efficiency at 70% full load.

Solution : The efficiency of the transformer is given as,

$$\% \eta = \frac{x \times kVA \times 1000 \times p.f.}{x \times kVA \times 1000 \times p.f. + W_i + x^2 W_{c(F.L.)}}$$

(i) When supplying full load, i.e.

$$V_2 I_2 \cos \phi = 450 \text{ watt}$$

$$0.89 = \frac{450}{450 + W_i + W_{c(F.L.)}}$$

$$W_i + W_{c(F.L.)} + 450 = 505.617$$

$$\therefore \quad W_i + W_{c(F.L.)} = 55.617 \quad \quad \quad ...(I)$$

(ii) When supplying half load,

$$0.89 = \frac{225}{225 + W_i + \frac{W_{c(F.L.)}}{4}}$$

$$W_i + \frac{W_{c\,(F.L.)}}{4} = 252.80 \qquad \ldots(II)$$

Solving equations (I) and (II),

$$W_i = 18.52 \text{ watt}$$

$$W_{c\,(F.L.)} = 37.08 \text{ watt}$$

∴ The efficiency at 70% of full load

$$\% \, \eta = \frac{0.70 \times 450}{0.70 \times 450 + 18.52 + (0.7)^2 \times 37.08} \times 100$$

$$= 89.567\%$$

Example 6.13 :

A 20 kVA, 3300 V/220 V, 50 Hz, single phase transformer has iron loss 200 W and copper loss at full load 400 W. Find the efficiency of the transformer at half load at 0.8 p.f. lagging. Also find the maximum efficiency and load at which it occurs.

Solution : Given : 20 kVA, 3300 V/220 V, f = 50 Hz, $W_i = 200$ W, $W_{c(F.L.)} = 400$ W,

p.f. = 0.8 lag

(i) Efficiency of the transformer is given as,

$$\% \, \eta = \frac{x \cdot kVA \times 1000 \times p.f.}{x \, kVA \times 1000 \times p.f. + W_i + x^2 \, W_{C(F.L.)}}$$

$$= \frac{0.5 \times 20 \times 1000 \times 0.8}{(0.5 \times 20 \times 1000 \times 0.8) + 200 + (0.5)^2 \, 400} \times 100$$

$$= 96.38\%$$

(ii) At maximum efficiency the iron loss = copper loss.

$$\therefore \qquad kVA_{max} = kVA_{(F.L.)} \sqrt{\frac{W_i}{W_{c\,(F.L.)}}}$$

$$= 20 \times \sqrt{\frac{200}{400}}$$

$$= \boxed{14.14 \text{ kVA}}$$

$$\therefore \; \% \text{ Maximum efficiency} = \frac{kVA_{max} \times \cos\phi \times 1000}{kVA_{max} \times p.f. \times 1000 + W_i + W_i}$$

$$= \frac{14.14 \times 1000 \times 0.8}{14.14 \times 1000 \times 0.8 + 200 + 200} \times 100$$

$$= 96.58\%$$

(iii) Load current corresponding to the maximum efficiency,

$$I_2 = I_{2\,(F.L.)} \sqrt{\frac{W_i}{W_{c\,(F.L.)}}}$$

But, $V_2 I_2 = kVA$

$$I_{2\,(F.L.)} = \frac{20 \times 1000}{220} = 90.909 \text{ A}$$

∴ $I_{2\,(m)} = 90.909 \sqrt{\frac{200}{400}} = 64.282 \text{ A}$

Example 6.14 :

50 kVA, 2200 V/220 V, 50 Hz transformer has an iron loss of 300 watt. The resistance of low and high voltage windings are 0.005 Ω and 0.5 Ω respectively. If the load p.f. is 0.8 lagging, calculate its efficiency on full load and half load.

Solution : Given : 50 kVA, 2200 V/200 V, f = 50 Hz, W_i = 300 watt, R_1 = 0.5 Ω, R_2 = 0.005 Ω, p.f. = 0.8.

(i) Efficiency of the transformer on full load,

$$\% \, \eta = \frac{x \times kVA \times 1000 \times p.f.}{x \times kVA \times 1000 \times p.f. + W_i + x^2 \, W_{c\,(F.L.)}}$$

But for full load copper losses,

$$W_c = I_1^2 \, R_1 + I_2^2 \, R_2$$

∴ $I_1 = \dfrac{kVA \times 1000}{2200} = \dfrac{50 \times 1000}{2200} = 22.727$ Amp.

∴ $I_2 = \dfrac{kVA \times 1000}{220} = \dfrac{50 \times 1000}{220} = 227.27$ Amp.

∴ $W_c = (22.727)^2 \times 0.5 + (227.27)^2 \times 0.005$

        $= 258.258 + 258.258$

        $= 516.516$ watt

∴ $\% \, \eta = \dfrac{1 \times 50 \times 1000 \times 0.8}{50 \times 1000 \times 0.8 + 300 + 516.516} \times 100$

        $= 97.99\%$

(ii) Efficiency at half load 0.8 p.f. (lagging)

$$\% \, \eta = \frac{x \, kVA \times 1000 \times p.f.}{x \, kVA \times 1000 \times p.f. + W_i + x^2 \, W_{c\,(F.L.)}} \times 100$$

$$= \frac{0.5 \times 50 \times 1000 \times 0.8}{0.5 \times 1000 \times 50 \times 0.8 + 300 + (0.5)^2 \times 516.516} \times 100$$

$$= 97.9\%$$

6.12 AUTO TRANSFORMER

An auto transformer is the one in which single winding is used as primary and secondary winding. It can be used as step up or step down transformer. The step down and step up transformers are as shown in Fig. 6.10 (a) and (b).

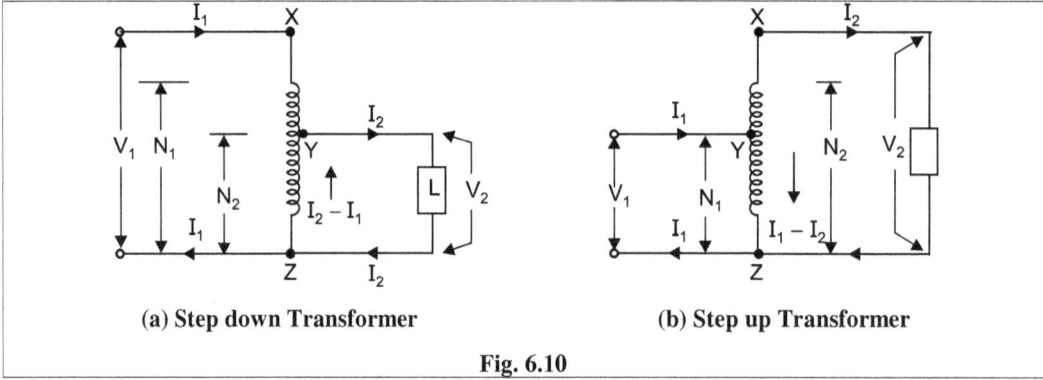

(a) Step down Transformer   (b) Step up Transformer

Fig. 6.10

As shown in Fig. 6.10 (a) the winding XZ forms the primary winding of the transformer having N_1 number of turns.

The winding YZ forms the secondary winding having N_2 number of turns. Similarly, in Fig. 6.10 (b) the portion XZ forms the secondary and YZ forms the primary winding. If the transformer losses are neglected then the same relationship holds good as in two winding transformer.

$$\text{i.e. } K = \frac{V_2}{V_1} = \frac{N_2}{N_1} = \frac{I_1}{I_2}$$

Advantages :

• Copper required in case of auto transformer is always less than the two winding transformer, it is always cheaper.

• Weight of copper required is less.

• The copper losses taking place in a transformer are less.

• Due to less copper loss, efficiency of the transformer is higher than that of two winding transformer.

• Auto transformer has better voltage regulation than that of two winding transformer.

Disadvantage :

There is always risk of electric shock, as the primary and secondary are not electrically separated.

Applications :

(1) It can be used as a starter for squirrel cage induction motor.

(2) It can be used as booster to raise the voltage in A.C. feeders.

(3) It can be used in industry as furnace transformers for getting required voltage.

(4) It can be used as dimmer for dimming the light.

6.13 DIMMERSTAT

Auto transformer can be used as dimmer for getting continuous variable supply voltage. It is also called as variac.

The core of the dimmerstat is in the form of toroid. Carbon brush is connected at the end of variable arm P. This variable arm slides over the winding. When the slider is at point x, the output voltage is zero

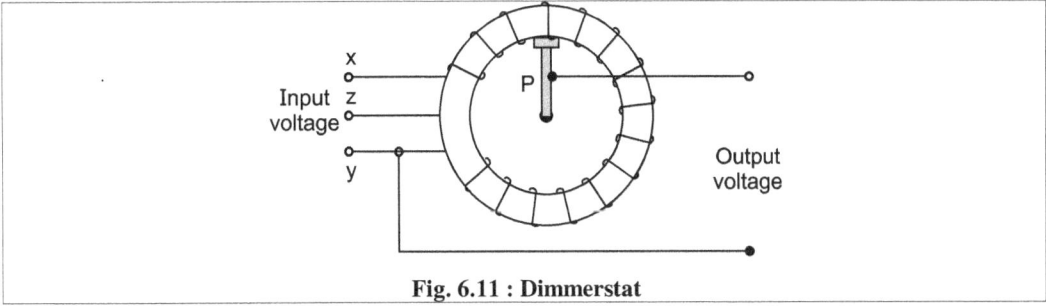

Fig. 6.11 : Dimmerstat

When it is changed towards Y the output voltage is equal to the supply voltage. If the slider is further moved from Y, then the output voltage is slightly greater than the input voltage.

Application :

It can be used in cinema theaters for dimming the light.

REVIEW QUESTIONS

1. A 5 kVA, 220 V/110 V, 50 Hz, single phase transformer has 50 turns on the secondary. Determine the number of turns in the primary the secondary and primary full load currents.   (**Ans. :** (i) 110 turns, (ii) 22.7 A, (iii) 45.45 A)

2. A 3000 V/200 V, 50 Hz single phase transformer has a cross sectional area of 150 cm² for the core. If the number of turns on the low voltage winding are 50, determine the number of turns on high voltage winding. Also calculate the maximum value of flux density in the core.   (**Ans. :** (i) 1200 turns, (ii) 0.75 Tesla)

3. Calculate the efficiency of half full and $1\frac{1}{4}$ load of a 100 kVA transformer for p.f. of (a) unity, (b) 0.8. The full load copper losses are 1000 watt and iron losses are 1000 watt.

   (**Ans. :** (i) 97.56%, (ii) 98.04%, (iii) 97.99%, (iv) 96.96%, (v) 95.23%, (vi) 93.98%)

4. A single transformer has 400 primary and 1000 secondary turns. The cross sectional area of the core is 60 cm². If the primary winding is connected to a 50 Hz, 500 V, supply. Find out (i) maximum flux density in the core, (ii) emf induced in the secondary winding.

5. A 40 kVA, 2000 V/250 V, 50 Hz, single phase transformer has efficiency of 97% at full load and 0.8 p.f. and the efficiency of 98% at half load and unity p.f. Determine

   (a) Iron and copper losses at full load, (b) Load at which copper losses are 400 W, (c) Efficiency at half load and 0.8 p.f. lagging.

   (**Ans. :** $W_i = 214.3$ W, $W_c = 775.4$ W, 28.73 kVA, 97.4%)

6. A 3 kVA, 1 phase transformer of 230/115 V has 60 turns on primary. Calculate

   1. Full load primary and secondary currents
   2. Number of turns on the secondary.
   3. Half load kVA (**Ans. :** $I_1 = 13.04$ A, $I_2 = 26.08$ A, $N_2 = 30$,

      $\frac{1}{2}$ load kVA = 1.5 kVA)

7. A 3300/110V, 50 Hz, 50 kVA transformer has full load copper loss of 1600 watt and iron loss of 1800 watt. Estimate the transformer efficiency at

   1. Full load 0.7 p.f. (lagging)
   2. Half load 0.8 p.f. (lagging)   (**Ans. :** 1. $\eta_{F.L} = 91.14\%$, 2. $\eta_{H.L.} = 90.62\%$)

UNIT - IV

Chapter 5

ELECTROMAGNETIC INDUCTION

5.1 FARADAY'S LAWS OF ELECTROMAGNETIC INDUCTION

First law: It states:

Whenever the magnetic flux linked with a circuit changes, an e.m.f. is always induced in it. OR

Whenever a conductor cuts magnetic flux, an e.m.f. is induced in that conductor.

Second law: It states:

The magnitude of the induced e.m.f. is equal to the rate of change of flux linkages.

Explanation : Suppose a coil has N turns and flux through it changes from an initial value of ϕ_1 webers to the final value of ϕ_2 webers in time t second. Then, remembering that by flux linkages means the product of number of turns and the flux linked with the coil, we have,

$$\text{Initial flux linkages} = N\phi_1$$

and
$$\text{Final flux linkages} = N\phi_2$$

$$\text{Induced e.m.f., (e)} = \frac{N\phi_2 - N\phi_1}{t} \text{ Wb/s or volt}$$

$$e = N\frac{\phi_2 - \phi_1}{t} \text{ volt}$$

Putting the above expression in its differential form, we get,

$$e = \frac{d}{dt}(N\phi) = N\frac{d\phi}{dt} \text{ volt}$$

Usually, a minus sign is given to the right side expression to signify the fact that the e.m.f. sets up current in such a direction that magnetic effect produced by it opposes the vary cause producing it. (Lene's Law)

$$\boxed{e = -N\frac{d\phi}{dt} \text{ volt}}$$

Lenz's Law : The emf induced during the process of electromagnetic induction set up a current in a particular direction such that it opposes the main cause producing it.

5.2 INDUCED E.M.F.

Induced e.m.f. can be either (i) Dynamically induced e.m.f. or (ii) Statically induced e.m.f.

5.3 DYNAMICALLY INDUCED E.M.F.

The e.m.f. induced in a conductor due to the relative physical movement with respect to steady magnetic field.

Explanation : Consider conductor A of length 'l' mtr. as shown in Fig. 5.1 within a uniform magnetic field of B Wb/m². Suppose the conductor moves through a small distance dx in dt seconds, across the right angle to the magnetic field. The area swept by the conductor is l dx.

Now,   Flux cut= Flux density × Area swept

$$= B \times l \times dx$$

$$= Bldx \text{ Wb}$$

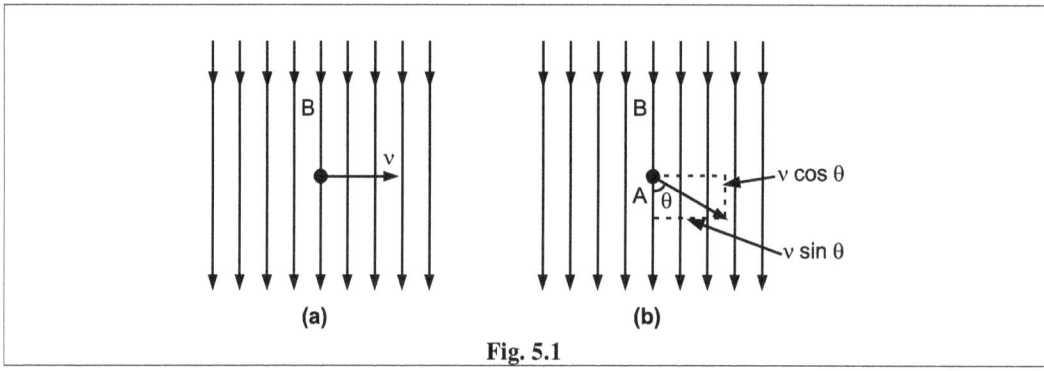

(a)   (b)

Fig. 5.1

According to Faraday's law of electromagnetic induction, e.m.f. induced in the conductor is given by,

$$e = N\frac{d\phi}{dt}$$

$$= \frac{Bldx}{dt} \qquad\qquad \dots \text{as } \frac{dx}{dt} = v$$

$$e = Blv \text{ volt}$$

If the conductor moves at an angle θ to the magnetic field then e.m.f. induced in the conductor,

$$e = Blv \sin \theta$$

The direction of the induced e.m.f. can be determined by Fleming's right hand rule.

Example : D.C. Generator.

5.4 STATICALLY INDUCED E.M.F.

The e.m.f. induced in a conductor when it links with time varying magnetic field without any relative physical movement with respect to magnetic field.

Statically induced e.m.f. is further divided into following types :

5.4.1 Self Induced E.m.f.

The e.m.f. induced in a conductor when it links with time varying magnetic field created by itself. E.m.f. induced in the primary winding of the transformer is a good example of statically self induced e.m.f.

Explanation :

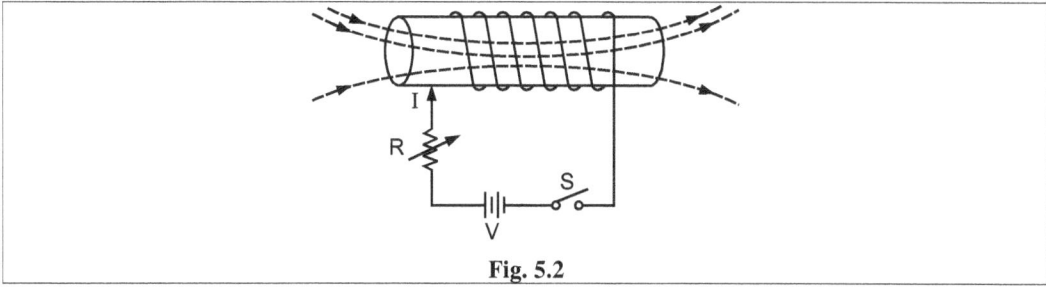

Fig. 5.2

As shown in Fig. 5.2, when the coil is carrying a current, a magnetic field is produced through the coil. If the current in the coil changes by varying the resistance, the flux linking the coil also changes. Hence the e.m.f. is induced in the coil. This is known as self induced e.m.f. The induced e.m.f. always opposes the cause producing it.

5.4.2 Mutually Induced E.m.f.

E.m.f. induced in a conductor when it links with time varying magnetic field created by some other coil.

Example : E.m.f. induced in the secondary winding of the transformer.

Explanation :

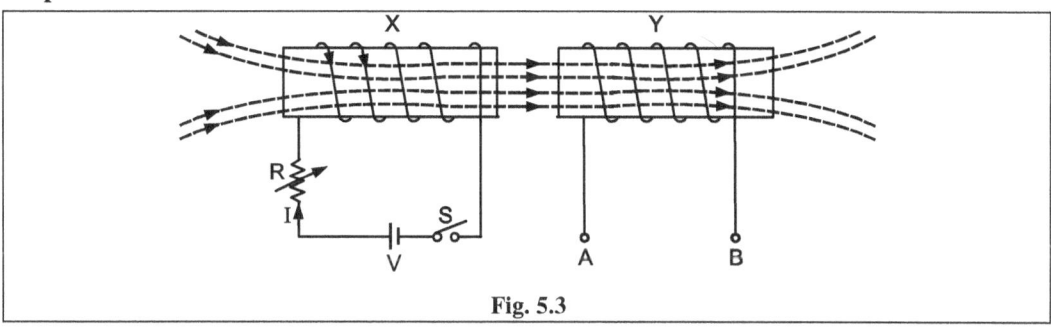

Fig. 5.3

Let us consider the two coils X and Y placed adjacent to each other as shown in Fig. 5.3.

A part of flux produced by coil X links the coil Y. If the current flowing through X changes, the flux produced by coil X also changes. Hence the flux linking to the coil Y also changes, thus e.m.f is induced in the coil Y. The e.m.f. induced in the coil Y is called as mutually induced e.m.f. The magnitude of mutually-induced e.m.f. is given by Faraday's law.

5.5 CONCEPT OF SELF INDUCTANCE (L)

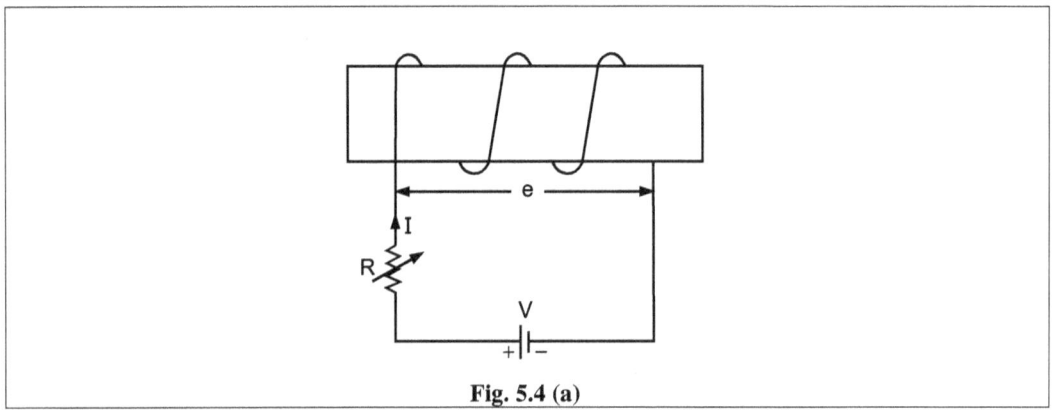

Fig. 5.4 (a)

When current in the coil increases, the changing magnetic field produced by the current links with coil, hence according to Faraday's laws an emf is induced in the coil. The emf induced in the coil opposes the cause producing it i.e. it opposes increase in current in the coil. When current in the coil decreases, the changing magnetic field again induces emf in the coil which opposes decrease in current in the coil.

From the above discussion it is clear that the induced emf always acts in the direction to oppose change in current in the coil. Actually the emf is induced in the coil and therefore you can say that the coil opposes the change in current flowing through it. This property of the coil which opposes change in current through it is called as self inductance or inductance of the coil.

5.6 EXPRESSIONS FOR SELF INDUCED EMF AND SELF INDUCTANCE

As current I is responsible to produce flux ϕ. Therefore,

$$\phi \propto I$$
$$\phi = KI$$
$$K = \frac{\phi}{I} = \text{constant}$$

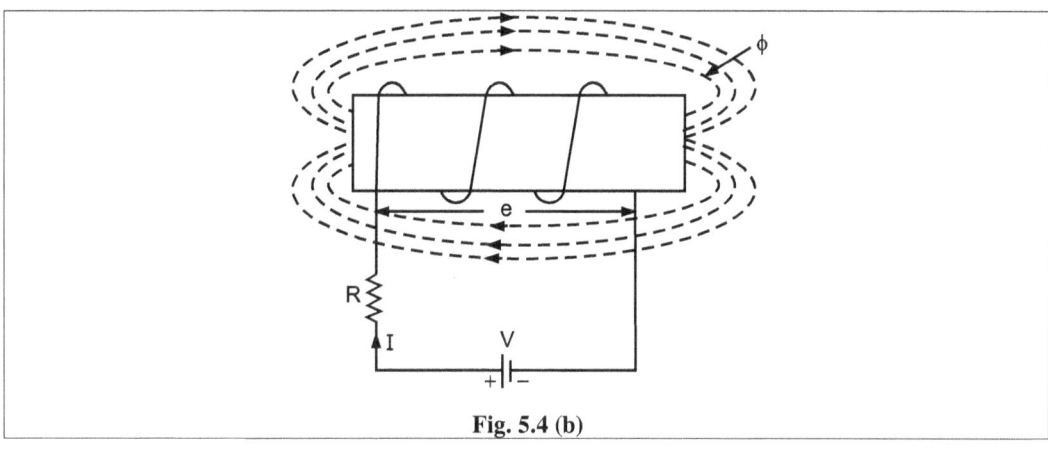

Fig. 5.4 (b)

The flux ϕ can be written as,

$$\phi = \phi \times \frac{I}{I}$$

$$\phi = \frac{\phi}{I} \cdot I$$

Differentiating, $\dfrac{d\phi}{dt} = \dfrac{\phi}{I} \dfrac{dI}{dt}$ ...(1)

When current I in the coil is changed e.m.f. induced in the coil is given by,

$$e = -N\frac{d\phi}{dt}$$

From equation (1), $e = -N\dfrac{\phi}{I} \dfrac{dI}{dt}$

$$\boxed{e = -L\frac{dI}{dt}}$$ ... (A)

where, $L = \dfrac{N\phi}{I}$ ...(B)

$\quad$ L $\rightarrow$ Self inductance of the coil

Expression (A) represents magnitude of self induced emf. From expression (B) self inductance can be defined as flux linkage to the coil per ampere change in current through it.

From equation (B), $\phi = \dfrac{\text{mmf}}{\text{Reluctance}}$

$$= \frac{NI}{S}$$

$\therefore$ $L = N \cdot \dfrac{NI}{S \cdot I}$, $L = \dfrac{N^2}{S}$

But,
$$S = \frac{l}{\mu_o \mu_r A}$$

$\therefore$
$$L = \frac{N^2 \mu_o \mu_r A}{l} \qquad \qquad ...(C)$$

Equation (C) is called expression for self inductance in terms of dimensions of the coil.

5.7 MUTUAL INDUCTANCE (M)

A coil possesses an inductance whenever the flux linking with it is changed. If the own flux link with the coil then the inductance possessed by the coil is called as self inductance. If the flux produced by some another coil get linked with coil then the inductance possessed by the coil is called as mutual inductance.

The mutual inductance is defined as it is flux linkage to one coil with respect to change in current in other coil. It is denoted by M and measured in Henry.

5.8 EXPRESSIONS FOR MUTUALLY INDUCED EMF AND MUTUAL INDUCTANCE

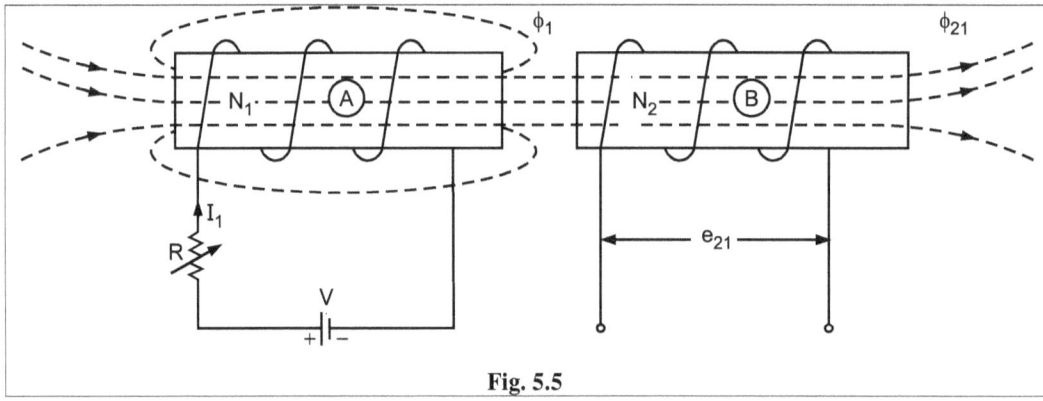

Fig. 5.5

Let, ϕ_1 : Flux produced by current I_1 again called as self flux of coil A.

ϕ_{21} : Part of ϕ_1 linking with coil B, again called as mutual flux.

As
$$\phi_{21} \propto \phi_1 \text{ and}$$
$$\phi_1 \propto I_1$$

$\therefore$
$$\phi_{21} \propto I_1$$
$$\phi_{21} = KI_1$$
$$K = \frac{\phi_{21}}{I_1} = \text{constant}$$

$$\phi_{21} = \frac{\phi_{21}}{I_1} \cdot I_1$$

Differentiating, $\dfrac{d\phi_{21}}{dt} = \dfrac{\phi_{21}}{I_1} \dfrac{dI_1}{dt}$ ...(1)

When ϕ_{21} links with coil B, according to Faraday's law a mutually induced e.m.f. e_{21} is induced in coil B given by :

$$e_{21} = -N_2 \frac{d\phi_{21}}{dt}$$

From (1) $e_{21} = \dfrac{-N_2 \phi_{21}}{I_1} \dfrac{dI_1}{dt}$

$$e_{21} = -M \frac{dI_1}{dt}$$ ...(A)

This is the magnitude of mutually induced e.m.f.

$$M = \frac{N_2 \phi_{21}}{I_1}$$

$$= \text{Mutual inductance}$$

As ϕ_{21} is part of ϕ_1

$\therefore$ $\phi_{21} = K_1 \phi_1$

K_1 indicates amount of flux linking with coil B

$\therefore$ $M = \dfrac{N_2 K_1 \phi_1}{I_1}$ ...(2)

If I_2 is the current flowing through coil B

ϕ_2 : Flux produced by current I_2, again called as self flux of coil B

ϕ_{12} : Part of ϕ_2 linking with coil A, again called as mutual flux

Then the mutually induced emf in coil A can be written as

$$e_{12} = -M \frac{d\phi_{12}}{dI_2}$$ ...(B)

where, $M = \text{Mutual inductance}$

$$= \frac{N_1 \phi_{12}}{I_2}$$

$$\phi_{12} = K_2 \phi_2$$

$K_2 \rightarrow$ Amount of flux linking with coil A

$\therefore$ $M = \dfrac{N_1 K_2 \phi_2}{I_2}$

If 100% flux linkage then

$$K_2 = 1$$

$\therefore$

$$M = \frac{N_1 \phi_2}{I_2}$$

But,

$$\phi_2 = \frac{N_2 I_2}{S}$$

And

$$S = \frac{l}{\mu_0 \mu_r A}$$

$\therefore$

$$M = \frac{N_1 N_2 \mu_0 \mu_r A}{l}$$

This is the expression for mutual inductance in terms of dimensions of coil.

5.9 FACTORS AFFECTING SELF AND MUTUAL INDUCTANCE

The self and mutual inductances are given by ...

$$L = \frac{N^2 \mu_0 \mu_r A}{l}$$

$$M = \frac{N_1 \, N_2 \, \mu_0 \, \mu_r \, A}{l}$$

(1) Self and mutual inductances are directly proportional to number of turns of the coil.
(2) Directly proportional to cross sectional area of magnetic circuit.
(3) Inversely proportional to length of magnetic circuit.
(4) It is directly proportional to relative permeability of core. Coils having magnetic material in a core possess large inductance whereas coils having non-magnetic material as a core like air possess less inductance.
(5) As μ_r varies with flux density, the inductance varies with respect to flux density.

5.10 COEFFICIENT OF COUPLING (K)

The mutual inductance between two coils is given by ....

$$M = \frac{N_1 \phi_{12}}{I_2} = \frac{N_1 K_2 \phi_2}{I_2} \qquad \qquad ...(1)$$

$$M = \frac{N_2 \phi_{21}}{I_1} = \frac{N_2 \phi_1 K_1}{I_1} \qquad \qquad ...(2)$$

Multiplying equations (1) and (2)

$$M^2 = \frac{N_1 \, N_2 \, K_1 \, K_2 \, \phi_1 \, \phi_2}{I_1 I_2}$$

$$M^2 = \frac{N_1 \phi_1}{I} \cdot \frac{N_2 \phi_2}{I_2} \cdot K_1 K_2$$

But,

$$L_1 = \frac{N_1 \phi_1}{I_1}$$

$$L_2 = \frac{N_2 \phi_2}{I_2}$$

$\therefore$

$$M^2 = L_1 L_2 K_1 K_2$$

$$M = \sqrt{L_1 L_2} \cdot \sqrt{K_1 K_2}$$

Let,

$$K = \sqrt{K_1 K_2}$$

$\therefore$

$$M = K \sqrt{L_1 L_2}$$

Whenever there is 100% flux linkage between two coils, the mutual inductance between the two coils is said to be maximum.

For 100% flux linkage, $K_1 = K_2 = 1 = K$

$\therefore$

$$M_{max} = \sqrt{L_1 L_2}$$

From equation (1),

$$K = \text{coefficient of coupling}$$

$$K = \frac{M}{\sqrt{L_1 L_2}}$$

But,

$$M_{max} = \sqrt{L_1 L_2}$$

$\therefore$

$$K = \frac{M}{M_{max}}$$

From equation (2) coefficient of coupling is defined as it is a ratio of actual mutual inductance between the two coils to maximum possible mutual inductance between two coils.

5.11 EFFECTIVE INDUCTANCE OF SERIES CONNECTION

Two inductances can be coupled in series. The inductances can be connected in series or in series opposition called as cumulatively coupled and differentially coupled respectively.

5.11.1 Series Aiding or Cumulatively Coupled Connection

Two coils are said to be cumulatively coupled if the fluxes are always in the same direction at any instant.

The winding direction of the two coils on the core must be same to carry current in the same direction. Fig. 5.6 shows cumulatively coupled connection.

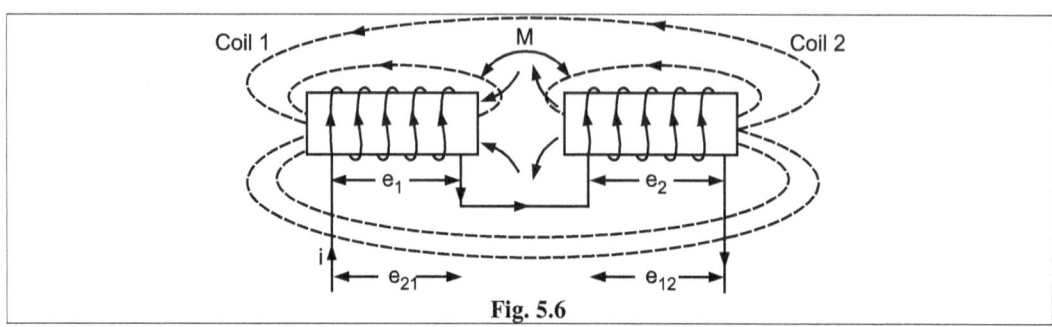

Fig. 5.6

Coil 1 has self inductance L_1 and coil 2 has self inductance L_2.

Both have mutual inductance of M.

If the current flowing the circuit changes at the rate of $\dfrac{di}{dt}$ then total e.m.f. induced will be self-induced e.m.f. and mutually induced e.m.f.

Due to flux linking with coil 1 itself, the self-induced e.m.f.,

$$e_1 = -L_1 \frac{di}{dt}$$

Due to flux produced by coil 2 linking with coil 1, there is mutually induced e.m.f.,

$$e_{21} = -M \frac{di}{dt}$$

Due to flux produced by coil 1 linking with coil 2, there is mutually induced e.m.f.,

$$e_{12} = -M \frac{di}{dt}$$

Due to flux produced by coil 2 linking with itself, there is self-induced emf.

$$e_2 = -L_2 \frac{di}{dt}$$

The total induced e.m.f. is addition of these e.m.f.s as all are in the same direction.

$$e = e_1 + e_{21} + e_{12} + e_2$$

$$= -L_1 \frac{di}{dt} - M \frac{di}{dt} - M \frac{di}{dt} - L_2 \frac{di}{dt}$$

$$= -(L_1 + L_2 + 2M) \frac{di}{dt}$$

$$= -L_{eq} \frac{di}{dt}$$

$$L_{eq} = \text{equivalent inductance}$$

$$\boxed{L_{eq} = L_1 + L_2 + 2\,M}$$

5.11.2 Series Opposition or Differentially Coupled Connection

Two coils are said to be differentially coupled if the fluxes produced by them are always in opposite direction. The connection is shown in Fig. 5.7.

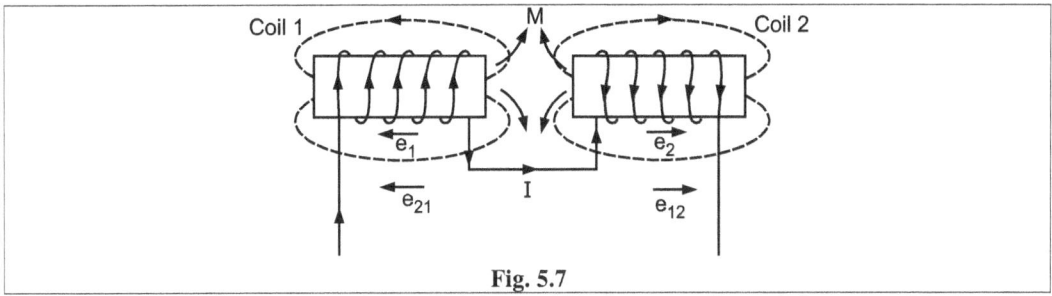

Fig. 5.7

Coil 1 has self inductance L_1, coil 2 has self inductance L_2 and the mutual inductance between the two is M.

The flux produced by coil 2 is in opposite direction to the flux produced by coil 1. If the current changes at the rate $\dfrac{di}{dt}$, the total e.m.f. will be the self-induced e.m.f. and mutually- induced e.m.f.

The self-induced e.m.f. will oppose the applied voltage and mutually induced e.m.f. will assist the applied voltage.

$$e_1 = -L_1 \frac{di}{dt}$$

$$e_{21} = +M \frac{di}{dt}$$

$$e_{12} = +M \frac{di}{dt}$$

$$e_2 = -L_2 \frac{di}{dt}$$

Hence, the total e.m.f. is the addition of these four e.m.f.s.

$$e = e_1 + e_2 + e_{12} + e_{21}$$

$$= -L_1 \frac{di}{dt} - L_2 \frac{di}{dt} + M \frac{di}{dt} + M \frac{di}{dt}$$

$$= -(L_1 + L_2 - 2M) \frac{di}{dt}$$

$$= -L_{eq} \frac{di}{dt}$$

where L_{eq} = equivalent inductance when two coils are connected in series opposition or differentially coupled.

5.12 ENERGY STORED IN A MAGNETIC FIELD

When the coil of inductance 'L' Henry is connected across supply, the lines of forces are created.

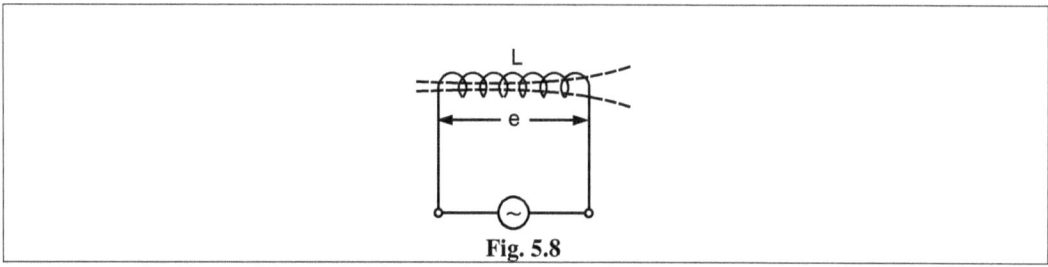

Fig. 5.8

Due to the lines of force linking to the coil, e.m.f. is induced in the coil. It is given as

$$e = -L\frac{di}{dt}$$

But $e = -v$ (as induced e.m.f. is always opposed by the cause producing it as per Lenz's law)

$\therefore$ $$-v = -L\frac{di}{dt}$$

$\therefore$ $$v = L\frac{di}{dt}$$

Multiplying both sides of equation (I) by idt, we have

$$vidt = Lidi$$

But $vidt = e$ be the electrical energy supplied to the coil by source.

Total energy supplied by the source to the coil when current varies from i_1 to i_2

$$E = \int vi\, dt = \int_{i_1}^{i_2} Li\, di$$

$$= L\left[\frac{i^2}{2}\right]_{i_1}^{i_2} = \frac{1}{2}L(i_2^2 - i_1^2)$$

If the current in the coil varies from zero to some final steady value 'I' ampere,

$$E = \frac{1}{2}L(I^2 - 0)$$

$$= \frac{1}{2}LI^2 \text{ joule}$$

Now $$L = \frac{N\phi}{I}$$

$\therefore$ $$E = \frac{1}{2}\frac{N\phi}{I}\cdot I^2 = \frac{1}{2}N\phi.I$$

But $B = \dfrac{\phi}{a}$ i.e. $\phi = B.a$

We have $\qquad\qquad\qquad E = \dfrac{1}{2} NB.a.I$

But M.M.F. i.e. $\qquad\qquad NI = H.l$

$\therefore \qquad\qquad\qquad\qquad E = \dfrac{1}{2} B.a\, H . l$

Where a.l be the volume,

Energy stored per unit volume $= \dfrac{1}{2}$ B.H joule

SOLVED EXAMPLES

Example 5.1 :

A coil of 400 turns has a flux of 0.5 mWb linking with it when carrying a current of 2 ampere. Determine the inductance of the coil.

Solution : N = 400, $\phi = 0.5$ mWb $= 0.5 \times 10^{-3}$ Wb, I = 2 amperes

$$L = \dfrac{N\phi}{I}$$

$$= \dfrac{0.5 \times 10^{-3} \times 400}{2} = 0.1\text{ H}$$

Example 5.2 :

A coil consists of 750 turns and a current of 10 A in the coil gives rise to a magnetic flux of 1.2 mWb. Calculate the inductance of the coil. If the current in the coil is reversed in 0.01s, determine the average voltage induced in the coil.

Solution : N − 750, I = 10 A, $\phi = 1.2$ mWb $= 1.2 \times 10^{-3}$Wb

$$L = \dfrac{N\phi}{I}$$

$$= \dfrac{1.2 \times 10^{-3} \times 750}{10}$$

$$= 0.09\text{ H}$$

Initial current $= 10$ A, Final current $= -10$ A.

Change in currents $= -10 - 10 = -20$ Amp. $=$ di

Time taken for this change $=$ dt $= 0.01$s

Induced voltage, $\qquad\qquad e = -L\dfrac{di}{dt}$

$$= -0.09 \times \dfrac{(-20)}{0.01}$$

$$= 180\text{ volt.}$$

Example 5.3 :

Calculate the inductance of a ring shaped coil having a mean diameter of 200 mm wound on a wooden core of diameter 20 mm. The winding is evenly wound and contains 500 turns.

If the wooden core is replaced by an iron core which has relative permeability of 600 when the current is 5 A, calculate the new value of inductance.

Solution : Mean diameter of the ring, d = 200 mm = 0.2 m

Mean length of magnetic path, $l = \pi d = 0.2\,\pi$

Diameter of the core,   d = 20 mm = 0.02 m

Cross-sectional area of the core, a $= \dfrac{\pi}{4}\,d^2 \ = \ \dfrac{\pi}{4}(0.02)^2 \ = \ \pi \times 10^{-4}\,m^2$

Number of turns in the coil,   N = 500

$$\mu_o \ = \ 4\pi \times 10^{-7}$$

For wooden core, which is non-magnetic, $\mu_r = 1$

Inductance of coil,

$$L \ = \ \frac{N^2}{S} = \frac{N^2}{l/\mu_o\mu_r a} \ = N^2\,\frac{\mu_o\mu_r a}{l}$$

$$= \ 4\pi \times 10^{-7} \times 1 \times (500)^2 \ \times \frac{\pi \times 10^{-4}}{\pi \times 0.2}$$

$$= \ 157 \times 10^{-6}\,H \ = \ 157\ \mu H$$

For iron core, $\mu_r = 600$

$$L \ = \ 4\pi \times 10^{-7} \times 600 \times (500)^2 \times \frac{\pi \times 10^{-4}}{\pi \times 0.2}$$

$$= \ 94.2 \times 10^{-3}\,H = 94.2\ mH$$

Example 5.4 :

Two coils having 150 and 200 turns respectively are wound side by side on closed magnetic circuit of cross section $1.5 \times 10^{-2}\,m^2$ and mean length of 3 m. The relative permeability of the magnetic circuit is 2000.

Calculate : (a) The mutual inductance between the coils.

(b) The voltage induced in the second coil if the current changes from 0 to 10 A in the first coil in 20 ms.

Solution : $N_1 = 150$, $N_2 = 200$, a = $1.5 \times 10^{-2}\,m^2$, $l = 3$ m, $\mu_r = 2000$

(a) $M = \dfrac{N_1 N_2}{S} = \dfrac{N_1 N_2}{(l/\mu_o\mu_r a)}$

$$= \frac{(N_1 N_2)\,(\mu_o\mu_r a)}{l}$$

$$= 4\pi \times 10^{-7} \times 2000 \times 150 \times 200 \times \frac{1.5 \times 10^{-2}}{3}$$

$$M = 0.377 \text{ H}$$

(b) $di = 10 - 0 = 10 \text{ A}$

$$dt = 20 \text{ ms} = 20 \times 10^{-3} \text{ s}$$

Voltage induced in second coil,

$$e_2 = M\frac{di}{dt} = 0.377 \times \frac{10}{20 \times 10^{-3}} = 188.5 \text{ volt.}$$

Example 5.5 :

A coil of 50 turns having a mean diameter of 30 mm is placed coaxially at the centre of solenoid 0.6 m long wound with 2500 turns and carrying a current of 2 A. Determine the mutual inductance of the arrangement.

Solution : Flux density produced by solenoid,

$$B = \mu_o \mu_r H = \mu_o H \qquad\qquad (\because \mu_r = 1 \text{ for air})$$

$$H = \frac{NI}{l}$$

$$B = \mu_o H = \mu_o \frac{NI}{l} = 4\pi \times 10^{-7} \times \frac{2500 \times 2}{0.6}$$

$$= 1.047 \times 10^{-2} \text{ T}$$

Diameter of inner coil, $d = 30 \text{ mm} = 30 \times 10^{-3} \text{ m}$

Area of c/s of the inner coil, $a_2 = \frac{\pi}{4} d^2 = \frac{\pi}{4} \times (30 \times 10^{-3})^2$

$$= 7.068 \times 10^{-4} \text{ m}^2$$

Flux linked with the inner coil, $\phi_2 = B \cdot a_2 = 1.047 \times 10^{-2} \times 7.068 \times 10^{-4}$

$$= 7.4 \times 10^{-6} \text{ Wb}$$

Mutual inductance of the arrangement,

$$M = \frac{\phi_2 N_2}{I_1}$$

$$= 7.4 \times 10^{-6} \times \frac{50}{2} \text{ H}$$

$$\boxed{M = 185 \text{ μH}}$$

Example 5.6 :

Two long single layer solenoids have the same length and same number of turns but are placed coaxially one within the other.

The diameter of the inner coil is 60 mm and that of outer coil is 75 mm. Determine the coefficient of coupling between the coils.

Solution : Suppose suffixes 1 and 2 are used for outer and inner solenoids respectively. Let N be the number of turns of each solenoid and 'l' the length of each solenoid.

$$L_1 = \frac{N^2}{S} = \frac{N^2}{l/\mu_o\mu_r a_1} = \frac{N^2\mu_o\mu_r a_1}{l}$$

$$L_2 = \frac{N^2}{S} = \frac{N^2}{l/\mu_o\mu_r a_2} = \frac{N^2\mu_o\mu_r a_2}{l}$$

Flux density produced by the outer solenoid,

$$B = \mu_o\mu_r H = \mu_o\mu_r \frac{NI_1}{l}$$

Flux linked with the inner solenoid is

$$\phi_2 = B \cdot a_2 = \mu_o\mu_r \frac{NI_1}{l} a_2$$

$$M = \frac{\phi_2 N_2}{I_1} = \mu_o\mu_r N^2 \frac{a_2}{l}$$

$$K = \frac{M}{\sqrt{L_1 L_2}}$$

$$= \frac{a_2}{\sqrt{a_1 a_2}} = \sqrt{\frac{a_2}{a_1}}$$

$$= \frac{\sqrt{\frac{\pi}{4} d_2^2}}{\sqrt{\frac{\pi}{4} d_1^2}} = \frac{d_2}{d_1} = \frac{60}{75} = 0.8$$

Example 5.7 :

When two identical coupled coils are connected in series, the inductance of the combination is found to be 80 mH. When the connections to one of the coils are reversed, a similar measurement indicates 20 mH. Find the coupling coefficient between the coils.

Solution :

$$L_{eq} = L_1 + L_2 + 2M$$

$$L'_{eq} = L_1 + L_2 - 2M$$

$$L_{eq} - L'_{eq} = 4\,M$$

$$M = \frac{1}{4}\,[L_{eq} - L'_{eq}] = \frac{1}{4}\,(80 - 20)$$

$$= 15\ mH$$

Since the coils are identical, $L_1 = L_2$

$$L_{eq} = 2\,L_1 + 2M$$

$$80 = 2\,L_1 + (2 \times 15)$$

$$L_1 = \frac{1}{2}(80 - 30) = 25 \text{ mH}$$

$$L_1 = L_2 = 25 \text{ mH}$$

Coupling coefficient, $K = \dfrac{M}{\sqrt{L_1 L_2}} = \dfrac{15}{\sqrt{25 \times 25}}$

$$= \frac{15}{25} = 0.6$$

Example 5.8 :

Two coils have self-inductances of 3H and 2H respectively and the mutual inductance is 2 H. They are connected in series and a current of 4 A is passed through them. Calculate the energy of magnetic field when the self and mutual fluxes are (a) in the same direction, (b) in opposition. Find also the coupling coefficient.

Solution : $L_1 = 3 \text{ H}, L_2 = 2\text{H}, M = 2\text{H}$

$$L_{eq} = L_1 + L_2 + 2M$$

$$= 3 + 2 + (2 \times 2) = 9 \text{ H}$$

$$L'_{eq} = L_1 + L_2 - 2M$$

$$= 3 + 2 - (2 \times 2) = 1 \text{ H}$$

(a) Energy $= \dfrac{1}{2} L_{eq} I^2 = \dfrac{1}{2} \times 9 \times 4^2 = 72 \text{ J}$

(b) Energy $= \dfrac{1}{2} L'_{eq} I^2 = \dfrac{1}{2} \times 1 \times 4^2 = 8 \text{ J}$

Coefficient of coupling, $K = \dfrac{M}{\sqrt{L_1 L_2}} = \dfrac{2}{\sqrt{2 \times 3}} = 0.816$

Example 5.9 :

A length of an air-cored solenoid is 1.7 m and area of cross section is 12 cm². The number of turns of coil is 1000. Calculate : (i) The self inductance, (ii) The energy stored in magnetic field when a current of 10 A flows through the coil.   **(Dec. 97)**

Solution : $l = 1.7 \text{ m}, a = 12 \text{ cm}^2 = 12 \times 10^{-4}\text{m}^2, \mu_o = 4\pi \times 10^{-7}, N = 1000, I = 10 \text{ A}$

$$S = \frac{l}{\mu_o a} = \frac{1.7}{4\pi \times 10^{-7} \times 12 \times 10^{-4}}$$

$$= 1.1273 \times 10^9 \text{ AT/Wb.}   \ldots \mu_r = 1 \text{ as air cored}$$

$$L = \frac{N^2}{S} = \frac{(1000)^2}{1.1273 \times 10^9}$$

$$= 8.87 \times 10^{-4} \text{ H} = 0.886 \text{ mH}$$

Now, if $E = \dfrac{1}{2} LI^2 = \dfrac{1}{2} \times (0.886 \times 10^{-3}) \times (10)^2$

$$= 0.0443 \text{ J}$$

Example 5.10 :

Two coils having 3000 and 2000 turns are wound on a magnetic ring. 60% of flux produced in first field coil links with the second coil. A current of 3 A produces flux of 0.5 mWb in the first coil and 0.3 mWb in the second coil. Determine the mutual inductance and coefficient of coupling.   **(Dec. 98)**

Solution : $N_1 = 3000$, $N_2 = 2000$, $\phi_1 = 0.5$ mWb, $\phi_2 = 0.3$ mWb.

$I_1 = I_2 = 3$ A and $\phi_2 = 0.6\ \phi_1$

$$M = \frac{N_2\phi_2}{I_1} = \frac{2000 \times 0.3 \times 10^{-3}}{3} = 0.2\ H$$

$$L_1 = \frac{N_1\phi_1}{I_1} = \frac{3000 \times 0.5 \times 10^{-3}}{3} = 0.5\ H$$

$$L_2 = \frac{N_2\phi_2}{I_2} = \frac{2000 \times 0.3 \times 10^{-3}}{3} = 0.2\ H$$

$$K = \frac{M}{\sqrt{L_1 L_2}} = \frac{0.2}{\sqrt{0.5 \times 0.2}} = 0.6324$$

Example 5.11 :

An iron ring 10 cm in diameter and 8 cm² in cross-section have flux density of 1.2 Wb/m² and relative permeability of 500. Find the exciting current, the inductance and energy stored.

Solution : d = 10 cm, a = 8 cm², N = 300, B = 1.2 Wb/m², $\mu_r = 500$

$$\text{Total mean length} = \pi \times d$$
$$= \pi \times 10$$
$$= 31.14\ cm$$
$$= 0.3141\ m$$

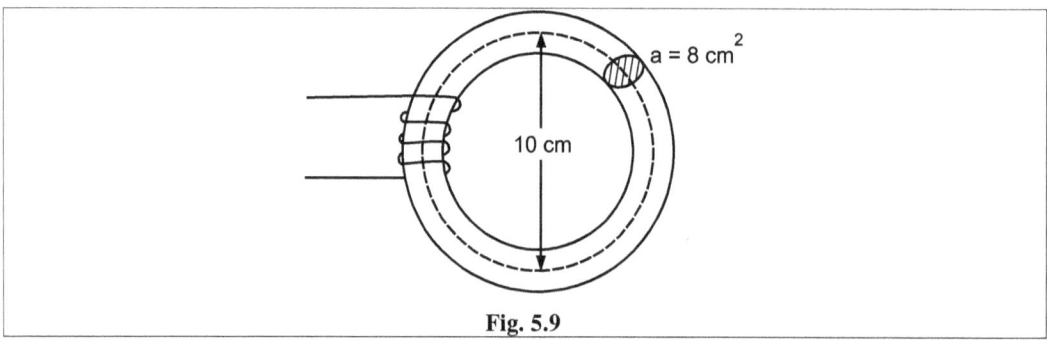

Fig. 5.9

$$S = \frac{l}{\mu_0 \mu_r a} = \frac{0.3141}{4\pi \times 10^{-7} \times 500 \times 8 \times 10^{-4}}$$
$$= 624.882 \times 10^3\ AT/Wb$$

$$\phi = \frac{NI}{S}$$

$$9.6 \times 10^{-4} = \frac{300 \times I}{624.882 \times 10^3}$$

$$I = 2 A$$

$$L = \frac{N^2}{S} = \frac{(300)^2}{624.882 \times 10^3} = 0.14402 \text{ H}$$

$$E = \frac{1}{2} LI^2 = \frac{1}{2} \times 0.14402 \times 2^2 = 0.288 \text{ J}$$

Example 5.12 :

Two coils A and B in a magnetic circuit have 600 and 500 turns respectively. A current of 8 Amp in coil A produces a flux of 0.04 wb. If the co-efficient of coupling is 0.2, calculate (i) The self inductance of coil A when B is open circuited, (ii) Flux linkage with coil B, (iii) Mutual inductance, (iv) Emf induced in B when flux changes from zero to full value in 0.02 sec. **(Dec. 2008) (5M)**

Solution : $N_1 = 600$ turns, $N_2 = 500$ turns, $I_1 = 8$ Amp, $\phi_1 = 0.04$ Wb, $K = 0.2$

(1)
$$L_1 = \frac{N_1 \phi_1}{I_1}$$

$$= \frac{600 \times 0.04}{8} = 3 \text{ H}$$

(2) Flux linkage with coil B $= N_2 \phi_2$

$$= N_2 K_1 \phi_1$$

$$= 500 \times 0.2 \times 0.04 \text{ (Assume coils are perfectly coupled)}$$

$$= 4 \text{ WbT}$$

(3) Mutual inductance M $= \dfrac{N_2 \phi_2}{I_1}$

$$= \frac{N_2 K_1 \phi_1}{I_1}$$

$$= \frac{500 \times 0.2 \times 0.04}{8}$$

$$= 0.5 \text{ H}$$

(4) EMF induced in coil B $e_2 = -N_2 \dfrac{d\phi_2}{dt}$ [where $\phi_2 = k_1\phi_1 = 0.2 \times 0.04 = 0.008$ Wb]

$$= -500 \times \frac{0.008}{0.02}$$

$$= -200 \text{ volt}$$

Example 5.13 :

A coil of 100 turns having a mean diameter of 5 cm is placed coaxially at the center of solenoid 50 cm long wound with 2500 turns and carrying a current of 3 Amp. Determine the mutual inductance of the arrangement.   **(Dec. 08) (6M)**

Solution : Given :

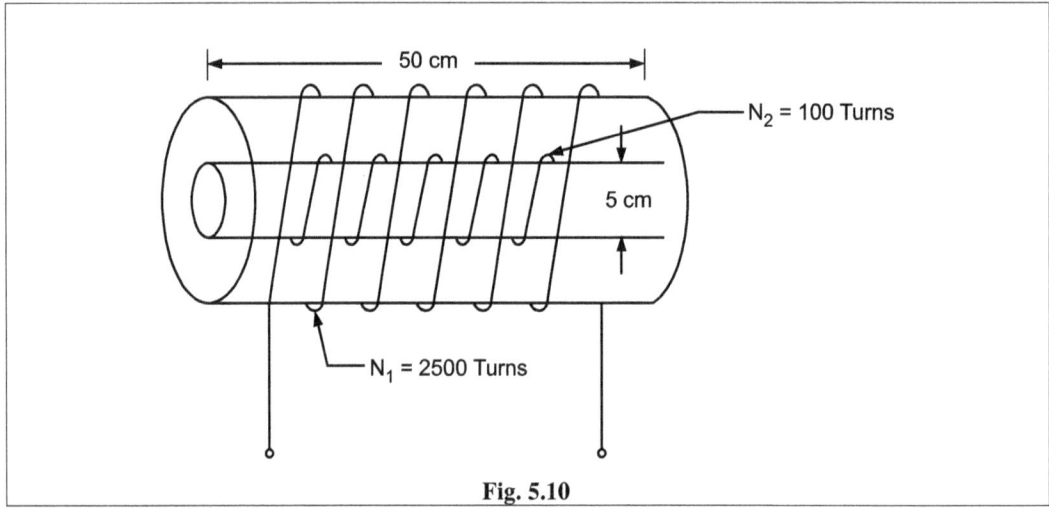

Fig. 5.10

Magnetic field strength at the centre of the coil

$$H = \frac{N_1 I_1}{l}$$

$$= \frac{2500 \times 3}{0.5}$$

$$= 15000 \text{ AT}$$

Magnetic flux density

$$B = \mu H = \mu_o \mu_r H$$

$$= \mu_o H$$

$$= 4\pi \times 10^{-7} \times 15000$$

$$= 1.89 \times 10^{-2} \text{ Tesla}$$

Area of the inner coil $a_2 = \pi \dfrac{d^2}{4}$

$$= \pi \times \frac{(0.05)^2}{4}$$

$$= 19.63 \text{ cm}^2 = 19.63 \times 10^{-4} \text{ m}^2$$

Flux linking with the inner coil, $\phi_2 = k_1 \phi_1 = B \cdot A_2$

$$= 1.89 \times 10^{-2} \times 19.63 \times 10^{-4}$$

$$= 37.12 \times 10^{-6} \text{ Wb}$$

$$M = \frac{N_2 \, \phi_2}{I_1}$$

$$= \frac{100 \times 37.12 \times 10^{-6}}{3}$$

$$M = 1.237 \text{ mH}$$

REVIEW QUESTIONS

1. An iron ring of mean length 1m and circular cross-sectional area 1000 mm² has an air gap of 3 mm and winding of 100 turns. Calculate the inductance of the coil if the relative permeability of iron is 500.   **(Ans. : L = 2.566 mH)**

2. A large electromagnet is wound with 1000 turns. A current of 2 A in this winding produces a flux through two coils of 0.03 Wb. Calculate the inductance of electromagnet.   **(Ans. : 15 H, 350 V)**

    If the current in the coil is reduced from 2 A to zero in 0.1 s, what average e.m.f. will be induced in the coil ?

3. A flux of 0.5 mWb is produced in a coil of 900 turns wound on a wooden ring by a current of 3 A. Calculate (a) inductance of the coil, (b) the average e.m.f. induced in the coil when a current of 5 A is switched off, assuming the current to fall zero in 1 ms. (c) The mutual inductances between the coils, if a second coil of 600 turns was uniformly wound over the first coil.   **(Ans. : 0.15 H, 750 V, 0.1H)**

4. A solenoid 500 mm long and 40 mm in diameter is uniformly wound with a coil of 2000 turns. Determine the self inductance of the coil assuming that is air cored.

    (Ans. : 12.62 mH)

5. A coil of 300 turns has a self inductance of 2.4 mH. If a second coil of 900 turns is positioned such that 25% of the flux produced by the first coil links with the second coil, determine the mutual inductance between the coils.   **(Ans. : 1.8 mH)**

6. Two inductors having self inductances of 0.1 H and 0.05 H are connected in series aiding. The total inductance of the circuit is 0.19 H. Calculate the mutual inductance and total e.m.f. induced if the current changes at a rate of 20 A/s.

    (Ans. : 0.02 H, 3.8 V)

7. An iron-cored coil of 1600 turns has an inductance of 0.1 H. Find the flux produced when 4 A current flows through the coil. If this current is reversed in 25 ms, calculate the average voltage induced in the coil. **(Ans. : 0.25 mWb, 32 V)**

8. The combined inductances of two coils connected in series are 0.75 H and 0.25 H depending on the relative directions of currents in the coils. If one of the coils when isolated has a self inductance of 0.15 H, calculate (a) mutual inductance, (b) coefficient of coupling.   **(Ans. : 0.125 H, 0.5455)**

9. Two coils of self inductances 0.2 H and 0.1 H are connected in series. If the mutual inductance is 0.1 H, calculate the effective inductance of the combination.

     (Ans. : 0.5 H or 0.1H)

10. Calculate the self inductance of an air-cored toroid 25 cm mean diameter and 6.25 cm² circular cross-section wound uniformly with 1000 turns of wire. Determine the induced voltage when a current increasing at the rate of 200 A/s flows in the winding.   **(Ans. : 1.0 mH, 0.2 V)**

UNIT - V

Chapter 7

A.C. FUNDAMENTALS AND A.C. CIRCUITS

7.1 INTRODUCTION

In the early days, direct current (d.c.) supply was used for supplying power to homes and small installations. The direct current is one which flows continuously in one direction with constant magnitude with respect to time. Fig. 7.1 (a) shows the graph of d.c. current with respect to time.

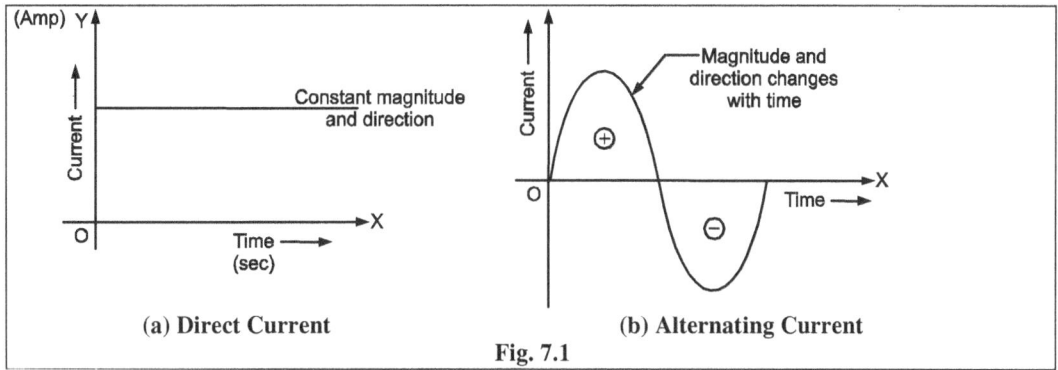

(a) Direct Current   (b) Alternating Current

Fig. 7.1

Fundamental variations, led to the extensive use of alternating currents. An alternating current (a.c.) is one which periodically passes through a definite cycle of changes in respect of magnitude and direction as well. Fig. 7.1 (b) shows the graph of alternating current with respect to time.

One cycle consists of two half cycles. During one half cycle, current flows in one direction and when second half cycle starts (polarity gets changed) current flows in opposite direction. When current flows in a particular direction, the magnitude of current also changes.

Uses of Alternating Current offers following advantages :

   (i) It is possible to build high voltage, high speed, a.c. generators with reduced cost per kW. But the same is not possible in case of d.c. generators.

  (ii) A.C. voltage can be stepped up or stepped down very conveniently by using static device called transformer. Such type of raising and lowering of d.c. voltage is not easy and economical.

(iii) Because of a transformer, A.C. voltage can be stepped up, leading to economical and efficient a.c. transmission system (for same power to transfer, if V is high, then I becomes low, $\therefore$ I²R loss is low and also volume of conductor material required is low).

(iv) A.C. motors are cheaper, simple in construction as compared to d.c. motors.

(v) Further, A.C. can be converted into d.c. by using rectifiers.

Because of all above advantages, A.C. system is extensively used. Therefore, the study of a.c. fundamentals is very important.

7.2   GENERATION OF ALTERNATING CURRENTS AND VOLTAGES

Alternating voltage may be generated by rotating a coil in a magnetic field or by rotating a magnetic field within a stationary coil. The magnitude of voltage generated depends upon the number of turns in the coil (N), strength of magnetic field (B) and the velocity at which either coil or magnetic field is being rotated. A.C. voltage may be generated by either of two ways stated above. Stationary magnetic field method is shown in Fig. 7.2.

7.2.1 Elementary Generator

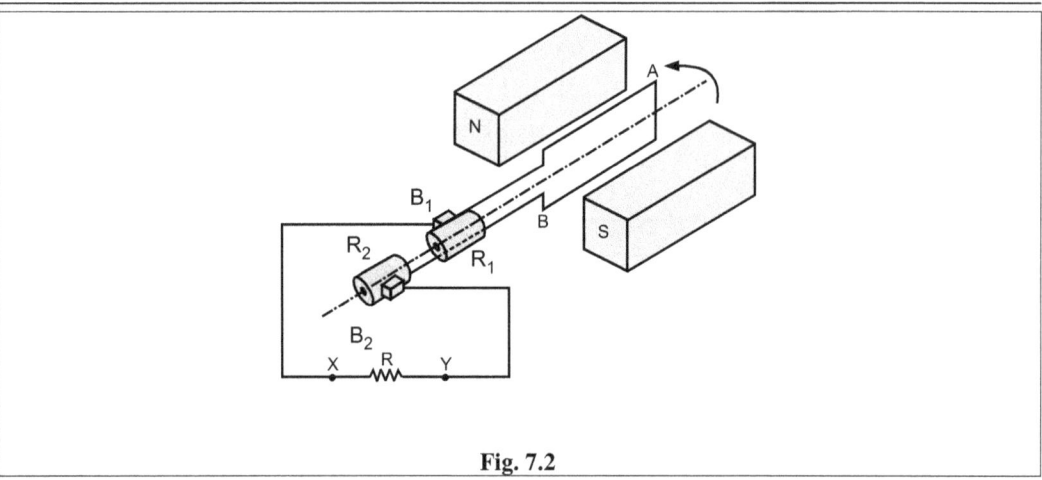

Fig. 7.2

Working : Assume that the coil AB is rotating in an anticlockwise direction. The conductors (A and B) of the coil cut the magnetic field while rotating and according to Faraday's law of electromagnetic induction, an e.m.f. is induced in them. This e.m.f. of induction causes a current to flow through the external circuit. The magnitude of this e.m.f. is dependent on the position of the coil AB in relation to the magnetic field. Let us, consider the few selected positions of the coil as shown in Fig. 7.3.

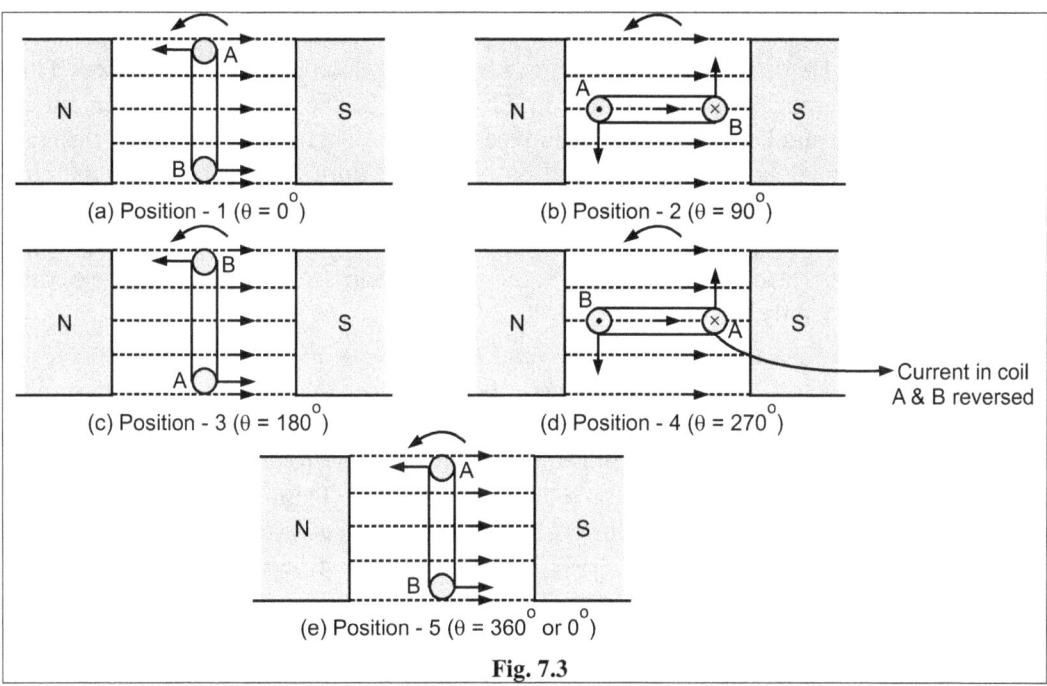

(a) Position - 1 ($\theta = 0^{\circ}$)

(b) Position - 2 ($\theta = 90^{\circ}$)

(c) Position - 3 ($\theta = 180^{\circ}$)

(d) Position - 4 ($\theta = 270^{\circ}$)

Current in coil A & B reversed

(e) Position - 5 ($\theta = 360^{\circ}$ or 0°)

Fig. 7.3

Position No. 1 : This is the initial position of the coil. The plane of the coil being perpendicular to the direction of magnetic field, the conductors (A and B) of the coil move parallel to the magnetic field. Since there is no flux cutting, no e.m.f. is generated in the conductors and therefore, no current flows through the external circuit. As this position of the coil is taken as reference therefore let us call it at $\theta = 0^{\circ}$.

Position No. 2 : As the coil rotates from Position 1 ($\theta = 0^{\circ}$) to Position 2 ($\theta = 90^{\circ}$), more and more lines of force are cut by the conductors. In the Position - 2, both the conductors of the coil move at right angles to the magnetic field and cut through a maximum number of lines force so the e.m.f. induced in them is also maximum. Thus, when coil moves from position 0° to 90°, the e.m.f. generated in the conductors builds up from zero to a maximum value. The e.m.f.s. in both the conductors being in series, the resultant coil e.m.f. is the sum of the two conductor e.m.f.s. It is therefore, twice that of one of the conductors, since the voltages are equal.

The current through the circuit varies just as the e.m.f. varies, being zero at 0° and rising to a maximum at 90°. In position - 2, according to Fleming's right hand rule, the direction of the induced current in conductor A is towards the observer (i.e. out of the plane of paper, dot convention) and in conductor B, it is away from the observer (i.e. into the plane of paper, cross convention) as indicated. Therefore, current flows through the external resistor from the terminal X to the terminal Y.

Position No. 3 : As the coil continues to rotate further from Position – 2 ($\theta = 90°$) to Position – 3 ($\theta = 180°$), the lines of force cut by the conductors gradually reduce. This decreases the generated e.m.f. in them. In Position – 3, the conductors again move parallel to the field and hence, no e.m.f is induced in them. Therefore, the current through the external resistor is also zero. It should be noted that during the rotation of the coil from 0° to 180° (i.e. during the first half revolution), the conductors of the coil move in the same direction through the magnetic field. Therefore, throughout this period, the polarity of the generated e.m.f. remains same and current flows through the external resistor form X to Y only.

Position No. 4 : As the coil rotates beyond Position – 3, the direction of the cutting action of the conductors through the magnetic field reverses. Now, the conductor A cuts up through the field and the conductor B cuts down through the field. In consequence, both the polarity of the generated e.m.f and the current flow reverse. To make it more clear consider the coil in Position – 4 ($\theta = 270°$). By applying Fleming's right hand rule, it is seen that the direction of induced current in conductor A is away from the observer and in conductor B it is towards the observer. As such, current flows through the external resistor from Y to X. Similar to Position – 2, e.m.f. in the coil is maximum in Position – 4 but only the direction of e.m.f. and current is reversed.

Position No. 5 : Here coil rotates from position $\theta = 270°$ to $\theta = 360°$ i.e. back to position 1 again. The lines of force cut by the conductors gradually reduce and thus decrease the generated e.m.f. in them. In general, the variations in the magnitude of e.m.f. of the alternator when the armature coil rotates from 180° to 360° are exactly similar to those in the first half revolution.

Thus, during the entire second half revolution, i.e. when the coil rotates from the Position – 3 to Position – 4 and back to Position – 1, the current flows in the opposite direction to that in the first half revolution.

Graphical Representation of E.M.F. or Current : The graph of e.m.f. or current for the complete revolution of the coil under consideration is shown in Fig. 7.1 (b).

7.3 IMPORTANT TERMS RELATED TO ALTERNATING QUANTITY

Before discussing further details, it is necessary to know some basic terms which are frequently used in relation to alternating quantities.

7.3.1 Instantaneous Value

The value of an alternating quantity at a particular instant is known as its instantaneous value, e.g. i_1, i_2 and i_3 shown in Fig. 7.4 are the instantaneous values of alternating current at different instances ($t_1 < t_2 < t_3$). The instantaneous values are always represented by small letters. e.g. v and i represent instantaneous voltage and current respectively.

7.3.2 Waveform

The graph of instantaneous values of an alternating quantity against time is called as its waveform. Fig. 7.4 shows the waveform of alternating current.

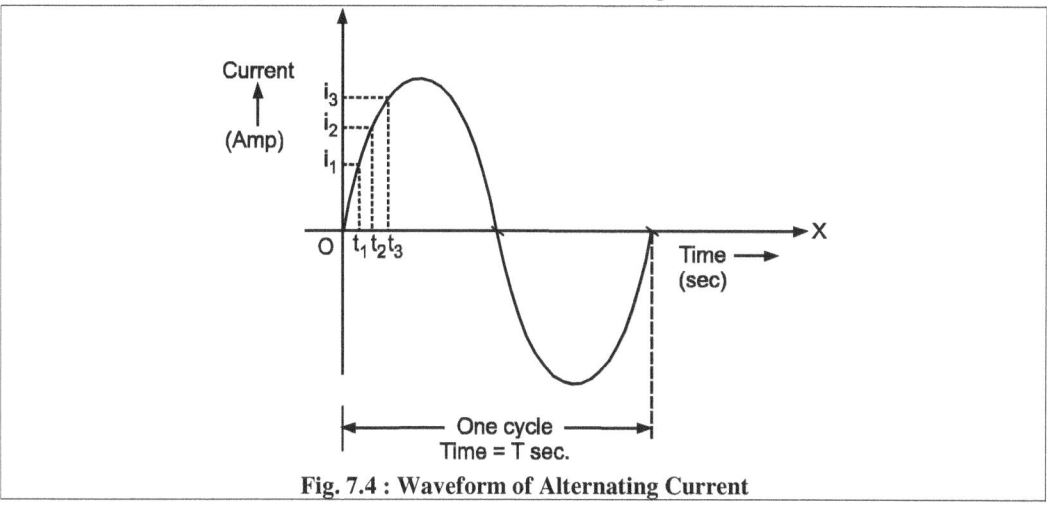

Fig. 7.4 : Waveform of Alternating Current

7.3.3 Cycle

Each repetition of a complete set of changes undergone by the alternating quantity is called cycle. These repetitions recur at equal intervals of time. One such cycle is shown in Fig. 7.4.

7.3.4 Time Period (T)

It is the time taken by the alternating quantity to complete one cycle. As we know cycles recur after every T seconds, the cycle of alternating quantity repeats.

7.3.5 Frequency (f)

The number of cycles completed per second by an alternating quantity is known as frequency. Its symbol is f and unit is cycles per second or Hertz denoted by Hz.

As time period T is time for one cycle (sec/cycle) and frequency is cycles/second, therefore we can say that frequency is reciprocal of the time period.

$$f = \frac{1}{T} \text{ Hz}$$

Our country has adopted a frequency of 50 Hz for alternating currents and voltages.

7.3.6 Amplitude

The maximum value attained by an alternating quantity during its positive or negative half cycle is called as amplitude or peak value. Fig. 7.5 shows the amplitude of A.C. voltage.

It is denoted by V_m or I_m where V_m represents peak value of voltage and I_m represents peak value of the current.

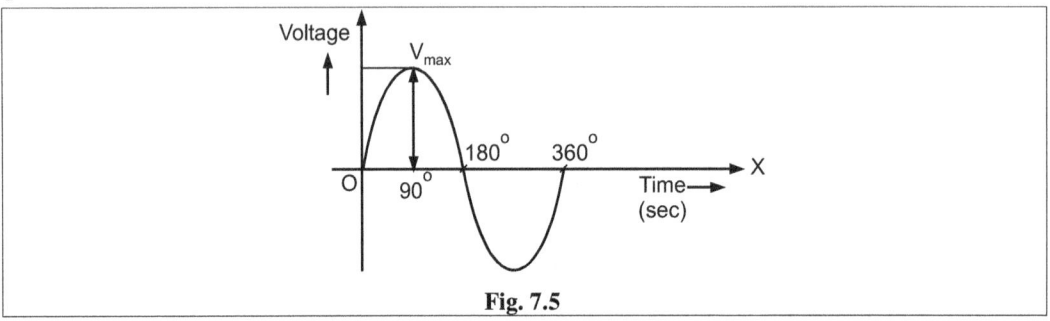

Fig. 7.5

7.4 EQUATIONS OF ALTERNATING VOLTAGES AND CURRENTS

Consider a rectangular coil of single turn placed in uniform magnetic field is rotated in anticlockwise direction with angular velocity ω radians/second as shown in Fig. 7.6. The flux linkages with the coil change and induce an alternating emf in it which follows a sine curve. Here we have to derive an equation for representation of such an e.m.f.

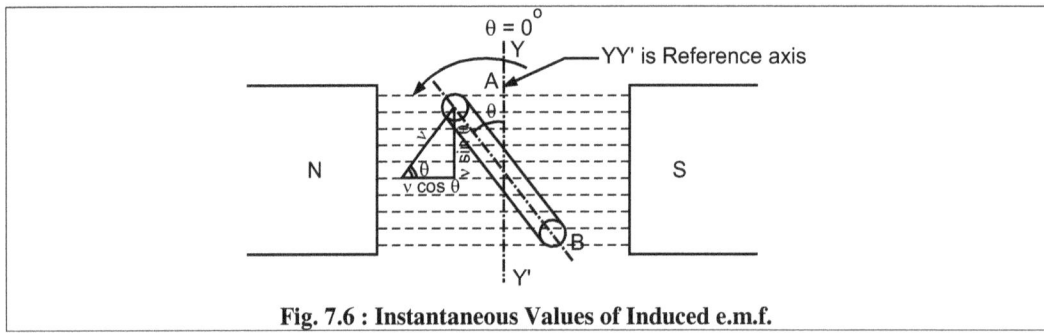

Fig. 7.6 : Instantaneous Values of Induced e.m.f.

Let,   B = Flux density of the magnetic field in Wb/m²

l = Active length of each conductor in meters.

ω = Angular velocity of coil in radians/second

v = Linear velocity of each conductor in m/sec

r = Radius of circular path traced by conductor in meters

v = r · ω

Consider, initially the coil is at position θ = 0° (i.e. on YY' axis) and from this it is rotated in anticlockwise direction in time 't' by an angle θ. So angle θ can be expressed as θ = ωt radians.

Fig. 7.6 shows the coil AB after it has rotated through an angle θ. At this instant, the peripheral velocity of each coil side can be resolved into two components, one perpendicular and other parallel to the direction of the magnetic flux.

The emf is generated in each coil side is entirely due to the component v sin θ of velocity. (∵ v cos φ is parallel to field, no emf is induced by it at any instant).

Emf generated in each coil side = B l v sin θ volts

∴   Total emf generated in the coil, e = 2 B l v sin θ volts   …(1)

When θ = 0°, total emf generated in coil = 0 volts   (i.e. along YY' axis)

When θ = 90° , total emf generated in coil = 2B l v sin (90°) = 2 B l v volts

Thus when θ = 90° coil lies in horizontal plane and attains maximum value i.e.

E_{max}= 2 B l v

When θ = 180° it again becomes zero. e = 0 and so on.

Equation (1) can be written as,

$$e \ = \ E_{max} \sin θ \qquad\qquad where\ E_{max} = 2\ B\ l\ v$$

$$= \ E_{max} \sin ωt \qquad\qquad where\ θ = ωt\ and\ ω = 2πf$$

$$= \ E_{max} \sin (2π\ ft)\ volt$$

Similar to equation (1) for instantaneous value of emf, we can write equation for instantaneous current as follows :

$$i = I_m \sin θ \ = \ I_m \sin ω\,t$$

$$= \ I_m \sin 2\ πft\ Amp$$

Example 7.1 :

A sinusoidal current of frequency 25 Hz has a maximum value of 100 A. How long will it take for the current to attain value of 20A and 50A starting from zero. Sketch the waveform and show the times and currents.

Solution : Given data,   f = 25 Hz

$$I_m \ = \ 100\ A$$

To find : time t for i = 20 A and i = 50 Amp.

frequency, f = 25 Hz, ω = 2πf = 2 × 25 = 157.08 rad/sec.

∴   Time period, T $= \ \dfrac{1}{f} \ =\dfrac{1}{25} \ = 40$ ms

Given current wave starts from zero.

$\therefore$ Standard equation is, $i = I_m \sin \omega t$

$$i = 100 \cdot \sin (157.08 \, t) \text{ Amp.}$$

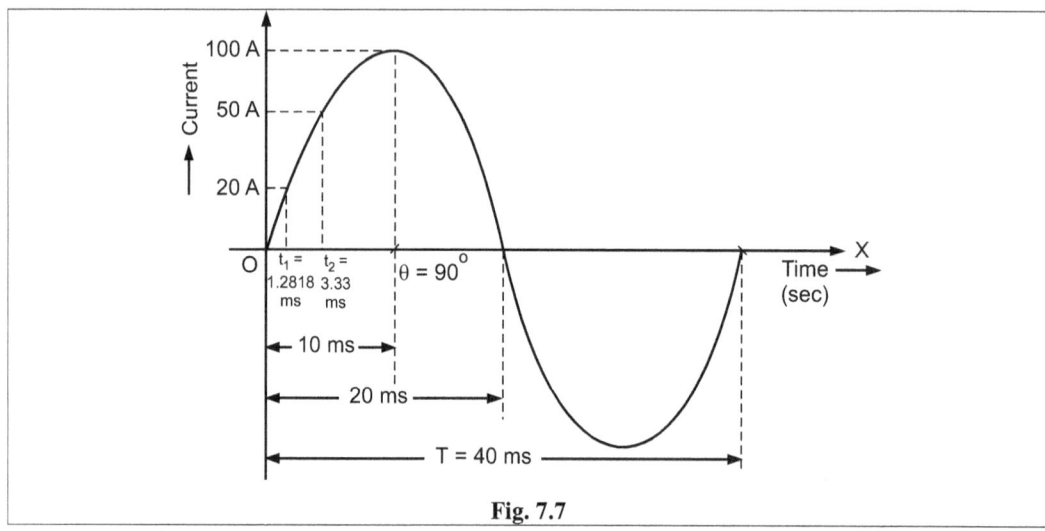

Fig. 7.7

(i) Now for $i = 20$ Amp time required is t_1

$\therefore$ $20 = 100 \sin (157.08 \, t_1)$

$\therefore$ $\sin (157.08 \, t_1) = \dfrac{20}{100} = \dfrac{1}{5}$

$$= 0.2$$

$\therefore$ $t_1 = \dfrac{\sin^{-1} (0.2)}{157.08} \text{ second}$

$$= \dfrac{0.20135}{157.08} \text{ second}$$

$$t_1 = 1.2818 \text{ m sec.}$$

(ii) When $i = 50$ Amp, let time is t_2. Put in equation (i)

$\therefore$ $50 = 100 \sin (157.14 \, t_2)$

$\therefore$ $t_2 = \dfrac{\sin^{-1} (0.5)}{157.08}$

$$= 3.333 \text{ m sec.}$$

Example 7.2 :

A sinsudoial wave of frequency 50 Hz has its maximum value of 9.2 Amp. What will be its value at (a) 0.002 sec after the wave pass through zero in positive direction. (b) 0.0045 sec. after the wave passes through positive maximum. Show the values of current in a neat sketch of the waveform.

Solution : Given : I_m = 9.2 A, f = 50 Hz,

$\therefore$
$$\omega = 2\pi f$$
$$= 2\pi \times 50$$
$$= 100\ \pi\ \text{rad/sec}$$
$$i = I_m \sin (\omega t)$$
$$= 9.2 \sin (100\pi \times t)\ \text{Amp}$$

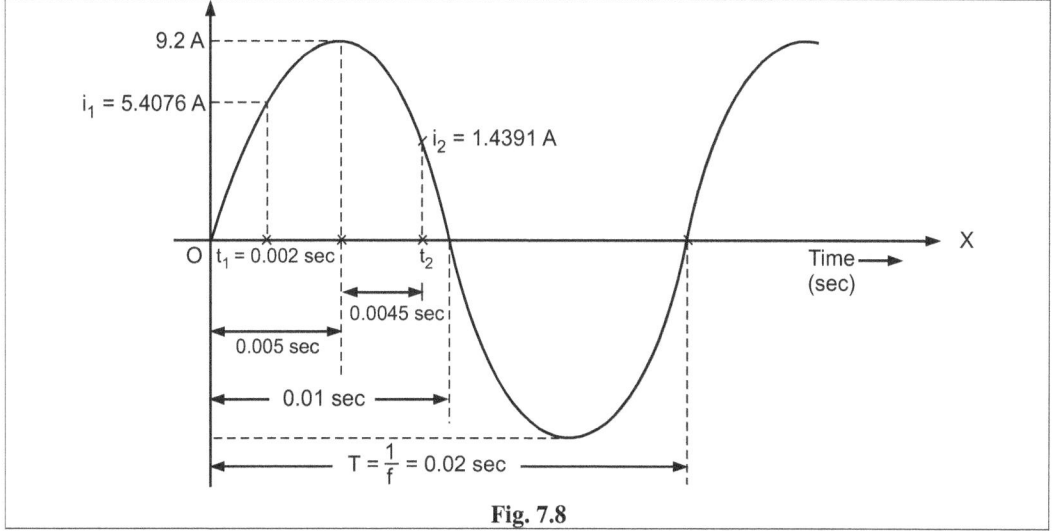

Fig. 7.8

(i) At t = 0.002 sec after passing through zero in positive direction.
$$i = 9.2 \sin (100\pi \times 0.002)$$
$$= 5.4076\ \text{Amp.} \qquad\qquad \text{[Use sin in radians]}$$

(ii) At t = 0.0045 sec after the wave passes positive maximum
$$f = 50\ \text{Hz}$$

$\therefore$ Periodic time, $\qquad T = \dfrac{1}{f}$
$$= 0.02\ \text{sec.}$$

Time for positive half $= \dfrac{0.02}{4}$
$$= 0.005\ \text{sec.}$$

After 0.005 sec, value is to be found out at 0.0045 sec. (positive half).

$\therefore$ Total duration from t = 0 is,
$$0.005 + 0.0045 = 0.0095\ \text{sec}$$

$\therefore$ i at t = 0.0095 sec, $i = I_m \sin (100\pi \times 0.0095)$

$$= 9.2 \sin (100\pi \times 0.0095)$$

$$= 1.4391 \text{ A}$$

Example 7.3 :

Draw a neat sketch in each case of the waveform and write expression of instantaneous value for the following :

(1) Sinusoidal current of amplitude 10 A, 50 Hz passing through its zero value at $\omega t = \pi/3$ and rising positively.

(2) Sinusoidal current of amplitude 8 A, 50 Hz passing through its zero value at $\omega t = -\pi/6$ and rising positively.

Solution : (1) Given : $I_m = 10$ A, f = 50 Hz, $\omega t = \theta = \dfrac{\pi}{3} = \dfrac{180°}{3} = 60°$

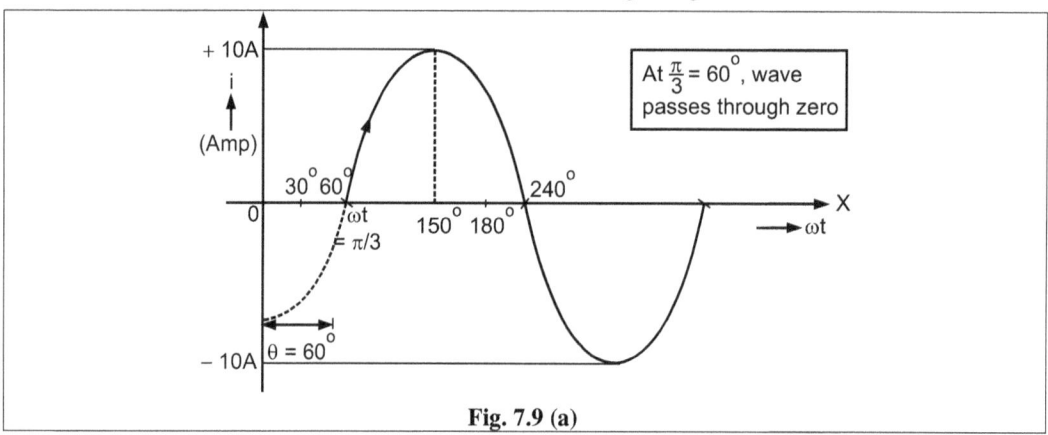

Fig. 7.9 (a)

The waveform starts at $\omega t = \theta = 60°$ then increases in positive direction as shown in Fig. 7.9 (a).

$\therefore$ Instantaneous current equation is,

$$i = I_m \sin (\omega t - \phi) = 10 \sin \left(\omega t - \frac{\pi}{3} \right)$$

$$= 10 \sin \left(100\pi t - \frac{\pi}{3} \right) \text{ Amp.}$$

(2) **Given:** $I_m = 8$ Amp, f = 50 Hz

Here, current wave passes through zero at $\omega t = \phi = -\pi/6 = -30°$ means it starts at 30° left to origin then rises positively as shown in Fig. 7.9 (b).

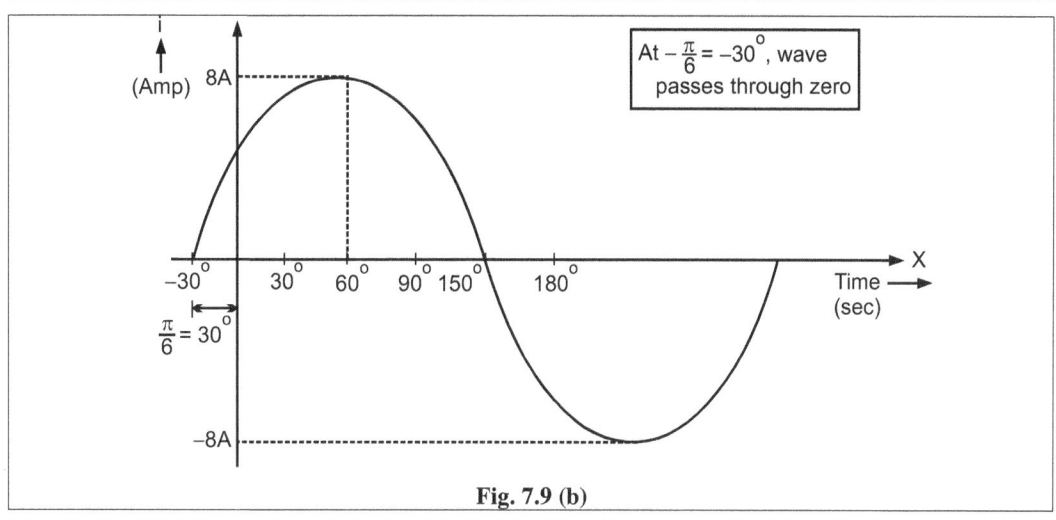

At $-\frac{\pi}{6} = -30^\circ$, wave passes through zero

Fig. 7.9 (b)

Instantaneous current equation is, $i = I_m \sin(\omega t + 30^\circ)$

$$= 8 \sin(2\pi \times 50 \times t + \pi/6)$$

$$= 8 \sin\left(100\pi\, t + \frac{\pi}{6}\right) \text{ Amp}$$

Example 7.4 :

In a certain circuit supplied from 50 Hz mains, the potential difference has a maximum value of 500 volt and the current has a maximum value of 10 Amp. At the instant t = 0, the instantaneous values of potential difference and current are 400 volt and 4 Amp. respectively both increasing in positive direction. State expressions of instantaneous values of potential difference and current at time 't'. Calculate the instantaneous values at time t = 0.015 second. Find the phase angle between potential difference and current.

Solution : Given data : $f = 50$ Hz, $V_{max} = V_m = 500$ V, $I_{max} = I_m = 10$ A.

It is given that when t = 0, v = 400 V and i = 4 Amp.

$\therefore$ $\qquad\qquad\qquad v = V_m \sin(\omega t + \phi_1)$

where ϕ_1 is angle made by v w.r.t. reference axis at t = 0

$$400 = 500 \sin(100\,\pi\,(0) + \phi_1)$$

$$4 = 5 \sin(0 + \phi_1)$$

$$\phi_1 = \sin^{-1}\left(\frac{4}{5}\right) = 53.13^\circ = 0.9272 \text{ rad}$$

$\therefore$ Instantaneous volt expression is,

$$v = V_m \sin(\omega t + \phi_1)$$

$$v = 500 \sin(100\,\pi\,t + 0.9272) \text{ V} \qquad\qquad\qquad …(1)$$

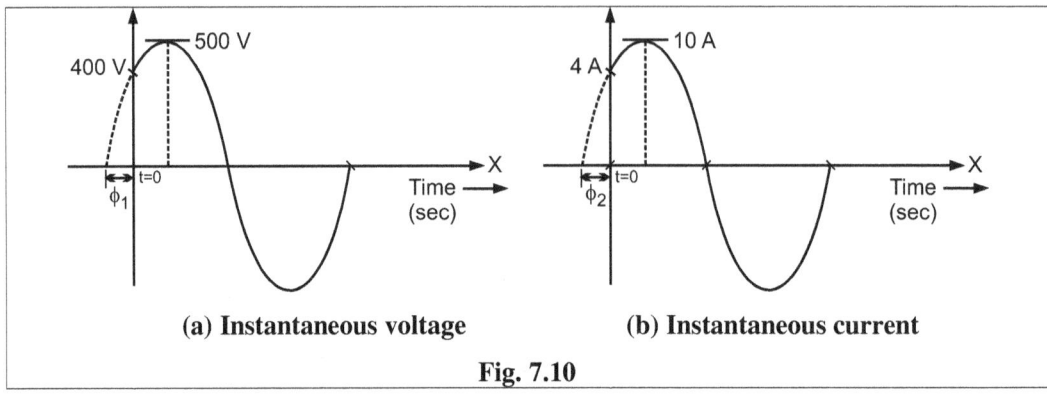

(a) Instantaneous voltage   **(b) Instantaneous current**

Fig. 7.10

When t = 0, instantaneous current, i = 4 Amp.

It has phase angle of ϕ_2 w.r.t. to reference.

$$i = I_m \sin(\omega t + \phi_2)$$

$$4 = 10 \sin(100\pi \times 0 + \phi_2)$$

∴ $$\sin \phi_2 = \frac{4}{10}$$

$$\phi_2 = 23.58° = 0.4115 \text{ rad.}$$

∴ Instantaneous current expression is,

$$i = I_m \sin(\omega t + \phi_2)$$

$$= 10 \sin(100\,\pi t + 0.4115) \text{ Amp.} \qquad\qquad ...(2)$$

(ii) Now, v and i at t = 0.015 sec.

substitute t = 0.015 in equations (1) and (2)

$$v = 500 \sin(100\pi \times 0.015 + 0.9272) = -300.038 \text{ V}$$

$$i = 10 \sin(100\pi \times 0.015 + 0.4115)$$

$$= -9.1652 \text{ A}$$

(iii) Phasor diagram of current and voltage is drawn in terms of rms value as shown in Fig. 7.10 (c).

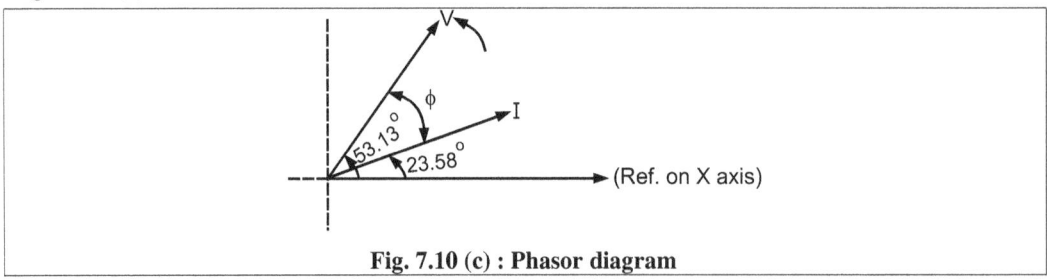

Fig. 7.10 (c) : Phasor diagram

ϕ_1 = 53.13 angle of V w.r.t. reference.

ϕ_2 = 23.58 angle of I w.r.t. reference.

Phase difference i.e. phase angle between

$$\text{V and I} = 53.13° - 23.58°$$
$$\phi = 29.55°$$

Thus, I lags behind V by 29.55°.

Example 7.5 :

For an A.C. circuit e = 100 sin ωt, calculate the value of e at t = 0.005 sec for (i) 50 Hz and (ii) 150 Hz. Sketch the waveform for e from t = 0 sec to t = 0.01 sec for both cases on the same time axis.

Solution :

$$e = 100 \sin \omega t$$

(i)
$$\text{for f} = 50 \text{ Hz}$$
$$e = 100 \sin 2\pi ft$$
$$= 100 \sin 2\pi \times 50 \times t$$
$$= 100 \sin 314 \, t$$
$$\text{at t} = 0.005 \text{ sec}$$
$$e = 100 \sin 314 \, (0.005)$$
$$= 100 \text{ volt}$$

(ii)
$$\text{for f} = 150 \text{ Hz}$$
$$e = 100 \sin 2\pi ft$$
$$= 100 \sin (2\pi \times 150 \times t)$$
$$= 100 \sin (942 \, t)$$
$$= 100 \sin (942 \times 0.005)$$
$$= -100 \text{ volt}$$

Waveform

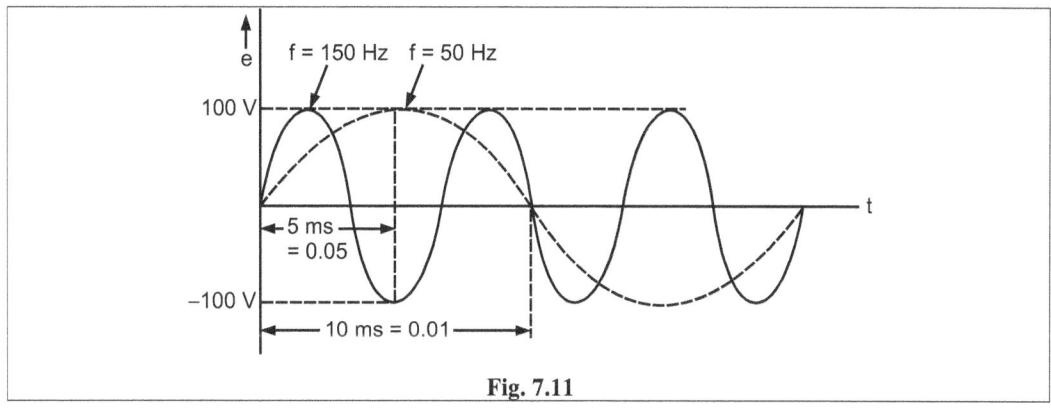

Fig. 7.11

Example 7.6 :

An alternating current varying sinusoidally at 50 Hz, has its r.m.s. value of 10 amp. Write the equation for its instantaneous value and find its value at

(i) 0.0025 sec after passing through positive maximum value.

(ii) 0.0075 sec after passing through zero and increasing positively.

Solution :

$$I_{rms} = I = 10 \text{ Amp}, \quad f = 50 \text{ Hz}$$

$$I_m = 10 \times \sqrt{2} = 14.14 \text{ Amp}$$

$$i = I_m \sin \omega t = I_m \sin 2\pi ft$$

$$= 14.14 \sin 2\pi \times 50 \times t = 14.14 \sin 314 \, t$$

$$T = \frac{1}{50}$$

$$= 0.02 \text{ s} = 20 \text{ ms}$$

(i) $$i_1 = 14.14 \sin 314 \, t_1$$

$$\text{where } t_1 = 0.005 + 0.0025$$

$$= 0.0075 \text{ sec.}$$

As the time required to achieve positive maximum value is 0.005 sec

$$i_1 = 14.14 \sin 314 \, (0.0075)$$

$$= 10 \text{ Amp}$$

(ii) After passing through zero and increasing negatively means after completing positive half cycle.

$$t_2 = 0.01 + 0.0075$$

$$= 0.0175 \text{ s}$$

$$i_2 = 14.14 \sin (314 \, (0.0175))$$

$$= -10 \text{ Amp}$$

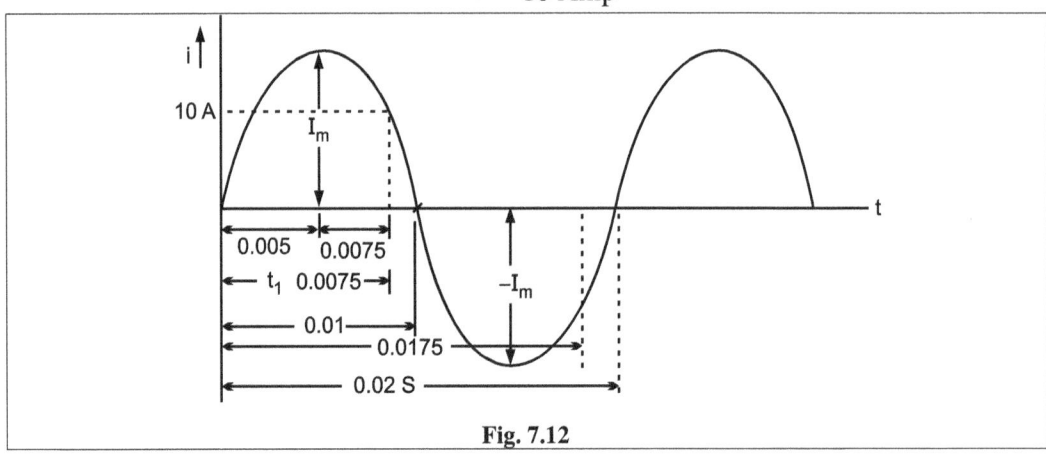

Fig. 7.12

7.5 ROOT MEAN SQUARE (R.M.S.) VALUE OR EFFECTIVE VALUE OF A.C. CURRENT OR VOLTAGE

From the definition of alternating current we know that, it varies from instant to instant, whereas the magnitude of direct current remains constant with time. For comparing the relative effectiveness of above two, the effect produced by two currents are compared and one such common effect is heating of resistance by the currents.

Based on comparison, r.m.s. value of current is defined as follows :

The r.m.s. value of an alternating current is given by that value of direct current which, when flowing through a given circuit for a given time produces the same amount of heat as produced by alternating when flowing through the same circuit for the same time.

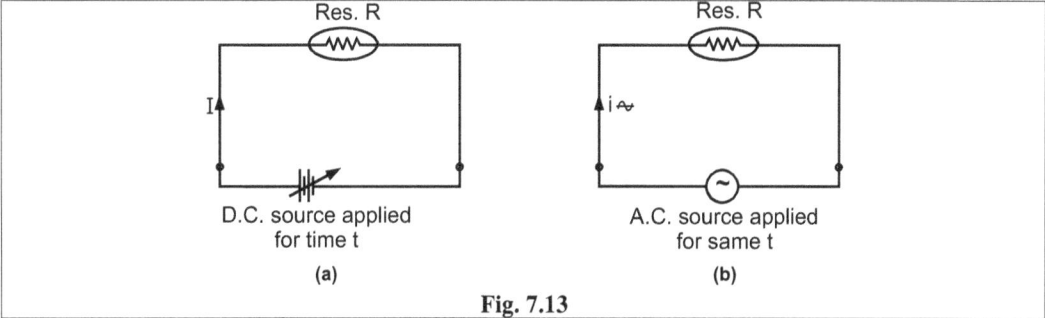

Fig. 7.13

R.M.S. value can be found by the following two methods :

(a) Graphical method, (b) Analytical method.

7.5.1 Graphical Method

To find r.m.s. value, as heating effect is considered which is proportional to the square of current therefore i^2 wave is non-directional. If both the half cycles are symmetrical then their square of current wave will be equal and in positive direction only. Therefore, considering only positive half cycle for finding the r.m.s. value, divide the **time base t into n-equal intervals, each of t/n seconds as shown in Fig. 7.14.**

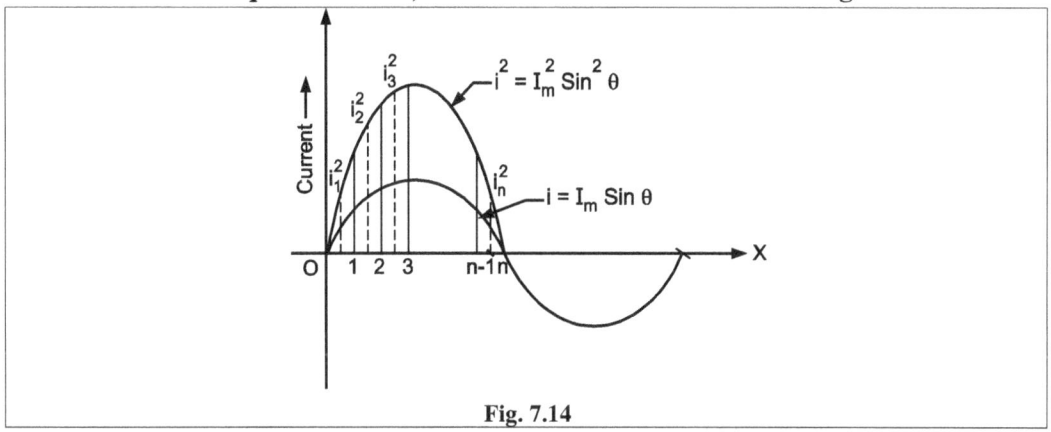

Fig. 7.14

The mid-ordinates i_1, i_2, i_3, ... i_n give the average value of instantaneous currents during these intervals. Let this current be passed through a resistance 'R'. Hence, heat produced can be calculated as,

$$\text{Heat produced in the first interval} = i_1^2\, R\, \frac{t}{n} \text{ joules}$$

$$\text{Heat produced in second interval} = i_2^2\, R \cdot \frac{t}{n} \text{ joules}$$

$$\text{Heat produced in the } n^{th} \text{ interval} = i_n^2\, R \cdot \frac{t}{n} \text{ joules}$$

$$\text{Total heat produced in t seconds} = R.t. \left(\frac{i_1^2 + i_2^2 ...... + i_n^2}{n}\right) \text{ joules.}$$

Now, let d.c. current I produce the same amount of heat when passed through same resistance for the same time t. Then expression for heat produced is $I^2\, R \cdot t$.

From the definition of rms value, the two heat produced must be same.

$$\therefore \quad I^2 \cdot Rt = Rt\left(\frac{i_1^2 + i_2^2 + ... + i_n^2}{n}\right)$$

$$I^2 = \frac{i_1^2 + i_2^2 + ... + i_n^2}{n}$$

$$\therefore \quad \boxed{I = \sqrt{\frac{(i_1^2 + i_2^2 + ... + i_n^2)}{n}} = I_{rms}}$$

I_{rms} = square root of mean of square of successive ordinates.

The effective value of an alternating current is also called as virtual value.

The expression for rms value of alternating voltage may be obtained similarly as,

$$V = \sqrt{\frac{v_1^2 + v_2^2 + ... + v_n^2}{n}}$$

7.5.2 Analytical Method

Alternating current can be expressed analytically as,

$$i = I_m \sin \theta$$

where, $\theta = \omega t$

Taking square of current, $i^2 = I_m^2 \sin^2 \theta$

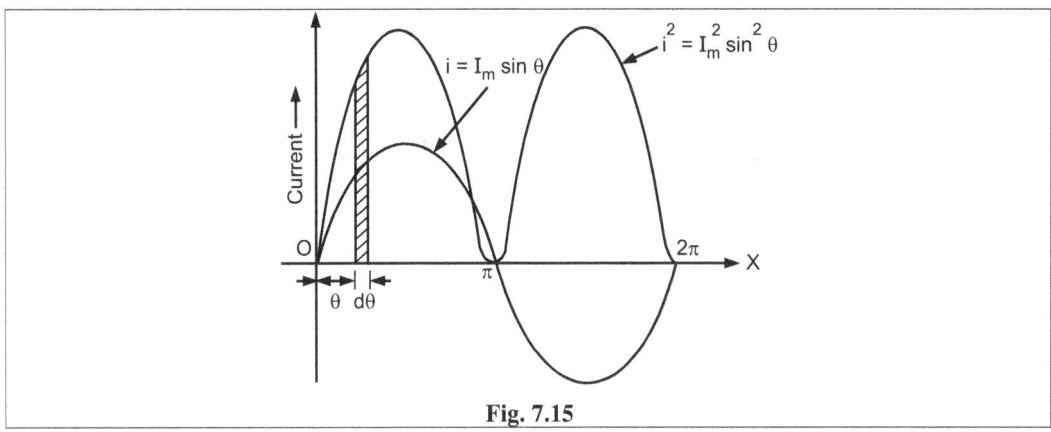

Fig. 7.15

Wave form for i^2 is plotted in Fig. 7.15 for an half cycle. To find the area under the curve (i^2), an interval of $d\theta$ is considered at a distance θ from origin.

$\therefore$ Area of squared curve over half cycle $= \int\limits_0^\pi i^2 \cdot d\theta$

The length of base is π. Therefore, mean value of squared curve of current over half cycle,

$$= \frac{\text{Area of squared curve over half cycle}}{\text{Length of base over half cycle}}$$

$$= \frac{\int\limits_0^\pi i^2 \cdot d\theta}{\pi}$$

$$= \frac{1}{\pi} \int\limits_0^\pi I_m^2 \cdot \sin^2 \theta \cdot d\theta$$

$$= \frac{I_m^2}{\pi} \int\limits_0^\pi \left[\frac{1 - \cos 2\theta}{2} \right] \cdot d\theta$$

$$= \frac{I_m^2}{2\pi} \left(\theta - \frac{\sin 2\theta}{2} \right)_0^\pi = \frac{I_m^2}{2\pi} (\pi)$$

$$= \frac{I_m^2}{2}$$

Hence, root mean square i.e. r.m.s. value can be calculated as,

$$I_{rms} = \sqrt{\frac{I_m^2}{2}} = \frac{I_m}{\sqrt{2}}$$

$$\boxed{I_{rms} = 0.707 \, I_m}$$

Thus, rms value of sinusoidal current is 0.707 times its maximum or peak value.

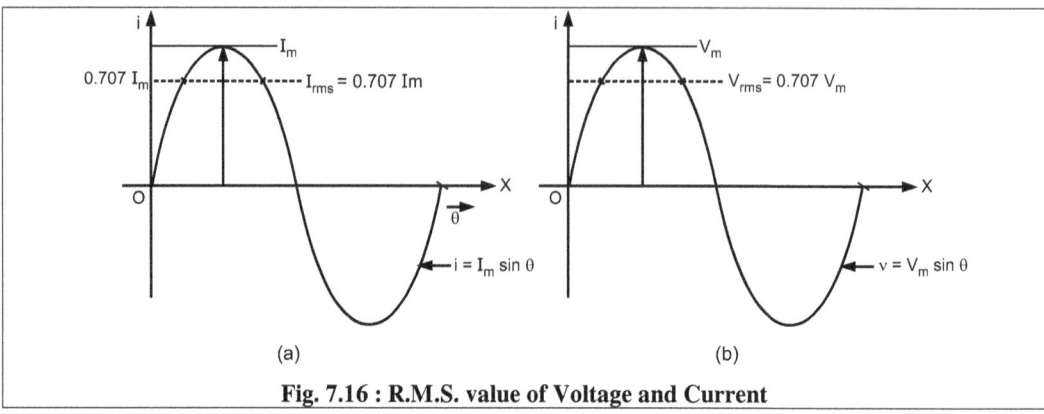

Fig. 7.16 : R.M.S. value of Voltage and Current

In similar way, it can be proved that rms value of sinusoidal voltage is given by,

$$V = \frac{V_m}{\sqrt{2}} = 0.707 \ V_m$$

In practice, r.m.s. value of alternative quantities are always represented by capital letters i.e.. V, I, etc.

Practical Importance of R.M.S. Value :

(1) The r.m.s. values are used to specify the magnitudes of alternating quantities. If given supply is mentioned as 230 V, 50 Hz or 110 V then unless and otherwise specified to be other, it should be taken as rms value.

(2) The ammeter and voltmeter indicate the rms values only.

(3) The heat produced due to a.c. is proportional to the rms value of current.

7.6   AVERAGE VALUE

Average value of an alternating quantity can be obtained by averaging all the instantaneous values of its wave over a period of half cycle. Only half cycle is considered because two half cycles being exactly similar, average value over a complete cycle is zero. Similar to r.m.s. value, average value can be obtained by either graphical or analytical method.

7.6.1 Graphical Method

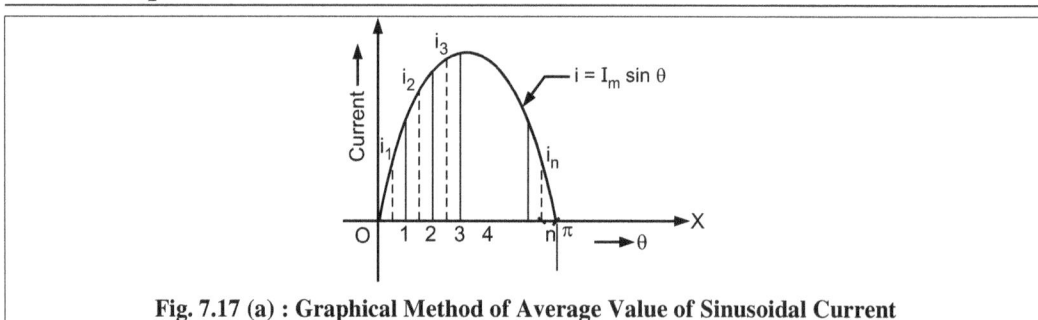

Fig. 7.17 (a) : Graphical Method of Average Value of Sinusoidal Current

Consider a half cycle of alternating current as shown in Fig. 7.17 (a). Divide the time base of this half cycle into n equal intervals, each of t/n seconds. Erect the mid ordinates $i_1, i_2, i_3, \ldots\ldots\ldots, i_n$ which give the average value of instantaneous current during these intervals. Now, average value of current over half cycle,

$$I_{av} = \frac{i_1 + i_2 + i_3 + \ldots\ldots\ldots + i_n}{n}$$

Similarly, for sinusoidal voltage,

$$V_{av} = \frac{v_1 + v_2 + v_3 = \ldots\ldots\ldots + v_n}{n}$$

7.6.2 Analytical Method

Alternating current can be expressed analytically as,

$$i = I_m \sin \theta$$

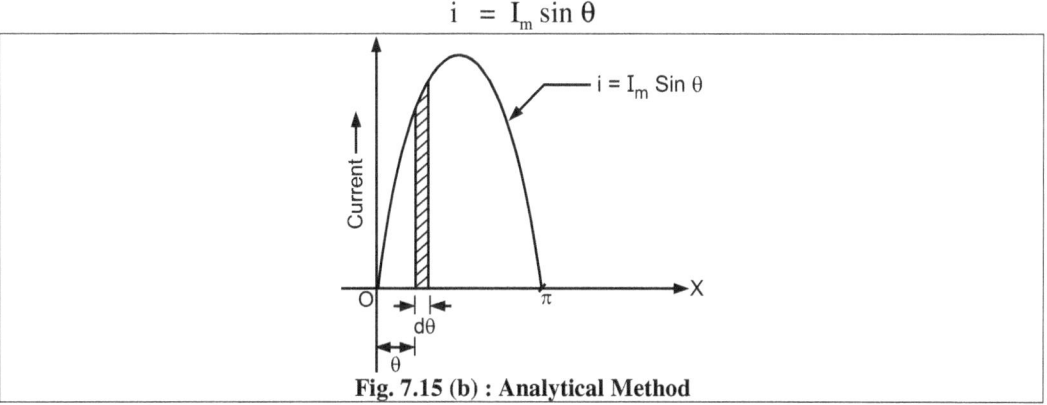

Fig. 7.15 (b) : Analytical Method

Fig. 7.17 (b) shows one half cycle for instantaneous current i. Here to find area under the curve i, consider an interval of $d\theta$ at a distance θ from the origin. Then total area under the curve (i) over half cycle $= \int\limits_{0}^{\pi} i \cdot d\theta$

∴ Average value of current over half cycle,

$$I_{av} = \frac{\text{Area under the curve over half cycle}}{\text{Length of base over half cycle}}$$

$$= \frac{\int\limits_{0}^{\pi} i \cdot d\theta}{\pi}$$

$$= \frac{1}{\pi} \int\limits_{0}^{\pi} I_m \sin \theta \cdot d\theta = \frac{I_m}{\pi} [- \cos \theta]_0^{\pi}$$

$$\boxed{I_{av} = \frac{2I_m}{\pi} = 0.637\, I_m}$$

Thus average value of sine wave is equal to 0.637 times the peak value.

Similarly,
$$V_{av} = \frac{2V_m}{\pi}$$

Example 7.7 :

Determine the average value, effective value and form factor of a sinusoidally varying half wave rectified alternating current as shown in Fig. 7.18.

Solution :

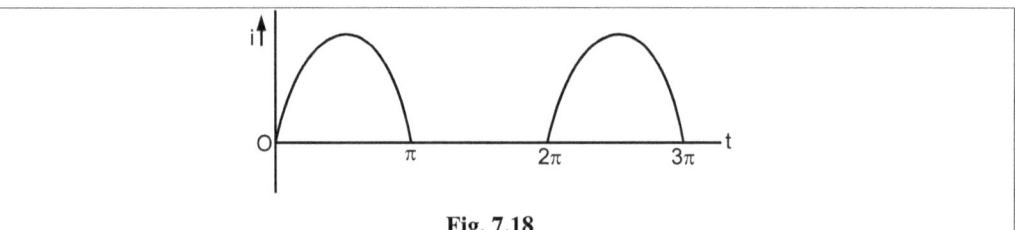

Fig. 7.18

$$\text{Average value} = \frac{\text{Area of the curve over a cycle}}{\text{Length of the base over a cycle}}$$

$$= \frac{1}{2\pi}\left(\int_0^{\pi} i\, d\theta + \int_{\pi}^{2\pi} 0\, d\theta\right)$$

$$= \frac{1}{2\pi}\int_0^{\pi} i\, d\theta$$

$$= \frac{1}{2\pi}\int_0^{\pi} I_m \sin\theta\, d\theta$$

$$= \frac{I_m}{2\pi}\left[-\cos\theta\right]_0^{\pi}$$

$$= \frac{I_m}{2\pi}\left[-\cos\pi + \cos\theta\right]$$

$$= \frac{2I_m}{2\pi} = \frac{I_m}{\pi}$$

$$I_{av} = 0.318\, I_m$$

$$\text{RMS value} = \sqrt{\frac{\text{Area of the curve over a cycle}}{\text{Length of the base over a cycle}}}$$

$$= \sqrt{\frac{1}{2\pi}\left[\int_0^\pi i^2\, d\theta + \int_\pi^{2\pi} 0\, d\theta\right]}$$

$$= \sqrt{\frac{1}{2\pi}\int_0^\pi I_m^2 \sin^2\theta\, d\theta}$$

$$= \sqrt{\frac{I_m^2}{2\pi}\int_0^\pi \left(\frac{1-\cos 2\theta}{2}\right) d\theta}$$

$$= \sqrt{\frac{I_m^2}{2\times 2\pi}\left[\theta - \frac{\sin 2\theta}{2}\right]_0^\pi}$$

$$= \sqrt{\frac{I_m^2}{4\pi}\, (\pi)}$$

$$= \frac{I_m}{2} = 0.5\, I_m$$

$$\text{Form factor} = \frac{\text{RMS value}}{\text{Average value}}$$

$$= \frac{0.5\, I_m}{0.318\, I_m}$$

$$= 1.5723$$

Example 7.8 :

The waveform of voltage has form factor of 1.15 and peak factor of 1.5. If the maximum value of voltage is 4500 V, calculate the average value and r.m.s. value of the voltage.

Solution : Form factor $= 1.15$, peak factor $= 1.5$, $V_m = 4500$

$$\text{Peak factor} = \frac{\text{Peak value}}{\text{RMS value}}$$

$$\text{RMS value} = \frac{\text{Peak value}}{\text{Peak factor}} = \frac{4500}{1.5}$$

$$= 3000 \text{ volt}$$

$$\text{Form factor} = \frac{\text{RMS value}}{\text{Average value}} = \frac{3000}{\text{Average value}}$$

$$= 1.15$$

$$\text{Average value} = \frac{3000}{1.15} = 2608.69 \text{ volt}.$$

Example 7.9 :

A 60 Hz sinsudoial current has an instantaneous value of 7.07 at t = 0 and r.m.s. value of 10$\sqrt{2}$ ampere. Assuming current wave to enter positive half at t = 0, determine (i) Expression for instantaneous current, (ii) Magnitude of current at t = 0.0125 second, (iii) Magnitude of current at t = 0.025 sec after t = 0.

Solution : Given data :

$$\text{frequency, f} = 60 \text{ Hz}$$
$$I_{rms} = 10\sqrt{2} \text{ Amp.}$$
$$i = 7.07 \text{ A at t} = 0$$

We know,
$$I_{max} = \sqrt{2} \cdot I_{rms}$$
$$= \sqrt{2} \times 10\sqrt{2}$$
$$= 20 \text{ Amps}$$

Given that, current wave when start at t = 0, enters in positive half i.e. (as per standard equation θ = 90° after is start, as shown in Fig. 7.19).

∴ Here, current equation is,

$$i = I_m \sin(\omega t + \phi) \text{ (since i is not zero at t = 0)}$$

where φ is the angle made by i w.r.t. reference axis.

$$7.07 = I_m \sin(\omega t + \phi)$$

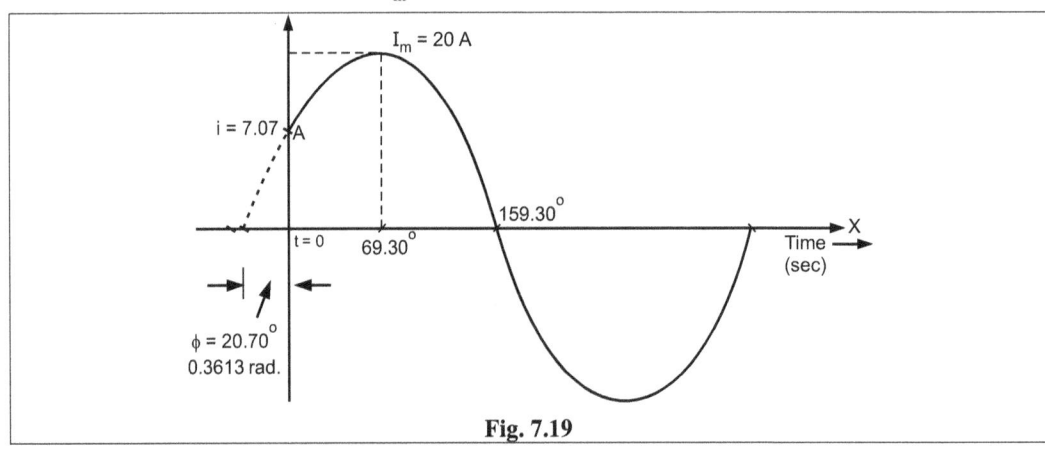

Fig. 7.19

$$7.07 = 20 \sin(\phi)$$
$$\phi = \sin^{-1}\left(\frac{7.07}{20}\right)$$
$$= \sin^{-1}(0.3535)$$
$$= 20.70° \text{ or } 0.3613 \text{ radians}$$

(i) $\therefore$ Expression for i, $i = I_m \sin(\omega t + \phi)$

$i = 20 \sin(2\pi 60 \times t + 0.3613)$ ...(1)

Putting $t = 0.0124$ sec in (1) we get

$i = 20 \sin(120\pi \times 0.0125 + 0.3613)$

$t = 0.0125$ sec

$i = -18.708$ Amp.

Putting $t = 0.025$ sec in (1) we get

$i = 20 \sin(120\,\pi \times 0.025 + 0.3613)$

$= -7.07$ Amp

7.7 PEAK FACTOR AND FORM FACTOR

Peak factor and form factor relate maximum average and r.m.s. values of an alternating quantity.

Peak Factor :

The peak factor of an alternating quaintly is defined as ratio of maximum value to the r.m.s. value. This factor may also be called as crest factor or amplitude factor.

For sinusoidal voltage and current,

$$\text{Peak factor, } K_p = \frac{\text{Maximum value}}{\text{R.M.S. value}}$$

$$= \frac{\text{Maximum value}}{0.707 \times \text{Maximum value}}$$

$$= 1.414$$

The knowledge of this factor is useful in applications like insulation testing and measurement of iron losses.

Form Factor :

The ratio of r.m.s value to average value of an alternating quantity is called as form factor.

Thus, for sinusoidal voltage and current :

$$\text{Form factor, } K_f = \frac{\text{R.M.S. value}}{\text{Average value}}$$

$$= \frac{0.707 \times \text{Maximum value}}{0.637 \times \text{Maximum value}} = 1.11$$

Example 7.10 :

A 50 Hz sinusoidal current has peak factor 1.4 and form factor 1.1. Its average value is 20 Amp. The instantaneous value of current is 15 Amp at t = 0 sec. Write the equation of currents and draw its waveform.

Solution : Given : f = 50 Hz,   peak factor = 1.4, form factor = 1.1

I_{av} = 20 Amp, i = 15 Amp at t = 0

$$\text{Form factor} = \frac{\text{RMS value}}{\text{Average value}} = 1.1$$

$$\text{RMS value} = 1.1 \times 20 = 22 \text{ Amp}$$

$$\text{Peak factor} = \frac{\text{Peak value}}{\text{RMS value}} = 1.4$$

$$\text{Peak value} = \text{Peak factor} \times \text{RMS value}$$

$$= 1.4 \times 22 = 30.8 \text{ Amp}$$

At t = 0,   i = 15 Amp

As the current has positive value at t = 0, so ϕ will be + ve.

$$\text{So,}\quad i = I_m \sin(\omega t + \phi) = I_m \sin(2\pi ft + \phi)$$

$$15 = 30.8 \sin(2\pi \times 50\, t + \phi)$$

$$= 30.8 \sin(314\,(0) + \phi)$$

$$\phi = \sin^{-1}\left(\frac{15}{30.8}\right) = 29.144° = 0.508 \text{ rad}$$

$$i = 30.8 \sin(314\, t + 29.144°)$$

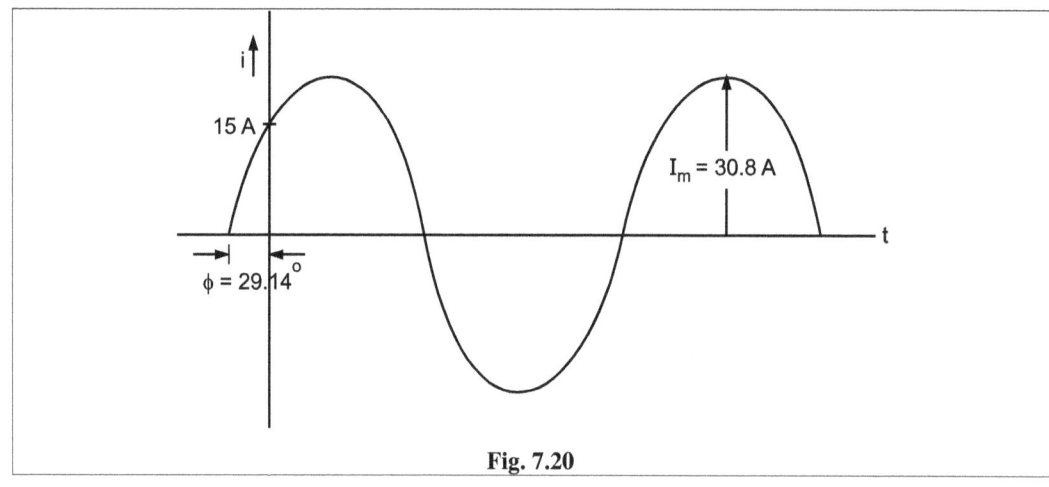

Fig. 7.20

7.8 PHASOR REPRESENTATION OF ALTERNATING QUANTITIES

We have to deal with many alternating quantities while studying a.c. circuits. It is, however, always cumbersome to handle these quantities in the form of their waves or mathematical equations (like $i = I_m \sin \omega t$, etc.). One of a standard method is to represent them with the help of rotating phasors. A phasor is a directed arrow analogous to vector used to represent the magnitude and direction of a quantity in space. Consider a phasor OA rotating in an anti-clockwise direction with uniform angular velocity (Fig. 7.21).

If the projections on Y-axis of this phasor in its different positions are plotted against the angle turned through (or time), we get a sine waveform. Therefore, the alternating quantity following a sine waveform can always be represented by such a rotating phasor.

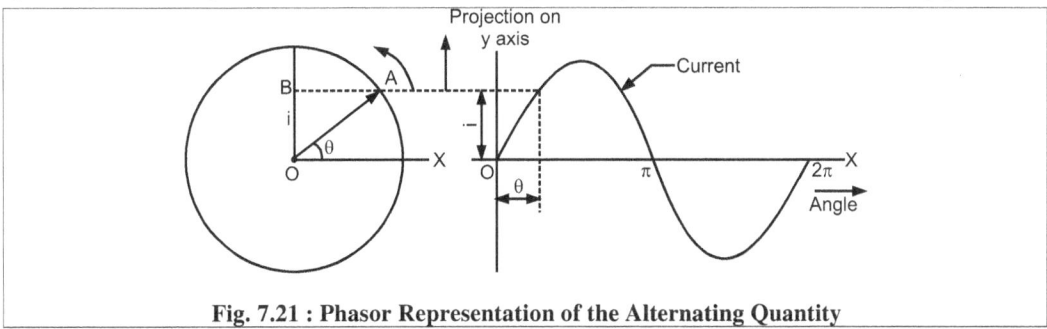

Fig. 7.21 : Phasor Representation of the Alternating Quantity

Let the phasor OA in Fig. 7.21 represent some sinusoidal alternating quantity, say current. If the length of OA is taken equal to maximum value, I_m of the sinusoidal current, then at any instant, the projection on Y-axis will be OB = OA $\sin \theta$ = $I_m \sin \theta$, where $\theta = \omega t$.

Hence, OB = i, the instantaneous value of the current. Thus, if the length of phasor is taken equal to the maximum value of the alternating quantity, then its orientation in space at any instant is such that the length of its projection on Y-axis gives the instantaneous value of alternating quantity at that particular instant.

We deal more frequently with the r.m.s. values of the alternating quantities, which bears a definite relationship to the maximum value $\left(V = V_m/\sqrt{2}\right)$. Therefore phasors are normally drawn to represent r.m.s. values of alternating quantities. It is important to note that the phasors are always assumed rotate in a counter-clockwise direction. This is purely a conventional direction which has been universally adopted. The phasor representation greatly simplifies the calculation work involved in a.c. circuits.

7.9 PHASE AND PHASE DIFFERENCE

7.9.1 Concept of Phase

In the analysis of alternating quantities it is important to know the position of the phasor representing that alternating quantity at a particular instant. Considering the instant when alternating quantity passes through zero and increases in the positive direction as reference point, the fraction of the time period (T) that elapses in achieving certain instantaneous value is known as **phase** of that alternating quantity. For example, in Fig. 7.22, phase of the alternating quantity at point S is T/4 seconds or when expressed in terms of angle, it is $\pi/2$ radians. In other words, the orientation in space at a particular instant (i.e. the angle turned through from reference axis) of the rotating phasor representing a certain alternating quantity also gives its phase. Considering again the case of point S (Fig. 7.22), the corresponding rotation of phasor OA will be through $\pi/2$ radians from reference axis OX. Therefore, phase at this point is $\pi/2$ radians.

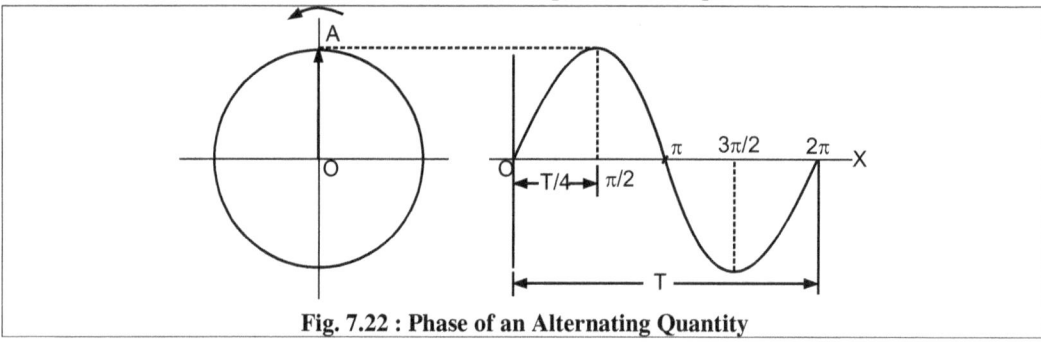

Fig. 7.22 : Phase of an Alternating Quantity

In practice, we are, however, more concerned with relative phases or phase difference between different alternating quantities rather than with their absolute phases.

7.9.2 Phase Difference

Consider, two single turn coils A and B of different dimensions arranged radially in the same plane and mounted rigidly on the common shaft as shown in Fig. 7.23 (a).

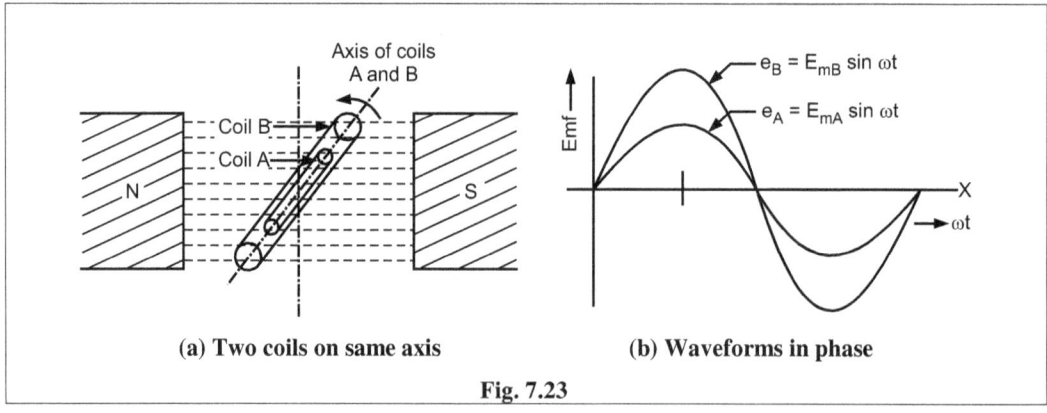

(a) Two coils on same axis   (b) Waveforms in phase

Fig. 7.23

Let the two coils rotate together with some constant angular velocity in the uniform magnetic field. Then, as seen in the case of an elementary alternator (Fig. 7.23), sinusoidal e.m.f.s will be induced in these two coils. These e.m.f.s. will have the same frequency but different values at every instant. **Even, if the values of these e.m.f.s. will be different at every instant, they would reach their respective maximum or zero values at the same time (Fig. 7.23 b), such e.m.f.s are said to in phase with each other.**

Thus, when two alternating quantities of same frequency attain their corresponding values (e.g. zero, positive maximum, etc.) simultaneously, they are said to be in phase with each other. The two alternating e.m.f.s in the coils A and B considered above can be represented by the following equations :

$$e_A = E_{mA} \sin \theta = E_{mA} \sin \omega t \qquad\qquad\qquad …(1)$$

$$e_B = E_{mB} \sin \theta = E_{mB} \sin \omega t \qquad\qquad\qquad …(2)$$

In some cases, it is not necessary that all alternating quantities must be always in phase. It is possible that one is achieving its zero value while other is having either certain positive or negative value. Now, to explain this let us assume that coil B is displaced from coil A by angle α as shown in Fig. 7.24 (a). In this, condition, it will be observed that the e.m.f.s' induced in the two coils will not reach their maximum or zero values at the same instant. **Thus, if two alternating quantities of the same frequency which attain their corresponding zero or maximum values at different instants are said to be out of phase.**

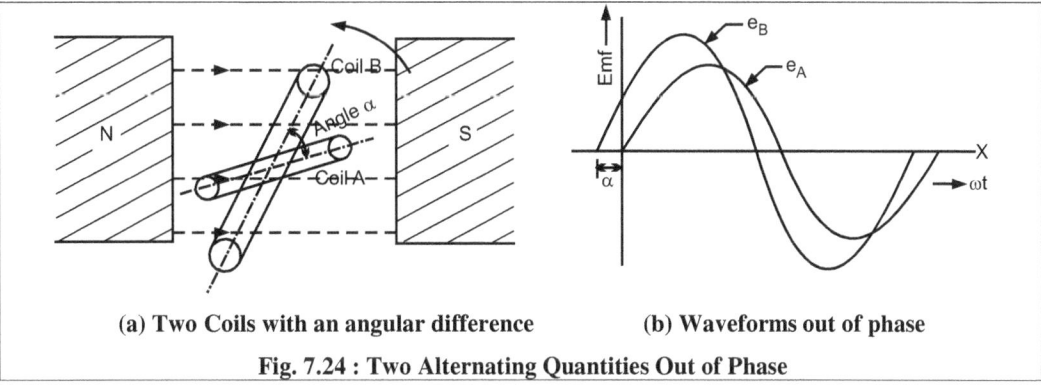

(a) Two Coils with an angular difference   (b) Waveforms out of phase

Fig. 7.24 : Two Alternating Quantities Out of Phase

Fig. 7.24 (b) shows the waveforms for the e.m.f.s induced in the two coils. It will be seen that there is an angular displacement of α between the two curves. **This angular displacement between the waveforms of two e.m.f.s. is known as phase difference between them.** When the phase difference between the two alternating quantities is $\pi/2$ radians (90°), they are said to be in quadrature, and when it is 180°, they are in phase opposition.

The waveforms shown in Fig. 7.24 (b) also reveal that the e.m.f. induced in the coil B attains its zero or maximum value earlier than the e.m.f. in the coil A by an angle α. Therefore, the e.m.f. in the coil B is said to be leading in by angle α with respect to the e.m.f. in the coil A or alternatively, the e.m.f. in the coil A is said to be lagging by an angle α behind the e.m.f. in the coil B.

Thus, we can define a leading alternating quantity as one which attains its zero or maximum value earlier as compared with the other quantity. Similarly, lagging alternating quantity is that which attains its zero or maximum value latter than the other quantity.

In the case considered above, if the e.m.f. in the coil A is represented by the equation,

$$e_A \ = \ E_{mA} \sin \omega t \qquad\qquad ...(3)$$

then the e.m.f. in the coil B will be represented by,

$$e_B \ = \ E_{mB} \sin (\omega t + \alpha) \qquad\qquad ...(4)$$

On the other hand, if the e.m.f in the coil B is taken as reference and represented by the equation, $\qquad e_B \ = \ E_{mB} \sin \omega t \qquad\qquad ...(5)$

then the e.m.f. in the coil A will be represented by the equation :

$$e_A \ = \ E_{mA} \sin (\omega t - \alpha) \qquad\qquad ...(6)$$

Thus, in connection with the phase difference, a plus (+) sign indicates lead whereas a minus (–) sign indicates lag in reference to the given alternating quantity.

7.10 PHASOR DIAGRAMS

The diagrams in which different alternating quantities (sinusoidal) of the same frequency are represented by phasors with their correct phase relationships is known as phasor diagram. The phasors representing different alternating quantities of the same frequency rotate in an anticlockwise direction with the same angular velocity ($\omega = 2\pi f$).

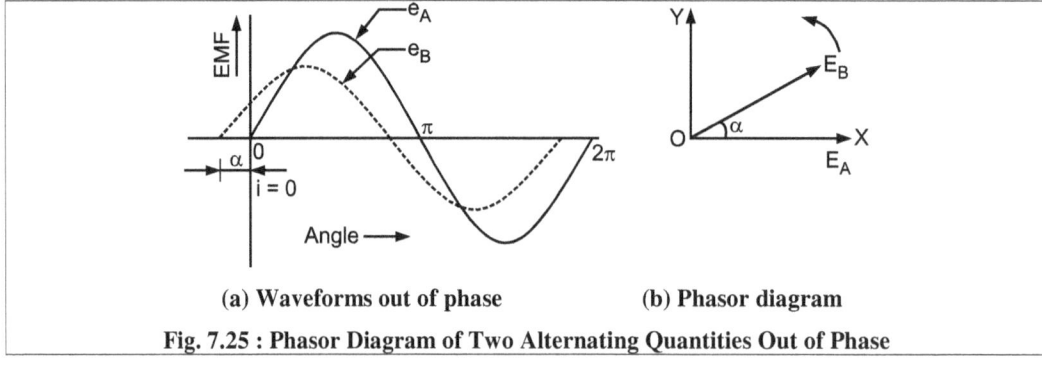

(a) Waveforms out of phase   (b) Phasor diagram

Fig. 7.25 : Phasor Diagram of Two Alternating Quantities Out of Phase

Let us, again consider the case of the e.m.f.s in two single turn coils A and B shown in Fig. 7.24 (a). If the e.m.f. wave for the coil A is supposed to pass through zero in upward in positive direction at the instant t = 0, the e.m.f. wave for the coil B already attains some positive value because of its advancement through an angle α from its zero value (Fig. 7.25 a). This can be shown with the help of phasors in the phasor diagram as illustrated in Fig. 7.25 (b). The angle α between two phasors is obviously the phase difference between the two e.m.f.s. In present case, e.m.f. in coil B leads the e.m.f in coil A by angle α.

Following few points should be remembered while drawing any phasor diagrams :

(i)   X and Y axis are fixed in space. Therefore, it is not necessary to include them in the diagram.

(ii) The phasors are drawn normally to represent r.m.s. values.

(iii) The phasor chosen as a reference phasor is drawn in the horizontal position e.g. the phasor E_A in Fig. 7.25 (b) is the reference phasor

(iv) Since the phasors representing different quantities are assumed to rotate in the counter clockwise direction, the phasors ahead in this direction from a given phasor are said to lead the given phasor, while those behind are said to lag the given phasor. e.g. in Fig. 7.25 (b), the phasor E_B leads the phasor E_A by an angle α. The angle between two phasors represents phase difference between two alternating quantities.

(v)   In order to distinguish between different alternating quantities like current, voltage or flux, different types of arrow heads may be used, e.g. the current phasors may be drawn with closed arrow heads while the voltage phasors with open arrow heads.

In this way, when different alternating quantities of the same frequency are represented by phasors in the same phasor diagram, their addition and subtraction becomes simple. It is similar to addition and subtraction of vectors in mechanics as seen in the next article.

7.11 ADDITION AND SUBTRACTION OF SINUSOIDAL ALTERNATING QUANTITIES

While analyzing the a.c. circuits, we are often required to add the two or more alternating quantities of the same frequency but of different magnitude and phase. These waves can be added by the use of trigonometric transformations or they are plotted and then added graphically. However, these methods are inherently cumbersome. Phasor representation of alternating quantities, as said earlier, greatly simplifies this addition. When the magnitude and phase angles of the various voltages or currents are known, the phasor diagram can be constructed. Once such phasor diagram is constructed, the addition of phasors becomes a simple geometric problem. For example, if two alternating e.m.f.s are to be added, the resultant is obtained by means of a parallelogram of e.m.f.s. or a triangle of e.m.f.s If there are several such e.m.f.s, then the resultant is given by the closing side of a phasor polygon. These graphical methods are rather inconvenient and often time-wasting. A more systematic method is to split each phasor into its components along the horizontal and vertical axes. The horizontal component of the resultant is then given by the algebraic sum of the individual horizontal components and the vertical component of the resultant is given by the algebraic sum of the individual vertical components. It should be remembered that the operation of subtraction of one phasor from the other is simply that of their addition with one of the phasors reversed.

7.12 COMPLEX NOTATION

Simple A.C. circuits can be solved with the help of phasor diagrams. But for solving more complex circuits this method is not much useful. In such case, complex algebra may be used. In this method, the phasor quantities, such as alternating voltages and currents, and their phase relationships are expressed in simple algebraic forms. The circuits are then solved by algebraic operations alone. The simple algebraic forms which are normally used to represent the phasors mainly include :

   (i)   Rectangular form,

   (ii) Polar form.

These two forms and the general principles of complex notation method are discussed in the following articles. The application of this method to A.C. circuits will be studied later on in the next chapter.

7.13 PHASORS IN RECTANGULAR FORM

Consider the phasor V at the angle θ with the reference axis as shown in Fig. 7.26 (a). The phasor V has two components, x along the reference axis and y at 90° to the reference axis. Thus, phasor V is the phasor addition of components x and y. This may be expressed symbolically as,

$$V = x + jy \qquad \qquad \text{...(7)}$$

Here, the actual magnitude of the phasor is,

$$V = \sqrt{x^2 + y^2}$$

while its phase angle, i.e. its inclination to the reference axis is given by,

$$\tan \theta = (y/x)$$

Thus, equation (7) completely specifies the magnitude and the position of the phasor. Phasors represented in this form are said to be in rectangular or Cartesian or symbolic form.

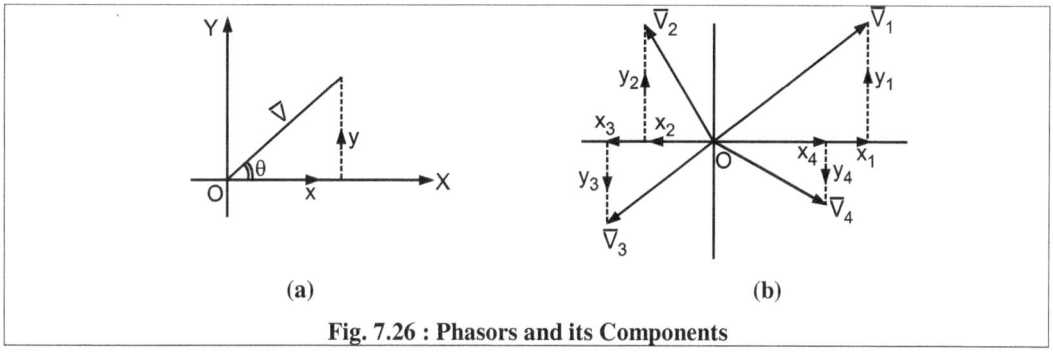

(a)   (b)

Fig. 7.26 : Phasors and its Components

7.13.1   The j Operator

The symbol j used in equation (7) indicates that the component y is perpendicular to the component x. In other words, the symbol j denotes rotation of the quantity to which it is attached through 90° in the counter-clockwise direction. The symbol j is thus a phasor operator indicating rotation through 90°. Hence, if applied twice, it turns the quantity through 180° e.g.,

$$jjy = j^2y = -y$$

This gives, $$j^2 = -1 \text{ or } j = \sqrt{-1}$$

The quantities when expressed in the form x + jy are called complex numbers. Complex numbers follow all fundamental laws of algebra. In all the algebraic operations with complex numbers, the operator j may be handled as if it were $\sqrt{-1}$. In mathematics, x is called the real and y the imaginary component of the complex number. However, in connection with A.C. circuits, these components are normally referred to as in-phase (or active) and the quadrature (or reactive) component respectively. While expressing the different phasors in the rectangular form due regard must be paid to the sign of their in-phase and quadrature components, e.g. consider the phasors,

V_1, V_2, V_3 and V_4 shown in Fig. 7.26 (b). These phasors can be expressed in their rectangular forms as given below :

$$V_1 = x_1 + j\, y_1$$

$$V_2 = -x_2 + jy_2$$

$$V_3 = -x_3 - j\, y_3$$

$$V_4 = x_4 - jy_4$$

7.13.2 Addition and Subtraction of Phasors in Rectangular Form

While adding two phasors in rectangular form, their in-phase and quadrature components are added separately. Similarly, while subtracting one phasor from the another, their in-phase and quadrature components are separately subtracted. However, it should be remembered that when phasors are added or subtracted, they must all represent quantities of the same physical kind.

Example 1 :

Two phasors are $\qquad \overline{V}_1 \ = \ 13 + j20$

and $\qquad \overline{V}_2 \ = \ 10 - j5$

Find (a) $\overline{V}_1 + \overline{V}_2$, (b) $\overline{V}_1 - \overline{V}_2$

Solution :
$$\overline{V}_1 + \overline{V}_2 \ = \ (13 + j20) + (10 - j5)$$
$$= \ (13 + 10) + j\,(20 - 5)$$
$$= \ 23 + j\,15$$

and
$$\overline{V}_1 - \overline{V}_2 \ = \ (13 + j20) - (10 - j5)$$
$$= \ 13 + j20 - 10 + j5$$
$$= \ (13 - 10) + j\,(20 + 5)$$
$$= \ 3 + j\,25$$

7.13.3 Multiplication and Division of Phasors in Rectangular Form

Multiplication of two phasors expressed in rectangular form is carried out as in ordinary algebraic multiplication, substitute –1 for j^2. While dividing one phasor by another, a process called rationalization is adopted to remove j terms from the denominator. In this process, numerator and denominator are multiplied by the conjugate of the denominator. The conjugate of complex number is obtained by reversing the sign of the j term. The process of multiplication and division is best explained by a numerical example.

Example 1 :

For the same phasors given in Example 7. (A) i.e. find : (a) $\overline{V}_1 \cdot \overline{V}_2$, (b) $\dfrac{\overline{V}_1}{\overline{V}_2}$

Solution :
$$\overline{V}_1 \cdot \overline{V}_2 = (13 + j20) \cdot (10 - j5)$$
$$= 13\,(10 - j5) + j20\,(10 - j5)$$

$$= 130 - j65 + j200 + (-100j^2)$$
$$= 130 + j135 + (100) \qquad \text{(since } j^2 = -1)$$
$$= 230 + j135$$

$$\frac{\overline{V_1}}{\overline{V_2}} = \frac{13 + j20}{10 - j5}$$

$$= \frac{13 + j20}{10 - j5} \times \frac{10 + j5}{10 + j5}$$

$$= \frac{(13 + j20) \cdot (10 + j5)}{(10)^2 - (j5)^2}$$

$$= \frac{130 + j65 + 200j + (-100)}{100 + 25}$$

$$= \frac{30 + j265}{125} = \frac{30}{125} + j\frac{265}{125}$$

7.14 PHASORS IN POLAR FORM

In this form, a phasor is specified by its magnitude and its angular position with respect to the X-axis taken as a reference axis. For example, the phasor V in Fig. 7.26 (a) can be represented in polar form as shown below :

$$V = V \angle \theta° \qquad\qquad ...(8)$$

where V is the magnitude of the phasor V and θ is the angle made by it with the X-axis. The magnitude of V is called the modulus or absolute value of the phasor V and θ is called the argument of this phasor. If the phasor is given in rectangular form, it can be easily converted into its polar form and its vice-versa. For example, we have seen that the phasor V shown in Fig. 7.26 (a) can be expressed in rectangular form as,

$$V = x + jy$$

This phasor can be expressed in polar form as,

$$V = V \angle \theta$$

where, from the geometry of Fig. 7.22 (a),

$$V = \sqrt{x^2 + y^2}$$

and

$$\theta = \tan^{-1}\left(\frac{y}{x}\right)$$

For reverse operation, $x = V \cos \theta$, $y = V \sin \theta$

Thus various ways of representing the phasor in algebraic forms are,

$$\overline{V} = x + jy$$
$$= V \angle \theta$$
$$= V (\cos \theta + j \sin \theta)$$

7.14.1 Multiplication and Division of Phasors in Polar Form

Multiplication of two phasors in polar form is done by taking the product of their magnitudes and the sum of their angles. On the other hand, their division is done by taking the quotient of their magnitudes and the difference of their angles.

Example 1 : Two phasors are $V_1 = 12 \angle 60°$ and $V_2 = 3 \angle -30°$.

Find : (a) $V_1 \cdot V_2$, (b) V_1/V_2

Solution :

$$V_1 \cdot V_2 = 12 \angle 60° \times 3 \angle -30°$$
$$= 12 \times 3 \angle (60° - 30°)$$
$$= 36 \angle 30°$$

$$V_1/V_2 = \frac{12 \angle 60°}{3 \angle -30°}$$
$$= \frac{12}{3} \angle (60° + 30°) = 4 \angle 90°$$

7.15 INTERCONVERSION OF RECTANGULAR AND POLAR FORMS

For addition and subtraction, phasors must be essentially in their rectangular forms. Multiplication, division, however, are less labourious in polar forms. The use of scientific calculator is very helpful in converting quantities from rectangular to polar form and vice versa. Following example, will illustrate how the use of complex notation method gives a more quick and accurate technique for finding the algebraic sum of sinusoidal alternating quantities. In the next chapter, this technique will be extended to permit the analysis of sinusoidal A.C. networks.

Example 7.11 :

Two currents $\overline{I}_1 = 10e^{j50}$ and $\overline{I}_2 = 5e^{-j100}$ flow in single phase A.C. circuit. Estimate

(i) $\overline{I}_1 + \overline{I}_2$ (ii) $\overline{I}_1 - \overline{I}_2$ (iii) $\dfrac{\overline{I}_1}{\overline{I}_2} \cdot \overline{I}_2$ (iv) $\overline{I}$ in complex form.

Solution : (i)

$$\overline{I}_1 = 10 \cdot e^{j50} = 10 \angle 50$$
$$= (6.4278 + j\,7.6604) \text{ A}$$

$$\overline{I}_2 = 5\, e^{-j100}$$
$$= 5 \angle -100$$
$$= (-0.8682 - j\,4.924) \text{ A.}$$

$\therefore$

$$\overline{I}_1 + \overline{I}_2 = 6.4278 + j\,7.6604 - 0.8682 - j\,4.924$$
$$= (5.5596 + j\,2.7364) \text{ Amp.}$$
$$= 6.196 \angle 26.21° \text{ Amp}$$

(ii) $\qquad \overline{I}_1 - \overline{I}_2 = 6.4278 + j\,7.6604 + 0.8682 + j\,4.924$

$\qquad\qquad\qquad = (7.296 + j\,12.5844)$ Amp

$\qquad\qquad\qquad = 14.5464 \angle 59.89°$ Amp

(iii) $\qquad \dfrac{\overline{I}_1}{\overline{I}_2} = \dfrac{10 \angle 50}{5 \angle - 100}$

$\qquad\qquad\qquad = 2 \angle 150$

$\qquad\qquad\qquad = (- 1.732 + j1)$ Amp

(iv) $\qquad \overline{I}_1 \cdot \overline{I}_2 = (10 \angle 50) \cdot (5 \angle - 100)$

$\qquad\qquad\qquad = 50 \angle - 50$

$\qquad\qquad\qquad = (32.13 - j\,38.30)$ A

Example 7.12 :

Find the resultant of three voltages given by

$V_1 = 10 \sin \omega t$, $V_2 = 20 \sin \left(\omega t - \dfrac{\pi}{4} \right)$, and $V_3 = 30 \cos \left(\omega t + \dfrac{\pi}{6} \right)$

Solution : This can be solved by vector or phasor addition as well as by adding them using complex notation.

(a) By using complex notation

$$V_1 = 10 \sin \omega t$$

$$V_2 = 20 \sin \left(\omega t - \dfrac{\pi}{4} \right)$$

$$V_3 = 30 \cos \left(\omega t + \dfrac{\pi}{6} \right)$$

$$= 30 \sin \left(\dfrac{\pi}{2} + \omega t + \dfrac{\pi}{6} \right) = 30 \sin \left(\omega t + \dfrac{2\pi}{3} \right)$$

$$\overline{V}_{m1} = \overline{V}_{m1} \angle 0 = 10 \angle 0 = 10 + j0$$

$$\overline{V}_{m2} = V_{m2} \angle -\dfrac{\pi}{4} = 20 \angle - 45° = 14.14 - j\,14.14$$

$$\overline{V}_{m3} = V_{m3} \angle \dfrac{2\pi}{3} = 30 \angle 120° = -15 + j\,25.98$$

Resultant maximum value

$$\overline{V}_{mR} = \overline{V}_{m1} + \overline{V}_{m2} + \overline{V}_{m3}$$

$$= (10 + j0) + (14.14 - j\,14.14) + (- 15 + j\,25.98)$$

$$= (10 + 14.14 - 15) + j\,(-14.14 + 25.98)$$
$$= 9.142 + j\,11.83$$
$$= 14.95 \angle 52.32° \text{ volt}$$

The expression for resultant voltage

$$v = V_{mR} \sin(\omega t + \phi)$$
$$= 14.95 \sin(\omega t + 52.32°) \text{ volt}$$

OR

(b) By using phasor addition

$$\overline{V_{m1}} = V_{m1} \angle 0 = 10 \angle 0,$$

$$\overline{V_{m2}} = 20 \angle -45°$$

$$\overline{V_{m3}} = 30 \angle 120°$$

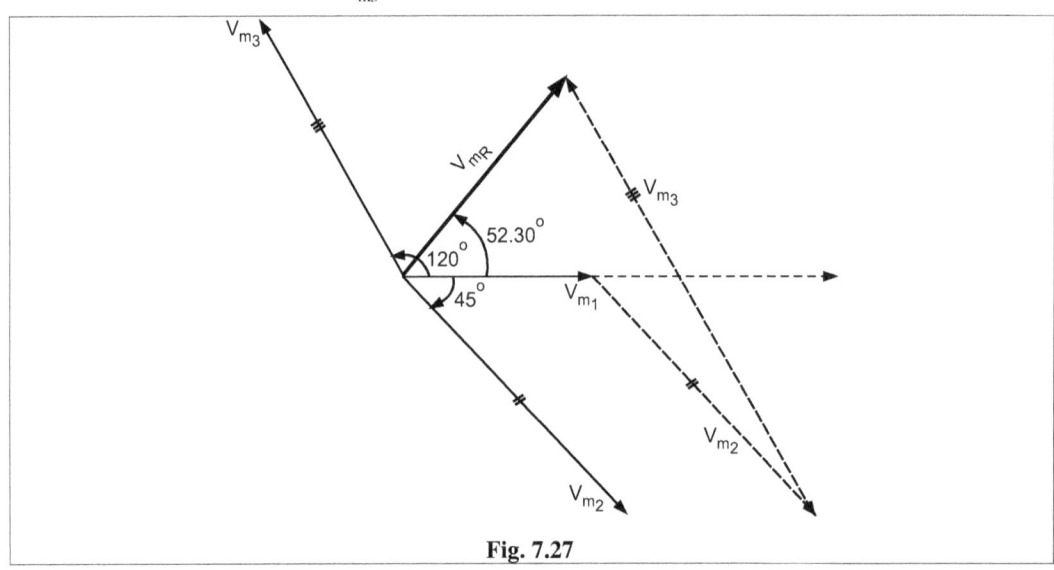

Fig. 7.27

$$\text{X component} = V_{m1} + V_{m2} \cos 45° + V_{m3} \cos 120°$$
$$= 10 + 20 \cos 45° + 30 \cos 120°$$
$$= 10 + 14.14 - 15$$
$$= 9.142$$

$$\text{Y component} = 0 - V_{m2} \cos 45° + V_{m3} \sin 120°$$
$$= -14.14 + 30\,(0.866)$$
$$= -14.14 + 25.98$$
$$= 11.83$$

$$V_{mR} = \sqrt{9.142^2 + 11.83^2} = 14.95$$

$$\phi = \tan^{-1}\left(\frac{11.83}{9.142}\right)$$

$$= 52.30°$$

$$v = V_{mR} \sin(\omega t + \phi)$$

$$= 14.95 \sin(\omega t + 52.30°) \text{ volt}$$

Example 7.13 :

Three voltages represented by

$$e_1 = 20 \sin \omega t$$

$$e_2 = 30 \sin\left(\omega t - \frac{\pi}{4}\right)$$

$$e_3 = 40 \cos\left(\omega t + \frac{\pi}{6}\right)$$

act together in a circuit. Find an expression for the resultant voltage. Represent them by appropriate vectors.

Solution :

$$e_3 = 40 \sin\left(\omega t + \frac{\pi}{6} + \frac{\pi}{2}\right)$$

$$E_{m1} = 20 \angle 0°, \ E_{m_2}$$

$$= 30 \angle -45°$$

$$e_3 = 40 \sin\left(\omega t + \frac{\pi}{6} + \frac{\pi}{2}\right)$$

$$= 40 \sin\left(\omega t + \frac{2\pi}{3}\right)$$

$$E_{m3} = 40 \angle \frac{2\pi}{3}$$

$$E_{m3} = 40 \angle 120°$$

$$\overline{E_{mR}} = \overline{E_{m1}} + \overline{E_{m2}} + \overline{E_{m3}}$$

$$= 20 \angle + 30 \angle -45° + 40 \angle 120°$$

$$E_{mR} = 20 \angle 0° + 30 \angle -45° + 40 \angle 120°$$

$$E_{mR} = (20 + j0) + (21.21 - j21.21) + (-20 + j34.64)$$

$$= (20 + 21.21 - 20) + j(0 - 21.21 + 34.64)$$

$$= 21.21 + j13.43$$

$$= 25 \angle 32.54°$$

$$e = F_{mR} \sin(\omega t + \phi)$$

$$= 25 \sin(\omega t + 32.54°) \text{ volt}$$

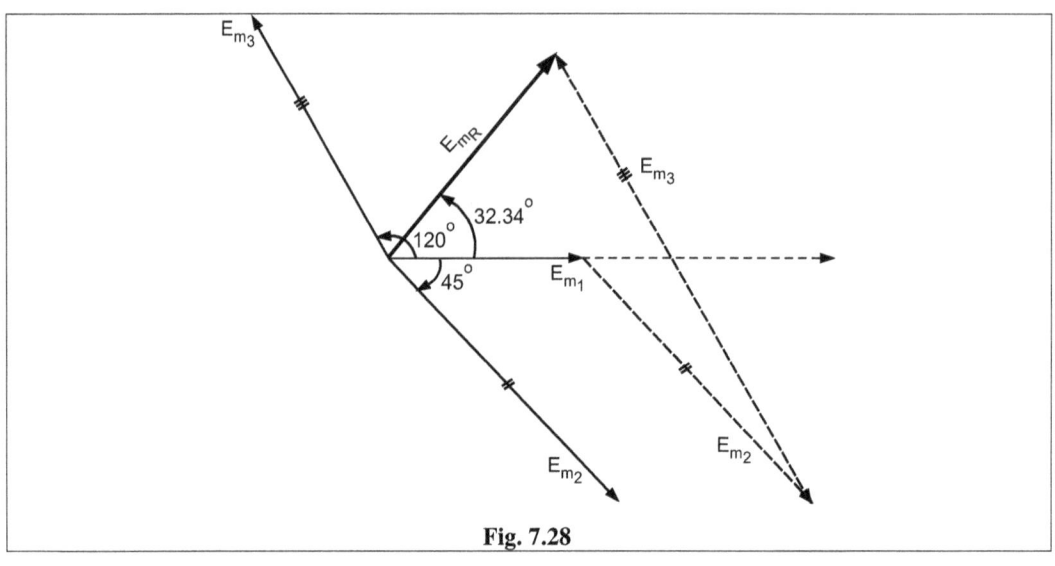

Fig. 7.28

or $\qquad \overline{E_m} = \overline{E_{m1}} + \overline{E_{m2}} + \overline{E_{m3}}$

x component $= E_{m1} + E_{m2} \cos 45 + E_{m3} \cos 120°$

$\qquad = 20 + 21.21 - 20$

$\qquad = 21.21$

y component $= 0 - E_{m2} \sin 45 + E_{m3} \sin 120$

$\qquad = 0 - 21.21 + 34.64$

$\qquad = 13.43$

$E_{mR} = \sqrt{x^2 + y^2}$

$\qquad = \sqrt{(21.21)^2 + (13.43)^2}$

$\qquad = 25.10$

$\phi = \tan^{-1}\left(\dfrac{y}{x}\right)$

$\qquad = \tan^{-1}\left(\dfrac{13.43}{21.21}\right)$

$\qquad = 32.54°$

$e = E_{mR} \sin(\omega t + \phi)$

$\qquad = 25 \sin(\omega t + 32.54°) \text{ volt}$

REVIEW QUESTIONS

1. What do you mean by sinusoidal alternating quantity ? Compare it with a direct current.

2. Define the following terms : Waveform, Cycle, Frequency, Amplitude and Periodic time of alternating quantity.

3. Explain the terms : Instantaneous and Maximum values of an alternating quantity.

4. Define r.m.s. value of an alternating quantity. Prove that in an alternating quantity varying sinusoidally, the maximum value is $\sqrt{2}$ times the r.m.s. value.

5. Explain the practical significance of the r.m.s. value of an alternating quantity.

6. Prove that for a sinusoidally varying current and voltage, the average value is $2/\pi$ times the maximum value.

7. Explain with the help of a sketch, how the average and r.m.s. values of an alternating current are obtained.

8. Define peak factor and form factor. State their values for a sinusoidal quantity.

9. Explain the meaning of the terms phase and phase difference.

10. What do you understand by the terms lag and lead in relation to alternating quantities ?

UNSOLVED NUMERICALS

1. An alternating voltage is mathematically expressed as :

   $v = 141.42 \sin (157.08 \ t + \pi/12)$ volts. Find its effective value, frequency and periodic time.   (**Ans. :** 100 V, 25 Hz, 0.04 sec)

2. A sinusoidal current of 7.07 A (r.m.s.) at 60 Hz flow a in a circuit. Write its expression and find its time period.   (**Ans. :** 10 sin 377 t, 0.0166 sec.)

3. The waveform of a voltage has a form factor of 1.15 and peak factor of 1.5 and if the maximum value of the voltage is 250 V, calculate the average and r.m.s. values of the voltage.

4. An alternating voltage $V = (160 + j\ 120)$ V is applied to a circuit and current flows, $I = -6 + j\ 15$ Amp. Find (i) Impedance of the circuit, (ii) Power factor of the circuit and (iii) Power consumed in the circuit.

    (**Ans.** : (i) 12.38 Ω, (ii) 0.25 leading, (iii) 839.25 W)

5. An alternating voltage is represented as $v = 141.42 \sin (628.42\ t + \pi/3)$ volts. Find its r.m.s. value, frequency and periodic time.

6. An alternating current, varying sinusoidally with a frequency of 50 Hz, has an r.m.s. value of 10 A. Write down the equation for instantaneous value and find this value of (i) 0.0015 s after passing through the positive maximum value, (ii) 0.0075 after passing through zero and increasing negatively.

7. In a circuit the equation of instantaneous voltage and current are given by $v = 35.35 \sin (\omega t - 2\pi/5)$ and $i = 7.07 \sin (\omega t - \pi/3)$ where $\omega = 314$ rad/sec. Sketch phasor diagram. Calculate impedance, average power, power factor instantaneous power at t = 0.04 second.   (**Ans.** : 5 Ω, 122.26 W, 0.978, 203.83 W)

UNIT - V

Chapter 8

SINGLE PHASE A.C. CIRCUITS

8.1 INTRODUCTION

Almost all electric circuits consist of combinations of three basic circuit elements namely Resistance (R), Inductance (L) and Capacitance (C). We have studied the A.C. fundamentals in the previous chapter. Now in this chapter, we have to study behavior of basic circuit elements on the application of A.C. supply. In each case, we will apply an alternating voltage of $v = V_m \sin \omega t$ and will proceed to find the equation and the phase of alternating current. With the help of current and voltage equations and their RMS values powers can be calculated.

8.2 A.C. THROUGH PURE RESISTANCE ALONE

Consider a circuit which consists of only a pure resistance R ohm as shown in Fig. 8.1(a).

Let, the applied alternating voltage is given by equation,

$$v = V_m \sin \omega t \qquad \qquad \dots(1)$$

As, voltage v is applied in a close loop so an alternating current will be set up in the circuit. At any instant, the value of current is given by Ohm's law as,

$$i = \frac{v}{R} = \frac{V_m \sin \omega t}{R}$$

$$\therefore \qquad i = \frac{V_m}{R} \sin \omega t$$

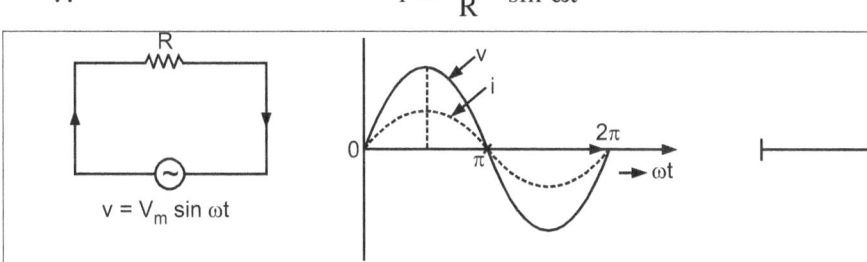

| (a) Circuit Diagram | (b) Voltage and Current waveforms | (c) Phasor diagram |

Fig. 8.1 : A.C. circuit containing pure R

The current will be maximum when sin ωt becomes unity.

$$\therefore \qquad I_m = \frac{V_m}{R}$$

$$\therefore \qquad i = \frac{V_m}{R} \sin \omega t = I_m \sin \omega t \qquad\qquad \ldots(2)$$

Thus, the current flowing through a purely resistive circuit is also sinusoidal. Comparing equations (1) and (2) and from Fig. 8.1 (b), we find that the voltage and current will achieve their zero and maximum values at the same instant. So the voltage and current are in phase as shown in Fig. 8.1 (c).

8.2.1 Instantaneous Power

In a.c. circuits, power at any instant is given by the product of instantaneous voltage and instantaneous current. In Fig. 8.2, waveform for voltage, current and instantaneous power is drawn.

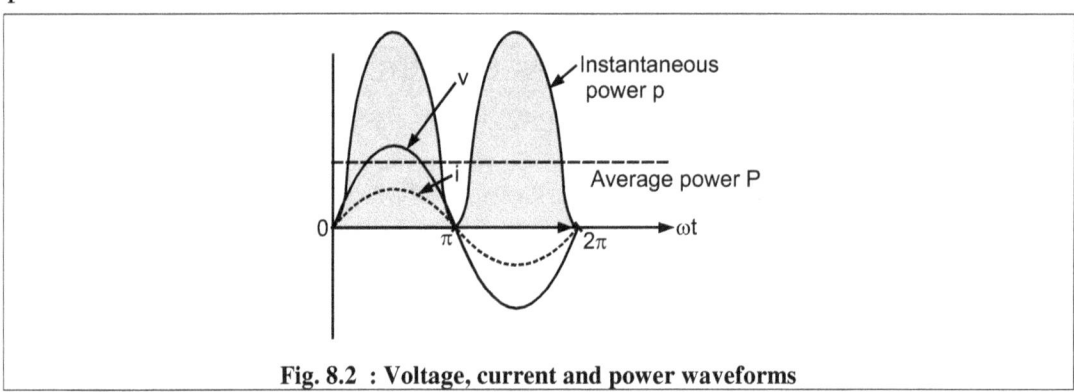

Fig. 8.2 : Voltage, current and power waveforms

Instantaneous power, $\qquad p = v \times i$

where for pure resistance, $\qquad v = V_m \sin \omega t$

and $\quad i = I_m \sin \omega t$

$$\therefore \qquad\qquad p = V_m \sin \omega t \times I_m \sin \omega t$$

$$= V_m I_m \sin^2 \omega t$$

$$= V_m I_m \left(\frac{1 - \cos 2\omega t}{2} \right)$$

$$= \frac{V_m I_m}{2} - \frac{V_m I_m}{2} \cos 2\omega t$$

Thus, instantaneous power consists of a constant part $\dfrac{V_m I_m}{2}$ and a fluctuating part $\dfrac{V_m I_m}{2}$ cos 2(ωt). The fluctuating part is a cosine curve of frequency double that of voltage and current waves. For one complete cycle, average value of $\dfrac{V_m I_m}{2}$ cos 2ωt is zero.

8.2.2 Average Power

Average power over a cycle,

$$P = \text{Average of} \left(\frac{V_m I_m}{2} \right) - \text{Average of} \left(\frac{V_m I_m}{2} \cos 2\,(\omega t) \right)$$

$$= \frac{V_m I_m}{2} - 0$$

$$P = \frac{V_m}{\sqrt{2}} \times \frac{I_m}{\sqrt{2}}$$

$$= V \times I \text{ watts}$$

Hence, in purely resistive circuit, average power is given by product of the rms value of applied voltage and current.

$$\therefore \qquad P = V \cdot I = V \times \left(\frac{V}{R} \right)$$

$$= \frac{V^2}{R} \text{ watts}$$

$$= (IR) \times I = I^2 R \text{ watts}$$

Note : All the wattmeters measure the average value of power over a cycle. Instantaneous power contains fluctuating part and therefore it pulsates between zero and certain maximum value with time (ωt).

Conclusions :

(1) In case of purely resistive circuit, total impedance of circuit is R i.e. Z = R.

(2) Here the applied voltage and current are in same phase i.e. phase difference between them is zero.

(3) As the phase difference is zero. i.e. $\phi = 0$ therefore power factor cos $\phi = 1$.

(4) Average power consumed by resistance R is given by,

$$P = VI \cos \phi = VI = I^2 R = \frac{V^2}{R} \text{ watts}$$

8.3 A.C. THROUGH PURE INDUCTANCE ALONE

Wherever, an alternating voltage of $v = V_m \sin \omega t$ is applied to a purely inductive coil of inductance L Henery, an alternating current starts flowing in the circuit. This current produces an alternating (changing) magnetic field which links with the same coil to produce an emf of self induction which is given by,

$$e = -L\frac{di}{dt}$$

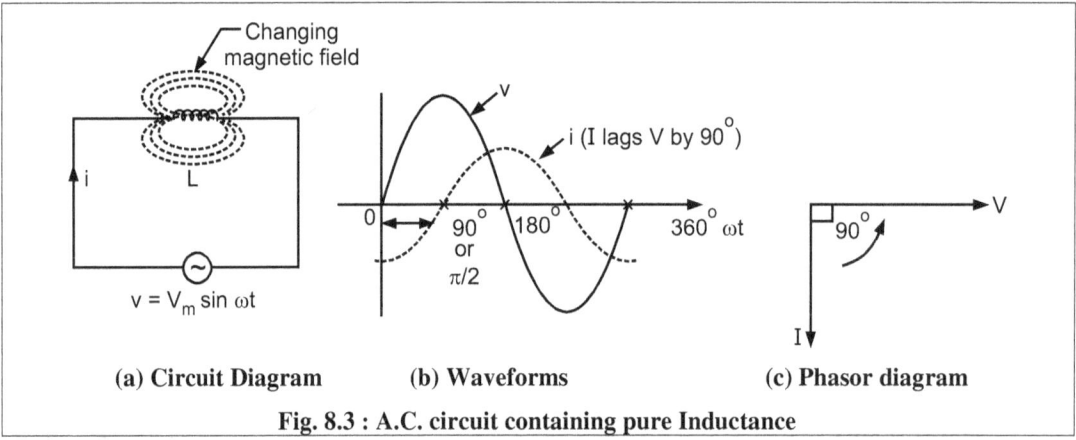

| (a) Circuit Diagram | (b) Waveforms | (c) Phasor diagram |

Fig. 8.3 : A.C. circuit containing pure Inductance

As circuit contains only L, therefore as per Lenz's law, e.m.f. of self induction will always oppose the applied voltage,

$$\therefore \qquad v = -e$$

$$= -\left(-L\frac{di}{dt}\right) = L\frac{di}{dt}$$

Substituting $\qquad v = V_m \sin \omega t$ ...(1)

we get, $\qquad V_m \sin \omega t = L \cdot \frac{di}{dt}$

$$L \cdot di = V_m \sin \omega t \cdot dt$$

$$di = \frac{V_m}{L} \sin \omega t \cdot dt$$

Integrating on both sides, we get,

$$i = \frac{V_m}{L} \int \sin \omega t \cdot dt$$

$$= \frac{V_m}{L}\left(-\frac{\cos \omega t}{\omega}\right)$$

$$= \frac{V_m}{\omega L} \sin (\omega t - \pi/2) \qquad ...(2)$$

When $\sin(\omega t - \pi/2)$ becomes unity, then current attains maximum value which is given by,

$$I_m = \frac{V_m}{\omega L} \quad \text{where } \omega L \text{ is called as inductive reactance, } X_L.$$

Substituting, $\qquad \dfrac{V_m}{\omega L} = I_m$ in equation (2)

we get, $\qquad\qquad i = I_m \sin(\omega t - \pi/2)$ $\qquad\qquad\qquad$ ...(3)

$$= I_m \sin(\omega t - 90°)$$

From the equation, and from Fig. 8.3 (b) we find that the current i will achieve its zero and maximum value 90° after the voltage. Fig. 8.3 (c) shows phasor diagram where V is taken on X-axis as reference and I is lagging behind V by 90°. Thus, the phase angle between voltage V and current I is 90°.

8.3.1 Concept of Inductive Reactance

We have seen that, $\qquad I_m = \dfrac{V_m}{\omega L} = \dfrac{V_m}{X_L}$

where $X_L = \omega L$ is called as inductive reactance which plays the role like a resistance and is measured in ohms (Ω). Thus, inductive reactance is defined as the opposition offered by the inductance of a circuit to the flow of current.

$X_L = \omega L = 2\pi f L$ where L = self inductance of coil in Henry. Thus, inductive reactance directly depends upon the frequency of the supply voltage.

Key Point : If D.C. supply is applied to an inductance, then inductive reactance is zero. Thus, an pure inductance offers zero reactance to the D.C. supply.

8.3.2 Instantaneous Power

Instantaneous power, $\quad p = v \cdot i$

$$= V_m \sin \omega t \cdot I_m \sin(\omega t - \pi/2)$$

$$= V_m I_m \sin \omega t \cdot (- \cos \omega t)$$

$$= - V_m I_m \cdot \sin \omega t \cdot \cos \omega t$$

$$= - \frac{V_m I_m}{2} \sin 2\omega t \qquad\qquad\qquad ...(4)$$

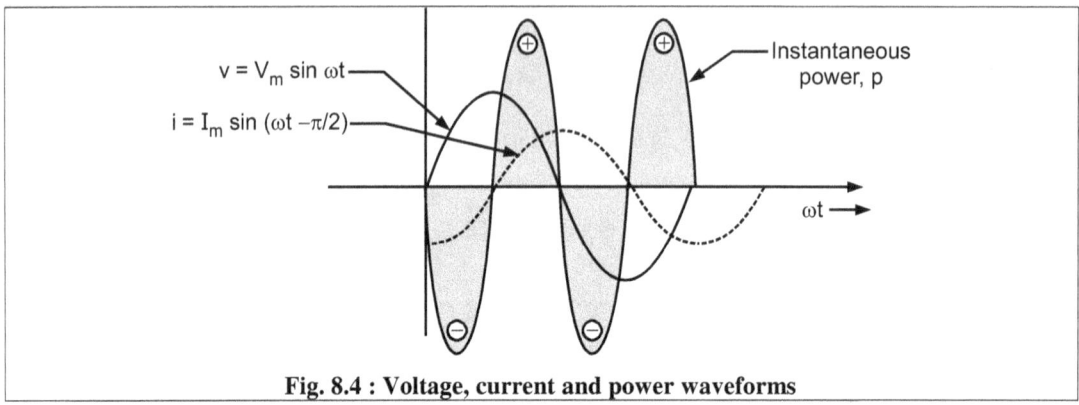

Fig. 8.4 : Voltage, current and power waveforms

Instantaneous power curve is shown in Fig. 8.4, which shows that it completes 2 cycles when alternating voltage or current completes one cycle. Hence, instantaneous power waveform is having double frequency than that of voltage and current wave.

8.3.3 Average Power

Average power over one complete cycle,

$$P = \text{Average of power}$$

$\therefore$ $$P = \text{Average of} \left(-\frac{V_m I_m}{2} \sin 2\omega t \right)$$

$$= 0$$

Hence, average power consumed by purely inductive circuit is zero. Actually when an instantaneous power curve becomes positive, energy is stored in magnetic field which is returned back to supply again when it goes in negative cycle. As positive and negative cycle equals, therefore, total power consumed over a one complete cycle is zero.

Conclusions :

(1) In purely inductive circuit, total opposition to the flow of current is called as inductive reactance and denoted by X_L.

(2) The applied voltage and current have a phase difference of 90° where current lags behind the voltage.

(3) As the phase difference between voltage and current is 90° i.e. $\phi = 90°$ therefore power factor cos $\phi = 0$.

(4) The nature of power factor is determined by the nature of current. Here as the current is lagging therefore power factor is zero lagging.

(5) Average power consumed by purely inductive circuit is zero.

Key Point : Unless and until the voltage or current given in numerical is mentioned as maximum or instantaneous value, always take it as RMS value.

Example 8.1 :

Find the current which will flow through the coil of negligible resistance and inductance of 0.8 H, when connected to 230 V, 50 Hz supply.

Solution : Given : V_{rms} = 230 V, f = 50 Hz, Self inductance, L = 0. 8 H.

$$\therefore \qquad\qquad\qquad \omega = 2\pi f = 314.28 \text{ rad/sec.}$$

(i) Inductive reactance, $X_L = \omega L = (2\pi f) \cdot L$

$$= 2\pi \times 50 \times 0.8$$
$$= 251.424 \ \Omega$$

(ii) We know, $\qquad\qquad V = I \cdot X_L$

$$\therefore \qquad\qquad I = \frac{V}{X_L} = \frac{230 \text{ V}}{251.424} = 0.91478 \text{ Amp.} \qquad\qquad \textbf{...(Ans.)}$$

8.4 A.C. THROUGH PURE CAPACITANCE ALONE

When a pure capacitor is connected across an alternating voltage of $v = V_m \sin \omega t$, capacitor is charged in one direction then in the opposite direction. Thus instantaneous charge q stored on the plates of capacitor depends on that instant (time t).

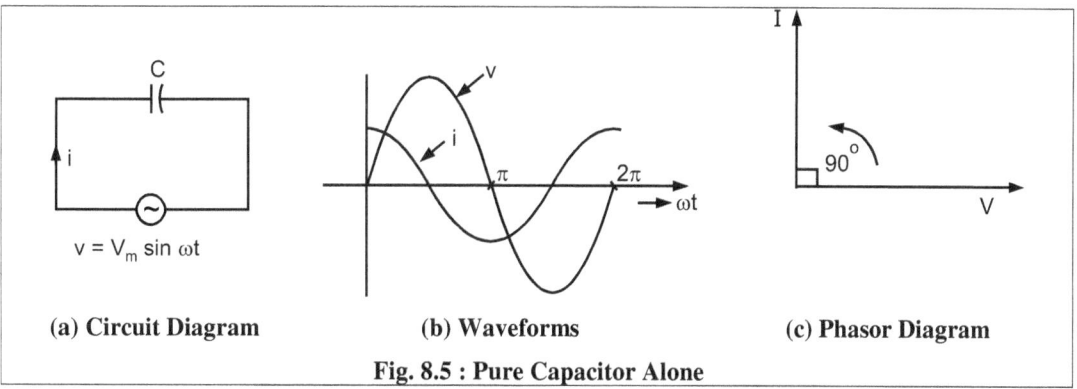

(a) Circuit Diagram	**(b) Waveforms**	**(c) Phasor Diagram**

Fig. 8.5 : Pure Capacitor Alone

The instantaneous charge (q) on the capacitor of capacitance value C is given by,

$$q = C \cdot v$$
$$= C \cdot V_m \sin \omega t$$

Let dq is the small charge which is stored on a capacitor plate, in small time interval dt second, when the instantaneous value of current is i.

Then, $\qquad\qquad$ Current i = rate of flow of charge

$$= \frac{dq}{dt} = \frac{d}{dt}(C \cdot V_m \sin \omega t)$$

$$i = C \cdot V_m \frac{d}{dt} (\sin \omega t)$$

$$= C \cdot V_m (\cos \omega t \cdot \omega)$$

$$= (\omega C) \cdot V_m \cdot \cos \omega t$$

$$= \frac{V_m}{1/(\omega C)} \cdot \cos \omega t$$

$$i = \frac{V_m}{1/(\omega C)} \cdot \sin (\omega t + \pi/2) \qquad \ldots(1)$$

Current reaches its maximum value I_m when $\sin (\omega t + \pi/2) = 1$

$$\therefore \qquad I_m = \frac{V_m}{(1/\omega C)} = V_m \cdot (\omega C)$$

where term $(1/\omega C)$ is called as capacitive reactance X_C,

Substituting $\qquad \dfrac{V_m}{1/\omega C} = I_m$ in equation (1),

$$i = I_m \cdot \sin (\omega t + \pi/2) \qquad \ldots(2)$$

Comparing equation (2) and $v = V_m \sin \omega t$, and from Fig. 8.5 (b) instantaneous current will achieve its zero and maximum value 90° before voltage. So the current said to be leading ahead the voltage by 90° Fig. 8.5 (c) is the phasor diagram for purely capacitive circuit. We find that current leads the applied voltage by 90°.

8.4.1 Concept of Capacitive Reactance (X_C)

Capacitive reactance $X_C = \dfrac{1}{\omega C}$ has similar nature of resistance and also measured in unit ohms.

We have, $\qquad\qquad I_m = \dfrac{V_m}{(1/\omega C)}$

$$= \frac{V_m}{X_C}$$

i.e. $\qquad\qquad V_m = I_m \cdot X_C$

$$\frac{V}{\sqrt{2}} = \frac{I}{\sqrt{2}} \cdot X_C$$

$$V = I \cdot X_C \qquad \ldots\text{(Ohm's law for purely capacitive circuit)}$$

Capacitive reactance X_C may be defined as opposition offered by the capacitance of the circuit to the flow of alternating current.

8.4.2 Instantaneous Power

Here, $\qquad\qquad i = I_m \sin (\omega t + \pi/2)$

Instantaneous power, $\qquad p = v \cdot i$

$$= V_m \sin \omega t \cdot I_m \sin (\omega t + \pi/2)$$

$$= V_m I_m \sin \omega t \cdot \cos \omega t$$

$$p = \frac{V_m I_m}{2} \sin 2\omega t$$

Thus instantaneous power wave has double frequency as that of applied voltage and current as shown in Fig. 8.6.

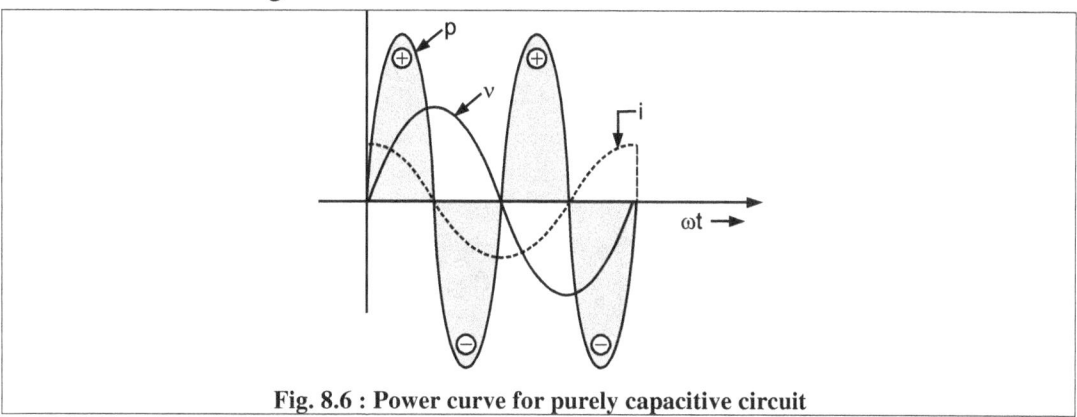

Fig. 8.6 : Power curve for purely capacitive circuit

8.4.3 Average Power

Average power power over a cycle = Average of $\left(\dfrac{V_m I_m}{2} \sin 2\omega t \right) = 0$

Thus, in purely capactive circuit, average power taken from supply is zero.

Conclusions :

(1) In purely capacitive circuit, total opposition to the flow of current is called as capacitive reactance X_C.

(2) The applied voltage and current have a phase difference of 90° where current leads to the applied voltage.

(3) As phase difference between voltage and current is 90° i.e. $\phi = 90°$, therefore power factor $\cos \phi = 0$.

(4) As the current is leading the applied voltage therefore power factor is zero leading in nature.

(5) Average power consumed by purely capacitive circuit is zero.

SOLVED EXAMPLES

Example 8.1 :

Find the current taken by a 100 µF capacitor when it is connected across single phase 230 V, 50 Hz supply.

Solution :

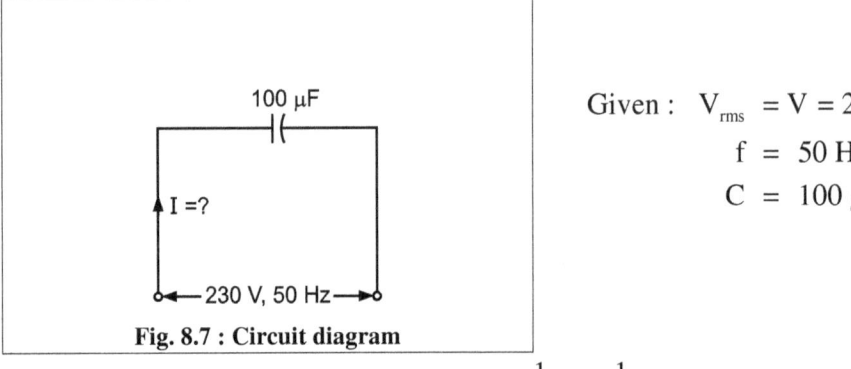

Given : V_{rms} = V = 230 V

f = 50 Hz

C = 100 μF

Fig. 8.7 : Circuit diagram

(i)   Capacitive reactance X_C = $\dfrac{1}{\omega C} = \dfrac{1}{2\pi fC}$

$$= \dfrac{1}{2\pi \times 50 \times 100 \times 10^{-6}}$$

$$= 31.83 \ \Omega$$

(ii)   Current drawn, $I = \dfrac{V}{X_C} = \dfrac{230}{31.83}$

$$= 7.23 \ A$$

Example 8.2 :

A 10 Ω resistor is connected across a voltage of v = 200 $\sqrt{2}$ sin ωt, find the equation for instantaneous current and instantaneous power. Also find maximum r.m.s. value of current. Draw the voltage and current waveform and phasor diagram.

Solution :

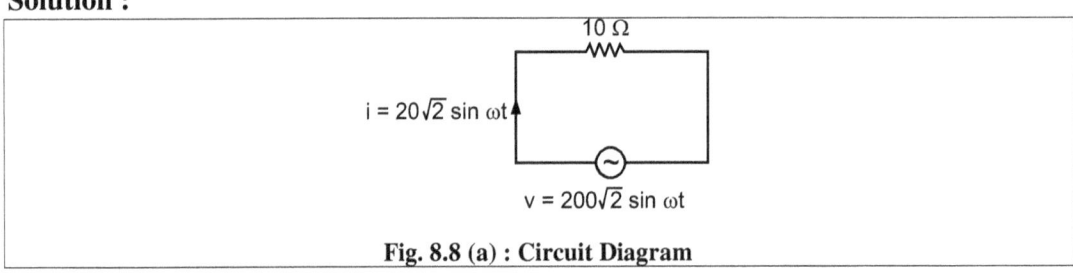

Fig. 8.8 (a) : Circuit Diagram

Given :   R = 10 Ω,

Voltage equation   v = 200 $\sqrt{2}$ sin ωt

Comparing with   v = V_m sin ωt

we get, V_m = 200 $\sqrt{2}$ V

(i) Now, $I_m = \dfrac{V_m}{R} = \dfrac{200\sqrt{2}}{10} = 20\sqrt{2} \ A$

Consider, f = 50, ∴ ω = 2πf = 314.28

∴   Instantaneous current, $i = I_m \sin \omega t$

$$= 20\sqrt{2} \sin (314.28\ t)\ \text{Amp}$$

(ii) Instantaneous power, $p = v \times i$

$$= \frac{V_m I_m}{2} (1 - \cos 2\omega t)$$

∴ $p = \dfrac{200\sqrt{2} \times 20\sqrt{2}}{2} (1 - \cos 628.56\ t)$

$$= 4000\ [1 - \cos (628.56\ t)]\ \text{watt}$$

$$V_{rms} = \frac{V_m}{\sqrt{2}} = \frac{200\sqrt{2}}{\sqrt{2}}$$

$$= 200\ \text{V}$$

(iii) $I_{rms} = \dfrac{I_m}{\sqrt{2}} = \dfrac{20\sqrt{2}}{\sqrt{2}}$

$$= 20\ \text{Amp.}$$

(iv) Voltage and Current waveforms :

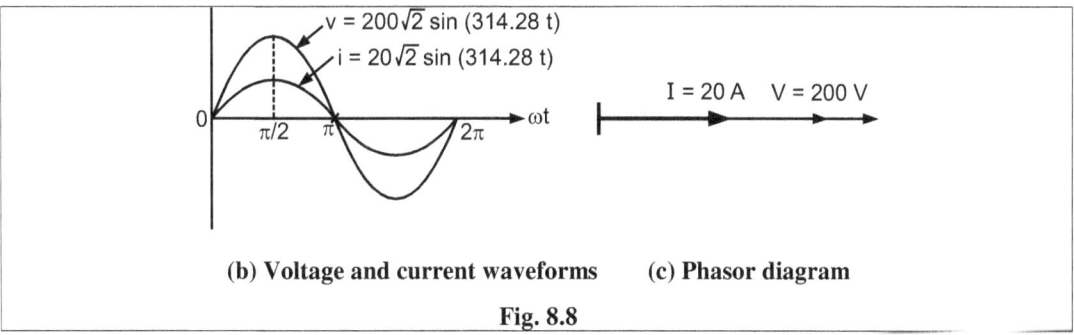

         (b) Voltage and current waveforms   **(c) Phasor diagram**

Fig. 8.8

Example 8.3 :

A pure inductance L = 0.1 H has an applied voltage v = 250 sin 314.28t. Find rms value of current, instantaneous power, average power. Write down equation for current and draw waveform and phasor diagram.

Solution : Given :   L = 0.1 H

Given circuit is purely inductive.   v = $V_m \sin \omega t$ is standard voltage equation

Given :   v = 250 sin 314.28 t

∴ V_m = 250 V

and   ω = 314.28 = 2πf

∴   f = $\dfrac{314.28}{2\pi}$ = 50 Hz

(i) Inductive reactance, $X_L = 2\pi fL$

$$= 2\pi \times 50 \times 0.1$$

$$= 31.43 \ \Omega$$

(i) $I_m = \dfrac{V_m}{X_L}$

$$= \dfrac{250}{31.43} = 7.95 \ \text{Amp.}$$

rms value of current, $I = \dfrac{I_m}{\sqrt{2}} = \dfrac{7.95}{\sqrt{2}} = 5.62 \ \text{Amp.}$

(iii)   In case of purely inductive circuit, current lags behind voltage by 90° or $\pi/2$ and equation of current is,

$$i = I_m \sin (\omega t - \pi/2)$$

$$i = 7.95 \sin (314.28 \ t - \pi/2) \ \text{Amp.}$$

(iv) Instantaneous power, $p = v \cdot i$

$$= -\dfrac{V_m I_m}{2} \sin 2\omega t$$

$$= -\dfrac{250 \times 7.95}{2} \sin (628.56 \ t)$$

$$= -993.75 \sin (628.56 \ t) \ \text{watt}$$

(v) Average power over a cycle, $P = 0$

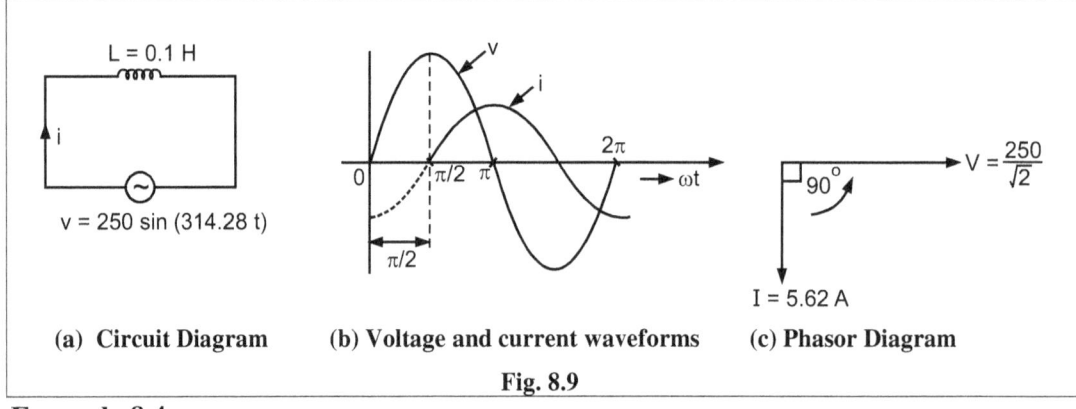

(a) Circuit Diagram   (b) Voltage and current waveforms   (c) Phasor Diagram

Fig. 8.9

Example 8.4 :

A 100 μF capacitor is connected across 250 V, 50 Hz supply. Find (1) capacitive reactance, (2) equation for current and voltage, (3) r.m.s. current, (4) instantaneous power.

Solution : Given : $V_{rms} = 250$ volts, $f = 50$ Hz, $C = 100$ μF

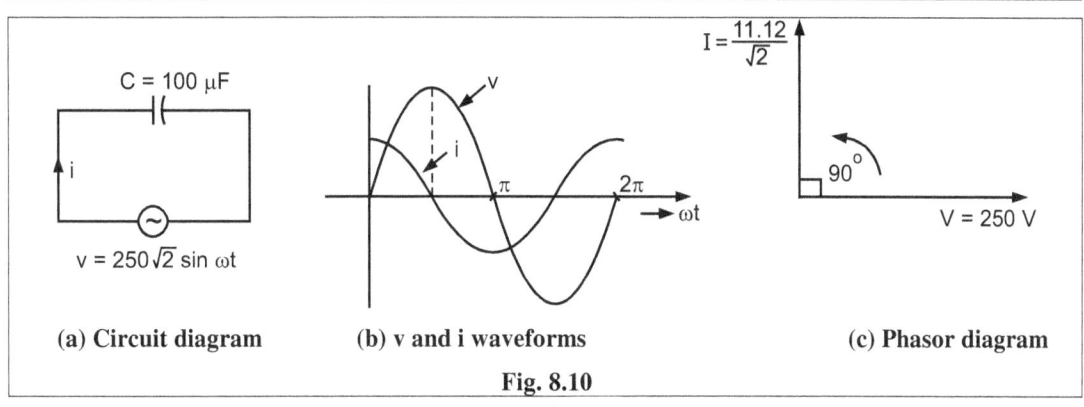

(a) Circuit diagram   (b) v and i waveforms   (c) Phasor diagram

Fig. 8.10

(i) Capacitive reactance, $X_C = \dfrac{1}{2\pi fC}$

$$= \dfrac{1}{314.28 \times 100 \times 10^{-6}}$$

$$= \dfrac{1}{31428 \times 10^{-6}}$$

$$= 31.8 \ \Omega$$

(ii) $V_{max} = V_{rms} \times \sqrt{2}$

$$= 250 \times \sqrt{2} = 353.5 \ V$$

(iii) $I_{max} = \dfrac{V_{max}}{X_C} = \dfrac{353.5}{31.8} = 11.12 \ \text{Amps.}$

rms value of current, $I = \dfrac{I_m}{\sqrt{2}} = \dfrac{11.12}{\sqrt{2}} = 7.863 \ A$

(iv) Now, instantaneous voltage equation is,

$$v = V_m \sin \omega t$$

$$= 250 \sqrt{2} \ \sin (314.28 \ t) \ V$$

(v) For pure capacitor, current leads the voltage by an angle of 90°.

∴ Instantaneous current equation is,

$$i = I_m \sin (\omega t + \pi/2)$$

$$= 11.12 \sin (314.28 \ t + \pi/2) \ \text{Amp.}$$

(vi) Instantaneous power, $p = v \cdot i = \dfrac{V_m I_m}{2} \sin 2 \omega t$

$$= \dfrac{250 \sqrt{2} \times 11.12}{2} \sin (628.56 \ t)$$

$$= 1965.76 \sin (628.56 \ t) \ \text{watts}$$

8.5 A.C. THROUGH RESISTANCE AND INDUCTANCE

A pure resistance R and a pure inductive coil of inductance L are connected in series as shown in Fig. 8.11 (a).

Let,   V = rms value of the applied voltage.

I = rms value of the resultant current.

Voltage drop across R,	V_R = IR	(V_R in phase with I)
Voltage drop across L,	V_L = IX_L	(V_L is leading I by 90°)

As resistance R and inductance L are in series, their individual voltage drops V_R and V_L also come in series. But they have phase differences, therefore total voltage, is found by phasor addition. Current I is taken as reference in series circuit as it is common in both the elements and it is drawn on positive X-axis as shown in fig. 8.11 (b).

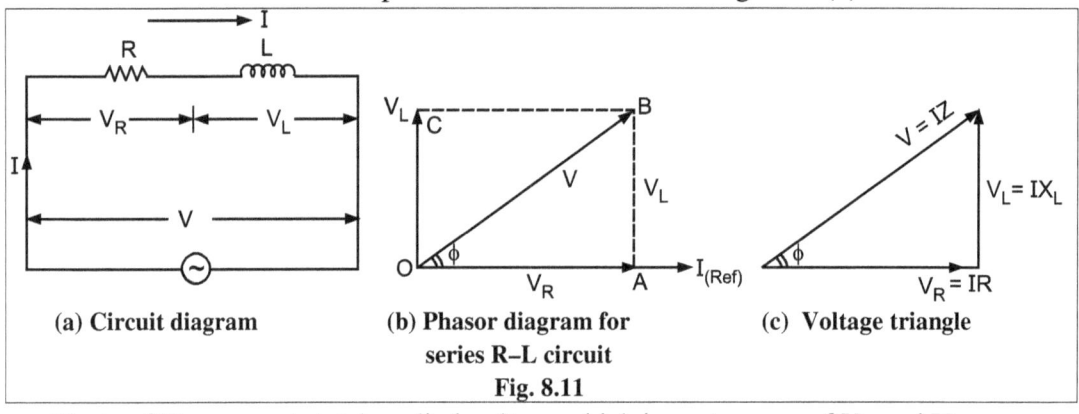

(a) Circuit diagram	(b) Phasor diagram for series R–L circuit	(c) Voltage triangle

Fig. 8.11

Vector OB represents total applied voltage which is vector sum of V_R and V_L.

$$\therefore \qquad \bar{V} = \bar{V}_R + \bar{V}_L$$

$$\therefore \qquad V = \sqrt{V_R{}^2 + V_L{}^2}$$

$$= \sqrt{(IR)^2 + (IX_L)^2} = I\sqrt{R^2 + X_L^2}$$

$$\bar{V} = \bar{I}\,.\bar{Z}$$

where,

$$Z = \sqrt{R^2 + X_L^2}$$

The quantity $\sqrt{R^2 + X_L^2}$ is known as the impedance (Z) of the circuit. As seen in the phasor diagram Fig. 8.11 (b), applied voltage V leads the current I by an angle ϕ such that,

$$\tan \phi = \frac{V_L}{V_R} = \frac{I \cdot X_L}{I \cdot R} = \frac{X_L}{R} \qquad \phi = \tan^{-1}\left(\frac{X_L}{R}\right)$$

In other words, current lags behind the applied voltage by an angle ϕ. Hence, if applied voltage is given by $v = V_m \sin \omega t$, then current equation is,

$$i = I_m \sin(\omega t - \phi) \qquad \text{where, } I_m = \frac{V_m}{Z}$$

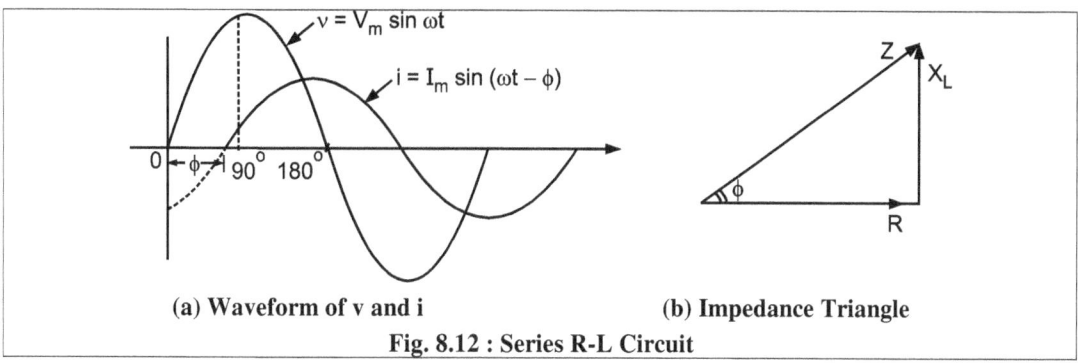

(a) Waveform of v and i   (b) Impedance Triangle

Fig. 8.12 : Series R-L Circuit

Key Point : For series A.C. circuit, generally current is taken as reference as it is common to both the elements.

8.5.1 Impedance Triangle

Fig. 8.11 (c) is called as voltage triangle and after dividing each side by I, we get a triangle called impedance triangle as shown in Fig. 8.12 (b).

From this triangle also, we have,

$$Z = \sqrt{R^2 + X_L^2}$$

$$\cos \phi = \frac{R}{Z} \qquad \text{and} \qquad \tan \phi = \frac{X_L}{R}$$

where, ϕ is the phase angle between applied voltage and circuit current.

For R. L. Series circuit, The impedance z in complex form can be written as :

(1) Rectangular form $\overline{Z} = \overline{R} + j \, \overline{X_L}$

(2) Polar form $\overline{Z} = z \, \angle\phi$ where, $z = \sqrt{R^2 + X_L^2}$ & $\phi = \tan^{-1}(X_L/R)$

8.5.2 Power Triangle

After multiplying voltage triangle by current I or by multiplying impedance triangle by I^2 we get a power triangle as shown in Fig. 8.13.

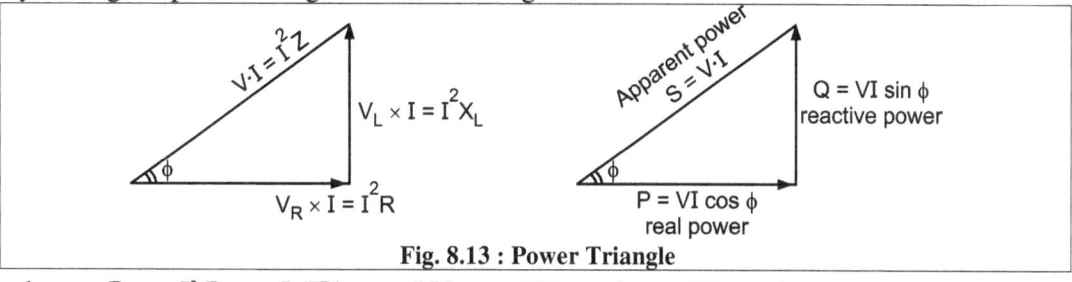

Fig. 8.13 : Power Triangle

where, $P = I^2 R = I \cdot (IR) = I \cdot V_R = I \cdot V \cos \phi = VI \cos \phi$ watts   (Real power)

$Q = I^2 X_L = I \cdot (X_L) = I \cdot V_L = I \cdot V \sin \phi = VI \sin \phi$ VAr (Reactive power)

$S = I^2 Z = I \cdot (IZ) = I \cdot V = VI \, \phi$ VA   (Apparent power)

Alternative Method : Let, voltage V is taken as reference on X-axis, then current I is drawn at an angle ϕ lagging. Current I can be resolved into its two mutually perpendicular components. I $\cos\phi$ along the applied voltage V and I $\sin\phi$ in quadrative with V as shown in Fig. 8.14 (a), Fig. 8.14 (b) obtained by multiplying ΔOAB by V.

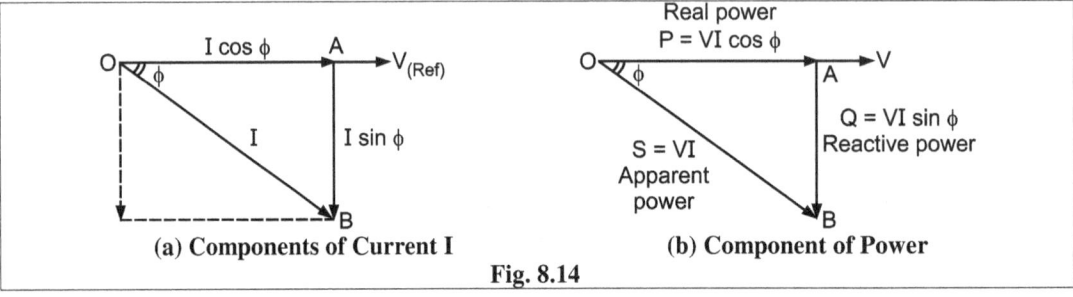

(a) Components of Current I   (b) Component of Power

Fig. 8.14

8.5.3 Active Power or Real Power (P)

Active power is the power which is actually consumed in the circuit and it is the product of voltage and in-phase component of current. It is measured in watts or kW and symbol is P.

$$\therefore \qquad P = V \cdot I \cos\phi \quad \text{Watt}$$

8.5.4 Reactive Power (Q)

Reactive power is not actually consumed by the circuit rather this power is taken and returned back to the source by components like inductance or capacitance. Reactive power is product of voltage and quadrature component of current. Symbol is Q and unit is VAr or kVAr.

$$\therefore \qquad Q = V \times I \sin\phi$$
$$= VI \sin\phi \quad \text{VAr}$$

8.5.5 Apparent Power (S)

The apparent power is the total power available at source. The product of r.m.s. value of voltage and r.m.s. value of current is called as apparent power. Symbol is S and unit is volt ampere or VA.

$$S = V \times I \quad \text{VA}$$

From Fig. 8.14 (b)

$$\text{Apparent power, } S = \sqrt{(\text{Real power})^2 + (\text{Reactive power})^2}$$
$$S = \sqrt{P^2 + Q^2}$$

8.5.6 Power Factor

It is the factor by which the apparent power must be multiplied in order to obtain the true power or it is the ratio of the true power to the apparent power.

$$\text{Power factor} = \frac{\text{True power}}{\text{Apparent power}}$$

$$= \frac{\text{VI cos } \phi}{\text{VI}}$$

$$= \text{cos } \phi$$

Power factor can be defined as cosine of the phase angle between the voltage and the current. From impedance triangle Fig. 8.12 (b), we have

$$\text{cos } \phi = \frac{R}{Z}.$$

$$\phi = \tan^{-1}\left(\frac{X_L}{R}\right)$$

Conclusions :

(1) In case of series R–L circuit, total impedance offered by the circuit is given by
$Z = \sqrt{R^2 + X_L^2}$.

(2) Here, applied voltage and current have a phase difference which is determined by
$\phi = \tan^{-1}\left(\frac{X_L}{R}\right)$ or $\phi = \cos^{-1}\left(\frac{R}{Z}\right)$.

(3) Due to presence of X_L, circuit is inductive in nature and current is always lagging by an angle ϕ.

(4) As the current is lagging in nature therefore power factor of the circuit is also lagging.

(5) Average power consumed by R – L series circuit is VI cos ϕ since pure inductor does not consume any power.

Key Point :

If the circuit contains pure resistance, then phase angle between voltage and current is zero and power factor is unity. If the circuit contains pure inductance L then phase angle is 90° and powerfactor is zero lagging.

As the present circuit is combination of R and L therefore depending on the value of them, angle ϕ is given by $\phi = \tan^{-1}\left(\frac{X_L}{R}\right)$ which lies between 0° and 90°. (0° < ϕ < 90° lagging). Also power factor lies between unity to zero lagging.

Example 8.5 :

A series R–L circuit with R = 25 Ω and L = 0.1 H is connected to a 250 V, 50 Hz source. Calculate, (1) impedance, (2) current, (3) power, (4) power factor and (5) draw vector diagram.

Solution : Given : R = 25 Ω, L =   0.1 H, V = 250 V, f = 50 Hz

Find : Z, I, P and cos ϕ.

$$X_L = 2\pi fL$$
$$= 2\pi \times 50 \times 0.1 = 31.416 \,\Omega$$

Impedance,
$$Z = \sqrt{R^2 + X_L^2}$$
$$= \sqrt{(25)^2 + (31.416)^2}$$
$$= 40.15 \,\Omega$$
$$\phi = \tan^{-1}\left(\frac{X_L}{R}\right) = \tan^{-1}\left(\frac{31.416}{25}\right)$$
$$= 51.5^\circ \text{ lag}$$

(2) Current,
$$I = \frac{V}{Z} = \frac{250}{40.15} = 6.226 \text{ Amp.}$$

(3)
$$\cos\phi = \cos(51.5^\circ)$$
$$= 0.6225 \text{ (lag)}$$

(4) Power
$$P = VI\cos\phi$$
$$= 250 \times 6.226 \times 0.6225$$
$$= 968.92 \text{ Watt}$$

(5) Phasor (vector) diagram is shown in Fig. 8.15 (b).

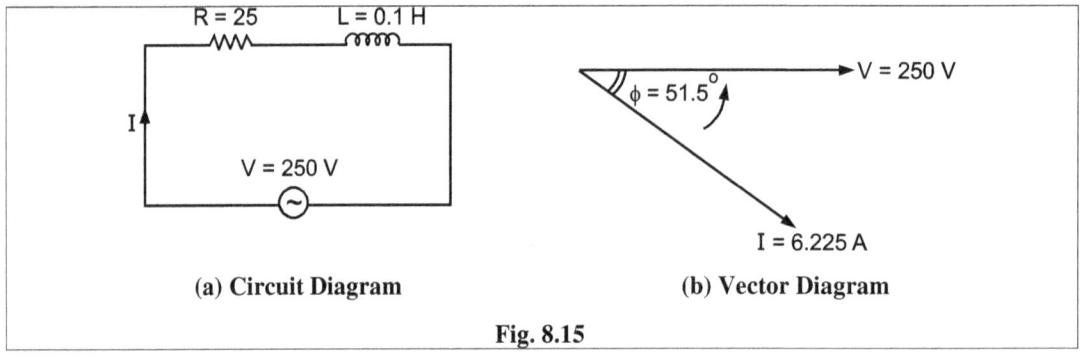

(a) Circuit Diagram   **(b) Vector Diagram**

Fig. 8.15

Note : Here phase angle $\phi = 51.5^\circ$ lags in between $(0 \angle \phi \angle 90^\circ$ lag) and power factor is between unity and zero lagging, due to R-L circuit.

Example 8.6 :

A coil has inductance of 20 mH and resistance of 5 Ω. It is connected across a supply voltage of v = 48 sin 314 t. Obtain the expression for current drawn by the coil.

Solution : Given : L = 20 mH, R = 5 Ω.

(1)   Supply voltage v = 48 sin 314 t

Comparing with, $v = V_m \sin \omega t$

we get, $V_m = 48$ V

                                     $\omega = 314$ rad/sec

(2) Inductive reactance, $X_L = \omega L$

                                     $= 314 \times 20 \times 10^{-3} = 6.28$ Ω

(3) Impedance, $Z = \sqrt{R^2 + X_L^2}$

                                     $= \sqrt{5^2 + 6.28^2} = 8.0273$ Ω

(4) Phase difference, $\phi = \cos^{-1}\left(\dfrac{R}{Z}\right) = \cos^{-1}\left(\dfrac{5}{8.0273}\right) = 51.474°$ lag

(5) $I_m = \dfrac{V_m}{Z} = \dfrac{48}{8.0273} = 5.9795$ A

(6) As power factor is lagging, therefore current i lags the applied voltage, by angle ϕ,

$\therefore$ $i = I_m \sin(\omega t - \phi)$

                                     $= 5.9795 \sin(314\,t - 51.474°)$ Amp.

8.6 A.C. THROUGH R-C SERIES CIRCUIT

Consider a resistance R and a capacitance C are connected in series across a rms voltage of V volts as shown in Fig. 8.16 (a). If the circuit current is I Amp. then,

Voltage drop across R, $V_R = I \cdot R$ (V_R in phase with I)

Voltage drop across C, $V_C = I \cdot X_C$ (V_C leads the I by 90°)

V_R and V_C are individual voltage drops which are not in same phase therefore total applied voltage V is the phasor sum of both as shown in Fig. 8.16 (b).

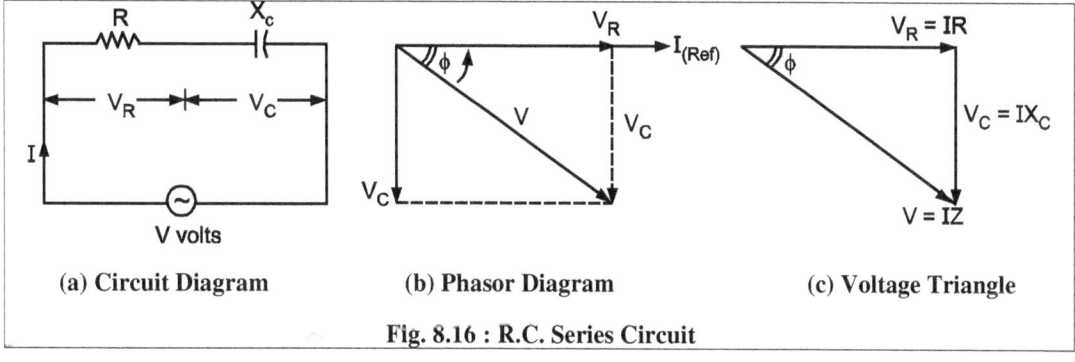

(a) Circuit Diagram   (b) Phasor Diagram   (c) Voltage Triangle

Fig. 8.16 : R.C. Series Circuit

Therefore, voltage V from voltage triangle (Fig. 8.16 c) is given by,

$$\bar{V} = \bar{V}_R + \bar{V}_C$$
$$V = \sqrt{(V_R)^2 + (V_C)^2}$$
$$= \sqrt{(IR)^2 + (I\,X_C)^2}$$
$$= I\sqrt{R^2 + (X_C)^2}$$
$$\bar{V} = \bar{I} \cdot \bar{Z}$$
$$\text{where, } Z = \sqrt{R^2 + X_C^2}$$

Impedance Z is the combined or total opposition by the circuit elements to the flow of alternating current and just like resistance has unit in Ω.

From voltage triangle, $\tan \phi = \dfrac{-V_C}{V_R} = \dfrac{-IX_C}{IR} = -\dfrac{X_C}{R}$

$\therefore$ $\phi = \tan^{-1}\left(\dfrac{-X_C}{R}\right)$

or $\cos \phi = \dfrac{V_R}{V}$

$$= \dfrac{I \cdot R}{I \cdot Z} = \dfrac{R}{Z}$$

$\therefore$ $\phi = \cos^{-1}\left(\dfrac{R}{Z}\right)$

where ϕ is the phase angle between voltage V and current I, we can say from Fig. 8.16 (b) that current I leads the voltage V by an angle ϕ, therefore power factor $\cos \phi$ is leading in nature.

8.6.1 Impedance Triangle

After dividing the three voltages of voltage triangle (Fig. 8.16 (c)) by current, we get impedance triangle as shown in Fig. 8.17.

From impedance triangle, $Z = \sqrt{R^2 + (-X_C^2)}$

$$\phi = \tan^{-1}\left(\dfrac{-X_C}{R}\right)$$

(X_C is taken negative, as it lies on negative Y axis)

$$\cos \phi = \dfrac{R}{Z}$$

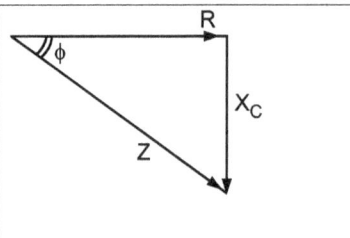

Fig. 8.17 : Impedance Triangle

In R-C series circuit, the impedance Z is written in complex form as

(1) Rectangular form $\bar{Z} = \bar{R} - j\,\bar{X}_C$

(2) Polar form $\bar{Z} = z \angle - \phi$ where, $z = \sqrt{R^2 + X_C^2}$ and $\phi = \tan^{-1}(-X_C/R)$

8.6.2 Power

Average power taken by circuit = Average power consumed by R + Average power taken by C.

But the average power taken by a pure capacitance over a complete cycle is zero, therefore average power P supplied to circuit is entirely consumed by resistance R only.

$$P = V I \cos\phi \text{ watts}$$

Conclusion :

(1) In case of series R-C circuit, total impedance offered by the circuit is given by $Z = \sqrt{R^2 + X_C^2}$.

(2) Series R–C circuit is capacitive in nature, such as applied current leads the applied voltage by an angle ϕ which is determined by $\phi = \tan^{-1}\left(\dfrac{-X_C}{R}\right)$ or $\phi = \cos^{-1}\left(\dfrac{R}{Z}\right)$.

(3) As the current leads the applied voltage, therefore power factor is leading in nature.

(4) Average power consumed by R–C series circuit is also VI cos ϕ.

Example 8.7 :

A resistance of 100 Ω and 50 μF capacitor are connected in series across a 230 V, 50 Hz supply. Find (1) the current in the circuit, (2) voltage across the resistance, (3) voltage across the capacitor, (4) power factor and (5) the power.

Given : R = 100 Ω, V = 230 V, f = 50 Hz, C = 50 μF.

Solution : Capacitive reactance, $X_C = \dfrac{1}{2\pi\,f \cdot C}$

$$= \dfrac{1}{2\pi \times 50 \times 50 \times 10^{-6}} = 63.66\ \Omega$$

Impedance, $Z = \sqrt{R^2 + X_C^2}$

$$= \sqrt{(100)^2 + (63.66)^2} = 118.54\ \Omega$$

(1) Current in the circuit, $I = \dfrac{V}{Z} = \dfrac{230}{118.54} = 1.94$ Amp.

(2) Voltage across the resistance, $V_R = I \cdot R = 1.94 \times 100 = 194$ volts

(3) Voltage across the capacitance,

$$V_C = I \cdot X_C = 1.94 \times 63.66 = 123.5 \text{ volts}$$

(4) Power factors of the circuit,

$$\cos \phi = \frac{R}{Z} = \frac{100}{118.54} = 0.8435 \text{ leading}$$

$$\phi = \cos^{-1}(0.8435) = 32.48°$$

(5) Power,

$$P = VI \cos \phi$$

$$= 230 \times 1.94 \times 0.8435$$

$$= 376.36 \text{ watt}$$

(6) Phasor diagram

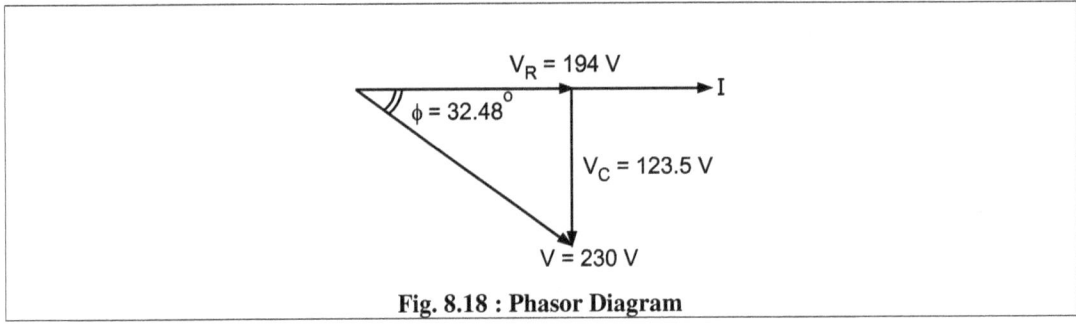

Fig. 8.18 : Phasor Diagram

8.7 A.C. THROUGH SERIES R-L-C CIRCUIT

Consider a resistance R, inductance L and capacitance C connected in series across alternating voltage whose r.m.s. value is V volt. When current I flows through these elements, then their individual voltage drops are given by,

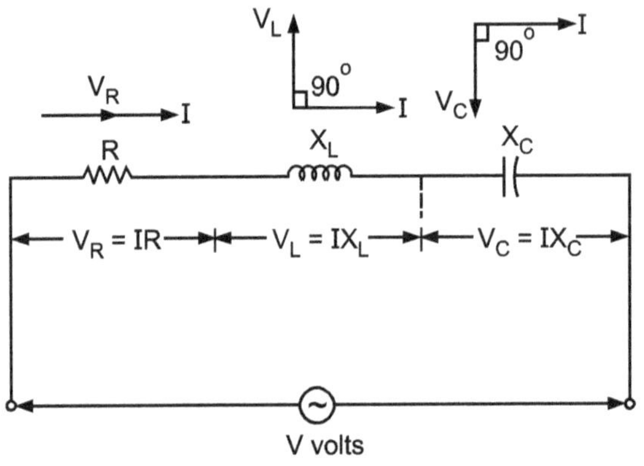

Fig. 8.19 (a) : R–L–C Series Circuit

$$V_R = I \cdot R, \qquad\qquad V_R \text{ is in phase with current I}$$

$$V_L = I \cdot X_L, \qquad\qquad V_L \text{ is leading current I by } 90°$$

$$V_C = I \cdot X_C, \qquad\qquad V_C \text{ is lagging current I by } 90°$$

where, $X_L = 2\pi fL = \text{inductive reactance}$

$$X_C = \frac{1}{2\pi fC} = \text{capacitive reactance}$$

The relative values of X_L and X_C play an important role in the behavior of R–L–C series circuit.

Let us consider three cases :

Case I :   Inductive reactance $(X_L) >$ Capacitive reactance, (X_C).

Case II :   Inductive reactance $(X_L) <$ Capacitive reactance, (X_C).

Case III: Inductive reactance $(X_L) =$ Capacitive reactance, (X_C).

Let us study each case separately and find the nature of circuit.

8.7.1 Case I : $X_L > X_C$

When $X_L > X_C$ then voltage drop across X_L is also greater than voltage drop across X_C i.e. $V_L > V_C$. To find the applied voltage, phasor addition is done as its component voltages are not in same phase. For phasor diagram shown in Fig. 8.19 (b), current I is taken as a reference phasor.

Since, V_L and V_C are in the direct phase opposition and $V_L > V_C$ therefore their resultant $(V_L - V_C)$ on +ve Y axis.

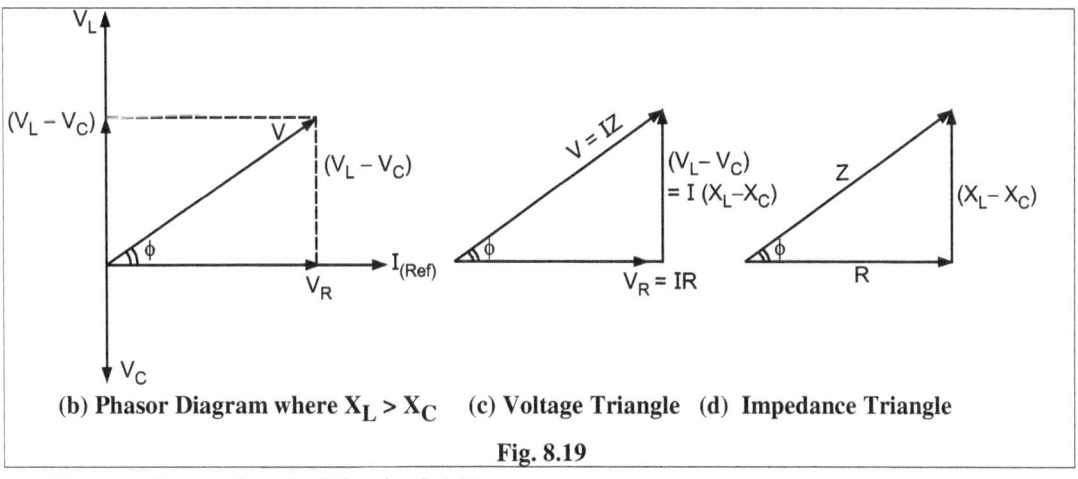

(b) Phasor Diagram where $X_L > X_C$ (c) Voltage Triangle   (d) Impedance Triangle

Fig. 8.19

From voltage triangle (Fig. 8.19 (c)),

Total applied, voltage, $\bar{V} = \bar{V}_R + (\overline{V_L - V_C})$

$\therefore$
$$V = \sqrt{V_R^2 + (V_L - V_C)^2} = \sqrt{(IR)^2 + (IX_L - IX_C)^2}$$
$$= I\sqrt{R^2 + (X_L - X_C)^2}$$
$$\bar{V} = \bar{I} \cdot \bar{Z}$$

where, $Z = \sqrt{R^2 + (X_L - X_C)^2}$ is called as impedance, which is combined opposition by circuit elements in R–L–C series circuit when $X_L > X_C$.

Fig. 8.19 (d) shows the impedance triangle.

$$\phi = \tan^{-1}\left(\frac{X_L - X_C}{R}\right)$$

In this case, when $X_L > X_C$, the circuit behaves like series R–L circuit and as the total current lags behind the total voltage by an angle ϕ, power factor will be lagging in nature.

The impedance in complex form can be written as,

(i) Rectangular form, $\bar{Z} = \bar{R} + j(\bar{X}_L - \bar{X}_C)$ where $X_L > X_C$,

    if $X_L - X_C = X$, $Z = R + jX$

(ii) Polar form $\bar{Z} = Z \angle \phi$,

    Where $Z = \sqrt{R^2 + (X_L - X_C)^2} = \sqrt{R^2 + X^2}$ and $\phi = \tan^{-1}\left(\frac{X_L - X_C}{R}\right)$

8.7.2 Case II : $X_L < X_C$

When $X_L < X_C$ obviously, $V_L < V_C$.

Phasor diagram as shown in Fig. 8.20 (a) is drawn to find the applied voltage. Here $(V_C - V_L)$ is resultant of V_L and V_C and it comes on –ve Y-axis.

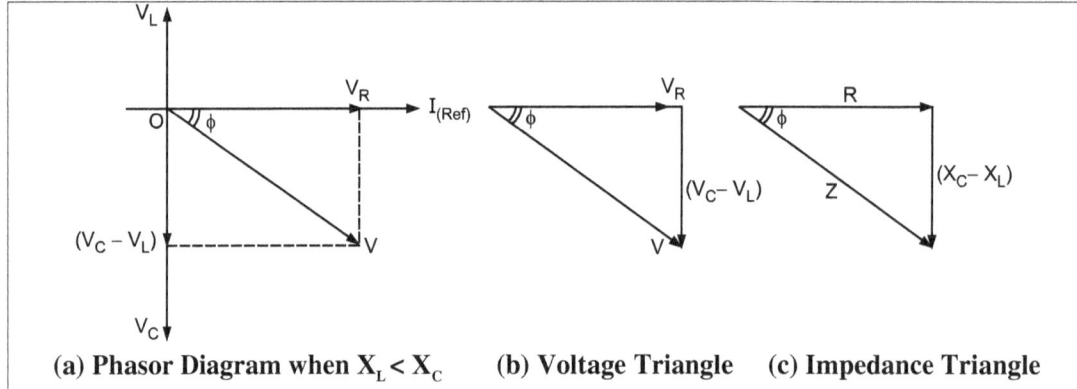

(a) Phasor Diagram when $X_L < X_C$ **(b) Voltage Triangle**   **(c) Impedance Triangle**

Fig. 8.20

From voltage triangle of Fig. 8.20 (b), we get,

$$\bar{V} = \bar{V}_R - (\overline{V_C - V_L})$$ [Phasor $(V_C - V_L)$ is –ve, as it is on –ve Y-axis]

$$= \bar{V}_R + (\overline{V_L - V_C})$$

$$\therefore \qquad |V| = \sqrt{(V_R)^2 + (V_L - V_C)^2} = \sqrt{(IR)^2 + (IX_L - IX_C)^2} = I\sqrt{R^2 + (X_L - X_C)^2}$$

$$\therefore \qquad \bar{V} = \bar{I} \cdot \bar{Z}$$

where, $Z = \sqrt{R^2 + (X_L - X_C)^2}$ which is impedance of R–L–C series circuit when $X_L < X_C$.

Fig. 8.20 (c) shows the impedance triangle.

$$\text{Angle } \phi = \tan^{-1}\left(\frac{-(V_C - V_L)}{V_R}\right) = \tan^{-1}\left(\frac{-(X_C - X_L)}{R}\right) = \tan^{-1}\left(\frac{+(X_L - X_C)}{R}\right)$$

Thus, when $X_C > X_L$ the overall circuit will behave like R–C series circuit and the total current leads ahead the voltage by an angle ϕ and power factor will be leading in nature.

The impedance Z, in complex form can be written as,

(i) Rectangular form, $\qquad\qquad \bar{Z} = \bar{R} + j(\bar{X}_L - \bar{X}_C) \qquad\qquad$ where $X_L < X_C$

    if $X_L - X_C = X$, $\qquad\qquad Z = R - jX$

(ii) Polar form $\qquad\qquad\qquad \bar{Z} = Z\angle -\phi,$

where $Z = \sqrt{R^2 + X^2}$ and $\phi = \tan^{-1}\left(\frac{X_L - X_C}{R}\right) = \tan^{-1}\left(\frac{-X}{R}\right)$

8.7.3 Case III : $X_L = X_C$

In this case as $X_L = X_C$, therefore voltages $V_L = V_C$. But as they are in direct phase opposition with each other, their resultant is zero as shown in Fig. 8.21 (a). Therefore, the applied voltage V is equal to the voltage drop across resistance R.

i.e. $\qquad\qquad\qquad\qquad\qquad V = V_R$

$$V = I \cdot R$$

$$\phi = \tan^{-1}\left(\frac{X_L - X_C}{R}\right) = \tan^{-1}\left(\frac{0}{R}\right) = 0^\circ$$

$$\therefore \qquad\qquad\qquad\qquad \cos\phi = 1$$

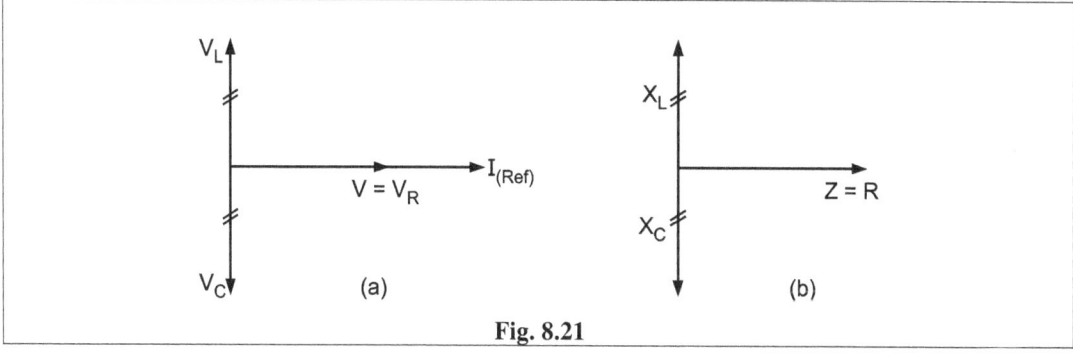

Fig. 8.21

Here impedance offered by circuit is only resistance R and whole of the R–L–C series circuit behaves like a purely resistive circuit. As current I and voltage V are in same phase therefore power factor is unity. In this case, as shown in Fig. 8.21 (b), X_L and X_C cancel out each other, therefore, net impedance offered is minimum and hence current is maximum under this case.

As the values of inductance L and capacitance C are constant, therefore X_L and X_C can be varied by varying the input supply frequency f so that X_L equals the X_C.

The impedance in complex form can be written as,

(1) In Rectangular form $\bar{Z} = \bar{R} + j\,(\bar{X}_L - X_C) = R$ as $X_L = X_C$

(2) In Polar form $\bar{Z} = z \angle \phi$ where, $Z = R$ and $\phi = 0$

Conclusions :

(1) In case of series R–L–C circuit, total impedance offered by the circuit is given by
$$Z = \sqrt{R^2 + (X_L - X_C)^2}$$

(2) Here applied voltage and current may have a phase difference which is determined by, $\phi = \tan^{-1}\left(\dfrac{X_L - X_C}{R}\right)$ or $\phi = \cos^{-1}\left(\dfrac{R}{Z}\right)$

(3) The relative values of X_L and X_C determine the nature of circuit.

   (i)   If $X_L > X_C$, then circuit is inductive predominant and it behaves like series R–L circuit where total current lags the applied voltage.

   (ii)   If $X_C > X_L$, then circuit is capacitive predominant and it behaves like series R–C circuit where total current is leading the applied voltage.

   (iii) If $X_L = X_C$ then overall circuit behaves like purely resistive as X_L and X_C cancel each other and here total current is in phase with the applied voltage.

(4) The cosine of phase angle gives the magnitude of power factor. The nature of power factor is determined by the nature of current, if current is lagging the applied voltage, the power factor is lagging and if current is leading the applied voltage then power factor is leading in nature.

Example 8.8 :

Derive the expression for instantaneous power, when voltage $v = V_m \sin \omega t$ is applied across the series R-L circuit. Draw the waveforms for voltage, current and power.

Solution : Let us consider the R-L circuit as shown in Fig. 8.22 (a).

Let $v = V_m \sin \omega t$

Now the current flowing through the circuit at any instant

$$i = I_m\,(\omega t - \phi)$$

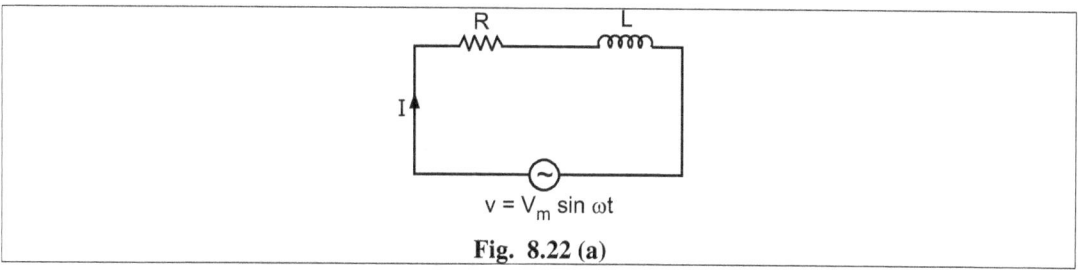

Fig. 8.22 (a)

Now the instantaneous power is given as,

$$p = v \cdot i = V_m \sin \omega t \cdot I_m \sin (\omega t - \phi)$$

$$= V_m I_m \sin \omega t \cdot \sin (\omega t - \phi)$$

$$= \frac{V_m I_m}{2} \left[\cos \phi - \cos (2\omega t - \phi) \right]$$

$$= \frac{V_m I_m}{2} \cos \phi - \frac{V_m I_m}{2} \cos (2\omega t - \phi)$$

In the above expression first term is constant and the second term having the double of the supply frequency. Hence the average power consumed over a cycle by second term is zero.

$$\therefore \qquad \text{Power} = \frac{V_m I_m}{2} \cos \phi$$

$$= \frac{V_{rms}}{\sqrt{2}} \cdot \frac{I_{rms}}{\sqrt{2}} \cdot \cos \phi = V. I. \cos \phi \text{ watt}$$

Note : When the voltage $v = V_m \sin \omega t$ is applied across series R–C circuit then expression for instantaneous power is as below,

Let $v = V_m \sin \omega t$ and $i = I_m \sin (\omega t + \phi)$

$$P = v \times i = V_m \sin \omega t \cdot I_m \sin (\omega t + \phi)$$

$$= V_m I_m \sin \omega t \cdot \sin (\omega t + \phi)$$

$$= \frac{V_m I_m}{2} \left[\cos \phi - \cos (2\omega t + \phi) \right]$$

In the above expression first terms is constant and the second term having double of the supply frequency, hence the average power consumed by the second term is zero.

$$\therefore \qquad \text{Power} = \frac{V_m I_m}{2} \cos \phi = V.I. \cos \phi$$

I. Waveform for series R – L circuit

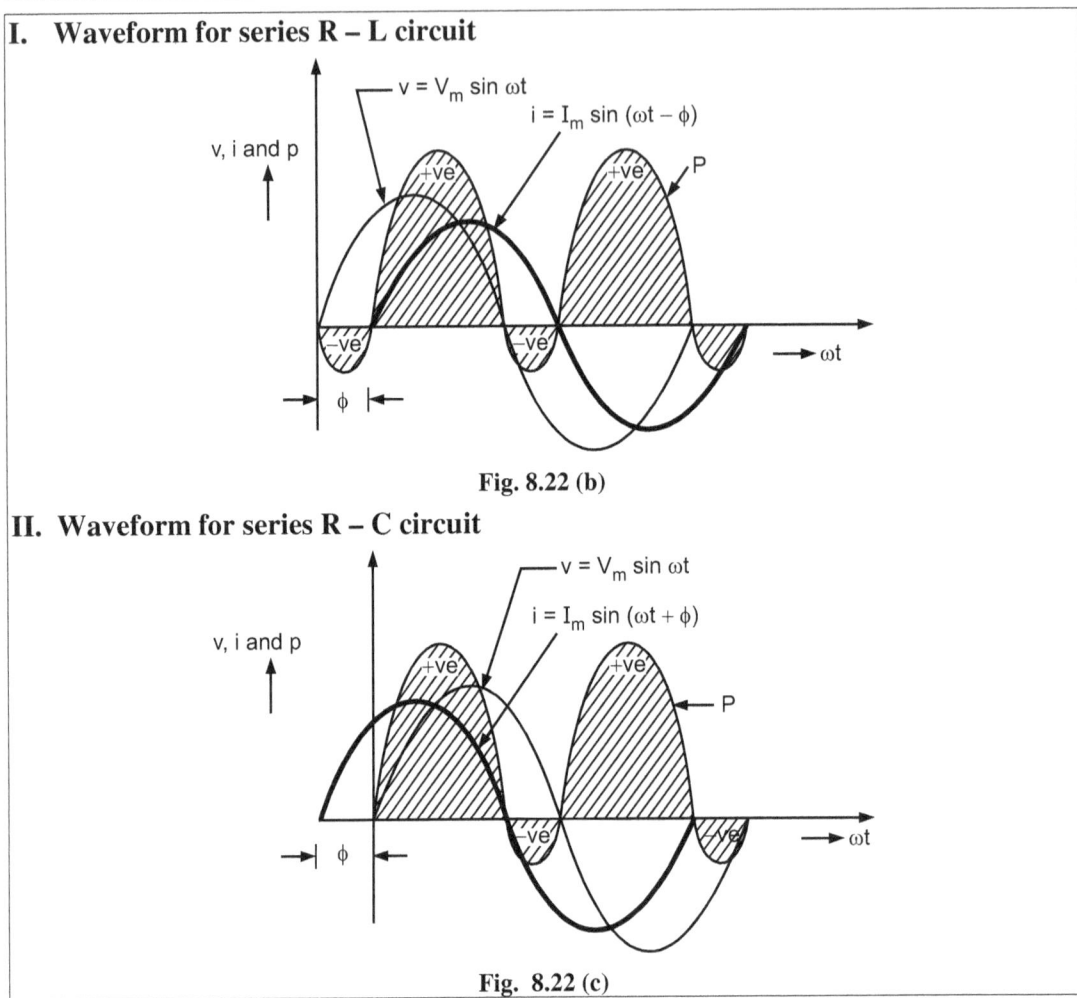

$v = V_m \sin \omega t$

$i = I_m \sin (\omega t - \phi)$

v, i and p

Fig. 8.22 (b)

II. Waveform for series R – C circuit

$v = V_m \sin \omega t$

$i = I_m \sin (\omega t + \phi)$

v, i and p

Fig. 8.22 (c)

Example 8.9 :

A resistance of 20 Ω, inductance of 0.05 H and a capacitor of 50 μF are connected in series. A supply voltage of 230 V, 50 Hz is connected across the series combination. Calculate the following :

(i)   Current drawn by the circuit.

(ii) Phase difference between the supply voltage and current.

(iii) Power factor of whole circuit.

(iv) Voltage drop across capacitor.

(v) Active and reactive power consumed by circuit.

Solution : Step 1 : Calculate values of X_L and X_C

$$X_L = 2 \pi f L$$

$$= 2\pi \times 50 \times 0.05 = 15.7 \ \Omega$$

$$X_C = \frac{1}{2\pi f C}$$

$$= \frac{1}{2\pi \times 50 \times 50 \times 10^{-6}} = 63.66 \ \Omega$$

Here, $X_C > X_L$ therefore, whole circuit is capacitive predominant.

Step 2 : Calculate the impedance of circuit,

$$Z = \sqrt{R^2 + (X_L - X_C)^2}$$

$$= \sqrt{(20)^2 + (15.7 - 63.66)^2}$$

$$= 51.96 \ \Omega$$

Step 3 : Calculate the current drawn by circuit,

$$I = \frac{V}{Z} = \frac{230}{51.96} = 4.426 \ \text{Amp.}$$

Step 4 : To find phase difference between V and I.

$$\phi = \tan^{-1}\left(\frac{X_L - X_C}{R}\right)$$

$$= \tan^{-1}\left(\frac{15.7 - 63.66}{20}\right)$$

$$= -67.36° \ \text{lead} \quad (\text{Here } X_C > X_L, \therefore \phi \text{ is leading})$$

Thus, current I leads the supply voltage by 67.36°.

Step 5 : To find power factor

$$\text{p.f.} = \cos\phi = \cos(-67.36°) = 0.385 \ \text{lead}$$

Step 6 : Voltage drop across capacitor

$$V_C = I \cdot X_C = 4.426 \times 63.66$$

$$= 281.76 \ \text{V}$$

Step 7 : Find P and Q

Active power, $P = VI \cos\phi$

$$= 230 \times 4.426 \times 0.385 = 391.92 \ \text{watt}$$

Reactive power, $Q = VI \sin\phi$

$$= 230 \times 4.426 \times \sin(-67.36°)$$

$$= -939.53 \ \text{VAr} \quad (\text{Capacitive})$$

Example 8.10 :

A coil of resistance 10 Ω and inductance 0.1 H is connected in series with a 50 μF capacitor across a 230 V, 50 Hz supply. Find the current taken and the phase difference between the supply voltage and current. Find also the voltage drop across the coil and capacitor.

Solution : Given that Resistance, R $=$ 10 Ω. Inductance, L $=$ 0.1 H

Capacitance, C $=$ 50 μF, V $=$ 230 V, f $=$ 50 Hz

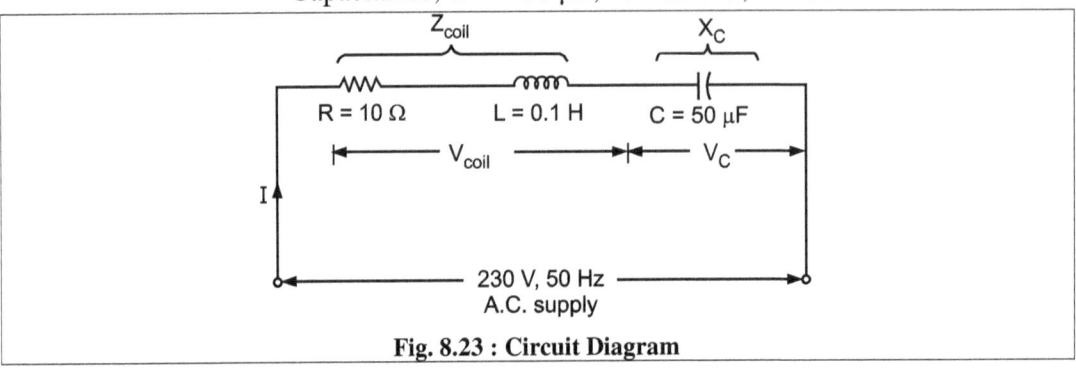

Fig. 8.23 : Circuit Diagram

Inductive reactance,

$$X_L = \omega L = 2\pi f\, L$$
$$= 2\pi \times 50 \times 0.1$$
$$= 314.16 \times 0.1 = 31.416\ \Omega$$

Capacitive reactance,

$$X_C = \frac{1}{\omega C} = \frac{1}{2\pi\, fC} = \frac{1}{2\pi \times 50 \times 50 \times 10^{-6}} = 63.66\ \Omega$$

Clearly here $X_L < X_C$, it means overall R–L–C series circuit behaves like series R–C circuit.

Impedance of the circuit,

$$Z = \sqrt{R^2 + (X_L - X_C)^2}$$
$$= \sqrt{(10)^2 + (31.416 - 63.66)^2}$$
$$= \sqrt{(10)^2 + (-32.244)^2} = 33.76\ \Omega$$

Now current taken by circuit,

$$I = \frac{V}{Z} = \frac{230}{33.76}$$
$$= 6.812\ \text{Amp.}$$

Now phase angle,

$$\tan\phi = \frac{X_L - X_C}{R}$$

∴.

$$\phi = \tan^{-1}\left(\frac{-32.244}{15}\right) = -\,65.05^\circ\,\text{lead}$$

Impedance of coil,

$$Z_{coil} = \sqrt{R^2 + X_L^2}$$
$$= \sqrt{10^2 + (31.416)^2} = 32.969\ \Omega$$

Voltage drop across coil, $V_{coil} = I \cdot Z_{coil} = 6.812 \times 32.969 = 224.58$ volts

Also voltage drop across the capacitor,

$$V_C = I \cdot X_C = 6.812 \times 63.66 = 433.65\ \text{V}$$

Example 8.11 :

A coil of power factor 0.6 is in series with a 100 μF capacitor. When whole circuit is connected across 50 Hz supply, the potential difference across the coil is equal to the potential difference across the capacitor. Find the resistance and inductance of the coil.

Solution : Given : $\cos \phi_{coil} = 0.6$, $C = 100\ \mu F$, $f = 50$ Hz.

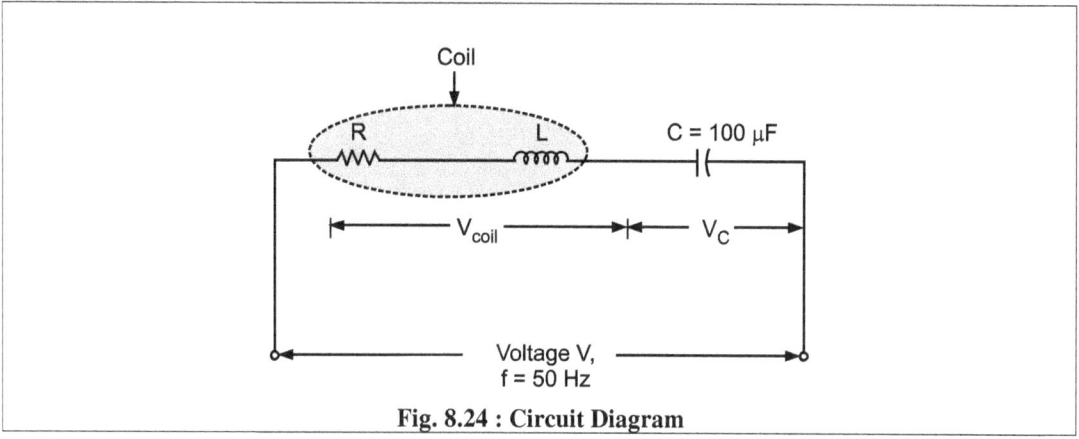

Fig. 8.24 : Circuit Diagram

Let R and L be the resistance and inductance of given coil and I be the current drawn from the supply.

(i) Capactive reactance,
$$X_C = \frac{1}{\omega C} = \frac{1}{2\pi fC}$$
$$= \frac{1}{2\pi \times 50 \times 100 \times 10^{-6}} = 31.83\ \Omega$$

Let Z_{coil} is the impedance of the coil. Given that voltage drop across the coil, V_{coil} and voltage drop across the capacitor, V_C are equal.

$$\therefore \qquad\qquad V_{coil} = V_C$$
$$\therefore \qquad\qquad I \cdot Z_{coil} = I \cdot X_C$$
$$Z_{coil} = X_C = 31.83\ \Omega$$

Also, power factor of the coil,

$$\cos \phi_{coil} = \frac{R}{Z_{coil}} = 0.6 \qquad\qquad\qquad \text{(given)}$$

$$\therefore \qquad\qquad R = 0.6 \times Z_{coil} = 0.6 \times 31.83 = 19.098\ \Omega$$

Now, $$X_L = \sqrt{Z_{coil}^2 - R^2}$$
$$= \sqrt{31.83^2 - 19.098^2} = 25.464\ \Omega$$

But, $$X_L = \omega L = 2\pi fL$$

$$\therefore \qquad\qquad L = \frac{X_L}{2\pi f} = \frac{25.464}{2\pi \times 50} = 0.081\ H$$

Example 8.12 :

A voltage given by $v = 100 \sin 100\pi t$ is impressed across a circuit consists of resistance of 40 Ω in series with 100μF capacitor and 0.25 H inductor.

Determine (i) RMS value of current, (ii) power consumed, (iii) power factor.

Solution : Given : R = 40 Ω, L = 0.25 H, C = 100 μf.

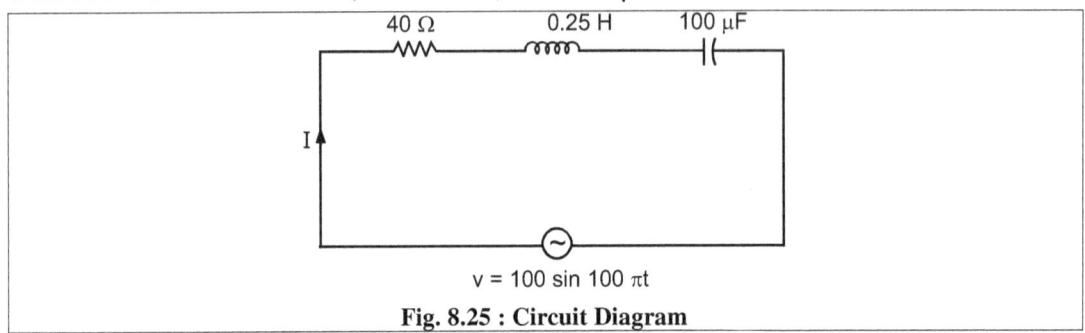

Fig. 8.25 : Circuit Diagram

Comparing the voltage with $v = V_m \sin \omega t$

we get, $V_m = 100$ V

and $\omega = 100\pi$ rad/sec

Now, $V = \dfrac{V_m}{\sqrt{2}} = \dfrac{100}{\sqrt{2}} = 70.7106$ volts.

(i) Inductive reactance, $X_L = \omega L = 2\pi f \times L = 100\,\pi \times 0.25 = 78.5398\ \Omega$

(ii) Capactive reactance, $X_C = \dfrac{1}{\omega C} = \dfrac{1}{100\,\pi \times 100 \times 10^{-6}} = 31.83\ \Omega$

(iii) Impedance, $Z = \sqrt{R^2 + (X_L - X_C)^2}$

$= \sqrt{(40)^2 + (78.5398 - 31.83)^2} = 61.496\ \Omega$

(iv)   r.m.s. value of current $= \dfrac{\text{r.m.s. value of voltage}}{\text{Impedance}}$

$= \dfrac{V}{Z} = \dfrac{70.7106}{61.496} = 1.15$ Amp.

Power consumed by circuit $= VI \cos \phi$ or I^2R

(v) Power factor of circuit, $\cos \phi = \dfrac{R}{Z} = \dfrac{40}{61.496} = 0.6504$ lagging

(vi) ∴ Power consumed by circuit, $P = VI \cos \phi$

$= 70.7106 \times 1.15 \times 0.6504 = 52.8887$ Watts

Example 8.13 :

A pure resistance R, a choke coil and a pure capacitor of 15.91 μF are connected in series across a supply voltage of V volts and carry a current of 0.25 Amp. The voltage across choke is 40 V, voltage across capacitor is 50 V and voltage across resistance is 20 volt. The voltage across the combination of R and choke coil is 45 volts. Calculate,

(i) supply voltage, (ii) frequency, (iii) power loss in choke coil.

Solution : Given : $V_R = 20$ V, $V_L = 40$ V, $V_C = 50$ V, and C = 15.91 μF, I = 0.25 Amp.

Let r and L be the resistance and inductance of choke coil. The circuit diagram is shown in Fig. 8.26.

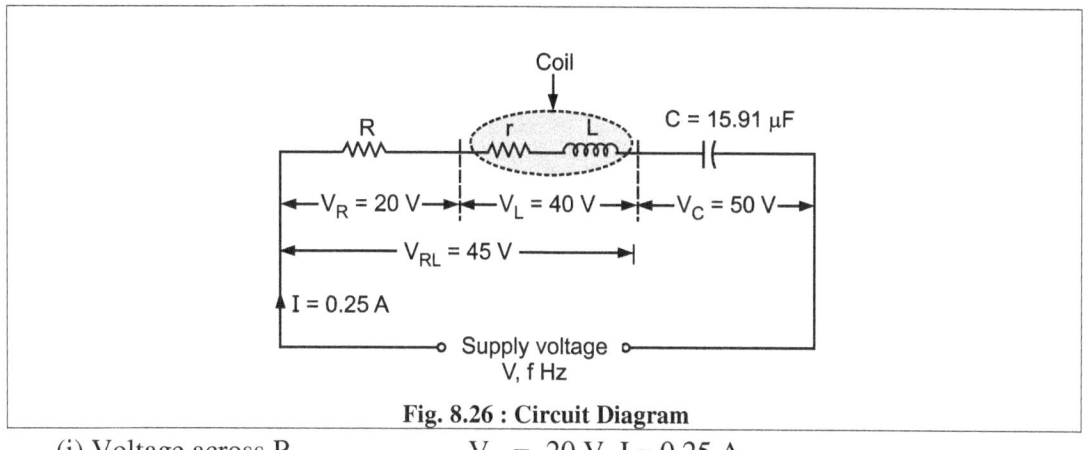

Fig. 8.26 : Circuit Diagram

(i) Voltage across R, $V_R = 20$ V, I = 0.25 A

$\therefore$ $R = \dfrac{V_R}{I} = \dfrac{20}{0.25} = 80\ \Omega$

(ii) Voltage across choke coil, $V_L = 40$ V, I = 0.25   (as series circuit)

$\therefore$ $Z_L = \dfrac{V_L}{I} = \dfrac{40}{0.25} = 160\ \Omega$

where, $Z_L = \sqrt{r^2 + X_L^2}$

$(160)^2 = r^2 + X_L^2$ ...(1)

(iii) Voltage across the combination of R and choke coil is 45 volts i.e.

$V_{RL} = 45$ volts

$\therefore$ $Z_{RL} = \dfrac{V_{RL}}{I}$

$= \dfrac{45}{0.25} = 180\ \Omega$

where, $Z_{RL} = \sqrt{(R + r)^2 + X_L^2}$

$180 = \sqrt{(R^2 + 2Rr + r^2) + X_L^2}$

$\therefore$ $(180)^2 = (R^2 + 2Rr + r^2) + X_L^2$

$(180)^2 = 80^2 + 2 \times 80 \times r + (r^2 + X_L^2)$ ...(2)

$\because$ $r^2 + X_L^2 = (160)^2$ put in equation (2)

$\therefore$ $(180)^2 = (80)^2 + 2 \times 80 \times r + (160)^2$

$\therefore$ $160r = (180)^2 - (80)^2 - (160)^2$

$\therefore$ $r = 2.5\ \Omega$

Put, r = 2.5 in equation, we get, $X_L = 159.98\ \Omega$

(iv) Voltage across capacitor C, $V_C = 50$ V

$\therefore$

$$X_C = \frac{V_C}{I}$$

$$= \frac{50}{0.25} = 200 \ \Omega$$

where,

$$X_C = \frac{1}{2\pi f C}$$

$$200 = \frac{1}{2\pi f \times 15.91 \times 10^{-6}}$$

$\therefore$

$$f = \frac{1}{2\pi \times 200 \times 15.91 \times 10^{-6}}$$

$$= 50 \ \text{Hz}$$

(v) Total impedance,

$$Z_T = \sqrt{(R + r)^2 + (X_L - X_C)^2}$$

$$= \sqrt{(80 + 2.5)^2 + (159.98 - 200)^2}$$

$$= 91.694 \ \Omega$$

(vi) Total voltage applied to the circuit,

$$V = \text{Current drawn} \times \text{Total impedance of circuit}$$

$$= I \cdot Z_T = 0.25 \times 91.694 = 22.923 \ \text{volts}$$

(vii) Power loss in choke coil, $\quad P_L = I^2 \times (\text{resistance of choke})$

$$= I^2 \cdot r$$

$$= (0.25)^2 \times 2.5$$

$$= 0.15625 \ \text{watt}$$

Example 8.14 :

A coil is connected in series with a non-inductive resistance of 30 Ω across 240 V, 50 Hz, supply. The reading of a voltmeter across the coil is 180 V, and across the resistance is 130 V. Calculate

    (i)   power absorbed by the coil   (ii)   inductance of the coil

    (iii) resistance of the coil   (iv) power factor of the whole circuit

Solution :

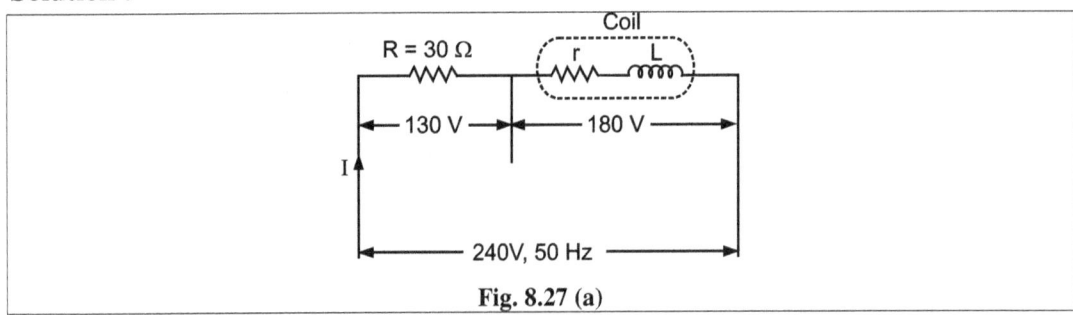

Fig. 8.27 (a)

$\therefore$ Circuit current I $= \dfrac{130}{30} = 4.33$ A

Phasor diagram :

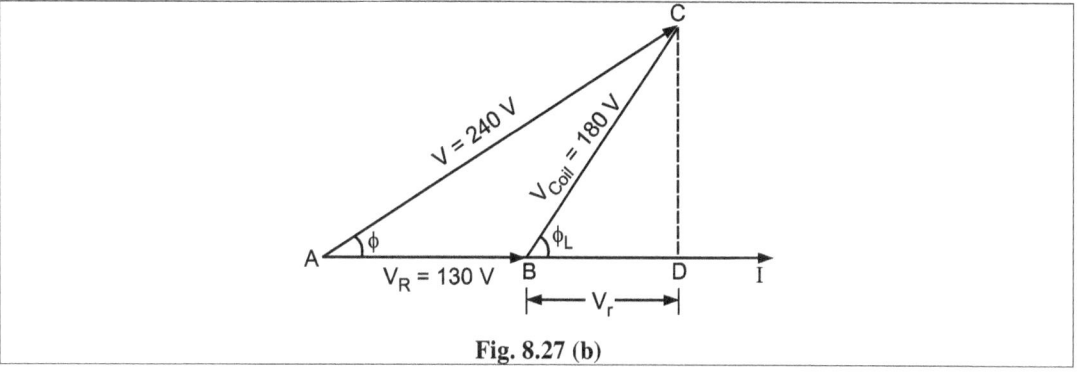

Fig. 8.27 (b)

From phasor diagram using cosine rule to $\triangle$ ABC.

$$AC^2 = AB^2 + BC^2 - 2 \cdot AB \cdot BC \cdot \cos(180 - \phi_L)$$

$\therefore$
$$240^2 = 130^2 + 180^2 + 2 \times 130 \times 180 \cdot \cos \phi_L$$

$$\cos \phi_L = \dfrac{240^2 - 130^2 - 180^2}{2 \times 130 \times 180}$$

$$= 0.177 \text{ (lag)}$$

(i) Power absorbed by the coil

$$= V_{coil} \cdot I_L \cos \phi_L$$

$$= 180 \times 4.33 \times 0.177$$

$$= 137.95 \text{ watt.}$$

(ii) Inductance of the coil

$$X_L = \dfrac{V_L}{I}$$

But
$$V_L = BC \sin \phi_L = V_{coil} \sin \phi_L$$

$$= 180 \times \sin(79.80) = 177.155 \text{ volt.}$$

$\therefore$
$$X_L = \dfrac{177.155}{4.33} = 40.913 \ \Omega$$

$$\text{Inductnace} = L = \dfrac{X_L}{2\pi f} = \dfrac{40.913}{2 \times \pi \times 50} = 0.130 \text{ H}$$

(iii) Voltage across coil resistance of the coil

$$V_r = BC \cos \phi_L = V_{coil} \cos \phi_L$$

$$= 180 \times 0.177 = 31.86 \text{ volt.}$$

$\therefore$ Resistance (r_{coil}) $= \dfrac{V_r}{I} = \dfrac{31.86}{4.33}$

$= 7.357 \; \Omega$

(iv) Power factor of the whole circuit

$$\cos \phi = \dfrac{AD}{OC}$$

$$\cos \phi = \dfrac{AB + BD}{AC} = \dfrac{130 + 31.86}{240} = 0.674$$

8.8   RESONANCE IN THE R–L–C SERIES CIRCUIT

Whenever the natural frequency of oscillation of a system coincides with the frequency of driving force, the two system resonate with respect to each other and the system has maximum response to a fixed magnitude of driving force. This phenomenon is known as resonance. This phenomenon may be useful or it may be disastrous for the system.

We have seen that both X_L and X_C are the functions of supply frequency. If the supply frequency is varied then both the X_L and X_C varies. At certain frequency, X_L becomes equal to the X_C. Such a condition where $X_L = X_C$ for a certain frequency is called as series resonance. The frequency at which resonance occurs is called as resonant frequency.

8.8.1 Characteristics of Series Resonance

Consider a series circuit of resistance R, inductance L and capacitance C (8.28 (a)).

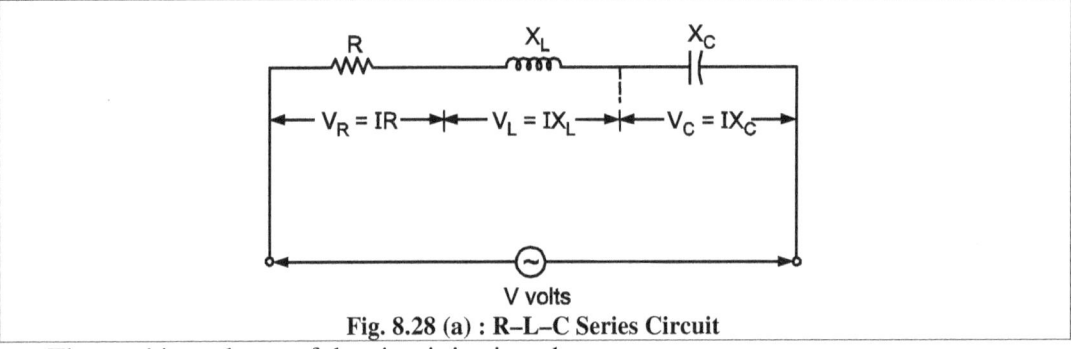

V volts

Fig. 8.28 (a) : R–L–C Series Circuit

The total impedance of the circuit is given by

$$Z = \sqrt{R^2 + (X_L - X_C)^2}$$

Now, if the supply voltage across the circuit is maintained constant and frequency is gradually increased from zero to a high value then inductive reactance, $(X_L = 2\pi fL)$, starts increasing from zero while capacitive reactance $\left(X_C = \dfrac{1}{2\pi fC}\right)$ decreases from its infinitely large value as shown in Fig. 8.28 (b). At a certain frequency f_r, the two reactances become numerically equal i.e. at this frequency, $X_L = X_C$

$$X_L = X_C$$

i.e.
$$X_L - X_C = 0$$

∴
$$\text{Impedance } Z = \sqrt{R^2 + (0)^2}$$

∴
$$Z = R \quad \text{and}$$

$$I = \frac{V}{Z} = \frac{V}{R}$$

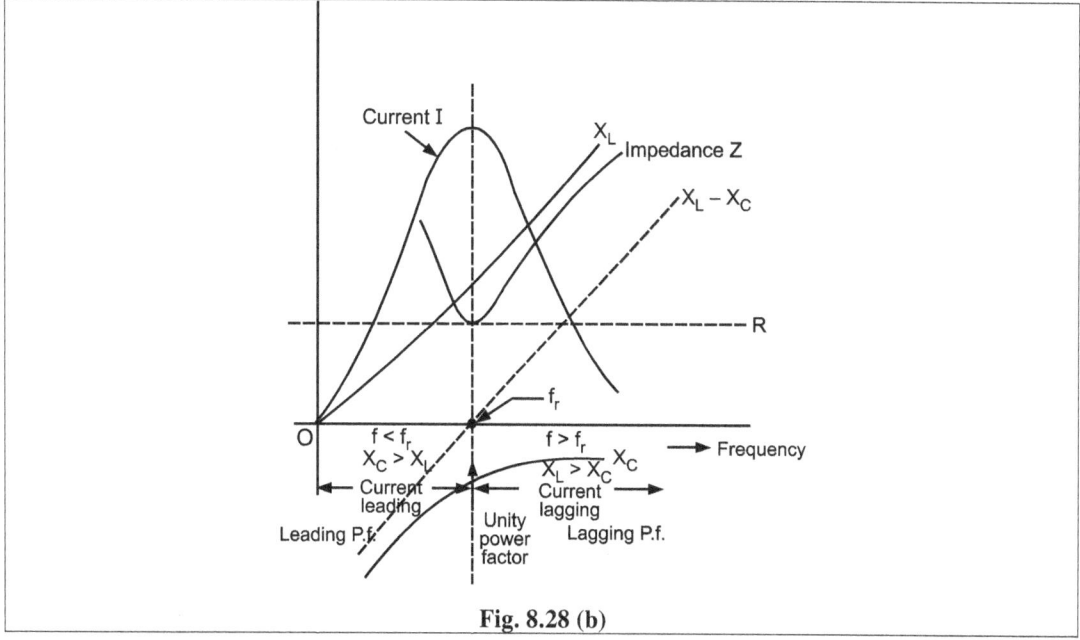

Fig. 8.28 (b)

Thus, under these conditions, the effects of the inductive and capacitive reactances completely neutralize each other. As a result, the impedance falls to a minimum value $(Z = R)$ and the current reaches a maximum value $\left(I = \dfrac{V}{R}\right)$ with unity power factor.

8.8.2 Resonant Frequency

Let, f_r be the resonant frequency. Then at this frequency,

$$X_L = X_C$$

$$\omega_r \cdot L = \frac{1}{\omega_r \cdot C}$$

$$2\pi f_r \cdot L = \frac{1}{2\pi f_r \cdot C}$$

∴
$$f_r^2 = \frac{1}{4\pi^2 \, LC}$$

∴
$$f_r = \frac{1}{2\pi \sqrt{LC}} \ \text{Hz}$$

Example 8.15 :

A series circuit consisting of coil and a variable capacitance having reactance X_C. The coil has a resistance of 10 Ω, inductive reactance of 20 Ω. It is observed that at a certain value of capacitance, current in the circuit is maximum. Find (i) the value of capacitance, (ii) impedance of the circuit, (iii) power factor, (iv) current, if applied voltage is 100 V, 50 Hz.

Solution : The current being maximum in the given R–L–C circuit, therefore circuit is under series resonance which occurs at,

$$X_L = X_C$$

(i) $\therefore$ Variable reactance, $X_C = 20 \, \Omega$

$$X_C = \frac{1}{2\pi fC} = \frac{1}{2\pi \times 50 \, C} = 20$$

$\therefore$ $C = 1.59 \times 10^{-4}$ farad

(ii) Impedance, $Z = \sqrt{R^2 + (X_L - X_C)^2}$ $(\because X_L - X_C = 0)$

$$= \sqrt{R^2 + (0)^2}$$

$$Z = 10 \, \Omega$$

(iii) Power factor, $\cos\phi = \dfrac{R}{Z} = \dfrac{10}{10}$

$$= 1 \text{ i.e. unity p.f.}$$

(iv) Maximum current, $I_{max} = \dfrac{V}{Z} = \dfrac{100}{10} = 10$ Amp.

Example 8.16 :

A coil having a resistance of 5 Ω and an inductance of 0.1H connected in series with a 50 μF capacitor. A variable frequency alternating voltage of 200 V is applied to the circuit. At what value of frequency will the current be become maximum ? Calculate the current and the voltage across coil and across capacitor for this frequency.

Solution : The current will be maximum when,

$$X_L = X_C$$

and in this case impedance, $Z = R$

$$= 5 \, \Omega$$

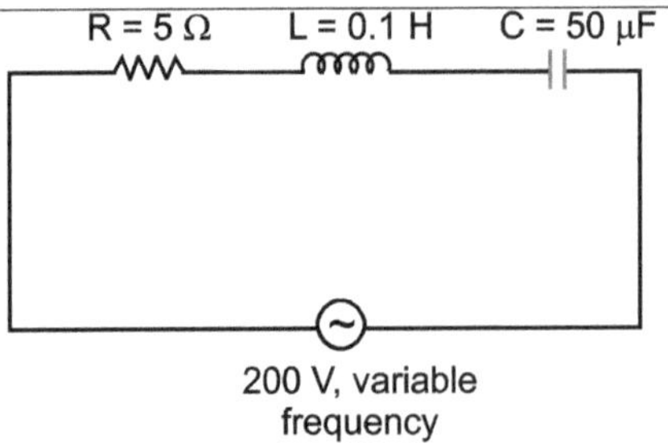

Fig. 8.29 : Circuit Diagram

Resonant frequency,
$$f_r = \frac{1}{2\pi\sqrt{LC}}$$
$$= \frac{1}{2\pi\sqrt{0.1 \times 50 \times 10^{-6}}} = 71.176 \text{ Hz}$$

Current under resonant condition, $I_{max} = \dfrac{V}{Z}$
$$= \frac{200}{5} = 40 \text{ Amp.}$$

Inductive reactance, $X_L = 2\pi f_r L = 2 \times \pi \times 71.176 \times 0.1 = 44.72 \ \Omega$

∴   Impedance of coil, $Z_L = R + j X_L = 5 + j\,44.72 = 45 \angle 83.62° \ \Omega$

Alternatively, $|Z_L| = \sqrt{R^2 + X_L^2} = 45 \ \Omega$

∴   Voltage across coil, $V_L = I \cdot |Z_L| = 40 \times 45 = 1800 \text{ volts}$

Under resonance, $X_L = X_C$

∴ $X_C = 44.72 \ \Omega$

∴ Voltage across capacitance,
$$V_C = I \cdot X_C = 40 \times 44.72 = 1788.8 \text{ volt}$$

8.9 PARALLEL A.C. CIRCUITS

A parallel A.C. circuits may consist of two or more series circuits in parallel across the same supply. The voltage applied across all this parallel circuit element is same and they are called as branches of the parallel circuits. The problems on parallel circuits can be solved by two basic methods :

(i) Phasor method,

(ii) Admittance method.

8.9.1 Phasor Method

In parallel circuits as applied voltage is common to all the branches of the circuit, therefore it is taken as reference phasor and drawn on positive X-axis. Here each branch of parallel circuit is analyzed separately as if as a series circuit then the effects of separate branches are drawn together with voltage as reference.

If the total current drawn by the parallel circuit is to be calculated, then following procedure is adopted:

(1) The current in the individual branches and their phase angles are determined using the following expressions, for each branch separately :
$$I = \frac{V}{Z} \quad \text{and} \quad \tan\phi = \frac{X}{R}$$

(2) The phasor diagram is drawn with voltage as refcrence. Then all the branch currents are drawn with their angle of lead or lag.

(3) Finally, the total current is calculated by a phasor addition of all branch currents either graphically or mathematically,

$$\bar{I} = \bar{I}_1 + \bar{I}_2 + \bar{I}_3 \qquad \text{... (Phasor addition)}$$

Note :

(1) The phase angle of resultant current I is power factor angle of whole circuit. Cosine of this angle is the overall power factor of the circuit.

(2) The voltage V is taken as reference and if the phase angle of resultant current comes out positive then it means current leads the voltage which is taken as a reference. Therefore, overall power factor of the circuit is leading in nature.

(3) If the phase angle of resultant current is negative, it means the current phasor lags the voltage and overall power factor of the circuit is lagging in nature.

Example 8.17 :

Two impedances $Z_1 = 30 \angle 45° \; \Omega$ and $Z_2 = 45 \angle 30° \; \Omega$ are connected in parallel across a single phase 230 V, 50 Hz supply. Calculate the (i) current drawn, (ii) p.f., (iii) power consumed by the circuit.

Steps to solve the example :

Step.1 : Find equivalent impedance of parallel combination

As the impedances of branch I and II are given, find out their equivalent impedance

as : $\bar{Z}_{total} = \dfrac{\bar{Z}_1 \times \bar{Z}_2}{\bar{Z}_1 + \bar{Z}_2}$.

Step 2 : Find the total current drawn by the circuit.

Take voltage as reference $\bar{V}$ (V $\angle$ 0°) and find the total current drawn by the circuit

by $\bar{I}_{total} = \dfrac{\bar{V}}{\bar{Z}_{total}}$.

Step 3 : To find the power factor

The angle in polar form of current I_{total}, represents the phase difference between I_{total} and applied voltage (taken as reference). Cosine of this angle gives us overall power factor. (i.e. cos φ).

Step 4 : To find power consumed by the circuit.

Total power consumed by the circuit is found by formula, $P_{total} = V \cdot I_{total} \cdot \cos \phi$

Solution : Fig. 8.30 shows the circuit diagram for example.

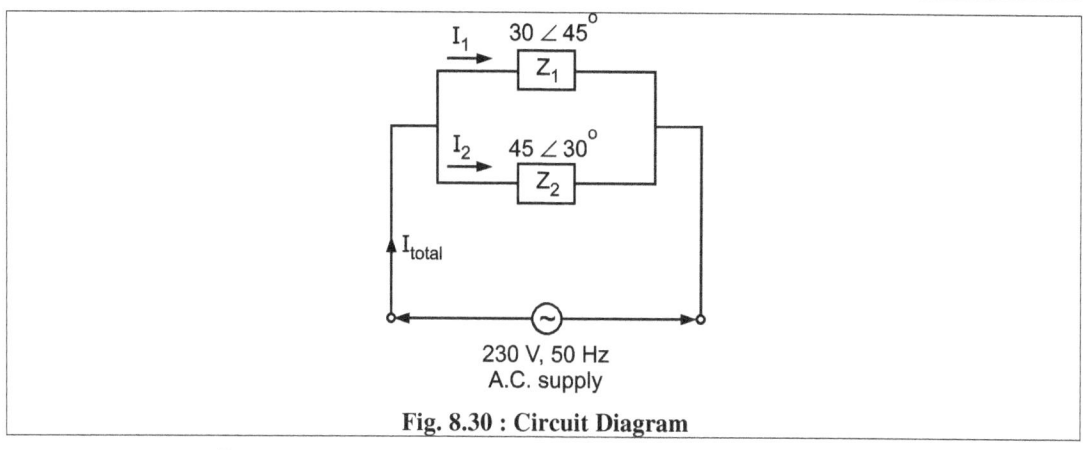

Fig. 8.30 : Circuit Diagram

Given data : $\bar{Z}_1 = 30 \angle 45^\circ\ \Omega$, $= 21.213 + j\ 21.213$, $\bar{Z}_2 = 45^\circ \angle 30^\circ\ \Omega = 38.97 + j\ 22.5$

$V = 230$ V, $f = 50$ Hz, $\omega = 2\ \pi f = 314.28$ rad/sec.

Now, $\bar{Z}_1 + \bar{Z}_2 = (21.213 + j\ 21.213) + (38.97 + j\ 22.5)$

$$= 60.183 + j\ 43.713 = 74.383 \angle 36^\circ\ \Omega$$

Step 1 :

As Z_1 and Z_2 are connected in parallel, therefore their equivalent impedance,

$$\bar{Z}_{total} = \frac{\bar{Z}_1 \times \bar{Z}_2}{\bar{Z}_1 + \bar{Z}_2}$$

$$= \frac{30 \angle 45^\circ \times 45 \angle 30^\circ}{74.383 \angle 36^\circ} = 18.15 \angle 39^\circ$$

Step 2 :

Taking voltage 230 V as reference,

$\therefore$ $\bar{V} = V \angle 0^\circ = 230 \angle 0^\circ$

$\therefore$ Total current, $\bar{I}_{total} = \dfrac{\bar{V}}{\bar{Z}_{total}} = \dfrac{230 \angle 0^\circ}{18.15 \angle 39^\circ}$

$$= 12.672 \angle -39^\circ$$

Step 3 :

$\therefore$ Power factor, $\cos \phi = \cos 39^\circ = 0.778$ lagging

Step 4 :

Total power consumed by the circuit,

$$P_{total} = V \cdot I_{total} \cdot \cos \phi$$

$$= 230 \times 12.672 \times 0.778$$

$$= 2264.61 \text{ watts}$$

Example 8.18 :

Two circuits, the impedances of which are given by $Z_1 = (12 + j5)$ Ω and $Z_2 = (8 - j4)$ Ω are connected in parallel across the potential difference of $(230 + j0)$ volt. Calculate (i) total current drawn, (ii) total power and branch powers consumed and (iii) overall power factor of the circuit.

Steps to solve the problem :

Step 1 : To find the equivalent impedance of parallel combination.

Two impedances are connected in parallel. First find out the total or equivalent impedance of the parallel combinations as

$$\bar{Z}_{total} = \frac{\bar{Z}_1 \times \bar{Z}_2}{\bar{Z}_1 + \bar{Z}_2} = |Z_{total}| \angle \phi°$$

Step 2 : To find total current drawn by circuit.

Take given supply voltage as reference $(V \angle 0°)$ then find the total current drawn from supply by,
$$\bar{I}_{total} = \frac{\bar{V}}{\bar{Z}_{total}}$$

Step 3 : To find the branch currents.

Find the branch currents as $\bar{I}_1 = \dfrac{\bar{V}}{\bar{Z}_1}$ and $\bar{I}_2 = \dfrac{\bar{V}}{\bar{Z}_2}$

Step 4 : To find power.

Find total power and branch power by using formula :
$$I^2 R \quad \text{or} \quad VI \cos \phi$$

Step 5 : To find power factor.

As voltage is taken as reference therefore cosine of phase angle of current phasor I_{total} will give the value of overall power factor.

Solution : Given impedances :

$$\begin{aligned}
\bar{Z}_1 &= 12 + j5 && \text{(R-L circuit)}\\
&= 13 \angle 22.62° \ \Omega \\
\bar{Z}_2 &= (8 - j4) && \text{(R-C circuit)}\\
&= 8.944 \angle -26.565° \ \Omega \\
\bar{Z}_1 + \bar{Z}_2 &= 12 + j5 + 8 - j4 \\
&= 20 + j1 \\
&= 20.025 \angle 2.862° \ \Omega
\end{aligned}$$

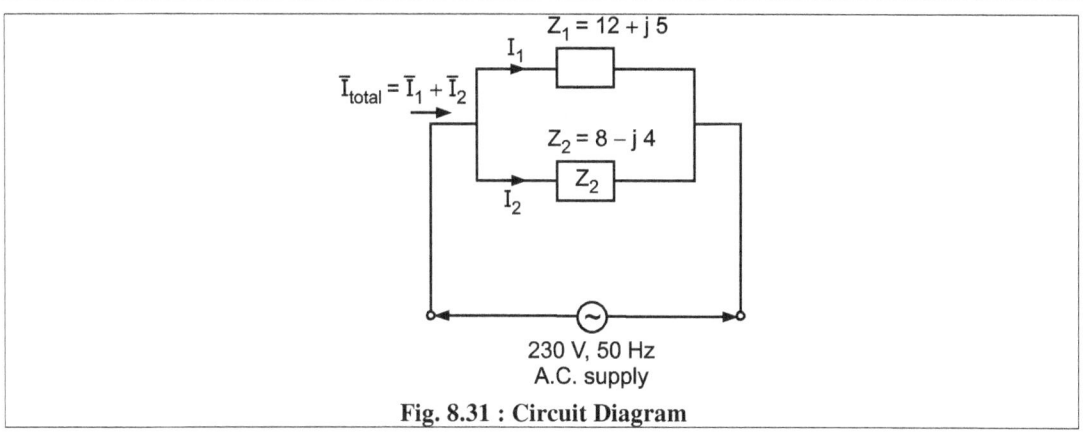

Fig. 8.31 : Circuit Diagram

(i) Total impedance,

$$\bar{Z}_{total} = \frac{\bar{Z}_1 \times \bar{Z}_2}{\bar{Z}_1 + \bar{Z}_2}$$

$$= \frac{13 \angle 22.62° \times 8.944 \angle -26.565°}{20.025 \angle 2.862°}$$

$$= \left[\frac{13 \times 8.944}{20.025} \angle (22.62 - 26.565 - 2.862)° \right]$$

$$= 5.8063 \angle -6.807° \ \Omega$$

(ii) Total current,

$$\bar{I}_{total} = \frac{\bar{V}}{\bar{Z}_{total}} = \frac{230 \angle 0}{5.8063 \angle -6.807}$$

$$= 39.6121 \angle 6.807° \text{Amp.}$$

(iii) Total power drawn by circuit,

$$P_{total} = V \cdot I_{total} \cdot \cos \phi$$

$$= 230 \times 39.6121 \cos (6.807)$$

$$= 9046.5 \text{ watts}$$

(iv) Branch current,

$$\bar{I}_1 = \frac{\bar{V}}{\bar{Z}_1} = \frac{230 \angle 0°}{13 \angle 22.62}$$

$$= 17.6923 \angle -22.62°$$

Power in branch 1,

$$P_1 = V I_1 \cos \phi_1$$

$$= 230 \times 17.6923 \times \cos (-22.62)$$

$$= 3756.2 \text{ watts}$$

Alternatively power,

$$P_1 = I_1^2 \ R_1$$

$$= (17.6923)^2 \times 12$$

$$= 3756.2 \text{ W}$$

Similarly,
$$I_2 = \frac{V}{Z_2} = \frac{230 \angle 0°}{8.944 \angle - 26.562°}$$

$$= 25.715 \angle 26.562° \text{ Amp.}$$

∴   Power in branch 2, $P_2 = V I_2 \cos \phi_2$

$$= 230 \times 25.715 \times \cos (26.562°)$$

$$= 5290.18 \text{ watts}$$

(v) With voltage as reference, phase angle of I_{total} is positive i.e. it leads the voltage.

Overall power factor, $\cos \phi = \cos (6.807)°$

$$= 0.9929 \text{ leading}$$

Example 8.19 :

A coil having resistance of 50 Ω and inductance of 0.02 H is connected in parallel with a capacitor of 25 μF, across a 200 volt, 50 Hz supply. Find the current in the coil and the capacitor. Also find total current taken from the supply, and overall power factor.

Draw a neat phasor diagram.

Solution : Given : R = 50 Ω,

             L = 0.02 H,

             f = 50 Hz,

             C = 25 μF,

             V = 200 V.

Find : I_{coil}, I_c and $\cos \phi$

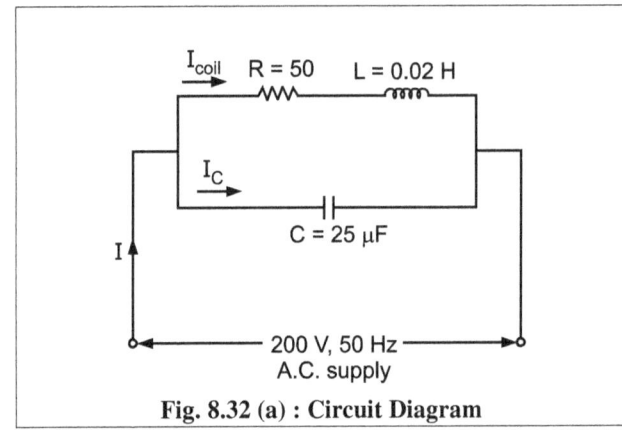

Fig. 8.32 (a) : Circuit Diagram

Inductive reactance, $X_L = 2\pi fL = 2\pi \times 50 \times 0.02$

$$= 6.283 \ \Omega$$

Capacitive reactance, $X_C = \dfrac{1}{2\pi fC} = \dfrac{1}{314.28 \times 25 \times 10^{-6}}$

$$= 127.3 \ \Omega$$

∴   Impedance of coil, $Z_{coil} = R + j X_L$

$$= 50 + j \, 6.283$$

$$= 50.3932 \angle 7.162°$$

Take supply voltage as reference.

∴ $\bar{V} = 200 \angle 0°$

∴   Current in the coil, $\bar{I}_{coil} = \dfrac{\bar{V}}{\bar{Z}_{coil}}$

$$= \dfrac{200 \angle 0°}{50.3932 \angle 7.162°}$$

$$= 3.9687 \angle -7.162 \text{ Amp.}$$

$$= (3.9377 - j\, 0.495) \text{ Amp.}$$

Impedance of capacitor, $0 - j\, X_C = 0 - j\, 127.3$

$$Z_C = 127.324 \angle -90° \ \Omega$$

∴   Current through capacitor, $\bar{I}_C = \dfrac{\bar{V}}{\bar{Z}_C}$

$$= \dfrac{200 \angle 0°}{127.324 \angle -90°}$$

$$= 1.571 \angle +90° \text{ Amp.}$$

$$= (0 + j\, 1.571) \text{ Amp.}$$

As the coil and capacitor are in parallel, therefore total current is sum of individual branch currents.

∴   Total current, $\bar{I} \;=\; \bar{I}_{coil} + \bar{I}_C = 3.9377 - j\, 0.495 + j\, 1.571$

$$= 3.9377 + j\, 1.076 \text{ A}$$

∴ $= 4.082 \angle 15.282° \text{ A}$

∴   Overall power factor, $\cos \phi = \cos (15.282)$

$$= 0.9646 \text{ leading}$$

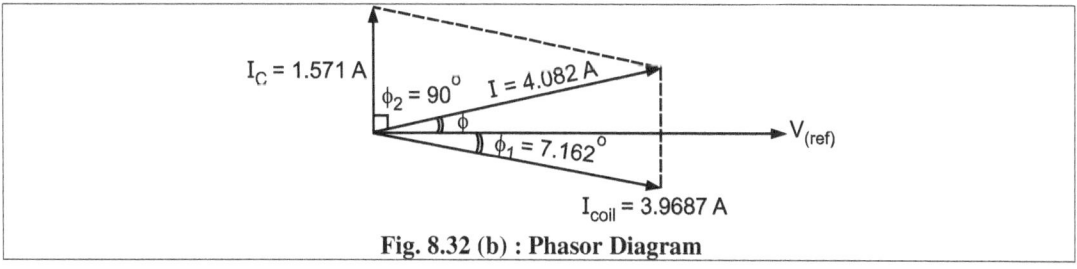

Fig. 8.32 (b) : Phasor Diagram

Example 8.20 :

Two circuits having impedances $Z_1 = 10 + j15 \ \Omega$ and $Z_2 = (6 - j8)$ are connected in parallel. If total current supplied is 15 A. Find (i) branch currents, (ii) power consumed in each branch, (iii) phasor diagram.

Solution : Given : $\bar{Z}_1 \;=\; 10 + j\, 15 = 18.0277 \angle 56.31° \ \Omega,$

$$\bar{Z}_2 \;=\; 6 - j\, 8 - 10 \angle -53.13° \ \Omega$$

$\therefore \qquad \bar{Z}_1 + \bar{Z}_2 = 10 + j\,15 + 6 - j8 = 16 + j7 = 17.464 \angle 23.63°$

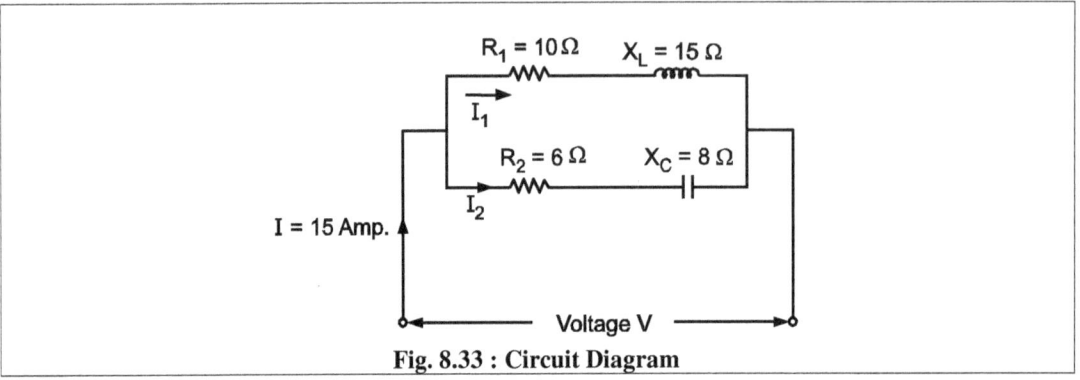

Fig. 8.33 : Circuit Diagram

(i) Branch Currents : Given total I as 15 Amp., let us take it as a reference

$\therefore \qquad\qquad\qquad I = 15 \angle 0°$

Using formula of current division in parallel circuit, we have,

$$\bar{I}_1 = \bar{I} \cdot \frac{\bar{Z}_2}{\bar{Z}_1 + \bar{Z}_2}$$

and

$$\bar{I}_2 = \bar{I} \cdot \frac{\bar{Z}_1}{\bar{Z}_1 + \bar{Z}_2}$$

$\therefore \qquad\qquad\qquad I_1 = 15 \angle 0° \dfrac{10 \angle -53.13}{17.464 \angle 23.63°}$

$$= \frac{150}{17.464} \angle (-53.13 - 23.63)°$$

$$= 8.589 \angle -76.76° \text{ Amp.}$$

$$I_2 = I \cdot \frac{Z_1}{Z_1 + Z_2}$$

$$= 15 \angle 0° \frac{18.0277 \angle 56.31°}{17.464 \angle 23.63°}$$

$$= 15.484 \angle 32.68$$

(ii) Power Consumed : Power in both the branches is consumed by their respective resistances alone.

$\therefore$ Power consumed by branch 1, $P_1 = I_1^2 \cdot R_1$

$$= (8.589)^2 \times 10$$

$$= 737.71 \text{ watts}$$

Power consumed by branch 2, $P_2 = I_2^2 \; R_2$

$$= (15.484)^2 \times 6$$

$$= 1438.544 \text{ watts}$$

(iii) Phasor Diagram :

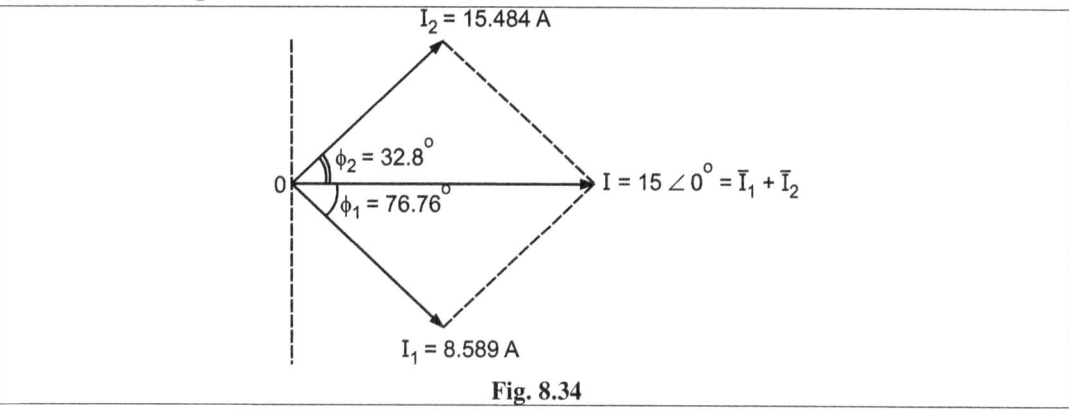

Fig. 8.34

Example 8.21 :

For the circuit diagram shown in Fig. 8.35, find the current supplied by the source. Use complex number method and sketch its phasor diagram. Also, find currents I_1 and I_2.

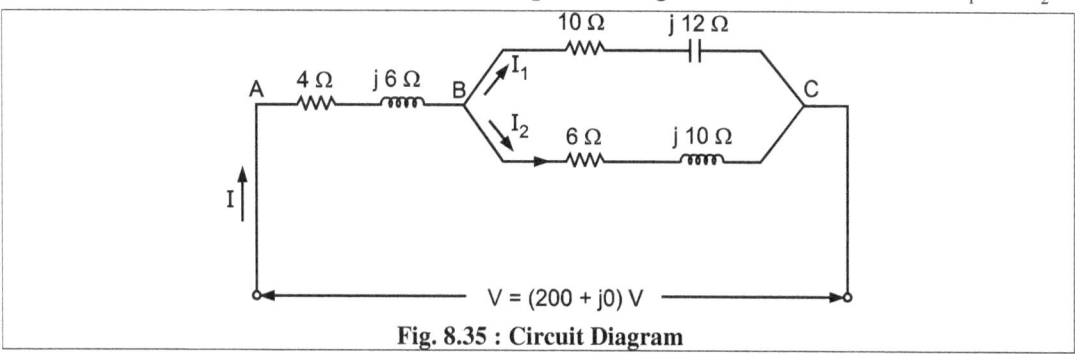

Fig. 8.35 : Circuit Diagram

Solution : Impedance, $\bar{Z}_1 = 10 - j12 \; \Omega$ (−ve sign is due to capacitive reactance)

$$= 15.62 \angle - 50.194° \; \Omega$$

Impedance, $\bar{Z}_2 = (6 + j \, 10) \; \Omega$

$$= 11.66 \angle 59.036° \; \Omega$$

$$\bar{Z}_1 + \bar{Z}_2 = (10 - j12) + 6 + j10$$

$$= 16 - j2$$

$$= 16.124 \angle - 7.125°$$

The two impedances Z_1 and Z_2 are in parallel. Therefore Z_p, impedance of parallel combination is, $\bar{Z}_p = \dfrac{\bar{Z}_1 \cdot \bar{Z}_2}{\bar{Z}_1 + \bar{Z}_2}$

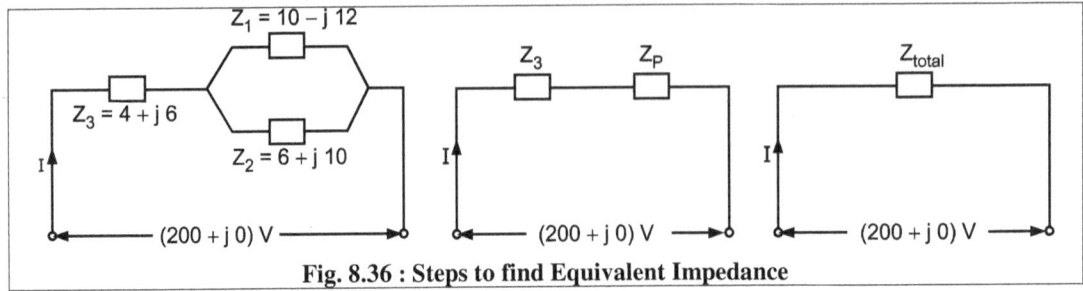

Fig. 8.36 : Steps to find Equivalent Impedance

$$= \frac{15.62 \angle -50.194 \times 11.66 \angle 59.036}{16.124 \angle -7.125°}$$

$$= 11.2954 \angle 15.967 \ \Omega$$

$$= (10.861 + j\,3.1077) \ \Omega$$

Z_p is in series with Z_3, $\bar{Z}_{total} = \bar{Z}_3 + \bar{Z}_p$

$$= (4 + j\,6) + (10.861 + j\,3.1077)$$

$$= (14.861 + j\,9.1077)$$

$$= (17.429 \angle 31.502°) \ \Omega$$

As shown in Fig. 8.37.

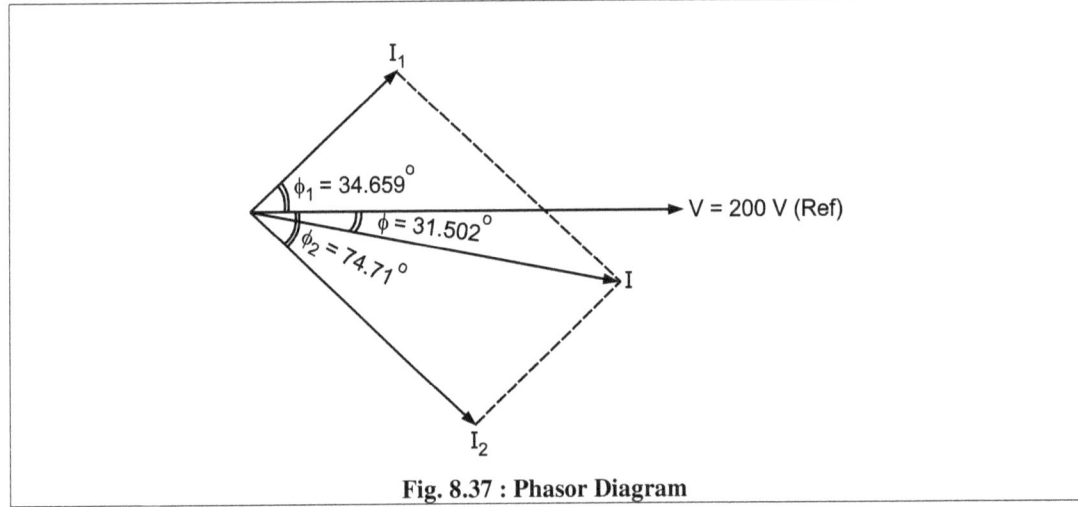

Fig. 8.37 : Phasor Diagram

$$V = I \cdot Z_{total}$$

$\therefore$ $$\bar{I} = \frac{\bar{V}}{\bar{Z}_{total}}$$

$$= \frac{200 \angle 0°}{17.429 \angle 31.502°}$$

$$= 11.475 \angle -31.502°$$

Using formula of current division in parallel circuit,

$$\bar{I}_1 = I \times \frac{\bar{Z}_2}{\bar{Z}_1 + \bar{Z}_2}$$

$$= \frac{11.475 \angle -31.502° \times 11.66 \angle 59.036°}{16.124 \angle -7.125°}$$

$$= \frac{11.475 \times 11.66}{16.124} \angle (59.036 + 7.125 - 31.502)°$$

$$= 8.3 \angle 34.659° \text{ Amp.}$$

Similarly,

$$\bar{I}_2 = I \times \frac{\bar{Z}_1}{\bar{Z}_1 + \bar{Z}_2}$$

$$= \frac{11.475 \angle -31.502 \times 15.62 \angle -50.194°}{16.124 \angle -7.125°}$$

$$= 11.1163 \angle -74.571° \text{ Amp.}$$

Example 8.22 :

Two circuits A and B are connected in parallel to a 115 V, 50 Hz supply. The total current taken by the combinations in 10 Amp. at unity p.f. Circuit A consists of a 10 Ω resistance and 200×10^{-6} F capacitor connected in series. Circuit B consists of a resistance and an inductor in series. Determine the following data for circuit B :

(1) current, (2) power factor, (3) impedance, (4) resistance and (5) reactance.

Step 1 : As total current and supply voltage is given with their phase difference f. Take voltage as reference and write current equation.

$$\bar{I}_{total} = |I_{total}| \angle \phi$$

Step 2 : Find the value of impedance of branch A and then the current of it.

$$\bar{Z}_A = R_1 - j X_C$$

$$\bar{I}_A = \frac{\bar{V}}{\bar{Z}_A} = |I_A| \angle \phi_1$$

Step 3 : As two branches are in parallel.

$$\therefore \qquad \bar{I}_A + \bar{I}_B = \bar{I}_{total}$$

$\therefore$ Find the current in branch B, $\bar{I}_B = \bar{I}_{total} - \bar{I}_A$

Step 4 : From the value of $\bar{I}_B$, find out impedance $\bar{Z}_B = \dfrac{\bar{V}}{\bar{I}_B}$ and angle ϕ_2

$$R_2 = Z_B \cos \phi_2$$

$$X_{L2} = Z_B \sin \phi_2$$

$$X_{L2} = 2\pi fL, \text{ find value of L}$$

Solution : Given : $V = 115$ V, f $= 50$ Hz,

$I_{total} = 10$ Amp at unity pf

i.e. $\cos \phi = 1$

$R_1 = 10\ \Omega$

and $X_C = 200 \times 10^{-6}$ F

$\omega = 2\pi f = 314.28$ rad/sec.

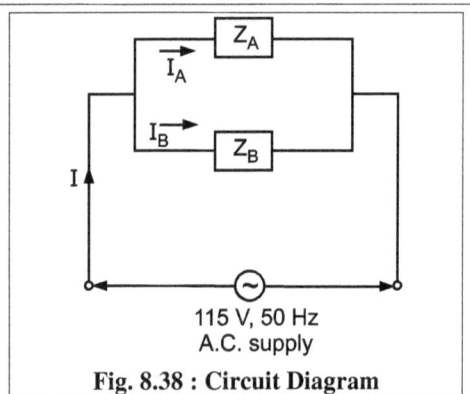

115 V, 50 Hz
A.C. supply

Fig. 8.38 : Circuit Diagram

Step 1 : Given that, total current, $I_{total} = 10$ A at unity p.f. i.e. $\phi = 0°$ between V and I_{total} taking voltage as a reference in parallel circuit,

$$I_{total} = 10 \angle 0° = 10 + j\,0 \text{ Amp}$$

Step 2 : Capacitive reactance, $X_C = \dfrac{1}{2\pi fC} = \dfrac{1}{2\pi \times 50 \times 200 \times 10^{-6}} = 15.9154\ \Omega$

$\therefore$ Impedance of branch A, $Z_A = R_1 + (-j\,X_C)$

[–ve sign is due to capacitive reactance]

$$= 10 - j\,15.9154 = 18.7962 \angle - 57.858°$$

$\therefore$ Current in branch A, $\bar{I}_A = \dfrac{\bar{V}}{\bar{Z}_A}$

$$= \dfrac{115 \angle 0°}{18.7962 \angle - 57.858°} = 6.118 \angle + 57.858° \text{ Amp.}$$

$$= 3.255 + j\,5.1804 \text{ Amp.}$$

(3) As branches A and B are in parallel,

$\therefore$ $\bar{I}_A + \bar{I}_B = \bar{I}_{total}$

$\therefore$ $\bar{I}_B = \bar{I}_{total} - \bar{I}_A$

$$= (10 \angle + j\,0) - (3.255 + j\,5.1804)$$

$$= (6.745 - j\,5.1804) = 8.5047 \angle - 37.52°$$

Power factor of branch B, $\cos \phi_B = \cos(-37.52°)$

$$= 0.7931 \text{ lagging (i.e. R + L circuit)}$$

Impedance, $\bar{Z}_B = \dfrac{\bar{V}}{\bar{I}_B}$

$$= \dfrac{115 \angle 0°}{8.5047 \angle -37.52°} = 13.522 \angle +37.52 \ \Omega$$

$$= (10.7247 + j\,8.2353) \ \Omega$$

Compare Z_B with $R_2 + j\,X_L$

∴ $R_2 = 10.7247 \ \Omega$

$$X_L = 8.2353 \ \Omega$$

∵ $X_L = 2\,\pi fL$

∴ $L = \dfrac{8.2353}{314.28} = 26.203 \text{ mH}$

8.9.2 Concept of Admittance

Admittance is defined as the reciprocal of the impedance. It is denoted by Y and is measured in unit seimens or mho. Consider a circuit shown in Fig. 8.39. The total current is phasor sum of individual branch currents.

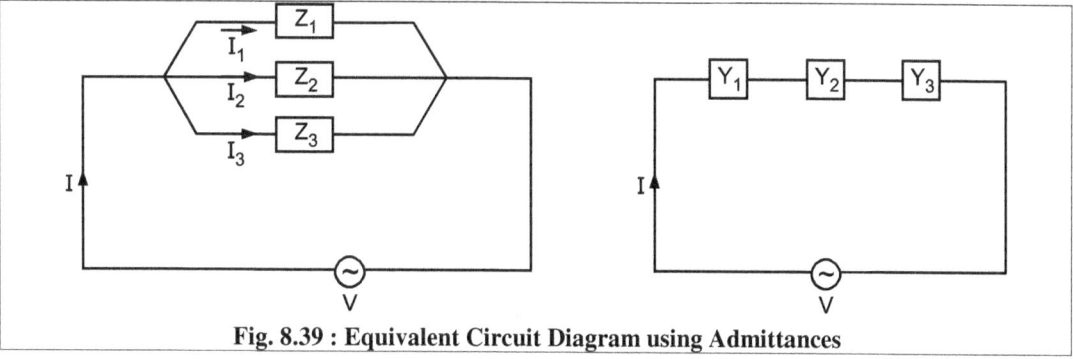

Fig. 8.39 : Equivalent Circuit Diagram using Admittances

∴ $\bar{I} = \bar{I}_1 + \bar{I}_2 + \bar{I}_3$

$$\bar{I} = \dfrac{\bar{V}}{\bar{Z}_1} + \dfrac{\bar{V}}{\bar{Z}_2} + \dfrac{\bar{V}}{\bar{Z}_3}$$

$$\dfrac{\bar{V}}{\bar{Z}} = \bar{V}\left[\dfrac{1}{\bar{Z}_1} + \dfrac{1}{\bar{Z}_2} + \dfrac{1}{\bar{Z}_3}\right]$$

$$\frac{1}{\bar{Z}} = \left[\frac{1}{\bar{Z}_1} + \frac{1}{\bar{Z}_2} + \frac{1}{\bar{Z}_3}\right]$$

$$\bar{Y} = \bar{Y}_1 + \bar{Y}_2 + \bar{Y}_3$$

where, Y is the total admittance of the circuit. The three impedances connected in parallel can be replaced by an equivalent circuit, where three admittances are connected in series.

Components of Admittance :

Consider an impedance Z given by, $Z = R \pm jX$

where +ve sign is for inductive reactance and – ve sign is for capacitive reactance,

$$Z = \sqrt{R^2 + X^2}$$

$$\phi = \tan^{-1}\left(\frac{X}{R}\right)$$

∴   Admittance, $Y = \dfrac{1}{Z} = \dfrac{1}{R \pm jX}$

Rationalizing the above expression, we get,

$$Y = \frac{1}{R \pm jX} \times \frac{R \mp jX}{R \mp jX} = \frac{R \mp jX}{R^2 + X^2}$$

$$= \frac{R}{(R^2 + X^2)} \mp j\frac{X}{R^2 + X^2}$$

$$= \frac{R}{Z^2} \mp j\frac{X}{Z^2} = G \mp jB$$

where, $G = \dfrac{R}{Z^2}$ = conductance

and $B = \dfrac{X}{Z^2}$ = susceptance

Conductance (G) : It is defined as the ratio of the resistance to the square of the impedance. It is measured in unit seimens.

Formula, $G = \dfrac{R}{Z^2}$ Siemens

Susceptance (B) : It is the ratio of the reactance to the square of the impedance. It is measured in the unit Siemens.

It should be remembered that with inductive circuit, the susceptance is negative, whereas reactance is positive ($Z = R + jX$). On the other hand, with capacitive circuit, the susceptance is positive and whereas the reactance is negative.

8.9.3 Admittance Triangle

The triangle in which sides are representing conductance, susceptance and admittance of the circuit is known as admittance triangle.

Admittance Triangle for R – L series circuit

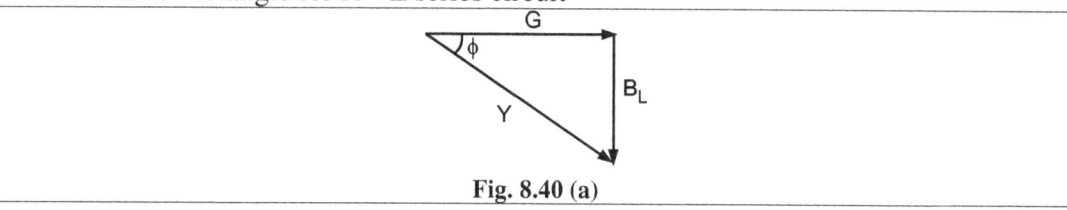

Fig. 8.40 (a)

where
$$\bar{Y} = G - j\, B_L$$

$$\bar{Y} = Y \angle -\phi$$

Admittance Triangle for series R – C circuit

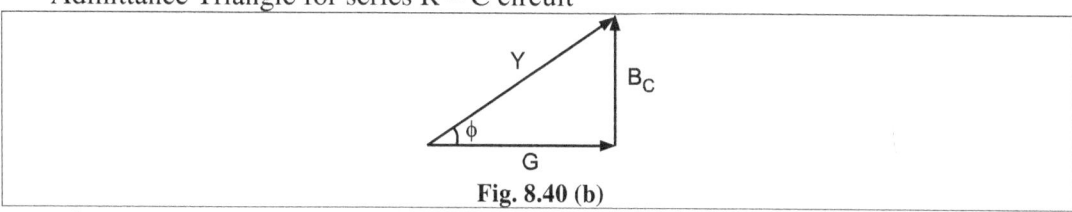

Fig. 8.40 (b)

where
$$\bar{Y} = G + j\, B_C$$
$$\bar{Y} = Y \angle \phi$$

Example 8.23 :

An A.C. circuit connected across 200 V, 50 Hz, supply has two parallel branches A and B. Branch A draws a current of 4 Amp. at 0.8 lagging power factor while the total current drawn by the parallel combination is 5 Amp. at unity power factor. Find (i) Current and power factor of branch B. (ii) Admittance of branch A, B and its parallel combination both in rectangular and polar form.

Solution :

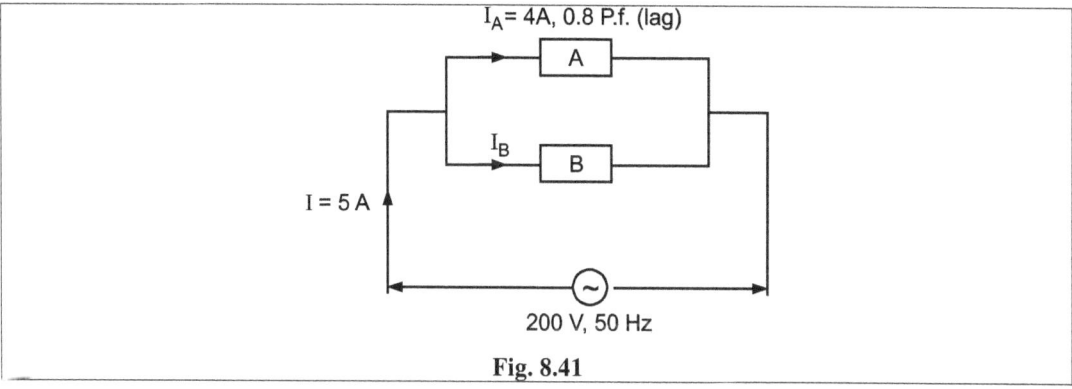

Fig. 8.41

Given : $I_A = 4 \angle - 36.86$, Amp., $I = 5 \angle 0$ Amp at unity p.f.

(i) Current and power factor of branch B.

$$\bar{I}_B = \bar{I} - \bar{I}_A$$
$$= 5 \angle 0 - 4 \angle - 36.86$$
$$= (5 + j0) - (3.2 - j2.39)$$
$$= (1.8 + j\, 2.39)$$
$$= 2.99 \angle 53.01 \text{ Amp.}$$

Power factor of branch B

$$\cos \phi_B = \cos (53.01) = 0.6 \text{ (leading)}$$

(ii) Admittance of branch A

Impedance of branch A i.e.

$$\bar{Z}_A = \frac{\bar{V}}{\bar{I}_A}$$
$$= \frac{230 \angle 0}{4 \angle - 36.86}$$
$$= 57.5 \angle 36.86 \ \Omega$$

$$\therefore \qquad \bar{Y}_A = \frac{1}{\bar{Z}_A}$$
$$= \frac{1}{57.5 \angle 36.86}$$
$$= 0.017 \angle - 36.86$$
$$= (0.0136 - j\, 0.01) \text{ siemens}$$

Impedance of branch B.

i.e.
$$\bar{Z}_B = \frac{\bar{V}}{\bar{I}_B} = \frac{230 \angle 0}{2.99 \angle 53.01}$$
$$= 76.923 \angle - 53.01$$

$$\therefore \qquad \bar{Y}_B = \frac{1}{\bar{Z}_B} = \frac{1}{76.923 \angle - 53.01}$$
$$= 0.013 \angle 53.01$$
$$= (0.0078 + j\, 0.01) \text{ siemens}$$

(iii) Net admittance of parallel combination

$$\bar{Y} = \bar{Y}_A + \bar{Y}_B$$
$$\bar{Y} = 0.0136 - j0.01 + 0.0078 + j0.01$$
$$= 0.0214 \text{ siemens}$$

8.9.4 Resonance in Parallel Circuit

Similar to a series a.c. circuit there can be resonance in parallel a.c. circuit.

- **Characteristics of parallel resonance :**

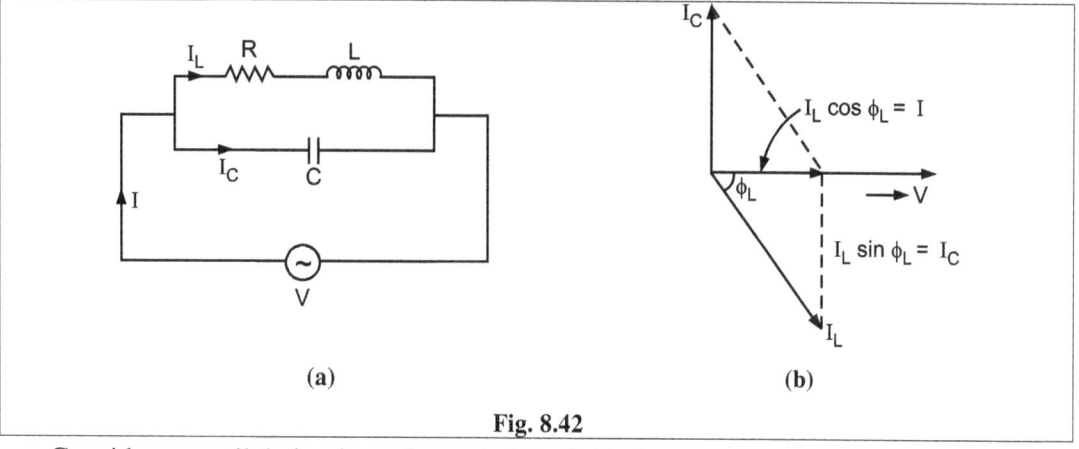

(a)   (b)

Fig. 8.42

Consider a parallel circuit as shown in Fig. 8.42 above.

In the above circuit one of the branch is resistance (R) in series with inductance (L) and other branch is pure capacitive with capacitor C. Both the branches are connected in parallel.

Let
$$\bar{Z}_1 = R + j\,X_L \text{ and } \bar{Z}_2 = -j\,X_C$$

∴
$$\bar{Y}_1 = \frac{1}{\bar{Z}_1}$$

$$= \frac{1}{R + j\,X_L} = \left(\frac{R}{R^2 + X_L^2}\right) - j\left(\frac{X_L}{R^2 + X_L^2}\right)$$

∴
$$\bar{Y}_2 = \frac{1}{\bar{Z}_2}$$

$$= \frac{1}{-j\,X_C} = \frac{j}{X_C}$$

Net admittance
$$\bar{Y} = \bar{Y}_1 + \bar{Y}_2$$

$$= \left(\frac{R}{R^2 + X_L^2}\right) + j\left(\frac{1}{X_c} - \frac{X_L}{R^2 + X_L^2}\right)$$

At resonance the imaginary part of the admittance becomes zero

Hence
$$\frac{1}{X_C} - \frac{X_L}{R^2 + X_L^2} = 0$$

∴
$$\frac{1}{X_C} = \frac{X_L}{R^2 + X_L^2}$$

$\therefore \qquad R^2 + X_L^2 = X_C X_L$

$\therefore \qquad R^2 + X_L^2 = \dfrac{L}{C}$

$\therefore \qquad R^2 + (\omega L)^2 = \dfrac{L}{C}$

$\therefore \qquad R^2 + (2\pi\, fL)^2 = \dfrac{L}{C}$

$\therefore \qquad f = \dfrac{1}{2\pi}\sqrt{\dfrac{1}{LC} - \dfrac{R^2}{L^2}}$

$\therefore \qquad f = f_r$ i.e. resonant frequency.

8.9.5 Dynamic Impedance

The admittance of circuit at resonance will be

$$Y = \dfrac{R}{R^2 + X_L^2}$$

But at resonance $R^2 + X_L^2 = X_L\ X_C$

$\therefore \qquad Y = \dfrac{R}{X_L\ X_C}$

$\therefore \qquad Z = \dfrac{1}{Y}$

$$= \dfrac{X_L\ X_C}{R} = \dfrac{L}{RC}$$

$\therefore \quad$ Z is called as dynamic impedance of the circuit.

Variation of current and impedance against frequency is as shown below.

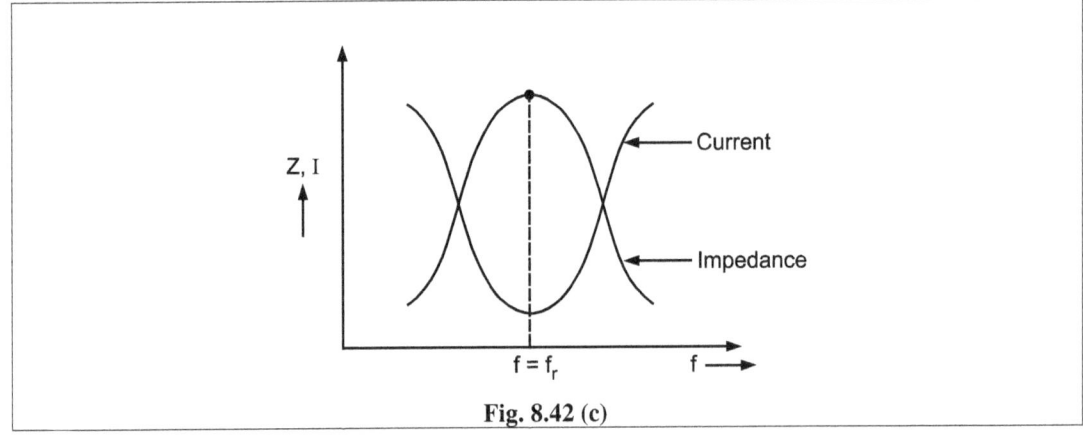

Fig. 8.42 (c)

8.9.6 Quality Factor

Quality factor of parallel circuit is defined as current magnification in the circuit at resonance it is given as.

$$Q \cdot factor = \frac{1}{R} \sqrt{\frac{L}{C}}$$

REVIEW QUESTIONS

1. Define inductive reactance of a coil and explain its variation with frequency.

2. What is the phase difference between voltage and current in purely capacitive circuit ? Justify your answer analytically ?

3. Derive an expression for the instantaneous current in a R–L series circuit when a sinusoidal voltage given by $v = V_m \sin \omega t$ is applied to the circuit.

4. Explain the term impedance of an A.C. circuit. Derive an expression for the impedance of an A.C. circuit consisting of a resistance, inductance and capacitance in series.

5. Sketch and explain the phasor diagrams of R–L–C series circuit for (i) $X_C > X_L$, (ii) $X_L > X_C$, (iii) $X_L = X_C$. Also explain why the current in such a R–L–C series circuit is taken as a reference ?

6. What do you understand by resonance in series R–L–C circuit ?

7. Deduce the expression of resonance frequency.

8. Explain the terms admittance, conductance and susceptance as applied to A.C. parallel circuits.

9. State why a parallel resonance circuit is called as rejecter circuit.

10. Define the following terms with their units (i) admittance, (ii) susceptance (iii) conductance.

UNSOLVED NUMERICALS

1. Find out the current taken by :

   (i) Pure resistance of 50 Ω, (ii) Pure inductance of 10 mH, (iii) Pure inductance of 100 micro farad. When each is connected across 230 volt, 50 Hz supply. Also calculate the power consumed when all are connected in series across the same supply.   (**Ans. :** (i) 4.6 A, 73.2411 A, 7.226 A and 795.96 W)

2. An alternating voltage v = 141.4 sin (157.08 t + π/12) volts is applied to a circuit and an A.C. ammeter, wattmeter and power factor meter are connected to measure the respective quantities. Reading of the ammeter is 5 Amp. and that of power factor meter is 0.5 lagging. Find : (i) The expression for the instantaneous value of current, (ii) The wattmeter reading, (iii) Impedance of the circuit in rectangular form.   (**Ans. :** (i) 7.07 sin (157.08 t – π/4), (ii) 250 W, (iii) (10 + j 17.32 Ω)

3. A circuit has a resistor of 10 ohms connected in series with a capacitor of 100 micro farad. If a variable frequency supply of 100 volt is connected across the circuit calculate voltage drop, across the resistor and capacitor for supply frequencies of (i) 50 Hz, (ii) 100 Hz. Calculate the circuit power factor for both conditions. What will be the new values of power factors if a pure inductance of 50 mH is connected in series with the circuit to form R–L–C circuit ?

   (**Ans. :** (i) 30 V, 95.4 V, 0.299, (ii) 53.2 V, 84.6 V, 0.5319, (iii) 0.526, 0.54)

4. A non-inductive load takes a current of 15 Amp. at 125 volt. An inductor is connected in series in order that the same current shall be supplied from 240 V, 50 Hz mains. Ignore the resistance of the inductor and calculate. (i) the inductance of the inductor, (ii) Impedance of the circuit, (iii) The phase difference between current and applied voltage.   (**Ans. :** (i) 0.043 H, (ii) 16 Ω, (iii) 58.6)

5. A coil of resistance 20 Ω and inductance of 1 Henry is connected in series with a condenser across 20 volt mains. What capacitance must the condenser have in

order that maximum current may occur at a frequency of 25 Hz ? Find also the current and voltage across condenser.   **(Ans. :** 4.05×10^{-4} F, 1 A, 157 V)

6. An A.C. circuit connected across 200 volt, 50 Hz, supply has two parallel branches A and B. The current in branch A is 4 at 0.8 lagging power factor. The total supply current is 5 amp. at unity power factor. Find current through branch B and phase angle.   **(Ans. :** 3 A, 53.15°)

7. A resistance of 15 Ω and inductance of 0.05 H are connected in series. If this is connected in parallel with 20 Ω, calculate branch currents and total current if this parallel combination is connected across 200 volt, 50 Hz, A.C. supply.

                                         (Ans. : 9.21 A, 10 A, 17.66 A)

8. Two impedances $Z_A = (4 + 3j)$ and $Z_B = (10 - j7)$ are connected in parallel and impedance $Z_C = (6 + j5)$ is connected in series with parallel combination of Z_A and Z_B. If the voltage applied across circuit is 200 volt at 50 Hz. Calculate :

    (i) Currents flowing in Z_A, Z_B and Z_C and

    (ii) The total power factor of the circuit.

    (Ans. : (i) 14.1972 $\angle$– 51.192°A, 5.8156 $\angle$ 20.677°A,16.9355 $\angle$– 32.137°A, (ii) 0.8467 lag)

9. Two impedances $Z_1 = 40 \angle30°$ ohm and $Z_2 = 30 \angle60°$ ohm are connected in series across single phase, 230 V, 50 Hz supply. Calculate the (i) current drawn, (ii) p.f. and (iii) power consumed by the circuit.

                (Ans. : (i) 3.399 $\angle$–42.807°A, (ii) 0.7336 lagging, (iii) 573.5064 W)

10. Two impedances are having equal magnitudes and power factors of these impedances are 0.7 lagging and 0.9 leading respectively. Calculate the power factor of their :

    (i) Series combination,

(ii) Parallel combination.   (**Ans. :** 0.985 lagging, 0.985 lagging)

11. A coil having a resistance of 4 Ω and inductive reactance of 3 Ω is connected in parallel with consisting of a resistance of 8 Ω in series with capacitive reactance of 6 Ω.

This combined circuit is then connected across a single phase A.C. supply if power loss in the coil is 1600 W. Calculate :

(i) The total current drawn and p.f. of the circuit and

(ii) Total power loss.   (**Ans. :** 24.74 A, 0.9701 lagging, 2400 W)

UNIT - V

Chapter **9**

THREE PHASE A.C. CIRCUITS

9.1 INTRODUCTION

Polyphase System :

A system with more than one phase is called as polyphase system. A polyphase system contains two or more than two phases of same frequency.

Most of the electrical power generated in the world today is three-phase. Three-phase power was first conceived by Nikola Tesla. In early days of electrical power generation, Tesla proved that three-phase power is the most efficient way that electricity could be produced, transmitted and consumed.

9.1.1 Three-phase Circuit

There are several reasons why three-phase system is superior to single-phase system.

(i) The rating of three-phase motor and three-phase transformer are about 150% greater than single-phase motor or transformer with a similar frame size.

(ii) The power delivered by a single-phase system pulsates. The power falls to zero, three times during each cycle. The power delivered by a three-phase circuit pulsates also, but it never falls to zero. So in three-phase system, power delivered to the load is same at any instant. This produces superior operating characteristics for three-phase system.

(iii) To transmit certain amount of power at a given voltage over a given distance, three-phase transmission line requires less amount of copper than single-phase line. This reduces the cost of material required, hence, becomes economical.

(iv) Power factor of three-phase motor is greater than single-phase motor for same rating.

(v) Three-phase motors are self starting, as the magnetic field produced by three-phase supply is rotating. But the magnetic field produced by single-phase system is pulsating, so most of the single-phase motors are not self starting.

(9.1)

9.1.2 Generation of Three-phase Voltages

When three identical coils are placed with their axes at $120°$ electrical apart from each other and rotated in uniform magnetic field, a sinusoidal voltage is generated across each coil. This is the basis of simple three-phase a.c. generator (alternator).

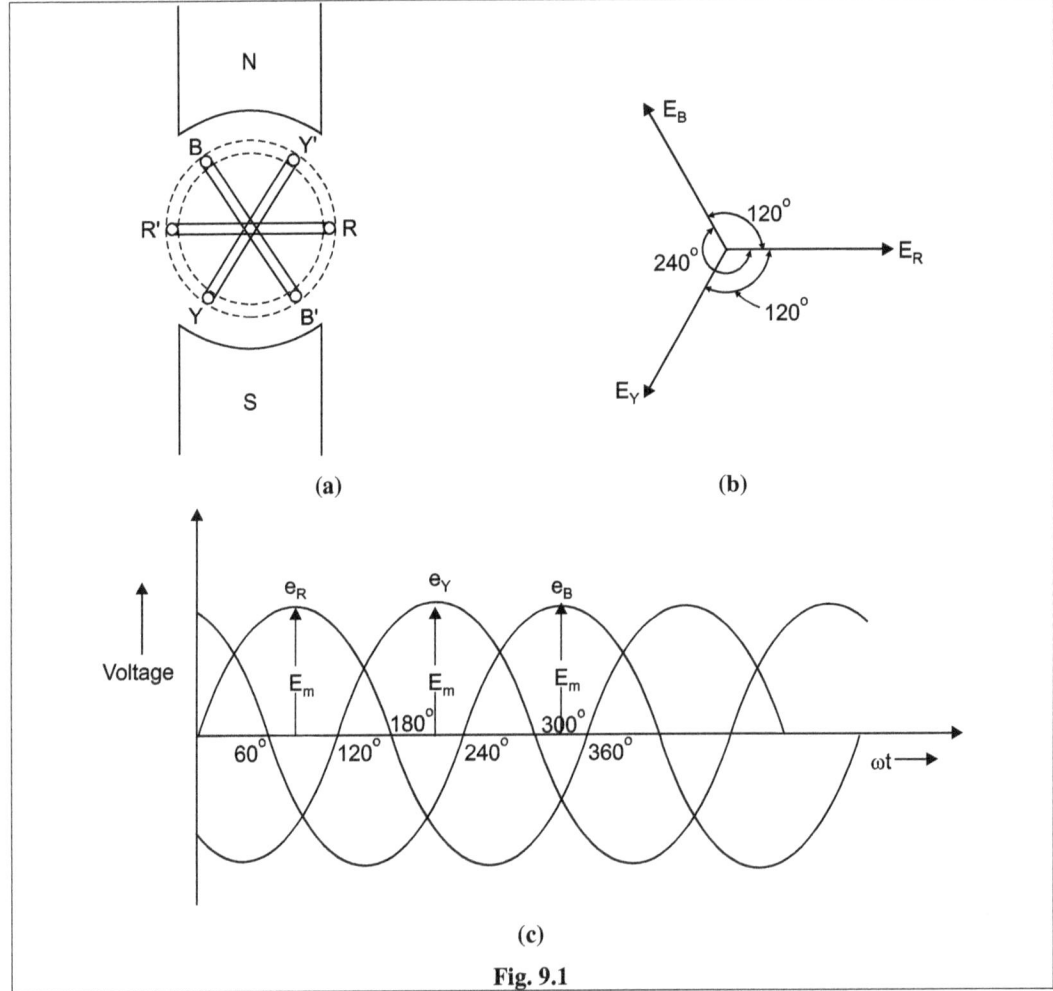

Fig. 9.1

Fig. 9.1 (a) shows a three-phase 2-pole generator. It has three sets of coils RR', YY' and BB' symmetrically mounted on rotor such that their axes are at $120°$ electrical from each other. When the rotor is rotated in anticlockwise direction at constant angular velocity ω radians per second, a sinusoidal voltage is generated across each coil. Since, the three coils rotate at same velocity ($\omega = 2\pi f$), the generated voltage have same frequency. Also since the coils are identical, the generated voltage have same magnitudes, but there is a phase difference of $120°$ between these voltages.

The instantaneous value of voltage generated in coil R-R' is

$$e_R = E_m \sin \omega t \qquad \qquad \text{... (i)}$$

The coils Y-Y' and B-B' lag behind the coil R-R' by 120° and 240° respectively.

So the instantaneous values of voltages generated in coils Y-Y' and B-B' are

$$e_Y = E_m \sin (\omega t - 120^\circ) \qquad \qquad \text{... (ii)}$$

$$e_B = E_m \sin (\omega t - 240^\circ) \qquad \qquad \text{... (iii)}$$

It is to be noted that a phase angle of (-240°) is same as $(+120^\circ)$.

In polar form, $\qquad \qquad E_R = E \angle 0^\circ$

$$E_Y = E \angle -120^\circ$$

$$E_B = E \angle -240$$

$$= E \angle 120^\circ, \quad \text{where } E = \frac{E_m}{\sqrt{2}}$$

Fig. 9.1 (b) shows position of three voltages by phasor diagram and Fig. 9.1 (c) shows sinusoidal voltage waveforms of three generated voltages.

9.1.3 Terms Related with Three-Phase System

(a) Symmetrical System : A three-phase system is said to be symmetrical when voltages of same frequency in different phases are equal in magnitude and displaced from one another by equal phase angles.

(b) Phase Sequence : A sequence in which three voltages will achieve their positive maximum values is called phase sequence.

For the arrangement shown in Fig. 9.1 (a) in which the coils are rotating in anticlockwise direction, the phase sequence is R-Y-B. If the rotor is rotated in clockwise direction, the voltages will reach their positive maximum values in the order R-B-Y. The sequence determines the direction of rotation.

(c) Balanced Load : The load is said to be balanced when loads in each phase are equal in magnitude and identical in nature.

9.2 METHODS OF CONNECTION OF THREE-PHASE SUPPLY

Since the voltage is generated in each coil, it may be considered as a source of voltage. The three coils together constitute a three-phase system and each coil is a phase. Let a load be connected across each phase. Fig. 9.2 (a) shows three loads supplied separately from the three phases.

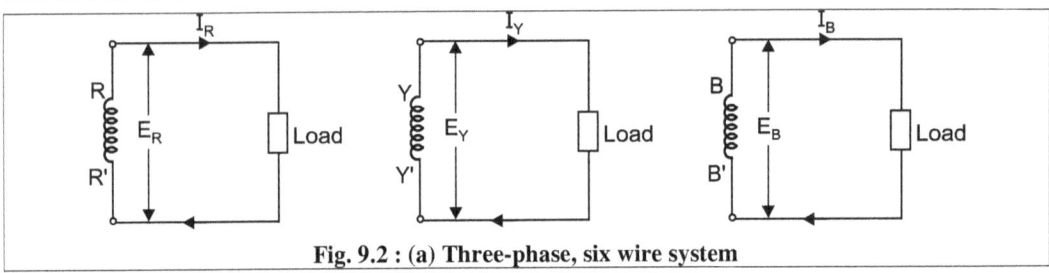

Fig. 9.2 : (a) Three-phase, six wire system

The end of coil where the current leaves may be called as starting end and the other end where the current enters the coil is called finishing end.

The ends R, Y and B are the starting ends while the ends R', Y' and B' are the finishing ends.

The arrangement shown in Fig. 9.2 (a) requires six wires to carry energy from coils (sources) to the loads. This is equivalent to three separate single-phase systems. Such a system is called a three-phase, six wire system.

The number of connecting wires may be reduced by the interconnection of the phases to form a single three-phase A.C. source. There are two methods of interconnecting the three phases.

9.2.1 Star or Wye (Y) Connection

In this type of connection, the finishing ends R', Y', B' are joined together at a common point N as shown in Fig. 9.2 (b) and (c). The free ends R, Y, B are connected to the external circuit through three conductors called lines. The point N is called as neutral point or neutral. It is also called as star point. The wire brought out from the neutral point is called neutral wire.

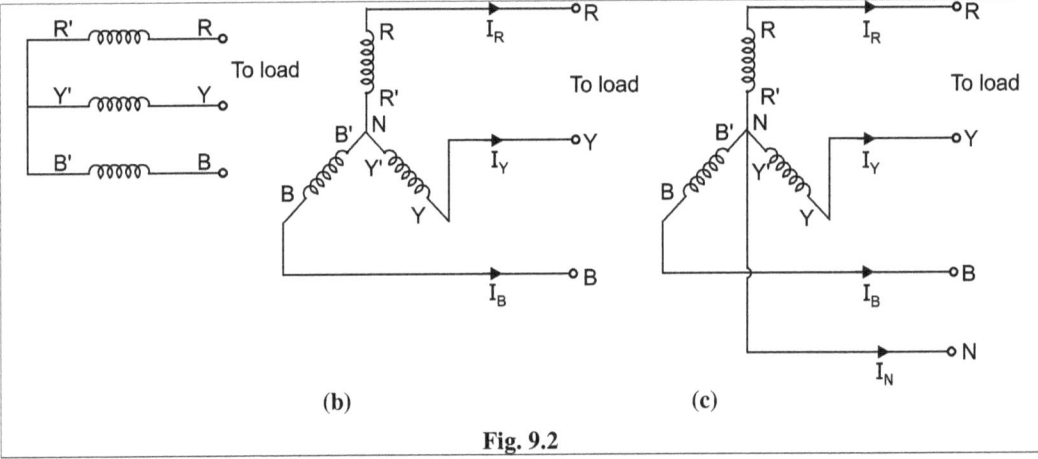

Fig. 9.2

The three line conductors and neutral wire provide a three-phase, four wire supply. It is common practice to connect the windings of three-phase alternator in star. The neutral point is connected to ground.

Phase : A phase is one of the three branches making up 3-phase circuit. In a Y connection, a phase consists of those circuit elements connected between one line and neutral.

9.2.2 Delta (Δ) or Mesh Connection

The three coils of the generator are connected such that finishing end of one is connected to the starting end of the next coil gives the delta connection. Fig. 9.2 (d) shows three-phase delta connection. Here R' is connected to Y, Y' is connected to B and B' is connected to R. Thus a closed mesh is formed, hence the name mesh connection.

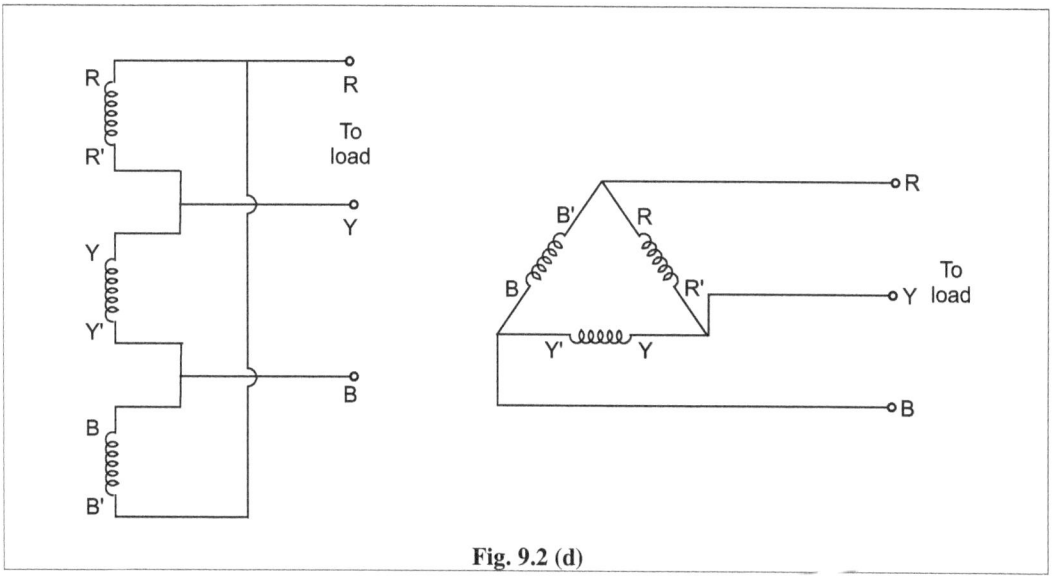

Fig. 9.2 (d)

The circuit resembles the Greek letter delta (Δ), hence the name delta connection.

In Delta, the term phase is used differently from that used in star-connected system. The phases are now connected between line terminals.

9.3 CONCEPT OF LINE VOLTAGES AND LINE CURRENTS

Line Voltage : The potential difference between any two line terminals of supply is called line voltage.

Line Current : The current passing through any line is called line current.

9.3.1 Line Voltage and Line Current in Star-connected System

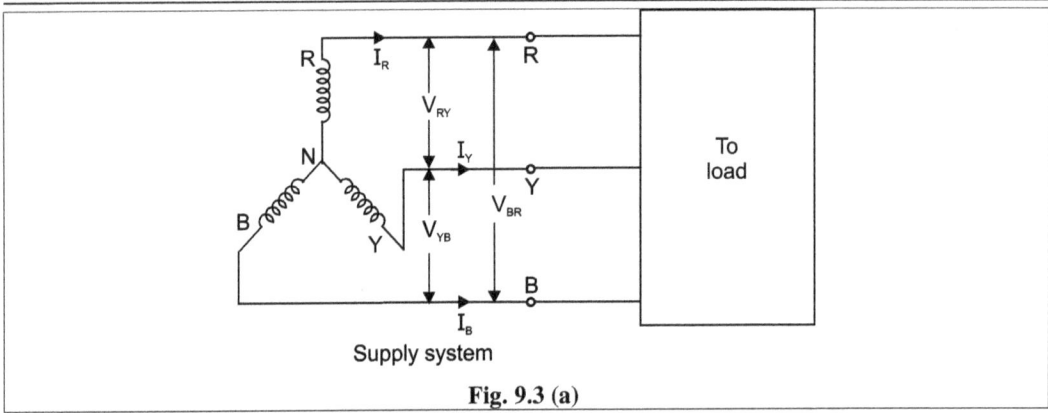

Fig. 9.3 (a)

Line voltages are denoted by V_L. These are V_{RY}, V_{YB} and V_{BR}.

Line currents are denoted by I_L. These are I_R, I_Y and I_B.

9.3.2 Line Voltage and Line Current for Delta-connected System

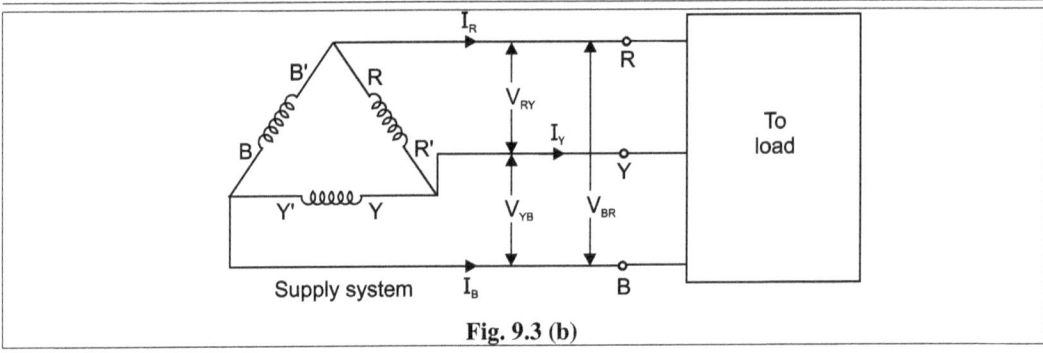

Fig. 9.3 (b)

Line voltages V_L are V_{RY}, V_{YB} and V_{BR}.

Line currents I_L are I_R, I_Y and I_B.

9.4 CONCEPT OF PHASE VOLTAGE AND PHASE CURRENT

To understand the concept of phase voltage and phase current, let us connect three-phase load to three-phase supply system.

The loads can be connected in two ways :

(i) Star connection, (ii) Delta connection.

Three-phase loads are nothing but three different single-phase loads (impedances) connected together in star or delta fashion.

Note : For voltage, symbol 'E' is considered on generation side and symbol 'V' is considered on load side.

9.4.1 Star-connected Load

The same ends (either starting or finishing) are connected together and remaining three ends are connected to supply terminals R-Y-B.

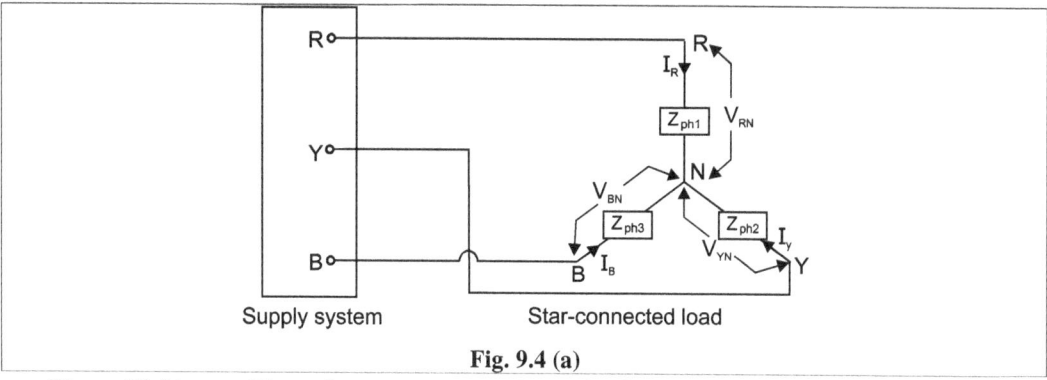

Supply system   Star-connected load

Fig. 9.4 (a)

Phase Voltage : The voltage across any branch of the three-phase load i.e. across Z_{ph1}, Z_{ph2} or Z_{ph3} is called phase voltage.

Phase Current : The current passing through any branch of three-phase load is called phase current.

In Fig. 9.4 (a), V_{RN}, V_{YN} and V_{BN} are phase voltages, while I_R, I_Y, I_B are phase currents.

The phase voltages are denoted by V_{ph}, while the phase currents are denoted by I_{ph}.

$$V_{ph} = V_{RN} = V_{YN} = V_{BN}$$

It can be seen from Fig. 9.4 (a),

$$I_{ph} = I_R = I_Y = I_B$$

This is possible if the loads are same in magnitude and nature. The line currents and phase currents are same.

$$\boxed{I_L = I_{ph}}$$

9.4.2 Delta-connected Load

If the three single-phase loads are connected such that finishing end of one is connected to starting end of the other to form a closed loop then it is called delta-connected load.

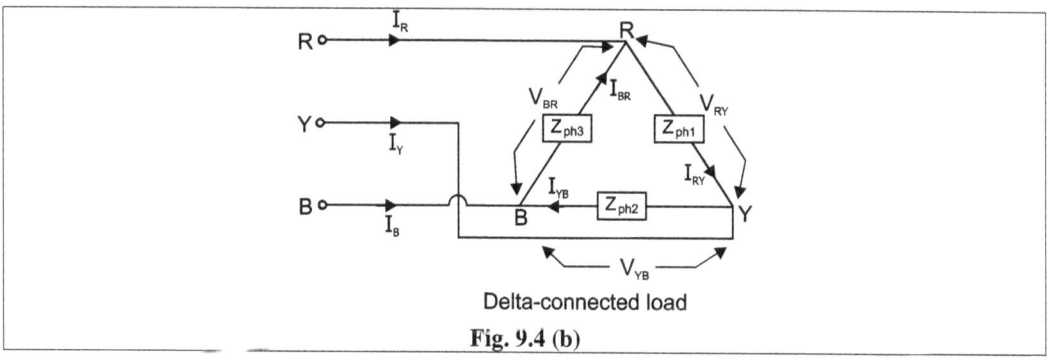

Delta-connected load

Fig. 9.4 (b)

The junction points are connected to supply terminals R-Y-B.

The currents I_{RY}, I_{YB} and I_{BR} flowing through branches of the load are phase currents. The line currents are I_R, I_Y and I_B flowing through supply lines. Thus, in delta connection, line current and phase currents are different.

The voltage across Z_{ph1} is V_{RY}, across Z_{ph2} is V_{YB} and across Z_{ph3} is V_{BR} and all are phase voltages.

$$V_{ph} = V_{RY} = V_{YB} = V_{BR}$$

The line voltage and phase voltages are same.

$$\boxed{V_L = V_{ph}}$$

9.5 BALANCED LOAD

The load is said to be balanced when loads in each phase are equal in magnitude and identical in nature, all are inductive or capacitive or resistive.

9.6 RELATION BETWEEN LINE VOLTAGE AND PHASE VOLTAGE, LINE CURRENT AND PHASE CURRENT FOR STAR-CONNECTED LOAD

Consider the balanced star-connected load.

Line voltages, $V_L = V_{RY} = V_{YB} = V_{BR}$

Line currents, $I_L = I_R = I_Y = I_B$

Phase voltages, $V_{ph} = V_{RN} = V_{YN} = V_{BN}$

Phase currents, $I_{ph} = I_R = I_Y = I_B$

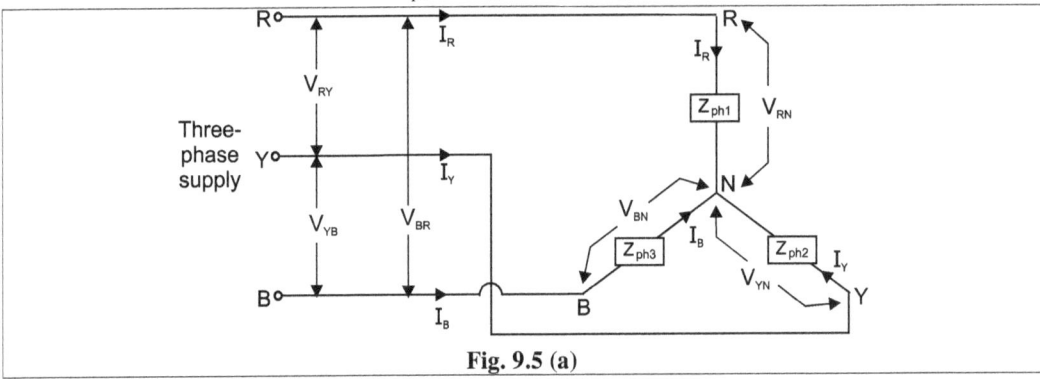

Fig. 9.5 (a)

As seen earlier, $I_L = I_{ph}$ for star-connected load.

To derive relation between V_L and V_{ph}, let us consider line voltage $V_L = V_{RY}$.

$$\overline{V}_{RY} = \overline{V}_{RN} + \overline{V}_{NY}$$

as $\qquad \overline{V}_{NY} = -\overline{V}_{YN}$

Hence, $\qquad \overline{V}_{RY} = \overline{V}_{RN} - \overline{V}_{YN}$ ... (i)

Similarly, $\qquad \overline{V}_{YB} = \overline{V}_{YN} - \overline{V}_{BN}$ ... (ii)

$\qquad \overline{V}_{BR} = \overline{V}_{BN} - \overline{V}_{RN}$ ... (iii)

The phasor diagram will give relation between line voltage and phase voltage.

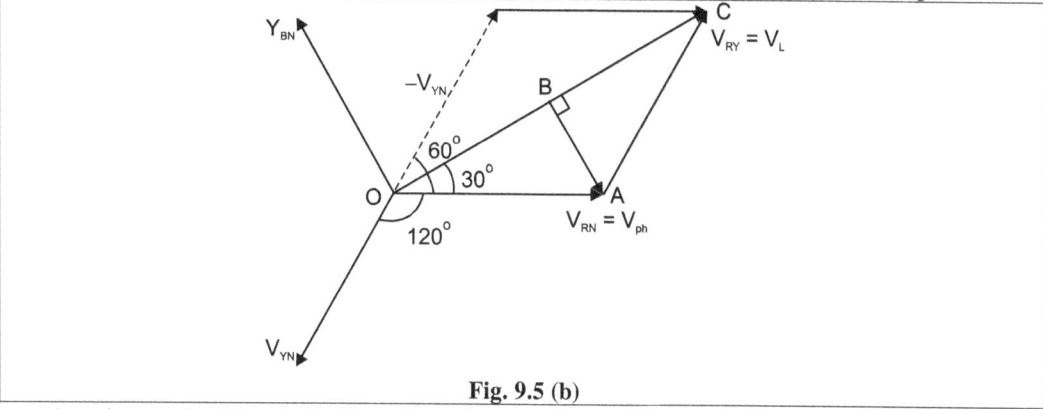

Fig. 9.5 (b)

As shown in Fig. 9.5 (b), take phase voltage V_{RN} as reference. The three-phase voltages are displaced by 120^0 from each other.

The phasor V_{RY} line voltage is addition of $\overline{V}_{RN}$ and $-\overline{V}_{YN}$, to get $-\overline{V}_{YN}$, $\overline{V}_{YN}$ is reversed.

The perpendicular is drawn from point A on phasor OC representing V_L. $OB = BC = \dfrac{V_L}{2}$

Angle between V_{RN} and $-V_{YN}$ is 60^0.

So $\angle AOB = 30^0$ (OC bisects $V_{\overset{\wedge}{RN}} - V_{YN}$)

From Δ AOB, $\qquad \cos 30^\circ = \dfrac{OB}{OA} = \dfrac{\dfrac{V_{RY}}{2}}{V_{RN}}$

$$\dfrac{\sqrt{3}}{2} = \dfrac{\dfrac{V_L}{2}}{V_{ph}}$$

$$\boxed{V_L = \sqrt{3}\, V_{ph}}$$ ... (i)

Thus, line voltage is $\sqrt{3}$ times the phase voltage and line current and phase currents are same.

$$\boxed{I_L = I_{ph}}$$ ... (ii)

The lagging and leading nature of current depend on per phase impedance.

- If Z_{ph} is inductive i.e. $R_{ph} + jX_{Lph}$, then I_{ph} lags behind V_{ph} by angle

$$\phi = \tan^{-1}\left(\frac{X_{Lph}}{R_{ph}}\right).$$

- If Z_{ph} is capacitive i.e. $R_{ph} - jX_{Cph}$, then I_{ph} leads ahead V_{ph} by angle

$$\phi = \tan^{-1}\left(\frac{-X_{Cph}}{R_{ph}}\right).$$

- If Z_{ph} is resistive i.e. $R_{ph} + j0$ then I_{ph} is in phase with V_{ph}.
- Remember ϕ is always angle of Z_{ph} i.e. between V_{ph} and I_{ph},

where $$|Z_{ph}| = \frac{|V_{ph}|}{|I_{ph}|}$$

9.6.4 Power

Power taken by each phase of load,
$$P_{ph} = V_{ph} I_{ph} \cos\phi$$
Three-phase power taken by load i.e. Active power.
$$\begin{aligned} P &= 3 V_{ph} I_{ph} \cos\phi \\ &= 3 \times \frac{V_L}{\sqrt{3}} \times I_L \cos\phi \\ &= \sqrt{3} V_L I_L \cos\phi \text{ watt} \end{aligned}$$ ... (iii)
Reactive power, $Q = \sqrt{3} V_L I_L \sin\phi$ VAr ... (iv)
Apparent power, $S = \sqrt{3} V_L I_L$ VA ... (v)

9.7 RELATION BETWEEN LINE VOLTAGE AND PHASE VOLTAGE, LINE CURRENT AND PHASE CURRENT FOR DELTA-CONNECTED LOAD

Consider the balanced delta-connected load.

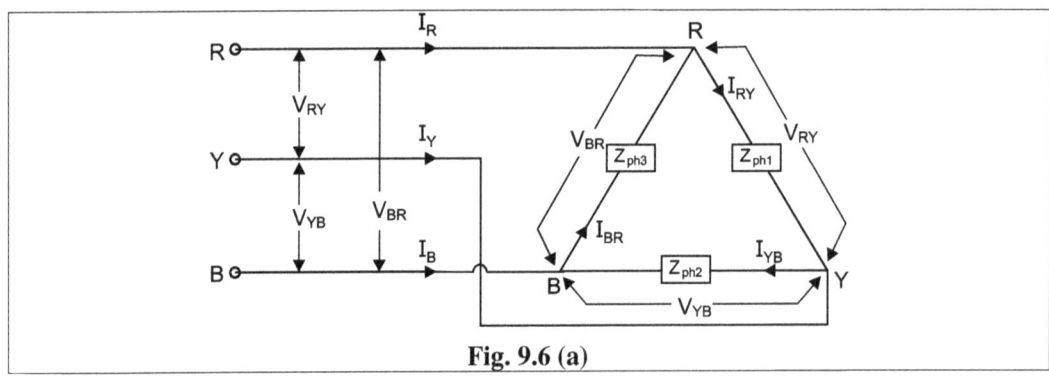

Fig. 9.6 (a)

Line voltages, $V_L = V_{RY} = V_{YB} = V_{BR}$

Line currents, $I_L = I_R = I_Y = I_B$

Phase voltages, $V_{ph} = V_{RY} = V_{YB} = V_{BR}$

Phase currents, $I_{ph} = I_{RY} = I_{YB} = I_{BR}$

As seen earlier, $V_L = V_{ph}$ for delta-connected load. To derive relation between I_L and I_{ph}, apply KCL at the node R of the load as shown in Fig. 9.6 (a).

$$\Sigma \text{ currents entering } = \Sigma \text{ currents leaving the node R}$$

$$\overline{I_R} + \overline{I_{BR}} = \overline{I_{RY}}$$

$$\overline{I_R} = \overline{I_{RY}} - \overline{I_{BR}} \qquad \text{... (i)}$$

Similarly, at node Y and node B, we get

$$\overline{I_Y} = - \overline{I_{RY}} \qquad \text{... (ii)}$$

$$\overline{I_B} + \overline{I_{BR}} = - \overline{I_{YB}} \qquad \text{... (iii)}$$

The phasor diagram will give the relation between line current and phase current.

As shown in Fig. 9.6 (b) take phase voltage V_{RY} as a reference. Three-phase voltages are displaced by 120° from each other.

Consider load as resistive $\overline{Z_{ph}} = \overline{R_{ph}} + j\,0 = R_{ph}$

Draw I_{ph} in phase with V_{ph}.

Angle between I_{RY} and $- I_{BR}$ is 60°.

OC will bisect $I_{RY} \overset{\wedge}{\ } - I_{BR}$

$\angle AOB = 30^\circ$

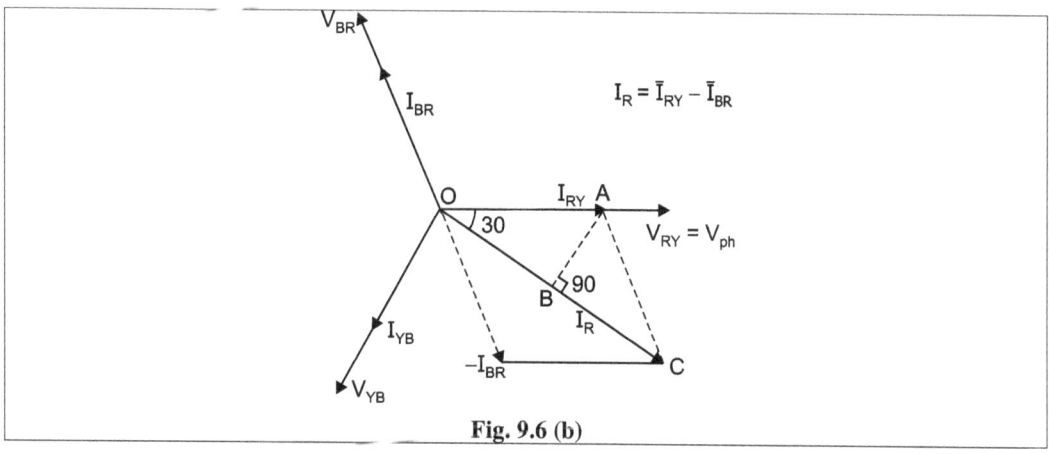

Fig. 9.6 (b)

Draw perpendicular on OC representing I_L.

$$OB = OC$$

$$= \frac{I_R}{2} = \frac{I_L}{2}$$

$$\cos 30^\circ = \frac{OB}{OA}$$

$$= \frac{\dfrac{I_R}{2}}{I_{RY}} = \frac{\dfrac{I_L}{2}}{I_{ph}}$$

$$\frac{\sqrt{3}}{2} = \frac{\dfrac{I_L}{2}}{I_{ph}}$$

$$\boxed{I_L = \sqrt{3}\, I_{ph}} \qquad \qquad \text{... (i)}$$

$$\boxed{V_L = V_{ph}} \qquad \qquad \text{... (ii)}$$

$$\text{Line current} = \sqrt{3} \ \text{phase current}$$

and $$\text{Line voltage } V_L = \text{Phase voltage } V_{ph}$$

The lagging and leading nature depend on per phase impedance.

Example 9.1 :

A balanced delta-connected load of $(4 + j\,3)$ Ω/phase is connected to a 3 phase 400 V supply. Calculate : (i) Phase current, (ii) Line current,   (iii) Power factor (iv) Active power, (v) Reactive power, (vi) Total volt amperes, (vii) Draw phasor diagram.

Solution : Given

$$\overline{Z}_{ph} = 4 + j\,3 = 5 \angle 36.86$$

$$V_L = 400 \text{ volt}$$

As the load is delta connected, $V_L = V_{ph} = 400$ volt, $\overline{V}_{ph} = 400 \angle 0$, $\overline{Z}_{ph} = 5 \angle 36.86^\circ$

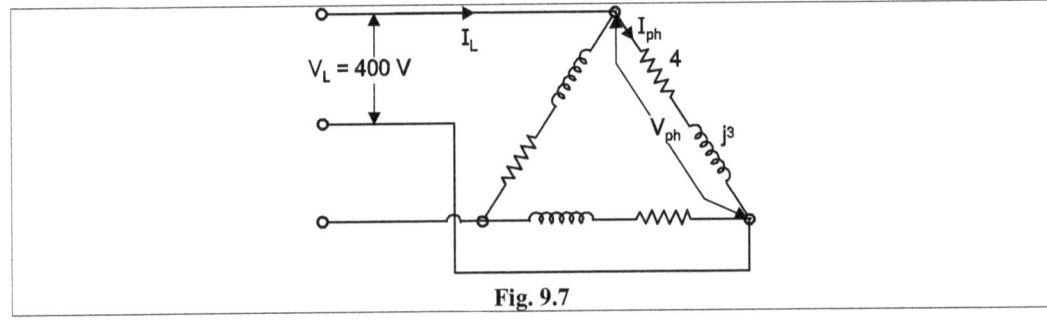

Fig. 9.7

(i) $$\overline{I}_{ph} = \frac{\overline{V}_{ph}}{\overline{Z}_{ph}} = \frac{400 \angle 0}{5 \angle 36.86^\circ} = 80 \angle -36.86^\circ$$

$$I_{ph} = 80 \text{ Amp.}$$

(ii) $\qquad\qquad\qquad\qquad I_L = \sqrt{3} \times 80 = 138.56 \text{ ampere}$

(iii) $\qquad$ Power factor $= \cos \phi = \cos (36.86^\circ) = 0.8 \text{ lagging}$

(iv) Active power or Total power $\quad P = \sqrt{3} \, V_L \, I_L \cos \phi$

      consumed $\qquad\qquad\qquad\quad = \sqrt{3} \times 400 \times 138.56 \times 0.8 = 76797.74 \text{ watt}$

(v) Reactive power, $\qquad\qquad Q = \sqrt{3} \, V_L \, I_L \sin \phi$

$\qquad\qquad\qquad\qquad\qquad\qquad = \sqrt{3} \times 400 \times 138.56 \times 0.6 = 57598.31 \text{ VAr}$

(vi) Total volt ampere, $\qquad\qquad S = \sqrt{3} \, V_L \, I_L = \sqrt{3} \times 400 \times 138.56$

$\qquad\qquad\qquad\qquad\qquad\qquad = 95997.18 \text{ VA}$

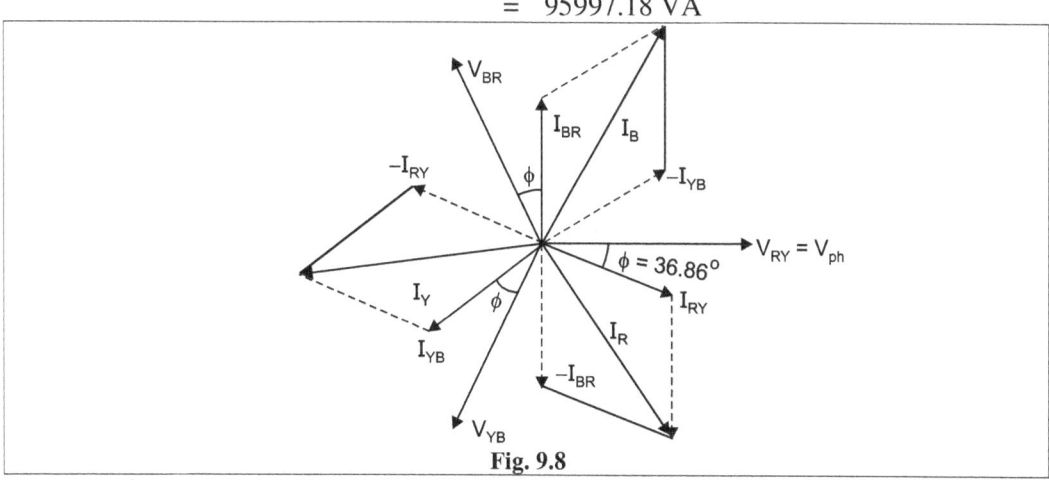

Fig. 9.8

Example 9.2 :

     A balanced star-connected load of $5 \angle 36.86^\circ$ Ω per phase is connected to a 3-phase, 400 V supply. Calculate :

(i)   Phase current,   (ii)   Line current,

(iii)   Power factor,   (iv)   Power consumed,

(v)   Reactive power,   (vi)   Apparent power,   (vii)   Draw phasor diagram.

Solution :

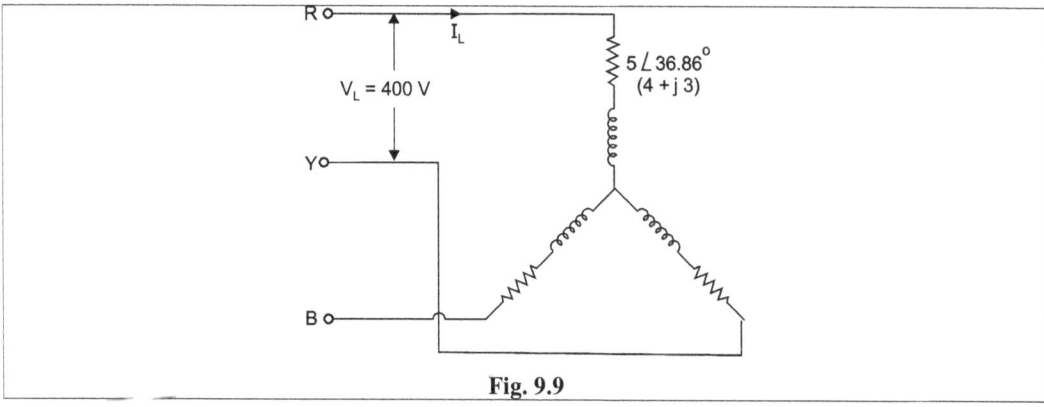

Fig. 9.9

Given $\bar{Z}_{ph} = 5 \angle 36.86° = 4 + j3$, $V_L = 400$ volt

As the load is star connected,

$$V_L = 400 \text{ V}, \quad V_{ph} = \frac{V_L}{\sqrt{3}} = \frac{400}{\sqrt{3}} = 230.91 \text{ volt}$$

$$\bar{V}_{ph} = 230.91 \angle 0°$$

(i) $$\bar{I}_{ph} = \frac{\bar{V}_{ph}}{\bar{Z}_{ph}} = \frac{230.91 \angle 0°}{5 \angle 36.86°} = 46.182 \angle -36.86°$$

(ii) $$I_L = 46.182 \text{ ampere} = I_{ph}$$

(iii) Power factor, $\cos \phi = \cos(36.86) = 0.8$ lagging

(iv) Active power = Power consumed

$$P = \sqrt{3} \, V_L \, I_L \cos \phi$$
$$= \sqrt{3} \times 400 \times 46.182 \times 0.8$$
$$= 25596.6 \text{ watt}$$

(v) Reactive power, $Q = \sqrt{3} \, V_L \, I_L \sin \phi$
$$= \sqrt{3} \times 400 \times 46.182 \times 0.6$$
$$= 19197.49 \text{ VAr}$$

(vi) Total volt ampere, $S = \sqrt{3} \, V_L \, I_L$
$$= \sqrt{3} \times 400 \times 46.182$$
$$= 31995.82 \text{ VA}$$

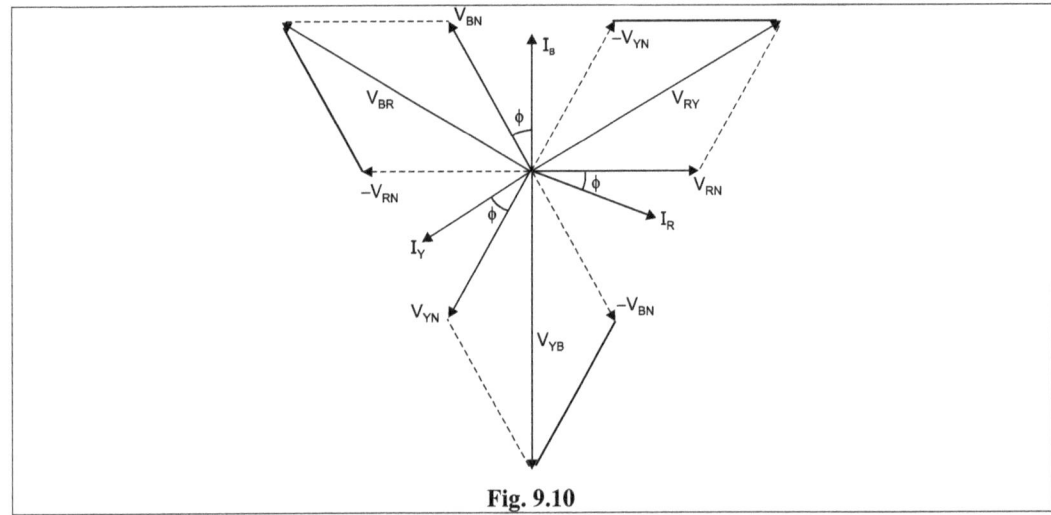

Fig. 9.10

Example 9.3 :

Prove that three-phase balanced load draws three times as much as power when connected in delta, as it would draw when connected in star. **(Dec. 07, 09) (4 M)**

Solution :

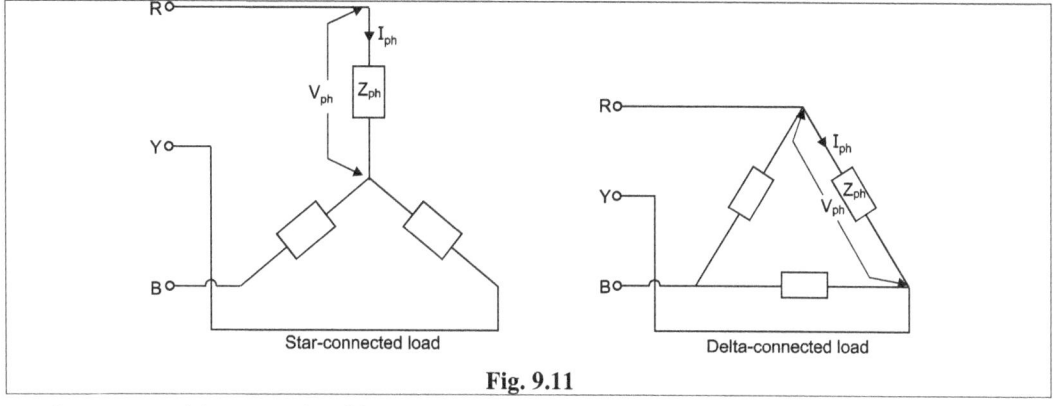

Fig. 9.11

Let us consider same load is connected in star and delta.

Star	Delta
$V_L = \sqrt{3}\, V_{ph}$	$V_L = V_{ph}$
$I_L = I_{ph}$	$I_L = \sqrt{3}\, I_{ph}$
$P = \sqrt{3}\, V_L\, I_L \cos\phi$	$P = \sqrt{3}\, V_L\, I_L \cos\phi$
$\quad = \sqrt{3} \times V_L \times I_{ph} \times \cos\phi$	$\quad = \sqrt{3} \times V_L \times \sqrt{3}\, I_{ph} \cos\phi$
$\quad = \sqrt{3}\, V_L \times \dfrac{V_{ph}}{Z_{ph}} \cos\phi$	$\quad = 3 V_L \dfrac{V_{ph}}{Z_{ph}} \cos\phi$
$\quad = \sqrt{3}\, V_L \times \dfrac{V_L}{\sqrt{3}\, Z_{ph}} \cos\phi$	$\quad = 3\, V_L \dfrac{V_L}{Z_{ph}} \cos\phi$
$\quad = \dfrac{V_L^{2}}{Z_{ph}} \cos\phi$	$\quad = 3\, \dfrac{V_L^{2}}{Z_{ph}} \cos\phi$

So power in delta (Δ) equals to three times power in star (Y).

Example 9.4 :

A three-phase, delta-connected load having an impedance $(30 + j40)$ Ω/phase is fed from star-connected transformer, which has a phase voltage of 231 volts. Draw the circuit diagram of the system and calculate :

(i) Magnitude of current in each phase of load.

(ii) The potential difference across each phase of load.

(iii) Magnitude of current in transformer winding.

(iv) Total power consumed by the load and its power factor.

Solution : $Z_{ph} = 30 + j\,40 = 50 \angle 53.13^\circ$, $V_{ph} = 231$ volts.

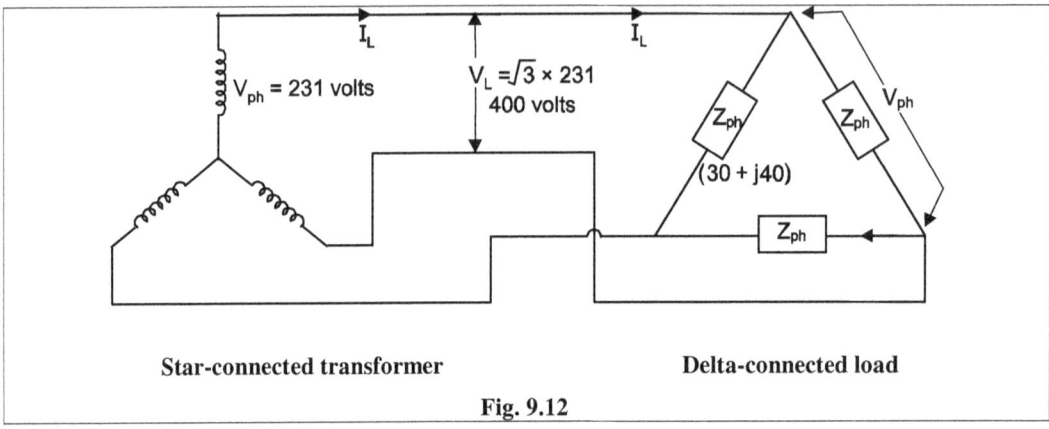

Star-connected transformer   **Delta-connected load**

Fig. 9.12

As transformer is star connected with $V_{ph} = 231$ volt, line voltage V_L from transformer is

$$V_L = \sqrt{3}\,V_{ph}$$
$$= \sqrt{3} \times 231 = 400 \text{ volt}$$

As the load is delta connected, $V_{ph} = V_L = 400$ volt

(i)
$$I_{ph} = \frac{V_{ph}}{Z_{ph}}$$
$$= \frac{400}{50}$$
$$= 8 \text{ Amp.}$$

(ii)
$$V_{ph} = 400 \text{ volt}$$

(iii) As transformer is star connected, current passing through transformer winding is same as line current I_L taken by load.

$$I_L = \sqrt{3}\,I_{ph}$$
$$= \sqrt{3} \times 8 = 13.856 \text{ Amp}$$

(iv) Total power consumed,
$$P = \sqrt{3}\,V_L\,I_L \cos \phi$$
$$= \sqrt{3} \times 400 \times 13.856 \times \cos (53.13^\circ)$$
$$= 5761.3279 \text{ watt}$$

Power factor $= \cos \phi = \cos (53.13^\circ)$
$$= 0.6 \text{ lagging} \quad \text{(as load is inductive)}$$

Example 9.5 :

A balanced star-connected load is supplied from a symmetrical 3-phase 400 V, 50 Hz system. The current in each phase is 30 ampere and lags 30° behind the phase voltage. Find :

(i) Phase voltage,   (ii)   Resistance and reactance per phase,

(iii) Load inductance per phase,   (iv)   Total power consumed.

Solution : Given : $V_L = 400$ V, $I_{ph} = 30$ Amp., $\phi = 30^\circ$ (lagging)

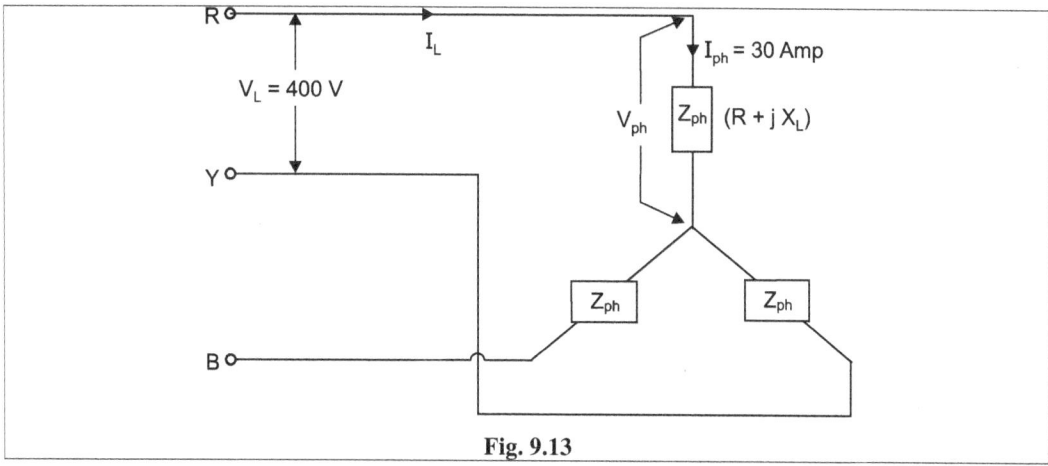

Fig. 9.13

(i) As the load is star connected, $V_{ph} = \dfrac{V_L}{\sqrt{3}} = \dfrac{400}{\sqrt{3}} = 230.9$ volt

(ii) $\overline{V}_{ph} = 230.9 \angle 0, \ \overline{I}_{ph} = 30 \angle -30^\circ$

$$\overline{Z}_{ph} = \frac{\overline{V}_{ph}}{\overline{I}_{ph}} = \frac{230.9 \angle 0}{30 \angle -30^\circ}$$

$$= 7.698 \angle 30^\circ \ \Omega$$

$$= (6.667 + j\,3.849) \ \Omega$$

$$\overline{Z}_{ph} = R_{ph} + j\,X_{Lph}$$

$$= (6.667 + j\,3.849) \ \Omega$$

$$R_{ph} = 6.667 \ \Omega, \ \ X_{Lph} = 3.849 \ \Omega$$

(iii) $X_{Lph} = 2\pi f L_{ph}$

$$L_{ph} = \frac{X_{Lph}}{2\pi f}$$

$$= \frac{3.849}{2 \times \pi \times 50}$$

$$= 0.01225 \text{ H} = 12.25 \text{ mH}$$

(iv)

$$P = \sqrt{3} \, V_L \, I_L \cos \phi$$

$$= \sqrt{3} \times 400 \times I_L \times \cos 30° \qquad \text{Here } I_L = I_{ph} = 30 \text{ A}$$

$$= \sqrt{3} \times 400 \times 30 \times \cos 30°$$

$$= 18000 \text{ watt} = 18 \text{ kW}$$

REVIEW QUESTIONS

1. A three-phase load consists of three similar inductive coils, each of resistance 50 Ω and inductance 0.3 H. The supply is 415 V, 50 Hz. Calculate :

   (a) Line current, (b) The power factor, (c) The total power when the load is,

   (i) star connected and (ii) delta connected.

   (**Ans. :** For star : $I_L = 2.25$ A, p.f. $= 0.469$ lagging, P $= 760$ watt)

   (For delta : $I_L = 6.75$ Amp., p.f. $= 0.469$ lagging, P $= 2277$ W)

2. A balanced delta-connected load of $60 \angle 30°$ per phase is connected across a 3-phase, 400 V, 50 Hz supply. Calculate the line current, power factor and power consumed.   (**Ans.:** $I_L = 11.53$ A, p.f. $= 0.866$ lagging, P $= 6928$ W)

3. A balanced 3-phase star-connected load of 120 kW takes a leading current of 100 A when connected across a 3-phase, 3.3 kV, 50 Hz supply. Determine the impedance, resistance, capacitance and power factor of the load.

   (**Ans. :** $\overline{Z}_{Ph} = 19.05 \angle -77.88° \, \Omega$, $R_{ph} = 3.99 \, \Omega$, $C_{ph} = 179.95 \, \mu F$,   p.f. $= 0.2099$ leading)

4. Each phase of delta-connected load has resistance of 25 Ω, inductance of 0.15 Ω and a capacitance of 120 μF. The load is connected across 400 V, 50 Hz three-phase supply. Determine the line current, active power, reactive power and apparent power.   (**Ans. :** 21.39, P $= 11439$ W, Q $= 9420$ VAr, S $= 14820$ VA)

5. A delta-connected load draws a current of 15 ampere at a lagging power factor of 0.85 from a 400 V, 50 Hz, 3-phase supply. Find the resistance and inductance of each phase.   (**Ans. :** $Z_{ph} = 46.2 \, \Omega$, $R_{ph} = 39.27 \, \Omega$, $X_{L_{ph}} = 24.34 \, \Omega$, $L_{ph} = 0.0775$ H)

6. (a) Three similar coils take a power of 3 kW at 0.6 power factor when connected in star to a 415 V, three-phase 50 Hz supply. Calculate the line current, resistance and inductance of each coil.

   (b) What would be the phase and line currents and total power if the coils were now connected in delta to the same supply ?

$$(\textbf{Ans. :}) \text{ (a) } I_L = 6.96 \text{ A}, R_{ph} = 20.66 \text{ }\Omega, L_{ph} = 0.08774\text{H})$$

$$((\text{b}) I_{ph} = 12 \text{ A}, I_L = 20.78 \text{ A}, P = 9 \text{ kW})$$

7. Three similar impedances are connected in delta across a 3-phase 400 V, 50 Hz supply. The line current is 12 A at a power factor of 0.8 lagging. Calculate the inductance and resistance of each impedance.   (**Ans. :** $L_{ph} = 0.11$ H, $R_{ph} = 46.2$ Ω)

8. Each phase of delta-connected load has a resistance of 50 Ω and a capacitance of 50 μF in series. Determine (a) line current and phase current, (b) the total power, (c) the kVA, when the load is connected to a 440 V, 3-phase, 50 Hz supply.

$$(\textbf{Ans. :}) \text{ (a) } I_{ph} = 5.46 \text{ A}, I_L = 9.46 \text{ A, (b) } 4480 \text{ W, (c) } 7.24 \text{ kVA})$$

9. A three-phase, star-connected alternator supplies a delta-connected load with 415 V, 50 Hz supply. Each phase of load has resistance of 15 Ω and reactance of 25 Ω. Calculate : (a) current in each phase of the load, (b) the alternator phase voltage and current, (c) the power factor of the load, (d) the total power taken by load. Sketch the circuit diagram and show on it phase and line voltages and currents.   (**Ans. :** (a) $I_{ph} = 14.24$ A, (b) $V_{ph} = 239.6$, $I_{ph} = 24.66$ A,

$$(\text{c}) \text{ } 0.5146, \text{ (d) } P = 9125 \text{ W})$$

10. Three chokes resistance of 40 Ω and reactance of 30 Ω are connected in (a) a star, (b) in delta to a 400 V, three-phase balanced supply. What is the line current in each case and total power dissipated ?   (**Ans.:** (a) $I_L = 4.62$ A, P = 2560 watt,

$$(\text{b}) I_L = 8 \text{ A}, P = 7680 \text{ watt})$$

11. A 3 phase, 400 V, 50 Hz, AC supply is connected to a delta connected load which has impedance of (15 + j 12) Ω in each phase. Find (1) Line current (2) Phase current (3) Active power (4) Apparant power.

$$(\textbf{Ans. :}) \text{ (1) } I_L = 36.06 \text{ A, (2) } I_{ph} = 20.82 \text{ A},$$

$$(3) \text{ } P = 19.49 \text{ kW, } (4) \text{ App. } P = 24.98 \text{ kVA})$$

12. A 3ph. 75 kW, delta-connected Induction motor operates at rated load in parallel with a star connected load having impedance of $(20 + j\ 15.66)\ \Omega$ per phase. The motor p.f. is 0.8 (lag). If the supply voltage is 440 V, 50 Hz, 3 ph. A.C. find

(i)   Line and phase current of motor.

(ii) Line and phase current taken by load

(iii) Total line current

(iv) Total power consumed

$$(\textbf{Ans.}:\ \text{(i)}\ (I_{L\ (motor)} = 123\ A,\ I_{ph\ (motor)} = 71\ A,\ \text{(ii)}\ I_{L\ (Load)} = 10A,\ I_{ph\ (Load)} = 10\ A,$$
$$\text{(iii)}\ I_{L\ (Line)} = 133.00\ A,\ \text{(iv)}\ P_{(line)} = 80.96\ kW)$$

13. A balanced star-connected load is supplied from a symmetrical 3ph, 400 V, 50 Hz system. The current in each phase is 30 A and lags 30° behind the phase voltage. Find (i) phase voltage, (ii) resistance and reactance per phase, (iii) load inductance per phase, (iv) total power consumed. Draw phasor diagram showing currents and voltages.

$$(\textbf{Ans.}:\ \text{(i)}\ V_{ph} = 230.94\ V,\ \text{(ii)}\ R_{ph} = 6.67\ \Omega,\ X_{ph} = 3.85\ \Omega,\ \text{(iii)}\ L_{ph} = 0.0122\ H,$$
$$\text{(iv)}\ P = 18\ kW)$$

14. A 3 phase delta connected load having an impedance of $(30 + j40)\ \Omega$ per phase is fed from the secondary of a 3 phase star connected transformer, which has a phase voltage of 230.94 V. Draw the circuit diagram and calculate

(i)   p.d. across each phase of load

(ii) phase current in load.

(iii) current in secondary of transformer

(iv) Total power consumed by load

(v)   Load p.f.

$$(\textbf{Ans.}:\ \text{(i)}\ 400\ V,\ \text{(ii)}\ 8.00\ A,\ \text{(iii)}\ 13.86\ A,\ \text{(iv)}\ 5.76\ kW,\ \text{(v)}\ 0.6\ (lag))$$

Chapter **10**

ELECTRICAL WIRING AND ILLUMINATION SYSTEM

10.1 ELECTRICAL POWER DISTRIBUTION SYSTEM

The electrical power distribution system provides power to individual consumer premises. Distribution of electric power is done by distribution networks. Distribution networks consist of following main parts

- **Service mains :** Different consumers are fed electric power by means of the service main. These service mains are tapped from different points of distributors. Service mains of the consumers may be either connected to distributors or sub distributors depending upon the position and agreement of consumers.

- **Distribution substation:** The transmitted electric power is stepped down at substations for primary distribution purpose. Stepped down electric power is fed to the distribution transformer through primary distribution feeders.

- **Primary feeder:** Feeder feeds power from one point to another without being tapped from any intermediate point. As because there is no tapping point in between, the current at sending end is equal to that of receiving end of the conductor. Overhead primary distribution feeders are supported by mainly iron pole. The conductors are stranded aluminium conductors and they are mounted on the arms of the pole by means of pin insulators. Sometimes, underground cables may also be used for primary distribution purposes.

- **Distribution Transformer:** Distribution transformers are mainly 3-phase pole mounted type. The secondary of the transformer is connected to distributors.

- **Distributors:** The distributors are tapped at different points for feeding different consumers; and hence the current varies along their entire length. The distributors can also be re-categorized by distributors and sub-distributors. Distributors are directly connected to the secondary of distribution transformers whereas sub-distributors are tapped from distributors.

Fig. 10.1 shows typical Power Distribution System. In Fig. 10.1, 'S' is the generating station or substation. MPO and MNO are distributors.

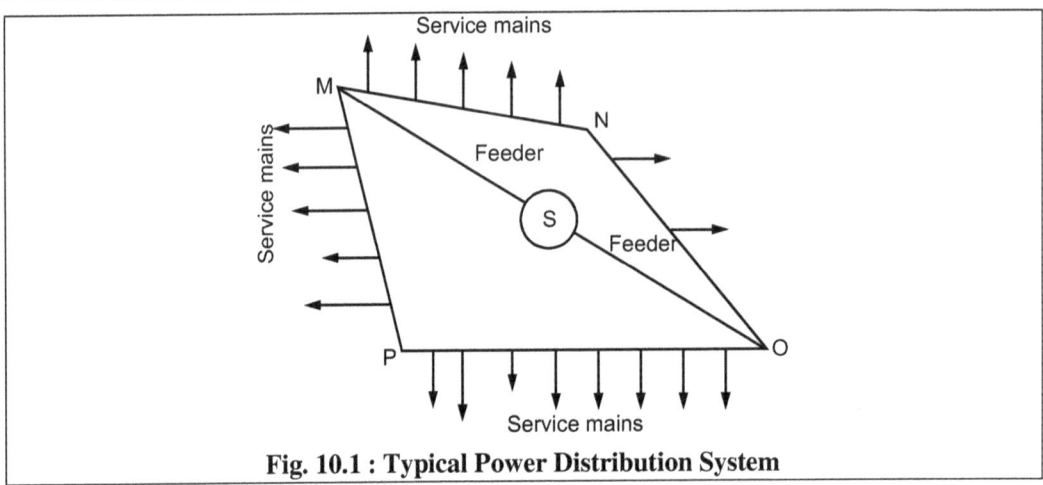

Fig. 10.1 : Typical Power Distribution System

10.2 TYPES OF DISTRIBUTION SYSTEM

1. Radial Electrical Power Distribution System :   Fig. 10.2 shows Radial Distribution System. In these systems, different feeders radially come out from the substation and connected to the primary of distribution transformer directly. These systems were used in early days of electrical power distribution system. But it suffered a major drawback as: when there would be any feeder failure, the associated consumers would not get any power as there was no alternative path to feed the transformer. The power supply is interrupted with transformer failure also. The consumer in the radial electrical distribution system would not get power supply until the feeder or transformer was rectified.

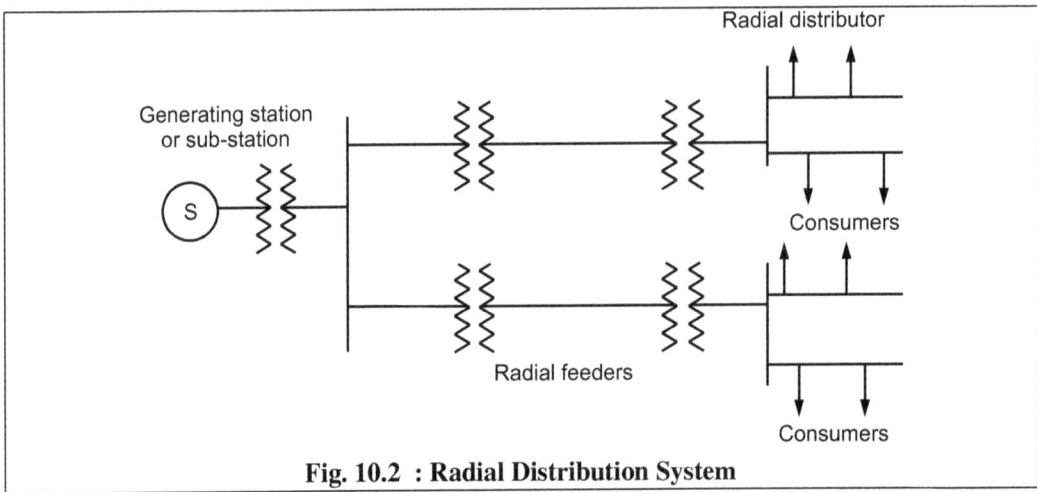

Fig. 10.2 : Radial Distribution System

Ring Main Electrical Power Distribution System :   Fig. 10.3 shows Ring Main Distribution system. In this system, one ring network of distributors is fed by more than one feeder. The sub-distributors and service mains are taken off, may be via distribution transformer at different suitable points on the ring depending upon the location of the consumers. Sometimes, instead of connecting service main directly to the ring, sub-distributors are also used to feed a group of service mains where direct access of ring distributor is not possible.

In this case if one feeder is under fault or maintenance, the ring distributor is still energized by other feeders connected to it. In this way the supply to the consumers is not affected even when any feeder becomes out of service. Thus the drawback of radial electrical power distribution system can be overcome by a ring main electrical power distribution system. The ring main system can also be isolated at suitable points. If fault occurs at any section of the ring then that section can easily be isolated by opening the isolators on both sides of the faulty zone. Supply to the consumers connected to the healthy zone of the ring, can easily be maintained even when one section of the ring is isolated. The number of feeders connected to the system depends upon the following terms:

1. If maximum demand of the system is more, then more number of feeders should feed the ring.
2. If length of the ring main distributors is more then to compensate the voltage drop in the line, more feeders are to be connected to the ring system.
3. The number of feeders connected to the ring also depends upon the permissible allowable, voltage drop of the line.

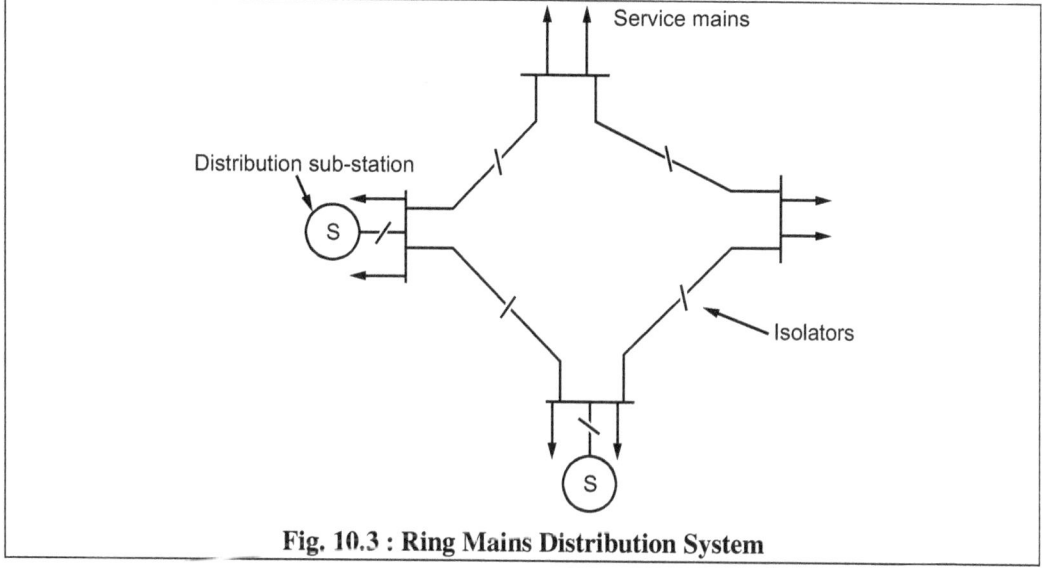

Fig. 10.3 : Ring Mains Distribution System

10.3 TYPES OF WIRING

Introduction : Electrical wiring refers to the system of conductors and other devices that are used to carry electricity. The different types of electrical wiring that are used vary according to purpose, quantity of electricity to be carried and location. The wire is also known as an electrical conductor. It is commonly made of copper and other materials that are good at transmitting current. The wire is usually insulated. Insulation can be made from materials such as plastics and fibers. Common insulators for outdoor wires include thermoplastics. Insulation on this type of system should also be resistant to ultra-violet rays.

- Stranded wires are a type of electrical wiring often employed in homes. It consists of number of small-gauge, solid wires that are wrapped around a central wire. The stranded wire can increase the amount of electrical power that can be carried in the wire. It is also commonly used because it is flexible and easy to shape, which is ideal for fitting electrical wiring behind the walls of homes.

- Fiber-optic and wireless, or Wi-Fi, systems may change the future of electrical wiring in residential homes. The Wi-Fi system uses radio waves that are carried through the air, and are received by a central receiving connector. For example, the traditional copper wire material could be replaced by fiber-optic systems, which use light pulses to carry electric current. This application is already used by some home computers to allow Internet use and replace the need for modems and many connecting wires.

There is an international standard for the types of wires and cables used in electrical wiring systems. For example, color coating is employed to help identify wires for safety, installation, and repair purposes. This enables electricians and laymen to know what kind of wires comprise an electrical system. These colors, however, are not the same everywhere. For example, a brown-colored wire usually denotes a live wire in European Union countries, Australia, and New Zealand. In contrast, a black brass color is used for these wires in the United States and Canada.

Domestic types of wiring are given below:

1. Cleat wiring : In this type of wiring, insulated conductors usually VIR, Vulcanized Indian Rubber are supported on porcelain or wooden cleats. The cleats have one base and the other cap. The cables are placed in the grooves provided in the base and then the cap is placed. Both are fixed securely on the walls by 40 mm long screws. The cleats are fixed 4.5-15 cm apart. This type of wiring is used for temporary purposes such as for marriages, functions, etc.

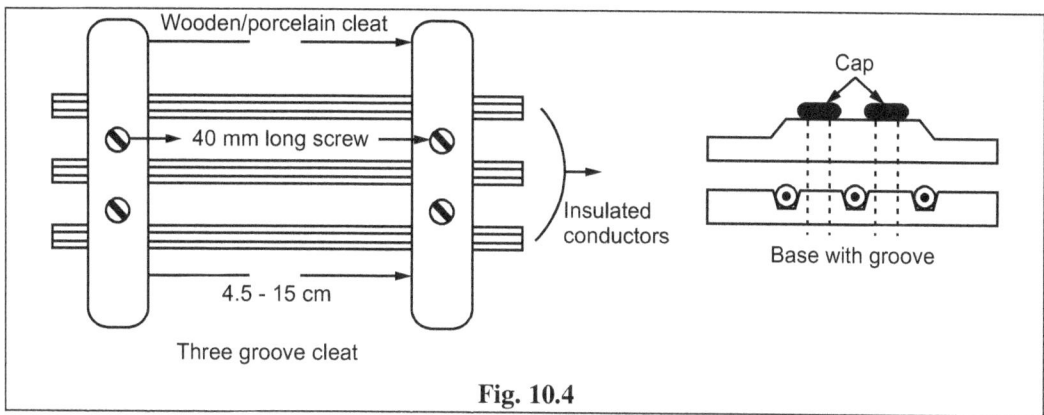

Fig. 10.4

Advantages:

1. Installation is easy.

2. Materials can be retrieved for reuse.

3. Flexibility provided for inspection, modifications and expansion.

4. It is economical.

5. Skilled manpower not required.

Disadvantages:

1. Open system of wiring requiring regular cleaning.

2. Appearance is not good.

3. Higher risk of injury.

2. Cable Tyre Sheathed (CTS) or Tough Rubber Sheathed (TRS) or   Batten Wiring : In this wiring system, wires sheathed in tough rubber are used. These cables are moisture and chemical proof. They are clipped on wooden battens with brass clips (link or joint) and fixed on to the walls or ceilings by flat head screws. They are suitable for damp climate but not suitable for outdoor use in sunlight.

Wiring with tough rubber sheathed cables is suitable for low voltage installations, and shall not be used in places exposed to sun and rain nor in damp places, unless wires are sheathed in protective covering against atmosphere and well protected to withstand dampness. Wiring with PVC-sheathed cables is suitable for medium voltage installation and may be installed directly under exposed conditions of sun and rain or damp places. This system of wiring is suitable in situations where acids and alkalies are likely to be present.

Advantages:

1. Easy installation and is durable.

2. Lower risk of short circuit.

3. Cheaper than casing and capping system of wiring.

4. Gives a good appearance if properly erected.

Disadvantages:

1. Danger of mechanical injury.

2. Danger of fire hazard.

3. Skilled workers are required.

4. Should not be exposed to direct sunlight.

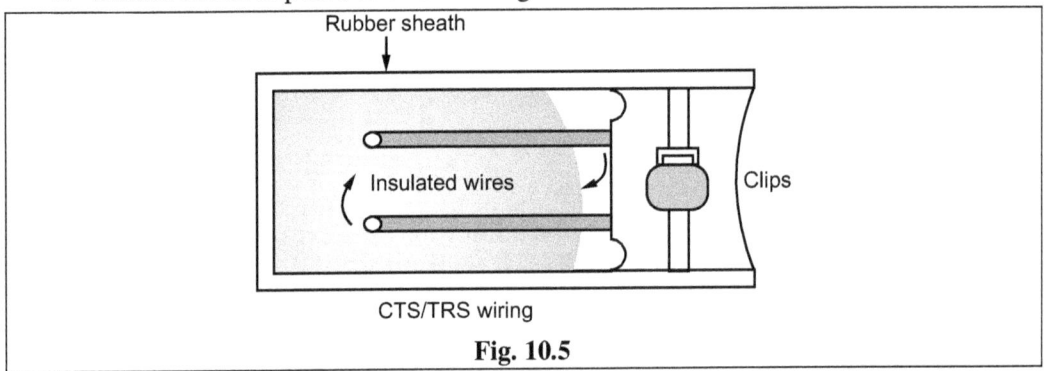

CTS/TRS wiring

Fig. 10.5

3. Metal Sheathed or Lead Sheathed Wiring : The wiring is similar to that of CTS but the conductors are individually insulated and covered with a common outer lead-aluminium alloy sheath. The sheath is earthed at every junction to provide a path to ground for the leakage current. The sheath protects the cable against dampness, atmospheric extremities and mechanical damages. They are fixed by means of metal clips on wooden battens. It is suitable for low voltage installations. The wiring system is very expensive.

Metal-sheathed wiring system is suitable for IGW voltage installations, and is not used in situations where acids and alkalies are likely to be present. Metal-sheathed wiring may be used in places exposed to sun and rain provided no joint of any description is exposed; this system may be installed in damp places with approved protection against dampness coming in contact with open ends of cables.

Advantages:

1. Easy installation and is aesthetic in appearance

2. Highly durable.

3. It is suitable in adverse climatic conditions provided the joints are not exposed.

Disadvantages:

1. Requires skilled labour.

2. Very expensive.

3. Unsuitable for chemical industries.

4. The clips used to fix the cables on battens should not react with the sheath.

5. Lead sheath should be properly earthed to prevent shocks due to leakage currents.

6. Cables should not be laid in damp places and in areas where chemicals are used as they may react with the lead.

4. Casing and Capping : The system is suitable for indoor and domestic installations. It consists of insulated conductors laid inside rectangular, teakwood or PVC boxes having grooves inside it. A rectangular strip of wood called capping having same width as that of casing is fixed over it. Casing is attached to the wall. Both the casing and the capping are screwed together at every 15 cm. Two or more wires of same polarity are drawn through different grooves.

Advantages:

1. Provides good isolation.

2. Cheaper than lead sheathed and conduit wiring.

3. Easily accessible for inspection and repairs.

4. Insulation is less affected by dust, dirt and climatic variations.

Disadvantages:

1. Highly inflammable.

2. Usage of unseasoned wood gets damaged by termites.

3. Skilled workers required.

5. Conduit wiring : PVC (polyvinyl chloride) or VIR cables are run through metallic or PVC pipes. It provides good protection against mechanical injury and fire due to short circuit. The conduits are buried inside the walls on wooden gutties and the wires are drawn through them with fish (steel) wires. They are either embedded inside the walls or supported over the walls, and are known as concealed wiring or surface conduit wiring respectively. The system is best suited for public buildings, industries and workshops.

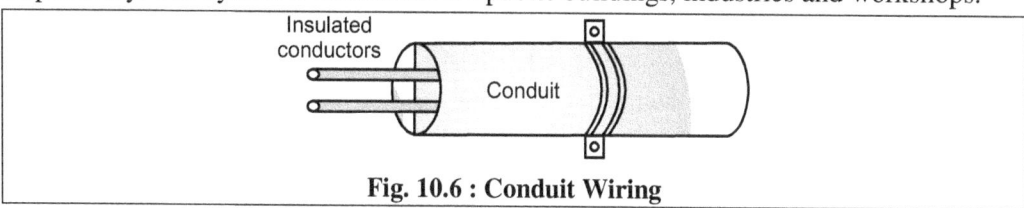

Fig. 10.6 : Conduit Wiring

Advantages:

1. No risk of fire.

2. The lead and return wires can be carried in the same tube.

3. Trouble shooting is easy.

4. Shock-proof with proper earthing and bonding.

5. Maintenance free

Disadvantages:

1. Very expensive system of wiring.

2. Requires good skilled workmanship.

3. Erection is time consuming.

4. Risk of short circuit under wet conditions.

10.4 TYPES OF CONDUIT

In general the conduits can be classified as:

(1) Thin Wall Conduits : These conduits are further sub-divided into:

(a) Close joint conduits : These are made out of light gauge steel strips, bent so as to form a tube. There is no mechanical adhesion between its two edges. It is the cheapest form of conduit, and provides only mechanical protection and covers risk against fire.

(b) Brazed conduits: These conduits are made similar to that of close-joint conduits, but the ends of the steel tubing are brazed together. This makes the conduits damp-proof. It has the main disadvantage that the brazing material is left projecting inside the tube which makes drawing in of the wires impossible.

(2) Rigid Conduits: These conduits are made out of heavy gauge steel and the tube edges are electrically welded. They are named as heavy gauge welded conduits. Solid drawn conduits are drawn from solids and have no joint throughout its section. They are heaviest and the best. They are a bit costlier.

These are available in about 3 meter length. They are threaded at two ends. The threads are usually tapered and are provided with a coupling on one side similar to that of plumbing pipe coupling.

There are two general types of finishes in which conduits are available.

(a) The black enamelled conduits have a coating of black enamel, baked in a heating furnace, so that it may not peel off easily. These conduits should be used only for indoors. Their use should be avoided where the location is damp and where they are liable to face acid fumes, and salt sea water atmosphere.

(b) The "galvanized conduits" have a coating of zinc which is usually applied by hot dipping process.

(3) Flexible Conduits: The flexible conduits are made from galvanized steel strips which are wound upon each other.

It is further sub-divided into following types:

(a) Concaved double strip: It consists of concave-shaped steel strips spirally wound one upon the other. A gasket is provided in between the strips to make the conduit moisture-proof.

(b) Flat double strip: The construction of flat double strip conduit is similar to that in except that the strips are flat.

Usually the double strip conduits are preferred to single strip conduits since

(1) They are more flexible.

(2) They are smoother from inside.

(c) Single strip: This type of flexible conduit is made from a single galvanized steel strip. Such strips are interlocked.

The type of wiring to be adopted is dependent on following factors :

(a) Durability

(b) Safety

(c) Appearance

(d) Cost

(e) Accessibility

(f) Maintenance cost

(g) Flexibility

(h) Reliability

10.5 WIRING ACCESSORIES

1. Romex cables: Wiring could be done with a conduit system or metal-sheathed cables, but in most places these plastic jacketed cables are the norm for houses and non-highrise apartments. These cables are to be secured to the home's framing every 4.5 feet at most. This support can consist of holes in the framing or approved staples or wire-ties. In addition, such support is to be provided within 12 inches of where the cables enter boxes. Within 8 inches of one-gang boxes which have no built-in clamps.

2. Electrical boxes: An electrical box is almost always required for mounting devices like switch and light fixtures, and also wherever circuit connections are made. They may be made of metal or plastic. Boxes are not only a mounting place but minimize shock hazard and the possible effect of sparks. The number and gauge of wires that may be installed in a box will be related to how many devices will be mounted in it and the volume of the box, which is stated inside it. They may be made of metal or plastic.

3. Connecting wires: At the terminals of switches and receptacles, wires may connect in a variety of ways. The means provided may include screws to loop wire around, holes to push wires into, and/or wire clamps to tighten down on the wire using a screw. It is important to strip enough insulation off the end of the wire that no insulation will be caught under the pressure of a screw or clamp or prevent a wire from inserting far enough in a hole. Stripping too much insulation off the wire could make accidental shorting or shocks a bit more possible. The practice of finally running tape around a device to cover its side-screws makes some sense when the box is metal or live parts of other devices are nearby, but not otherwise.

4. Circuit breakers: Breakers come in different brands, sizes, and number of poles. When a breaker is available in skinnier sizes, it is often a unit with two breakers together. 2-pole or double-pole breaker is for 240 volt circuits or for two 120 volt circuits that share a neutral. Most commonly, only one wire will be held under a breaker's screw terminal. Unless the fine print of the breaker allows two, installing more than one wire per terminal called as "double-tapping" will prove unreliable. A 20 amp breaker is never allowed to run any circuit whose wires are 14 gauge. But a 15 amp breaker's wires out on the circuit may be 14 gauge, 12 gauge, or even a mixture.

5. 15 amp versus 20 amp: Most circuits and devices in a home are rated as 15-amp or 20 amp. 14 gauge wire is the smallest allowed for the permanent wiring of a circuit. It is rated as able to carry upto 15 amps of current. 12 gauge wire is the next size larger and is allowed to carry upto 20 amps.

6. Electrical panel: A circuit breaker panel has two kinds of capacities -- its amperage and its space for breakers. Panel cannot be determined by its individual circuit breakers. Even a 200 amp panel is not "overloaded" just because the sum of its circuits' ratings is, say, 500. In such a case, if you could purposely load down every branch circuit to its full rating, the main breaker would trip. If there is no mains, the power company's fuse could blow.

7. Couplings: Since the conduits are available in smaller lengths, so to obtain and continuous length of the conduit the two are coupled together by means of coupling.

8. Conduit Box: The conduit boxes are also called as outlet boxes since they are usually used for outlets. The boxes are provided with a cover held by screw on it. The rigid conduits are always terminated at outlets into a box. There are different types of boxes; it may be round, square or octagonal. Boxes provide following functions :

   (a) outlet boxes to provide connections for lights, fans, heaters etc.

   (b) inspection boxes to facilitate the pulling of conductors in the conduits

   (c) junction boxes to house the junctions of the conductors,

   (d) to provide snap switches.

9. Conduit Fittings: The conduit fittings have projections and have female threads. The use of boxes are generally limited to the concealed type wiring as the conduit fittings are rarely used for that, but for the surface work both fittings and boxes can be used.

10. Conduit Saddles or Clamps or Straps: The conduit straps or saddles are used to fix the conduit to the wooden plugs in the wall. The conduit saddle may have one or two such saddles are made from sheet steel.

11. Box Connector Bushings for Flexible Conduits: The connectors so used are usually made of cast iron; one end of it clamps the flexible conduit while the other threaded end enters the bore where it is fixed to the box with the locknut represents the bushing to be used when the flexible conduit enters the box.

12. Elbows: The change of direction in conduit wiring is always made by means of an elbow which provide a 90° bend. Radius of the bend must be about 6 times the internal diameter of the conduit. Usually the standard elbows are available in the market, but it is always a practice to bend the conduit at the site by means of hickey or by hand in pipe vice.

13. Conduit Bushings: It is either made from a malleable iron ore from a formed sheet steel. These are used when the rigid conduit enters the conduit box or when the conduit enter a hole which is not threaded. There is another closed type of bushing which is used during the construction of the building. Such type of bushing is provided with a cap. It prevents the moisture entering the conduit system during construction. The bushings serve a double purpose.

(i) Firstly it prevents the insulation on the cables from being peeled off due to rubbing against the sharp edges of the conduit when they are pulled in.

(ii) Secondly it helps in securing the rigid conduit to conduit box when no locknut is placed on the inside of the box. Generally the collared bushing is used since it covers the hole in the board.

14. Locknuts: The locknuts are punched out of thin steel sheets. Locknuts are either hexagonal or octagonal. When the conduit enters a box, it is necessary that the look nut should be screwed on the conduit as it makes the connection to the box rigid and electrically continuous.

15. Thin Wall Conduit coupling: The thin wall conduits cannot have threads, so coupling cannot be done in an ordinary way. When a flexible conduit is to be connected to a right conduit, a combination coupling is used. The combination coupling is similar to that of a split coupling with 4 screws, but one end of such a coupling is provided with threads for rigid conduit coupling represents such type of coupling.

10.6 EARTHING

Earthing is basically a part of electrical wiring which is being done on initial level in order to connect the electrical system with general mass of earth so as to have discharge of electrical energy. The process of connecting metallic bodies of all the electrical apparatus and equipment to huge mass of earth by a wire having negligible resistance is called Earthing. Earthing or grounding means to connect any electrical appliance, machine or equipment at zero potential of general mass of earth with wire connected with the earth electrode burried in the earth at the moistened place. Earthing is important to make the electrical fitting safe and secure from the immediate shock or thunder storm that may affect building.

Equipment earthing is a connection done through a metal link between the body of any electrical appliance, or neutral point to the deeper ground soil. The metal link is normally of MS flat, CI flat, GI wire which should be penetrated to the ground earth grid.

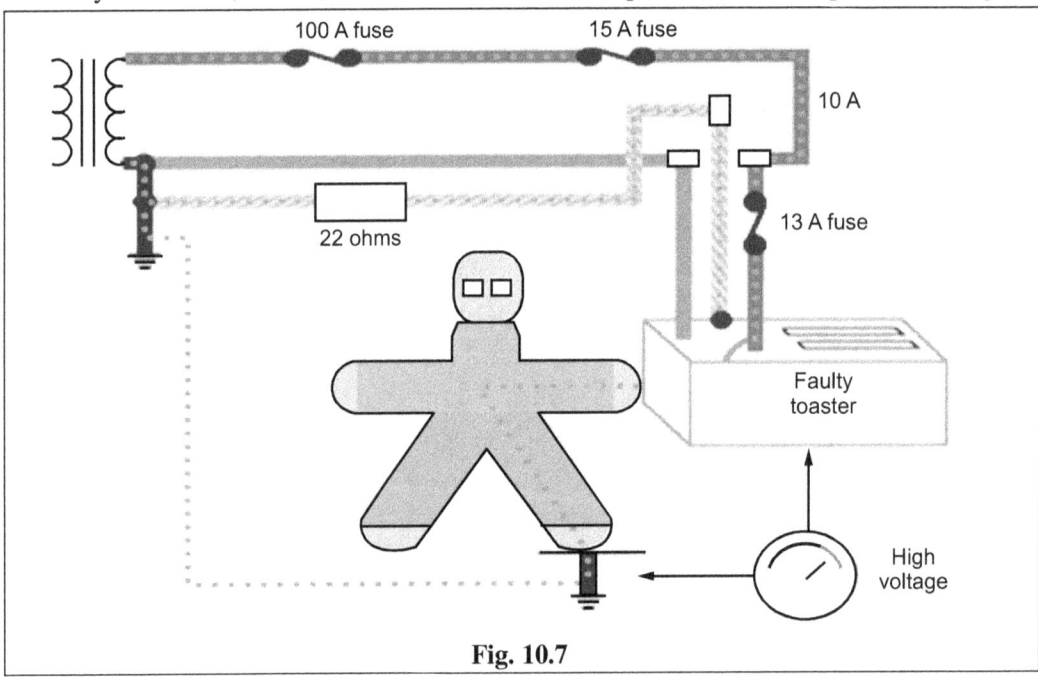

Fig. 10.7

The earthing is divided as

(a) System earthing: It is connection between part of plant in an operating system like LV neutral of a power transformer winding and earth.

(b) Equipment earthing: It is connecting bodies of equipment like electric motor body, transformer tank, switchgear box, operating rods of air break switches, LV breaker body, HV breaker body, feeder breaker bodies etc to the earth.

10.7 OBJECTIVES OF EARTHING

- Provide an alternative path for the fault current to flow so that it will not endanger the user.

- Ensure that all exposed conductive parts do not reach a dangerous potential.

- Maintain the voltage at any part of an electrical system at a known value so as to prevent over current or excessive voltage on the appliances or equipment.

Definitions

1. **Earth :** The conductive mass of the earth, whose electric potential at any point is conventionally assumed and taken as ZERO.

2. **Earth electrode:** A conductor or group of conductors providing electrical connection to earth.

3. **Earth electrode resistance:** The electrical resistance of an earth electrode to the general mass of earth.

4. **Earthing conductor:** A protective conductor connecting the main earthing terminal to an earth electrode or other means of earthing.

5. **Equipotential bonding:** Electrical connection putting various exposed conductive parts and extraneous conductive parts at a substantially equal potential.

6. **Potential gradient:** The potential difference per unit length measured in the direction in which it is maximum.

7. **Earth grid:** A system of grounding electrodes consisting of interconnected connectors buried in the earth to provide a common ground for electrical devices and metallic structures.

8. **Earth mat:** A grounding system formed by a grid of horizontally buried conductors.

Following are few of main points to be followed before implementation of earthing :

1. Earthing connection is done using galvanized wire or copper wire as they are considered good conductor of electricity.

2. When the soil is corrosive then copper ripe or plate must be used during earthing.

3. Earthing work is ideal in moist earth.

4. It is better to do earthing near the place of water drain, main water pipeline etc. to enhance the effects of earthing and resistance.

5. It is better to spread or fill pit for earthing with salt or some charcoal pieces.

Permissible Values of Earth Resistance

a) Power stations - 0.5 ohms

b) EHT stations - 1.0 ohms

c) 33 kV Substation - 2 ohms

d) DTR structures - 5 ohms

e) Tower foot resistance - 10 ohms

10.8 CLASSIFICATION OF EARTHING

1. Conventional Earthing: The conventional system of earthing calls for digging of a large pit into which a GI pipe or a copper plate is positioned in the middle layers of charcoal and salt. It requires maintenance and pouring of water at regular interval.

2. Maintenance Free Earthing: It is a new type of earthing system which is readymade, standardized and scientifically developed. It requires no maintenance. No need to pour water at regular interval- except in sandy soil. Maintain stable and consistent earth resistance around the year. The conductive compound creates a conductive zone, which provides the increased surface area for peak current dissipation. It has long life and easy installation.

10.9 METHODS OF CONVENTIONAL EARTHING

1. Plate Earthing: In plate type earthing, cast iron plate of (600 mm × 600 mm × 6.3 mm) thickness is being used as earth plate. This is connected with hot dip GI main earth strip of size (50 mm × 6 mm thick × 2.5 meter long) with nut, bolts and washers of required size. The main earth strip is connected with hot dip GI strip of size (40 mm × 3 mm) of required length upto the equipment earth or neutral connection. The earth plate is back filled and covered with earthing material. Earthing material is a mixture of charcoal and salt which covers 150 mm from all six sides. The remaining pit is back filled with excavated earth. Rigid PVC pipe of 2.5 meter long is also provided in the earth pit for watering purpose to keep the earthing resistance within specific limit.

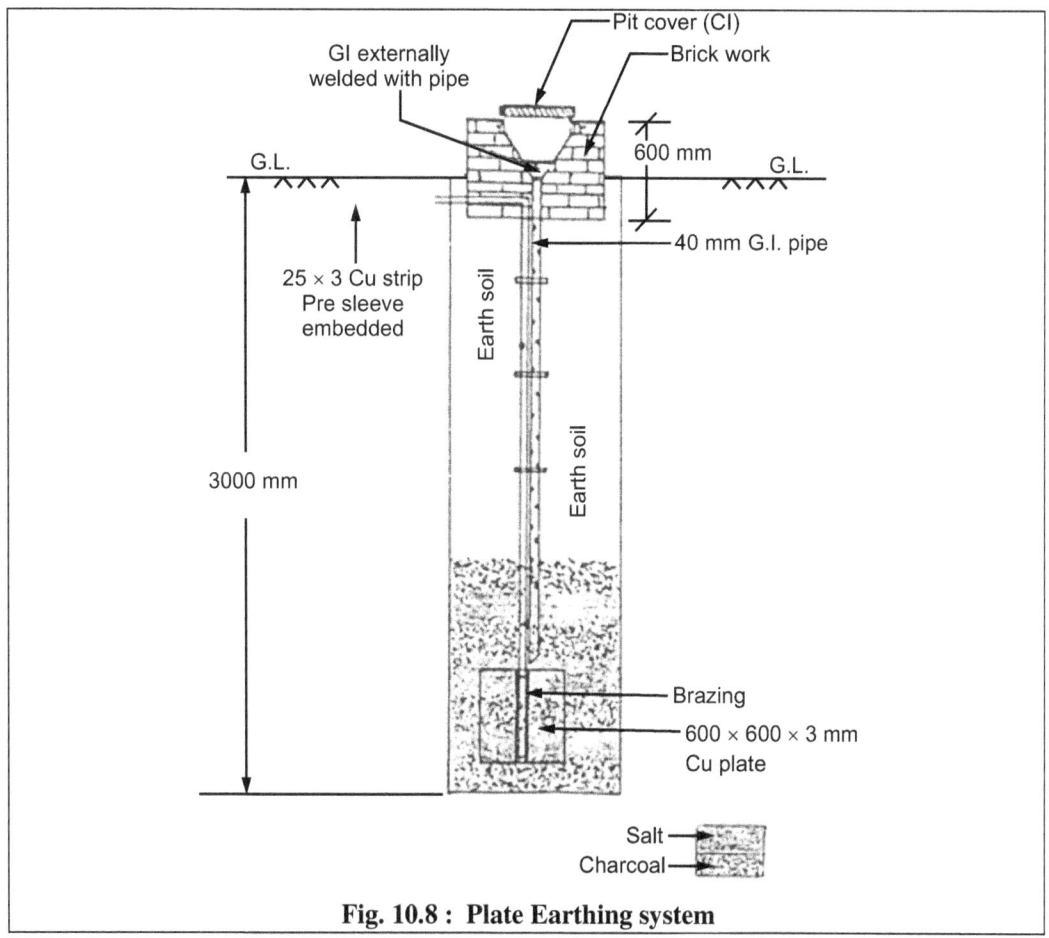

Fig. 10.8 : Plate Earthing system

2. Pipe Earthing : In pipe type earthing hot dip GI pipe of size 40 mm × 2.5 mm is being used for equipment earthing. This pipe is perforated at each interval of 100mm and is tapered at lower end. A clamp is welded with this pipe at 100 mm below the top. It is done for making connection with hot dip GI strip of size 40 mm × 3 mm of required length as per the site location upto the equipment earth or neutral connection. Funnel is being fitted for watering purpose at its open end. The earth pipe is placed inside 2700 mm of pit. A "farma" of GI sheet or cement pipe in two halves is placed around the pipe. Then the angular space between this "farma" and earth pipe is back filled with alternate layer of 300 mm height with salt and charcoal. The remaining space outside the "farma" will be backfilled by excavated earth. The pit is being filled upto 300 mm below the ground level. This remaining portion is covered by constructing a small chamber of brick so that top open end of pipe and connection with the main earth pipe will be accessible when required. This chamber is closed by wooden or stone cover. Water is poured into the pipe through its open end funnel to keep the earthing resistance within specific limit.

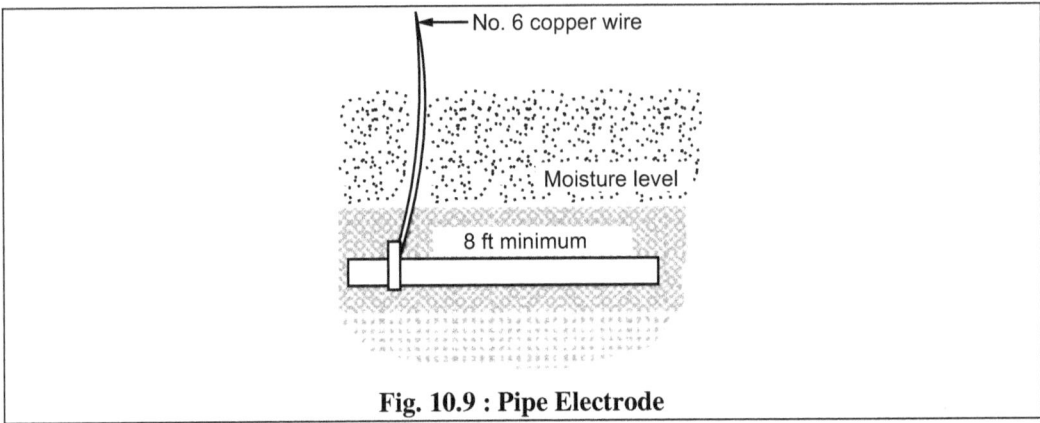

Fig. 10.9 : Pipe Electrode

3. Rod Earthing : This system of earthing is very cheap. In this system of earthing 12.5 mm diameter solid rods of copper 16 mm diameter solid rod of GI or steel or hollow section of 25 mm GI pipe of length not less than 3 meters are driven vertically into the earth. This system of earthing is suitable for sandy area.

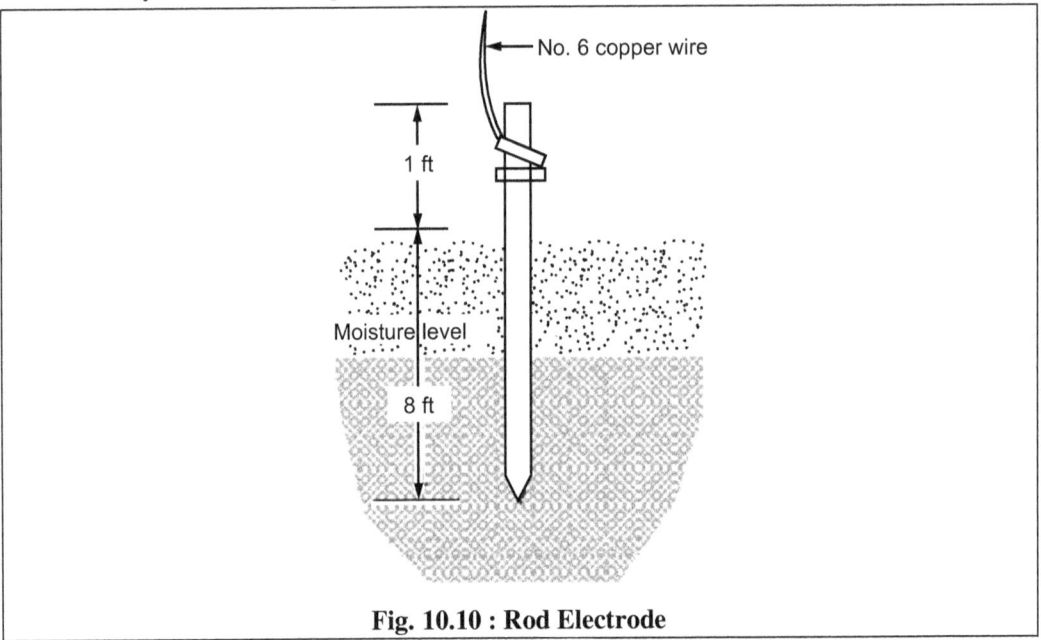

Fig. 10.10 : Rod Electrode

4. Strip Earthing: This type of earthing is used in rockey soil earth bed. In this system of earthing strip electrode of cross section not less than 25 mm into 1.6 mm of copper or 25 mm × 4 mm of GI or steel are buried in horizontal trenches of minimum depth of 0.5 m. The length of buried conductor shall be sufficient to give the required earth resistance (about 0.5 Ω to 1.5 Ω). The electrode shall be widely distributed as possible in a single straight or circular trenches radiating from a point.

10.10 NECESSITY OF EARTHING

The necessity for earthing is to ensure that the metal work of electrical equipment, other than current carrying parts, should not have a potential above earth in the event of a fault which might otherwise cause danger of an electric shock. When fault occurs, then unearthed metalwork of a piece of electrical equipment is charged to a level of very high potential. Any person touching the metal and at the same time comes in contact with earth will receive a severe electric shock. If the metal is effectively earthed, then very low resistance of the circuit would result in a flow of current sufficient to blow the fuse or to operate the protective device. A person does not get a shock as metal work of electrical equipment is at zero potential.

10.11 FACTORS AFFECTING ON EARTH RESISTIVITY

1. Soil condition: Most of the soils are very poor conductors of electricity when they are completely dry. Different soil conditions give different soil resistivity. Soil plays a significant role in determining the performance of electrode. Soil with low resistivity is highly corrosive. If soil is dry then soil resistivity value will be very high. If soil resistivity is high, earth resistance of the electrode will also be high.

2. Soil resistivity: It is the resistance of soil to the passage of electric current. The earth resistance value of an earth pit depends on soil resistivity. It varies from soil to soil. It depends on the physical composition of the soil, moisture, dissolved salts, grain size and distribution, seasonal variation, current magnitude etc. It depends on the composition of soil, moisture content, dissolved salts, grain size and its distribution, seasonal variation, current magnitude.

3. Moisture: Moisture has a great influence on resistivity value of the soil. The resistivity of a soil can be determined by the quantity of water held by the soil and resistivity of the water itself. Conduction of electricity in soil is through water. The resistance drops quickly to a more or less steady minimum value of about 15% moisture. And further increase of moisture level in soil will have little effect on soil resistivity.

4. Dissolved salts: Resistivity of soil depends on resistivity of water which in turn depends on the amount and nature of salts dissolved in it. Pure water is poor conductor of electricity. Small quantity of salts in water reduces soil resistivity by 80%. Common salt is most effective in improving conductivity of soil.

5. Effect of grain size and its distribution: Grain size, its distribution and closeness of packing are also contributory factors, since they control the manner in which the moisture is held in the soil.

6. Effect of seasonal variation on soil resistivity: In dry weather, the resistivity will be very high and during rainy season the resistivity will be low.

7. Effect of current magnitude: The thermal characteristics and the moisture content of the soil will determine if a current of given magnitude and duration will cause significant drying and thus increase the effect of soil resistivity.

8. Area available: Single electrode rod or strip or plate will not achieve the desired resistance alone. If a number of electrodes could be installed and interconnected the desired resistance could be achieved.

9. Obstructions: The soil may look good on the surface but there may be obstructions below a few feet like virgin rock. In that event resistivity will be affected. Obstructions like concrete structure near about the pits will affect resistivity. If the earth pits are close by, the resistance value will be high.

10. Current magnitude: A current of significant magnitude and duration will cause significant drying condition in soil and thus increase the soil resistivity.

10.12 LAMPS

Artificial luminous radiation can be produced from electrical energy according to following two principles:

- **Incandescence:** It is the production of light via temperature elevation. The most common example is a filament heated to white state by the circulation of an electrical current. The energy supplied is transformed into heat by the Joule effect and into luminous flux.

- **Luminescence:** It is the phenomenon of emission by a material of visible luminous radiation. A gas subjected to an electrical discharge emits luminous radiation which is called as electroluminescence of gases. The discharge is produced by generating charged particles which permit ionization of the gas. Nature, pressure and temperature of the gas determine the light spectrum.

Photoluminescence is the luminescence of a material exposed to visible or almost visible radiation (ultraviolet, infrared). When the substance absorbs ultraviolet radiation and emits visible radiation which stops a short time after energization, this is fluorescence.

Following characteristics are to be considered when choosing a lamp for an application.

(a) Luminous efficacy which includes
- Luminous flux
- Lamp power and ballast losses

(b) Lamp life which includes
- Lumen depreciation during burning hours
- Mortality

(c) Quality of light which includes
- Spectrum
- Correlated color temperature (CCT)
- Color rendering index (CRI)

(d) Effect of ambient circumstances which includes
- Voltage variations
- Ambient temperature
- Switching frequency
- Burning position
- Switch-on and restrike time
- Vibration

(e) Luminaire which includes
- Lamp size, weight and shape
- Luminance
- Auxiliaries needed (ballast, starter, etc.)
- Total luminous flux
- Directionality of the light, size of the luminous element

(f) Purchase and operation costs which include
- Lamp price
- Lamp life
- Luminous efficacy
- Lamp replacement costs
- Electricity price and burning hours are not lamp characteristics, but have an effect on operation costs.

10.12.1 Incandescent Lamp

Incandescent lamp is also called General Lighting Service Lamp (GLS). In this lamp, light is produced by leading current through a tungsten wire. Working temperature of tungsten filaments in incandescent lamps is about 2700 K. Main emission occurs in the infrared region. The typical luminous efficacy of different types of incandescent lamps is in the range between 5 and 15 lm/W.

- **Standard Incandescent bulbs :** These contain a tungsten filament and are filled with an inert gas (nitrogen and argon or krypton).

- **Halogen Incandescent bulbs :** These also contain a tungsten filament, but are filled with a halogen compound and an inert gas either krypton or xenon. This halogen compound is responsible for the phenomenon of filament regeneration. This increases the service life of the lamps and avoids them blackening.

Advantages of incandescent lamps:

(i) It is inexpensive.

(ii) It is easy to use.

(iii) It does not need auxiliary equipment.

(iv) It is easier to dim by changing the voltage.

(v) It has excellent color rendering properties.

(vi) It can work at power supplies with fixed voltage.

(vii) It is free of toxic components.

Disadvantages of incandescent lamps:

(i) It has short lamp life (1000 h)

(ii) It has low luminous efficacy

(iii) Its heat generation is high

(iv) It is dependent on the supply voltage

(v) Costs are high due to high operation costs.

10.12.2 Fluorescent Lamp

A fluorescent lamp is a low-pressure gas discharge light source. In this lamp light is produced predominantly by fluorescent powders activated by ultraviolet radiation generated by discharge in mercury. It is usually in the form of a long tubular bulb with an electrode at each end. It contains mercury vapour at low pressure with a small amount of inert gas for starting.

In a glass tube small drop of mercury and small amount of argon gas are placed for initiation of discharge. Pressure, voltage and current are so adjusted that 253.7 nm line is excited. Radiation from low pressure mercury vapour is impinged on luminescent materials and re-radiated at longer wavelengths of visible spectrum. This re-radiates at longer wavelength. Maximum sensitivity is around 250-260 nm. Various types of fluorescent lamps are:

1. Day Light Fluorescent Lamps

2. Standard white Light - 3500°K suitable for general lighting.

3. 4500°K white lamp – It is between standard white light and day light lamp.

4. Soft white lamp – Pinker light. It is suitable for residential lighting and restaurants.

Reliable starting is achieved by having preheated cathodes / hot cathode. Dimension and voltage depend on luminous efficacy, brightness, lumen output and lumen maintenance. Lamp voltage decides the arc length, bulb diameter and lamp current. Half the open circuit voltage should be used by the lamp and the other half by the ballast. Hot cathode lamps operate at lower voltage. Typically cold cathodes have 70-100 V drop at the cathode.

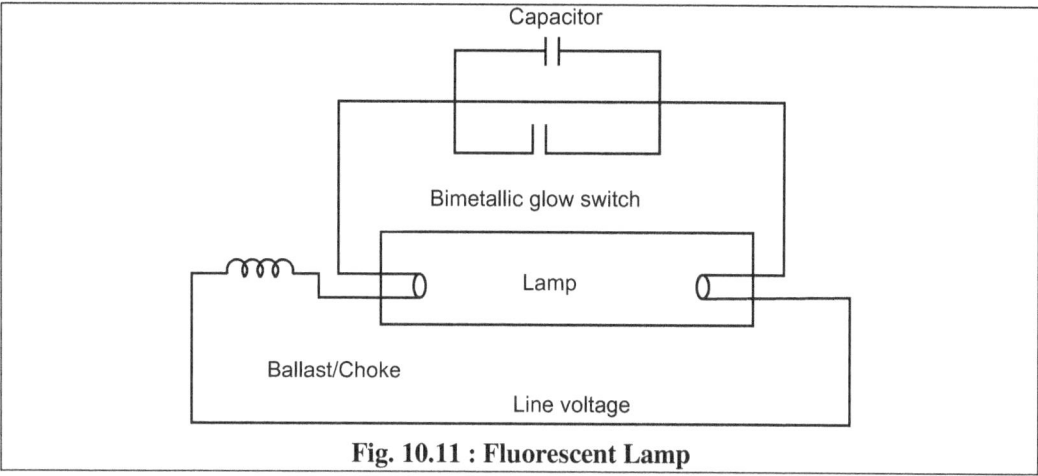

Fig. 10.11 : Fluorescent Lamp

Compact Fluorescent Lamps (CFLs)

CFL is a compact variant of the fluorescent lamp. The luminous efficacy of CFL is about four times higher than that of incandescent lamps. For a direct replacement of tungsten filament lamps, such compact lamps are equipped with internal ballasts and screw or bayonet caps. There are also pin base CFLs, which need an external ballast and starter for operation.

The overall length is shortened and the tubular discharge tube is often folded into two to six fingers or a spiral.

CFLs have following properties:
- Different shapes
- With bare tubes or with an external envelope
- Different CCT (warm white, cool white)
- Diminished sensitivity to rapid cycles

Advantages of compact fluorescent lamps
- It has good luminous efficacy.
- It has long lamp life (6000-12 000 h).
- It has reduced cooling loads when replacing incandescent lamps.

Disadvantages of compact fluorescent lamps
- It is expensive.
- Its light output depreciates with age.

- It has short burning cycles and shorten lamp life.
- The current waveform of CFLs with internal electronic ballast is distorted.

10.12.3 Mercury Lamps

In mercury lamp light is produced with electric current passing through mercury vapour. An arc discharge in mercury vapour at a pressure of about 2 bars emits five strong spectral lines in the visible wavelengths at 404.7 nm, 435.8 nm, 546.1 nm, 577 nm and 579 nm. The red-gap is filled up by a phosphor-layer at the outer bulb.

10.12.4 Light-Emitting Diodes (LEDs)

Solid-state lighting (SSL) is commonly referred to lighting with light-emitting diodes (LEDs), organic light-emitting diodes (OLEDs) and light-emitting polymers (LEPs).

LEDs work similarly to a semiconductor diode, allowing current flow in one direction only. An LED is a p-n junction semiconductor which emits light spontaneously directly from an external electric field known as electroluminescence effect. The diode structure is formed by bringing p- and n-type semiconductor materials together in order to form a p-n junction. p and n materials will naturally form a depletion region at the junction, which is composed of ionized acceptors in the p-side and ionized donors in then-side forming a potential barrier at the junction. External electric field applied across the junction will allow electrons in the conduction band, to gain enough energy to cross the gap and recombine with holes on the other side of the junction emitting a photon as a result of the decrease in energy from the conduction to the valence band. This is radiative recombination. Radiative recombination is characteristic for direct bandgap semiconductors. Therefore, direct bandgap semiconductor alloys are commonly used in optoelectronic devices such as LEDs.

Examples of direct bandgap semiconductors that have bandgap energies within the visible spectrum are binary alloys composed of elements in the groups III and V of the periodic table (e.g., InP, GaAs, InN, GaN and AlN). The present high-brightness LED-industry is based on ternary and quaternary alloys containing a mixture of aluminium (Al), gallium (Ga), and/or indium (In) cations and either one of arsenic (As), phosphorus (P), or nitrogen (N) anions. The three main relevant material systems for LEDs are AlGaAs, AlGaInP and AlInGaN.

This energy efficiency potential of LED is referred to as radiant or wall-plug efficiency η_e. It is defined as the *ratio between the total emitted radiated power and the total power drawn from the power source.* The radiant or wall plug efficiency of an LED depends on several internal mechanisms regulating light generation and emission processes in the semiconductor and LED package. These mechanisms are commonly characterized by their efficiencies, commonly referred to as feeding efficiency η_f, external quantum efficiency η_{ext}, injection efficiency η_{inj}, radiative efficiency or internal quantum efficiency η_{rad} and optical efficiency or light-extraction efficiency η_{opt}.

$$\eta_e = \eta_{ext} \times \eta_f$$

$$\eta_f = h\upsilon/qV$$

$$\eta_{ext} = n_{inj} \times \eta_{rad} \times \eta_{opt}$$

Luminous efficacy η_υ is obtained by multiplying the radiant efficiency with the luminous coefficient k_m.

$$\eta_v = \eta_e \times k_m$$

White LEDs can be realised by mixing the emission of different colored LEDs or by the utilisation of phosphors. Phosphor-converted white LEDs are usually based on blue or ultraviolet LEDs. The white light results from the combination of the primary blue or ultraviolet emission and the partially downward-converted emission created by specific phosphor layer or layers located over the semiconductor chip.

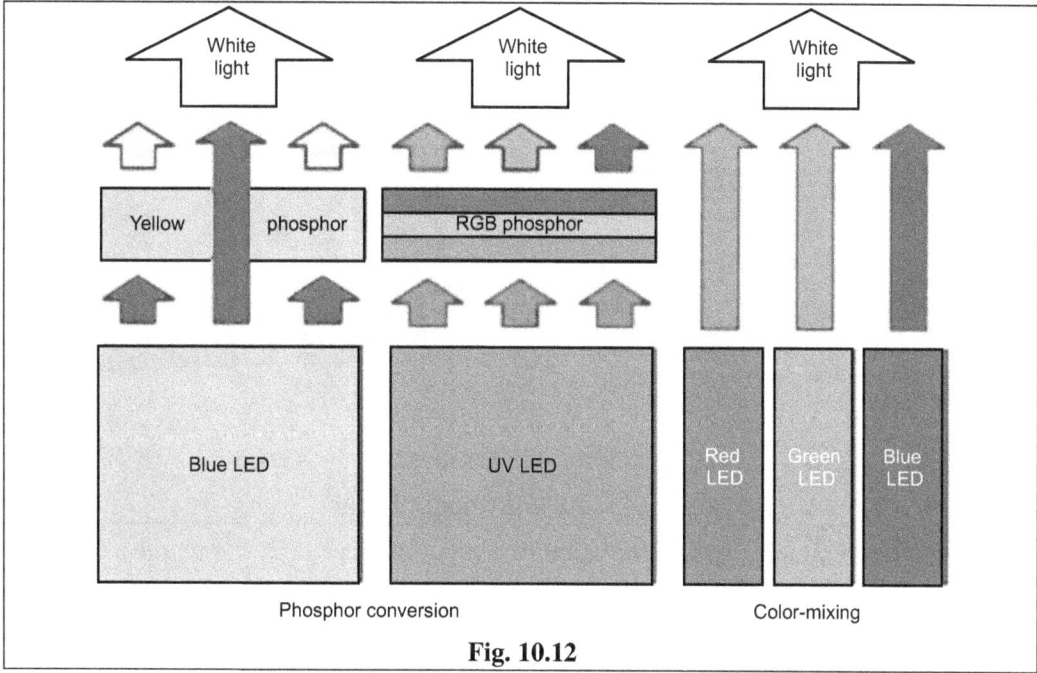

Fig. 10.12

Advantages of LEDs:

- It comes in small size.
- It is robust.
- With proper thermal management, long lifetime is expected.
- Switching has no effect on life.

- Very short rise time.
- It does not contain mercury.
- Excellent low ambient temperature operation.
- High luminous efficacy.
- Possibility to change colors.

Disadvantages of LEDs:
- Need for thermal management.
- High price.
- Low luminous flux / package.
- Risk of glare due to high output with small lamp size.

10.12.5   Sodium Vapour Lamp

It was commercially introduced in 1932. The low pressure sodium lamp has consistently maintained its enviable position as the most efficient light source available. The construction of a typical LPS lamp is given below.

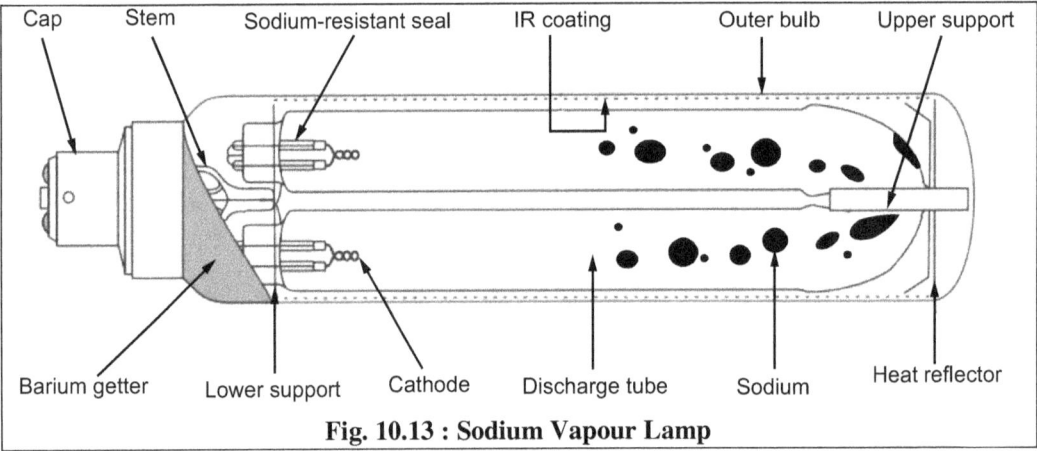

Fig. 10.13 : Sodium Vapour Lamp

To achieve optimal efficacy the sodium vapour is kept at low pressure. It has a discharge tube of large dimensions having a relatively low operating temperature. A protective layer of special borate glass is blown onto the inner surface of the glass tube so as to reduce the rate of attack by the chemically corrosive sodium vapour. The discharge tube is closed with metallic sodium and also contains a rare gas filling, usually neon-based, which facilitates starting. To reduce the length of the long discharge tube, it is customary to fold it into a U-shape, although linear designs also exist. The electric current is supplied via thermionic electrodes at either end. The discharge tube requires thermal insulation to ensure a high lamp efficacy, and this is provided by mounting it inside a secondary outer bulb. The outer bulb is equipped with either a bayonet or pin-type cap to ensure the correct alignment of the discharge tube in the optical system of the luminaire.

Basic Characteristics

The reason for the remarkably high efficacy of the low pressure sodium discharge is due to the wavelength of light it radiates which is very close to the peak sensitivity of the human eye under normal viewing conditions. Fig. 10.14 shows the energy balance of a typical low pressure sodium lamp. It tells that in fact only about 30% of the input power is converted into visible light. This percentage is comparable with other modern discharge lamps.

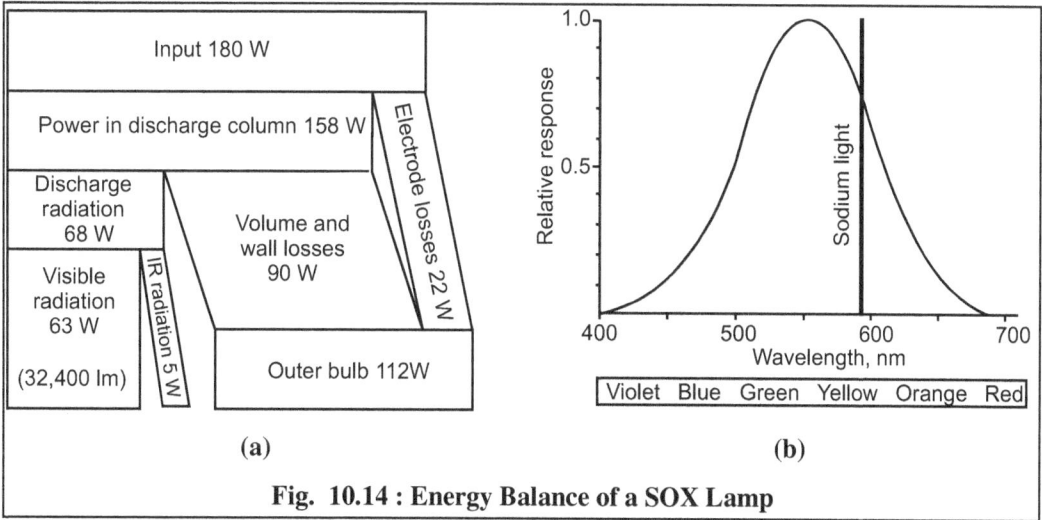

(a)   (b)

Fig. 10.14 : Energy Balance of a SOX Lamp

The lamp has been subjected to continual improvements in materials and manufacturing technology over the years, which has allowed it to unfailingly maintain its position as the most efficient light source available.

Advantages

1. Most suitable light source for road lighting.
2. The large physical size of the lamp means that it has a low surface luminance, so it is less likely to give rise to glare.
3. Low operating temperature permits the use of compact optical systems and lightweight plastic lanterns.
4. They are used for tunnel illumination, particularly in Japan and Korea.
5. It is relatively inexpensive.
6. Can be operated on low cost electrical control gear.
7. It contains zero mercury.

8. Can be easily disposed off as non-toxic waste without incurring extra expense at its end of life.

9. In the case of a momentary power supply interruption, the lamp will restrike as soon as the power is restored and no cooling down period is required.

Disadvantages

1. No colour rendering is possible under its monochromatic light.

2. Its rated life is shorter than other types of discharge lamps.

3. Typical installations have to be re-lamped every two years.

4. Expensive maintenance schedule can be extended to three or four years with high pressure sodium, and the reduced maintenance cost of the latter can totally offset the cost of energy savings with low pressure sodium.

10.12.6   Mercury Vapour Lamp

The mercury vapour lamp is a high intensity discharge lamp. It uses an arc through vaporized mercury in a high pressure tube to create very bright light directly from its own arc. This is different from fluorescents which use the mercury vapour arc to create a weaker light that mainly creates UV light to excite the phosphors. It has been used for society, lighting streets, factories and large areas for over 100 years.

Advantages

- Good efficiency.

- Colour rendering is better than that of high pressure sodium street lights.

- Life is good. Some lamps last far longer than the 24000 hour mark, sometimes 40 years.

10.12.7 Metal Halide

Traditional quartz MH arc tubes are similar in shape to mercury vapour (MV) arc tubes, but they operate at higher temperatures and pressures. Metal halide (MH) lamps consist of an arc tube within an outer envelope, or bulb. The arc tube may be made of either quartz or ceramic and contains a starting gas which is usually argon, mercury, and MH salts. The gas in the MH arc tube must be ionized before current can flow and start the lamp. MH lamps start when their ballast supplies a high starting voltage higher than those normally supplied to the lamp electrodes through a gas mixture in the arc tube. The ballast also regulates the lamp starting current and lamp operating current. Metal halide (MH) ballasts are required to start the lamp, regulate the lamp starting and lamp operating currents, and provide appropriate sustaining supply voltage.

The gas in the MH arc tube must be ionized before current can flow and start the lamp. As pressure and temperature increase, the materials within the arc tube vaporize and emit light and ultraviolet (UV) radiation. A bulb is usually made of borosilicate glass .It provides a stable thermal environment for the arc tube, contains an inert atmosphere that keeps the components of the arc tube from oxidizing at high temperatures, and reduces the amount of UV radiation that the lamp emits.

Some MH lamps have a coated finish on the inside of the bulb that diffuses the light. Often a phosphor coat is used to both diffuse the light and change the lamp's color properties.

The ballast regulates the lamp operating current flowing through the lamp after the lamp has been started. The ballast is set to deliver relatively stable power to the lamp while regulating the lamp current despite typical line voltage fluctuations. This maximizes lamp life and ensures other performance characteristics such as color and light output. MH ballasts must maintain suitable voltage and current wave shape to the lamp. MH lamp voltage typically increases over time, and the ballast must continue to provide sufficient voltage to the lamp as it ages.

Advantages:

- It has bright crisp, white light output suitable for commercial, retail, and industrial installations.
- Ceramic arc tubes are now predominantly used in low wattage (20W to 150W) lamps, though new designs up to 400W have emerged in recent years.
- Ceramic arc tubes provide improved Colon consistency over lamp life.

(b) Applications of lamps

Type	Application
Standard Incandescent bulbs	Domestic use, Localized decorative lighting
Halogen Incandescent bulbs	Spot lighting, Intense lighting
Fluorescent tube	Shops, offices, workshops, outdoors
Metal halide	Large areas, Halls with high ceilings
LED	Signaling traffic lights, "exit" signs and emergency lighting.
Low-pressure sodium	Outdoors, Emergency lighting
HP mercury vapour	Workshops, Halls, Hangars- Factory floors

10.13 STUDY OF ELECTRICITY BILL

Important terms to be revised before studying Tariff are as follows:

1. Connected Load : It is sum of the continuous ratings of all the equipments connected to the power system

2. Maximum Demand : The greatest of all the load which occur during a given period is called maximum demand.

3. Demand Factor : The ratio of maximum demand on the system to the rated connected load to the system is called demand factor. The actual maximum demand is always less than the rated load connected to the system , therefore, demand factor is always less than unity.

$$\text{Demand Factor} = \frac{\text{Maximum demand}}{\text{Connected load}}$$

4. Load Factor : The ratio of average load to the maximum load is called load factor. Load factor is generally used for determining the average load or energy delivered by the generating station in a given period.

$$\text{Load factor} = \frac{\text{Average load}}{\text{Maximum load}}$$

Average load is always less than maximum load , therefore, load factor is always less than one.

10.13.1 Tariff

The electrical energy produced at the generating station is delivered to a large number of consumers. The rate at which energy is sold to the consumers is called tariff. Tariff is fixed by the supplying company. The supply companies invest money to generate, transmit and distribute electrical energy. While fixing the tariff, the supply companies should not only recover the total cost of producing the energy but also earn some profit. The cost of generation depends upon the magnitude of energy consumed by the consumers and his load conditions. The profit should be minimum possible so that electrical energy can be sold at reasonable rates and the consumers encouraged to use more electricity.

Before understanding tariff of electricity system in detail a slight overview of the entire power system structure and hierarchy in India should be understood. The electrical power system consists of generation, transmission and distribution. For generation of electrical power we have many PSUs and private owned generating stations. The electrical transmission system is mainly carried out by central government body Power Grid Corporation of India limited. India is divided into 5 regions : Northern, Southern, Eastern, Western and North eastern region to facilitate this process. Further within every state we have a SLDC (state load dispatch centre). The distribution system is carried out by many distribution companies and State electricity board. There are two tariff systems, one for the consumer which they pay to the distribution companies and the other one is for the distribution companies which they pay to the generating stations.

Tariff for the Distribution Companies: The tariff system in India for the distribution companies is regulated by central electricity regulatory commission. This tariff system is called availability based tariff (ABT). It is a tariff system which depends on the availability of power. It is a frequency based tariff mechanism which tends to make the power system more stable and reliable. Mechanism of ABT is as follows:

1. The generating stations commit a day ahead about the schedule power which they can provide to the regional load dispatch centre (RLDC).

2. The RLDC conveys this information to various state load dispatch centre which collects the information from various state distribution companies about the load demand from various types of consumers.

3. State load dispatch centre sends load demand to regional load dispatch centre. Regional load dispatch centre allocates the power accordingly to the various states.

    But practically one or more state overdraws one or more generating stations under supplies. If demand is more then supply frequency dips from normal and vice verse. This led to deviation in frequency and system stability.

4. If the frequency is less than 50 Hz, implies demand is more than supply, then the generating stations supply more power to the system. If frequency is above 50 Hz, supply is more than demand, incentives are provided to generating station for backing up the generating power.

Tariff of electricity for the consumer: This is the cost which consumer pays to the distribution companies. The total amount paid by the consumer depends on its maximum demand, actual energy consumed plus some constant sum of money.

Total cost of electrical energy = fixed cost + semi fixed cost + variable cost

$\quad = ₹ (a + b \times kW + c \times kW\text{-}h)$

where

$\quad$ a = fixed cost independent of the maximum demand and actually energy consumed. This cost includes the cost of land, labour, interest on capital cost, depreciation etc.

$\quad$ b = constant which when multiplied by maximum kW demand gives the semi-fixed cost.

$\quad$ This includes the size of power plant as maximum demand determines the size of power plant.

$\quad$ c = a constant which when multiplied by actual energy consumed, kW-h gives the running cost. This includes the cost of fuel consumed in producing power.

10.13.2 Objectives of Tariff

The main objective of the tariff is to ensure the recovery of the total cost of generation and distribution. Tariff should include the following items:

(1) Recovery of cost of electrical energy generated at the generating system.

(2) Recovery of cost on the capital investment in transmission and distribution system.

(3) Recovery of cost of operation and maintenance.

(4) Recovery of cost of metering equipment, billing and miscellaneous services .

(5) Profit on the capital investment .

10.14 TYPES OF TARIFF

1. Simple Tariff : In simple tariff, the rate per unit of energy is fixed. This is a simplest possible tariff. The rate per unit of energy consumed by the consumer is fixed irrespective to the quantity of energy consumed by a consumer. This energy consumed is measured by installing an energy meter. Since it is very simple form of tariff, it is generally applied to tube wells which are operated for irrigation purposes

Advantages are:

- Consumer has to pay as per his consumption.
- It is in simplest form and easily understood by the consumers.

Disadvantages are:

- Consumer has to pay the same rate per unit of energy consumed irrespective of the number of units consumed by him.
- The cost of energy per unit delivered is high.

2. Flat Rate Tarrif : The tariff in which different types of consumers are charged at different per unit rates is called flat rate tariff. Consumers are grouped into different classes and each class of consumer is charged at a different per unit rate. For example, flat rate for fan and light loads is slightly higher than that for power loads.

Advantages :

- It is good for different types of consumers.
- It is simple in calculations.

Disadvantages :

- Separate meters are required to measure energy consumed for light loads and power loads.
- Consumers are not encouraged to consume more energy because same rate per unit of energy consumed is charged irrespective of the quantity of energy consumed.

3. Block Rate Tariff : The tariff in which first block of energy is charged at a given rate and the succeeding blocks of energy are charged at progressively reduced rates is called block rate tariff. The rate per unit of energy for the first block is the highest and reduces progressively with the succeeding blocks. For example, the first 100 units may be charged at the rate of ₹ 3.00 per unit; the next 100 units may be charged at the rate of ₹ 2.50 per unit and the remaining additional units may charged at the rate of ₹ 2.00 per unit. This type of tariff is mostly applied to domestic and small commercial consumers.

Advantages :

* By giving an incentive, the consumers are encouraged to consume more energy. This increases the load factor of the power system and hence reduces per unit cost of generation.
* Only one energy meter is required to measure the energy.

4. Two-Part Tariff: In this tariff electrical energy is charged on the basis of maximum demand of the consumer and the units consumed by him. The total charges to be made from the consumer are split into two components namely fixed charges and running charges. The fixed charges are independent of energy consumed by the consumer but depend upon the maximum demand, whereas the running charges depend upon the energy consumed by the consumer. The maximum demand of the consumer is determined on the basis of the kW capacity of all the electrical devices owned by a particular consumer or on the connected load. Thus

$$\text{Total charges} = ₹ (a \times kW + b \times kWh)$$

where,   a = charges per kW of maximum demand

                          b = charges per kWh of energy consumed

In this tariff, the charges made on energy consumed, recovers operating cost which varies with variation in generated (or supplied) energy. The charges made on maximum demand recover the fixed charges of generation such as interest and depreciation on the capital cost of building and equipment, taxes and a part of operating cost which is independent of energy generated.

Advantages

* It is easily understood by the consumers.
* The supplier gets the return in the form of fixed charges for the connection given to the consumer even if he does not consume any energy in a particular period.

Disadvantages

* If a consumer does not consume any energy in a month still he has to pay the fixed charges.
* The maximum demand of consumer is not measured, therefore, there is always conflict between consumer and the supplier to assess the maximum demand.

5. Maximum Demand Tariff: The tariff in which electrical energy is charged on the basis of maximum demand of the consumer and the units consumed by him is called maximum demand. In this tariff the maximum demand is actually measured by installing a maximum demand indicator meter. Thus the drawback of two-part tariff is removed. This tariff is mostly applied to bulk supplies and large industrial consumers.

6. Power Factor Tariff : The tariff in which power factor of the consumer's load is also taken into consideration while fixing it, is called power factor tariff.

SOLVED EXAMPLES

Example 10.1 :

A consumer has a constant load of 200 kW at power factor of 0.8 lagging for 16 hours per day and 300 days per annum. Estimate his annual payment if charged at 40 paisa per kWh plus ₹ 800 per kVA per annum.

Solution :   Maximum load in kVA = Maximum load in kW/p.f.

$$= 200/0.8 = 250 \text{ kVA}$$

Energy consumed per year = Average load × Number of hrs/year

$$= 200 \times 16 \times 300 = 960\,000 \text{ kWh}$$

Annual payment = $40/100 \times 960000 + 800 \times 250$

$$= ₹\,584000$$

Example 10.2 :

A company has a maximum load of 300 kW at 0.72 p.f. The tariff is ₹ 300 per kVA of maximum demand plus 20 paisa per unit. It has annual consumption of 4 × 104 units. Find out the average price per unit.

Solution : Data : Maximum demand of factory = 300 kW

Power factor = 0.72

Number of units consumed = 40000

Maximum demand in kVA = $300/0.72 = 416.67$

Annual bill = $300 \times 416.67 + 0.2 \times 40000$

$$= ₹\,133000$$

Average price per unit = $133000/40000 = 3.32$ ₹

Solved University Question Paper of
Fundamentals of Electrical Engineering (BVDU)

Dec. 2014

2012 Pattern

Time : 3 Hours   **Max. Marks : 60**

1. (a) Define resistance temperature coefficient with usual notations. Prove that   **[05]**

$$\alpha_2 = \frac{\alpha_1}{1 + \alpha_1 \,(t_2 - t_1)}.$$

Ans.   Please Refer to Article No. 1.4 on Page No. 1.6.

(b) An electric pump lifts 12 m^3 of water per minute to a height of 15 meters. If its overall efficiency is 60%. Find the input power. If the pump is used for 4 hours a day, find the cost of energy for the month of April.   **[05]**

Ans.   Please Refer to Article No. 1.6.2 on Page No. 1.14.

OR

(a) Define and explain : (i) Ohm's Law (ii) Potential difference   **[05]**

Ans.   Please Refer to Article No. 1.1.3 and 1.2 on Page No. 1.1 and 1.3.

(b) The resistance of copper wire is 70Ω at temperature of 45°C. If the wire is heated to a temperature of 90°C. Find its resistance at that temperature. Assume $\alpha_0 = 0.00427/°C$.

Ans.   Refer Similar to Example 1.8 on Page No. 1.11.

2. (a) Obtain the equations to convert delta connected resistive Network into equivalent star connected network.   **[05]**

Ans.   Please Refer to Article No. 2.7.1 on Page No. 2.28.

(b) Apply Kirchhoff's laws and calculate current flowing in 2 Ω resistance for the circuit shown in Fig. 1.   **[05]**

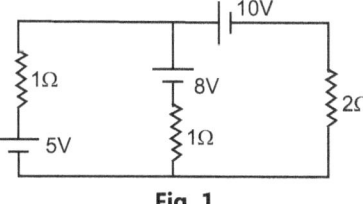

Fig. 1

Ans.   Refer Similar to Example 2.1 on Page No. 2.10.

OR

(a) State and prove maximum power transfer theorem as applied to d.c. resistive circuit.
   [05]

Ans.   Please Refer to Article No. 2.8.3 on Page No. 2.80.

(b) Using Thevenin's theorem find the current flowing through the 2 Ω resistance as shown in Fig. 2   **[05]**

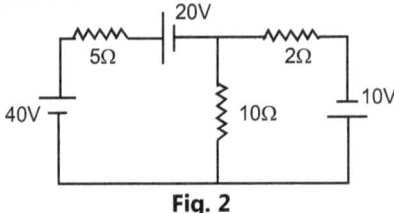

Fig. 2

Ans.   Refer Similar to Example 2.32 on Page No. 2.63.

3. (a) With neat sketch, explain construction and working of Lead Acid Battery.   **[05]**

Ans.   Please Refer to Article No. 3.18 on Page No. 3.25.

   (b) Two capacitors of 8µF and 2µF are connected in series across 400 V supply.   **[05]**
   Calculate : (i) Resultant capacitor (ii) Charge on each capacitor (iii) Voltage across
   each capacitor.

Ans.   Refer Similar to Example 3.7 on Page No. 3.22.

OR

   (a) Derive the expression of energy stored in capacitor.   **[05]**

Ans.   Please Refer to Article No. 3.12 on Page No. 3.15.

   (b) A series combination having R = 2MΩ and c = 0.01 µF is connected across a d.c.
   voltage source of 50 V. Determine

      (i)   Capacitor voltage after 0.02 sec.

      (ii) Charging current after 0.02 sec.

Ans.   Refer Similar to Example 3.8 on Page No. 3.23.

4. (a) Define the following terms and state their units :   **[05]**

      (i)   Flux density   (ii) Magnetic field intensity

      (iii) Absolute permeability   (iv) Relative permeability

      (v)   Coercivity

Ans.   Please Refer to Article No. 4.2.8 and 4.4 on Page No. 4.5 and 4.12.

   (b) Explain and derive the emf equation of transformer.   **[05]**

Ans.   Please Refer to Article No. 6.5 on Page No. 6.5.

OR

   (a) Draw the equivalent circuit of a transformer on load and explain each parameter. **[05]**

Ans.   Please Refer to Article No. 6.6 on Page No. 6.7.

   (b) An iron ring of mean diameter 10 cm and an area of cross section of 2.5 cm^2 has a
   saw cut of 2 mm in it. The ring is wound with a coil of 1000 turns, carrying a current
   of 0.1 A. Assuming a relative permeability of iron to be 800, determine the flux
   density in the air gap.

Ans.   Refer Similar to Example 4.6 on Page No. 4.25.

5. (a) What is the form factor and peak factor ? State these values for standard AC.   **[04]**

Ans.   Please Refer to Article No. 7.7 on Page No. 7.23.

(b) A pure inductor, a non-inductive resistor and a capacitor are all connected in series. The supply e.m.f is 85V at 50 Hz the p.d across inductor is 40V and that across resistor and capacitor together is 85 V. The current is 5A. Calculate the value of all components and p.f. of the circuit.   **[06]**

Ans.   Refer Similar to Example 8.9 on Page No. 8.28.

OR

(a) Define the following terms and also state their units :   **[04]**

(i)   Apparent power   (iii) Reactive power

(ii)   Active power   (iv) Power triangle

Ans.   Please Refer to Article No. 8.5 on Page No. 8.16.

(b) A coil having a resistance of 5Ω and an inductance of 0.02 H is connected in parallel with another coil having a resistance of 1 Ω and inductance of 0.08 H. Calculate the total current and power absorbed by the circuit when a voltage of 100 V at 50 Hz is applied.   **[06]**

Ans.   Refer Similar to Example 8.14 on Page No. 8.34.

6. (a) Draw the fluorescent lamp circuit and describe its working principle.   **[05]**

Ans.   Please Refer to Article No. 10.12.2 on Page No. 10.20.

(b) Explain the scheme of wiring for one lamp to be operated by two switches (staircase wiring).   **[05]**

Ans.   Please Refer to Article No. 10.3 on Page No. 10.4.

OR

(a) What are different types of earthing ? Explain each in detail.   **[05]**

Ans.   Please Refer to Article No. 10.8 on Page No. 10.14.

(b) What are different wiring accessories ? Explain any three in detail.   **[05]**

Ans.   Please Refer to Article No. 10.5 on Page No. 10.9.

Notes

www.ingramcontent.com/pod-product-compliance
Lightning Source LLC
Chambersburg PA
CBHW081326090726
47907CB00010B/2386